MIDNIGHT SOUL

THE FANTASYLAND SERIES
BOOK FIVE

KRISTEN ASHLEY

A LOVE IS EVERYTHING SAGA BY

KRISTEN

NEW YORK TIMES BESTSELLING AUTHOR

ASHLEY

FANTASYLAND BOOK FIVE

MIDNIGHT SOUL

Midnight Soul

Cover Image: Pixel Mischief Designs

I

WOULDN'T EVEN BLINK

Franka

That day had been one I wished to quickly forget.

Indeed, the months since those witches took my Antoine had been time I wished I had the power to erase from my memory.

I had power.

I did not have that kind of power.

These thoughts on my mind, I moved down the hallway of the Winter Palace seeking my room where I planned to pull the cord, ring a servant and request several bottles of Fleuridian wine.

Wine might not make me forget, but I'd found of late that it served well to dull the pain.

I turned the corner, my eyes to my slippers, but my senses made me lift my gaze to the passageway.

At what I saw, I halted and grew still, then slowly and quietly retraced my steps and ducked behind the corner, peering back around.

Oh my.

The Prince Noctorno of the other world was in the doorway to a bedchamber.

Although, he was not actually a prince. Not in this universe. Apparently they had very few princes in that other world. A world that existed on a parallel plane where all beings had twins to my own world.

This I thought was rather mad (everything about it, obviously), but with few princes, that meant there were few kings, so who ruled?

He reported that he was instead a member of the city guard, an occupation he referred to as being "a cop." A rather surprising statement considering all that was him.

He was no member of a guard.

He was a prince.

And he called himself Noc for some unknown reason, as Noctorno was a fine name, a strong name, a regal name (this last was true as his counterpart in this world *was* a prince).

And right now, he had his back to me.

He was wearing a pair of trousers the like that couldn't be found in my world. They were made of a rough, sturdy, faded-blue material. He also had a shirt that was not the fashion in this world. It was attractive and made of an equally attractive plaid. And it was a shirt that fit his broad shoulders magnificently.

His thick, black hair was untidy (this also attractive).

And I could see his light-blue eyes but only in my imagination as he had his back to me.

They were not eyes you were likely to forget. With his dark hair and skin browned in the sun, those eyes were deliciously striking.

There was a day, though now that day seemed lifetimes ago, when a sight such as Noctorno Hawthorne of another world (or indeed this one) would have caused me to have a much different reaction, not only to him, but to my plans for the imminent future.

That was before Antoine.

That was before I met the man who introduced me to, well...*me*.

Now I stood peeking around a corner, my body hidden (something I would *never* do before Antoine, unless it served a purpose, of course), but it wouldn't matter if I was around the corner or dancing a jig in the corridor.

The two people standing in the doorway of the bedchamber just down the hall wouldn't know I was there unless I shouted.

For Noctorno of the other world was not alone.

He was standing with Circe. Circe of this world, my world, but she'd spirited herself through magic to the parallel universe and decided to stay.

She was facing Noctorno, and once I could tear my eyes from his shoulders, his hair, his arse in those trousers, I looked at her face.

And again went still.

There was much I read in her look.

I was Franka Drakkar of the House of Drakkar. And if any member of the

House of Drakkar was clever (and I was clever, very clever, but not clever enough), they learned early how to take in anything they could in order to read a situation and then manipulate it to their advantage.

Therefore, I saw the sated look on her face, and I knew why Noctorno was standing there in her bedchamber door, his big body loose, relaxed, his hand lifting so he could gently stroke her jaw with his thumb.

And what I knew as I watched this was that they'd just had relations, and at least for Circe now of the other world, she'd enjoyed it.

Greatly.

But there was more to her look. More that would have given me, the woman I used to be, everything I needed to cut her to the quick for social sport, or bring her low in order to cow her to my every whim.

Relief. Acute relief.

And gratitude. Extreme gratitude.

I felt something stirring in the region of my belly, looking at her lovely face, knowing her story.

Knowing how she'd been misused since she was a child. Her parents slaughtered by a king who then made her his plaything in all the ways he could do that, every one of them despicable. Knowing of her escape from his captivity, which only brought her into the hands of pirates (and further misuse). Knowing her exceptionally unfortunate luck took her from said pirates to the savage land of Korwahk where she was entered into the Wife Hunt—a heinous practice, its simple name stating exactly what it was, if not relaying the information that when the "wives" were captured, they were violated.

Awaiting the Hunt, that had been the end for her. She'd used her considerable magic, *all* of it, and sent herself to a different realm. Another world. That parallel universe. One, from the snippets I'd heard, that was very different from my own.

Circe had exchanged herself for her twin. And the Circe of the other world was now the Golden Warrior Queen of Korwahk, beloved, even revered, not only by her people but her husband, King Lahn.

No one would know if the Circe I saw now, standing with Noctorno, would have earned that adoration from a ruler and his people if she'd chosen to remain after all that had befallen her since childhood.

Therefore it didn't matter.

Now was now.

And that very day, the evil triumvirate of witches that threatened two continents had all been dispatched.

Executed.

This made it safe for the most powerful men on those two continents to live out their days in harmony with the loves they'd found across universes.

Found them and impregnated them.

All four of them.

It was the way of men.

Quite tedious. Lay claim and then *lay claim*: planting their seed so they could bind their women to the servitude of motherhood and the men could live eternal through their spawn.

As far as I knew (and I was not privy to much), none of these men (save Frey Drakkar, my cousin) had been with their loves for more than a few years (and in some cases it was only months).

And yet all the women were expecting; three of them with their second child.

This had naught to do with me.

I was going to drink wine. Sleep. Wake.

Leave.

I tried not to be in Lunwyn—my icy country, my beautiful home—very often. Not only because, to many of those I knew, I wasn't welcome.

Even so, I didn't wish to return to Fleuridia where I had apartments and spent most of my time either.

They were apartments I'd shared with Antoine.

I needed to be rid of them.

Where I would go, I had no idea.

Of course, it was a must I first visit with Kristian, my brother, who, after what I was forced to do in the hopes of saving my lover, had suffered.

My brother was bountiful of heart but weak of character. He needed looking after. He needed protecting.

I'd see to him.

As I always did.

Then...

I had no idea.

But now was not the time to decide that.

Now, as I stood watching Circe press her jaw into Noctorno's touch, I knew he'd taken care of her. In so doing, I knew he'd been immensely gentle, took great amounts of time and paid tremendous attention.

All of this I understood from the replete expression on her face.

The relief I witnessed in her visage was likely, after all she'd endured, that she didn't think any man could offer that kind of pleasure, and she was delighted to know they could.

The gratitude was not for the gentleness, time, attention and the undoubted climax he'd given her.

It was simply for him being him.

The kind of man who had all of that in him.

One man in billions.

In two universes.

My vision went hazy as memories flitted through my brain.

I closed my eyes at the colossal pain those memories caused.

I had that, didn't I, my love. We *had that. Didn't we?* I grew uneasy even through the pain, wracked with uncertainty. *Did I give you that, my Antoine?*

As had been the case every time I sent my messages blindly to the gods in hopes they'd feel generous and send them where they were meant to be received, even before he expired after enduring such cruelty, I had no reply.

I couldn't allow the images the witches had sent of his torture to come to my mind's eye. If I did, it would be crippling. So I only let them through when I was alone at night in bed and could be crippled by them, tossing and turning, sleepless for hours.

Days.

Weeks.

I opened my eyes, and again swiftly and quietly, turned and made my way back down the hall, leaving Circe and Noctorno to their moment.

As I did this, I felt my lips curl in a scornful smirk.

Look what's become of me, Antoine. I called out silently to the ether. *Walking away from that touching scene without even catching Circe's eyes to share I'd seen what I'd seen and I knew what I knew. You did this to me,* mon cœur. *I must get back to who I am. If only to have something diverting in the years to come that don't have you in them.*

I halted again, halfway down the passageway, when Antoine's deep, polished voice sounded in my head in answer.

That is not you, mon ange, *and I would be most annoyed if you went back to impersonating that woman you never were.*

Mon ange, his angel.

All those months we'd spent together...

Did he even know me?

This was a vague thought.

A more crucial one came to my lips.

"Are you there, beloved?" I whispered to the empty hall.

I heard no reply.

"Antoine, *mon cœur*, are you there?" I called and winced when I heard the urgency and desperation in my own voice.

Even so, there was no more from Antoine.

And if a servant, or (as if I hadn't already been cursed by the goddess Adele to endure the unendurable), the dire happenstance of being caught by Noctorno (either of them), my cousin Frey, his Finnie, the king of Korwahk, his Circe (or the other Circe), Prince Noctorno's Princess Cora, Apollo or Madeleine, should they walk down this corridor, they'd think me deranged.

And I couldn't have that.

I'd shown them weakness.

With the loss I'd suffered, what I'd been forced to do to my Lunwyn, my family's House, my brother, I no longer had it in me to show them strength.

And I'd learned when that was the case. When you were brought low, escape was the wisest course.

I hurried toward the steps, deciding to find my wine somewhere else.

I knew Queen Aurora was enjoying refreshments with the green witch of the other world, a woman who went by the name Valentine (and I approved that she pronounced it in the Fleuridian manner, Val-ehn-*teen*) as well as Lavinia, Lunwyn's most powerful witch.

And all of them indisputably deserved those tonics, what with the palace having all its windows blown out by evil magic, the green witch instigating her layering of plans in order to save our realm, and Lavinia having actually died at the hands of the wicked triumvirate, necessitating her being resurrected by the elves.

They'd been at it since everyone was transported back to the Winter Palace and the short debriefing had occurred.

They were all women I admired—intelligent, powerful, shrewd. In Aurora's case, cold and strategic, in Valentine's case, smug and calculating and in Lavinia's case, nurturing and gracious.

I would never tell them I thought any of that.

This was not because they wouldn't give me the opportunity, not seeking or desiring my company.

I just wouldn't.

I was a Drakkar. Even a compliment earned was withheld, regardless if that compliment had to do with saving the world.

I finished my descent down the stairs to the first floor and caught a scurrying servant as I did.

As was habit, I lifted my chin slightly, kept it aloft and looked down my nose at her.

"I shall be in the morning room. Have two bottles of wine delivered to me, some bread and cheese. *Des Champs du Sauvage*, if the queen has that in her cellar."

"Right away, Lady Drakkar."

I didn't even nod. I moved sedately to the morning room as the servant, who had also endured the attack that day, not to mention they had a house full of visitors to see to due to the cancelled Bitter Gales that was to happen that night, if the world had not been threatened.

I worried the morning room would have some of these visitors occupying it and was relieved to find it didn't.

Aloneness.

What I needed.

Loneliness, my mind whispered.

What no one needed.

I drew in breath as I entered the room, seeing it was lit. The sun had long since set, as it was late evening, but regardless, the windows had to be boarded. I was equally relieved to see that the debris from the blast that shattered them had been neatly cleaned away.

Yes, the servants were all likely dead on their feet.

That was the last I thought of that as I pulled the cord and found my seat.

To my fortune, a male servant came in swiftly. I wasted no time with pleasantries (as was my wont) and ordered a fire laid and lit.

He did this as another servant hurried in with my wine, bread and cheese.

Perhaps due to the amount of wine I'd ordered they'd brought two glasses.

Uncharacteristically of me, after the girl poured, I did not bid her to take the extra wineglass away. I didn't need a reminder I would be drinking alone.

She more didn't need an extra errand this day.

You've made me soft, I told Antoine. *Too soft*.

I waited, taking the filled glass and bringing it to my lips for a sip, my body held tense, expectant, hoping to hear his beautiful voice in my head again.

It did not come.

The servants left me with all I'd asked and a roaring fire that was quickly warming the space. However, when the male made to close the door behind him, thus closing me in and keeping the draught from the hall from cooling the room, I lifted my hand lazily his way.

"No, leave it open," I bid.

He bobbed his head, did a slight bow and disappeared out the door.

I ordered the door left open for I had no company and it'd be quite dire to sit in a closed room all by myself, brooding.

With the door open and the comings and goings of a busy palace, at least there would be something that could take my attention.

I sipped. I allowed the soft cheese to soften further in the warming room. I sipped more. And more. I replenished my glass. I spread the cheese on the bread and nibbled.

And through this, I found myself alone in a room, staring at the fire, brooding.

"Hay," I heard and started at the strange word that pertained to barns and horses being uttered in a deep voice that was not suave, even on that short word, but rough, as if hewn through granite.

I turned my head to see Noctorno of the other world (and his appealing faded-blue trousers), moving into the room with immense masculine grace, his gaze on me.

But as he walked toward me, I took in his expression, which, like Circe's, was sated.

There was, however, no relief or gratitude.

Instead, even if some time had passed, he seemed invigorated most assuredly by his recent activities inside Circe's bedchamber, and at the sight of it I felt my breath catch in my throat.

I remembered that look.

I *relished* that look.

Not only on my Antoine but any lover I'd had (but, obviously, getting it from Antoine was far more rewarding).

It was a look I worked toward, putting great energy and imagination into it, losing myself in these endeavors, feeling free of my name, my history, my secrets, my responsibilities, and reveling in my success as if I'd scaled mountains.

It was my greatest talent: bringing a man to climax and making utterly certain it was one he wouldn't forget.

This was my greatest talent outside, of course (as any good Drakkar would excel), homing in on any vulnerability and manipulating it for the greatest possible gain—coin, jewels, furs, favors, silence, information, or simply for amusement.

Seeing the look on Noctorno in that moment, I knew Circe too had performed well (admirably well, I might add, considering her dismal past).

I also recognized—focusing on it keenly—what Circe might have missed, or perhaps what Noctorno hid from her understanding, or simply just sensing, how she came to him.

He was not done.

Oh no.

If she had not given indication she wished him out of her bedchamber, he'd still be in it.

Indeed, he might be in it all night, and not to sleep.

He might have been in it, perhaps, for days.

As these thoughts flitted in my mind, I became aware he'd fully entered the room, was stopped not far from my chair, and was standing, chin tipped down, eyes regarding me with a scrutiny that I found so uncomfortable I actually shifted in my seat.

I ceased this reaction the instant I became aware of it, appalled at myself.

Giving something away so easily? Especially something like discomfiture?

You've ruined me, I snapped silently at Antoine.

My dead lover had no rejoinder.

"You okay?" Noctorno asked.

"Am I what?" I asked in return.

His head gave a slight twitch before he went on, "You okay? All right?" His voice lowered. "It's been a tough day, babe, for all of us. Including you."

I looked beyond him to the fire, lifting my wine to my lips but not sipping it until after I murmured, "I'm perfectly fine."

"Yeah, right," he stated, and the disbelief veritably dripping from his tone made my gaze flick immediately back to him.

This meant I watched as he sauntered right in front of me to the chair accompanying mine, threw his lengthy frame in it and reached for the wine at the table that separated our seats.

He also reached for the extra glass.

These were seats, I shall add, that were turned at corners to each other with a small, round table in between, so my knee was nearly touching his.

He poured.

It was on the tip of my tongue to share that I had not invited him to attend me.

Alas, I became distracted by his long fingers, and the words died in my mouth.

"That shit was whacked," Noctorno declared, easing back in his chair, lifting the red wine to finely-molded male lips while I watched. "Glad it's done," he finished before he drew in a sip.

With some effort I refused to acknowledge, I turned my eyes back to the fire.

"Franka, right?" he asked my name.

"Correct," I answered, thinking that one of the other universe women claimed by men in this one should have shared with this man, princely or not, that as a member of the guard he was well beyond his station *tossing* his (long, powerful) body in a chair, *helping himself* to *my* wine and *introducing* himself *to me* with a, "Franka, right?"

Inexcusable.

Perhaps this was how they did it in his world.

It was not how we did it in mine.

I was of the House of Drakkar. I was aristocracy. My cousin, Frey Drakkar was *The* Frey, *The* Drakkar. He commanded elves *and* dragons. He was married to the Ice Princess of my snowy country (even though she actually wasn't the *real* princess, she was from a parallel universe, I had no earthly idea what had become of the real Princess Sjofn, but everyone seemed to be disregarding that so I had no choice but to do so as well, and frankly I'd never liked the woman much anyway, her replacement, however, was quite spirited).

Not to mention, my cousin, Frey, had already sired the future king on her, for Adele's sake!

I was, however, not going to offer myself up for etiquette lessons to this man.

I would sip my wine and hope he'd get the indication I wished no company through my manner. If he didn't, I would leave (though, I couldn't figure out how to do that and take the other bottle of wine with me without this appearing undignified).

As I turned this quandary in my brain, he said in that gentle voice, "Hay," again, but he added at the end, for some unknown reason and for the second time in the short period he'd been addressing me, "babe."

I turned to him and informed him condescendingly, "You speak strangely."

That got another twitch of his head before he asked, "Pardon?"

"Hay. Babe," I said. "What do these words mean?"

"You...uh, don't have the words 'hey' and 'babe' in this world?"

I lifted my chin a smidge.

"Of course we do. Hay is fed to horses. And babes are wee. Newborns. I simply don't understand why you utter them to me."

He grinned.

My heart squeezed, the pain so immense it was a wonder I didn't double over, fall to the floor, dead before I hit.

So handsome. That light in his striking eyes.

My Antoine had been handsome.

But when he'd smiled...

"Not saying 'hay,'" Noctorno told me. "I'm saying 'hey,' with an e. It's how people say hello, greet each other in my world."

I battled the pain, hid the severity of the fight and nodded my head once.

"And 'babe?'" I prompted, though I shouldn't have. Engaging in discourse would not get him to leave.

"It's what guys call chicks in my world."

I drew up a brow.

He watched it go and his striking eyes lit brighter.

"Chicks?" I asked, ignoring the amused light in his eyes.

"Girls. Women."

"Girls and women?" I asked.

"Well, you wouldn't call a girl-girl, like a little kid, a babe or a chick. You'd call women that."

"So it's an endearment," I deduced, thinking that I might, indeed, expend the effort to have a word with one of the women in this world who were of his world to share with him a few important things.

Precisely that he shouldn't be referring to anyone he barely knew, and certainly not his superior, with an endearment.

"That, though chick is more slang," he shared.

"In other words, in your world, you refer to the female gender with words indicating to said female every time you use them that you think they're as vulnerable and weak as a newborn child or the like, but that of a species of fowl."

Without hesitation, his mirth surged forth, filling the room, warming it, drawing me out of my mood, away from the events of that day, of the last months, of the loss of the only man I'd ever loved, and silently I watched and listened.

I gave no indication I enjoyed it.

But I enjoyed it.

He controlled his joviality but didn't stop smiling or watching me as he asked, "What do you call dudes here?"

"Dudes?" I responded to his query with a query.

"Men," he explained, still smiling. "Guys."

"We call them men or gentlemen."

"No, I mean endearments or slang."

"*I*, personally, *do not* engage in uttering *slang*."

He studied me like I was a highly entertaining jester who'd come to court before he inquired, "Okay, what do you call a man you're in with?"

"In with?"

"Who means something to you. Your guy. Your man," he stated.

I looked to the fire again, feeling my face freeze.

The instant I did, he bit off, "*Fuck*." There was a slight pause before, "Babe... Franka, Tor told me about the shit that went down...fuck." I felt strong fingers curl around my wrist, a wrist I was resting on the arm of the chair, before he finished, "That was stupid. I'm so sorry."

With a delicate twist, I freed myself from his touch, lifted my wineglass to my lips, and before I took a sip I murmured, "It's nothing."

"Bullshit."

This odd word made my gaze move back to him.

"I beg your pardon?" I snapped.

"Bullshit," he repeated.

"I don't understand this word."

Though I had a feeling I did.

There was no smile on his face. No humor in his eyes. He was regarding me closely again, but this time I was prepared and didn't shift in my seat.

"You're full of it," he explained. "You're not giving me the entire truth. You're saying something to get past something you don't want to be talking about."

"And if I did this, considering what we both know I'm moving us past, it's customary to allow the awkward moment to *pass*."

He leaned slightly toward me. "You're in here all alone, drinkin' wine by yourself, lookin' like the world just ended. And I get why you'd feel that way. I don't understand, when all the others are so tight, why you aren't tight with them. But that's not my business. All I know is, you put your ass on the line today to save four women's lives and the life of every being in this universe. It took courage to do that, babe. You suffered a big loss losing your man and I'm sorry for that. But at least for tonight you should be proud of what you did for your country, for four good women and the men who love them, for the memory of the man you lost. It's time to celebrate. The good side won and *you*," he pointed a finger at me (insufferably *rude*!), "were a part of that."

Again, on the tip of my tongue, words hovered to share precisely, in a calculated way, how I knew he had celebrated with Circe.

Those words did not drop off my tongue.

They vanished completely as I simply turned my attention back to the fire.

"And that kinda situation does not say wine," he carried on. "It says whiskey, vodka, or better yet, tequila."

I could not argue with that (regardless of the fact I had no idea what tequila was).

"To that, I heartily agree," I declared, deigning again to glance at him and wishing I hadn't, for his smile had returned, making me further wish I could snatch my words back.

"I'll go find something," he announced, putting his hands to the arms of the chair in order to heft his big frame out of it, and I felt my brows draw together as, once he was up, it seemed he was moving toward the door.

"You simply have to pull the cord and demand it of a servant," I explained.

He was now standing, staring down at me, appearing bemused.

By the powers of Adele, if she reigned in his realm, she gave him more than his fair share of *everything*.

He even looked delectable bemused!

I really had to leave as quickly as I could without giving anything away.

"Uh...what?" he asked.

I gestured indolently with a hand to the cord in the corner of the room. "Pull the cord. A bell sounds..." I didn't have the information of where it sounded as I didn't concern myself with such matters, and continued with, "somewhere. A servant comes. We tell him we want whiskey. He brings it."

His lips quirked.

I drew in an annoyed breath for that was delectable too.

"Right," he muttered and began to stride toward the cord.

I twisted in my chair and called to his back, "When they arrive, share with them more fuel needs to be added to the fire."

He stopped and turned back to me while I was speaking.

When I was done, he looked to the fire and then back to me.

"Babe, there's a pile of logs right there," he stated.

"Indeed, there are," I agreed, though I hadn't concerned myself with that matter either and had no idea if he spoke truth.

"So I can put more *fuel* on the fire."

By Adele, he again looked amused.

I needed to find a way to exit this situation with all due haste.

"If you wish to dirty your hands..." I left it at that but added a slight shrug.

He shook his head, his mouth again quirking, and he turned back to the cord.

Fine.

He would order whiskey.

I would imbibe a bit (or perhaps more than a bit). Then I'd find a way to purloin the extra bottle of wine and the glass and remove myself to my rooms.

This was my plan.

As Franka Drakkar of the House of Drakkar, I was very good with plans, making them and executing them to their fullest.

However, that night, not for the first time, I would not succeed.

"You jest," I declared.

I was leaning across the arm of my chair (rather inelegantly) toward Noctorno, who was lounged (rather negligently) in his chair, whiskey in hand, dancing, startling light-blue eyes on me.

"Nope," he stated.

"Nope" I had learned through the fullness of our discourse these past hours in his world meant "no."

Incidentally, we'd had a good deal of whiskey.

We'd also finished all the wine.

And I was sure I was likely to lament how deep in my cups I was at that present juncture.

I just didn't have it in me to care.

"You can speak to any being you want in the entirety of your universe, as long as you have this...*number* you describe? By just entering it into a gadget and putting it to your ear?" I asked.

"Yep," he replied. "And as long as they also have a phone."

"Yep" I'd learned meant "yes."

So did "Yup," but we had that in my world too.

I examined his face.

He looked relaxed and amused.

He did not look as if he was dissembling.

Even so, he *had* to be dissembling.

Therefore, I moved back an inch on my accusation. "You lie."

He shook his head, leaning forward and reaching behind him, stating, "Nope."

He then pulled out a thin, rectangular piece of what looked like metal and glass. It had rounded edges. It was simple but somehow exceptionally handsome.

He leaned toward me, holding this thing my way, and as I watched the little window illuminated, showing a variety of tiny pictures on it, all lined up precisely in rows, up and down.

"By the gods," I whispered, reaching toward it but stopping, struck immobile by the fantastical.

"Yep," he said, moving his thumb on the window. A white screen came up with a listing of text. "That's email. You can send mail to anyone too, if you have their address. And it gets to them in a couple of minutes. Of course I can't do that now, seeing as I'm *way* outside service. But if I wasn't, I could call 'em, mail 'em, text 'em."

I turned my gaze from his gadget to his face.

"Text them?"

"Type in a message," he said, my eyes dropped back to his contraption as his thumb moved over it. "Hit send, it goes to someone else's phone, bings, they get the message within minutes. Seconds even."

"That's *extraordinary*," I breathed, reaching out yet again but stopping before I touched the little box of magic.

"You can take it, Franka. It won't bite you."

Laughter laced his words and I again looked at his handsome face.

I didn't take his gadget.

I asked, "Is it magic?"

"We don't have magic in our world like you do."

I sat back in shock. "How bizarre."

"We do," he went on to clarify. "It just isn't *out*. As in, practiced openly."

He could not be serious.

"That's very dangerous," I stated primly (perhaps in order to hide I also did it uncomfortably).

"It probably fuckin' is," he muttered.

"You should do something about that," I informed him with authority. "It's my understanding you're in the city guard. You should speak to your constable. Perhaps he can speak to your...whatever title your ruler bears. They can surely do something about that. And as you can imagine with your activities here, it's advisable."

He shook his head. "If the president went on record making folks come forward to register that they're witches and sorcerers...or whatever...he'd be removed from office in about twenty-four hours."

"That's ludicrous."

A small grin flirted at his lips as he shook his head again. "It's the truth."

"Odd," I murmured, looking back to his...*phone*.

He shook it side to side in a coaxing way. "Take it, babe. You can't hurt it. It can't hurt you. There's games on it if you want me to show you how they work."

I again caught his eyes. "Games?"

This time, he nodded. "Solitaire. Tetris. Trivia Crack. Think there might be Fruit Ninja on there still."

"Fruit...*ninja*?" I asked the question like I was trying out the words.

He simply chuckled at that, but he did it in a way I knew he was being gracious for he appeared to be fighting roaring with laughter.

I ignored this and told him, "I don't know these games."

He again smiled. "That would be me showin' you how they work."

I took in his smile.

I looked in his eyes.

There was amusement there (as there seemed to be since he entered the room, something I'd never encountered in my life, such good humor).

There was also intelligence, a great deal that could not be hidden even if, for some reason, he were to wish to try.

And there was kindness, so much, there was more than enough to exploit should one have that in mind.

But there was no guile.

Even Antoine had an agenda when it came to me. To anyone. That was how one lived in my world. Not just my universe, the world I lived in due to the status I carried.

Noctorno Hawthorne of the world of magical gadgets had none.

And staring in his eyes, I felt a sensation gathering behind mine I hadn't felt since I was a young child.

"You should not be kind to me," I whispered.

His expression changed.

It did not go wary.

It warmed with a gentleness that made it feel my insides were unravelling.

"Franka," he whispered back.

"You should not be kind to me," I repeated.

"Babe—"

"I've done terrible things."

He said nothing, just stared right into my eyes, unafraid, without judgment, holding my gaze steady.

"I love my frosted country," the whiskey (or the wine) made me whisper. "They don't think so. They don't know. I can't..." I shook my head, enough of my faculties still intact not to give him that. "I don't let that be known. I've traveled the Northlands extensively. But there's nothing like the air in Lunwyn. I prefer it in the many months it's covered in snow. I prefer the chill. I prefer the cold air carving through your innards, washing them clean."

Something flickered in his gaze.

Curiosity.

"Franka—"

"I would do nothing...*nothing*...to betray my country." My voice dropped beyond a whisper to nearly nothing. "But for him."

"I get it."

I shook my head. "You don't." I lifted a hand weakly then dropped it in my lap. "They don't."

I was referring to Queen Aurora. Frey and his Finnie. King Lahn and his Circe. Prince Noctorno and his Cora. Apollo and his Madeleine. The green witch Valentine. Lavinia.

Everybody.

"They get it," he returned.

"No, they don't."

"They get it, sweetheart. You don't think if those men had the same choice as you, their women taken, tortured, living in the pits of hell every day for weeks, fucking *months*...or those women had that choice with their men...they wouldn't make the same choice as you?"

"I shared this exact sentiment with them and they—"

He leaned deeply across the seat over the table that separated us, very close to me, and his voice was the lash of a whip when he interrupted me to state, "*Lied*."

He did not move away as he continued, and when he did his voice was no less strong.

"They fuckin' lied, Franka. I know those are good men who have done remarkable things for their countries. I also know they wouldn't hesitate to do anything in their power to keep their women safe and free from harm. So, since they weren't in your position, they can say whatever the fuck they wanna say. But today, when Cora and Circe and Maddie and Finnie were taken, if they weren't made safe as quickly as they were, if you think for one fuckin' second each one of those men wouldn't make a deal with the goddamned devil to make that so, you...are...*wrong*."

He jerked a finger at his chest and didn't cease talking.

"I know, 'cause I'm a man like that. And if I had a woman I loved like those men love their women, I'd do it and I wouldn't fuckin' *blink*."

That sensation behind my eyes became stronger as I asked, "You would?"

"Fuck yes," he stated inflexibly. "And I wouldn't even blink."

It had started, and for the first time in decades, I couldn't stop the flow of words coming out of my mouth.

"I'm a traitor," I admitted.

"You were and you aren't the first to make the decision you made for someone you loved. Worse has happened when people made that same decision. And what you did, in the end, no one got hurt. But today, even if that's the case, you made up for it. Those bitches could have cut you down with a snap." He lifted his hand and made that noise with his fingers, the sound so loud I jumped. "You knew it. You still walked in there. I know vengeance, I get the need for that. I know that's what pushed you to make the decision you made. But there was more. Loyalty. To the country you think you betrayed, to your family, 'cause I know you and Frey are blood. I get with the way he looks at you, the others too, that there's no love lost, and I don't give a fuck why. You changed the course of history, baby, and every citizen of this nation should be grateful."

"I walked into a room and cast a spell," I reminded him. "I hardly wielded swords, and it wasn't even my magic."

"And saved lives doin' that. *A lot* of them."

"You make me sound like a hero," I scoffed.

He edged slightly back, a cloud coming over his expression.

"There is no such thing as a hero. Just a person doing the right thing in more than the usual, extreme circumstances."

It was my turn to consider him curiously.

Once I'd taken long moments to do this, I asked quietly, "Why do I think that declaration is self-effacing?"

"I'd answer that, if I knew what the fuck 'self-effacing' meant."

I felt my lips curl slightly up at the edges.

"Modest," I explained.

"It isn't," he stated. "It just is what it is."

As he would say, *bullshit*.

I did not share this sentiment.

I also did not share my immense gratitude at the relief his words made me feel.

I simply continued to look into his remarkable eyes.

"You're good at it," he said softly, tipping his head my way. "That game you got goin' on. Those walls you built that you hide behind. The distance you keep with every look, every word, every fuckin' breath." His gaze tipped down to the table then back to me. "When you aren't drinking whiskey, that is."

"Noctorno—"

"No one calls me Noctorno," he stated flatly and leaned toward me again. "It's Noc. Especially to friends, and Franka, I help save a universe with a woman then down a coupla bottles of wine and a whatever this is called..." he motioned with a flick of his wrist to the nearly depleted whiskey, "of hooch."

"A decanter," I shared.

"Whatever," he muttered then spoke up when he spoke on. "You're a friend. So call me Noc."

I pressed my lips together.

He let that go and continued.

"So now I'm a friend. I'm also the man who sees you for what you are, sugarlips. You don't fool me. And those other men," his eyes flicked to the door briefly, his indication of Frey, Lahn, the other Noctorno and Apollo, "if they didn't have the end of the world as they knew it breathing down their necks and took the time to *see*, you wouldn't fool them either."

I drew in a breath, burying his words, words I'd heard (of a sort) from another man, in fact, from the only other person I'd come across in my years on this earth who'd expended the energy to *see*.

However.

He'd called me *sugarlips*.

I felt my brows snap together and I couldn't control the sneer in my, "Sugarlips?"

It was then his gaze dropped to my mouth before it came back to my eyes and he whispered, "Baby, you got the prettiest mouth I've ever seen."

This flirtation after that very evening he'd succeeded in bedding a woman who had been repeatedly violated for over two decades.

The gall.

"Cease flirting with me," I clipped.

He blinked, again looking perplexed, before he stated, "I'm not. I'm just sayin' it like it is."

I stared at him angrily.

And again saw no guile.

This was not a man who would flirt with a woman who he knew had just lost the only man she'd ever loved in a heinous, drawn-out way, the pain of which would never die.

Gods.

How mortifying.

"I...I, well..." By the gods, I was stammering! "I apologize." And apologizing! Gods, what had become of me? I finished it quickly, "I mistook your words."

"I like lookin' at you, Franka, and you're cute when you stop tryin' so hard to be a hard-ass bitch. But no decent man would make a play on a woman in your situation." He grinned, "He succeeds in getting her shitfaced drunk or not."

Shitfaced?

I did not ask.

"I am not drunk," I lied haughtily on a toss of my head.

"Bullshit."

I narrowed my eyes at him declaring, "I dislike this word."

He continued to appear amused. "I get it you think you can rule the world with a flash of those gorgeous blues, a pout on that pretty mouth and a pissed-off look, baby, and there are men who'd likely break their backs to cater to your every whim. I'm just not one of those who falls for that shit." He leaned in mock-suggestively. "I do it the other way around, minus the pouting and pissed off parts."

I pressed his way. "You *do* flirt."

He shrugged, clearly continuing to be entertained—by *me*—and not hiding it.

"It's just me."

There was a time when I'd wish he would. When I would play with Noctorno Hawthorne in ways we'd both like.

Those times were dead for me.

Forever.

I wrapped my fingers around my mostly-drunk glass of whiskey on the table, turned to face the fire, sat back and emptied its contents down my throat.

"Hey," he called.

I allowed only my eyes to slide his way.

"Just messin' with you, sweetheart," he explained.

I looked back to the fire and decided, with all that I'd already given him, there was no reason to stop doing it.

With this man, one of only two I'd ever met, it would cause no harm.

Therefore, I shared, "I miss him."

"Bet you do," he said gently.

"Their deaths were too quick," I declared, speaking of Minerva, Edith, Helda, the witches who had all deservedly perished that day.

The witches who had taken my Antoine from me and then treated him to a slow, agonizing death.

"Mm-hmm," he murmured soothingly.

"But it's over," I concluded.

"That's the rub, am I right?"

I turned my head to give my attention to Noctorno. "The rub?"

"Without vengeance to concentrate on..."

I understood him even if he left it at that, and I shifted my gaze back to the fire.

"Got all night, Franka," he told me. "Goin' to Apollo and Maddie's wedding in a few days, hangin' here, taking some time to be in a place not a lot of people from my world could hit for a vacation. So if you want me to pull the cord and get us more whiskey, just say the word."

He *was* kind.

Too kind.

"I wish for the bread and lovely cheese I consumed earlier to remain in my stomach, not be expressed onto the carpet," I told him.

"Think that's a good plan," he muttered.

I set my glass on the table and pushed out of my seat, looking down at him.

"I should find my bed and allow you to find yours."

He stood too, putting him nearly toe to toe with me.

I was a tall woman, unusually tall, and I found myself wondering if it was the same in his.

But he towered over me.

Suddenly, and in a strange way I found oddly enjoyable, I felt delicate.

Vulnerable.

He was closer than he'd been to Circe in the doorway to her bedchamber.

Thus he could easily lift his hand and sweep his thumb along my jaw.

"You gonna sleep?" he asked quietly, and I tore thoughts of his thumb on my jaw out of my mind, now feeling no joy but deep guilt for a disloyal thought so soon after I'd lost Antoine.

"Since I haven't done that well since he was taken, I doubt tonight will be any different, regardless of the whiskey," I answered.

"They got things you can take here, you know, that help you with that?" he asked.

"Are you referring to sleeping draughts?" I inquired.

"Probably," he answered.

"Yes," I said on a succinct nod. "However, I avoid them. There are those who use them who become dependent on them. I don't wish to hazard that."

"Good call, Franka. But one night? A couple?" He leaned infinitesimally closer. "I can see it in your eyes, babe, the shadows under them. I can see exactly how much you haven't been sleeping. Pull the cord, sweetheart. Get someone to bring you some. Get some good sleep. Yeah?"

Why he ended his statement with a "Yeah?" (another form of "yes" from his world) as if he was asking for my agreement when he'd uttered a command right before that (I gentle one, but one nonetheless), I had no idea.

What I did know was that my head was swimming from the drink, lack of sleep, the activities of the day, and regardless that I knew I wouldn't sleep, I was exhausted and had been exhausted, down to my bones, for months.

Further, I'd spent far too long in his intoxicating company already.

So I agreed by lying, "I'll pull the cord, Noctorno."

"Noc, babe," he corrected.

"Of course," I murmured.

"You want, I'm around, you're still around the next couple of days, I'll teach you Tetris," he offered.

I wanted to learn Tetris even though I had no idea what it was. I wanted him to show me everything his gadget could do.

I wanted to be in his soothing company where no games were played.

Where it was just him and me.

"I'll be leaving imminently."

He studied my face, sobered and nodded.

Inebriated or not, my mask was back in place, and Noctorno didn't miss it.

"I'll bid you goodnight," I said crisply, stepping back, dipping my chin into my neck and buckling my knees in a slight curtsy.

A slight curtsy.

To a commoner.

What was becoming of me?

"'Night, Franka."

I should thank him for the evening. Thank him for the words he said. Thank him for spending time with me when he could be with others that were better company.

I didn't do that.

I rose to my full height, gave myself the gift of one last look in his eyes, turned and swept from the room.

Once in the bed in said room I tossed.

And I turned.

Leaving my trusted lady's maid to her own slumber, I eventually got up and pulled the cord.

A servant brought me a sleeping draught.

It took some time to work.

But once I fell asleep, I slept for twelve hours.

2

THERE ARE NO SUCH THINGS AS HEROES

Franka

The next afternoon, following one of the royal guards, I strode sedately down the halls toward the queen's study.

I'd been summoned.

I'd had my bath, my hair arranged, my personal lady's maid, Josette, working miracles (as she normally did) doing the work of three maids quietly with no complaint and great talent.

I had never told her this, of course. Though I did pay her wages and they were more than others in her position, so I suspected she knew.

If I saw him again, I would also not tell Noctorno that I took his advice about the sleeping draught and now felt more refreshed than I had in months.

Further, I would not tell him that our conversation of the evening before had been most helpful.

It had not alleviated the pain or the guilt. However, it offered me ways to cope with, at least, the latter.

I had no idea why the queen was summoning me, but I hoped whatever it was didn't take too long. I'd had no food since my bread and cheese (and wine and whiskey) of the night before, and for the first time since Antoine was taken, I was famished.

I also needed quiet and concentration to plan my next steps, those being the ones I took after I visited Kristian to make certain he was healthy and well.

I followed the guard down the hallway thinking all of this as well as the fact I wished to be away from the Winter Palace as soon as I could.

I thought this because I simply wished to be away as soon as I could. It was never safe for me in Lunwyn. Every visit there was a risk.

But also, with the windows being boarded, no natural light could come in, and it made the Winter Palace, a normally beautiful dwelling, eerie in a way I did not like.

The guard stopped at the closed door to the queen's study, rapped on it sharply with his knuckles, waited for the command of, "Come," and I felt my lips curl with suppressed delight.

No queen had ever ruled Lunwyn.

Nor Hawkvale.

Nor Fleuridia or the city-state of Bellebryn. And certainly not any of the savage nations of the Southlands—Korwahk, Keenhak and Maroo.

Women did not rule.

And yet, when Aurora's Atticus, Lunwyn's king, had been murdered during hostilities some time past, the most powerful man in our country (that man, incidentally, was my cousin, Frey) installed his mother-in-law on the throne.

He did not do this as an act of nepotism.

He did this because Atticus was the king he was (a good one) mostly (to my way of thinking) due to the woman at his side.

Queen Aurora was savvy, watchful, deliberate and guarded as well as outwardly attractive and stately of demeanor.

All excellent qualities in a ruler.

It was not a surprise since her coronation that much news had come to me. News that shared she was excelling in her new role.

Our first queen.

Long may she reign.

Of course I thought this, but would never say it out loud.

No, when I followed the guard through the door, my smile died, and with ease born of decades of practice in order to face whatever was next, as I always did, I slipped one of my many masks into place.

This one: Loyal Subject.

As the guard stepped out of the way, in front of me I saw Queen Aurora's large desk. She sat behind it. Sitting atop and situated at the outer edge of the desk, closest to me, I distractedly noted that there were three chests, one rather small, one somewhat sizeable, one in between.

But this did not take but scant attention.

As ever, I needed to identify the players and act accordingly.

Therefore I saw surrounding Aurora on both sides were my cousin, Frey, and his wife, Princess Sjofn, or as Frey and all who knew her (that she felt affection for) called her, Finnie.

Close to Frey stood Apollo Ulfr, the queen's general and chief strategist.

At his side was Ilsa, though they called her Madeleine, the other-world woman who'd taken the place of Apollo's dead wife. Indeed, this Madeleine was going to do that two days hence in an official manner, becoming his actual wife.

I'd met his previous Ilsa prior to her expiring.

The women were the spitting image of each other.

I did not understand this, Apollo carrying on with this new Ilsa. It seemed sordid to me. Disrespectful of Ilsa's memory.

Even knowing there was another Antoine in the other world, I would never seek to go there to find him or bring the other him here to be with me.

There was no replacing him.

There was only one *true* Antoine.

However, it appeared Apollo held genuine affection for her.

He was a man of emotion. He'd grieved his wife openly and he'd done that for years.

But he was not a man ruled by emotion. He would never take to wife a woman who had not found her way into his heart.

This mattered naught to me.

One thing I had managed to decide that day during my bath, with my head refreshed and my thoughts clear, was that the concerns of others were no longer any concern of mine.

My life from that day forward would be quiet.

No more machinations.

No more intrigue.

This decision was Antoine's fault too. I knew it.

However, despite it not being my character, I couldn't stop myself from looking to a future such as that, perhaps not with relish as that future held no Antoine, but with a sense of serenity.

I thought this as I turned my head to take in the rest of the room.

On the other side of Finnie stood the mighty (and *large*) Dax of Korwahk, their king, Lahn, his Circe, and close to them stood Prince Noctorno and Princess Cora.

Taking him in, I found I wished I had the time to study Prince Noctorno more closely. But even with the brief glance I gave him, I noted the resemblance to the man who called himself Noc was uncanny.

Prince Noctorno of Hawkvale had a scar on his face that didn't mar but instead enhanced his features, which Noc did not have.

But that was the only difference.

As I came to a halt at the front of the desk, I sensed more and looked over my shoulder.

When I did, I felt an odd pang hit my belly.

Circe was sitting in an armchair (and it was more than disconcerting, though I'd never allow it to show, the present Ilsa looking like a dead Ilsa, two of the same Circes and two of the same Noctornos in that room).

Noc was standing beside her, leaning into her chair in a way that made me question my read of the situation the evening before.

It seemed with the way he appeared now that what they'd had was not a tryst.

His position, the closeness of it, would suggest something else.

That odd pang came again, stronger, when I saw he was regarding me, a look of familiarity on his face, warmth in his eyes.

He was the only one in the room who was showing even a modicum of cordiality. The rest were regarding me with unconcealed impatience (even if I had just that moment arrived) and even (in the case of Frey and Apollo), dislike.

It wasn't cordiality Noc was displaying, however.

It was friendliness.

It took me off guard, mostly because, outside my friend Valeria, the only true friend I had in the Drakkar House (or anywhere), no one looked on me with friendliness.

"It's good you were able to rise from your bed. Or Sjofn's bed, as the Winter Palace is the home of Lunwyn's Ice Princess."

Queen Aurora's cool greeting turned my attention back to her.

I didn't trouble myself with a reply.

It was not lost on me that my behavior (in more than being forced to turn traitor against my country, indeed an adulthood (and then some) of behaving precisely like a Drakkar) had earned me this kind of enmity.

Any other person, even our queen (who rarely showed any emotion) would be aware of all they'd lost, all they'd suffered, all they'd known Antoine had suffered, and thus she would deduce sleep would not have been easy.

Indeed, by the gods, day in, day out, simply finding the strength to throw my legs over the side of the bed and face another day plagued with the pain was an extraordinary endeavor.

But I had not earned that regard.

I had earned the frosty look in her eyes that accompanied the chill in her voice.

And as ever, I withstood it, but this time, I had no venomous rejoinder.

I just stood there silently.

"In order to save you the energy of making your play, Franka," she continued. "And as we've all got much more important things to move on to, we've discussed recompense for your activities of yesterday and we're seeing about doling that out without delay."

I stood silent, but inside I went still.

How much I had changed.

Even playing my small part in saving the world, it hadn't occurred to me to use that happenstance to better my circumstances. Prior to Antoine, this very thought would be the first thing on my lips before I'd actually go to Spectre Isle to face the three most evil, most powerful witches in our entire hemisphere.

I'm not slipping, Antoine, my love, I thought in horror. *I've lost it completely!*

Queen Aurora swept out a hand slightly to her right, indicating the small chest on her desk.

"Lunwyn's Sjofn ice diamonds," she declared, and I felt my knees lock.

Even that size chest, filled with Lunwyn's highly sought after ice diamonds, was not a small fortune.

It was a magnificent one.

"This from Lunwyn, as thanks," Aurora uttered her last word as if it was difficult for her to say. She then gestured to the largest chest that lay in the middle of the three. "Korwahk emeralds, rubies and sapphires."

By the gods!

It took grave effort not to allow my eyes to widen.

"From the Dax," she turned her head toward King Lahn and Queen Circe and tipped it their way, "his Dahksahna and the people of Korwahk, in gratitude." She looked back to me and indicated the last chest. "Gold coin, in appreciation of your efforts from King Ludlum of Hawkvale, his son, Prince Noctorno, ruler of Bellebryn, and, of course," a small amount of warm infused her features as she looked to Princess Cora, "his princess."

I turned my gaze their way and saw distaste in Prince Noctorno's eyes, eyes that were on me.

Princess Cora, however, was studying me as if I was a curiosity.

"And last, from the House of Ulfr," Queen Aurora went on, and I looked back to her to see she had her arm straight out. I turned my attention to where she was indicating, directing it at one of the chairs that sat in front of her desk, a chair that was piled high with luxurious pelts, "sable, chinchilla and mink, the finest, of course, as they're Ulfr."

My eyes moved from the dizzying spectacle of that beauty back to my country's queen as she kept speaking.

"As I know you, Franka, I can safely assume, for your part in the difficulties that played out yesterday, this will be enough. I do hope you consider this a debt fully paid."

The coin from Hawkvale alone, I could tell from the size of the chest, was more than enough.

This more than enough being the fact that I could live on that quite well (in other words, get Josette a much-needed assistant for the care of my person and belongings). I could also get far better appointed apartments in Fleuridia (or wherever I chose to go). Further, I could have not only a butler, a cook and two lady's maids (all that I already had in Fleuridia, save the second lady's maid) with help coming in every two weeks to clean and tidy, I could hire an actual house maid on staff who'd clean and tidy every day.

By Adele, I could hire fifty if I wished!

With the riches that lay before me (and on the seat beside me), I could live in extreme luxury until I took my last breath.

More, I could share them with Kristian. He could then be safe from the House of Drakkar, independent, his own man. He could make his wife safe, his son. He, through me, could make them *all* safe from the secrets that had plagued us since we were children.

Indeed, if he had a mind to, he could take them away. He could even go live in a realm across the Green Sea where nothing could touch them.

Nothing.

No one.

Not even magic (maybe).

This, I would share with him. He listened to me. I'd heard things about those realms. There was great beauty in the countries of Airen, Firenze, Wodell.

Perhaps I'd go with my brother and his family.

And yet, as these thoughts raced through my mind—along with feeling the sensation of relief, the knowledge that I no longer had to connive and manipulate to obtain the lifestyle to which I was accustomed, the understanding I could make my brother and his family safe with a finality that would mean decades of worry would disappear—I tasted a sourness in my mouth.

I do hope you consider this a debt fully paid.

Were they showering Noctorno and Circe with riches for the parts they'd played?

Or was it simply me they wished to pay off for they thought (due to my own actions over the years, it must be said) it would be expected.

"And I do hope this extraordinary show of generosity," Queen Aurora carried on, "will mean that you feel yourself well taken care of and we will find there is some time, *a great deal of it*, before we're again in your company."

They might be showering Noctorno and Circe with riches.

But they were showering me with them to be rid of me.

For good.

The queen studied me, and I endured her scrutiny even as I tried to understand what I was sensing in the room.

I knew I had everyone's attention. However, it seemed far keener than this insignificant chore would need. The magnitude of the offering was astounding. But the chore of being done with me surely was felt by all (save Noc) as insignificant.

And yet I sensed they were all watching me closely.

I didn't like the feeling. It seemed dangerous.

And in a room filled with people who either disliked me greatly or didn't think much of me, that danger was considerable.

I knew that kind of danger.

And I knew the play that had to be made when I found myself in it.

I needed to retreat immediately.

"My gratitude, your grace," I said quietly. "May I beg the favor of a servant to carry these generous gifts to my rooms?"

"I appreciate you voiced this request, as you haven't seemed to concern yourself with ordering about servants who've been scuttling around the Palace now for weeks preparing for the Bitter Gales, not to mention after the rather dire and miraculous events that occurred yesterday, in order for them to cater to your whims," Queen Aurora returned.

I fought my back snapping straight.

That was not cold.

It was spiteful.

Any guest in this palace would not hesitate to do the same.

And I'd ordered wine, bread, cheese and a fire. Noc had ordered the blasted whiskey.

Oh, and I'd asked for a sleeping draught and a bath to be brought up that morning.

But that was all.

I hadn't even requested breakfast.

"But, yes," Aurora went on to answer my request. "We'll see they're safely delivered to your rooms immediately. Now, can I further offer the services of the palace staff to assist you in packing and being certain the horses are put to your sleigh so that it's waiting for you early on the morrow?"

In other words, *get out*.

I didn't fight back lifting my chin a smidge. "Yes. You may. And I would be grateful."

"Excellent," she murmured, casting her eyes to her daughter (who was not her daughter), somehow communicating at the same time she was casting me out of her mind.

I was to leave.

Immediately.

I did not bow or drop into even a slight curtsy, although this was a considerable breach of protocol.

I'd been dismissed.

Therefore I turned to leave.

"As I said," I heard Frey mutter.

Apollo's words came right after. "Yes, Franka Drakkar would never do something for naught."

I heard this, but it was what I was feeling coming from Noc that made my gaze shift to him.

And the pang came back, ten times the strength, searing a swath of pain through my middle as I saw disappointment and even mild aversion in his eyes as he watched me move through the room.

Looking at him, I knew. I knew he'd told them of our time together last night. He'd likely shared he thought more of me than they ever would.

Undoubtedly, this was met with incredulity.

Or, perchance, hilarity.

But I knew he'd also told them I would not accept remuneration for the part I'd played in saving my universe.

Or, perhaps, not that extraordinary amount.

And I knew just looking at him, looking at the carefully blank expression on Circe's face, which I caught when I cast a swift downward glance in her direction, that they may have been offered their rewards.

But they'd declined, or at the very least eschewed such extravagance.

They'd done what they'd done out of care and concern. They'd put their lives at risk because it was the right thing to do.

They'd done it because they were good, kind people right down to their bones.

Unlike me.

I'd been born with the black soul of a Drakkar and no matter how hard Antoine had worked to cleanse it, it would forever remain midnight.

"As you said, Noctorno," I spoke haughtily, looking right in his eyes as I kept moving toward the door, "there are no such things as heroes."

Except, I thought but did not say, *you*.

And with that, I pulled my gaze from his, kept my head lifted and swept out of the room.

~

Valentine

"SHE IS NOT A GOOD PERSON," Lavinia declared.

"Mm..." Valentine murmured, her attention aimed at the large sphere sitting on its emerald-green velvet pillow on the table between Valentine and her fellow witch.

"I can understand your fascination with her, my friend, she's quite fascinating. As a snake lying coiled in the sun would be fascinating. But get too close, the snake strikes."

Valentine lifted her hand to her crystal ball, twisted her wrist and skimmed the blood-red tips of her fingers across the cool glass.

The image in it of Franka Drakkar walking with head held high from the queen's study drifted away in a mist of green smoke.

She looked up to Lavinia.

"There's more to that one," she stated.

"I'm uncertain you wish to discover it," Lavinia returned.

Valentine wasn't uncertain.

"Perhaps you forget," Valentine returned, "the rose grows amongst thorns."

"This is true," Lavinia retorted, "and I have not had any direct dealings with the woman, but I've heard much. So much, it indicates not only is Franka Drakkar a thorn, her particular thorn is dipped in poison."

Valentine studied her friend and wondered if she didn't sense it.

Lavinia was nowhere near as powerful as Valentine was.

However, she held great power. She should be able to sense it.

Where she sat across from Lavinia in the warm comfort of her rooms in the palace, she asked, "Do you not sense it?"

"I sense it," Lavinia replied.

As Valentine thought.

"Unusual in your world, no?" Valentine asked.

"Unusual and unlawful," Lavinia replied shortly.

Yes, from what Valentine had learned, it was.

Intriguing.

Valentine's gaze drifted back to her crystal as she purred, "Hmm..."

"The only reason I like that look on your face, Valentine, is because I sense your interest in Franka Drakkar will mean you will not leave our world as you'd planned after Apollo and Maddie's wedding. I enjoy your company. Over the last months, I prayed to the gods our troubles would end without too much destruction and heartache. But with the fondness I hold for you, I still faced the end of those troubles with a heavy heart for I knew it would take you away, for there would no longer be any reason for you to come back. Therefore, even if the reason you'd stay, or return, is Franka Drakkar, I'll take it."

Valentine nodded, touched in spite of herself at Lavinia's words.

Valentine made a habit of not connecting with mere mortals. Not that she was a goddess, but she was also no mere mortal. This, a habit she'd broken of late, precisely when she'd started dabbling in travel between the worlds, her own and the women she'd brought here.

"No, indeed, I do believe things will continue to be interesting in this world," she raised her eyes to Lavinia. "The *good* kind of interesting this time."

Lavinia shook her head, a smile playing at her mouth, and Valentine knew if she didn't feel it was beneath her, she would have rolled her eyes.

Valentine felt her lips curl at her friend's reaction, but her thoughts strayed.

There had been much that had happened over the last years in this universe. It took a great deal of attention. So it wasn't a surprise that the few people she knew in this world, most of them quite clever, had not taken the time to scratch under the surface of Franka Drakkar.

The truth of the matter was Valentine would have been interested in her even if she was as vile as they all thought she was.

In this world, much more than Valentine's own (even though it was still prevalent in her own, irritatingly), a woman had very little power.

In this world, she had to rely solely on her cunning and wits, her looks, her sexuality, anything at her disposal, in order to get what she needed, grasp hold of what she wanted, wield as much power as she could amass.

These were not weak weapons in any arsenal, a woman's or a man's.

It was just, for some reason Valentine didn't understand, the organ swinging between a man's legs put him at an advantage.

In this world, where wars were still fought with swords, bows and arrows, it was understandable physical strength was valued.

Understandable but still unacceptable, as the successful reign of Queen Aurora would attest.

And from what Valentine knew, Franka Drakkar enjoyed a good life with no paid occupation, traveling the Northlands, flitting from ball to ball in fine dresses, wreaking havoc as sport as she injected her venom, her aim so true there were many who actually feared her.

Yes, Valentine found Franka Drakkar very interesting.

She had business to attend to, amongst other, more intimate needs to be met, at home. Those intimate needs she hadn't seen to in a long time.

She needed to return to New Orleans, see to that business, then spirit back for the wedding.

She was in the mood to do a little scratching, dig beneath the surface.

And it was what lay under the skin of Franka Drakkar that she wished to discover.

Noc

"You're brooding."

"I'm not brooding."

"You're totally brooding."

"Who even *says* brooding?"

"They do here."

Noc scowled at Cora.

Princess Cora, to be precise. Her twin was an evil and now a dead one, a casualty of yesterday's dramas, and not a big loss.

Her body had been spirited to her parents in Hawkvale.

Fucking *spirited.*

Apparently they grieved.

But they were the only ones.

Jesus, this place was fucking crazy.

It was also crazy interesting.

But it was still fucking crazy.

The woman sitting next to him had to seriously love her man to give up their world to live in what seemed to Noc like a Renaissance Festival run amuck. A really good one. But with all that snow outside, a really *cold* one.

Though Cora had told him Bellebryn, where she lived, was much farther south and had a different climate.

"We have weather like Florida. Cool winters, warm summers, sunshiny days," she'd said then shot him a huge smile. "Without the humidity, which makes it totally perfect."

Noc shook himself out of his thoughts and carried on the conversation.

"She's not that girl," he stated as to the reason of why he was "brooding."

Cora's beautiful face got even more beautiful when she openly showed her concern.

"I don't know her, but from what Frey and Apollo say, she is, as in she *really* is," she replied. "And Maddie told me the story of what she'd said to her, right to her face, and, Noc, it was *not* nice."

"It's an act, Cora. All a big show," he told her.

"Maybe so, but if it is, from what I've heard, it's a good one." She leaned his way where she was sitting beside him at the dinner table. "And Noc, okay, she helped save the world. That was a big deal. But Frey explained to you what they gave her in the queen's study. In our world value, it's worth millions." She leaned closer. "Maybe even billions. No joke."

"She put her ass on the line, babe," he returned. "And maybe she needs it."

"Perhaps the furs, some coin." She shook her head, moving away and tipping her eyes back to her plate. "But all that?" She kept shaking her head, speared a buttered, herbed new potato and looked back at him. "She's a member of a House. In Lunwyn, they take care of each other in aristocratic families. She'll have an allowance. And that allowance will be handsome. You can't know this, but her clothes are of superb quality. She clearly has more than one maid, the way she's tended to. She wasn't hurting before. Her taking all that, well, I don't need to know her to know it's greedy, Noc."

"I'm a cop, Cora, I read people for a living. And I'm tellin' you, that woman who walked into that room today is not the woman that woman is."

"I know," she muttered, lifting the potato to her mouth. "You told us all that before she showed."

She ate the potato, and Noc looked to his own plate to spear one too, because this world might be crazy, but they had great food, and he didn't know how those potatoes were made, but they fucking rocked.

"Maybe she was, I don't know...playing you," Cora suggested softly.

Noc turned his eyes to her. "I don't get played."

"From what I hear, she's a master."

"I don't get played," he repeated.

"Okay, then maybe she's more likeable when she's drunk," Cora tried.

Noc chewed and swallowed his potato then turned fully to the gorgeous princess at his side, his dinner partner, as Cora explained, something that was important in any seating arrangement in this world.

Crazy.

"There's more to that woman than meets the eye," he stated.

Her head twitched. "Are you...I mean, I thought...uh, well, you know, you and Circe seem like...are you...do you...?"

He put her out of her misery by sharing, "Circe and me, that was what it was, and what it was was between us. She's an amazing woman. We'll keep in touch when we go back to our world. But she doesn't want that and I'm not looking for it either. We both knew that going in. We both knew what we wanted going in. We both got that. And that part's done."

"I don't actually get any of that," she admitted.

Noc gave her a grin that he hoped took any sting out of his next words. "Not yours to get, babe. That's what I'm tryin' to say."

"Right," she replied.

"And straight up, different time, different world, I'd be into Franka," he glanced up at Cora's phenomenal, thick, shining, dark-brown hair, looked back to her and winked. "She's my type."

And she was.

He'd dated gold, and Circe was a blonde.

But he knew the one he'd pick in the end would be a brunette.

Cora had great hair, but Franka's was even more thick and shining and a deeper, richer brown.

Not to mention the woman's eyes were fucking amazing. That deep blue. Goddamned gorgeous.

She also had a beautiful neck.

No, not beautiful.

Slim.

Delicate.

Elegant.

But it was her mouth that drew him. She was what a cosmetic surgeon would use to create a million different sets of lips. Pink. Full. They looked soft, even pillowy.

Noc had to admit it'd suck, leaving this world and not being able to put his mouth to those lips.

But he was not going to kiss those lips.

He wasn't about to get in deep with a woman from this world and he knew himself; the way she looked, her manner, the way she was both before and after they got drunk last night, she'd draw him in.

But he'd already done that and it got his ass in a sling in a variety of ways, including him being magicked to a parallel universe, dropped onto some remote island in order to face down three witches who wanted to take over the world and wouldn't have hesitated to wave their wands or snap their fingers (or whatever witches did) and waste him like blowing out a match.

He wasn't going to go there with Franka.

That was why he knew they were all wrong about her.

It wasn't her playing him. It wasn't her being drunk.

It was that she loved the man who'd been killed by those witches and she'd done it deeply.

The woman they all described didn't feel anything deep, except for herself.

But the pain behind those blue eyes of hers, she could try to hide it, but it was so immense, that was impossible.

The thing was, Noc didn't get why he cared so much what they thought.

They'd talked about how much they were giving her, doing this way overkill because they wanted rid of her for good and sneered at the fact she'd take it.

He'd told them she wouldn't, and the way they'd been when they disagreed was not ugly or mean, just definite.

Then she'd taken it.

He was not that guy who always had to be right and he'd only spent a few hours with the woman.

But he'd felt like she'd personally slapped him in the face when she'd accepted all that treasure from Queen Aurora. He'd been certain, and shared it with Frey and Apollo, after their time drinking whiskey, after she'd admitted how she felt guilt about what she'd done to betray her country, she'd decline.

He didn't feel like the asshole who had lost a bet. That moron who was in the position to take the hit of *I told you so.*

He'd felt like she'd betrayed *him* by not being who he was certain she was by doing what he was sure she wouldn't do.

All of this meant it was probably good she was leaving tomorrow.

First, she needed to get away from folks who didn't like her and didn't mind in the slightest sharing that with her. No one needed that.

And second, Noc needed her away from him.

He was going to go to Apollo and Maddie's wedding.

After that, he was going to sail with Frey and Finnie as they took Cora and Tor back to Bellebryn.

When they'd offered him his own chests of jewels and gold, he'd bartered instead for that. A few months in this world, taking it in, seeing as much of it as he could see.

Before he'd come here, discussing his involvement with Valentine, he'd already put in notice at work.

And then Valentine had assured him she would find him a position in New Orleans and he was all for that. A big adventure where he didn't have to worry about reporting for duty, any cases he'd left open, nothing.

Then afterward, a new place, new job, new start.

And the good news was, Circe would be there because she lived in New Orleans, so he'd have someone to hang with.

Valentine lived there too, but Noc didn't see that woman hanging with anyone. Though he suspected if they found a place that made good martinis, she might stoop to throw a couple back with them.

Queen Aurora (and Frey, and when Noc kept refusing, the kicker, Cora) had insisted he take a small bag of those ice diamonds and a small chest of gold. And with his adventure in this crazy place, that was all he needed. More than he needed (Circe had taken more, but she'd had a seriously fucked-up life, was trying to make a go of it in NOLA as an office manager of a towing company, and after all she'd had done to her, she deserved some cush and the means to spoil herself).

And that was what he was going to get, what he was going to do, what was up next for Noc.

The beautiful, but grieving, Franka Drakkar with her pretty mouth didn't factor.

"So she's your type," Cora said, taking him back into their conversation, "But you're not gonna go there."

Noc shook his head. "She's from here, I'm from home. I'm *going* home. But it isn't even about that, babe. Tor got you back. Frey got Finnie back. Won't go on because you were there, you know. Franka didn't get her man back."

"Don't say that in front of Apollo," she whispered. "Maddie suggested that and it pisses him off. He thinks she's incapable of any emotion, much less love."

"You four couples aren't the only ones who've known love, Cora," he returned. "Not bein' a dick, but that's the way it is. And she's stone cold on the outside, babe, but inside the woman is in some serious pain. She's capable of emotion, just like you and me, and I know that because I saw it."

What he didn't share was that Franka Drakkar might be capable of more of it, with the pain he saw in her eyes, the guilt that seemed to visibly weigh on her at what she'd done.

She just, for some reason, wouldn't allow herself to let it show, even maybe fully feel it.

That reason was a mystery and Noc was a cop. Cops were big on mysteries. Solving them, to be precise.

Fuck.

Another reason he had to steer clear of Franka Drakkar.

Cora nodded. "I think your perception of her is right, at least the way she is with you, for whatever reason she gave you that particular Franka. What concerns me, honey, is that it seems to mean so much to you."

That was what concerned him too.

"Woman's in pain, she gave me that, she gave me time," he tried to explain it. "Tomorrow, she'll be gone and eventually she'll be just another memory of this place. But you spend hours with a woman drinking whiskey and watching her face light up, the pain she's trying to hide clearing clean away because she's never seen a phone before. We'll just say that'll be a memory I won't forget."

"I'll bet," Cora replied, the concern shifting out of her expression, understanding replacing it.

Noc grabbed his knife and started cutting into the tender, moist, perfectly-cooked steak on his plate.

Cora changed the subject.

"I can't wait to show you my world, Noc. It's gonna be *awesome*. You're gonna *love it*."

He looked to her, meat in his mouth, and chewing and smiling he said, "Can't wait either, babe."

Her face lit up too.

And seeing it, Noc knew that'd be another memory he wouldn't forget that he'd take home from this crazy world.

There it was.

They were having dinner and Franka wasn't invited.

Tomorrow morning, she'd be leaving.

So she was a memory of this world.

A mysterious one.

A sad one.

But just a memory.

And Noc had to live with that.

What he wouldn't admit was that he didn't like it.

3
ENDURE

Franka

I sat curled in an armchair by the fire in my room wearing my silk nightgown, my lacy-knit wool shawl held tight around my bared shoulders, staring at the fire, thinking that Kristian's home was an eight-day sleigh ride from Fyngaard, where the Winter Palace was located.

A long, cold ride for me and Josette, but as much as I wished to get to my brother, I would savor it, for it would likely be the last time I'd sled over my Lunwyn.

Over a lonely day and a lonely dinner, I'd made my decision.

I was going to Airen, across the Green Sea. I'd heard the sky city was marvelous. Dark and austere, but it opened onto a bay with stunning views, and the Sky Citadel was made of the glinting black stone that could only be found on that continent, but I'd heard it was extraordinary.

And I'd heard Firenze had barely taken its first steps into the civilized world, but their city of fire, and the barbarians who lived there, might be to my taste, if only to see one (or several).

Not to mention, there was the magical sisterhood of the Nadirii, who lived shrouded by enchantments, a warrior class of women who dwelled solely amongst their own, using males only for purposes of procreation...and pleasure.

I was no warrior. But I had other attributes and no need for male companionship. Not anymore. I'd never been good at being a member of the sisterhood.

But facing a new life and new adventures, it was worth a try. Perhaps they'd allow me behind their enchantments.

Therefore, even if I couldn't talk Kristian into going with me, I was going.

And perhaps I could find a way to dull the pain through adventure.

Before I left, however, I'd give my brother plenty of jewels and coin to make him safe. He loved his wife, his son. He might not be as sharp-witted as most of the Drakkars (a boon for him, for without that sharp wit he also did not have sharp claws, and that was something of a lovable anomaly for our House—none of this, of course, I'd ever told him, or ever would), but he'd definitely desire to have the means to keep his family safe.

I'd sent a bird to share I was arriving so he'd know and could prepare.

I just hoped the bird made it.

I didn't like communicating by bird. It obviously took much less time to do so than sending post by land or sea. But it was easy to intercept a bird, or other things befell the creatures, and half the time they didn't make it to their destination.

And alas, for Kristian, after what had befallen him when he'd helped me with my traitorous plans, my arrival would not be a pleasant surprise.

Therefore, I decided to send another bird prior to my departure in the morning, just in case.

The door to my dressing room opened and Josette moved through it.

"All's packed and ready for our departure on the morn, milady," she said, walking toward me.

"Thank you, Josette," I replied.

She stopped several feet in front of me. "Is there anything you need?"

I shook my head, turning my attention back to the fire. "No. You may seek your bed."

To my surprise, moments passed and I didn't feel her presence leave.

I turned back to her.

"Is there more?" I asked.

"He's alone, back in the morning room."

I knew to whom she was referring and at the thought I felt a warmth hit my belly at the same time a cold chill slid over my skin.

"I think...well, milady," she went on nervously, "I think he might be there waiting for you."

Providing Josette with an elevated salary was not only because she was very good at doing what she did. It also didn't solely have to do with the fact she did the job of three lady's maids.

It was because no one knew what was happening in a house better than the servants.

For years, Josette had been my eyes and ears in places I'd never be privy, providing information I'd never have without her, much of it of great use.

She was not the only lady's maid who offered these services. Indeed, I suspected they all did if they were any good at their jobs.

But she made a point of ascertaining all I might need to know (and some I didn't but it didn't hurt to hold the knowledge) and sharing it with me.

Yes, she earned her elevated salary in a number of ways.

Therefore, it was not surprising that, even though I didn't share with my maid what had transpired with Noc the night before, she would know.

However, now, as I gazed up at her, I did not see the usual. A petite, pretty, plump, ash-blonde girl with blank, hazel eyes looking down at me and awaiting my response because she was doing her job.

I saw a pretty girl with kindness and concern in her hazel eyes, looking down on me, knowing all I'd lost and that I had not one single true friend in the world.

That look only made me feel warmth.

Touch her hand, mon ange, *show her what her compassion means to you.*

Antoine's voice sounding in my head made me blink and lose focus.

"Lady Franka," Josette called, and I forced my attention from waiting to hear more in my head from my dead lover to my maid. "I'm happy to assist you back into your gown."

Noc sitting alone in the morning room very well might mean he was waiting for me. That he'd enjoyed our time together (which I knew he did). That he wanted more before I was to leave.

Or perhaps it meant he wanted an explanation of what transpired earlier in the queen's study.

Either way (especially the latter), I would not go to him.

It would be better he leave this world when he eventually did with nary a memory of Franka Drakkar of the midnight soul.

It was better anyone was not touched by that blackened spirit.

Now I'm just feeling sorry for myself, which is dire as well as boring, I thought.

What I said to Josette was, "We have a long ride ahead of us on the morrow. We should both get a good night's rest."

She looked disappointed before she covered her expression and nodded.

"Would you like another sleeping draught?" she inquired.

I didn't need to sleep twelve hours again (although I actually did). I needed to be up, as I'd instructed Josette to wake me, at half past five so we could see to my toilette and be away before the palace woke and became bustling. This meaning (I hoped) we'd be away without running into anyone I didn't wish to see.

And one of those primary "anyones" was Noctorno Hawthorne of the other world.

Therefore I shook my head.

Josette nodded again and she seemed to be moving to leave before she hesitated and turned back to me.

"You'll sleep?" she pressed.

I studied her, noting she couldn't quite hide her feelings of worry...for me.

Thus I continued studying her, thinking, *Gods, did she actually like me?*

I'd never been cruel to her. I'd never been overtly kind. I respected her talents, demonstrated that in more ways than monetarily, but never told her so.

Perhaps that was just her way. I wouldn't know, for outside her sharing gossip while she was attiring me or doing my hair, or I was giving her orders, we didn't speak very much. But there were many, for reasons unfathomable, who were thoughtful and benevolent to just about anybody.

It appeared my maid was one of those many.

I didn't know what to do with this. Outside Antoine—and Kristian when I allowed him to do so—no one had ever shown concern for me.

Or kindness.

Not in my life.

"Yes, Josette, I'll sleep," I felt safe in assuring her.

To my surprise at this juncture I endured my lady's maid studying *me*, seemingly to determine if I spoke truth, before it became clear she approved of what she saw. When she did, she nodded again and made her move to leave, this time following through.

"Goodnight, Lady Franka," she said as she walked to the dressing room door.

"Goodnight, Josette," I replied and watched her open the door, move through it, but she gave me one last, long look before she closed it behind her.

The instant I heard it click, I turned back to the fire and whispered, "Antoine, are you there?"

I waited. I listened.

I heard nothing. I felt nothing.

I studied the flames dancing in their grate and came to the understanding Antoine was not coming to me as a spirit to keep me company in the only way he could.

It was just my conscience.

Gods, my conscience came to me in Antoine's voice.

I supposed it would considering I'd never had one before him.

I sighed and uncurled my legs from under me, putting my bare feet to the thick rugs on the floor.

The morrow heralded the beginning of an eight-day ride to my brother through cold and snow.

Even though it might be, after having had a good sleep the night before, having been given chests of gold and jewels, new trunks filled with the finest furs, the safety wealth provided me, a plan for the coming days, months, years, that I would sleep, I was not counting on it.

So I might as well get down to it.

Whether it bring victory...

Or what I'd grown accustomed to.

Defeat.

ATTEND YOUR FATHER.

The hiss sounded in my ear and my eyes flew open.

I saw nothing but a dark room cut only by the faint dancing of firelight from the grate.

Attend your father!

Oh no.

Gods no.

I shot up to sitting and threw the covers off me, my gaze darting through the room.

She wouldn't come to the Winter Palace. She'd *never* come to the Winter Palace.

But *he* would.

He most definitely would.

He did whatever he wished.

And she did whatever she had to to make that so.

Thus, worse, she'd make it safe so he *could.*

The buttery at the end of the hall off the kitchens, the voice instructed.

I felt the snake of panic and fear coil up my throat, but I didn't even waste the time to snatch my shawl from the end of the bed after I jumped out of it and hurried to the door.

I just asked the room, "Do you have him?"

I'm near.

Oh gods. Gods.

Never safe. Even with trunks of jewels and gold I was never safe.

And worse, neither was Kristian.

"I'm going to him directly. Let Kristian be," I demanded as I put my hand to the doorknob.

Accept your punishment, endure the length of it, and your brother will be safe, the voice replied.

At what I knew was to come, I felt saliva fill my mouth and swallowed it down as I pulled open the door.

The hall was lit with lantern sconces on the walls, but faintly. Hesitating only a second, I made the decision to seek the servants' stairs, a more direct route and one where I was sure not to run into one of my kind. I had no idea where those stairs were but moved instinctively away from the main stairwell to the back of the hall.

I found them and rushed down the flights. The light even more dim there, I held on to the banister to guide my way, my bare feet making no noise on the risers.

I made the kitchens, shifting through the barely-illuminated, deserted area on darting feet, this being an area I'd been made familiar with during Frey's first interrogation of me after a woman was poisoned at a past Bitter Gales.

I found the door at the end of the hall closed. Even knowing what lay beyond, I hesitated not even a second in opening it.

This room was lit brightly, blinding me the instant I stepped through.

I struggled to become accustomed to the light as I swiftly closed the door behind me.

Too soon, my eyes adjusted and I saw him. Standing tall and strong amongst the casks and shelves of bottles, the Drakkar good looks stamped on his proud features, even through age.

"Papa," I whispered, fighting the shiver seeing him caused to slither over my skin.

It had been years.

But I was never safe. I knew I was never safe. Not in Lunwyn.

Her magic didn't reach Fleuridia. And thus I counted on the fact it definitely wouldn't reach the realms across the Green Sea.

But in Lunwyn, I knew, *knew* I was never safe.

"You and your brother have behaved very badly, Franka," my father declared.

"I—" I started to explain.

"*Silence!*" he barked, leaning toward me, and as used to it as I was, the verbal strike of his loud word still made my body lurch in surprise and fear.

It was then I saw the lash coiled in his grip.

I didn't take a step back. I never did. Weakness was not tolerated. I'd learned. I'd learned if I showed weakness, Kristian received the punishment and it would be twice as bad.

He could not endure it. We'd discovered that when we were children in a way so heinous, I buried it so deep I couldn't even remember it, just the feelings it caused.

But we'd learned.

Kristian broke. He did it easily.

Soft heart. Weak will.

Thus I had to endure it. Every last strike. If I broke, they'd turn to Kristian and wouldn't stop until the blood flowed in streams down his legs while he hung unconscious, receiving his punishment through oblivion.

"What have you done to our House, Franka?" my father asked, but didn't allow me to answer. He continued on, "The mighty House of Drakkar could have been brought down to nothing, and *would have* if this generation didn't see the resurgence of The Frey within The Drakkar."

How had he heard?

"Please, Papa, if you'd allow me to—" I began.

"There's no explanation for *treason*," he bit out.

Gods! *How had he heard?*

"Papa, if you'll let me share. I assisted Frey and the others with—"

"You," he interrupted me, "are at least a Drakkar. Headstrong. Whip-sharp. I can imagine you have a reason for what you did, though I don't bloody give a damn what it was. Your brother, however, had no reason. None at all. Except to do as you told him. Always minding you, like a brainless pup. It's revolting," he spat his last, the expression twisting his face sharing just how revolting he thought his son was. "I wished to punish him. Your mother, though, she has a soft spot for that boy. So I'm here."

I was uncertain my mother had anything soft about her. In my estimation, it was less her caring for Kristian and more the enjoyment she got from inflicting pain on me.

"The hook is ready, Franka. Prepare and make your way to it," he ordered.

I cast a glance to my right and up, seeing the hook was indeed ready, as in times like these, it always was.

But I didn't prepare and move to it.

I looked back to my father.

"I endure, she leaves him alone," I stated.

That was the arrangement. It had always been the arrangement. And they had never reneged.

But there was a reason I carried a midnight soul, for the evil contained in both my parents set their souls to cinders years ago. It was not a wonder I'd inherited the blackness.

"You committed treason, daughter," my father reminded me.

"I endure, she leaves him alone," I repeated.

Panic threatened to paralyze me when I saw the cruel sneer curl at his mouth, the excitement light in his eyes, the same in the rush of pink to his cheeks.

He enjoyed this. I'd learned that as well. In the past, there needn't even be a transgression for Kristian or I to earn a punishment. No, our father simply had to be in the mood.

And to our misfortune, he was in the mood often.

"You endure, my daughter, she leaves him alone," he agreed.

But I knew by his expression. I knew my transgression, Kristian's, had earned a punishment even I might not be able to survive.

Regardless, I nodded. On shaking legs I focused all efforts on keeping me upright, I moved to the hook.

I was twelve when they'd stopped binding my wrists and hanging me from the hook. From that point, it was part of the punishment to keep my fingers curled around, hold myself up, not fall.

Never fall.

And tonight, I definitely could not fall.

When I arrived below the hook, I turned my back to my father and pulled the thin straps of my silk nightgown down my shoulders and arms. I felt the material drift down my skin to catch on my hips.

Bare up top, I took in a deep breath, closed my eyes tight then set my jaw.

I opened my eyes, lifted my hands and curled my fingers around the cold steel of the hook.

"I begin, my sweet," I heard my father say and knew he was communicating with my mother. A mother who was not there but could be in a blink if there weren't enchantments protecting the Winter Palace.

No, she was close to Kristian, ready to complete the punishment should I fall.

On that thought, my fingers gripped the hook tighter.

He did not delay in doing as he said he would.

The first lash I barely felt. Years of this, the scar tissue ran deep.

He would get there, though. He always did.

No, at that point it was the whip whistling through the air, the crack, the sinister whisper as it snaked against my flesh that could unravel my mind.

In order to fight it, I thought of Antoine. His smile. The sound of his laughter. The change in his eyes when I'd bare even an inch of flesh to him. The touch of his fingers as they drifted over my skin.

Another lash came and I kept hold of these thoughts.

Then another. And more.

But I'd closed my eyes and I saw only Antoine. Felt only Antoine's touch.

Until the first rivulet of blood glided over the upper swell of my hip to soak into the silk of my nightgown.

Then, suddenly, I saw Noc and the fierceness in his face when he'd said he wouldn't even blink at turning traitor to save the woman he loved.

The next lash came, and the next, the pain intensifying with each strike, but I focused on Noc and his fierceness, focused further on something alien to me.

Hope.

In this instance it was the hope that he found a woman he could love that much, but more, a woman worthy of that kind of love.

I kept this focus through the next lash.

And the next.

It continued and I could no longer think of Noc. Or Antoine. Or anything but keeping my hands curled around that hook, trying to block out the sweat of that effort mingling with the blood trailing down my body. Attempting to force my shallow panting into deeper breaths to beat back the pain. Blinking rapidly as dull cloudbursts exploded behind my eyes threatening to blind me, take me to a blissful, painless oblivion.

There was none of that for me. Not Franka Drakkar. I'd been born to agony, and as ever, simply had to endure.

More lashes and I feared I couldn't withstand it. It was worse than ever before. Far worse. As my transgression had been.

My hands had gone beyond clammy, they were slipping on the hook and I was terrified I'd lose hold.

I couldn't lose hold.

Mother was close to Kristian. She could be with him in seconds.

He'd *never* endure.

Another lash, and for the first time I cried out as it hit, tearing through my flesh, feeling like it glanced across my spine.

When it was done, my heated body all of a sudden iced over with fear that I'd lost consciousness when I heard the impossibility of a shocked feminine gasp and right on its heels an enraged, "Fucking hell. What the *fuck*?"

Noc's voice.

He couldn't be here. I had to have blacked out.

"Who are you?" my father asked.

"Get Frey," Noc's voice ordered.

"You'll do no such thing!" my father snapped, his deep voice no longer astonished but annoyed.

"Fucking *get Frey*!" Noc demanded.

"You'll mind your betters," my father hissed.

A moment of nothing before, "Goddamn...*get*...*Frey*."

The pain drove deep as I chanced looking over my shoulder and saw Josette disappear from the doorway.

I also saw Noc, fury carved in his handsome features, moving to me.

How was he there?

Why was he there?

The pain remained, I couldn't have slipped into oblivion.

Thus, he was bloody *there*.

"Know your place!" my father commanded on a near-shout. "Remove yourself from this room this instant!"

Noc didn't remove himself from the room. He arrived at my front, his eyes holding mine.

His voice came as a shock, precisely the gentleness running through it that belied the look of wrath seated deep in his eyes. "Let go of the hook, baby."

"This is beyond the pale, a servant intruding on private matters of members of the most powerful House in Lunwyn!" my father decreed loudly.

"Frannie, sweetheart," Noc whispered, ignoring Papa, and I felt his hand touch light at my waist, "let go of the hook."

"Intolerable!" my father bit out. "Franka, is this domestic your lover?" he demanded.

"No," I answered my father hoarsely. "You must go, Noc," I whispered to Noc, not wishing to whisper, but I had the strength for nothing more. "Please. You must. It will be worse if he doesn't get to finish. I need to complete my punishment."

A flare of rage blazed in his eyes, but he simply repeated, "Let go of the hook. Hold on to me."

"I need to endure or they'll turn to Kristian," I told him.

"Please, baby, let go. I got you," Noc replied.

"Stand back," my father ordered.

"You must go," I went on.

"Promise, Franka, I got you," Noc said.

"Stand bloody *back*!" my father commanded, his voice no longer affronted and annoyed.

No, it was much worse.

At the warning of it, sheer terror coursed through me, almost paralyzing.

"You *must* go," I declared. "*Now* or he'll—"

As I spoke my last, my father thundered, "*Stand back!*"

But through his thunder, I heard the whistle of the whip.

I knew he'd repositioned and I knew his aim.

It was not me.

Therefore I did what I did next automatically, without thinking. I did something I never did. Not since I was a youngster. Not since I'd learned how vile it was, what I had in me, what my mother gave to me, what I took great pains to hide, using intrigue and torment like weapons not only as was expected of a Drakkar, not only as a way to hold others at bay so they wouldn't be touched by the darkness of my soul, but as a way to conceal the true power I held.

I let go of the hook and twisted. Unable to bury my cry of pain when the fire of the movement seared through my back, I lifted a hand and swept it wide and high, the sapphire glow bursting forth, the tip of my father's lash glancing against it, sending it back where it tore through the skin of his face.

He fell back in surprise and pain, his feet slipping from under him, landing on his arse.

That would not mean good things for me.

But at least he'd not landed the whip on Noc.

"Holy fuck," Noc whispered.

I turned back to Noc urgently.

"You must go. I've done wrong. Kristian has done wrong. I must endure or they'll turn their attention to Kristian and he *won't* endure, Noc. He *won't*. And I must protect him."

"Franka, who the fuck is that guy?" Noc asked.

His look of shock barely penetrated when I answered, "My father. And I must complete the punishment. I *must*."

"Baby, this shit is whacked." He started to unbutton his shirt. "Let's get you covered. Frey can deal with him. Let's see if this place has a doc—"

I'd heard my father scramble up, felt his fury sparking the air, and I instantly lifted my hands to the hook, curling my fingers around.

"I'll endure," I announced to Papa. "Don't hurt Noc. I will not fall. Tell her. Tell her I'm still standing."

Noc's hand returned to my waist and curled in. "Baby—"

I looked in his eyes. "He'll break. Kristian will break. I must—"

"She's used her magic, Anneka," my father said from behind me and terror gripped me because I knew he was sharing this with my mother.

"No!" I cried. "Recommence! I will not fall!"

"Go to the boy," my father ordered.

Gods!

Kristian!

"*No!*" I shrieked.

"What the bloody hell?" Frey's voice came from the direction of the door.

I let go of the hook and whirled to my cousin.

Lifting my arms crossed in front of me to cover my bared breasts, I beseeched, "You must stop her! You must command the elves! You must bring the green witch! She's going to Kristian. He'll break. The green witch must go there and *stop her*."

Frey's face was a picture of disbelief and distress as he stood in the doorway staring at me, Josette cowering behind him.

"Explain what's happening," he bit out tightly.

"We need a doctor, Frey," Noc stated.

"She's committed treason and so has her brother. For that, she's being punished," Papa explained.

Frey turned to my father.

"And that punishment would come at the command of your queen if your daughter hadn't moved to make amends," Frey clipped, twisted at the waist and ground out to Josette, "Get Valentine. And find a bloody physician."

Josette nodded at the same time she turned and vanished from sight.

I rushed across the room to my cousin, curled a hand into his sweater at his chest and begged, "You must go. You must take Noc. If I withstand what he wishes to mete, they'll leave Kristian alone."

I was too deep in my state to notice my cousin for the first time in our lives addressing me gently.

"And how long has this been the understanding, Franka?"

I simply replied on a plea. "*Please*, Frey, let him finish."

Frey looked in my eyes but a moment before his went over my head.

"Cover her, Noc, and take her from here."

"No!" I cried as I felt careful hands on my shoulders pulling me from Frey.

The pain at my back was too immense to struggle so I didn't. I watched Frey look to my father.

"You're communicating with Anneka?" he asked.

"Family business is family business, Frey," my father returned.

Frey's tone deteriorated while Noc turned me to face him. I saw his chest bare and felt the agony of the whisper of material of his shirt hitting my back.

"Are you...*communicating with Anneka*?"

"I don't have to answer that," Father retorted.

"Kristian is more than a week's sled ride away. If she's taking guidance from you, that means you're a sorcerer or she's a witch. Either way, you or she are undeclared. Which is it?" Frey demanded.

"This is none of your concern, nephew," my father snapped.

I flinched as Frey roared, "*Which is it?*"

At this juncture, my tortured cry slashed through the room as Noc lifted me to cradle me in his arms.

"Sorry, Frannie, so sorry, baby," he cooed. "Stick with me. Hold on just a little longer until I can get you to a bed."

I battled the pain of his arm against the torn flesh of my back and looked into Noc's eyes. "He must finish."

Noc's face turned hard as he stated, "He's not gonna fuckin' finish."

"Noc—"

"Quiet, Frannie. Frey's got this."

I shook my head fervently as Frey moved out of our way and Noc took us toward the door. "No, you don't understand."

"No, sweetheart, *you* don't understand," Noc declared, striding through the door and into the hall. "They didn't get it. Now they'll get it. And, baby, that means you are no longer alone."

My panic overwhelming me, I barely heard a word he said as we moved down the hall.

I shifted my gaze over his shoulder toward the door, hearing Frey demand on an enraged bellow, "Talk, Nils. *Now*!"

But that was all I heard as Noc quickly carried me down the passageway.

"This isn't good," I whispered.

"It's gonna be fine," Noc assured.

I closed my eyes tight. "You don't know."

"What on...?"

This was a female voice, and I opened my eyes and turned my head to see the green witch rushing toward us.

"Frey needs you," Noc grunted, not pausing a step, meaning Valentine needed to jump to the side as he forged right ahead, passing her. "Room at the back," he finished.

I turned my attention over his shoulder and watched Valentine disappear in a tall, thin spiral of green smoke.

Noc kept moving.

I took in a deep breath, closed my eyes again, and for the second time that night, the second time in decades, I used my power, opened my senses and sought my brother.

I was out of practice and in immense pain. I couldn't sense him.

Either that or she'd already broken him. With Kristian, it never took long.

"I can't sense him," I told Noc, still trying to do so and feeling us ascending stairs.

"Franka, just focus on you, yeah?"

"This could mean she might have already broken him."

"Frey and Valentine have this."

I opened my eyes only to narrow them at him. "What do those words even *mean?*"

Noc blinked as he kept climbing stairs, and when he was done with his blink, his lips quirked.

"There's my sugarlips," he muttered.

I didn't have it in me to cut him with a reply. The pain jarred through my conscious and I felt bile drive up my throat.

I swallowed it down but whispered a horrified, "I may be sick."

"Please, fuck, wait ten seconds until I have you in my bed," Noc begged.

"I'll try," I promised, and fortunately, after what felt a great deal longer than ten seconds, I was able to keep that promise.

I bit back a moan as he carefully extricated his shirt from me and gnashed my teeth silently as he rolled me to my belly. Once he'd positioned me, I felt the covers being pulled up over my bottom.

I then watched as he reached to the cord beside the bed and tugged on it.

"How did you know to come to the buttery?" I asked.

He looked down at me. "Your girl. She woke me up, totally freaked."

I felt my brow furrow. "Freaked?"

"Panicked," he explained. "Worried about you."

"How did she know?" I asked.

"I don't know, babe. She woke me, she was freaked way the fuck out, said you were in danger. I didn't take time to interrogate her. I put some clothes on and hauled ass."

I decided to leave that alone. I'd speak with Josette about how she knew later, after I was assured Frey and the green witch "had this."

Therefore, I changed the subject as I watched Noc stride purposefully across the room. "Why did you pull the cord?"

He disappeared through his dressing room door but still called out, "Gonna need clean towels. And more water. And one of those sleeping drinks you talked about. And a bunch a' other shit, this place has it."

Being slightly twisted to observe the door to the dressing room was causing too much pain, so I rested my cheek on my arms crossed under me and demanded loudly so he could hear (meaning indecorously, which I found irritating), "You need to go back to Frey. Ascertain he has things in hand."

Noc came back wearing another shirt, this one odd, seeming to be one piece of material, no buttons, long sleeves, the fabric looking soft and fitting snug at his chest and shoulders.

He was also carrying a drying cloth that looked wet but wrung.

"Your cousin's got dragons on call, Frannie, I think he's good," he denied my demand.

"I—" I began just as he stopped by the bed.

"Please be quiet, baby," he said in a soothing tone. "Try to relax. I'm gonna lay this on your back, maybe the cool will give you some relief, and we'll hope a doc gets here soon."

He said that and I had no response, just kept my eyes tipped up to him, fascinated that the soothing tone of his voice was reciprocated by the look on his handsome face.

After some time, he asked, "You good with that?"

"Pardon?"

"Me putting this on your back, Frannie, you ready?"

I felt my face pucker. "I dislike this name you call me."

He bent at the waist so his face was much closer to mine.

Confronted in that proximity by his striking good looks, I felt my face unpucker.

"Franka's a good enough name, I guess. But it's hard and that's not you."

I mentally pulled my famous Franka Drakkar bravado around me and would have tossed my head if I didn't know it would cause intense pain. "You don't know me."

His voice got lower when he returned, "You know I do."

That made me shut my mouth, for oddly and with not a small amount of panic at the mere thought, I imagined he did.

"You ready for the towel, sweetheart?" he asked.

I did not bite my lip. I did not tense (for tensing made the pain worse, I'd learned that long ago). I did nothing but nod.

Noc nodded back, straightened, and with a tenderness that made my nostrils sting in order to fight back a different reaction, he laid the cool, wet cloth along my burning, ravaged back.

I closed my eyes.

"There," he whispered.

When I opened my eyes, he was crouched low close beside the bed so he was all I could see.

"How long's he been doin' this to you?" he inquired softly.

"That's hardly your business," I replied, though I couldn't infuse even a small measure of condescension in my voice after the care he'd taken of me.

His glance slid in the direction of my back before it came again to me.

"He got that far, no one could take that shit without passing out. Unless they had practice," he remarked.

He was correct.

I didn't answer.

He lifted a hand, used the tip of a finger to slide my hair away from my temple and my cheek as he spoke.

"You're a grown woman, Frannie. You don't have to take that. Why didn't you put a stop to it? Hell, why'd you go down there at all?"

That, I answered.

"Because my brother wouldn't be able to take it."

There was a change in his gaze. A glittering hardness that I found fascinating.

And that hard was now in his tone when he declared, "You are not one fuckin' thing like they think you are, are you?"

"I'm exactly what they think I am," I retorted.

"Keep tellin' yourself that, babe. See you believe it. But it's utter bullshit," he returned.

Before I could get in a rebuttal, there was a knock at the door.

I watched Noc straighten from his crouch, move quickly and with masculine fluidity to the door and open it.

A palace maid was beyond it.

Her eyes flicked to me and I drew breath in through my nostrils at the indignity of my position and her attention.

Damned, bloody *Noc.*

"I need towels, please," Noc stated. "Lots of them. Hot water. Mild soap. You got a bad bottle of whiskey around, bring that too. If you don't, bring a good one. And one of those drinks that puts you to sleep. Her girl was sent for a doctor," Noc went on, doing this jerking his head back to indicate me. "If you could find out where he is and have him come to us as soon as he can, that'd be awesome."

The maid nodded and dashed away even though I suspected there were several things he said that she didn't understand.

He closed the door and turned to me.

When he again got close and hunkered beside me, I tried to take a different tack.

"It would mean a good deal to me, Noc, if you were to return to Frey and ascertain what's happening with my father, my mother and my brother."

"I'll do that, once the doc's here and you're good."

"Noc—" I began to protest but he again leaned closer.

"Frey know you got magic?"

Uncharacteristically, I allowed my eyes to slide away.

"Frannie," he called.

My eyes slid back and I snapped, "Cease calling me this."

He ignored my demand and asserted, "I gotta know. You don't want me to say anything, I gotta know."

I felt my lips part in surprise at the fact that he'd just shared he'd keep my secret.

"And if your dad says shit, I gotta be on the ball with that too," he carried on.

Oh balls.

I should have thought of that.

"I don't practice," I told him swiftly, lifting my head slightly but lowering it when the numbness in my back disappeared and fire shot through my mutilated flesh. "I don't ever use it. I just...inherited it from my mother. *She* uses it."

Noc nodded. "Gotcha."

"You must believe me, Noc, for I'm telling the truth." For some reason I persevered. "When I was young, I experimented with it. But seeing what she did, how she used hers." I shook my head. "I didn't want a thing to do with it."

He lifted a hand and cupped my cheek, saying comfortingly, "I said gotcha, baby. That means I get you. I understand you. It's all good. I got your back. Okay? You get that?"

I wasn't sure but I thought I did, therefore I gave a slight nod.

"Now, relax for me, yeah? I'm gonna go get another towel, take this one off, change it." Even as his mouth got tight, his voice turned into a mutter while his attention wandered to my back. "Blood's soaked this one through."

Humiliation belatedly stole through me, and I closed my eyes against the sight of his fine-looking face set with anger that warred with concern.

"You good with that, Frannie?" he asked.

This name, it was common. I detested it.

I didn't say that.

I sighed, kept my eyes closed and replied, "Whatever you wish to do, Noc."

"Babe," he said.

I lay there, unmoving.

"Sweetheart, look at me."

I didn't wish to but felt it would be a show of weakness if I didn't.

Therefore I did.

"Gonna take care of you," he promised, the look in his eyes now one of warmth and determination. "Get you back to fit. And I'm gonna see he's taken care of too. Do you believe me?"

I wished to do that.

But that would not happen.

"He's a member of a powerful House, Noc. You may not understand this but that means something. He's detested by Aurora, as he was by Atticus, for reasons I don't know but it wasn't surprising. The king and queen felt even less for my mother. They do not consort with the royals and only allowed Kristian and I to do so when we were younger through my uncle, Frey's father. Regardless of that, his position, and hers, gives them leeway. And further, I went to him uncoerced."

"When'd it start?" he asked.

"Pardon?"

"Got scar tissue he didn't get to opening up this go, Frannie, so don't think you can pull one over on me. This is not your first time. How old were you when it started?"

"I don't understand the import of that information," I declared haughtily.

"Just tell me how old," he pushed.

"If it's that interesting to you, five."

He rose.

Immediately.

Coming straight out of his crouch in a powerful surge, he stood towering beside me on the bed.

And now, at the expression on his face, I fought cowering before him.

"Five?" he whispered.

I fought the pain as I pushed up on my forearms, beginning, "Noc—"

"*Five?*" he snarled.

I stared up at him, unable to speak in the face of his fury.

Fury on my behalf.

Something that had never happened, not from Kristian, not from Antoine.

Not from anyone.

"You were coerced, Franka, whether you know that shit or not," he bit off, and before I could utter a noise, even if I had no intention of doing so, a knock came at the door and Noc barked, "*Come in!*"

He then prowled to the door as a maid came through with towels.

He did this continuing to bark, just not as loudly, and dispensed with the "pleases" and ludicrous "that'd be awesomes" and behaved like the man he would be if he was of this world.

In other words, he issued commands.

"Change the towel with a clean, cool one on her back. Give her the goddamned sleeping drink so she can get some relief from the pain. And get the *fucking doctor in here.*" He was at the door the maid had scurried through and he turned to me. "You move from that bed, baby, I'm gonna be fuckin' pissed. Let her take care of you, drink the goddamned drink, get some rest. I'll be back."

I had no earthly clue what "fuckin' pissed" meant.

I still nodded.

Noc watched me do it.

Then he swept out the door.

4
HOW IT WAS GOING TO BE

Noc

It took three of Frey's guys to pull Noc off the man.

Even accomplishing this, he still struggled against their hold, knowing every blow he'd dealt didn't make him feel better, but that didn't mean he didn't get gratification each time his fist landed in the asshole's flesh.

"I understand your anger, Noc, but this is not helping," Frey said from close.

"It defies belief you'd allow that...that...*man* to lay his hands on me."

At Franka's father's words, Noc went still.

His entire body.

But not his mouth.

"It defies belief you took that fuckin' *whip* to your daughter since she was fuckin' *five* without anyone stopping you," he spat, feeling no joy as he watched Franka's father swipe blood from his mouth seeing as Noc's repeated blows to his face where the whip had caught earlier tore that wound long and wide.

He felt no joy mostly because he also felt the job was not even close to done.

It took a while for the vibe in the room to hit him, but when it did he jerked away from Frey's boys and turned his attention to the man himself.

Frey's face was carved from stone, his eyes directed at his uncle, and they were blazing with hellfire.

"Since she was *five*?" he whispered, his tone heavy with disbelief and disgust, not to mention rage.

Noc shifted his attention back to the older man when he replied, "It's none of your concern, nephew, what I do with my children."

"It's bloody *law* in Lunwyn that corporal punishment of minors does not go beyond a simple spanking or a paddle," Frey shot back.

"She's now an adult," the man retorted.

"Which does not negate the crime of child cruelty, but adds the crime of assault," Frey declared.

"I'm a member of a House, *your* House, may I remind you," Franka's father returned.

"You're a monster," Noc clipped.

The man turned his gaze to Noc. "And you're a peasant who I've not given leave to speak to me."

Noc opened his mouth but Frey got there before him.

"Are you unfamiliar with the Prince of Hawkvale?" he asked.

"I know of these secrets," the asshole fired back, a sneer twisting his lips, "and this is not the heir to the throne of Hawkvale." He indicated Noc with his arm. "This man is nothing."

"This man saved you from slavery at the hands of Minerva and her minions," Frey retorted. "This man has the ear of the Queen. The Princess. *And* The Drakkar. This man is twin to the heir of Hawkvale. This man is far from nothing."

"You can pretty him up as much as you like, nephew, but his manner, his speech. He may look like a prince of our world, but he's far from that. He's simply common," Franka's father returned.

"Cease speaking," Frey ordered.

"You are who you are, Frey, but I'm your uncle, your elder, and you *never* have leave to speak to me in that manner," Franka's father retorted.

"Cease..." Frey leaned forward and thundered, "*speaking*."

"I—"

That was all the asshole got out before Frey was across the room with his hand wrapped around the guy's throat, his feet lifted two feet from the ground, and he was slammed into a shelving unit so hard, all the bottles swayed and four crashed to the ground.

"I said...*cease speaking*," Frey repeated through clenched teeth.

Franka's father opened and closed his mouth like he was fighting for air at the same time he clawed at Frey's arm at his throat.

"You better hope Valentine returns with Anneka, reporting Kristian and his family are safe, healthy and whole, or I swear to the gods, *uncle*, I'll press for you to fucking *swing*," Frey warned.

Franka's father made a gurgling noise and Frey dropped him to the ground where he crumpled, landing on a hand and his knees.

Frey turned immediately from him to one of the men standing close to Noc.

"Thad, go to Finnie. Franka's maid woke her along with me and no doubt she's still awake seeing as she wasn't keen on not accompanying me to the kitchens. Ask her to go to Noc's room, attend Franka as the physician sees to her and ask her to stay there," he ordered.

Thad nodded and took off.

Frey looked to one of the other men close to Noc and demanded, "Lund, fetch the constable. Nils Drakkar is being arrested tonight for child cruelty and assault."

Lund didn't nod. He smiled a humorless smile and then he left the room.

"Arrested?" Nils Drakkar asked in a choked voice, still on his knees, only his head was tipped back to look at his nephew.

"You've been committing crimes for decades, uncle. You'll stand trial for those crimes and pay the penance," Frey announced.

Nils pushed himself to his feet, declaring, "That's absurd."

"It's the law," Frey returned.

The older man's back shot straight. "I'm a Drakkar!"

"You're a gods damned useless piece of shite," Frey bit out, turning again fully to his uncle. "I still cannot grasp what I saw when I walked into this room. I don't even *want* to. How could you mark your child that way? It's unfathomable to do to a son. But it's unconscionable to do it to a *daughter*."

Nils tossed his head. "You know Franka. She earned many punishments."

"And her punishment was tearing open her flesh?" Frey asked with incredulity.

"As her father, it's *my* decision what her punishment would be."

"And that decision you made will land you in a cell," Frey fired back. "And if I have anything to do with it, and in case you haven't grasped this, uncle, I have a great deal to do with *everything*, you'll stay in that cell until your dying day."

Nils expression filled with disdain as he snapped, "You cannot mean that."

"Look at my face," Frey demanded, "and tell me if I do or I do not."

Nils obviously looked at Frey's face because his paled.

Even so, he fought his corner. "I cannot believe you stand in defense of her after she committed treason."

"Excellent," Frey weirdly replied, crossing his arms on his chest in a way it looked like he was settling in. "Let's talk about that. How, precisely, did you know of that?"

The older man lifted his chin.

"Anneka and I keep informed about our children," Nils informed him.

"Not surprisingly you do this likely with spies, paid sneaks and unlawful magic, because I've noted that for years neither of your children have had anything to do with you," Frey retorted. "Now I know why."

"I'll remind *you*, nephew, she came to this buttery of her own accord," Nils shared.

It was time for Noc to butt in and he did just that.

"She came to this buttery to protect her brother."

Nils's eyes went to Noc. "Weakness. The both of them. My bloody son, I've no idea how he makes it through a night, petrified of his own shadow. And her. My daughter. Twisting herself in knots to hide her brother's affliction from me and her mother, like we wouldn't notice it *and* lament it. Putting *herself* in line for his punishments because the boy faints and cries and begs, and she can't bear it. Even going so far as misbehaving, courting our ire, so we'll turn our attention to her. It's obscene. A flaw in her character."

"And I'm sure you punished her for that too," Frey said in a quiet, dangerous voice.

"Of course I did," Nils snapped. "She's a Drakkar. She was taught to know better. And that boy..." He sniffed before he declared, "*My* son should have ascended to Head of the House. *You* didn't want it and neither of your soft-hearted brothers deserved it. Instead, my son attached himself to a sniveling woman who pushed out a worthless child, causing his mother and myself inexpressible shame."

Noc watched as Frey held his uncle's eyes, and he did this for a long time before he turned away and dropped his head. Lifting his hand to the back of his neck, he wrapped it there and squeezed.

He released his neck, his hand falling, his gaze coming to Noc's.

"How is she?" he asked.

"In pain, but still uppity as all hell and worried sick about her brother," Noc answered.

Frey nodded.

"The other Heads of the Houses will not stand for my incarceration," Nils declared.

Frey turned back to him. "This is a delusion. When they hear of what you've done, they'll stand in line to condemn you. But even if what you believe were to be the case, I would not care."

"You hold great power, nephew, but you do not rule this land," Nils fired back, his face twisted.

"You are correct," Frey agreed. "But my mother-in-law does and it was me who seated her on that throne."

Nils drew in a long, loud breath through his nose.

"Bloody hell," Frey muttered, looking to the ceiling. "I can't stand to be in his presence much longer. Where's that bloody witch?"

"You called?"

Both Noc and Frey turned toward the feminine drawl, and they did this just in time to see the green smoke start to dissipate and Valentine lift her hand in an indifferent gesture. This movement caused the handsome but frightened-looking woman she'd brought with her to tumble back. She slammed into Nils Drakkar, taking them both into the shelves where more bottles fell and smashed on the ground.

"Pity, waste of good liquor," Valentine noted casually.

"Kristian and his family?" Frey asked.

Valentine looked to him. "Frightened, but no harm had been done. Though I arrived just in time."

"She's a witch," Frey informed Valentine.

"She *was* a witch," Valentine returned. "I've stripped her of her powers."

"What?" Nils whispered.

Noc looked to him. He was now holding his wife in a protective embrace Noc didn't think the man had in him.

"It's true, my love," his wife said in a trembling voice. "My magic, she took it." Her gaze wandered fearfully to Valentine. "Her power is...I've never felt anything like it."

"This is...it is...it's," Nils sputtered, "*unspeakable.*" He speared Valentine with his eyes. "Return it immediately."

"If you don't cease speaking to me in this manner, you odious man, you'll find yourself without a tongue," Valentine retorted.

"Who do you think you are?" Nils demanded, pulling his wife behind him and taking a step toward Valentine.

When he did, the witch lifted her hand and snapped.

Nils stopped immediately. Both his hands shooting to his mouth, his eyes getting huge, his facing losing all color, he staggered back and Noc watched as his eyes got even more huge and he rolled his jaw around in a bizarre way that was also creepy as fuck.

"Valentine," Frey sighed.

"I'll give it back," she promised, but finished with, "eventually."

Noc stared at her. "You took his tongue?"

She tipped her head to the side. "I didn't fancy how he was using it."

"Bloody hell," Frey muttered.

Frey's last man in the room, a guy named Ruben, chuckled.

"I assume you have plans for these two cretins that I'll approve of?" Valentine asked Frey.

"I'm uncertain you'll approve of them, but I can assure you they'll be punished," Frey answered.

She shifted only her eyes Nils and Anneka's way. "Punished seems a tame word in this instance."

"They're going to be inhabiting a cell for the rest of their days," Frey shared. "Does that suffice?"

"You can't be serious." Anneka's words sounded forced out.

Frey looked to his aunt. "I can't?"

She took in his face and shrunk away.

"I suppose that'll do," Valentine murmured.

Having turned fully to them, she was eyeing them like she would eye a pesky rodent she intended to trap by breaking its back and then dispose of.

"I'm done here," Frey stated and looked to Ruben. "Keep an eye on them until Lund gets back with the constable."

"Right, Frey," Ruben answered.

He turned to Valentine. "Give him back his tongue."

She gave him a small smile. "Can't I keep it?"

"Give it back, Valentine."

"Just for a little while," she coaxed.

"Valentine, there's Franka to see to," Frey reminded her.

That took the witch's attention. She lifted her hand, snapped, and Nils instantly whispered a relieved yet horrified, "By the gods."

Frey wasted no time sweeping an arm out for Valentine to precede him, something she did. He glanced at Noc. Noc lifted his chin. Frey moved and Noc followed him.

They were through the kitchens and heading to the main stairs when Frey spoke.

"I've known her since she was a little girl. But you were right."

Noc stopped. Valentine stopped. And they both found that Frey had stopped.

His attention was to Noc.

"There's great substance to anyone who would endure what she did, doing it for decades to protect her brother," Frey continued.

Noc said nothing.

Valentine also remained silent.

"Kristian is not as Nils described him," Frey went on. "But his wit is not as sharp as his sister's. And his will definitely not as strong. I cannot imagine how he would cope even with the threat of the lash, much less feeling the bite of it. But Franka, what I saw, I don't even know how she remained standing."

"She remained standing so her brother would not fall," Noc pointed out.

Frey shook his head. "I would never think she had this in her."

"The two people who, from birth, were meant to love her, look after her, protect her, but for Franka they were those two fuckwads," Noc jerked his head in the direction they came, "it's no surprise she did everything she could to make certain no one got close. This guy, the one who died, had to be something to tear off the mask she'd been wearing for so long it's a wonder it didn't fuse with her skin."

"I see this now," Frey said softly, and it didn't take a cop who could read people to read he was kicking his own ass for not seeing any of this earlier.

"Man, she was a master," Noc told him something he knew. "Twice, I've been around her, and she's always trying that shit with me even though she knows I see right through it. Don't beat yourself up. You were feeling for her exactly what she wanted you to feel."

Frey continued to look into Noc's eyes as he nodded.

"You two should feel free to stand here in the hallway of a palace in the middle of the night and dissect how Franka Drakkar's childhood traumas have affected the woman she's become," Valentine drawled. "I, however, am going to go see to the woman herself."

With that, no other way to put it, she flounced away, but elegantly, as Noc was noticing was the only way that woman did anything.

Noc and Frey started moving after her a whole lot slower. Noc wanted to go a fuckuva lot faster but he felt Frey's mood, so he kept his strides in line with the other man's.

"Looking back," Frey started reflectively as they began to walk up the stairs, "outside, of course, what she did for her lover, and that's explainable considering he's the only person she's allowed to see behind her mask, she never did aught truly amiss, except be catty and forcefully unlikeable. She even came forward with helpful information when Finnie and I were having our troubles when my wee one came to me."

"Frey, brother, you can knock yourself out trying to find the signs you missed that'd lead you to her true character," Noc replied. "But that secret was a secret well kept. You didn't know what was happening to her so you couldn't do a damned thing about it. Just count yourself lucky you know now."

"Yes," Frey muttered. "Difficult to do. But wise."

When they made the top of the stairs, Noc started to move faster and thankfully Frey came out of his thoughts and moved with him.

They'd barely cleared the door before Finnie was at her husband.

"Frey—" she began.

"Not now, my wee wife," Frey said gently, his arm going around her waist but his eyes went to Franka. "I'll explain all later."

Noc just went to Franka.

She was out. Her eyes closed. Her breaths even. Her beautiful face peaceful. And he saw strips of gauze with some kind of milky gunk laid across her back.

He lifted his gaze to a man who was bending over a leather case sitting on one of the chairs by the fire.

"How is she?" he asked.

The man raised his head and caught Noc's gaze.

"Mutilated," he bit out and turned his attention to Frey. "I hope, sir, that whoever perpetrated this outrage has been detained."

"He has," Frey told him.

"What's this stuff on her back?" Noc asked, and the guy who was obviously the doctor looked back to him.

"Willow salt," he stated. "I've left a jar and clean dressings," he went on.

He dipped his chin to a variety of shit that was sitting on the table beside the chair.

Then he closed his case with a pissed-off snap and lifted it, ordering, "In the morning, if you can get her to eat, do so. But I've also left some willow tea to assist with the pain. It needs to be seeped until it's dark. And the dressings need to be changed as well. On the morrow, mix these jars." He pointed to the jars on table. "As the bleeding will be staunched, willow salt will no longer be needed. Simply mix the lavender oil with the honey salve and the willow paste." He glanced at Franka. "There's nothing to be done with stitches, considering the extensive scar tissue she already has. But even if that were not the case, there's little skin left to stitch. But the salve will be soothing and hasten healing."

He started marching to the door but stopped and looked up at Frey.

"I'll return late morning to check on her," he announced.

"That would be appreciated," Frey replied.

The doctor gave Frey a short nod, didn't look at anybody and stomped out the door.

"Can you do more, Valentine?" Finnie asked, she and Frey moving closer to the bed where Valentine was standing opposite it from Noc.

"I'm not a healer, my goddess of love," she stated, her gaze directed at Franka. She looked to Finnie. "I know some, but they would not be able to do much more than the doctor did. Even if we brought her to our world, outside of managing the pain, I'm not even certain a cosmetic surgeon could find results. Unfortunately, the damage has long been done."

Finnie looked up at Frey. "The elves?"

Frey nodded. "I'll call to Nillen."

"I caution you, my *chéries*, do not act in haste without Franka's input. Your kindness might not be considered the same to her," Valentine warned.

"I mean no offense, Valentine, but that's daft," Frey returned, jerking his head toward the bed. "I know her state has far from escaped you."

"There are many of us who find strength and even honor in our scars, those within," she dipped her head to Franka, "and those without."

"Begging all your pardons," a timid voice came at them, and Noc turned his head in its direction to see that the girl who had woken him to tell him Franka was in danger was coming out of the shadows by the windows and toward the bed, "but Lady Franka should continue to rest and I fear, the lights on, conversation happening..." she trailed off, but they all got her gist.

"I'm staying," Noc said, turning to the lamp by the bed and twisting it so the flame within died. "You all go."

"I can stay with my lady," the girl offered.

"You have a name, honey?" he asked.

"Josette."

"Right, Josette, you'll need to have it together to take care of her when she's up. So you should probably get some shuteye."

She bit her lip, looked to Franka, made her decision and nodded.

But she didn't leave. She started moving around, turning out the lamps.

Frey, Finnie and Valentine did move to leave.

"You need anything, you call," Finnie said as she paused at the door. "We're three rooms down, other side."

"Right, babe. Thanks," Noc muttered, gave her a smile, gave Frey a look, and they moved out.

Valentine didn't say anything. She just smiled that small, weird smile of hers that he didn't know if it was cute, smirky or sexy, but taking it in it was all three.

Noc went to the fire, threw a couple of logs on and settled in a chair.

"Goodnight, Lord Noctorno," Josette said quietly as she made her way to the side door.

"I'm not a lord, Josette, and everyone calls me Noc."

She made a shy, self-conscious noise, avoided his eyes and disappeared behind the door.

The room was dark, except for the fire.

But thank fuck, the chair was comfortable.

So Noc stretched out, stared at the fire, didn't think he'd get a wink of sleep, but was unconscious in minutes.

~

Franka

I barely woke before I heard Josette's hushed, "I think she's awake."

I opened my eyes and tilted them up to see Noc and Josette standing by the bed, Josette looking anxious, Noc looking gentle.

Bloody hell.

"Yep, she's awake," Noc murmured and started grinning. "How you doin', Frannie?"

I began to push up to my forearms, surprised that the pain in my back was dull rather than sharp, doing this snapping, "I'll be excellent, when you cease calling me this crude name."

Noc's grin got bigger but he did it bending closer.

"Move another inch, sugarlips, and I'll sit on you."

I was groggy from the sleeping draught but I was also Franka Drakkar.

Therefore I was relatively certain the glare I sent his way was scorching.

Apparently I was wrong, for the glare had no effect except to make him stop grinning and start smiling.

He had excellent teeth.

Oh, but the goddess Adele did not like me.

Our eyes locked in a battle of wills I was physically incapable of winning, though mentally I could best him (perhaps), but movement made the dull pain sharpen and thus I decided (for my own sake, of course) to settle back down to my front.

Noc nodded like he was pleased and straightened, turning to Josette. "Can you make her some of that tea?"

"Right away," Josette whispered and scurried away.

"Kristian?" I said my brother's name as a question.

Noc looked back down at me. "Your brother's good, babe. His wife, kid, they're all good. Valentine got to them in time."

Thank the goddess.

"My father?" I asked.

"Your dad and mom are both currently sitting in a jail somewhere, on a variety of charges."

That was...

It was...

I couldn't even decide what it was before Noc continued speaking.

"And Valentine stripped your mother of her magic. Frey's pissed, babe. I mean seriously. They're not gonna hurt you anymore. They're not gonna hurt your brother anymore. They're not gonna hurt anyone anymore."

My mother was stripped of her magic?

I couldn't help it, I felt my mouth curve into a gleeful, malicious smile.

"I know," Noc stated, and I focused again on him for I had no idea why he said this. "Wish you'd been there, sweetheart. Valentine magicked out your dad's tongue at one point so he'd shut the fuck up. If I wasn't so pissed, I would have bust a gut laughing."

I couldn't fight my eyes going wide.

"She magicked out his tongue?"

"You shoulda seen his face, Frannie. It was creepy as all get out, but still, I'll never forget it...in a good way."

I thought of the other punishments that my father had given me, hundreds of them, perhaps thousands, none of which involved a whip. But they did involve the verbal lashings of his tongue.

Yes, I too wish I'd been there.

"She gave it back but only 'cause Frey made her," Noc shared.

In speaking, he regained my attention and I made an immediate decision.

Kristian well. My parents neutralized.

Onward.

"You need to leave," I declared.

His brows drew together a moment before his expression showed clearly that comprehension had dawned.

Sadly, comprehension might have dawned but he didn't leave.

He crouched by the bed and offered in a soft voice, "You need me to carry you to the other room so you can have a bit of privacy?"

Dear goddess.

He thought I needed a chamber pot.

But...

What was happening to my face?

Dear goddess!

The heat I felt in my cheeks could be nothing other than me blushing.

I didn't *blush*. I'd *never* blushed. Not even when I'd set about seducing my first lover at age sixteen.

I needed to be quit of this man as soon as possible.

"No...I...do...*not*," I bit out.

"Sure?" he asked kindly.

"I need you to leave, Noctorno," I used his full name in an effort to irritate, something that worked if the flare in his eyes was any indication, "so Josette can prepare me. We're away to Kristian's this morning."

Another drawing of his brows before he asked, "What?"

"After my toilette, Josette and I are to my sleigh so we can begin our journey to my brother's home."

His eyes got bigger as his mouth inquired peculiarly, "Are you high?"

"No," I answered his ridiculous question unnecessarily, "Indeed, I'm low. As you can see since I'm lying abed."

For a second, he just stared at me.

Then he threw his head back and burst into loud, deep, beautiful laughter.

I wanted to throw something at him.

Unfortunately, in my current position, this was not an option open to me.

"I fail to see what's amusing," I noted.

He controlled his mirth only to mutter, "I'll explain it later." He went on more distinctly, "Frannie, you're not goin' to your brother's today. Or tomorrow. Or until you're fit. Then, maybe Valentine will spirit you there, or whatever the fuck that's called. But for the foreseeable future, your ass is in that bed and you're resting so you can heal."

Well!

Who did he think he was, telling me what I would or would not do?

"As you've determined," I began, "this is not the first time I've been in this condition so I do believe that *I* know best what I'm capable of and..."

I stopped speaking because he came slightly out of his crouch so he could put his face into my face and he was no longer looking mirthful.

He was looking angry.

Very angry.

"That was when you had no one lookin' out for you, but that's not the case anymore. So this is how it's gonna be," he announced.

He then, to my shock, irritation and outrage, *announced how it was going to be.*

Like he had the right to tell *me* how it was *going to be*!

"First, like I said, you're gonna hang tight, rest and heal. Second, once you start feelin' better, *then* we'll discuss what's gonna happen after that. And the last is the most important, baby, so listen up. You're gonna take care not to remind me your mom and dad are such motherfucking assholes because I got a few solid shots to his face last night, but I let Frey's boys pull me off before I did the damage I intended to do. You keep remindin' me, I'm gonna find those two monsters and do somethin' that'll mean my time here won't be about discovering a parallel universe but memorizing every inch of a jail cell."

There were a large number of things to discuss regarding his announcement. So many, on the fly, I couldn't decide a priority, so I said the first that came to mind.

"You struck my father?" I asked.

"Repeatedly," Noc answered. "But not repeatedly enough."

Oh my.

Warmth was filling my belly.

I decided to focus on the second thing that needed to be discussed and not on that feeling.

"I think it's important to note that I barely know you, thus you're nothing to me. Although I appreciate your efforts last night, you have no say in what I do or where I go. And even if I were to wish to stay in the Winter Palace for a day or two in an effort to be in better condition to make the journey I *fully* intend to make, that will be *my* decision and what happens after that will *not* be discussed with *you*."

"Think that, babe," he said, moving out of my face and back into his crouch by the bed, "but we'll see, and I'll just say what we'll be seein' is your ass is not leaving that bed."

"I can't believe I need to remind you that I'm hardly welcome to remain at the palace," I pointed out.

"Figure that's changed, Frannie."

I ignored him calling me that dreadful name and said in a scoffing voice, "You would think wrong."

"Babe, had to have a chat with Frey last night, he was kickin' his own ass, thinkin' shit about you that wasn't the way it was. But more, the man is so far *not* about what went down with you last night, what you and your brother been dealin' with for years, probably thought if he read it right, he coulda done something about it."

"That's preposterous," I retorted.

"That's the thinking of a good guy who's loyal to his men, loves his wife beyond measure and feels the same about the kid they made." Noc smiled a gentle smile. "Know you're not used to that kinda shit, but stick with me, sugarlips, you'll learn."

I felt a skip in my heart at this offer. At his smile. At his words and knowing they likely not only described Frey Drakkar, but also Noctorno Hawthorne of the other world (when he had a woman to love that was).

I decided to end this conversation at once.

"I've no desire to discuss this further with you, Noctorno—"

He interrupted me with, "Noc."

I disregarded his interruption and carried on, "But I've asked you to leave. Please do so that I can go about my business."

"Frannie, baby, you are not gettin' this," he stated, leaning into me, but thankfully not so close his face was in mine this time. "I'm not goin' anywhere. If I gotta go somewhere, someone else will be here to make sure *you* don't go anywhere. You are resting. You are healing. And that's just the way it's gonna be."

"Perhaps I'll pull the cord, ask a servant to request that Queen Aurora attend me and we'll see what she has to say about your plans for me."

He directly straightened and reached to the cord, tugging it.

I stared at his actions and continued staring when he cast his gaze down at me.

"Yeah, good call. We'll request Aurora shows and see what she has to say," he agreed.

Hmm.

He seemed more certain than I about the outcome of said engagement.

Truthfully, without Josette's help (or his) I actually *could* go nowhere and do nothing. Not simply because I was in pain, and movement without assistance I knew would be agony (even with assistance, it would be agony), but also because I was naked.

Not that I had any qualms with that, just that it was *me* who made the decision about who saw me and he'd seen enough without my making that decision already.

In other words, I was stuck.

And this was maddening.

Therefore I did the only thing I could.

I glared at him again.

He grinned at me again.

The gall!

"Now we got that straight, you sure you don't want me to carry you to the other room?" he asked.

In truth, at that juncture I could have used the chamber pot.

Of course, this was not what I shared.

I said, "Absolutely not."

"Gonna be right here, you need me," he stated.

"To my everlasting distress," I murmured, right then doing the only other thing I could do, pathetic as it was.

I turned my head away from him.

He did not let that happen unnoted.

Oh no.

He chuckled.

Insufferably *rude*.

I ignored that and stared at heavy curtains that hid the dull wood that covered the blasted-out windows.

The good news was, my parents incarcerated, my mother's magic stripped so she couldn't use it to foil any efforts of castigation or to rain further misfortune on my brother and me, Lunwyn was safe for me again.

And Kristian.

The bad news was, my back was a mess, my secret had been revealed (both of them!), and I seemed to be at the mercy of a dictatorial member of an other-world city guard, of all outlandishness.

I could not allow this to concern me.

I would ignore him in the short term and deal with whatever befell me in the long term.

Because I had no choice.

And such was my life.

Drat.

~

"You can hardly hold me at the Palace against my will," I asserted.

"I can't?" Queen Aurora asked with a raised brow.

It was undignified in the extreme that I was lying abed, staring up at my queen, having any conversation, much less this one.

Even so, one could say there was a single answer to her question.

She could.

"This is not to be born," I groused.

Yes!

Me!

Franka Drakkar reduced to *grousing*.

The mortification of it all!

She glanced to my back and I could not merit (but there it was, right in her expression) the slight softening of her features before she looked again at me.

"A week, I think," she murmured pensively. "And then we'll see what the physician says."

"With respect, your grace, I'm aware of what I'm capable of in this condition or any," I stated, avoiding Noc's eyes.

A Noc, I will note, who was leaning negligently against the wall beyond the nightstand, arms crossed on his chest, foot crossed at the ankle, regarding this like it was an enthralling melodrama.

"I can imagine even you, Franka, would admit that a physician is far more capable of making that judgment than you," Queen Aurora replied.

I could not argue that.

Therefore, I didn't.

"You've consumed your willow tea?" she asked, like a strict but concerned nanny.

Yes.

The queen speaking to me like a strict but concerned *nanny*.

Me!

"I have, my queen," I muttered.

"Excellent. I believe I'll give you the day. Tomorrow is the wedding, the perfect time for you to rest and mend uninterrupted. The eve after that, I'll dine with you. Myself and Finnie, and, of course, The Drakkar."

I wanted to dine with the queen, her other-world daughter and her son-in-law, a cousin who hated me, like I wanted someone to stick knitting needles in my eyes.

But did one refuse a queen?

No.

One did not.

"It would be my most fervent wish, your grace," I replied, my voice betraying it was what it was, absolutely the opposite.

"And Noc as well, I'm sure," Queen Aurora went on.

I ground my teeth and glanced to Noc.

He was again grinning.

"I'll be there," he assured.

"Lovely, I'll check in on you later. Rest, Franka," the queen ordered.

"As you wish, my queen." I had no choice but to agree.

With a short nod, she turned, and with no further ado, swept out of the room.

I frowned at the door.

Noc pushed away from the wall and moved to fill the space the queen had been occupying by my bed.

"I'm thinkin' that's that," he noted, his lips still curled up.

"As I've been ordered to rest by our sovereign, perhaps you'll leave me so I can do just that," I suggested tetchily.

He shrugged. "Sure."

"My gratitude," I bit out.

"Be back to have lunch with you, though."

Really.

I might have lived a life of malice and intrigue, but surely all I'd done hadn't earned me *this*.

"I can't wait," I gritted.

"Bet you can't," he murmured, his voice shaking with mirth.

I lifted my brows. "You were leaving?"

"Right," he replied, but did not move.

"The sooner you do that, the sooner I can rest and mend," I prompted.

"Fuck, don't know if you're more cute than you are funny or the other way around."

"Just so you're aware, I take neither as a compliment," I shared.

He burst out laughing, the sound filling the room and warming it better than the biggest, most blazing fire could achieve.

I decided my best course of action from that point was silence.

When his hilarity calmed, he decreed, "Right now, funnier than you are cute. But just barely."

I simply stared up at him blankly.

His expression changed to serious. "You're in pain, you say. Josette or someone will be close. We'll get you more of that tea."

I remained silent.

"Doc's comin' later," he told me.

I tipped my head the best I could as it was resting on my arms.

"You good, sweetheart?" he asked gently.

I was not.

"Fine," I bit out.

That got another curl of his lips.

"Right then, Frannie. See you later."

Stop calling me that appalling name! my mind screamed.

My mouth said nothing.

I should have said something. I should have even screamed my thoughts at him.

But since I didn't, he was open to shift closer and bend so near he was able to brush his lips at my temple at the same time he swept the hair from my neck.

"Rest good," he whispered in my ear.

I fought new warmth in my belly, tilted my eyes to catch his as he moved away and attempted yet again to scorch him with a glare.

It glanced off him as his lips quirked, he turned, and I watched his arse in another, more faded-blue pair of his attractive other-world trousers.

When he disappeared beyond the door, I tilted my eyes so far to the side, I could see the ceiling.

"If I promise to be the soul of charitability and kindness, will you release me of my torment?" I asked the gods, any of them, I didn't care which one was listening.

"What's that, Lady Franka?" Josette called.

"Nothing," I muttered, foiled at every turn, including the fact I knew my maid was sitting by the fire in one of the armchairs in my room, mending some of my clothing, thus she would hear I was reduced to verbally begging the gods for a reprieve.

Oh, but it was so much easier when no one cared a whit. It'd only been hours when they did and I already knew that as a certainty.

I sighed.

I stared at the pillow.

I considered making more promises to the gods (but silently).

My mind wandered to Noc's arse in his trousers.

And thus, unbeknownst to me, I fell asleep with a curl on my lips.

I WOKE SUDDENLY, feeling strange.

I saw vague firelight glinting on my pillow but the room was lit by naught else.

It was night.

I'd been sleeping.

Now I was awake.

Awake and I could see the shadow of a large man sitting in a chair by my bed.

Disoriented but feeling alarm course through me at this realization, my back raged with pain as I abruptly pushed up to my forearms.

"Calm, Franka," Frey's voice came to me quietly. "It's only me."

I tried to put a whip in my voice, but I was drowsy and confused so it came only as a minor bite when I asked, "And what, pray, are you doing sitting by my bed in the middle of the night?"

"It's barely eight in the evening."

Blast my father and his abuses. I'd drifted off after my (delicious, amazingly so considering what it was) broth, bread and wine.

"I presumed you'd wake and then we could talk," Frey continued.

"I do hope you understand I'm really in no mood," I replied.

He leaned toward me, putting his elbows on his knees, and ignored my assertion completely.

"I was wrong about you," he told me softly.

"You were not," I returned briskly. "I am precisely who you thought I was."

"You realize the game is over?" he inquired.

"I realize nothing of the sort, considering there *was* no game," I retorted. "I am Franka Drakkar now. I was Franka Drakkar a week ago, two months ago, ten years ago. Nothing has changed."

"Everything's changed."

I could take no more.

"Frey, my darling cousin," I started on a drawl, "it seems I've procured one stubborn, annoying male in my life for the foreseeable future. I'd very much appreciate it if you didn't double that number for I don't even want the one I already have."

He again ignored me, something both the stubborn, annoying males in my life were clearly very adept at doing.

"I wish you'd told me."

That was not relayed in a quiet voice. Or a soft one.

It was gentle and it was melancholy.

And, damn all the gods, I felt it touch my heart.

As *I* was adept at doing, I triumphed over the weakness of such a feeling.

"And how would that conversation have gone, Frey?" I asked. "Perhaps the *first* time you accused me of treason, I should have played that card by playing on your sympathies. 'Oh, but Frey, I'd never do that, not because I'm a Drakkar and it'd be foolish beyond reason. But because, poor little me, my father is fond of a lash and has been since I was wee.'"

"Derision is no longer a weapon you need to use, Franka," he shared.

"It's served me well much of my life. I've honed my talent with it quite keenly, so if it's all the same to you, I think I'll keep it," I rejoined.

I could not make his face out well in the shadows and firelight, but he didn't seem to be getting annoyed.

If my eyes didn't deceive me, it seemed he was smiling.

"As you wish, cousin," he murmured. "Understanding what lies beneath the mask, it will surely cease to be irritating and prove quite enjoyable."

Things seemed to continue to get worse.

"I can call the elves, Franka," he said low. "Ask them to see to your back."

The elves of our realm had healing powers beyond comprehension, as evidenced by the fact they'd brought a dead Lavinia back to life. It was lore the dead person needed to be freshly dead for this to prove a successful, rather than a highly disturbing endeavor (and thus the elves no longer did such a thing). Luckily, Lavinia was only in that sad state for a few hours.

And Frey had command of the elves.

But I thought *not*.

"My back will heal," I declared.

"It will, but they can—"

"They're mine," I bit out. "I earned them in a way you can't comprehend and I'm keeping them, Frey. And with respect, that's the end of that discussion."

He was silent for a moment and I felt his contemplation.

But fortunately, he let that subject go.

"Do you need anything before I return to Finnie and send Noc back to you?" he queried.

"I need you not to send Noc back to me," I answered.

There was a timbre to his voice that betrayed his amusement when he returned, "Yes, I see this is going to prove quite enjoyable."

I fought gnashing my teeth.

Frey stood.

"Rest well, Franka. I'll poke my head in after the wedding tomorrow. See how you're faring."

"I await this visit with bated breath, cousin," I murmured sardonically.

"Yes," he whispered. "Most amusing."

I did not look but I feared he stood, grinning down at me for a long moment (because he stood by my bed for a long moment) before he finally bid me good-night and took his leave.

There it was.

Proof.

The gods had forsaken me.

I understood that from a wee girl but it seemed since then I'd held on to a vein of hope.

That hope was dashed.

My cousin Frey *liked* me and found me amusing.

Him and others besides.

I was a disgrace to my House.

Blast.

5

GET WITH THE PROGRAM

Franka

"Is everything all right, my lady?" Josette asked.

I turned my head from my contemplation of the view outside the newly-installed window, in front of which my chair was resting, and looked to my maid, trying not to be annoyed at her hovering concern.

"Everything is just fine, Josette. Except perhaps you can bring me my book?"

She jumped as if she'd been asleep and just awoken before she dashed to the book sitting on the nightstand, like procuring it was of grave import. Once this crucial task was accomplished, she dashed directly to me.

"There you go," she said, offering me the slim volume.

"My appreciation," I murmured tightly, taking it.

"Anything else?" she inquired. "Do you feel pain? Would you like me to brew some willow tea? Are your dressings chafing? Would you like me to assist you back to the bed?"

"I'd like, my dear, some quiet and peace in order to read," I replied with forced composure.

"Yes," she returned swiftly. "Of course. I'm just in the other room should you need to call."

As she had been for the last three days, only a slight raise of the voice away.

I watched as she made her way to my dressing room door, a small antechamber of that room where her narrow bed was located, but I stopped her before she vanished behind it.

"Josette?"

She turned to me.

I continued, "We haven't discussed it, but I'd like for you to share how you knew to awaken Noctorno and take him to the buttery."

Her inquisitive look turned guarded and it took a moment for her to answer.

As this moment passed I sought patience, something of which I'd once had a profuse amount at my disposal. Patience was important when one engaged in plentiful amounts of intrigue.

Something I'd found slipping of late.

When I was on the cusp of prompting her, she declared, "I sleep light."

"This is not quite an explanation," I noted when she said no more.

"I've been in service almost all my life. When my employers have need of me, night or day, I'm trained to be awake and aware."

"You're an excellent maid, Josette. Are you saying something woke you, you found my bed empty and went in search of me?"

"Actually, you woke me, closing the door to your room. I worried about you, your...well, state of mind being...well..." She shook her head. "That doesn't matter. The thing is, I was worried so I followed you."

How curious.

I hadn't heard her. I hadn't even sensed her.

Then again, my mind had been on other things.

"And thus, you saw it all," I remarked. "Or heard it, when you weren't bustling to go tell Master Noctorno what was happening."

She visibly swallowed.

I studied her, and as I did so I watched her anxiety escalate.

As noted, she'd been an excellent maid for some time.

The past several days, however, she'd been more.

Therefore, I found myself assuring her softly, "I'm not angry with you, Josette."

"He was..." she shook her head again, "Master Noc was the only one I was certain would...help," she finished feebly.

"I'm certain you're quite right," I replied.

She took a step toward me and stopped. "I'm very pleased you're not annoyed with me, Lady Franka. I thought...when the subject came up, you'd..." she trailed off and didn't continue.

There was much about this to consider and I'd most assuredly considered it over the last few days.

Namely, the filthy secret of Nils, Anneka, Franka and Kristian Drakkar being out.

And the end of the domination, fear and torment.

It was unexpectedly not easy to come to terms with.

Considering my mother's magic, and the life I'd led where memories started with suffering in a way I knew nothing else, I'd never pondered a life without Nils and Anneka meting out their brand of ruthlessness. A life not living under the cloud of it happening again, doing my best to escape it and finding ways to keep safe from the minute I could.

I should have been relieved. Even joyous.

And yet I was not.

I felt a good deal of humiliation, but more of shame with an underlying uneasiness.

Kristian, I'd learned (from Finnie during one of her many visits), wanted to settle his wife and child after the fright of Mother appearing, and then they were journeying to the Winter Palace to see me. Valentine had offered to bring them there much quicker, that was to say in an instant, but Kristian had declined, fearing his young son's reaction to such a happenstance.

Though mostly, I'd decided, it was probably that this offer was extended right after Valentine interrupted my mother's preparations so my brother was likely more concerned about the state of mind of his family than travel plans.

It was highly unusual (and if they were to journey by sleigh, which it seemed they were going to do, meaning I'd be at the Winter Palace even longer than the queen decreed), but I was keen for my brother's visit.

It wasn't unusual because I wished to see him and ascertain if he was indeed well in mind and spirit.

It was unusual because I wished to talk with him about *his* reaction to our lifelong misery coming to an abrupt, unanticipated end.

Discussing my feelings was not something I was adept at doing. That was to say, since I put a stop to Kristian and I whispering together as children because we were repeatedly punished for it, I'd never done it, not even with Antoine.

Therefore looking forward to such discourse was farcical.

But it could not be denied I did.

"My lady, is there aught else?" Josette called, and I started, losing track of our conversation and even forgetting she was there.

"I'm so sorry, Josette. My mind wandered. No, thank you. Nothing else."

She did not move.

All she did was blink.

I found that odd until I realized what had come out of my mouth.

Dear goddess, I'd *apologized.*

And...

I peered closer at my maid, squinting my eyes across the distance...

It appeared she was on the verge of tears!

Bloody hell.

I wasn't an ogre, but she'd been with me for five years.

Five years with someone who was distant, respectful, but not kind.

Not to mention, the very idea of living a life at the beck and call of anyone was revolting.

Further, as my parents had taught me—that servants were beneath my notice—living a life not once considering that dreadful fact was even *more* revolting.

Which meant *I* was revolting!

You're learning, mon ange, Antoine said in my head.

Bloody bleeding *hell.*

Bugger off, I snapped.

"I...you're...I..." Josette cut into my demented thoughts and this time she visibly gulped, "I'll check in on you later, milady."

I decided to keep my mouth shut and simply lift my chin.

She finally vanished behind the door.

I watched this and did not beat back my sigh of relief.

I then found the ribbon in my book and opened it to the next chapter I should be reading.

However, I knew this was a wasted effort, for regardless of the copious time I'd had to *rest* and *mend,* that time had been broken repeatedly, mostly by Josette, but also with irritating frequency by Noc and even by a solicitous Frey and an openly pleasant and sociable Finnie.

And just that morning, the first I'd been out of my bed, she'd brought Circe and Cora (Madeleine was now celebrating wedded bliss with Apollo, on their way to one of his houses by some lake somewhere, this I knew due to the chitter-chatter of the two princesses and queen who'd attended me, all of whom gabbed like scullery maids).

I had found that ignoring Noc or giving him monosyllabic answers did not deter him in his friendliness. In fact, he found it amusing and did not hesitate not only to demonstrate this by smiling, chuckling or out and out laughing, but also sharing this with me verbally. As if not only could I read he found this so by his smiling, chuckling and laughing, but also he wished to assure me of the veracity of these acts like this was the most sought after attribute.

I also found that one did not have to be sociable and forthcoming around sociable and forthcoming people. One could be virtually silent and even sullen and they just carried on being social and forthcoming.

It was grating on my nerves.

I'd even pulled the real Franka out, saying something cutting to Finnie right in front of Aurora (although Frey had left my room—I was frustrated, not foolish), and if it could be credited, Finnie had just smiled at me and declared, "Franka, I swear, you're a stitch."

Yes.

That was precisely what she said.

I'd never forget it.

And now, as I should be averting my mind to a book, I was not. Instead, I was on tenterhooks awaiting who might come through the door.

I would not admit that I wished it to be Noc even as I did know that, with the frequency of his visits, he was the most likely candidate.

Indeed, I would not admit I wished it to be *anyone*, because, damnably, sociability and outgoingness was nauseatingly pleasing to be around.

I turned my attention from my book to the window and asked it, "If I looked in the mirror, would I even recognize me?"

This is who you've always been, love, Antoine answered.

I'm quite pleased you're dead, I lied irritably.

I know this is not true. Though, this being what you think, you'd be free to explore the feelings you have growing toward Noc.

At these words in my head, my back shot straight so fast a swell of pain rose that was so fierce I had to bite my lip in an effort not to moan.

During this effort, I heard a sharp rap on the door, and heralding Noc's arrival (as this was always the case), before I bid entry (or denied it, this effort always unheeded), the door opened and he sauntered through.

"Hey, babe," he greeted.

I did not greet back.

I glowered.

This was because he was wearing those trousers again. It seemed he had a number of pairs, all the same fabric but all different shades of blue, all of them an impossibility to decide which pair suited him the best.

He was also wearing a shirt that looked of the same material, except more lightweight and almost completely faded, only a nuance of blue was left. And this shirt managed to do remarkable things not only to his chest, but also his narrow waist, his broad shoulders and his extraordinary eyes.

Yes, if I hadn't already come to that conclusion, the last three days it had been made clear the gods had utterly forsaken me.

I looked to the window attempting to call up the vision of Antoine. His lanky frame. His refined features. The thickness of his dark-blond hair. The vividness of his green eyes.

But all I could see was Noc in his trousers.

And all I could hear was Noc dragging a chair over to mine.

"You good?" he asked.

"I am," I answered the window.

"Should you be sitting up?" he asked.

"The physician seemed to think so, considering it was his suggestion."

"Is that pillow you got behind you fluffy enough?" Noc pressed.

Proof.

Friendliness and sociability, not to mention kindness, were frustrating.

And nauseating.

(I told myself).

Slowly, I turned my eyes to him. "No, it's hard and chafing. But considering I've just ordered Josette to bring me a hair shirt so I can continue my self-flagellation at higher levels of discomfort, I think it will suffice."

Noc flashed me a smile. "You're bein' funny so I see you're good."

Somehow, I continued to give myself away.

I sighed heavily and turned my attention back to the window, announcing, "I had intended to read."

"Then read."

I looked back at him. "*Alone.*"

"Then read alone. I'll run down to the library, find a book, come up and do it with you."

I tipped my head to the side. "You do have the word *alone* in your world, do you not?"

"Sure we do," he replied amiably. "But figure, you got your head in a book, you're always alone, even if someone's with you."

If one did indeed have their head in a book, he was quite right.

I shifted my gaze back to the window.

"Your book's not out the window, Frannie."

Gods, that *name.*

"The green witch has disappeared," I stated, my curiosity at said disappearance getting the better of me for I knew I should say nothing that might strike up discourse. Even though I needed to say nothing to strike up discourse, Noc was adept at doing that all on his own.

"She has. According to the others, this is her way. She comes and goes as she pleases."

I did not turn away from the window when I asked, "With the troubles over, is she gone for good?"

"According to Lavinia, she reckons Valentine will be back. When? That's anybody's guess."

I said nothing for a long time, struggling with my thoughts that I found the green witch fascinating, and of all my visitors these last days, she was the one I'd actually wish to have.

I became cognizant of my reflection in the window, the chill coming off the glass, cooling my shoulder.

I needed my shawl.

I needed peace and quiet.

I needed my own company.

I needed...

"I can't picture him," I declared for reasons unknown, likely because taking in all this sociability and outgoingness was making me daft.

"Say again?" Noc asked.

"I can't picture him," I shared insanely. "Antoine. It's difficult to call him up. I might focus in on a feature, but it's elusive. The rest, hazy."

"Right, see you might not be good," he muttered.

He was correct.

I fought my shoulders slumping, and not simply because that minute movement might cause pain, but of what it would betray to Noc. A physical habit, this subterfuge, for even as I fought it, my mouth kept giving him what was in my head.

"I should have hired a portrait artist," I said faintly to the window. "Twenty of them. Hundreds of them. I don't have a single image of him and my mind is failing too soon." My voice fell to a whisper. "Too, too soon."

I was startled when Noc took my hand. I looked down to it and up to him to see he'd drawn his chair even closer, we were but inches away, and he was holding my hand in a warm, firm grip.

"He wasn't what he looked like, baby," he said gently. "He was always only what he made you feel. And I bet that isn't failing."

Looking into his startling blue eyes, eyes I knew instinctively I'd never forget, not for a moment, I feared he was wrong.

I slipped my hand from his grip, placed the ribbon back into the book, shut it smartly and again turned to the window.

"Am I right?" Noc pushed.

"He deserves more," I replied, not looking at him. "He deserves to have every memory held precious."

"Memories are what they made you feel too, sweetheart. But Franka," not attempting to grab my hand again, he curled his long fingers around my knee, "if you hold on too tight, you won't let go. You don't let go, you don't move on.

You gotta hold on to what you can have, the good you got from him, how that made you feel, but hold on loose, baby, so you don't miss out on what might be in store."

I felt a tinge of pain in my back as my attention jerked again to Noc.

"And you assume I wish to move on?"

"Not now, maybe," he said. "It's too fresh. But someday, yes."

"Well, you'd be wrong," I snapped.

"And what would Antoine think of that?"

I shut my mouth and yet again diverted my gaze to the window, for I knew exactly what Antoine would think of that.

And it wasn't much.

He lived life to its fullest. He loved life. He taught me to do the same (when I was with him).

He'd be disappointed if I did not continue on in that vein, now even more so without the threat of my parents clouding my every move.

Noc gave my knee a squeeze. "This shit, it's not for now, Frannie. This shit, you think on in the future. They say there're five stages of grief. Wasn't around you to know if you hit the first, which is denial. But I know you worked through anger with the revenge you played out on those witches. Maybe you did the bargaining but it seems to me you're in the depression stage now and you just gotta feel it. Don't fight it. It's gonna suck. But then you'll get through that, get to the last stage, and accept it."

I turned back to Noc, declaring, "That's utterly preposterous."

"Tell me you haven't touched on all of those, babe. Say it right to my face," he dared.

"I haven't," I retorted.

His lips quirked. "Think on it and repeat that."

"This is a ridiculous exercise, Noc," I announced instead of "thinking on it."

This earned me a half smile and a muttered, "Right, maybe you're still in the anger stage."

"Weren't you going to go to the library and get a book?" I reminded him.

His brows went up. "Is that an invitation to come back and read with you?"

"Absolutely not. However, Frey had the rail taken out of the door so I can't bar it against you, so you, and everyone else in the palace, are free to come and go as you wish, something you, and everyone else in the palace, feel free to do. What *I* wish is that you'd go, and if it's simply to find a book, this would not be unwelcome."

He released my knee and sat back. "Don't be pissed at Frey for that, sugar-lips. I asked him to do it so you wouldn't get up to anything stupid."

"I've never been stupid a single day in my life," I rejoined.

"I bet that's true," he whispered, his eyes never leaving mine.

I drew in breath through my nose then stated, "As you seem determined to spend time in my presence, and you and Frey seem to have a good deal of accord, it would be prudent on my part to make you useful. Thus, prior to my brother arriving at the Winter Palace, I'd like you to request of Frey that I'm allowed to see my parents in jail."

He did an odd blink where he closed his eyes, lifted his brows keeping his eyes closed, then opened his eyes only to share his were filled with disbelief.

"Say what?" he queried just as oddly as the elongated blink.

"I'd like you to request of Frey that I'm allowed to see my parents in jail, doing this prior to Kristian and his family arriving here," I repeated.

"I heard you, babe, I'm just wondering if you've lost your mind in the last two minutes."

I found this offensive and foolishly straightened my back, controlled the wince that move should have caused and pierced him with a glare.

"I fail to see how desiring a visit with my parents is losing my mind."

"Frannie, you never have to see them again."

I carefully straightened my shoulders as I felt my mouth purse.

Then through it, I declared, "A barter, kind sir, my entire chest of Hawkvale gold if you never call me Frannie again. And while I'm mentioning that, my entire chest of Korwahkian jewels *and* the furs if you never call me sugarlips again."

A light hit his eyes I was coming to know so I braced for what was next.

"Seein' as tickin' you off makes you cuter *and* funnier, no matter how killer a deal that is, I gotta say no."

"I was being quite honest," I lied. Even if the danger no longer lurked, I was absolutely not giving him chests of gold and jewels for the favor of not calling me names I loathed.

Perhaps *a* fur and *a* jewel and *several* coins (that's how much I loathed those names for the truth was, I didn't even wish to part with that).

But not all of them.

"Liar," he returned.

I waved a hand in front of me and moved us back to the pertinent subject, but did it getting a cut in because I was, well...*me*. Or at least a shadow of me. But there was still that.

"I see. So I request you not call me these names. You decline. I request you speak to Frey in my stead to procure a visit with my parents. You decline that as well. This meaning you're not only annoying, you're also not useful."

He leaned again toward me, reaching out one hand to touch my knee before he asked carefully, "If you don't have to see them again, after all they've done to you, your brother, why on earth would you see them again, sweetheart?"

"Because I'm still standing."

He sat back in his chair and studied me.

But as he did so, a smile I'd never seen on him curved his mouth.

It was filled with viciousness and glee.

It was astonishing.

And mouthwatering.

"I'll talk to Frey for you," he agreed.

"I'd be most obliged."

He leaned forward again and declared, "Just so you know, you aren't going alone."

I wasn't?

"Whyever not?' I queried.

"Because I'll be with you."

"Why?" That word came higher pitched.

"You're sharp as a tack but slow to pick up a few things, so I'll explain again," he started and promptly finished. "You no longer have to go it alone."

"I'm not being slow, Noc," I returned. "I *want* to go it alone and I'll explain that further. I don't want you with me."

"I give a shit about you," he stated suddenly sharply, speaking in a way he'd never spoken to me, something which made me fall silent. "You don't know how to cope with that and I get it, babe. I absolutely do. And you can take all the time you need to wake up and see what's happening around you. Through that, I'm gonna stick with it, and in case you haven't noticed, so are Frey and Finnie. In other words, Frannie, buckle up. You don't get with the program, it's gonna be a wild ride."

There was much I understood in his speech.

There was also much I didn't.

"I do believe I understand the word shit," I retorted. "And it means excrement."

His sharp mood was failing as a smile broadened his mouth. "Yeah."

"So why would you give an excrement about me? Isn't that saying you *don't* think much of me?"

"It's slang," he explained.

"Everything you utter is slang."

"Not everything."

"The vast majority," I replied.

His next came in a mutter. "Not gonna argue that."

"Are we done speaking on this topic?" I queried.

"You don't fight me on goin' with you to your parents, then yeah."

"I'm not in the mood to argue. I'm in the mood to read," I lied about the latter.

I was in the mood to brood, something I wasn't going to do in front of him, and I was assuming whatever came next for me would be done with him at least in the room.

"I take that back," he stated strangely. "One more thing on that topic."

"Yes?" I prompted.

"Why don't you ask Frey yourself?"

"When I'm around him he's friendly and sociable."

Noc stared at me for some time after I finished speaking before he asked, "And?"

"I find it nauseating."

He burst out laughing.

I rolled my eyes.

When he was controlling his mirth, I was done rolling my eyes.

He caught them and declared, "You're so full of shit."

"What an offensive thing to say," I snapped.

"It's slang too, babe, as you know. But yeah. I just essentially called you a liar. Though, in a teasing way."

With nothing else for it, I looked to the ceiling and begged of the gods who had abandoned me, "Deliver me."

"You gonna read?" he asked.

I turned my attention to him. "The next item on my day's agenda is practicing my skill at ignoring you. So yes, Master Noc, I'm going to read."

"Great, I'll go get a book," he muttered, pushed out of his seat and came to me.

He then bent close in order to kiss the top of my hair.

Kiss the top of my hair!

Like he was a doting uncle.

The gall!

Even as the aristocrat in me was insulted beyond measure, I felt a shiver glide down my spine and it was the first thing that felt good in that area for three days.

"Be back," he said.

Deciding to put my plan into action, I didn't respond.

I simply opened my book, removed the ribbon and pretended to read.

~

Late that evening, after dinner, I sat on the chaise in the dressing room next to the bedroom (both decidedly masculine, but then Noc and I had exchanged rooms due to my situation), bent slightly forward for comfort. My robe was draped low at the back but I held the edges of it up in front to cover me.

Josette was sitting behind me, attending my wounds.

After a day I'd spent completely in the company of others (Noc, reading, Noc, lunch, Noc and Finnie, afternoon chat, Circe and Cora joining us for afternoon tea—we'll just say it was a great relief when they were away to prepare for dinner), we'd just completed my evening bath.

"The physician wants the lavender and honey on them tonight, milady, but he spoke to me and believes you should do your best to leave them to the air tomorrow. The moistness isn't allowing scabs to form. We can dress them prior to bed, but during the day leave them. Do you think you can do that?"

As I'd never sustained a beating from my father in my life where anyone attended my wounds, I had a feeling I could.

These were not the words I used to answer my maid.

I stated, "We'll try it, Josette."

"Good," she mumbled.

I sat, feeling the restfulness of her ministrations, and seemingly unable to stop my mouth from speaking that day, more words poured forth.

"There are matters of our future to discuss," I informed her.

"Our future?" she asked.

"Indeed," I replied. "Losing Master Antoine, the situation as it stands here, things are quite up in the air."

Her voice sounded surprised. "Won't we return to Fleuridia?"

Fleuridia was her home.

I knew from her *curriculum vitae* she'd been in service in both Hawkvale and Lunwyn prior to coming to being in my employ, which was why I assumed the lovely lilt of her Fleuridian accent was not pronounced and her Valerian was superb.

It had not occurred to me, uncomfortably, but she might be wishing to return home.

"Will this be a problem for you?" I asked.

"I...well, I go where you go, milady."

She did indeed.

But that had never been across the Green Sea.

"Can you sit up?" she requested. "I need to wrap the dressings around."

I did as she asked, dropping my arms to give her the access she needed.

"Josette?" I called.

"Right here, Lady Franka."

"You do know..." By the gods, how did one go about doing such things? "That your service...the way you perform your duties...that I quite...*value* it."

There was a pause in her movements before she answered me, her voice lower, not with emotion, or at least not soft emotion.

She sounded like she wished to be laughing.

"I do get that impression, milady."

"Excellent," I stated brusquely. "In understanding that, you can imagine in future I'd like to keep you in my employ."

She wound the gauze around my front and back as I spoke and continued to do so as she did the same. "I would hope so."

"And for your loyalty and level of performance," I persevered, feeling drattedly awkward, "which has always been at a high standard, I shall be giving you a rise in pay."

"That'd be lovely, thank you," she said quietly from behind me, still wrapping my naked front with gauze, but sounding like she meant those words.

The intimacy of our situation was not lost on me.

The fact I'd not once considered how I'd entrusted such intimacies to Josette without thought (until then) was also not lost on me.

I struggled with feelings of shame and hoped Antoine's voice didn't sound in my head as I persisted.

"I'm also in a position to add to our numbers. However, if you agree to accompany me as I carry out my plans for the future, then I'd like you not only to see to employing someone you feel you'll work well with, but overseeing that someone once I've hired them."

"Help with my duties?" she asked, the pitch of her voice rising in surprise.

"You've worked diligently for some time. I'm in a position to remunerate you to show you my appreciation as well as retain some help for you with said duties."

"I would...that would...I would be grateful for that, Lady Franka."

"Excellent," I murmured as I felt her tying the dressing in place.

"I'm done," she announced.

I carefully pulled my robe up my back, closed it at the front and cinched it loosely at the waist before turning to sit properly on the chaise.

Josette had already bustled away and was dealing with wet bathing cloths, organizing jars and bottles and gathering my spent clothing.

I'd never once observed her in these duties. I actually didn't know what became of my attire and items of my toilette after I'd swanned from the bathing room. But now I saw the end of my toilette, as the duration of it, not to mention the time prior to it, heralded nothing but work for Josette.

"Josette," I said softly and her eyes darted to me as she stopped moving. "Come sit with me, please," I requested.

Having said "please," I felt that was enough of a kindness and stopped myself from patting the cushion beside me, which was a bizarre urge I had in that moment.

She threw my clothing over a beautifully-appointed clotheshorse and moved my way. Her step was tentative but her gaze held mine.

She sat next to me, and in deference to my wounds, I turned carefully to her.

"I've made a decision about what's next for me and our earlier discourse was done in order for me to share that, in what I've decided, I'd like you to remain with me. However, I'll say what's next, what I have planned, is most unusual, and of course your life is your own so your decision to accompany me, or not, is also your own."

"All right, Lady Franka," she said hesitantly.

"And obviously, from what I've already shared, I'll give you an excellent reference and a healthy stipend should you decide against continuing with me. Enough that perhaps you can take some time to yourself. Travel or..." I flipped a hand, "whatever you enjoy doing. Or you may wish to learn an additional trade. It will be your coin to do with as you wish. But regardless, there will be no need to fret if you don't find alternate employment immediately. You'll be safe."

As I spoke, I ignored her mouth falling open.

I continued to ignore it as I prompted, "Do you understand that?"

She nodded slowly and said, "Yes, milady."

"Good," I replied, shifting in my seat, ready to get on with it. "Now I'll share that I've had time to reconsider the plans I had prior to my parents being incarcerated, and even though this means my options for my future are now more extensive in the Northlands..."

Her look turned from astonished to confused, but I ignored that too and carried on.

"I still feel an adventure would be just the thing. With the loss of Master Antoine, Fleuridia—"

Josette didn't make me utter it, saying swiftly, "I understand, Lady Franka."

I nodded smartly and declared, "So I've decided to cross the Green Sea."

At this, not only did her mouth drop open, but her eyes grew large.

"That's quite an adventure for anyone," I went on, even though her expression shared she knew that and then some. "So I do understand if you'd rather not. If you have ties to Fleuridia, family or..." I shook my head, having no idea what she had, "acquaintances you'd not like to be that far away from."

"My family's dead, milady."

That was when I finally shut my mouth and stared at her.

I stopped doing that to inquire, "All of them?"

She nodded. "Mother, father, sister."

Bloody hell.

"I...well," I stammered, pulled myself together and asked, "If you wish to share, would you like to tell me how such a thing came about?"

"A bridge crumbled under their sleigh," she informed me readily. "The sleigh fell through and somehow flipped as it descended. My father got free, but my mother and sister were trapped under it at the bottom of the river." She shrugged as if this mattered little to her, but I could see the pink in her cheeks that seemed pronounced due to the sudden pallor of her skin. "My father died because he stayed in the water trying to pull them free."

This was...

Well...

Unthinkable.

With naught else in my power to do, I simply whispered, "Josette."

She shook her head like doing so could negate the pain of these memories.

"It was a long time ago. As I had an interest in music that they did not, I was at a concert at our Dwelling of the Gods with friends. A traveling choir that was quite good. They'd gone into town to have dinner at a local pub. The pub was known for excellent stew." Another shrug and she finished, "At least they had a lovely last dinner."

"Cease that nonsense," I ordered and watched my maid blink.

"I beg your pardon?"

"This is horrific, this story," I announced something she knew much better than me. "I know you wish to make little of it and move on, though I don't know why, except perhaps you don't want to trouble me with it, or you wish to deny the feelings you still feel about it."

"Well, of course I don't wish to trouble you with it. You have enough to concern you," she replied ridiculously.

"And my maid who's been loyal, hard-working and attentive, and these last days, exceptionally kind, having this history doesn't concern me?" I queried with one raised brow.

After a careful pause, she reminded me just as carefully, "It hasn't for years, milady."

She was damnably right.

I lifted my chin. "Well it does now," I stated crisply and continued in the same tone. "And I'm sad for you. Were you close?"

She nodded.

"Then that makes me even sadder for you," I declared.

"Thank you," she replied.

"Is this how you came to service, or was your family in service before you?"

"I was...well, I needed to find work. I was thirteen. It was an orphanage or service. I think I chose rightly," she answered.

She'd been thirteen.

Yes.

Unthinkable.

"I've no idea if you did or did not but that matters not now," I told her. "Here you are. In service to me. And there I'd like you to remain, with another maid for you to oversee and assist you as we travel over the Green Sea for whatever awaits us there."

I found after making my proclamation that I was anxious to hear her reply.

Travel across the Green Sea was unusual because it wasn't entirely safe. Indeed, travel anywhere wasn't safe by land or by sea. Pirates. Highwaymen. Intemperate weather.

But from my knowledge (which was not vast), there were other dangers lurking along that passage.

In other words, this wasn't your average adventure.

This was an *adventure*.

Therefore, I knew what I was asking, and these were partly the reasons why I was offering her a rise in salary but also every opportunity to break out of my service without any stress or concern about her future should she wish to decline.

I did actually think after my visit with my brother and his family and my back had healed enough to make the journey, rather than remaining in Lunwyn, which was now safe for me, that an adventure was just the thing.

But to embark on it with someone familiar would be beneficial.

And if I only admitted it to myself (for, even though I seemed to be sharing with alarming frequency), embarking on it with Josette would be beyond beneficial and maybe prove to make the journey and any ventures we had enjoyable.

"It would be an honor to go with you," she said.

I was stunned by her ready acceptance (as well as heartened and perhaps flattered) thus had to fight the mad desire to cheer out loud.

Even so, I needed to be certain Josette was certain.

"And Fleuridia? Do you leave no one else behind? Friends? A lover?" I asked.

"No, milady."

I narrowed my gaze at her. "You're certain."

She nodded fervently and it was then I noted a light of excitement in her eyes.

"Yes, I'm sure. Very sure." She hopped a little on her cushion and reached out to grab my hands that were folded in my lap. "This might be fun!"

I looked down at my hands and barely caught sight of hers holding mine before she wrenched hers away.

"My apologies for the forwardness, milady," she murmured as if I'd chastised her.

I looked back at her face to see she'd averted her gaze.

"Josette," I called.

It took time but she eventually turned her attention back to me.

Or, to be exact, my nose.

"You've cared for my person for years. I do think it's quite all right in a moment of excitement to touch my hands, don't you?"

Her focus shot from my nose to my eyes.

"I...yes, if you don't mind, milady."

"I surely don't," I decreed then promptly stood, because frankly, I'd had enough.

Truly, the ease of participating in friendliness and sociability was troubling.

"Would you like your nightgown, Lady Franka?" Josette asked.

"Yes, please."

She assisted me in divesting me of my robe. She assisted me in donning my nightgown. She then assisted me putting my robe back on. She even saw to the unnecessary task of holding me steady as I slid my feet into my slippers. And she hovered close as I moved back into the bedroom.

Not done, she fervently plumped the pillows before I climbed into bed and threw the soft, woolen throw over my legs after I'd managed that feat.

"Is there aught else?" she asked.

"Yes," I answered.

She waited patiently but I could see that light of excitement still there in her eyes.

She did indeed like me.

She also liked adventure.

"Milady?" she prompted when I did not speak on.

"Do you hope we make Airen or would you rather we journey inland and seek Firenze?"

A gleaming smile spread on her face even as she shook her head. "I actually hope we find Mar-el."

Mar-el, an island nation that was said to be heavily guarded, for reasons that were an even more heavily-guarded secret. An island nation where it was also said its citizens, who were deliciously dark of skin, actually spent the vast majority of their time on magnificent galleons wreaking havoc on the seas.

"Hmm," I murmured. "I'd not considered that." I tipped my head to the side. "We'll have to put that on our agenda."

"That'd be *marvelous*," she breathed, her excitement visibly escalating.

I nodded, actually fighting back an indulgent smile.

Winning that, I beat back rolling my eyes...at myself.

"Indeed," I murmured in a way I hoped she knew she was dismissed, but kindly.

Gods.

Perhaps I should allow Noc to call me the revolting *Frannie* and ask everyone else to do the same for it would seem I was Franka Drakkar no more.

"I'll just see to sorting everything for the night," Josette said.

"Thank you, Josette," I replied, reaching for my book.

"No."

At her peculiar response, I turned my attention back to my maid.

"Pardon?" I queried.

"No," she said softly. "Thank you, Lady Franka. Thank you *bunches*."

This put me in the awkward and unpleasant position of feeling emotion swelling up the back of my throat.

Fortunately, Josette was very good at her job.

So before I embarrassed myself (further), she turned on her slipper and scurried to the dressing room.

I looked down at my book but didn't open it.

Josette was accompanying me across the Green Sea.

I allowed my lips to curl up minutely.

Marvelous.

6

I SMILED. HUGE

Valentine

Valentine Rousseau's eyes opened and she stared at the dark ceiling.

Then she slid out of bed, leaving the young, slumbering, firm, naked male form in it.

Bending gracefully, her red-tipped fingers tagged the slip of green silk and lace off the floor. She pulled it over her head and the soft material slithered down her body.

She moved out of her bedroom, down the hall and to the room with the salmon-colored walls.

She did not bother herself with turning on a light. She knew every inch of the room, her house, for not only did she live in it, she'd been born to it.

She glided through the dark to stand at the small, round table on which the large, clear, smooth, crystal sphere sat on top of a bed of emerald-green velvet.

The tips of her fingers skimmed the ball and instantly a wisp of jade smoke curled inside the crystal.

She stared at its glow through the dark and felt her mouth get soft.

Just as she thought.

What she didn't understand was why she cared. Cared so much it woke her.

On this thought, her mouth grew hard.

"Annoying," she murmured as the smoke twisted, coiled and curved.

Valentine took in a delicate, displeased breath.

For years, she cared about very little. In fact, nothing.

But herself.

Then came her little goddess of love, Seoafin, Finnie.

Now, caring seemed to be all she did.

And not just about herself.

In fact, all the troubles were sorted in that other world, but was she quit of it?

No.

She was not only not quit of it, she was home in New Orleans and still checking in frequently to see how things progressed with not only Franka and Noctorno, but Seoafin and Frey, Circe and Lahn...

All of them.

This going so far as to wake her in the night so she'd seek her crystal just to make certain all was well.

She cared, there was no denying it.

This didn't mean she didn't lament doing just that.

Valentine studied the smoke, sighed and watched Noc laughing and Franka glowering as they sat together in Franka's chamber.

It was no surprise he'd made little headway. Not only Franka's history would inhibit things moving forward, she'd lost a lover in a dramatically sad way.

There were many wounds Franka Drakkar needed healed but only some of them Noc could assist in this effort.

The loss of her lover she'd have to come to terms with on her own.

Suddenly, Valentine tipped her head to the side as she felt it. Within seconds, the room turned green. Not Valentine's green, which shaded emerald to jade. No, Lavinia's green. The green of Lavinia's goddess of the other world, Alabasta, which was the color of a fertile meadow.

Every witch with any amount of power had their own color.

It represented their soul.

Thus Lavinia's was fresh and nurturing.

And Valentine's was rich and precious.

Valentine directed her eyes to the vortex forming and watched Lavinia appear.

"My friend," Lavinia greeted when her feet were planted on Valentine's priceless Persian rug.

"It's late," Valentine replied.

Lavinia, accustomed to Valentine, took no offense at her reply and smiled but looked to the sphere on the table.

Her eyes moved back to Valentine.

"The knight of your world is making progress," she noted.

Valentine swept a hand to her crystal ball.

"This, I've noticed," she drawled.

Lavinia nodded. "What you may not have noticed is that her mother's magic was revealed, but Franka's was not. We both felt the swell of it that terrible night some days ago, but she has not come forward as a witch. No one else is aware of it, save perhaps Noctorno. This concerns me."

"She's coping with a good deal, Lavinia, perhaps you'll give her more than a few days," Valentine suggested.

"It's my duty to my country to share that I hold this knowledge, my friend," Lavinia replied.

Valentine sighed a delicate, displeased sigh.

"It would be nice if you would come," Lavinia urged. "I do think she's of your..." her friend's lips tipped up, "*kind*, and you will speak well together." Her voice dipped quieter. "In times such as these, she may need something just as that."

"I'll return," Valentine replied.

Lavinia nodded. She knew if Valentine said she would be there, she would be there.

Unfortunately, Lavinia knew Valentine would be there because she *cared*.

"You came to my world just for this?" Valentine asked.

Lavinia looked through the dark room but shook her head doing it, stating, "I was curious."

"Do be curious at another time," she invited. "When it's not the dead of night and I don't have a lovely body, not mine, obviously, currently warming my bed."

Lavinia eyed Valentine. "Now I see why you returned home."

Valentine shook her head. "You see nothing. He's just a body. A trifle. A useful one, but only that."

Lavinia eyed her far more closely. "No one is *just* a body, Valentine."

"He is," Valentine sniffed.

"Have you had another who meant more?" Lavinia asked.

"Ah," Valentine breathed out. "I see you've come in the middle of the night not only because you were curious, but to discuss my love life, which means you're not simply curious. You're nosy."

"It's morn in my world," Lavinia reminded her.

"I do know that, *chérie*," Valentine sighed.

"I know you know. I also know you didn't answer my question," Lavinia pressed.

"When the time comes, I'll choose a man to make me round with a daughter. But even then he'll just be a body, though he'll also be his seed, so rest assured, I'll select him with great care."

"That's wretched," Lavinia said gently.

Valentine lifted her brows in surprise. "You wish to be tangled up in a *relationship?*"

"I've lived a life where I was quite content with my own company. But I must say, watching Finnie and Frey, Maddie and Apollo..."

"That was about magic. And destiny," Valentine eschewed.

"All love has its own magic," Lavinia returned, her eyes sliding toward the door, her words the truth, of course, with caveats. "Even love that doesn't span universes."

"It also can be used for ill, if turned into a weapon," Valentine retorted. "And this happens often, in both worlds."

Lavinia returned her gaze to her friend.

"Quite right, my dear," she whispered. "Odd, we seem to have this conversation often. With varying results. This suggests love is foremost on our minds most of the time. Including yours."

Valentine didn't deign to reply.

"You must come soon," Lavinia urged, wisely changing the subject. "I've only visited with Franka once, and I didn't know her before, but from what I knew of her, she's much changed, though I think she's discomfited by it."

Valentine knew *very* well how that felt.

Lavinia spoke on. "Not to mention, when I'm with the others, they speak of her already not simply with compassion for what she's endured, but with humor and even growing affection."

This, Valentine had seen in her crystal, finding herself looking on...*happily*, doing so hoping it would continue.

"I'll be there," Valentine replied.

She then wondered when she started hoping about anything.

Caring *and* hoping.

How vile. Both were so very *vulgar*.

"Until we meet in my world," Lavinia called, and Valentine watched as she faded away.

With an agitated gesture, Valentine shook her sleek red hair out of her face and looked back to her crystal. She lifted a hand and trailed her fingers over it, searching, and she found someone she'd discovered some days ago when she'd decided that meddling with Franka and Noc would not be enough.

There was another.

And as she watched the large man go about the business of sleeping in his own bed, her jaw set and she trailed her fingers over the crystal again.

The smoke vanished.

There she went, *caring* about someone else.

And worse, doing something about it.

Valentine Rousseau rarely expended effort on anything someone didn't compensate her for, except, of course, one of her trifles.

She *definitely* expended effort on her trifles.

Her thoughts moved to what she'd just seen in her crystal and she was pleased in this world, as in the other, he was such a fine specimen. A plaything such as him would be—Valentine drew in a wistful breath—*delicious.*

Alas, such as him, she had found, didn't tend to like the way Valentine played.

He would be perfect for his intended.

An intended he didn't know he had (yet). And that intended had no idea what Valentine had planned for her future.

A warm curl swirled in her belly.

Valentine sighed yet again as she shook off her uncharacteristically soft, romantic thoughts.

She was losing her touch.

She needed to find it again.

To do that, her thoughts moved to the young, naked, firm, male form asleep in her bed, and in the dark, Valentine smiled her cat's smile.

She walked back to her bedroom, went to the nightstand, opened it and took out a box of matches. She struck one and lit the three candles on the night table.

She brought the match to her lips, blew out its flame and touched the glowing ember against her tongue where it sizzled.

She dropped it to the nightstand with a small smile curving her lips.

She then tossed the matchbox back into the drawer and closed it.

And then Valentine turned with languid but definitive purpose to the form in the bed.

Franka

I WALKED down the front steps of the Winter Palace somewhat stiffly, but I managed it, hoping I hid the stiffness by twitching my fur cloak closer around me.

That stiffness became more pronounced when I saw what awaited me at the bottom of the steps.

I was headed to the jail to see my parents.

Noc had told me he'd be accompanying me.

However, at the bottom of the steps, milling about at the side of not *my* sleigh but one of the queen's sumptuously-appointed *royal* sleighs, stood not only Noc but also Finnie, Frey, Circe, Lahn, Cora and the Noctorno of my world (who allowed those close to him to call him Tor, something he invited I do at my command attendance at dinner last night with the lot of them and the queen).

What, by the gods, were they *all* doing there?

No.

No.

I didn't care.

In my estimation from the message delivered by the bird my brother sent sharing when they'd left his home, Kristian and his family would arrive at the Winter Palace on the morrow.

It had been nine days since the drama in the buttery. Due to a physician's care (and Josette's), my back still ached, but it was healing far more rapidly than normal.

Noc and the rest had not ceased being friendly and sociable in this time. In fact, the more I was able to get up and about, the friendlier and more sociable they became.

This didn't matter to me.

I wanted this final visit with my parents done and behind me. I wanted to see my brother. After that, Josette and I (and whatever maid she selected to accompany us, the task of finding said maid something Josette had thrown herself into with abandoned glee) were off to cross the Green Sea.

Therefore, whatever befell me at this present moment, and the next, and the next, I would endure.

Until I was away.

Perhaps the others were preparing to go into town. There were two royal sleighs waiting and a variety of horses.

That was likely it.

But due to the fact that they were friendly and sociable, for whatever reason traits like that made you behave in ways like this, they were milling about waiting to see Noc and I off.

Noc noticed me making my descent, and not surprisingly he broke off from chatting with Cora and Tor and jogged up the steps toward me.

"How you doin', sweetheart?" he asked, his face a picture of concern, his hand capturing mine, and before I could pull it free he tucked my fingers around the inside of his elbow, drew me close to his side, kept his fingers snug around mine in a way I could not escape, and thus he assisted me down the steps.

"How I'm doing is being quite capable of descending a flight of steps on my own," I replied.

"I'll take that sass as you doin' good," he muttered.

I had learned from the very beginning that Noc decided to take whatever I said in whatever manner he wished to take it.

Hence in response I simply sighed.

Noc led us to the side of the sleigh where Cora and Tor were standing, and I noted Frey ceased speaking with Finnie, Lahn and Circe and came our way.

We stopped by the sleigh and Frey stopped at our grouping.

He was looking down on me with the same concern Noc showed.

"You're certain you wish to do this, Franka?" he asked.

"Absolutely," I answered.

He studied me a moment before he nodded once and declared, "We'll be there with you in case something upsetting happens."

At his words, I felt my body jolt and knew the extent of recovery in my back for I only felt a vague twinge of pain.

"I...sorry?" I asked.

Frey indicated the assemblage with a sweep of his proud head, which now included Circe, Lahn and Finnie, all of whom had joined us, before he repeated, "We'll all be with you in case something upsetting happens."

Dear goddess.

They were going to the jail with me.

But...

Why?

"That isn't necessary," I stated swiftly.

"A sister has a sister's back," Cora decreed. "And a sister's man has *her* back."

I looked to her. "Rest assured I mean no offense, princess, but we aren't sisters."

"We totally are," she returned.

"But..." I felt my brow furrow. "Are you, that is to say, is the other me your sister in your world?"

I heard Noc chuckle and saw grins and smiles all around while Cora answered (through her own grin), "No, babe. What I'm saying is, we're both chicks and all chicks are sisters, blood or not. And we have to look out for each other."

How peculiar. She, too, used these slang words "babe" and "chick" to refer to her own gender.

Mad.

And women looking out for women?

That wasn't mad. It was delusional.

It was my experience (and not experience due to my participation in such vulgar goings-on, they were so vulgar, they were even beneath *me*) most women, at least women of my ilk, didn't look out for each other.

They seduced one another's men and uttered cruel things about clothing, hairstyles, excess of weight or not enough of it, not to mention homing in on and dissecting with malicious glee anything else that might be perceived as a weakness or unattractive. Or they would harp on it to make it *seem* unattractive (mostly due to jealousy or spite). The sound of a voice. An ungainly talent at a dance. A gaucheness with social discourse.

These were not the cuts I had once relished, and not because it was all too easy.

Mostly because if a woman had a man, it was lower than low to set your sights on him. And tearing apart anyone for things they could not control wasn't sport. It was simply vicious.

But I'd lived my life with women behaving in this manner. Josette had even shared tidbits of female servants doing the same.

Three women giving up a morning where they could be at their leisure to do anything they wished in order to accompany me to a bloody *jail* just in case I got *upset*?

Unheard of!

"There's really no need," I persisted. "I'll only be there a short while."

"There's a need," Circe put in.

"Absolutely a need," Finnie agreed.

I didn't understand this.

However, this discussion was prolonging a situation that I'd like to see done. Precisely getting in the sleigh, getting to the jail, seeing my parents and returning to the palace.

So I gave in, murmuring, "As you wish," pulled free of Noc and turned to the sleigh.

I felt movement as Noc reached in front of me to open the door to the open-topped sleigh. I also felt his hand at my hip steadying me as if I couldn't climb into a bloody sleigh on my own, something I'd been doing since I'd gained control of my legs and feet.

I clenched my teeth in frustration, attempted to ignore his touch, which was firm enough that I felt it even through my furs, my gown and my warm undergarments, and found my seat.

Noc found his beside me and Cora had entered the sleigh and was settling beside him.

I didn't stoop to looking around to see where the others had gone. I simply grabbed the fur throw that was at the ready for us on the floor of the sleigh to pull over my lap. It was large and long and while I did this, Noc adjusted it over his lap as Cora did the same.

All of us tucked in the sleigh together like bosom buddies on a jaunt (laughable), Noc reached forward to take hold of the reins secured before him.

I looked at the four horses attached to the sleigh.

For the horse's sake, two was optimal to share a load, even on a long distance ride.

Four to sledge through town was ludicrous.

Unless you were a royal.

And since Cora was, I supposed it wasn't outlandish.

What surprised me was that Noc took the reins when I was relatively certain that the other men mounted steeds.

I turned to him and asked, "Do you not ride?"

I heard him click his teeth and watched him snap the straps, lurched with the forward movement of the sleigh, and then saw him look down at me.

"Ride?" he asked.

"A mount," I explained.

"Not much of that kind of riding in my world, babe," he stated, and I felt myself blink in surprise. "Though I do ride, just not a horse. A hawg. As in a Harley."

Cora piped in at this juncture.

"You have a Harley?"

Noc looked to his other side. "Yeah."

"Wow. Cool. Wish I'd gotten a ride with you before I had to leave our world," she remarked.

"Didn't get to get on it much in Seattle," Noc remarked. "Figure that'll change in NOLA. Least I hope so."

I heard this conversation but I was still back where it started.

"You ride a pig?" I asked with disbelief.

Both Noc and Cora's attention came to me and they stared at me mutely for a second before they both burst out laughing.

Well.

How rude.

I looked forward.

"Not laughin' at you, sweetheart," Noc said gently, through laughter that was, indeed, *at me*. "But you were bein' funny. We're talkin' about motorcycles. You don't have them here. We have automotive vehicles powered by gas. Move on wheels called tires. No animals needed. They go a lot faster. Most of them are enclosed, but not bikes, what motorcycles are sometimes referred to as, a brand of which is Harleys. That's what I've got. Those have two wheels, not four, and are open to the elements. You ride them kinda like a horse, except they're motor-powered."

"Interesting," I said like it was not.

However, it was.

What kinds of machines would these be, no animals needed? They seemed implausible and fanciful, just like what he'd shown me that first night we spoke—his "phone."

And yet that was real.

I had often thought of his gadgetry since, in the rare alone times I'd had, wishing I'd taken hold of it, inspected it, tested its magic.

Animal-less "vehicles" powered by gas I would adore the opportunity of seeing.

"It's cute, you not getting it," Noc went on to explain, noting my continued mood (as he always did, he just often chose to ignore it). "If you went to our world, you'd understand it."

I did not share that I'd be quite interested in going to his world and seeing these fantastical contraptions at work.

I also did not share that it was not cute to laugh at someone who was ignorant about something for reasons not in their control.

I just looked out the side of the sleigh, not noticing the houses and buildings and people we sledded by, and barely noticing the whoosh of our transport, the one behind us, and the clomp of the many horses' hooves in the snow.

But I did vaguely sense that many watched us pass.

Then again, we were a grand procession with a king, a queen, a prince, princesses and The Drakkar. But even if it was only Dax Lahn, the fellow was such a sight to see with his large body, long, bunched hair, fierce face with its abundant dark beard and unusual clothing made of hide, all would stop to watch.

Truth be told, I wished to watch him ride. I was certain he'd be good at it (though, that wasn't the only reason I wished to do this, as fierce as he was, he was most assuredly pleasing to the eye).

"You're right," Noc muttered, pulling me from my thoughts of the Dax, and I felt his arm round my waist so my head snapped around to look up at him again, seeing he appeared contrite. "Wasn't cool, us busting a gut like that. You don't know. And there's all sorts of shit about your world that I don't get or know about. I probably wouldn't like it much if I said something you thought was funny and you laughed in my face."

"Yeah, that wasn't cool, Franka, really sorry," Cora chimed in.

I did not know how to take this. Outside of a servant making a mistake and apologizing to me for doing so (as they should), I didn't think anyone had ever apologized to me. Certainly not when they'd done something wrong or hurtful. And absolutely not admitting they understood they'd done so and moving verbally to rectify that hurt.

"You cool?" Noc asked.

In that moment I did not wish to get into the fact that their usage of "cool" was like Noc's usage of "shit" and "fuck" and a variety of others. In other words, these were all used frequently but with what seemed like different meanings.

We spoke the same language but it still felt like I was cast adrift in a foreign land with only a modicum of understanding of the native tongue and I had to decipher all with only the barest of foundations.

Nevertheless, the way they'd both used "cool," I could only assume he meant to ask if I was over my pique.

I was not, of course, but that didn't factor.

"Yes, Noc, I'm fine," I lied.

His lips quirked, his eyes didn't leave mine, and he murmured, "You so aren't."

I faced forward again.

This allowed Noc's lips a direct line to my ear, and I fancied I could actually feel them whisper against the skin there, causing a chill to race down my spine that was not chilly in the slightest as he said, "Also cute."

Considering where his mouth was, he couldn't see my face. Therefore, I rolled my eyes.

I felt him pull away.

I decided silence was my best course of action for the rest of the journey (and the return one).

However, this was the wrong decision.

Although Noc and Cora chatted amiably together the entire distance, both of them made frequent attempts to draw me into their conversation, to which I was not rude, just short or monosyllabic, and they eventually let me be, leaving me in my head.

This was not a good place to be, especially these last nine days.

If I was honest with myself—something I tended not to be for reasons of self-preservation, but even more so the last week—I would have admitted that their company, any of them, was a boon. It kept me out of my head. It kept me away from melancholic, ashamed or anxious thoughts of what had befallen me and what was to come.

But now, as we sledged ever closer to the jail (a place I had no idea where it was so I didn't know exactly how close it was, just that we were moving, so naturally we were getting closer), I wondered why I'd decided to visit my parents.

Yes, I was where I was. Healing. Standing. Free. And they were where they were, imprisoned, their rights stripped, my mother's magic stripped, their abundance of pride and conceit likely (hopefully) being chipped away day to day.

But what was to be gained from this visit?

And further, what could be lost?

They had power over me. They always did. I didn't have to admit that to myself. It was a fact I'd lived with since I could ruminate. That power they wielded whether I was young or old, near or far.

Would their being in a jail change that?

Would my confronting them somehow be turned on me and cause more shame?

These were the thoughts that plagued me not only during our journey but at the end of it, through Noc assisting me out of the sleigh and while we made our way to the jail.

Frey opened the door, Finnie on his arm. They swept through followed by Lahn and Circe, then Noc and I, and we were trailed by Tor and Cora.

By the time we made our way inside, Frey was speaking with someone who looked official and was wearing a city guard uniform of brown leather shorts, thick brown stockings, high brown boots and a warm-looking brown sweater with deep-red epaulets stitched in along the shoulders.

The moment Noc and I entered, both men's eyes came to me.

Unexpectedly, I had the instant desire to bolt. In order not to do it, I made my body lock.

Noc felt it.

"Frannie?" he called quietly.

My gaze shot to his. "Do I look all right?"

In the many "nevers" that I'd experienced happening recently, this was another.

I'd never asked a soul that question.

And in my heart I knew I looked nothing but like I always looked. Josette made sure of that, going extra distance considering where I was heading, fashioning the lovely chignon she'd fastened at my nape and selecting the perfect accessories for my ensemble. It was also she who'd decided on the wine-colored gown that skimmed my figure beautifully, showing only a hint of cleavage at the square neckline, the subtle, thin, vertical cable-knit at my midriff, waist and hips giving the impression that entire area was nipped in and tiny.

She'd also chosen my most expensive, most fabulous cloak. A luscious, luminous sable, its high collar when flipped up (as it was not now) covered not just my neck but up beyond my ears.

I knew all this.

But I did not.

And when I asked this question of Noc, he had an odd reaction.

His expression grew soft and kind(er) and he turned into me so we were front to front, close, dipping his chin into his throat to bring his face near, all the while holding my eyes.

"You look beautiful, Franka. You always look beautiful. Your cheeks flushed from being out in the cold, your eyes brighter because the pain is subsiding, you look more beautiful than yesterday and the day before, and I could go on with that." His hand that was covering my fingers he'd curled inside his elbow tightened as his lips tipped up reassuringly. "It's all good."

I heard his words and yet I did not.

And it didn't matter that I did and did not.

I promptly and fretfully asked him another question.

"Can you tell I still have pain? When I move," I hastened to add. "Or even stand," I kept at it. "Can you tell," I got up on my toes, "*at all?*"

"No, baby," he whispered hearteningly. "You can't tell at all. Where you were, where you are now, every day I've thought it. You may just be the strongest woman I've met."

My hand reached up and clamped over his sweater at his biceps, curling around, but in my state I didn't notice the hardness of muscle underneath his wool.

"You aren't saying these things just to soothe me, are you?" I pressed.

He shook his head. "No way. Truth. All of it, Frannie. Swear to God."

I stayed right where I was, *this close* to Noc, holding on to his arm, but I turned my head toward where Frey was still standing, beyond which was a passageway that seemed dim and bleak.

Noc's free arm slid carefully along my waist and my attention returned to him when he stated firmly, "If you're having second thoughts, we're outta here."

I stared up into his eyes.

They'd all come. Out in the cold, they'd all come. To be there with me.

To be there *for* me.

And Noc was right there, close, holding me, reassuring me.

For his part, he wouldn't have let me go without him.

I might be a new Franka Drakkar, and she was a woman I didn't yet understand.

What I did understand was that I had to do this.

But this time it was not for my brother.

It was for me.

"You wanna do it, we're with you," Noc went on, and I again focused on him. "The final chapter, Frannie. The end of that book. Period. Dot. You're done. You do this, you show them they didn't break you, they *never* broke you, sweetheart, you walk away, close that book and move on."

I heard every one of those words said in his strong, deep, rough but luxuriant voice, and they somehow seemed to sink into my flesh, my muscle, my heart, lungs, innards, all this forcing my scabbed-over back straight.

They'd never broken me.

I was free. My brother and I were safe.

And they were there. In that dismal, bleak place, a version of which they'd be in for the rest of their lives.

"You're correct, Noc," I stated smartly.

"Fuck yeah, I am," he replied on a grin.

I squared my shoulders. "I'm ready."

"Right." This came as a determined growl, and he bent his face even closer to mine. "Then let's do this."

I nodded. Noc took that in, slid his hand from my waist and turned us both toward Frey, Finnie and the guard. As he did, he lifted his arm where I held his elbow and drew it and my hand in to hold them tight to the front side of his chest.

"She's good to go," he announced to Frey.

Frey watched Noc say this before he turned his eyes and studied me.

And then he said something that, if Noc wasn't holding me up, would have set me on my behind.

"For the first time in my life, you've made me proud to be a Drakkar."

I heard a little pip that I assumed came from Cora, who had closed in at my left side. It sounded like she was fighting back a sob.

What I saw was Finnie smiling at me so largely it had to hurt her face.

My eyes drifting from Finnie, Frey's words warming my belly, my anxiety fully left me and my surroundings came to me.

I saw the building was not made of wood but cold, dull, colorless stone. There were iron bars that stood as a door to the passageway. The room we were in had several wooden chairs that lined the walls but did not invite you to relax and pass the time. There was also a high desk at an angle in the right corner where two men wearing city guard uniforms (but with black epaulets) were clearly on a riser for they towered feet above us, lording over the small room. And there were intermittent, round iron hooks on the walls, some with chains and manacles hanging from them, obviously where prisoners were shackled prior to being led to their accommodation in the back.

Thinking that there was a great likelihood my parents had been fettered thus, I felt a swell of wicked glee surging up my throat that I felt no shame about whatsoever.

The guard Frey had been speaking with moved to the bar door, jingling a large loop filled with keys.

He found one, opened the door, and with Noc and I following Frey and Finnie, the rest following us, we walked through.

The first section beyond the doors had two more guards in their guard clothing, one on each side of the space behind desks. Behind the men there was cabinetry, one side looking like it held drawers where files were kept, the other side with an abundance of locks, which meant they likely housed weapons.

They looked up at us and stood instantly, at first putting their fist to the underside of their chin, a salute to The Drakkar, then pressing themselves into bows in deference to their Ice Princess, Finnie.

They stayed in this position as our procession walked by their desks and into the wide walkway beyond.

In this area there was a line of cells to each side.

The first two sets of cells, left and right, were empty.

The third to the left held a man who appeared (and an unsavory whiff of him and the unconscious belch he emitted with poor timing as we passed proved this assumption) to be sleeping off a drunken binge.

Another two sets of cells were empty, which I found vaguely surprising. Fyngaard was not a small city. Surely there must be more ruffians running amuck than this.

There was only one other cell filled with a man wearing bad clothes, having clearly not taken care of his teeth over the years, as openly shown to us as he sneered at us from his bunk. This also was apparent in the care of his hair, which was long and lank but looked like the last time it had been clipped, this had been done haphazardly with the side of a knife.

A dull one.

I only viewed him curiously before I looked again to Frey's and Finnie's backs as we made our way down the passage.

I had warning when we'd neared my mother and father, this a glance by Frey over his shoulder at me.

I lifted my chin. His lips tilted up. He looked forward then right.

I looked right as well.

Noc drew me even nearer.

My mother lay in that cell, her finery gone, no soft lamb's wool, angora or cashmere gown covering her still-youthful figure. She was wearing a rough, boxy shift with long sleeves, belted with what appeared to be rope, visibly coarse stockings and crude, tie-up leather boots.

On sight of us, she pushed up to her bottom, her lustrous hair that had only threads of lovely silver in it was plaited in a long braid falling over one shoulder and tied with what looked like a dirty scrap of cloth.

"Daughter," she whispered, her eyes locked to me.

I said nothing.

Furthermore I *felt* nothing at the sight of her.

How odd.

Frey led us beyond her cell but stopped us at the wall between hers and the one next to it. There I saw my father in the last cell in the hall.

He was similarly attired as my mother, except no stockings, rather rough breeches. The only thing that looked clean on him was the bandage that had been tied on a slant to his face with a strip of white gauze that ran along his jaw to the wounded cheek opposite and up over his crown.

I noted they both had thin woolen blankets on their narrow bunks (though no sheet over the slim pallet atop it) and wooden buckets to serve as chamber pots.

Other than this, there was naught else in their cells.

Nothing.

"Frey!" my father snapped, and at his voice I pressed closer to Noc. "When he gets here, my solicitor will be having a word with the queen. Being *in* this building is outrageous. These clothes," he plucked at his shirt furiously, having strode to the bars before his cell and stopping in front of them. "No creature comforts. Barely a passable blanket to keep the chill away that veritably *whistles* through the walls. Not even a book to pass the time. And I demand that Anneka be moved into my cell with me, or at the very least across from me so we can see each other as we converse."

"I do believe, uncle, it's escaped you that you're not in a position to make demands," Frey replied calmly.

Papa's voice was rising. "Wait until your father hears of this!"

I held my ground even as I sensed my mother approaching the bars.

"It shocks me how little you've paid attention, Nils," Frey returned. "Although you're correct. My father will undoubtedly be outraged by your current circumstances. I just don't give a fuck what he thinks, and I never did."

"Franka," my mother called softly.

I made certain my features were arranged as I wished them, blankly, before I gave her my attention.

"You cannot wish this on your father and I." She continued to speak in that quiet, timid, beleaguered tone, which obviously I'd never heard.

Even with my first real glance at her, I saw she was broken. Without her husband's name, his House, his self-importance and her magic to stand behind, it had been but days and she was a ghost of the spiteful, conceited, pitiless, evil woman I knew.

I'd endured torture at their hands to mind, body and spirit for thirty-four years and there I was.

There I was.

And in nine days she'd all but wasted away.

She'd never survive a life in prison. Or, more accurately, her life imprisoned would be a life significantly shortened.

"Frey, if you would," I began, looking to my cousin who in turn directed his attention to me. "Order they be given another blanket. A pillow. And a flannel sheet to cover their pallets and help to beat back the chill. Perhaps they both should also have a book."

Frey didn't hide his surprise but he inclined his head and turned to the guard.

"See that it's done."

"Of course, my lord," the guard murmured.

"A bloody blanket and a book?" my father asked furiously. "Franka, demand our release *at once*," he ordered.

I ignored him and again looked at my mother.

When I caught her eyes, she dropped hers and said, "Your kindness is appreciated, daughter."

"Do not mistake it as kindness," I declared, and startled, her gaze came again to mine. "I do not request this as a kindness, Mother," I explained. "I request this in an effort to keep you healthy. It would not do for you to catch a deathly chill and shorten your penance."

She blanched, taking a step back from the bars.

"Franka," my father growled in a warning tone.

I again ignored him and took a step toward my mother's cell.

"You reap what you sow," I said quietly, not tearing my eyes from her horrified ones. "For years, you taught me nothing but callousness and cruelty. You taught me strength was in manipulating others' weaknesses for my gain. You taught me arrogance was a point of pride and a weapon to add to my arsenal. You taught me loyalty was to be punished. Fear was to be unrelenting. Pain was to be expected. I only hope that in the remaining years of my life I've got enough light in the midnight soul you shadowed inside me to burn the seed you've sown to cinders and plant a new one that will take root and grow. But even if that isn't to be the case, as you've taught me my entire life to live my own with heartlessness and selfishness, knowing you live a life of fear and torment will suffice to see me through to my own end."

Her hand snaked up to her throat, her eyes wide as saucers, dread wafting from her in physical ways I could not only feel, but could smell, and it reeked. My father bellowed, "You'll rue those words when we're released, you ungrateful bitch!"

I shifted, letting go of Noc to approach my father's cell but feeling Noc move with me, close to my back.

I tipped my head back to look up at Papa.

The wrathful, persecuted look on his face and burning from his gaze shared he had not broken. He was quite certain his position and name would change his circumstances in the near future.

He was misguided.

No.

He was a fool.

"And what, pray, Papa, should I be grateful for that you and Mother have given me?" I asked.

He tipped his head angrily toward my body. "That fur you're wearing, for one."

"This fur was purchased when the quarterly Drakkar stipend was forwarded to me, something that's increased now that Frey's brother is head of the House and managing it capably, rather than your brother running it straight into financial ruin."

"And the *Drakkar name* was given to you by *me*," he spat.

"Alas," I murmured.

"The impudence," he bit off.

I stared at him.

Without Mother's magic, outside of retaining his handsomeness, which had nothing to do with him and everything to do with the strength of the Drakkar line, he suddenly seemed like an old, blustering buffoon.

And indeed, without Mother's magic that was all he'd ever been.

"This is the last you'll see of me, Papa. Any loving words you wish to say?" I invited.

"If you don't speak to the queen on our behalf, Franka—" he began to warn.

I lifted my brows and interrupted him. "You'll what, Papa?" I then lifted a hand and touched the bars that separated us with the tip of my index finger, reminding him of his situation. "What will you do?"

Faster than his years, which had always been the way, his hand darted up and he caught my finger in an excruciating hold, his own fingers tightening, crushing mine against the bar even as he pressed his face between them.

"I'll break you, you revolting harlot," he hissed.

He was able to get that out before I found my finger suddenly released.

I heard the terrible noise of bones breaking, then my father's pained howl sounded against the stone walls, and finally Noc's order of, "Step back, Franka."

He'd torn my father's fingers from mine and bent them back, using a bar to leverage his hold, a hold he still had on my father so even now I could see they were at an unnatural angle that had to be excruciating.

I felt it prudent to step back. This I did.

When I did, Noc released my father and took his own step to return to my side.

Father retreated from the bars and held his damaged hand in his other, bent over them both at his chest protectively.

"You might wish to call for a physician to set those," Frey suggested to the guard.

"You'll hear from our solicitor," Papa snarled angrily, his head bent back to glower at us, but his voice betrayed his pain.

"And I'm sure whatever he says will be most amusing," Frey drawled.

My father sent a scowl his way then asked, "Have you humiliated us enough, bringing the Winter Princess here to see our degradation? The bloody ruler of Bellebryn and his bride? The savage king and his Middlelandian queen? Have you, nephew? For if you have, I'd thank you to leave us to our ordeal further unmolested."

Frey didn't answer my father. He turned to me.

"Are you finished, Franka?"

I looked at Papa, pain starting to twist his face, ire still blazing in his eyes.

I then looked to my mother. She'd retreated to stand against the back wall beside her bed, both her elegant hands lifted and clasped at the base of her throat, her eyes on me.

Finally, I looked to my cousin.

"I am indeed, cousin."

"Let us be away then," Frey stated, sounding relieved and proving he was by moving all of us immediately to retreat.

Neither of my parents called a farewell.

I did the same, not even giving them my regard as I walked from view of their cells.

Noc took my hand and curled it at once around his elbow, bending to me and asking, "Your finger okay, sweetheart?"

"Quite all right, Noc," I answered, my eyes straight ahead.

"You kicked ass back there, baby. Wish I had that on video. Fuckin' brilliant," he decreed.

I had no idea what "on video" meant, but I didn't ask.

I also did not even try to fight back the urge to do what I next did.

I simply did it.

This being turning my head and tipping it back.

Once that was done and I'd caught Noc's gaze, I did my last.

Slowly, and with great delight I did not hide, I smiled.

Huge.

"Master Noc broke his fingers?" Josette asked incredulously.

"At least three of them," I informed her.

She stared at me a moment looking horrified but this dissolved as her body started shaking and then a loud giggle erupted from her mouth.

I felt my lips curling up.

When she controlled her mirth, she mumbled, "I wish I was there."

"I do as well," I replied.

I ignored her blinking at me in shock, having decided over the past days when I did something kind that Josette found unexpected and she showed her surprise, she'd eventually get used to it.

For I had found that guarding myself from this variety of camaraderie, sharing moments and news and snippets of life, and even feelings with the woman with whom I spent most of my time, was not only draining and tiresome, but also unnecessary.

Josette had not a cruel bone in her body. She'd remained steadfast to me even when I wasn't as I'd begun to be.

She was now blossoming under my warm regard.

And I found witnessing it most pleasant.

Thus, it was late afternoon and we were now sharing prior to her assisting me in my preparations to attend another dinner with the queen and the others.

"Now, tell me, how goes your search for a new maid?" I asked.

She settled her behind deeper in the chair opposite me and stated, "I've narrowed it down to three, Lady Franka. They all seem quite capable, have much experience, excellent references, good dispositions and are keen to go on an adventure by crossing the Green Sea."

At her words, I frowned.

I'd found of late (that "of late" being the last several days) that the "Lady Franka" business, something of which I hadn't thought of in the slightest in the past, was grating.

I was, of course, a lady.

Josette reminding me of it every time she spoke my name was superfluous.

I didn't call her "Maid Josette." The very idea was ludicrous.

"Josette, if you please," I said on a sweep of my hand in front of me, "I'm tiring of 'Lady Franka.'"

"I...well," her expression turned perplexed, "what, milady?"

"That too," I replied. "'Milady.' Of course when we're in company, you'll need to continue to address me thus. But when we're on our own, I see no reason for you to consistently utter my title. Franka will do."

She said nothing, likely because her mouth had dropped open and her stare had become vacant.

"Is this something that offends you?" I asked when her look persisted, as did her silence.

She snapped her mouth closed, opened it, closed it and finally got down to it.

"As you know, my, uh...well, as you know, no other maid *I* know addresses her lady that way. It just isn't done."

"I'm not just any lady and you are definitely not just another maid. If the Winter Princess herself knew of your talents, she'd try to steal you from me."

A blush of pleasure pinkened her cheeks as she said, "I'd never leave you."

I tipped up my chin. "And I know this and prize it. So let's dispense with some of the formalities, shall we?"

"I...all right," she agreed, a tentative smile forming on her face.

"Excellent," I murmured. "Now that's done, I'll meet your final candidates tomorrow. Once I do, we'll discuss them and decide. But I need to give you another task."

"And that would be?" she asked.

"Your gowns, stockings, cloaks, boots, slippers, etc. You'll need to visit a local clothier, cobbler and milliner as you'll require clothing suitable for a variety of climes and a good deal of it. When we're aboard a ship, I'm not certain there are laundry facilities, and I don't like the idea of you donning dirty clothing because you have no spare. And please, increase the quality of the pieces you choose. You are a maid of a lady of the House of Drakkar, but further, we've no idea what we'll be encountering. It would be good for those who look upon us to think you're my ward, and thus have some protection of a certain class, rather than my maid."

"Really, Lady...I mean, Franka?" she breathed, her mouth now working, but her eyes had again gone wide.

"If I didn't mean it, I wouldn't say it," I retorted.

"I would...would...would..." she finally spit it out, nearly bouncing in her seat, "*adore* that."

"I change my mind," I stated and her face fell. "We'll go together. I want to make certain you don't do anything frugal out of habit. Once my brother has arrived and I've greeted him, he'll want to settle his family and probably rest. We'll go out after he arrives."

Bright-eyed again, Josette replied, "That would be most lovely, erm, Franka."

"Indeed it would," I agreed, regarding her thoughtfully. "With your coloring, I think greens. Perhaps pinks. You've excellent skin, roses and creams, pink would suit you." I tipped my head to the side. "I do believe red would also become you, but we'll have to see."

She sniffled and I stopped scrutinizing her and looked in her eyes.

They were wet.

"Josette," I chided softly. "You really cannot rush from the room under the threat of tears every time I show a kindness."

"My Lady," she said in a choked voice.

"I thought we dispensed with that," I reminded her gently.

"No," she stated. Lifting her hand and coughing delicately behind it, she dropped it and straightened in her chair. "That's the last time I'll say it, I promise. But I just want you to know, you're My Lady."

These words made me blink rapidly three times, feeling the sting hit my eyes.

I then straightened in my own chair and declared, "It would vex me greatly if our growing relationship meant we degenerated into simpering ninnies, weeping at every pleasantry that passed between us."

"I'll endeavor to be more hardened, Franka," she promised.

"See to that," I ordered smartly.

She fought it. I watched it. But she couldn't control the strangled giggle that passed her lips.

I smiled at her indulgently.

I did not berate myself on doing this or doing it indulgently.

I was getting used to it.

7
IT WAS GONE

Franka

I was abed with my breakfast tray the next morning when there came a rap on the door.

I turned my head that way only to see said door open and Noc stroll through.

I narrowed my eyes at him.

Truly.

The nerve.

I wasn't even out of bed yet!

"I'm having my breakfast," I snapped.

"Good morning to you too," he replied, not hiding his amusement in the face of my frustration and sauntering across the room but not coming to my bedside.

No.

He walked across the foot of the bed to the other, vacant side, and I watched in stunned silence as he put his arse to it, twisted, put his *whole body* to it, stretched out and settled on his side but with his body up on his forearm, facing me.

Noc in those bloody *trousers* and a blue shirt that did nice things to his eyes, stretched out in bed beside me.

He was *impossible.*

Once settled, he then reached out and selected a cantaloupe ball from my crystal bowl of fruit and popped it into his mouth.

"That's my melon," I kept snapping.

"Chill, baby," he murmured, grinning at me.

"Chill?" I asked, knowing this was his-world slang, just not able to fathom what it meant.

"Relax," he explained.

Oh.

Hmm.

That was actually quite clever, considering my ire was heated.

I didn't relay this sentiment to him.

I declared, "I'll relax when you get *out* of my bed, *leave* my room and allow me to eat my breakfast in *peace*."

"I'll do that when you tell me how you're doin' this morning and what's up for your day," he returned.

I turned slightly his way and queried, "Has it occurred to you how irritating it is that you consistently ignore my wishes?"

"Has it occurred to you that I know your act is bullshit so I'm gonna keep ignoring the bullshit and get on with things?" he retorted, but he wasn't quite finished. "You like me. You like spending time with me. Stop pretending that you don't."

He was correct, of course. He was excellent company. Engaged. Amusing. Affectionate. Attentive. Thoughtful. Caring. And very much not hard to look at.

I was not about to share those sentiments with him either.

I turned back to my tray, picked up a triangle of buttered toast and my knife and started slathering marmalade on it as I mumbled (me! mumbling!), "It'll be good when I'm away on a ship."

"What?" Noc asked.

"Nothing," I kept mumbling and continued spreading as I raised my voice and answered his question. "I'm quite all right this morning, Noc. As concerns my back, better than yesterday. And I would imagine, just in case on the morrow you find yourself curious about the same, it will be even better as healing tends to go that way."

"Glad to hear it, sweetheart," he said softly. "But I meant that gig with your folks yesterday and your brother probably showin' today."

I turned my head his way, lifting my toast and inquiring, "The *gig* with my parents, if I'm to understand you, is done. Behind me. And my brother and I might not have a close, loving relationship, but we've been through a good deal together so I'm looking forward to his visit."

I then put the toast between my lips, sunk my teeth into it and munched.

"Big stuff like what happened yesterday can mess with your head, Frannie. Feels like a relief at the time, then the demons everyone fights in their heads start playing with you," he noted.

The demons *everyone* fights?

He had demons?

This I found surprising. And intriguing. He seemed confident in all matters. The way he held and used his body. The way he spoke. The way he communicated with others.

I suddenly felt hungry for something I'd given up on doing.

This being gathering all the information I could on a certain subject and not caring how I had to obtain that information.

This time the subject was Noc.

Fortunately, after Kristian left, Josette and I would be away so I couldn't indulge in this pastime.

"There are no demons playing with my mind," I assured him. "I had some unease prior to yesterday's visit but it couldn't have gone better if I'd planned every second prior to entering that jail."

"Good to hear that too," he muttered, reaching out and snatching more of my cantaloupe.

I sighed.

I then shared, "As you've spoken it repeatedly, you know my name is pronounced Frahn-kah."

His brows drew together, he swallowed *my* melon and he said, "Well...yeah."

"So should I wish to have one, which I don't, the nickname Frannie is not only abhorrent, it doesn't make sense. It should be Frahnnie and that's just ridiculous. Or more ridiculous than Frannie."

"Could call you Koko," he remarked, and I felt my lip curl. I then felt the bed slightly shake with his chuckle as he said, "Okay, that's out."

"How about calling me Franka?" I suggested.

"Can't call you Kaka because that's just wrong," he went on his own bent, as was his wont, completely ignoring my suggestion because it went against what *he* wished to do.

But my curiosity got the better of me.

"Not that I desire you to call me Kaka either, but why is that just wrong?"

"In my world that's shit. As in it means *shit*, crap, *excrement*."

The lip curl that earned was more pronounced.

Noc exploded with laughter.

I sighed yet again and nibbled more toast.

"So it's Frannie," he said when he was done laughing.

"I suppose," I murmured, finishing my toast and going after my fork to spear some scrambled eggs.

"So you're good with the visit to your folks and you're lookin' forward to your brother showin'. What else is up for your day?" Noc asked.

I chewed and swallowed eggs, still curious (it must be said, the queen's cook was superb, even the eggs were delicious).

"May I ask why you wish to know?"

"Why wouldn't I wish to know?" he answered my question with a question.

Yet it was still an answer.

He was interested in me. Even the mundane goings-on of my day. He came in first thing in the morning for no reason whatsoever, except, it seemed, to be in my company.

I felt my throat start closing, cleared it daintily and turned my attention back to my tray.

But I did this speaking.

"Josette and I are going to be making the final selection of a new lady's maid. After that and also after my brother arrives, we'll be sledding into town to order some clothing for her. It's time we start preparing for our journey and the seamstresses who'll be making her new attire will need to get to work on it as soon as possible. I don't suspect Kristian will wish to stay long. He tends to prefer to be at home."

"What journey?" Noc queried, and I looked to him.

"Pardon?"

"You said you're preparing for a journey. What journey?"

I took hold of a rasher of bacon, raised it and answered, "Once Kristian leaves, Josette, the new maid we select and I will be on our way to Sudvic to see about purchasing passage across the Green Sea."

"Come again?"

My bacon held aloft, I turned my attention back to Noc.

"We're sailing across the Green Sea," I repeated. "Not many people journey there so I imagine we'll be in Sudvic some time, waiting for a galleon that makes that journey to return, or to prepare to make the journey, as I can imagine that takes some doing as I hear it's many weeks. In truth there may be no galleons who sail the Green Sea that harbor in Sudvic. We may need to find another port city, perhaps even travel to Hawkvale, passage across the green waters is so unusual. But we'll find our way over," I finished decidedly.

I crunched bacon, chewed, swallowed and started mumbling again, this time mostly to myself.

"I hope we can make the island nation of Mar-el, for Josette's sake. But then I dearly wish to see Airen."

I finished my bacon, had eaten more egg and was slathering marmalade on another corner of toast when I realized Noc hadn't said anything for some time.

I looked his way to see he had his gaze fixed to my tray but his eyes were distant.

"Have you had breakfast?" I asked.

He said nothing.

"Noc," I called, his head twitched and his ice-blue eyes came to me.

"Sorry," he muttered. "What?"

"Have you had breakfast?"

"Yeah."

"Are you still hungry?"

"Not really."

"Then will you explain why you're staring at my tray like you wish to nick my bacon?"

His mouth spread in a grin that for the first time I didn't believe was real.

"No one can have enough bacon," he quipped.

This was quite true, bacon was delicious.

However I had the uncomfortable feeling he was lying and I didn't like this. I'd lied and been lied to by many people, starting from so far back I didn't even remember when it actually began.

But Noc, I knew instinctively, had never lied to me.

And thinking that he was now, about bacon of all things, troubled me far more than I'd care to admit.

"You can have my bacon," I said quietly.

"Baby, I don't want your bacon. Honest," he replied in my tone.

I studied him closely before asking, "Is all well?"

"I just got something on my mind."

I shouldn't extend the invitation.

Nevertheless, I extended the invitation.

"Would you like to share it with me?"

His gaze on my face warmed and his words made my chest do the same when he replied, "Yeah."

I put my cutlery down, the wedge of toast, and twisted to him to give him my full attention.

Even so, he carried on by saying, "Just not now. Seems you have a full day. But can I ask that we end it together?"

"End it together?"

"Yeah," he gave me a genuine grin that time. "You and me in a room somewhere with a bottle of whiskey."

I wanted that very much, this something I would never share.

Though I did agree to this assignation.

"We can do this, Noc."

"Great, Frannie. Gotta go," he declared and immediately made a move to go, however, quick as a flash, his hand darted out and he pinched my last rasher of bacon.

"Noc!" I snapped.

But he was out of bed, smiling at me cheekily as he munched my bacon and sauntered around my bed toward the door.

He arrived at it, eyes to me, swallowed a bite of *my* bacon and said, "Later, babe."

I rolled my eyes.

He kept smiling at me a moment before he closed the door behind him.

Noc

"Hey," Noc greeted Finnie as he walked into the room one of the servants had told him she was in.

She was alone and looked like she was writing letters, but she stopped doing this the minute she lifted her head and saw him approach.

She set everything aside on the cushion of the couch where she was sitting and replied, "Hey."

"Don't want to interrupt you—" he began.

She cut him off. "Interrupt me. Please. People bring gifts to the Bitter Gales for Frey and me and I'm writing thank you notes. I tried to share with the queen that doing this was killing too many trees. She thought I was losing my mind, told me so and also told me to stop procrastinating. A princess writes thank you notes. And trees are a hell of a lot more plentiful here than in my old world. So I really don't have any excuse not to do it," her eyes lit, "except to talk to you."

While she spoke, he moved to a couch, sat and grinned at her when she was done.

"Pleased to be of service."

She tipped her head to the side.

Not dim by a long shot, she read him and asked, "Do you have something you wanted to talk to me about?"

He did.

A couple of somethings.

"Do you know how to get in touch with Valentine?"

"Not in any definitive way, no."

Fuck.

Finnie went on, "But she's back."

That was news.

"Back?" Noc requested confirmation.

"Unh-hunh." Finnie nodded. "She's back. She checked in with Frey a couple of days ago."

"I haven't seen her," Noc shared.

"I haven't either, actually. Apparently, she's rented some manor house close by. Don't know why. When she's here, she likes to be in the thick of things. But she did and Frey knows where she is, so he can send a message to her."

"I'd like to get a message to her," Noc told her.

Finnie nodded. "Sure. I'll find Frey and—"

She'd started to push up from her seat but he lifted a hand and stalled her.

"No, babe. I'll talk to Frey. There's something else I wanna ask you."

"Shoot," she invited, settling back into her seat.

"The Green Sea, that's the big ocean to the west, right?" Noc asked.

She nodded. "Yep. Big body of water. Green, like its name," she said on a smile. "But a green you wouldn't believe, Noc. It's beautiful. I'm really looking forward to you seeing it. I traveled widely in my old world and even the emerald waters in some of the Caribbean don't hold a candle to the vast beauty of the Green Sea."

"And you've traveled widely here too, yeah?" Noc asked.

She nodded again. "I have."

"Over the Green Sea?"

She looked confused. "Over it?"

"Over it. To a place called Mar-el, or Airen, or something like that."

She shook her head. "Oh no. We've traveled up and down the coast of the Northlands, over the Winter Sea, the Marhac Sea too, but never across the Green."

"Has Frey traveled across?"

More nodding from Finnie.

"Yes. Twice. As a diplomat for my dad when he was alive and because there were some Lunwynian treasures that should never have left Lunwyn soil that had made their way over there." Her eyes lit, telling him there was more to the story of what she said next. "Frey has a habit of collecting those."

"So it's a doable journey, not unsafe," Noc pushed.

She again looked confused. "Do you want to voyage across the Green Sea?"

"No, Franka does."

Her lips parting in a knowing way, she sat back, murmuring, "Ah."

"Is it safe?"

Finnie held his gaze. "The journey is long. Very long. I never asked Frey just how long but I think it takes months. Easy to run out of supplies, especially if you don't know where you're going or get cast adrift by a storm. And Frey told me there are lots of islands that are inhabited, not all of them with friendly people, and some of those unfriendly people have boats. There are reefs that are difficult to negotiate if you don't know they're there to avoid them. And there are pirates in this world with the addition of raiders. Raiders tend to wreak havoc by land, anchoring close to shore and raiding from there. Pirates are about ship to ship takeovers. Raiders usually simply steal and don't create a lot of collateral damage. Pirates take booty and women and the rest feel the length of a saber or go down with the ship they usually set fire to, if they don't decide to steal that as well."

"Jesus," Noc whispered.

"Yup," Finnie agreed. "I've seen a couple of pirate ships. They've tried to come up on Frey's galleon. But they see his flag and back off." She smiled proudly. "Not many people fuck with Frey. You do, suddenly a dragon's overhead and you're toast. Literally."

Noc felt his eyes crinkle. "Yeah, I suppose that would put most people off, even pirates."

Finnie settled in, crossing her legs under her long, sweater gown and continued, "In fact, I don't think there are any passenger ships I know of that make that voyage. Merchants, definitely. There's a bunch of stuff from that side of the world that's highly valued here and costs a whack, so it's worth the risk of the journey. They have a kind of wool that's amazing. I have dresses and throws made of it and I've never felt anything like it. Firenzian rubies are spectacular. Frey got me a necklace and earrings made of them and they're extraordinary. Exotic spices. Tons of stuff."

"And you dig travel so if it was safe to take you..." he didn't finish because she was nodding.

"Yeah, if it was safe, we'd go. I haven't even asked because I read between the lines when he told me all he told me. No reason to get into a discussion about it. Frey spoils me a lot. But when it's time to put his foot down, he doesn't have a problem with doing just that. Since that sometimes pisses me off, I've learned to read when it's important to him and I shouldn't push it, so I won't push it."

Noc shot her a grin. "Good plan."

Finnie's lips twitched at his reply, but then her face got serious. "She shouldn't go."

Noc's grin died.

This was what he thought not only from all Finnie just shared but from the minute Franka mentioned she was doing it.

What he didn't think about was why it perturbed him so much she seemed to be totally okay with taking off after her brother left like she was leaving nothing behind.

The "leaving something behind" part and precisely what bothered him about that was the part he wasn't thinking about.

"I'm gettin' that impression," he said.

"What I'd want to know is why she'd want to go," Finnie remarked.

"Because she's lost the man she loves, her parents are dead to her and never were much to write home about, she wants to put it all behind her and that's a surefire way to do just that. She won't run into anything familiar on an entirely different continent."

"Surefire, true. Dramatic, definitely. A little bit crazy, also definitely," Finnie returned. "And that's being nice because in truth it's a whole lot of crazy."

Fuck.

"You can't let her go, Noc," Finnie stated.

"Not sure once she's fighting fit I'm gonna have a lot of say about that, Finnie."

Her mouth got soft as it tilted up, and looking at her normally, all that white-blonde hair, her fantastic figure, her pretty blue eyes, Noc got why Frey went all out to keep her at his side.

Shit, when she looked like that, he got why Frey would kill and die for her.

"Think she's got a soft spot for you, honey," she said quietly. "Hard to miss the way you two were at the jail yesterday."

The way they were at the jail yesterday.

No, it was more the way Franka was at the jail yesterday. All of it.

Fuck, he'd been so damned proud of her, it was scary how much emotion he felt for a woman he really barely knew.

But when she'd turned to him, vulnerable, and latched on to him like she needed his strength, looked to him to allay her fears, that caused even more emotion, he was so fucking happy he could be there for her. And more, that she had the strength to show her weakness, she showed it to him and she let him be there for her.

"She's definitely finding it easier to let the mask slip on occasion," he replied. "But she's stubborn and I get why she wants to go. Why she wants to put her past where it belongs and get somewhere nothing reminds her of it."

"I see why she wants that but it's still not the right choice."

"There's a world nothing like hers she can go to where no pirates will take her as booty," Noc pointed out.

Finnie's eyes got bigger as she sat forward.

"Holy cow, there is," she whispered.

"Not sure I can talk Franka into coming with all of us when I go with you guys while you take Tor and Cora back home. Not sure I can even talk her into coming back with me. What I am sure of is that I can't take her back unless Valentine does it for me."

"She'll do it. She seems like a cold fish but she's all heart."

That was what Noc was counting on.

"So, bringing us back, I gotta talk to Frey and get Valentine a message."

Finnie was out of her seat before he even finished talking.

"Let's go find him," she said.

Nope.

That look on her face where she didn't hide her excitement was probably what did it for Frey. That look you'd want to see every day. That look was another look you'd kill and die for.

Noc enjoyed taking it in the only way he could as he pushed out of the couch.

Then they took off together to find Finnie's husband.

~

Franka

Late morning I sat with Josette in a small sitting room the queen's secretary set aside for Josette and myself to do our final interviews of prospective maids.

It was a lovely room, the best part of it being it was one of the growing number that had already had its glass replaced, so it was bright, sunny and cheerful.

I'd read all the *curriculum vitae* and references of the candidates. There were several references written by people I knew or knew of (only one I knew to trust every word as the girl had been employed by Norfolk Ravenscroft, an honest, intelligent man and cousin to the queen). We'd spoken to all the candidates. I'd asked a few questions, but Josette had asked many more, her follow-up questions.

And now I was being mostly silent.

She didn't seem to notice, she was chattering up a storm in a way that was thinking out loud.

"The second one, Deona, I think she's keen for the job just because she wants to catch the eye of a Firenz savage," she stated. "Man crazy could cause problems."

"Mm..." I murmured rather than saying it like it was.

She was absolutely right.

She continued babbling.

"The first one had a problem meeting your eyes. Not sure what that was about. Timidity is one thing, but we spoke with her for over half an hour and not once did she get herself together to look you straight in the face. I think that would annoy you over time if she eventually didn't snap out of it, and I'm worried she won't."

"Mm..." I murmured again, because again she'd hit it on the nose.

"Not to mention, if she doesn't have the courage to meet your eyes, how is she going to have the courage to board a galleon and venture across the Green Sea?"

"Good question," I said softly.

She either didn't hear me or was deep into her bent for she chattered on.

"But the last, I like her. She even brought stitching samples with her and she's talented with a needle. Almost more than me," Josette went on.

This last was untrue, Josette's talent with a needle, in my experience, was unsurpassed, but I said nothing.

"I think that was smart, doing that," Josette continued. "I should have thought to bring my own samples when I interviewed with you. She also has no ties here that would make her homesick and melancholy, which I think we would both find trying."

She was again very correct.

"And her eyes lit up at the idea of crossing the Green Sea," Josette prattled on. "It seemed genuine. Not many would have that reaction. Both one and two said they'd be fine with it, but I didn't quite believe them. Candidate three, well, I get the sense she's like Princess Sjofn...and you, of course. A female but with a hint of a raider's spirit."

I spoke not and waited.

"I think three," Josette declared.

She'd chosen well. Petite and slender though number three was (a girl by the name of Irene), she carried herself well, had ready answers, stated she relished being busy and she was younger and less experienced than Josette so there wouldn't be a future where I had one maid attempting to perform a coup to take the status of my other.

"What do you think?" Josette queried.

"Three," I stated.

"You liked her?" she asked uncertainly.

"I don't know her. I liked her for the job. And you two seemed to converse well."

"I like her," Josette shared.

"Then it's three."

"But you have to like her," she returned.

I drew in breath to calm my sudden impatience and held her eyes.

"Okay, it's three," she said, reading my look, her lips quirking.

I dipped my chin in an affirmative. "Send your missive. We'll need to prepare her for our adventure as well. She might as well start planning now."

Josette jumped from her chair and started to rush from the room, doing this talking.

"I'll be back to go shopping."

I was certain she would.

"Until then," I said to her back.

The door closed.

I smiled.

That task complete, onward to the next.

Whatever that turned out to be.

One of the palace servants came to me to share that Kristian had arrived.

I didn't pay any heed to what it might communicate that I abruptly rose from my seat and left Cora and Circe alone in the sitting room as I dashed out the door.

The hallways seemed interminable.

But finally I made the front hall and there he was, allowing his cloak to be taken by a footman while his wife's cloak was taken by her own maid.

She saw me first.

Brikitta Drakkar.

A mouse of a woman with nondescript hair and features and a too-thin frame, my brother was far more attractive than she.

That said, except in her presence, I'd never seen Kristian smile as much.

Or laugh.

I saw the frozen look on her face I knew was her attempt to hide the fear she had of me.

It was safe to say I had been far from kind to her.

I had not at first because I didn't wish her with my brother. Not because she looked a mouse of a woman. Because she behaved as one. I wanted him to have a strong mate by his side who could help him endure the threat he lived under and get beyond the suffering of his past. But also to bolster his tendency toward leading with his heart, not thinking with his head, something in our world, and especially in our House, that was considered a weakness and thus preyed upon.

Though it was more.

She made my brother smile and laugh. She had kind eyes. She spoke softly and didn't hide her affection not only for my brother, but her family, with whom she was close. She was even demonstrative with her servants.

My parents could break Kristian.

If I had ever fallen and they'd turn to Kristian and his own, they would have destroyed her.

I'd wanted to scare her away. When I'd failed at that, I'd wanted her to develop a thick skin.

But now I'd done nothing but make her fear and likely detest me.

In the few days I was sure they'd remain at the palace, I could do nothing lasting about that, of this I was relatively certain.

But that did not mean I shouldn't try.

Well thought, mon ange, Antoine said in my head, and I very nearly tripped over my own slippers, his voice was such a surprise as I hadn't heard it in days.

I'd thought he was gone.

I'd even so far as *hoped* he was gone, a hope that caused me guilt as well as angst.

"Brikitta," I greeted, not quite warmly because I did not yet have the skills to pull that off.

"Franka," she replied stiltedly.

"And where is Timofei?" I asked, glancing around as my brother rounded his wife to come toward me.

It was Kristian who answered me.

"Your nephew fell asleep in the sleigh right before we arrived. He's having a difficult time sleeping so we didn't want to rouse him. He's under furs outside with his nanny."

I looked up at my brother, into kind blue eyes that had never been anything but, even when they rested on me.

"Brother," I whispered.

"Sister," he whispered back.

Bloody hell.

I was going to weep.

Right in the grand hall of the Winter Palace, for the first time since I was a wee child, *I was going to weep*.

My brother there, tall, handsome, healthy and safe.

Me with him, perhaps not healthy, but also safe.

Our ordeal over.

The relief of it all surged over me and I didn't know if I could withstand it.

I needed to escape.

Immediately.

Before I could do so, Kristian tore his glove from his hand and lifted it.

Cupping my cheek, he moved close to me, dipping his face to mine.

"Franka," he said softly.

"I'm glad you're well," I forced out in a voice that was not my own. It was hoarse and unpolished.

He continued to speak in his quiet voice as if he only wished me to hear.

"It was bad."

"It was," I affirmed, wanting to touch him, to pull him to me, to wrap my arms around him and have him wrap his around me like we did when we were youngsters, before my mother and father put a stop to it.

Now his voice was gruff. "Sister."

"I endured," I shared the obvious.

His eyes started to get bright with tears when he replied, "You always did."

I delicately cleared my throat and stepped back far enough away from him so his hand dropped.

"You need to settle your family. Rest. Have some luncheon. We'll talk more when you're revived from your journey."

I included Brikitta in this invitation and noted she was staring at me like she'd never seen me, or indeed anything like me before.

"Yes, Franka. Of course," Kristian said.

"Ah, they've arrived. Excellent." We heard from behind us, and we all turned to the voice to see Queen Aurora moving our way.

Brikitta and I dropped into curtsies. Kristian bowed.

"Rise, rise," Aurora murmured. "Delighted you made it safely, Kristian, Brikitta," she stated, sweeping them with her glance. "Your room awaits, one of the rooms with a nursery attached. Thus Timofei's cot also awaits."

"Our gratitude, your grace," Kristian replied.

"Not at all," she stated, turning and motioning to a hovering footman. "See them to their rooms and please see that their trunks are brought up and send a maid to them."

"Yes, your grace," the footman replied, doing a slight bow then extending a hand out to Kristian and Brikkita.

"We'll sit together later, yes?" Kristian asked as he put his hand to his wife's elbow.

"Of course," I replied. "Pleased you're all here safe."

Brikitta nodded and her eyes skittered away. Kristian gave me a smile and then turned to Brikitta's maid, "Please would you see how Nanny's faring with Tim?"

"Yes, Lord Kristian."

She promptly made her way to the front doors.

Kristian and Brikitta followed the footman.

Aurora made her way to me.

"You're well, Franka?" she asked.

"Very well, my queen," I answered.

"Lovely," she said and began moving away, declaring, "Much looking forward to your lively discourse at dinner."

I stood still and stared after her.

Then I felt the mirth bubble up my throat and only just managed to swallow it down.

I barely said anything at dinner. During the first dinner I'd been commanded to attend once I was well enough to do so, this was because I had no intention to. Last night it was because the conversation was so fast and furious between the men and women, I couldn't get a word in.

I had a feeling that was my queen's subtle way of telling me to fit my words in.

She really shouldn't press for that. There was much surprising me recently and most of it had to do with my own behavior.

Therefore even I didn't know what would happen.

IT WAS SURPRISINGLY NOT me who caused a stir at dinner that evening.

It was my always mild-mannered brother.

This happened promptly after I informed him, once he and his family left the Winter Palace, I was journeying with Josette and our new acquisition across the Green Sea.

He was my dinner partner, sitting to my right, and I thought we had a cocoon of privacy thus it was safe to share this information without others inputting their opinions.

Until he shouted, *"Have you gone mad?"*

"Kristian," I murmured, shocked at his reaction, including the sheer volume of it, and acutely aware of all eyes coming to us, particularly Noc's, who was sitting directly across the table from me, his dinner partner Brikitta.

"The very idea is daft, Franka," my brother bit out (still loudly). "I'll not allow it."

My surprise faded and I felt my jaw tighten.

He'd not allow it?

Kristian would not allow me to do something I wished to do?

It was not I who had gone mad. It was him.

No. That was inaccurate.

The entire world had gone mad all around me, taking me with it.

My parents were imprisoned, never to breathe free again.

I was being kind to my maid, asking her to call me my given name and calling upon her to make decisions on matters of great import, like who was going to attend *my person* and *my clothing* and *my bedchamber*.

I was allowing Noc to interfere in my life at any given moment, these moments chosen by *him*.

My cousin Frey *liked* me. His wife also liked me. Further, their *friends* liked me.

Those friends, the female *and* male ones, had accompanied me on a trying engagement simply in order to be near should I become upset.

My dead lover's voice sounded in my head.

The queen of the entire bloody country had spoken to me like she was my nanny and later *teased* me like I was a fond friend of her daughter's she'd known since they were in the schoolroom.

And worst of all, it seemed I had no control, not a whit, over *any of it*.

"What's this?" Aurora queried.

I opened my mouth to intervene in hopes I could get my brother to remain silent, but he spoke before I could make a sound.

"My sister wishes to journey across the Green Sea," he declared. "She intends to leave right after Brikitta and I depart for home, your grace."

Queen Aurora assumed a severe expression. "Franka, is this true?"

I clenched my teeth, managed not to grind them and turned my torso to face the head of the table.

"Yes, my queen."

"She won't be doing it," Kristian railed on, looking from Aurora to me. "If you don't wish to return to your apartments after you've lost Antoine, which is understandable, Sister, then you'll travel back with Brikitta and me. You can stay with us until you've made a *sane* decision about where you wish to go next. Hell, you can stay with us for good, as far as I care. The house is big enough and I know you like it, no matter what you've said."

Brikitta made a noise during my brother's latest that I deciphered as fear and panic, and I found myself intervening not only on my behalf but on hers as well.

"Brother, you know that's not a good idea. I'm much better living on my own," I replied swiftly, wishing I didn't have to and further wishing that such private matters weren't being shared in public.

But again having no choice.

"You'll turn over a new leaf," he sniffed, looking to his consommé and dipping his spoon into it, stating, "And that's a matter sorted."

"It is not," I retorted, doing my all to keep the snap out of my voice and not exactly succeeding. "I'm quite keen on my plan and have no intention to alter it."

Kristian rudely dropped his spoon in his consommé and turned back to me. "I believe you'll change your mind when the pirates board your vessel."

"No pirates will board the vessel," I scoffed.

"Tell that to the many sailors who never returned, who likely felt the same *before the pirates boarded their vessels*," Kristian retorted.

"Merchants make that journey often," I replied.

"Merchants *try* to make that journey often," Kristian responded and didn't allow me time to counter. He looked to Frey. "What say you, Drakkar? How many go and how many come back?"

Frey was looking amused, which I was certain made me look annoyed since I felt that but didn't feel like hiding it, as he answered, "I'd like to say the stakes are fifty-fifty. But I'd wager it's more like thirty-seventy."

I blew out an exasperated breath before I asked my cousin, "Have you been across those waters?"

"Yes," he answered.

"How many times?" I inquired.

"Twice," he stated.

I sat back in my chair smugly. "Then I'd say the stakes are far better than thirty-seventy, surely."

"I'm a good seaman," Frey retorted. "I'm handy with a variety of blades. Not to mention bows. My men are arguably better than me...at both. My ship is fast. And I have less scruples than a pirate when it comes to saving my men and my necks." His lips formed a slow, superior grin. "Oh, and there's the small fact I command dragons."

I huffed and took up my spoon, requesting, "Can we please move on from this topic? I'm sure we all agree it's no one's business but my own."

"My sister taking, at *best*, a fifty percent chance with her life to cross an expanse of water only to perhaps best that challenge, if she's fortunate, to arrive in lands most of us know nothing about?" Kristian asked, his tone dripping in disbelief. "I think it's anyone's duty to talk her out of such foolhardiness."

I didn't even attempt to keep the snap out of my, "It's *not* foolhardy."

"It is," Kristian returned heatedly. "Sheer folly. And reckless. And, frankly, absurd."

It was me who rudely dropped my spoon in my consommé as my voice rose when I demanded, "How dare you!"

"I dare very easily when I've finally gotten my sister back only for her to decide to do something rash and idiotic that might make me lose her again," he replied.

I snapped my mouth shut as my throat completely closed at his words in a way it was a miracle I didn't immediately start gasping for air.

"You're going to come home with us," Kristian decided. "You're going to get to know my wife and my son and the child my wife now carries once he or she comes," he went on, and my gaze flew to Brikitta who was now blushing.

But my brother had not finished.

"And if you don't, you'll be somewhere near, the furthest away Fleuridia, so you can visit us or we can visit you. I'll hear no more talk about your ridiculous impulses. In fact, I'm determined you return with us. It's clear with all you've endured recently your mind isn't right and you need time to get it right again."

I had many cutting retorts on the tip of my tongue.

But the new Franka turned her gaze to her sister-in-law and inquired, "You're with child?"

"I..." more blushing from Brikitta, "yes."

"I'm pleased for you, sister. Very."

Her eyes grew large.

"As for you," I looked back to my brother, "we'll finish this discussion later."

"We won't, for the discussion is already finished," he decreed.

"It is not."

"It is."

"It is *not.*"

"It is *so.*"

"Not!" I cried.

"So!" he shot back.

I heard laughter erupt all around us, but through it I also heard Queen Aurora's shuddering with amusement (shuddering!) command of, "Franka, no more talk of this nonsense. Kristian is right. Your plans are far too risky and you've decided them at a time when you're vulnerable to making poor decisions. I forbid you to cross the Green Sea. At least for a year. Should you continue to wish to do so, perhaps it can be discussed again after that time."

I stared at my sovereign, speechless.

The Queen of Lunwyn was not speechless.

She carried on.

"Your choices are to return to your brother's home with your family or journey with me to Rimée Keep. With Frey, my Finnie and my wee Viktor off to Bellebryn, I'll be quite alone and you'll be lovely company."

I would be lovely company?

Me?

I remained speechless.

Aurora did not.

"You have until Kristian and Brikitta depart five days hence to make your decision. Now," she looked around the table, "that's done. Allow us to toast Kristian and Brikitta's lovely news and move on from sibling squabbles."

She picked up her wineglass and all followed, including me. When a queen toasted, you didn't demur.

But I was fuming because, apparently, the unexpected end to my parents' years of torment caused me to be uncertain of my feelings and my future and my entire bloody nature and grow soft. However it caused my brother to grow a backbone. Not to mention an open willingness to engage in inappropriateness by drawing me into what could be described as none other than what the queen had deemed it.

A sibling bloody squabble.

At the royal bloody dinner table.

I sipped my wine, ignoring the smiles all around that I was sure had something to do with the fact my brother's family was growing, but more to do with mirth at my brother and my antics.

Thus I did this frowning.

However, I noted the only one not seeming to have enjoyed our display was Noc. He was not smiling. He was regarding me intently.

When I caught his eyes, he mouthed, "All right?"

"Fine," I mouthed back.

He continued studying me before he nodded.

"I do hope," Aurora called out as everyone resumed eating, and I looked to her to see her attention set on Brikitta, "that your wee Timofei was able to get a good nap in this afternoon. Prior to Franka taking her maid shopping, she was quite thorough in addressing the servants to request that they practice quiet around your rooms as your wee one has been having trouble sleeping recently."

By the goddess Adele, were my cheeks flaming?

Brikitta's eyes darted to me and they were again large.

Yes, my cheeks were flaming.

Blast!

"A phase, I'm sure," Aurora went on. "He'll stop fretting and return to good sleep soon, mark my words."

"I say, Franka," Kristian began after the queen finished, speaking in my ear. "It's too strange, gazing upon this gentleman who's the vision of Prince Noctorno. Uncanny. I'm glad the prince has a scar or I wouldn't be able to tell them apart."

I turned my head and blasted my brother with an icy glare, stating without words I, unlike he, was not over our very recent spat.

He grinned at my glare and asked in a teasing tone, "Did you enjoy shopping with *your maid*?"

My glare intensified.

My brother took it in and did not cower.

He started chuckling and returned to his consommé.

With no other choice open to me, I also turned to my place setting, thinking I was not losing my touch.

It was gone.

And I had no choice as to what to think of that.

Except, so be it.

8
MY VALIANT

Valentine

Valentine stood at the window of her lovely little house in the countryside outside of Fyngaard and looked to the shadowed frosty wonderland of snow and ice sparkling in the moonlight.

Frey Drakkar stood in the middle of the room behind her and he did this speaking.

As he spoke, Valentine fought the urge to smile.

"We're willing to make it worth your time," Drakkar declared as he concluded stating what he wished to request from Valentine.

She'd do what he requested for free.

However, he didn't need to know that.

"I'm sure your wife has shared much, though you cannot understand the extent of it, Drakkar," she said to the window. "But suffice it to say that it's an understatement when I note that my world is much different than this one."

"I do get this impression, Valentine, and thus that world holds no interest to me outside those things I pay you to bring for my wee one that she misses," Frey replied. "It sounds busy and crowded, overcomplicated, and from what I've heard from Finnie, the majority of those who inhabit it live lives mistaken as to what's important."

Valentine turned toward the man. "And yet you wish to send Franka there?"

"She needs to be rid of bad memories. She also needs a challenge," he responded. "But I sense she'll be seeking ones much different than what she's sought in the past. And with you and Noc and perhaps Circe to guide her way, she'll not get lost again, even in that world."

"I see your point," Valentine murmured.

Frey gave her a short nod. "And her riches, you've mentioned they'd be considerable there as well, but they'd also be suspect if discovered by those in positions of authority. Franka is accustomed to a certain standard of living and will expect that in any land she inhabits. She also has lived a life of independence, outside the threat of her parents' actions. I can't imagine that'd change, and with that threat eradicated, I can only imagine her desire for autonomy will increase. She'll not like her standard of living lowered or her new liberty threatened with, for example, the need to seek employment or the like. Both would most assuredly sway her decision in the wrong direction about whether or not to go."

Valentine's lips curled. "I've ways to assist her in converting her parallel universe resources to my-world currency, not to mention other issues she may have, such as finding and paying for appropriately appointed accommodation. She'll live very well, Drakkar, and do it not having to ask if someone wishes 'fries with that.'"

"Good," he murmured then asked, "Fries with that?"

Valentine lifted a hand and flipped it languidly, "The explanation to that is truly beneath your notice, Frey."

The Drakkar didn't reply.

Valentine tilted her head, querying, "And this was Noc's idea?"

Frey gave another short nod. "Yes, and I believe a good one." At that point his lips twitched. "We discovered at dinner tonight that she intends to cross the Green Sea. The queen forbade it, of course, but it indicates Franka is up for an adventure, the bolder the better."

"And would it be me or Noc that will suggest this to her?" Valentine went on.

"It's my understanding that Noc's speaking to her this evening."

Valentine's smiled a small smile. "Excellent. Well, do keep me informed, Frey. When she's agreed to leave this world for mine, I'll be certain to put all the pieces in place for her to do so and enjoy her position when she arrives."

His brows rose. "There's the matter of payment, Valentine."

"Of course," she said quietly. "And you'll be seeing to this? Or will Franka be expected to compensate me for my services? Perhaps Noc?"

"This is a gift from Finnie and I," Frey answered.

That was what Valentine hoped he'd say.

"If that's the case, I request an audience with the elves in their realm under the ice," she shared and watched his mouth grow tight.

"This is a grand request," he stated shortly.

"Even I don't have the power to visit the elves, and I've a feeling it would be most interesting."

"You would be right, Valentine, but they hold their realm dear and may not grant this request."

"You rule them, Frey," Valentine reminded him.

"I do, but I do not do it through tyranny as one of my predecessors did, resulting in losing them for centuries," he returned. "I take their desires and concerns into account, and if something is important to them, I consider it gravely."

He lowered his voice and his gaze never left hers as he continued.

"You know I appreciate all you've done for my Finnie, myself and my country, even if, for most of it, you were paid handsomely. Your life as well was often in danger and you showed courage and loyalty, which I admire. You also know because of this I hold a fondness for you as does my wife. But even so, the elves have free will and can retreat to their underground dominion, not to return until there's a new Frey who does not rule them with an oppressive hand. If they refuse your visit, Valentine, I can offer you time speaking with Nillen and his council by calling them up to the ice. This would cause no umbrage and it, too, I would hope would be interesting."

"I would prefer my own adventure in the elfin realm, Drakkar, but if I must accept the alternative, I would do that as well," she granted.

"My thanks."

Valentine looked to the door then back to Frey. "I don't wish to be rude, and you know I always enjoy your company, but even if the hour grows late, I have things to see to."

"Of course," he murmured, moving her way.

Valentine stayed where she was.

When he arrived at her, he bent to brush his lips against her cheek and pulled back, again catching her gaze. "I'll deliver a message when I know of Franka's decision."

"In the meantime, I'll hope she makes the right one."

This time, Frey's lips curled. "With what I see growing between her and Noc, I've no doubt she will."

Valentine hoped that was true as well.

"Our gratitude, Valentine," Drakkar said as he began to move away from her.

Valentine watched him go, relished doing so for he was quite the specimen, and she did it replying, "I enjoy being at your service."

He stopped at the door to the room and looked back at her, now fully smiling.

"You enjoy being paid," he retorted, a teasing note to his voice.

"That too," she agreed.

He shook his head, lifted a hand and bid, "Farewell."

Valentine said nothing. She simply stood where Frey left her and watched the door, pleased that things were progressing so well and so swiftly with Franka and Noc, even without her meddling.

But now she had an actual invitation to meddle, and Valentine looked forward to doing just that.

Thinking of meddling, she turned her attention from the door to her crystal that lay on its bed of emerald velvet.

She moved to it, drifting her fingertips across the orb, watching the smoke swirl inside, her mind taken not only from Franka and Noc but also what was in that very house upstairs waiting for her attention, and Valentine directed her thoughts to what was in the sphere.

She again wafted the tips of her fingers across the crystal and watched the smoke change direction and a new vision formed.

She should not dally. If left to their own devices, it would never happen simply due to location and circumstances. She further couldn't court either of them finding another.

She'd done her research. She'd been thorough. She knew she'd made the right decision. There was nothing further to do.

Except find the perfect time.

And then intervene.

In fact, with the plans she had for Franka, it might be agreeable that they work together to see Valentine's other scheme to fruition.

An excellent idea.

She snapped her fingers and the wisps in the crystal disappeared.

She then looked at the clock on the mantel.

Frey had arrived a quarter of an hour after she'd given her instructions. He had not stayed long. If she wished to make her test a more onerous one, she'd wait another half hour, or longer.

But thinking what awaited her, Valentine found uncharacteristically that she didn't wish to wait even a minute longer.

No.

She was quite keen to see the results of how her instructions had been carried out.

Thus, it was time to see to things.

And this Valentine walked leisurely to the door to make her way to what awaited her in her bedchamber in order to do.

Franka

"There you are."

I turned at my brother's voice and saw him sauntering into the room.

I turned back to the window where I was staring out at the snow-covered back garden of the palace, concocting elaborate schemes of packing up Josette and myself, finding Irene and making a clandestine escape.

Alas, I feared if I attempted any of the many maneuvers I'd dreamed up in the hours that had elapsed after dinner, the queen herself would order me found. She'd likely send her son-in-law after me and we'd be on the run for, my guess, a day and a half before we were dragged back.

I sighed at the window.

"It's very late, Franka, and I wish to join my wife in bed," my brother said, and I could hear now he was close. "But I didn't want to do so without making certain you were over your pique from earlier."

That made me cut my gaze to him and arch a brow. "My *pique*?"

He grinned. "Surely even you," his eyes slid to the window and back to me, "after hours of brooding can't still think a voyage across the emerald waters is a good idea."

I looked back to the window, suggesting, "Perhaps we can cease discussing this topic."

"Perhaps that's wise," he murmured.

He said nothing more.

I continued giving him the cold shoulder, doing so getting colder and colder myself, standing at the window.

"Franka," I heard from closer. "It was only worry that made me react that way at dinner."

This was true.

It was also irritating in the extreme mostly because it *was* true.

"It's been my whole life you looked after me," he went on, his voice quieting. "Now, it's my turn."

Even more irritating because he was so bloody *endearing*.

And he always had been.

"I've left it too late, but at least now I have the chance," he finished, and I finally turned back his way.

"I don't need looking after, Kristian."

"I know, Franka. But I still desire that privilege."

I shifted so I was fully facing him. "Brother, the beauty of what's happened is that now we can both live our lives without bothering with such nonsense."

His face grew hard in a way that most assuredly did not suit him.

And yet it very much did.

At least it suited the new Kristian.

"As your brother, it's always been my job to look after you, it'll always be my job and it's not *nonsense*. Until now, I've failed. From now I will not. It's my time and I'm taking it."

I studied him but was careful not to show how intently I was doing so in order not to make him uncomfortable.

I did this for some time before I noted gently, "You're much changed."

"As are you," he replied.

I nodded my acceptance of that.

"Do you..." I subtly cleared my throat and started again, "I went to see them in jail."

His head moved in an abrupt and uncomfortable manner. "Cousin Frey informed me of this."

I lifted my chin and carried on, "I found before doing that I was not quite at peace with how things had changed."

Kristian's expression turned baffled at the same time concerned. "I cannot imagine how that could be, sister," he whispered.

I shook my head and readjusted my position, turning my gaze back to the window.

In other words, hiding in the only way I could from my brother even as I gave him everything.

"I did not know who I was without my existence being the way it was."

"Franka," he said quietly in a way I knew he was no longer baffled.

"I still am uncertain," I admitted. I looked over my shoulder at him. "Do you...or perhaps *did* you feel the same?"

"No, love," he stated quietly. "When that witch stripped Mother of her magic and shared with me Father had been detained by Frey, I felt like great stones had been weighing me down for centuries and they'd suddenly been lifted so not only could I take my feet, I could lift my arms and fly."

This made me feel something I'd never felt.

My heart taking flight for my brother.

Without thought, my hand darted out to find his.

Our fingers curled around each other's.

"I'm happy for that, brother," I told him.

"You'll find your way, sister," he told me.

I hoped so.

Though I'd thought my way was an adventure across the sea, but Kristian had done something about that.

Now I needed to find another way.

Oh well, I would. Eventually my back would be fully healed and the shocking knowledge of what had been before for Kristian and I would mean all the attention I was receiving would fade. People (I assumed) would feel less protective (or, by my way of thinking, *over*protective). And then I (and Josette, not to mention Irene), would be at liberty to go about our business again.

I just needed patience and I'd had that once. I'd find it again. Utilize it.

And onward we'd go.

"Shit, sorry to interrupt."

This came from the door, and Kristian let me go to step aside as we both looked to see Noc backing out of the space.

"No, Sir Noc, or...um, Master Noc," Kristian called clumsily but quickly rallied. "If you seek Franka, you've found her and I'm off to join my wife." My brother looked to me. "We'll breakfast together?"

I nodded. "That would be lovely."

He smiled and moved toward me leaning in.

He touched his cheek to mine and whispered, "Goodnight, my valiant."

I felt my mouth tighten because his words vexed me. And they vexed me because they meant the world to me and I found this constant overflowing of feeling decidedly *annoying*.

This meant when he pulled away and looked at my face, his head jerked before his mouth broke into a wide smile.

"And with gratitude, some things never change," he murmured, still smiling as he moved away.

I watched him leave, hearing him bid goodnight to Noc as he did so, Noc returning that gesture.

My attention moved to Noc only when my brother disappeared from view.

Noc was now in the middle of the room, looking at me, and he didn't appear to be in a good mood.

"Is aught amiss?" I queried, hoping to sound innocent of the wrongdoing I knew I'd done, which he knew as well for it was written all over his face.

"Aught's definitely amiss," he stated shortly. "Babe, we had a date and I've been sittin' in our room for the last two hours waitin' on your ass."

Drat it all, his using the words *our room* made warmth flood my belly.

"Our room?" I asked, even though I knew precisely what he was referring to.

"Babe," he growled low, knowing I knew.

All right, onward from that.

"Why didn't you ask a servant where I was?" I inquired.

"Why didn't you come to our room like we agreed?" he fired back.

"We agreed on an assignation, Noc, we didn't agree on a location."

This, at least, was true.

He tossed an arm out wide. "Have you been waitin' in here for me?"

No, guiltily I had not. I had been in that room somewhat avoiding him but doing it in order to brood and lick my wounds from dinner, which turned into me madly planning a variety of elaborate escapes I wouldn't be able to execute and losing track of time.

But mostly I was avoiding him, and I was doing this because he did simple things, like say two innocuous words, and doing such made warmth flood my belly.

"Well..." I said that word slowly and trailed off, attempting to find an inoffensive, slightly factual answer.

"Fucking hell," he muttered, prowling to the cord in the room and tugging on it. He then turned again to me and crossed his arms on his chest. "You gonna get your ass over here and sit with me by the fire or are you gonna stand in front of that window until the cold coming through freezes you to death?"

"There's no need to be surly," I noted (although there was), shifting from the window (which was indeed cold) and moving his way where there were two chairs with a table between them angled toward a hearty fire.

"Frannie, I waited *two hours for you.*"

Gods, the guilt assailing me was going to make me bite my lip!

I managed not to do something so ridiculous and simply stopped in front of a chair, keeping my gaze on him.

I opened my mouth to say something flippant.

But, "I'm sorry, Noc, I've got much on my mind," came out instead.

Some of the ire in his face faded as me moved toward me.

I expected him to stop in front of his own chair but he was Noc. He didn't do the expected.

He did the affectionate.

This meant he stopped half a foot from me so I could smell his cologne, a fresh, spicy scent I quite liked, his head tilted down so his eyes could hold mine.

"This gig, you know, the one I'm tryin' to help you get used to?" he began.

I nodded.

"Part of it is bein' in a place where, when you got shit on your mind and you got someone who cares about you, they're there for you to unload it on," he explained.

"There are things I need to work through myself."

"I hear you, sweetheart, but from what happened at dinner, thinkin' that you might wanna stop doin' that for a while, unload your shit on me, someone who's thinking a whole lot clearer, and let me help you work through those things, maybe give you ideas of where you could go from here."

I drew in breath to calm the additional warmth that pronouncement caused in my belly.

One could say that Antoine was many things, nearly all of them good, and part of those many things was that he was intelligent and he was strong.

However, he did not have that kind of strength. There was much he depended upon me to do. His upkeep, for one, as before he came to be committed only to me, he was a Fleuridian prostitute. Decisions about our home, servants, travel, money matters were other matters he looked to me to see to. He had a good deal saved from his earnings when he'd plied his trade, something which he was in great demand to do. Earnings I'd demanded he keep saved for no one knew what the future would bring and I was capable of taking care of us both, this something he had no qualms about accepting.

Antoine had been sensitive. He'd been caring. He'd been decent and kind to all, not only me. He'd had a flippant sense of humor I relished. And he, like Noc, had a way of seeing deeper inside me than I'd wished (at first) for him to see.

And he was exceptional in bed (obviously).

But he was not that man. He was not Frey to my Finnie, Lahn to my Circe, Tor to my Cora, Apollo to my Madeleine.

He might listen to my problems, but then he'd ask, "So what do you intend to do, *mon ange*?"

He would never say, "This is what you should think about doing." And definitely never, "This is what you're going to do because this is what's best for you."

Living my life, I would never admit, even to myself, that I found making every decision—from the small to the grand—draining, and the very idea of living the whole of my life with that burden mine alone was exhausting.

To share a burden not simply with someone to listen to it, but to assist me in seeing past it, felt like a gift so precious, it outshone chests five times as large as the one I owned filled with Sjofn diamonds.

"Frannie," Noc called, and I focused on his face.

"I had my plans," I blurted, "and now they're thwarted."

His expression grew understanding as he gently commanded, "Sit down, baby, I'll order some whiskey and tell you my idea."

He had an idea, and I assumed it was not aiding me in an intricate scheme to spirit Josette, Irene and I into the night taking us someplace no one would find us (until Frey found us, of course).

I sat.

Noc, bizarrely determined to carry on doing mundane things I suspected he had to do in his world but he didn't have to do in mine, went to the windows and drew the drapes. He then stirred the fire, added a couple of logs on it, and whilst doing this, ordered our whiskey from the servant who'd arrived.

I understood why he went about these efforts when the warm glow of the fire became a radiating blaze, taking away any chill, enveloping us in snug intimacy in a way neither of us would have to call for a servant (or in Noc's case, get up and do it himself) to add more fuel to the fire for some time.

The decanter of whiskey came quickly and the servant had barely laid the tray on the table between our chairs before Noc thanked him and started pouring.

"And close the door behind you, would you?" he called.

"Yes, sir." We heard murmured and the door clicked.

Noc handed me my cut crystal glass filled with two fingers of whiskey.

Quite a dose.

And it was a dose that made me wonder with even more curiosity about his idea.

"All right, Noc, you stated you had an idea, so perhaps you'll break the suspense and share," I prompted as he took a sip from his own glass.

I did the same as he lowered his and started speaking.

"Finnie and Frey have a few things they gotta sort out here before we take off, which I think is mostly her way of delaying 'cause she likes spending time with her mom," he declared.

"This doesn't exactly end the suspense," I replied when he shared no further.

He grinned at me. "What I'm sayin' is, we're probably gonna be around awhile and that while will take us until at least the time your brother leaves."

This meant five more days of being able to spend time with Noc.

I found it alarming just how much this pleased me.

Really, did I not adore my Antoine *at all*?

I fought shifting uncomfortably in my chair as Noc continued talking.

"And you've got another choice other than going with your brother or going with the queen," he said then promptly announced, "You can come with us."

I felt my body start in surprise at this offer.

"I—" I began.

"Givin' you this idea to think on, Frannie," he interrupted me to say. "Not make a decision right here and now."

I took a sip of whiskey to sort my thoughts.

After I'd swallowed, carefully, I shared, "Noc, this is a kind offer and I'm glad for it. But my plan of going across the Green Sea was not as foolhardy as people believe. There was a reason I made that choice and I did so even understanding the risks it brought. Josette chose to accompany me understanding those same risks."

"You wanna get away from anything that reminds you of your parents or Antoine."

I closed my mouth, astonished he'd guessed so accurately.

I opened it to say, "I've been to Bellebryn and I've been with Antoine. We took a holiday there once. He'd never been. He enjoyed it greatly."

"Babe—"

I spoke over him. "There was more to Josette and my adventure than eluding my past. I've deduced that it's likely on an adventure you're experiencing so many things, you can think of nothing but what you're experiencing."

"You can't escape your problems, sweetheart, or your emotions," he told me gently. "They got a way of not letting go."

He was undoubtedly right.

"Yes, but when other things are prevalent and they are that for a good period of time, those emotions have a way of fading away."

"You got me there," he muttered.

"In other words, I did know what I was doing, Noc, and now I don't. Now my options are limited. And although I'd enjoy spending time with my brother, meeting my niece or nephew when he or she arrives, something I did not know which I now have to take into account, I think both of us can agree the time is ripe for a variety of changes in my life. And I feel, the sooner I see to them will be the better."

"Come home with me."

I froze in my seat, my eyes locked on him.

Noc did not freeze.

He continued.

"Valentine says she'll take care of it all. And maybe we can give her some of the gold we got to bring us back if you get homesick. I can take a vacation, experience more of this world then. But now, or after your brother leaves, I won't go with Finnie and Frey and instead take you back to my world with me."

I sat mute and immobile, unable to take my eyes off him, but my mind was awhirl with hundreds of thoughts.

Maybe thousands.

But the one that repeatedly churned through the others was Noc's attractive voice saying the words, *Come home with me.*

"Frey already asked her," he carried on. "It's all set. You gotta get away, there's no further away than there, Frannie. And if you want an adventure to get your mind off shit, that'll be the biggest adventure you can have, there aren't any pirates and I'll be there to keep you safe."

I'll be there to keep you safe.

By the goddess, he must stop.

"Noc—" I began in an effort to make him do that.

He reached across the table between us, caught my hand that was resting on the arm of my chair and laced his fingers through mine.

He had very long fingers. Competent-looking. Most appealing.

Bloody hell.

"Don't decide on that right now either," he urged. "You got time to think about it. But, babe," he smiled and that was most appealing too. Always. "I'd love to show you my world. And you won't be alone there. You'll have Valentine. And Circe lives where we live too. She's already gone back, and from what she's said, she can use a few friends who know her like we'd know her. You'll have people. You'll have resources. You'll be good. You'll be safe." His smile got wider. "And you'll be in New Orleans so you'll have good music, great fucking food and every opportunity to have a shit ton of fun."

I finally managed to string a thought together.

"I couldn't ask you not to take your adventure in order to give me mine."

"I get vacation days, toss a couple gold coins Valentine's way, I'm back and I'll get it."

"Noc, that's most kind, but it'd be selfish of me even to consider."

"Happily give up my adventure for a different one, that bein' givin' you yours."

It appeared he was going to be difficult to dissuade.

Worse, as I was able to string together further thoughts, I was wondering why I would try.

I did manage to note, "There's Josette to consider. And my new maid, Irene."

"Don't know about this Irene, Frannie. Havin' a lady's maid isn't something people have in my world, much less having two. As for Josette, she's your girl and I'd get you'd want her with you. But she was willing to cross the Green Sea with you, don't think she'd back off from traveling to a parallel universe."

Troublingly, I suspected Josette would follow me straight to hell if I guided her there. I treasured that loyalty even if I didn't know how I'd earned it.

A place with such fanciful things as motorcycles and phones, if she was right there in the room with us, she'd say yes for the both of us before I could utter another noise.

"Frannie, it's a good deal and you know it," Noc pressed. "Better than whatever you wanted to see on another continent in this world. Hell, you eat a bite you'll wonder why you didn't say yes before I finished making the offer when you have pizza."

I knew I shouldn't ask.

But I asked.

"What's pizza?"

"Tangy tomato sauce, smooth cheese, spicy sausage, all baked on top of a doughy crust with crispy, chewy edges. You got killer food here, Frannie, but the minute I get home, I'm getting a slice, and if you're with me, I'm getting you one too. Extra cheese and pepperoni."

I liked tangy sauce, smooth cheese and sausage.

I also liked bread.

No, I *adored* bread.

Drat.

"I must think on this, Noc," I told him, and it was true.

What also was true was that there was no reason *not* to take this alternate adventure, except I'd be even further away from my brother.

Though, if Valentine was but a coin or two away from bringing me home, I had many of those and I could be back with him and his family faster and safer than I could return across the Green Sea.

No, it was Noc that was the concern.

Noc and just how much I liked spending time with him.

And just how wrong that was.

"More options," he stated and my focus sharpened on him. "I go do my thing with Finnie and Frey and the rest, you go back with your brother. Few months, maybe after the baby's born and you know it's all good with that, Valentine takes us home. I get my gig here, you get your time with your family, then we take our adventure."

My.

Now *that* might be workable.

Months away from Noc would mean I could get my head sorted about him, for surely it was his attention and kindness all bundled in the alluring package that was him and handed to me at a time when I was at my most vulnerable that was muddling it.

I missed Antoine. I'd lost him forever.

Perhaps as a coping mechanism, my mind was searching for an alternate, even if this was wrong and disloyal.

That had to be it.

"Yeah?" Noc prompted.

"Yes," I replied. "I'll think on that option too, Noc."

A grin from him and a heartfelt, "Great, baby."

Looking pleased with himself, he gave my hand a squeeze, let it go and turned to the fire, lifting his glass.

I did the same.

"Pizza. Phones. Bikes," Noc's voice came again. "TV. Movies. Computers. Football." I turned my head to him just in time to see him do the same my way. "And you know I like you when I promise to take you to the shoe department at Nordstrom."

"Do they have a nice selection of slippers?" I queried.

His grin this time was different. It made my breath catch and my nipples contract.

Worse, he did it leaning across the table toward me and his voice was lower, deeper, like he was sharing a delicious secret when he spoke next.

"Baby, just you wait and see."

My.

I gave myself a hearty inward shake and pulled myself together.

"I do believe, Master Noc, that you're taking unfair advantage by applying not-so-subtle pressure for me to fall in with your plans."

He sat back, lifted his glass and warned, "You don't come to me after you have breakfast with your brother tomorrow and tell me you're in, get used to that over the next few days, Frannie."

Wonderful.

I looked from him in a patented Franka Drakkar dismissive way and took another sip of my whiskey, only to do this hearing Noc's chuckle.

Gods.

"You're gonna look good in spike heels," Noc remarked.

Spike heels?

Intriguing.

"Cease," I demanded.

He ignored me.

"And a little black dress."

"Cease," I snapped.

"Wearin' both at midnight sittin' across from me at Café du Monde after we did the town, kicked back listening to live jazz, got drunk on Bourbon Street, eating a beignet caked with powdered sugar and drinking coffee with chicory."

Jazz? What was that?

And a beignet? I had no clue what that was but anything caked with a substance called "powdered sugar" had to be delicious, didn't it?

I turned my head to glower at him.

"Noc. Cease!" I insisted.

"Shrimp étoufée."

I loved prawns.

"Quiet."

"Avenues lined with five hundred-year-old oak trees and graceful antebellum mansions."

I definitely loved mansions.

"Quiet!"

"Spicy-hot jambalaya."

I'd had enough.

"Would you care to wear my whiskey?" I asked mock sweetly.

"No, baby," he muttered amusedly.

"Then kindly cease speaking."

"Like a cat, curious, aren't you, Frannie?" he teased. "Gonna eat you up, you don't come home with me."

Come home with me.

Blast!

I turned again to face the fire, announcing, "I'm ignoring you now."

"Give that five minutes, which is as long as you can keep that shit up," he accepted, doing so to my frustration because I suspected he was right.

And he was right.

Though, fortunately, when he pulled me back into conversation, he did so not tempting me with strange words that piqued my curiosity, but instead with thoughtful ones that coaxed me to talk about how I felt about my brother's behavior at dinner and how we were both getting on otherwise since he'd arrived.

Thus we spent a pleasant hour drinking whiskey but not doing so becoming inebriated. Just enjoying pleasant company.

But this time, when it was over, I didn't sweep from the room.

Noc walked me to the door to my bedchamber and kissed my temple before he opened it and scooted me in with a light hand on the small of my back.

And last, he gave me a soft smile that I could swear held a promise I didn't quite understand before he closed the door behind me and I lost sight of him.

9
STRICT LIFE EDICT

Franka

The next morning, I walked into the breakfast room to see only Brikkita there, finishing up her crêpes.

She looked up at me, startled, as if she had no idea I would be arriving at breakfast when Kristian and I had made that plan the night before, something I would assume he'd share with his wife.

"Good morning, Brikkita," I greeted, selecting a seat across from her at the oval table.

"Good morning, Franka," she replied timidly, the manner in which she always spoke to me, a manner I'd always found irksome, but one I now understood was a manner I'd earned.

Therefore, hearing it now, I was irked at myself.

I'd barely sat and tossed the napkin at the waiting place setting over my lap before a footman came forward to pour my coffee.

I prepared it with cream and one sugar and had taken a sip, regarding my sister-in-law, who kept her head studiously bent to her plate as she fixedly scraped up the last of her crêpes.

"Did you sleep well?" I asked.

She lifted her eyes to me for a scant second before returning them to her plate and answered, "The palace has comfortable beds."

I decided that meant yes.

"And Timofei? Did he have a good night?" I queried.

Her glance lasted longer before she put down her fork and reached for her coffee cup, avoiding my eyes. "He was restless. He's not woken us like this repeatedly in the night since he was first born. I hope the queen was right, and he'll grow out of it."

"I'm sure she is. She's raised her own child, as you know," I replied, though the child she'd raised was not the one currently abiding at the palace, but that was beside the point.

"Of course," Brikkita mumbled, taking a sip of coffee, her eyes aimed away from me.

"Is Kristian arriving at breakfast soon?" I pressed on.

"I hope so," she said, and this, I was sure had more than one meaning.

"Mm," I murmured, having used all my available discourse and finding myself in the uncomfortable position of having no more, considering the fact I knew not what interested her because I'd never bothered to find out.

The footman saved me, asking, "Would you like me to tell Cook to prepare crêpes for you, milady, or do you wish to attend the buffet?"

"The buffet, I think," I decided. "But fresh toast would be well received."

The footman nodded, gave a slight bow with one arm behind his back and retreated to a door that undoubtedly led to stairs that went to the kitchen.

I took another sip of my coffee, exited my chair, walked to the buffet and made my selections.

I was back at my seat, nibbling my food, the footman having returned with my toast, and I was finding I was not enjoying breakfast in the slightest. For having your sister-in-law sit opposite you, alone together for the first time when I had no ulterior motives but instead wished to find some avenue to start a different sort of relationship, was exceptionally awkward.

It would not be surprising, but utterly shocking when Brikkita piped up, and instead of me doing it, she took up these same reins.

"I hope you don't mind me saying..." she began, and my eyes went to hers.

She was casting a quick peek at the footman and I waited as patiently as I could for her to continue.

Finally, she seemed to feel safe in turning her attention to me, but when she spoke again, her voice had lowered.

"My husband has shared with me much of his history."

I put down my fork, reached again to my coffee cup and held it aloft, keeping my gaze locked to hers. I nodded once, slowly, an indication for her to go on.

She did so.

"When I say much, what I mean is all of it," she clarified.

"You are his wife," I stated carefully. "This comes as no surprise."

"In doing so," she sallied forth swiftly, still speaking low but now doing it like she wished she wasn't, "he of course had to share about you."

"Of course," I agreed.

She licked her lips and pressed them together.

I took a sip of coffee, giving her time.

"I...it's not my place," she eventually carried on.

"What isn't your place?" I inquired when she didn't explain.

"To say what I wish to say," she finished.

I drew in breath and put my cup in its saucer. Once I'd done that, I folded my hands in my lap and straightened my shoulders minutely in hopes she wouldn't see this effort at bracing for what I suspected she felt was not her place to say was that now, as her husband had started to blossom out from under the oppression of oppressive parents, she felt secure enough to do the same.

But her oppression had come at my hands.

And therefore now she felt it was time to share a few choice things with me about how I'd treated her, and even Kristian, not the least of which was dragging my brother into my treachery, in doing so putting him, her and their son at risk.

Things I'd not only earned having to hear, but I deserved.

I would not relish it, of that I was certain.

But I deserved it.

When she didn't speak further, I felt it was my place to invite her to do so.

This I did.

"I have not treated you thus, Brikitta, and there were reasons for this that may at this juncture seem feeble and still cruel, so I'll not insult you by attempting to explain them, but in the end you are my sister. The sister my brother chose to add to our family when he fell in love with you. I'm sure I don't have to remind you that in the past I've not hesitated in saying a great many things to you, most of them unwelcome. I'm sure you've sensed much has changed in the last weeks. Thus, I'd like to encourage you at this time to return that favor, no matter what you wish to say. All I can say at this time to reassure you is that you have my vow no matter what you say, there will be no ramifications, to you or my brother."

She stared at me, her eyes widened, her lips parted in astonishment.

She did this but she did not snap out of it and say what she wished to say.

Therefore I added, "In other words, Brikitta, you are my sister. You are my family. And thus it's absolutely your place to say whatever is on your mind."

"Thank you," she whispered.

I shook my head. "You don't need to thank me for sharing that you're free to speak your mind."

"No, what I wished to say that I didn't think was my place to say was... thank you."

I stared at her, puzzled.

"Pardon?" I asked.

"You...I love my husband," she stated.

"This I know," I told her.

"And you kept him safe. For years, you kept him safe. Thank you."

Suddenly, it was me turning my eyes away. Indeed, I turned my whole head away, giving her my profile. And for no reason, I lifted my napkin to touch it to my lips as I fought for composure.

"Franka," she called softly.

"A moment if you don't mind," I replied, and damn it all, my voice was thick.

"Certainly," she murmured.

I drew in breath, put the napkin to my lap and again faced my sister-in-law.

The instant I caught her eyes, I saw hers were not timid or frightened. They were bright with emotion, undoubtedly just like mine.

"That is done. We move on from here, yes?" she asked, her tone also quite husky.

I nodded, not trusting my voice not to give me away.

"Good," she said and carefully cleared her throat.

I again took up my fork and used it to slice into a fat, juicy sausage.

"I also would like to extend my invitation for you to journey back and stay with us at our *aateliskartono*," she said. "Kristian is right, we have much room and I think he'll quite enjoy his sister close for a while. Not to mention, watching you get to know your nephew better."

I had never much thought of children except the fact that I never intended to have any. I had not had good examples of parenting and the very thought of being in that position (I did not admit to myself, but it was true) terrified me.

But one could definitely say that Timofei was the handsomest child I'd ever laid my eyes on, and from what little I'd noted, he was exceptionally bright, and I was certain that was not a prejudiced assessment in the slightest.

"I would enjoy both," I told her. "With the addition of spending time getting to know my sister better."

She flushed at my words and then awarded me the first smile I think she'd ever given me, except the one she gave upon meeting me, something to which I said something foul that wiped it clean from her face.

I curved my lips up in return.

"My two favorite girls in the world at the breakfast table together," Kristian declared, and I twisted in my seat to watch him walk in. "This heralds the beginning of an excellent day."

He was late for reasons unknown.

Until then.

He'd orchestrated what just occurred, perhaps at Brikitta's behest, perhaps for his own ends.

And there it was.

It would seem my brother was also blossoming in the art of intrigue.

"Good morning, brother," I greeted.

"Sister," he greeted back, smiling brightly at me and stopping at my seat to bend and sweep his lips along my cheekbone.

When he straightened and moved toward his wife, his smile changed a nuance as he said, "My wife."

"My husband," she replied.

He arrived by her seat and she tipped her head back for him to touch his lips to hers. He lifted but an inch away and they shared a look that made me cast my eyes from them for it was intimate and not for me to see even if it was across a breakfast table.

But in witnessing it, abruptly I felt much like Kristian had explained he felt when he heard what had become of our mother and father.

He had Brikitta. Someone who loved him. Who gave him children. Who made him smile and laugh. Who clearly fretted for his safety and had the courage to thank a woman who had not once been kind to her because she made that husband safe. And she was a woman who gave him that intimacy it was clear he not only savored but cherished.

The feeling all that gave me was as if a weight had been lifted and I could struggle to my feet, and perhaps not fly, but be free to allow my feet to take me wherever they wished to take me.

Not to mention, I'd never thought my sister-in-law attractive, but at what I'd beheld, I changed my mind.

Love created beauty, it would seem.

Following these thoughts, I also realized with some discomfort that I'd never had that with Antoine. There was intimacy, of course, and affection. He knew me well, better than I knew myself, it was true. We shared many moments of humor and also moments of quiet togetherness that I treasured.

But he was my kept lover.

He'd never been my partner.

I'd never had that. Not from Antoine, not from anyone.

But I was pleased I could go forward with my future plans content my brother did.

"So, I hope you'll remain with us even if you've finished your breakfast, my love," Kristian said, and I turned back to them to see him sitting at the foot of the table, his wife to his right, me to his left, his eyes on his beloved.

He had his napkin in his lap and the footman was pouring his coffee.

"For a spell, Kristian," Brikitta replied to his request. "Then I'd like to get to Timofei."

"Of course, darling," Kristian murmured, smiling at her fondly then turning that look to me. "I ran into your Noc in the passageway on the way here."

I felt my breath turn shallow simply at the mention of his name, but also at the way my brother referred to him as "your Noc."

"He's hardly *my* Noc, brother," I returned.

"Hmm..." Kristian mumbled noncommittally and again gave his attention to his wife. "He'd just returned from being outside, running. Odd that. Out in the snow wearing curious shoes that I must admit look rather comfortable, the most peculiar loose-fitting pants and a sweater made of fleece material that appeared rather warm. But along with all that, he was running, of his own accord just to do so, out in the cold. He was breathing heavily because of it but seemed rather invigorated." He shook his head in bewilderment. "Such an unusual thing to do."

Naturally, both Brikitta and Kristian had been fully informed about the parallel universe—save Princess Finnie not being the real one, and Princess Cora not being the real one either, the same with Queen Circe, those were regarded as state secrets.

"Most unusual," Brikitta agreed.

I said nothing, trying to visualize Noc's attire and what he looked like "invigorated."

I'd seen him "invigorated" once before, so just as swiftly as I tried to visualize this, I attempted to banish such thoughts from my brain (and failed).

"He shared with me his plan to take you back to his world after Brikitta safely delivers, and I wholeheartedly agreed."

My mind was wiped of visions of Noc in loose-fitting pants looking invigorated and my eyes cut to my brother at his words.

"I beg your pardon?"

Kristian didn't repeat himself.

He declared, "We decided that's what you'll do. Return with us Älvkyla. Once the baby comes, Master Noc will have concluded his explorations in our world and you'll return with him to the other world. An excellent idea. We spent not much time with that world's witch, but even in the short time we spent with her, she seemed most capable, and it was shared she'd be your champion. Not to mention, Master Noc shared he'd look after you, and he may not be a prince in his world, but he still has a princely bearing. Thus, I'm confident you'll be safe with him and the witch."

Although I'd been leaning toward the same decision, I found Noc's sharing with my brother and my brother's declaration more than a little vexing.

"I'm sure I don't have to remind you that where I go next is my decision to make, Kristian," I informed him tartly.

"It's lost on no one that you've grown quite close with this man and he does not hide the fact that he holds great affection for you, Franka," Kristian returned. "He'll have your best interests at heart and seems to trust this witch. If you desire a complete change of scenery, this is much preferable to your other plans. Further, Master Noc informed me that you can return when you please for but a few gold coins, and in but moments, not months."

"I've not spoken to this witch so I'm actually not aware of what the cost of travel would be," I retorted.

Though, that said, I undoubtedly had whatever the cost, even if it was extravagant.

And this reminded me I had yet to speak to my brother about that as well for I intended to give him a healthy portion of what I had.

That would happen, of course, but at that juncture I wasn't feeling the need to share my intended generosity.

Kristian pushed his chair back and began to move to the buffet, stating, "We'll talk more of it later. Brikitta wishes to get to our boy and I wish to join them. He had a fitful night. Perhaps later we'll all sledge into Fyngaard and get Timofei some liquid chocolate." He gave his wife a tender look. "And my Brikitta as well, as you so love the chocolate from Esmerelda's."

"I would enjoy that, Kristian," Brikitta agreed.

"Then it's sorted," Kristian decided and scooped up eggs.

"Well, if you both will excuse me," I announced, pushing my own chair back, having not finished my breakfast, not caring but instead standing, "I have some fuming to do and I'd prefer to do that alone."

Brikitta grinned down at her plate.

Kristian appeared to be fighting his own amusement as he lifted his brows. "Fuming?"

"Don't pretend you don't know your dictatorial ways aren't especially welcome, brother."

His expression grew serious. "I'm looking out for you."

"And this is annoying too," I shared.

His amusement came back as he turned to the heated silver chafing dish filled with sausages, muttering, "You'll get used to it."

I sighed.

"Excellent, we thought we'd be late and miss company at breakfast."

This came from the direction of the doorway, words uttered by Circe as she and Lahn came into the room, Circe first, Lahn needing to duck his head to get through the door, such was his height.

"Too late for Brikitta, as she's off to see to our son," Kristian declared. "And Franka as well, as she's off to fume."

Lahn and Circe both looked to me, but it was Circe who asked, "Fume?"

"I'll allow my brother to explain as he feels free to discuss me and my activities and my future with just about anyone," I replied then arched a brow to my brother. "Would you like me to go round up the servants? Send them here so you can ask their opinion about what I should expect my next days and months to contain?"

Kristian started chuckling as he took his seat. Brikitta looked away and made no noise but her shoulders were shaking.

Lahn gave Circe a severe look that would be quite frightening if I had not seen him do it before, not to mention their many moments of open tenderness and affection, this look I took as his version of confusion even as she smiled brightly at me.

Truly, wouldn't anyone be annoyed by all this?

"I bid you all good day," I stated, turned and began to flounce from the room, and I felt no shame whatsoever flouncing.

If ever there was a flouncing moment, that was it.

"We'll see you at the sled to go for liquid chocolate," Kristian called as I continued to do just that.

I made no reply even if I fully intended to go with them.

I'd spent no time with my nephew at all since they'd arrived.

But it wasn't just that.

I had a strict life edict I never broke.

I didn't turn down chocolate in any form.

Ever.

Valentine

Once bathed, attired and her hair arranged, Valentine nodded to her maid who left her and then she wasted no time moving through the house to her sphere resting on its bed of velvet. She called up a vision of Franka in its depths, ascertained her location and she spirited herself right there.

Sitting in a chair in her bedchamber, appearing like she was trying to read the book in front of her but her mind had wandered, Franka started in her seat as her eyes flew to Valentine.

"By the gods," she whispered, "you're here."

"I am," Valentine replied, smoothly moving to the chair that was angled opposite Franka in front of the toasty fire. Without invitation she sat, her eyes never leaving the lovely woman in the room with her. "I'm pleased to note you're in a much better state than when we last saw each other."

"I'm pleased as well," Franka replied, having swiftly gotten over her surprise at Valentine appearing, her regard was steady as she flipped shut her book with a snap.

"I've been informed that they're taking good care of you," Valentine noted.

"You would be correct, as annoying as it's been," Franka returned crisply.

Valentine smiled her small smile.

"Kindness is, of course, kind, even if it's often most irritating, that being when it's intrusive and unceasing."

A quickly hidden look of relief flashed through Franka's remarkable blue eyes, an indication she felt soothed to be in the presence of a kindred spirit. This came before she nodded smartly.

"I'm told you've been invited to journey to my world," Valentine remarked.

"I have," Franka confirmed.

"Have you made your decision to come?" Valentine asked.

"I have not."

Hmm.

"May I ask why not?" Valentine pressed.

"Because I fully intend to do it, but I also fully intend not to let on that's been my decision because everyone is being so damnably insistent about me doing it. And you can take that to mean they feel the decision has been made without *me* making it, and I intend to make clear that when the decision is official, it was *my* decision that was made."

"I approve of this course of action," Valentine murmured and watched Franka lift her chin.

"With respect, I don't care if you do or don't."

"I approve of that too," Valentine replied and at that she watched Franka's lips twitch. With no ado, she then announced, "You have magic."

Franka was not able to hide her response to that, quickly or otherwise. She stiffened visibly and her expression went guarded.

"Calm, my sister," Valentine said softly. "It is your secret, and as your sister, it's also mine."

Franka didn't calm immediately. She studied Valentine warily and it took her some time before she nodded her acceptance even if Valentine sensed she didn't fully give it.

"I have your mother's magic, as you know," Valentine continued.

"Pardon?" Franka asked.

"Your mother's magic. I have it," Valentine explained. "I could absorb it, such as it is. I don't need it, though one can never have enough magic. However, I've not done that. I'm waiting on you to tell me what you wish done with it."

It took a moment for Franka to answer, but then she did.

"In honesty, as I didn't know such could occur, I cannot say what you should do with it except that I want no part in whatever is done."

As Valentine suspected, Franka Drakkar held magic, but she did not use it or even understand it.

"You have options, *chérie*," she began, deciding to ignore the last of what Franka said. "I could give it to you, augment the power you have. I sense your power is significant, especially as you inherited it from your mother and haven't used it, so it grows inside you in great stores. Your mother's was used often, randomly and for ill. It wasn't meager, but it is no match to yours."

This was not welcome news, clearly causing Franka to wonder if she knew how to use her power if she could have done so to save herself, her brother and her lover from harm.

Franka shared all of this with Valentine by looking to the fire.

"That wouldn't have helped," Valentine told her sympathetically. "It's an assumption, but I've seen others of little experience make such attempts with much less at stake. They backfired and made matters far worse. So do not concern yourself with that, sister. There was nothing you could have done, not for you, your brother, but most particularly, for your lost lover."

Franka lifted her chin but said nothing.

Therefore Valentine carried on, "You should have been trained. It should have been something beautiful, something precious, time spent together with your mother that you didn't look on fondly, you looked on lovingly, remembering the beauty she shared with you as she taught you to harness and wield your power. Much like every moment I shared with my mother and my grandmother when they guided me in how to wield mine."

Franka turned back to her.

"This, she did not do."

"I know," Valentine replied. "But it would be my honor to do so, sister."

A flash of interest quickly buried before she returned, "I want nothing of hers."

"It's the only good she's given you," Valentine retorted. "And no woman should eschew any power she holds rightly, or that she's earned, or even that she's wrested from a defeated foe. Your mother was a waste to this world. But your magic should not be wasted, and magic is sacred, so what's left of hers shouldn't either."

"What are the other options for her magic?" Franka asked.

Although she admired the trait, at this moment Valentine found Franka's stubbornness frustrating.

"I could expel it into the earth," Valentine answered. "Close to an adela tree, which would assist all of them across Lunwyn in growing."

"As the adela were nearly made extinct during the war, they hold great beauty and provide the same when their power is used, and they take decades to grow, I think that's the better option, don't you?"

"Although it would hasten growth, it would not shave decades off, but only perhaps a few months," Valentine replied.

"A few months are just that and that's something."

Valentine was not pleased with how this conversation was going.

It was time to take another course with the willful witch.

With that in mind, abruptly, she declared, "In my world, when you are with me there, I not only wish to train you to use your magic, but I wish for you to join me as I perform the services I perform for my clients in order to eventually take on your own." She leaned closer to her witch-sister. "I can assure you, the intrigues in which I'm enlisted are often quite delicious."

Finally, she'd caught Franka's attention.

"Indeed?" she asked.

"Indeed," Valentine said as she sat back. "In fact, I have some meddling I intend to do. And it would assist me greatly if I had a partner."

Franka made no reply, she simply continued studying Valentine.

"I would like you in my world. I think it would suit you. I think you'd blossom there. And I hope you'll also blossom under my tutelage," Valentine coaxed.

"That decision has been made, as I've shared," Franka reminded her. "I'll be journeying to your world."

"It has, I'm talking about your magic and you absorbing your mother's."

Franka started to shake her head but Valentine spoke again.

"You are aware there are twins of nearly everyone in both worlds."

"Yes," Franka affirmed.

"And Dax Lahn's twin lives in New Orleans."

Valentine was satisfied to see a slight widening of Franka's eyes and a definite look of heightened attentiveness in them.

"As does this world's Circe, of course," Valentine carried on.

"My," Franka whispered, her sister-witch far from dim, Valentine had to explain no further.

Instead, she shared, "I've paid some attention to him. I've decided they'll suit."

It took a moment, but after that moment Franka's lips curled in a way Valentine found very familiar for she'd felt that same curve on her own lips many a time.

"My," she repeated.

"It may take some time, it's important for you to be comfortable in your magic, but do you fancy some meddling?" Valentine invited.

Franka took another moment and this one was longer.

Valentine waited.

It was worth the wait when she received her answer.

"Absolutely."

Franka

"I WOULD LIKE for you to put that down and come here," I said to the child.

My nephew looked up at me but did not do as I said.

Instead, he put what he was holding right in his mouth.

"I'll repeat," I carried on speaking to the child. "Please put that down and come here."

Timofei just stared at me.

Then he let out a giggle that made the precarious purchase of steadiness he had on his own two feet disappear. He wobbled, fell, and the bangle Josette had given him to distract his attention from his parents leaving him with me (this being right before Josette left him completely alone with me) flew from his hand only to roll on its thin side under a couch.

I sighed.

Timofei adjusted himself so he was on his nappy-covered bottom, looked where the bangle had disappeared, looked to me, his face started to crumple, and I knew what was coming.

Thus, I stood swiftly and stated commandingly, "Do not even consider weeping."

He blinked up at me.

I bent with only a small pang of pain, experiencing another one as I picked up the toddler who was barely a year and a half old but who was also a very big boy (he would grow straight and tall, like his father, I was certain) and planted him so one of his legs was hitched on my hip, the rest of him was wrapped around my belly.

"There will be many times to weep in life, child," I declared as if I was a tutor giving a lesson to her pupil, one that was much older than the one who was staring up at me with wide eyes that looked like mine, and wet, rosy lips that were more endearing than I cared to admit. "I can assure you, a lost bangle is not one of those times."

He slapped my chest and I decided to take that as his agreement to my declaration.

"Quite right," I stated, and moved with him, instinctively bouncing him on my hip.

I took him to the mantel, pointed at a rather unattractive, but I knew nearly priceless *objet d'art* resting there, and instructed, "If this were to break, no weeping."

For some reason he was smiling up at me now, so I bounced him higher and that produced another giggle.

Odd.

Oh well.

I pointed to his chest and pressed in, saying in a softer voice, "Now, if this were to break, you should weep. And don't let anyone tell you differently. I don't care if you're male. A broken heart deserves tears. In truth, I do believe it's the only way to mend it."

"Think you're right, sugarlips."

I jumped at Noc's teasing voice coming to me and whirled with my nephew to face the door.

His voice had been teasing.

As he regarded me across the room by the fire holding my nephew, his face did not say playful.

It said something quite different and I blocked it before I could come to an understanding of just what it said.

"Can I assist you with something?" I queried.

"You comin' home with me?" he returned my query with his own.

Dear goddess, I wished he'd cease referring to it like that.

Home.

With him.

"I've not decided yet."

"Bull," he decreed.

I looked down to Timofei, "It's quite coarse and rude to speak this way, nephew. I know you're young, but it's never too early to bear that in mind."

He looked up at me and bounced himself on my hip. I took my cue and gave him a hearty spring, and he giggled again.

I found that quite pleasant.

"Babe," Noc called.

I turned to him and arched my brows.

"I'm also here to tell you they're ready to take off for Esmerelda's."

"Ah," I looked down to Timofei. "It's time for chocolate."

He knew few words, but I learned he knew that one for he let out an excited shriek, bounded in my arms repeatedly, banged my chest with his fist, and once done shrieking, screeched, "Choc choc!"

"Come on, sweetheart, get your cloak. You're riding in my sleigh with me," Noc said.

I looked to him as I moved to him. "Will you be vexing me with your attempts to encourage me to go to your world in said sleigh?"

"Probably."

"Then I shall ride with my brother," I told him as my nephew and I arrived at him in the doorway, a position he didn't move from when we did.

"His sleigh is full, baby."

"Tosh, he can fit me." I looked again to Timofei. "Can't he, nephew?"

"Choc choc!" was his answer.

I turned again to Noc. "That means yes."

"It so doesn't," Noc replied, his lips quirking.

"It absolutely does," I returned.

Noc gave up the fight, grinned, shook his head and then plucked my nephew right out of my arms with a practiced ease I found both astounding and bizarrely pleasing. In the same manner he planted Timofei on his hip, reached to grab my hand, his fingers tight around mine, and thus, he dragged me into the hall carrying my nephew and speaking.

"Dig you bein' cute, babe, always. But everyone's talking about this liquid chocolate so I wanna get some in me. To do that you need your cloak, I need my coat, and this little one needs to get bundled up. So let's get a move on, yeah?"

I had no choice of whether or not to agree to *get a move on*.

Noc moved me by keeping hold of my hand and pulling me with him.

Again with no choice, as Josette was at the grand entryway awaiting me with my cloak, I accepted it and my gloves and hat.

Noc shrugged on his other-world coat, a nice, dark-blue, double-breasted wool that Finnie shared later was a, "Navy pea coat...*hot*," (her words exactly).

Timofei was bundled by his nanny.

And away we went.

With me in Noc's sleigh.

He did not attempt to press me to go to his world during our trip. Nor during our time at Esmerelda's. Nor much later, when he was my dinner partner at dinner (something Queen Aurora seemed intent on doing, only Kristian had taken his place but once in all the dinners I'd shared with them).

And yet he did.

And he did it simply by being Noc.

~

Valentine

VALENTINE STUDIED Lavinia with unconcealed distaste.

After her friend swallowed a bite of her sidewalk-hot dog-vendor hot dog while standing on a street in New Orleans, Valentine shared, "I can introduce you to much more sumptuous delicacies, my friend."

Lavinia took another bite of the chili, onion and mustard slathered hot dog and said through a full mouth that had Valentine's lip curling, "But this is *delicious*."

She was quite wrong.

Valentine didn't share this.

She looked across the street.

It was nearly time.

"I've decided you'll come to my world more often and the next time you come, I'll take you to Arnaud's."

"Do they have these at Arnaud's?" Lavinia asked, and Valentine turned again to see her lifting the remaining quarter of her hot dog.

"No," Valentine drawled disgustedly.

Lavinia grinned, took another bite, glanced away from Valentine and promptly choked on her hot dog.

Valentine's attention went to where her friend's eyes were aimed and she saw Dax Lahn walking out of the handsome building wearing his exceptionally well-tailored suit.

She would not have thought a man such as him would wear a suit well, but she was wrong.

"You brought the Dax here?" Lavinia asked incredulously.

"No, *chérie*, I did not," Valentine answered.

There was a moment's silence before Lavinia queried, "That's...that's...*this world's Dax*?"

"It is, indeed."

Through this, her friend didn't tear her gaze from Dax Lahn as he walked to the waiting sleek, gleaming-black Mercedes parked at the curb.

"He's an attorney, known as 'the Savage,'" Valentine informed her fellow witch. "He's quite feared in the courtroom, it's said. Razor-sharp. Shrewd. Sly. A cunning strategist. And ruthless."

The man under discussion got in the car while Valentine spoke, and both women watched as the vehicle smoothly moved away from the curb.

They continued to watch until it disappeared from sight.

Only then did Valentine feel Lavinia's eyes on her and she turned her attention back to her friend.

"He's wealthy, *very*," she stated. "Unmarried, obviously. And he gives not only generously of money but also of the expertise of his firm, of which he's the founding and managing partner, to a local domestic violence shelter. This for reasons I can't fathom, outside the fact he's simply a good man, for his mother and father had a long, loving relationship that only ended when his father died in a tragic car accident."

"Valentine—" Lavinia started.

Valentine didn't allow her to continue.

"And he moves in circles that are such it's unlikely he'll run into the office manager of a towing company."

Light had already dawned in Lavinia's eyes, but with that she moved closer to Valentine.

"With our Circe, I'm not sure this is wise," she declared.

"You would be wrong," Valentine sniffed.

"My dear—"

"It is, as it can't have escaped you, the natural order of things," Valentine reminded her.

Lavinia's focus wandered to the street where they last saw Dax Lahn's car.

She then whispered, "The Savage."

"Perfection," Valentine decreed.

Lavinia's attention cut back to her. "I hope you know what you're doing."

Valentine tried not to be offended.

And failed.

"I know precisely what I'm doing," she said with a slight snap.

"I think you believe that down to our emerald soul, I just hope you're right."

"I'm absolutely right."

Lavinia held her gaze and shook her head.

Really, her friend's misgivings were quite insulting.

"It's late in Lunwyn and I have things to see to there," Valentine announced. “Are you finished with that... *fare*?” She tipped her head to the remains of Lavinia’s repulsive hot dog.

To that, Lavinia shoved the last bite in her mouth and followed that by chewing at the same time smiling.

Valentine controlled her lip curling in derision.

She then moved them both to an alley close by that was deserted and there were no eyes on them.

And with verdant green smoke mixing with jade, the two witches disappeared.

10

Always but Always

Franka

"Goodness, almost a bullseye."

I jumped at Cora's words and looked to her to see I was so engrossed in what I was watching out the window, I hadn't even sensed her coming close.

And what I was watching out the window was Finnie and Frey, with some of Frey's men and Lahn looking on, teaching Noc how to go about using a bow and arrow.

I'd been watching for some time, and I'd noticed in this time he not only took very little of it to feel comfortable with the weapon but to start shifting back further and further from the target with his aim each time quickly coming more and more true.

"You want to get our cloaks and go out with them?" Cora asked, turning her eyes to me.

"Certainly not," I sniffed and forced myself to move sedately from the window to take a seat on one of the two couches sitting parallel to each other by the fire. The couch I selected was empty. The one across from it had Circe and Brikitta sitting on it, Circe grinning knowingly at me, Brikitta regarding me closely.

I ignored both of them and reached forward to the tea service that had been laid for us to pour myself some tea.

"She so does," Circe declared, and I knew she was talking to Cora.

I also knew it was a tease.

But my deep-seated feelings of guilt and shame surfaced, and struggling with them now for some time I was unable to push them back.

Therefore, I looked to Circe and snapped, "You do realize that not long ago my lover was tortured to death."

Circe's lovely face went stricken, and at the sight of it, my guilt and shame increased.

"I'm so sorry," she said quickly. "I do know that. I shouldn't have said anything."

"No," I stated, looking away, feeling my embarrassment in the heat in my cheeks and bringing my teacup to my lips but not sipping. "There was no reason for me to be curt when you were simply teasing."

I sipped and hoped that was where the matter would lie.

My hope was in vain.

"It's sweet, you and Noc," Cora said, coming to sit next to me. "And it's not bad, you and Noc. He's a good guy, Franka. And he gets it. I don't know, I've never lost what you've lost, but he's that good of a guy, he's just trying to be there for you, as we all are. And you should take that, babe. People caring. Let him in. Let *us* in. We might be able to help."

"He is a..." I hesitated before I tried out the words, "*good guy*. It's not like I don't know this."

She scooted closer to me.

"What I'm saying is, if you want to get your mind off things, it won't hurt anything or anyone to put your cloak on and go out and be with people who like being around you and who want to be there for you," Cora further explained.

"I've feelings for him," I blurted.

Gads!

Now I was blurting my thoughts willy-nilly.

Cora stared at me, and as she did I felt the room grow still.

Why I said it I didn't know, but as was happening quite often of late, I couldn't stop it and further, I couldn't stop myself from continuing to share.

And this is precisely what I did.

"It's wrong and it's shameful and it's disloyal to Antoine's memory. He's barely made his way to the lap of the gods, and here I am, admiring another man."

"There's a lot to admire about Noc, Franka," Circe said carefully. "The guy is hot."

"As I understand this word in your vernacular," I replied to her, "you are very right. That makes it no less shameful and disloyal."

"I understand your struggle," she murmured.

"It's more," I stated.

Drat.

Why couldn't I stop speaking?

"More?" Brikitta asked, her regard of me kind.

I fastened on that and kept bloody speaking.

"These past days, in being with you and Kristian, and these past weeks, being with the others and their mates, I've realized the inadequacies of my relationship with Antoine. My mind conjures them frequently, doing so as if trying to find some excuse for the feelings I have for Noc."

"Shit," Circe murmured.

She understood.

Why did that feel so good?

"Indeed," I replied.

"Okay, listen to me," Cora demanded, and I looked her way. "Hot guys have power. Trust me. My hot guy looks *exactly* like Noc so I know. When we, uh..." she paused, only her eyeballs slid Brikitta's way, and then she looked back to me and went on, "first met, he hated me. Like *loathed* me. Seriously. And he made no bones about it. I still thought he was hot and totally got into it any time he touched me. And forget about it if he actually kissed me."

I found this confusing.

"Why was he touching and kissing a woman he loathed?" I queried.

"Well, because he liked doing it, and of course, he kinda wanted an heir." She looked fully to Circe and finished on a slight grin, "He didn't mess about getting that taken care of."

"So you're saying," I began, calling her attention back to me, "simply because a man is exceptionally attractive, I should feel no compunction about my utter faithlessness to a lover I committed treason for in order to attempt to protect?"

"The way you say it makes it sound really not good," Cora mumbled, but her eyes were still lit with good humor. "Though," she carried on, "what you didn't get about what I said is that obviously," she put her hand to her belly, inside of which the second child she would give Prince Noctorno was growing, and it was put there not simply because he desired another heir, "something was there between us. Something in the end that was really, *really* good."

By the goddess Adele, this was true.

"What inadequacies?" Brikitta asked.

I looked to her, still shaken by Cora's words. "Pardon?"

"You say your mind conjures inadequacies in your relationship with Antoine. What are these conjurings?"

"I kept him," I informed her.

"What?" Circe asked.

I looked to her. "He was a prostitute. We suited. In order for him to be solely mine and give up his employment, I kept him housed, fed, clothed, entertained, etc., and I did so in a way in which he was accustomed. He was not a partner in my life, even though in some senses he was. To all intents and purposes, however, he was my paid lover."

"Mm..." Cora mumbled.

"This is not unusual, Franka," Brikitta stated quietly, and I watched both Cora and Circe turn surprised expressions to her and knew from their reactions that this was not the same in their worlds.

As they'd grown accustomed, they both hid those reactions before Brikitta caught them.

Then again, her attention was fixed on me.

Still kindly.

"And such arrangements are oft not long lasting," Brikitta went on. "That does not mean there is not affection between the two players. Or even, as in your case, love. And it does not lessen your grief, no matter what feelings you have for a man who shows you attention, is sensitive to your circumstances and is very attractive. To end, what I'm trying to explain is, you're declaring these thoughts as 'conjuring' as if you're making them up, when in fact they're quite true."

I didn't wish to believe it, but it couldn't be denied she was right.

However.

"It was not solely the fact that he was not a partner in the traditional sense. He was not thus in other ways as well," I pressed on. "For instance, Antoine did not assist me in making life decisions. Or any decisions at all. It was not only not his place, it was not his nature. He was not a pillar to lean on when times were difficult, though," I said the last vaguely, as I'd just recalled it, "I was that to him when he had some familial problems, and, of course, the troubles his friends caused when he left the life they all shared and committed to me."

I realized after some time when the silence became prolonged in the room that I'd fallen into my thoughts.

I focused, cleared my throat and kept speaking.

"He could be a sounding board when it was needed, but advice would not be forthcoming. Noc is both. He's very strong, and although I dislike admitting it, he's seeing far more clearly than I at this juncture in my life and provides excellent advice. He sees options I do not think of. And he has ways that are both annoying and heartening in sharing all this with me."

"Antoine is not here at this time to provide such things to you," Brikitta said gently.

"But I knew him, and if he was here, he would not," I returned.

"As you knew him, I cannot say," Brikitta conceded.

"It's like I didn't love him at all, having these thoughts about him, doubts about what we had," I shared.

Brikitta sat up straighter, stating in a sharp way I would never have thought she could speak, "It isn't any such thing."

"I disagree," I retorted.

"Could it be, sister, that in the presence of a man who gives you things you prize, without Antoine here, you're simply coming to conclusions you would have come to if he actually still was, though experiencing shame at coming to them because he is lost?" Brikitta inquired.

"I don't understand what you're saying," I told her.

"Did you think you'd spend the rest of your life with Antoine?" she queried.

"I've no idea," I answered, though the truth was I didn't often think far in the future. I lived in the present. My future was always murky and swirling with menaces I didn't wish to consider so I didn't peer too closely into those depths.

But the truth was, Antoine loved me, as I loved him, but he was who he was and I was who I was. We were both always honest about that, nothing hidden, a freedom he gave me that I cherished.

He did what he did for employment because he was good at it and because he enjoyed it. There was a good possibility he would eventually seek other amusements.

And as discomfiting as it was to realize, there was an equally good possibility I would as well.

That said, I knew in my heart if there ever was to be a parting, that parting would be sweet, not bitter, and he would remain in my life in some manner, even if he no longer was my lover, for the length of it.

"And say Antoine was alive," Brikitta pushed, "and you met Master Noc and found he gave you these things you prized and you were attracted to him. Perhaps doing this in a way you wished to explore. Would you not think on the current relationship you were in, knowing you'd never get these things which, Franka, are not things to prize but things you *need*? They are things any woman *needs*. They are not of value. They are precious. Knowing this about a kept lover or any man you were spending your time with, you would reconsider doing that—"

"Throw him over for something better?" I interrupted to ask incredulously.

"End the relationship so you can be in one to get not only what you want but what you *need*," she clarified.

"That, too, is offensive to Antoine's memory," I told her sharply.

I told her this, but I could not say she was incorrect in her words.

"That, sister," she said softly, "if Antoine were alive, is the way of the world. Even more so as he was your kept lover. He would know this even better than you and would undoubtedly be planning for it."

She's right, Antoine said in my head.

Quiet, I snapped.

"This is but another excuse, Brikitta," I said out loud. "And I appreciate your efforts to try to make me feel better—"

"You're torn up," Cora cut in, and I turned to her. "And I get it, Franka, honey, *damn*. If all that had happened to you had happened to me and Tor came into my life like Noc came into yours, my head would be totally messed up about it too."

"Mine too, totally," Circe chimed in.

"You're all simply being kind," I declared.

"Yeah, we girls do that for each other," Cora stated. "But, Franka, what you're dealing with, we would not blow sunshine. No way. If I didn't agree with Brikitta, I'd keep my mouth shut."

"Me too," Circe added.

"It also could be that you're denying what's growing between you and Master Noc, what we all can see quite vividly, because you wish to punish yourself as your parents have done for decades, not believing you deserve to be happy," Brikitta put in.

"I wish to cause no offense, but that's absurd," I told her, truly not wishing to cause offense, believing it *was* absurd. "Lest I remind you, I committed *treason* for Antoine."

"Nothing we're saying negates your feelings for him, Franka," Brikitta returned. "I know as fact you love your brother, and if he were to be taken by those witches, you would have done the same. Love makes us behave in a variety of manners we never would expect. You honored Antoine greatly with your action."

I blinked in utter shock at this declaration, but my sister-in-law was not done.

"What I wish to make clear is that you don't dishonor him by living your life, feeling your feelings, thinking the thoughts you've had now that he's gone. They're natural. And you shouldn't punish yourself for them. And it should be noted that no relationship, no matter how much love there is or how strong it may be, is perfect. I've no doubt you wish to think back on Antoine and what you had with him only with a rosy hue." Her face softened. "But I think, my sister, that it's also a natural progression in the process of grief to come to the realization that what you had was strong and beautiful, but it was not what nothing ever can be...perfect."

She was not incorrect about that either.

It would seem for years I'd missed not only the fact my sister-in-law was quite pretty in her own way and gave my brother many precious things, but she was also quite wise.

"Not to mention, you put your life on the line to rectify that." Circe did her own reminding.

My attention moved to her.

"And I put my brother and his family's lives on the line while committing the treason I committed," I continued my own reminding.

"Babe, you're churning through history," Cora noted. "History is *history*. Break free."

"You think it's that easy?" I asked her.

"I think it would be harder than hell," she answered instantly. "But I also think Brikitta's right. Your parents," she shook her head, "not good people. I don't know what they made you believe about yourself but I was there in that jail. I heard what you said to them. I heard how they taught you to be. And I heard that you want to be something different. Don't let them hold you back. Okay, you were how you were. You did what you did. But that's over. Let that go. Let *them* go. And be who *you* want to be."

I looked away from all of them, lifted my forgotten teacup and took a sip of the now-cool contents.

"Just be his friend," Cora advised, reaching out a hand and wrapping her fingers around my thigh to give me a squeeze that I found quite bolstering. "He wants that. You *need* that. Don't fight it. And whatever happens from here..."

She trailed off and I saw her compassionate smile and slight shrug.

Staring in her eyes, allowing all their words to penetrate, I realized in some ways I was still agitated.

An uncertain future had a way of causing that.

But in more important ways, I was far less.

They did not think my thoughts shameful. They didn't think any less of me after sharing them.

They were caring. And supportive.

And it couldn't be escaped.

It felt nice.

And damn it all, I had to thank them for it.

"I appreciate you listening," I murmured, leaning forward to put my cup in its saucer.

"Anytime," Circe said.

"Definitely," Cora said.

"With pleasure, sister," Brikitta said.

I looked at them in turn, my lips tipped slightly up.

"Right, I want my babies. Naptime should be over. Should we pull the cord and have the nannies bring in the kids?" Circe asked, deftly changing the subject.

"I'd love that," Brikitta declared.

"I'm on it," Cora stated, jumping up and moving to the cord.

Now this was something to look forward to. The last several days, I'd spent some time with Timofei, and in that time I'd been proved irrevocably correct. He was an almost unbearably handsome child, would most certainly grow up tall and straight like his father, and he was exceptionally intelligent.

I'd not seen him that day.

His arrival would take my mind from my troubles, much more than watching Noc excel with a bow.

Or at least I told myself that.

~

Prior to going down to *avant*-dinner drinks that evening, I stood in my dressing room with my brother, the doors to the locked wardrobe open, the chests also open, the furs folded, stacked and on display.

And my brother was speaking.

"Out of the question."

I'd just offered him his share.

"Kristian—"

He turned a severe look to me and I closed my mouth.

"You went before the evil she-god *Minerva*, your life most definitely on the line, she could have cut you low in a *snap*," he lifted his hand and did just that, "as penance for what you did. For my penance, I cowered in very well-appointed accommodations that, it's true, I was not at liberty to leave, but there was no danger to life and limb."

"You did what you did because of me," I reminded him.

"Stop that," he clipped.

I blinked in utter shock at his angry tone.

"You asked my assistance. I gave it to you," he stated sharply. "I was under no duress to do so. You didn't threaten me or my family. It was *my* choice,

Franka, to help my sister who was in distress and I wanted to do something to alter that. *I* committed treason and I did it knowingly because I care about you. You bear no responsibility for that and I don't wish to upset you, love, but it's offensive you think me that weak that you feel you need to shoulder it for me."

"I didn't mean to offend," I replied in a feeble voice I'd not heard pass my lips, not ever, not even when my father was doling out his punishments.

"I know you didn't," Kristian responded, his tone now gentle. "But, sister, you did it all the same so I'm asking you to stop."

I tried a different tack.

"I certainly don't need all this, Kristian," I flicked a hand to the wardrobe, "and you know it's true. I could give you but a quarter of it and you and Brikitta would want for nothing for the rest of your lives."

"We did not earn that treasure," he retorted.

"Fine, if you believe I did, then it's mine to do with as I wish, and I wish to share it with you. *And*," I said my last word tersely, "if you refuse it again, then I'll bestow it on Timofei, then, when he or she arrives, I'll bestow more on your unborn child. That you *cannot* refuse."

He scowled into my face for a long moment before he muttered, "You're very stubborn."

"Do not say this as if you haven't known it about me the extent of your life," I returned.

He looked to the treasure displayed.

I waited.

My brother said nothing.

I grew impatient.

"I've just decided to visit a goldsmith and have him immediately begin work on a set for Brikitta, earrings, necklace, bracelets, rings, at least one hundred Sjofn ice diamonds, with perhaps a few Korwahkian gems thrown in," I declared.

Kristian looked to me, grinning and shaking his head.

"You've always been impossible," he declared.

I tossed my head. "A trait of which I'm most proud."

His next came abruptly, with no warning.

Though, even warned, it was one thing all my life I knew I could never endure without breaking.

"You know I love you."

I took a small step back.

My brother did not take this nonverbal cue.

"From the first memory I have of you, I fell in love with you. As a child, you were so beautiful, dazzling, and that never changed. And even then, I felt your strength."

"Please, Kristian," I whispered.

"I would not be here without you."

"That's not true."

"You know it is. My mind would have broken. They'd have driven me literally mad."

I shook my head. "Kristian, don't."

He ignored my plea.

"I will love you until my dying breath. And I will tell my children stories of your courage and strength and the depth of love you had for me so often they will love you until their dying breath. And they will share this with their children in a way that the name Franka Drakkar will never die, but will be spoken with devotion and reverence until my line ceases to exist."

I felt them, cold and wet, hovering on my cheekbones. The burn in my throat threatened to consume me as I fought to keep them back, but I failed.

They fell down my cheeks.

"Please go to this other world and find happiness, sister," Kristian whispered.

I nodded, swallowed, and more tears fell.

He opened his arms and continued whispering.

"Now please come here so I can hold you."

My feet moved me directly to him, right into his arms.

They closed around me.

The instant they did, the sob wracked through me.

It was painful, pain so deep, there was no cure.

And it was cleansing, a clean so thorough, I'd never, not once in my life, felt so pure.

"I wish I had magic like you do," he said into the top of my hair. "I'd wipe away the scars that mar your beauty with ugly memories and remind you that you were never allowed to be happy. Doing this making you believe you have that right and you should reach for it."

"Y-you...m-must...stop," I stammered through my weeping.

"For you, Franka, I will stop."

And he did as promised, holding me as the wet poured forth. Years of tears I was not allowed to shed, I did so, letting them leak into my brother's shirt, dousing it, giving him the privilege for once, of returning the favor and absorbing *my* pain.

When I quieted to unladylike hiccoughs I didn't have the energy to feel mortification over, his arms tightened and he said quietly, "You give Brikitta and I what you wish to give from your treasure, love, and we'll accept it with glad hearts."

I nodded.

One of his arms left me so he could put a fist light to the underside of my chin. He leaned back as he lifted it and looked down at me.

"I shall call Josette to see to you. Would you like me to share with the others that you'll need to miss drinks and will join us at the dinner table?"

This meant I looked a fright.

Gods.

I nodded again.

He smiled at me tenderly. Shifting his fist so his hand cupped my jaw, he swept his thumb through the wet there. Once he'd done this, he bent and touched his lips to my forehead.

He straightened, gave me another squeeze with his one arm and held me steady until I made a slight move to share I was all right to stand on my own.

He let me go and went to the cord that would send Josette to me.

He pulled it and moved to the door.

Stopping at it, he turned to me. "I'll see you at dinner, sister."

I again nodded and replied, "You will."

Another tender smile before he started to close the door behind him.

"Kristian," I called.

He stopped and tipped his head to the side.

"You know I love you too," I told him.

He stood solid in the doorway, eyes on me, and I watched them grow bright with wet.

I also watched the one tear fall.

And I heard the hoarse of his voice that was so beautiful, if it held healing power, the scars on my back would vanish in but an instant, when he replied, "That, my beloved sister, you truly must know I always, but always, knew."

And on that, he shut the door, disappearing behind it.

Averting my face from Noc (who was my dinner partner, *again*) an hour later, with Josette's assistance, feeling and more importantly *looking* refreshed, I sat down at the table as Noc held my chair.

Regardless, I averted my face, for I looked refreshed but Noc had a way of seeing beyond the surface, and tonight of all nights, this was something I didn't wish him to see.

I busied myself with my napkin, my jaw tilted away from him as Noc took his own seat.

My efforts were instantly foiled when he barely got his arse in his chair before his lips were at my ear.

"Baby, what the fuck?"

Damn.

And he hadn't even properly seen me!

I smoothed my napkin over my lap.

"Pardon?" I asked with an effort at innocently, failing miserably because this trait was something my parents stripped from me when I was five, so I had no idea how to pull it off.

"Look at me."

Oh blast.

I couldn't demur, he'd force the issue. At the dinner table. And it was safe to say I'd already endured enough mortification at this dinner table.

I turned to Noc and he pulled his head away while I did.

His eyes traveled my face and I fought both a blush and shifting in my chair.

He looked at me and his repetition was this time growled.

"Baby, what *the fuck*?"

"I'm returning to your world after Brikitta delivers my future niece or nephew safely," I announced.

Noc did one of those odd blinks that was slow and included his eyebrows lifting.

"Say again?"

"I'm going to your world," I stated. "And when I shared this with my brother earlier, he and I had a..." I struggled to find a word, "*moment*. I found it..." more struggling, "*affecting*. I needed some time to collect myself. I'm collected. Now I need wine."

"Great. And now *I* don't know whether to go high five Kristian for pulling that off or punch him in the face," he declared.

My shoulders straightened with affront. "Why would you punch him in the face?"

"Because you look emotionally wasted by whatever was *affecting*, and he was the one who did that to you."

"Noc—"

"But you're goin' home with me so I should probably keep my shit."

"There's no probably about that," I stated tartly.

Finally, the harshness in his face disappeared and he grinned.

That was worse.

Drat.

I moved past that and queried, "What does 'high five' mean?"

Inexplicably, he grabbed the wrist of the hand sitting in my lap and lifted it up in front of me.

"Palm out, fingers straight," he ordered.

I did as told.

He kept hold of my wrist, and with his other hand, slapped mine.

I jumped in surprise at this preposterousness.

He then slid the hand holding my wrist up so his fingers were laced in mine and he brought both our hands down to rest on the table, like we were lovers out at an intimate dinner by ourselves, not sitting at a table in a palace surrounded by royalty.

By the gods.

Bloody Noc.

"High five," he declared.

"Pardon?"

"Five fingers, slapped high, high five."

Oh.

Well that explained the name of said maneuver.

But it did not explain the absurdity of it.

"Why would one do that?" I asked.

"To celebrate," he answered.

"You do know that's absurd," I shared.

He grinned again. "You're comin' home with me, sugarlips. That means I'm gettin' you into the Seahawks. We'll be in Saints country, but you and me, we'll keep our allegiance true. And when they kick ass, you'll get the high five."

"You do know that all those words are understood by me and yet all of them are *not*."

His grin grew.

I sighed.

"Wine, milady?" the footman asked, and I pulled my hand from Noc's to look over my shoulder at him.

"Absolutely."

He nodded and poured. He barely got to Noc's other side before I had a healthy dose down my gullet.

I took the glass from my lips, drew in a large breath, let it go and relaxed.

I ceased relaxing when Noc's hand wrapped around my thigh under the table and squeezed.

This was not bolstering, as Cora's squeeze had been.

It was something else entirely.

"Pleased as fuck you're comin' home with me," he declared, thankfully letting my thigh go.

"Mm..." I murmured.

"It's gonna be culture shock, trust me, *huge*. But you'll get over that and love it."

I hoped so.

I said nothing and took another sip of wine.

"Baby?" he called.

I looked his way and nearly downed the glass at the happiness warming his face and making his handsome so much more handsome it was almost unendurable to lay witness to.

"You made the right decision," he decreed.

"I hope so, Noc."

"I know so, Frannie."

I nodded.

He smiled.

Hesitantly, I smiled back.

~

LATE THAT EVENING, after Josette had prepared me for bed and gone to seek her own, I stood in front of the mirror in the dressing room and closed my eyes.

It had been so long since I'd tried this—and the last time I'd done it my mother had sensed it and punished me for it—I was quite certain it wouldn't work.

But I needed to do what had to be done and I'd made a variety of decisions that day.

It was time to carry them all out.

Therefore, I sought it and it wasn't hard to find, the quickening I felt in my innards, always there in truth, but vague, and it having been there for so long, I'd learned to live with the sensation.

And ignore it.

Now, I focused on it, and the instant I did, to my astonishment, I felt it sparking up my spine, the sensation like the light touch of a lover, stirring tickles of awareness all over my skin.

I opened my eyes and saw the muted glow of the one lamp I'd lit had a sapphire hue, and the mirror in front of me had gone from clearly showing my visage to cloudy.

"By the gods, it worked," I whispered, staring at the clouds in front of me as they started to swirl, those too, tinted blue.

I'd managed that, it was time to try my next.

"I wish to speak to you," I said into the mirror.

I stood there and waited.

The clouds swirled languidly.

I waited longer.

Nothing but clouds.

Over time, I noted it was actually quite mesmerizing in a relaxing way.

But after more time elapsed, I noted it was also quite boring.

All right then, maybe it didn't work.

I started to turn away, seeing the tinge of blue in the room begining to dissipate, when suddenly, the entire room turned jade green.

My eyes flew to the mirror and I saw Valentine's reflection there, not my own.

"I'm impressed," she declared.

I'd done it!

"This delights me, my sister," she stated. "It would seem you do have some instinctual understanding of how to harness your power."

It seemed I did.

Excellent.

"I'm pleased you're delighted," I replied.

"Though, I have things to do," she told me. "And although I'm communicating to you on the astral plane, it is taking my attention and I wish my attention on something else at this moment. That something is very good at waiting. But I'm in the mood not to do the same. So you had something to share with me?"

"Yes," I replied. "I've informed my brother and Noc, and neither delayed in sharing it with the others that I will return with my brother and sister-in-law to their home, await the birth of their child and then journey to your world."

This reminded me I hadn't spoken of any of this to Josette, including the fullness of understanding the parallel universes (something I knew she understood, of a sort, considering the twins wandering around the palace, something I had not gotten into with her in any direct way).

Not to mention sharing with her I had magic.

I needed to rectify that first thing in the morning.

"But I must also note, where I go, if my maid agrees to go with me, she goes as well," I added.

"Of course," Valentine murmured. "I'm pleased this has progressed."

I nodded. "And in an effort not to keep you, I shall also share that I'm agreed to learn how to use my magic and absorb what you stripped from my mother, but only on the contingency that you assure me it is not tainted with her malice."

"Magic is never dark, Franka, only the bearer of it makes it so."

I found that most interesting.

"So you have no fears with that, and I'll set up the ceremony as soon as I'm able," she carried on.

That made me somewhat anxious.

Valentine sensed it, even through a mirror.

"It will be glorious, Franka, and you will savor the memory of it until your dying breath."

I lifted my chin. "Then I look forward to it."

"As do I," Valentine replied. "Is there more?"

Outside of wondering what an astral plane was, there was not.

I could ask that later.

"No, and I thank you for coming to me."

"To receive this news, it was my pleasure. Goodnight, *chérie*, and you know I feel this way, but I will say it again, you chose rightly."

With that, she faded from sight and her magic receded from the room.

But I stood there staring into the mirror that was now just a mirror.

And I did it hoping she was correct.

The next morning, first thing, before my breakfast tray even came, incongruously and in a way that would make my mother apoplectic and my father spit fire, I sat cross-legged on my bed opposite Josette, who was in bed and cross-legged as well.

I did this sharing with her I held magic and informing her of how my future plans had changed and that I desired her to change hers with me.

"It's unlikely we'll be able to bring Irene," I finished. "Though, it's my understanding things are much different there so it's also my understanding we won't need her."

Josette simply sat still and stared at me.

"Josette," I called.

She blinked but said nothing.

"Josette, my dear," I called again, reaching out and wrapping my fingers around hers.

The instant I did, hers twisted and captured mine.

"We'll not have an adventure, we'll have an *adventure*," she breathed. "And how exciting! You're a witch!"

There were many witches in our world so I really had no concern she'd react badly to me being one.

But I was so worried that she would refuse to undertake something infinitely unknown, the light I did not see was budding in her eyes bloomed, and I fancied it lit the room with its brilliance.

"You'll journey with me?" I queried to confirm.

"Anywhere, Franka." Her hand held mine all the more tightly. "Everywhere."

My heart felt light, and thus, as I was learning happened, my mouth started moving.

"I don't know what caused you to gift me such loyalty, Josette, but what I want you to know is that it means much to me."

"My position means there were scars I could assist you with your clothing to hide from others, but you couldn't hide them from me," she shared readily.

"I don't..." I shook my head. "How did that gain loyalty?"

Josette studied me with curiosity, asking me, "How would it not?"

"Many people have many scars for many reasons."

"And all of them I admire," she returned. "But you most of all, for you lived your life and you did as you pleased and whatever caused those scars did not beat you. My father prized strength and taught my sister and me to do the same. He was himself so strong he refused to believe he could not save his family from icy waters. He didn't stop believing, even dying because of it. This makes me sad. But that sadness has never cobbled me because I'm far more proud that he was that man and he died displaying that strength. And I didn't allow it to cobble me for I knew if my father knew I had, he'd be disappointed in me. So," she shrugged, "that's it, I guess."

After this, it was I staring at her.

"Oh no," she whispered. "Are you going to become a simpering ninny? Because...you mustn't, seeing as if you do, I will."

I sniffed and pulled my hand from hers, declaring, "Certainly not."

She grinned.

I curled my lips up at her and then stated, "I'm hungry, Josette."

"Of course," she replied, jumping off the bed.

"Josette?" I called, and she stopped her dash to the door and turned to me. "Tell them to prepare a tray for you as well. I wish to share breakfast with you this morning, and every morning I take it in bed in future. When you bring mine up, ask one of the other servants to bring up yours."

Her eyes grew very large. "But...Franka, I...they'll...this will be quite shocking to the palace staff."

"And I care about this because...?"

This did not grant me a grin but instead a wide, bright smile.

"I'll be back," she declared.

"I'll be here."

The door closed behind her.

I looked to my lap.

"Finally," I murmured. "It's all sorted."

I drew in a breath and lifted my head to let it out.

And then it was me whose mouth spread into a wide, bright smile.

11
WIRED

Valentine

Valentine was sitting, her legs crossed, in the darkened apartment, Circe's cat in her lap, a long-haired ginger with intelligent eyes (as all cats were, considering they were spirit creatures and had long since been smart enough to allow themselves to be the familiars of witches).

She'd timed it precisely.

Enough time had passed where she remained aggravated.

Not enough time had passed where she could get exasperated.

She wasn't angry any longer. This, she found, her lovely companion had the power to curb by performing so beautifully and being quite capable of giving as well as receiving.

For this, Circe was lucky.

She was also lucky that Valentine heard the lock click and the door open before Valentine had to wait any longer.

"Really? You sit in the dark waiting for me?" Circe asked.

This greeting was not a surprise. Valentine knew better than to think she could sneak up on a witch.

"You're blocking me." Valentine found herself in the annoying position of wasting energy to share something that didn't need to be said.

The door closed, a switch was flipped and several of the lamps in the relatively-attractive-but-sparsely-furnished room illuminated.

Really, Circe should use some of her treasure, something Valentine had noted she hadn't touched, simply to decorate.

But the witch could actually purchase a home, if she so desired, one that provided far superior accommodation than...*this*.

Valentine did not declare these thoughts aloud.

She watched Circe toss her purse into a chair and then cross her arms, leveling her eyes on her sister-witch.

"You're doing something that needs to be blocked," she finally replied.

"I'm simply looking after you, *chérie,*" Valentine lied.

"I've been in this world for some time, Valentine, I hardly need looking after."

Valentine lazily flipped out a hand as she suggested, "Why don't we look at it as a mother bear taking care of her cub?"

"Please, no offense, my sister, but we both know you are no mother. And you bear no responsibility for me. I brought myself to this world and it was my decision to stay. You had nothing to do with any of that."

At Circe's mention of Valentine and "mother" in the same sentence, strangely, disturbingly, and lastly, pleasantly, visions of little girls with lovely blue eyes and thick blonde hair danced in Valentine's head.

Her trifle, who somehow she'd allowed to turn into her companion, had lovely blue eyes and thick blond hair.

He'd once been simply a body.

Now he was...

Not.

Merde.

"And we both know with my magic restored, especially having that and being in this world where it isn't often wielded, I need no one taking care of me," Circe continued.

"Is there something you don't wish me to see?" Valentine asked, forcing her mind from her thoughts back to their conversation.

"I simply don't wish the intrusion, and I have that right, as you know."

She did.

Bother.

"Though, I might be moved to stop blocking you if I knew why you were suddenly watching me," Circe went on with her own lie.

No witch, or non-witch for that matter, liked someone interfering in their lives.

Certainly not observing them.

It would not do to tell her she was watching in order to start meddling, doing this to magically maneuver a meeting with the future love Circe was destined to have, her aim to see them married, creating children, doing such enjoyably and living happily ever after.

Circe was fiercely independent, something of which Valentine approved, though the reasons life had given her to make her bent on protecting this trait at all costs was something Valentine despised.

A history where she had nothing like it. No independence. Not even free will.

Nearly her entire life she'd lived imprisoned and enslaved by a despotic ruler who took advantage of a beautiful young witch and her powers in every way he could.

Goddess, she hoped this world's Dax Lahn could handle such a challenge.

Valentine's mind wandered to the fact that, interestingly, his first name was Dax in this world, Lahn his last, proof the Dax in the other world would hold his kingly title as prophesied until he passed it to his son on his death.

This meant the Circe and Dax of this world would likely name their son the same.

Lovely.

"Valentine?" Circe called, and Valentine focused on her again, feeling her frame slightly tighten.

She'd just gone sentimental.

Hoping.

Caring.

Worrying.

And now being sentimental.

She shivered in revulsion.

Another shiver of revulsion followed at the very thought that she'd have to give up magical meddling and do something a mundane human would need to do in this situation when magic was not an option.

Fix the two of them up.

How revolting.

"It would seem you're holding an entire conversation to which I'm not privy since you're having it silently with yourself," Circe observed.

At this, Valentine stood, dropping the cat gracefully to her feet as she did.

"Franka has decided to come to our world to start her life anew," she declared, and went on further, sharing about Franka's growing connection with Noc and the friendships she was making in the other world.

Circe looked astonished and moved to her couch, seating herself on the arm, her cat slinking elegantly to her momma, jumping on the seat and rubbing against Circe's thigh.

"This surprises me," Circe stated.

"I see that. I have, of course, shared with you all that has occurred and the knowledge she's our sister. Thus this decision pleases me. She's also decided to accept my training. Unlike *you*," Valentine stressed, "it seems she has no qualms with using her magic for enjoyable purposes once she learns to wield it."

"I've had my magic manipulated nearly all my life, Valentine," Circe reminded her. "I like it to be my own, to use it when I will, how I will."

"That's understandable," Valentine murmured, annoyed to have to concede that point.

"I'm pleased she's made this decision too," Circe said. "This is an odd realm, but it's a good one to make a new start. Very easy to get lost in the sheer numbers of people, and because of this you can focus on the person you wish to be."

"There are nearly the same numbers in both worlds," Valentine reminded her. "With scant variation."

"I've assessed that my old world has nearly twice the land mass as this one, which allows much more space for people to spread out," Circe returned.

Valentine knew this to be true.

She didn't concede that point.

She stated, "She's awaiting her sister-in-law's safe delivery of a new child. I cannot assess when this will be, but calling up the woman and the little she's showing, my assumption would be that this will happen in five to six months' time."

"I will welcome her and assist her in any way whenever she arrives, my sister."

"That's good to hear," Valentine replied.

"This is not why you're watching me."

Valentine tilted her head. "Do you think for even a second I do it for malicious reasons?"

Circe grinned. "I think *you* think you're quite wicked when you have a soul of emerald but a heart of pure gold." When Valentine opened her mouth to object to that ridiculousness, Circe lifted a hand, kept grinning and continued speaking. "Don't deny it. Actions speak louder than words, my green witch, and with all of yours, you could talk, as they say in this world, until you're blue in the face, or green," her grin got bigger, "and I wouldn't believe you."

Valentine lifted her hands, declaring, "I feel this visit is at an end."

Before she could conjure her magic, Circe spoke on.

Gently.

"I'm happy, my sister, please know that with whatever your golden heart is speaking to you to do."

Valentine halted her spell that would spirit her back to the other world and regarded the witch closely.

Then she stated, "You will be happier."

And at that juncture, before Circe could open her mouth to speak, Valentine finished casting her spell and disappeared.

When the hour had struck midnight in Lunwyn, Valentine appeared at the appointed place seeing a sleigh close by, four horses hitched to it, blankets covering the steeds' coats to protect them in the cold, her two compatriots already there and waiting.

As she'd asked, Lavinia had brought their charge.

The witches had decided to perform Franka's ceremony close to an adela tree. It was just a sapling, but its power could still be felt, and its place in this world for anyone with magic was sacred.

Franka stood beside the adela sapling wearing a glorious cloak of Prussian-blue fine wool lined with ermine, her hands encased in blue kid gloves, no cap on her head to cover her glorious hair that had a healthy sheen, even in the moonlight.

And there was no anxiety in her eyes. Her shoulders were straight, her chin up.

Valentine sensed no fear from her.

She also sensed no excitement.

This would change.

"Are you ready, my sister-witch?" Valentine asked, moving through the snow toward her, her own green cloak lined with red fox keeping her warm.

"Of course," Franka replied.

Valentine stopped close and cast her gaze to Lavinia, who was moving to them. She waited for her fellow witch to arrive and catch her eyes.

When she did, Valentine nodded to her.

Lavinia returned this gesture.

They both looked to Franka.

"Take my hand in one of yours, Lavinia's in the other," she ordered.

Without hesitation, Franka did as told.

Valentine felt her power through her touch and realized, even if she'd already sensed it was substantial, she'd been in error at just how substantial it was.

This power Franka Drakkar held had not simply fed on itself and grown over the years with no use.

She, too, like Valentine (as well as Lavinia) was a legacy. And from what Valentine could feel, it was not one or two generations in Franka's line who had practiced the craft, but centuries of them.

This was superb news. So much so, it made Valentine smile and look to Lavinia, who she knew felt it too, not only because it would be impossible to miss, but also from the answering smile on the witch's face.

"Would you care to share what you find so pleasing?" Franka drawled.

Both of them turned back to her. "Your power is already substantial."

"And you can tell that how?" Franka asked.

"Do you not feel it?" Lavinia queried softly, and Valentine knew she squeezed her hand when Franka looked down at their two hands clasped together. "You must feel it," Lavinia prompted.

The tip of Franka's tongue came out and touched her lower lip briefly before she turned her gaze to Lavinia and answered, "I feel it. From you," her gaze went to Valentine, "and much more from you."

"We feel it too," Lavinia told her. "From each other...and you."

"You come from a long line of witches," Valentine put in, this gaining Franka's attention, and her altered expression showing unconcealed surprise. "The last, not a very good one. Sadly, she didn't share this proud heritage with you so that you both could enjoy the satisfaction of having such, *ma sorcière*. But as you stand with two of your own with the same noble lineage, we will teach you exactly this."

"I've never been proud of anything to do with my *noble* lineage," Franka shared.

"This is because your lineage was superior as self-decreed, not noble, save the magic it offers the Freys and Drakkars it produces," Valentine explained.

Franka nodded her understanding of this then asked, "Will all future sessions such as this be conducted in the dead of night, thus the worst of any day's chill, and carry on a good deal of time? If so, I'll be forewarned for them and dress warmer."

Valentine had the odd desire to laugh out loud.

Oh, but she liked this witch. She liked her very much.

"She's impatient," Lavinia noted with kindred humor.

"I'm cold," Franka returned but took a breath and went on, her voice lower, her gaze going between them, direct and steady. "And when this is done, I can be done with her."

She could indeed.

And that should be seen to immediately.

"Then let us delay no longer," Valentine decreed.

She looked to Lavinia and nodded.

When she did, Lavinia turned her gaze to Franka.

"Magic is nature. Nature is magical," she began to enlighten their charge. "What you have flowing through you, millennia ago, was drawn from the earth. From the sky. The air, the dirt. From the seas, the winds, the rains, the rays of the sun. Our originators worshipped these things, walked, breathed, sowed, all with reverence. The elements shared their beneficence for this veneration, offering them power, allowing them to manipulate the magicks they celebrated, to internalize them, to utilize them. And more, they strengthened them through sisterhood, rewarding loyalty, building them along magical lines, enhancing power when used amongst other sisters, communing with them."

"Covens," Franka whispered.

"Indeed." Lavinia smiled. "And here," Valentine felt Lavinia's hand tighten, knowing her other did the same with Franka's, "we sisters stand, in nature, in magic, and now, Franka, my sister-witch, my daughter, my mother, my ally, my friend, I bid you to feel the cold. Feel the snow beneath your boots. The sting of ice in the air against your skin. The cool freshness of it in your nose, down your throat, in your lungs. The strength of the adela growing in the nurturing embrace of the earth. The whisper of the gentle wind in your ear. Close your eyes, my friend, and open your senses. Feel the magic all around you. Celebrate it for it is beauty, and the fact that beauty lives inside you."

Valentine watched Franka close her eyes.

When she did, Valentine did the same.

It was time.

"We are one," Valentine declared quietly.

"We are one," Lavinia repeated after her.

Valentine squeezed Franka's hand as a prompt.

"We are one," she whispered, taking her cue.

"We are earth," Valentine stated.

"We are earth," Lavinia repeated.

"We are earth," Franka said.

"We are air," Valentine decreed, her voice rising.

"We are air," Lavinia echoed, her voice doing the same.

"We are air." Franka followed suit.

"We are the sea," Valentine said, now on a low cry, the winds through their words kicking up as that element, too, celebrated the power in that glade. The cold now biting, their heavy cloaks beginning to sway, their hair getting mussed, and after she spoke, her witches followed with the same words.

And with each additional chant, their voices carried into the air louder and louder, the pine rustling, the powder of snow under their feet catching in the wind and drifting up, swirling around them.

"We are wind."

"We are rain."

"We are the rays of the sun."

And on this decree, the three witches started chanting together. Franka drawn into the magic through her sisters, knowing the words by instinct, their voices ringing straight to the heavens, their words carried up on tufts of wind and whirls of snow glittering in the moonlight.

"We are the light of the moon. We are *power*. We are *strength*. We are the *dark*. We are the *light*. We are *magic*. *We...are...sisters!*"

And with that, a burst of emerald, grass green and sapphire shot in a twisted circle from their boots into the sky, and the three women were thrown back several steps. Losing their connection, they opened their eyes to see the glade around them swirling with wafting clouds of greens and blue shimmering off the gentle, floating flurries settling around them.

But Franka was standing, hands lifted before her, blood-red sparks glinting from them, illuminating her face, a face now tainted with alarm.

"Do not fear, Franka," Lavinia said gently, again edging close. "She burns away. Your sapphire soul is good, it's strong, it's pushing out the wickedness and spite. It won't take long, it'll cause no pain and then it will be gone."

Lavinia was quite right and was proved so when, in mere moments, the last of the red sparked with trails of cobalt until there was nothing but blue, and finally, the glimmers died away.

Valentine and Lavinia stood silent as Franka remained still and staring at her hands.

It took time but she eventually lifted her head.

And Valentine felt the soft curve lift the corners of her mouth as she saw the wonder in her sister's expression.

"It's beautiful, isn't it?" she asked quietly, feeling that same beauty. The beauty she felt any time she called up her craft or was around a sister using hers. The tingle of it on her skin. The warmth of it through her insides. The thrill of it up her spine. The heat of it in her sex. The sumptuous taste of it down her throat. The glorious energy of it in her fingertips.

Oh, but it was good her companion was waiting for her at the cottage and she had planned what she had planned, as for once she could take these feelings and exalt in them just as she should do, joyously and uninhibitedly.

"It's...well, nothing like I've ever known," Franka replied.

"But beautiful, yes?" Lavinia prompted.

Franka shook her head and Valentine felt her brows draw together.

"That isn't the word," Franka explained, crossing her arms at her front. Not protectively, she'd curled her hands around her biceps and was stroking them as if she was trying to keep the feeling close, hold it to her, not lose it. "There is no word to describe this beauty," she finished reverently.

Valentine relaxed and again smiled.

"I..." Franka went on and shook her head again, this time shorter, sharper shakes, like she was clearing it, but her gaze was steadfast on Valentine. "I thank you. I...*thank you*, my sister," she finished on a heartfelt whisper. "I would not think I'd wish anything from her. Anything that was hers. But..." she swallowed and finished, "you were right. I'll remember this night always, her end, my beginning."

Oh yes, Valentine very much liked this witch.

Both Valentine and Lavinia approached and all of them again clasped hands.

"It was my honor," Valentine shared the truth.

"And mine to be here," Lavinia added.

"I wouldn't have chosen this, not if you hadn't advised it," Franka told Valentine. "And you will have my gratitude for as long as I remain breathing."

"It's most appreciated," Valentine accepted before she gave her a small smile. "And it's also cold. We will soon meet again. Your training now commences."

It was not blinding, but there was excitement in Franka's eyes that she didn't hide.

Progress.

Excellent.

"The sisterhood," Lavinia said on a tightening of her hand.

"The sisterhood," Valentine repeated, doing the same.

"The sisterhood," Franka trailed, her hand tightening and her lips twitching.

Valentine broke away.

"And now to warmth," she declared, *and warm, firm, naked male bodies with handsome faces, beautiful blue eyes, charming smiles and mouths that could utter sweet words*, she did not say.

"To warmth," Lavinia agreed. "Until we see you again, farewell, my friend."

Valentine nodded to Lavinia and Franka.

It had been beautiful, as she knew it would be. It had been an honor, as she knew as well. It would be something, like Franka, and she was certain Lavinia, Valentine would never forget.

But now it was done and time to go home.

Time to get warm.

Time to celebrate not only what had just occurred but much more.

It was time to celebrate and continue to nurture what was growing between her and...

Not just a body.

Not a trifle.

Not her companion.

With *Laurent.*

Franka

I WAS PACING MY ROOM, the only illumination the fire that was also providing warmth.

My feet were bare, but not cold. No, I was far too stimulated to even think of cold feet.

I should be in bed.

But the quickening inside had not died down. I felt like I had too much energy. As if I could run around the palace again and again (like Noc did nearly every day for reasons he stated were, "keeping fit," whyever anyone would do something like *that*).

And I was just *bursting* to tell someone all that had occurred and just how beautiful it was.

Unable to stop myself, regardless of the fact it was late, I knew in my heart he wouldn't mind, I dashed to the door, opened it and hastened down the hall to Noc's room.

I knocked. Not loudly, I didn't want anyone to hear.

Seconds later, I did it a little louder because Noc surely was sleeping, and I did want *him* to hear.

I was still doing it when the door flew open.

The firelight was illuminating Noc's room as well, not to mention the lamplight from the hall.

And thus I saw quite clearly that he was shirtless, wearing a pair of loose, lightweight trousers with a string tied under his navel to hold them up.

At the sight of all of it (though I had to admit, my eyes got stuck on his flat stomach, the ridges that defined it, and the trail of thick, black hair that led from his unusual sleeping trousers to his navel), my mouth went dry.

"Baby, you okay?" Noc asked.

I jerked my eyes up to his face, saw his hair mussed and fought the urge to lift my hands and smooth it.

Or muss it further.

With effort, I stayed focused.

"The ceremony was tonight."

I was standing in the hall and then I was not.

Noc grabbed my hand, yanked me into his room and closed the door. He didn't hesitate to guide me straight to the fire to stand in front of it so it could warm us both.

Once he got us there, he also didn't hesitate to draw me near to him and say, "I know. That's why I asked if you're okay. You look..." his head tipped to the side as his scrutiny on my face intensified, "wired."

"Wired?"

"Jazzed. Hyper. Agitated. Edgy. Alert."

I leaned closer to him. "I do think I am all of those, Noc. But in a good way."

He continued to study my face. "So it went okay?"

I nodded fervently. "It was...I was..."

How to explain the unexplainable?

There was no way except understanding Noc would listen and do so closely even if I couldn't find the right words.

Thus I sallied forth, "I was very anxious. I did not wish to have anything of hers but the word 'absorb'..." I shook my head. "That concerned me the most. To have her inside me in any way..." I didn't finish that thought, but Noc's expression told me he understood what I was communicating, so I carried on, "But it was...I felt her and...and then it was me, it was what's inside me..." Again, I couldn't finish so I pulled slightly away, lifted up my hand and whispered, "Here, I'll show you."

I focused on the quickening inside and that was all I had to do before I felt it surge up my spine, through my frame, tingling in my scalp and fingertips and the blue sparks drifted up lazily from my palm.

"Gotta say, sweetheart, as freaky as that is, it's still fuckin' cool," Noc muttered, and I looked from my hand to his face, now illuminated in blue, making his eyes even more extraordinary, his gaze riveted to my palm.

"It sparked red when it happened," I shared, and he looked to me. "When Valentine gave the magic to me. It was her. It was Mother. I felt her. The ugliness. The darkness. But it was me," I lifted my hand, the blue still sparking, "that forced her out. Took over. See?" My hand rose another inch. "That's just me. No red. All blue. It's all mine. And look, Noc," my hand rose further but my voice lowered with reverence, "don't you think it's beautiful?"

He only glanced back to my hand before his gaze again caught mine.

"Yeah, baby," he whispered. "It's fuckin' gorgeous."

I smiled at him.

He smiled back and his attention drifted again to the sparks.

"Can I touch it?" he asked, and instantly I closed my hand and the magic disappeared.

Noc returned his eyes to me.

"I don't know much about it," I explained hastily as I didn't want to hurt his feelings or deny him anything he wished to have. "It could be dangerous and I don't wish to harm you."

He nodded. "I get that."

I smiled again. "Maybe when I know more, when I know if it's safe, I'll conjure it again and you can."

Noc smiled again too. "That'd be cool."

"I just, well, I just had to share." I leaned back into him, lifting the hand that had sparked blue and wrapping it around the warm, silken skin covering hardness at his biceps. "It's impossible to explain. Being out there with Valentine and Lavinia. Being given a gift I didn't want but the instant I received it I knew how precious it was. Understanding more of who I am, what's inside me, that there are women who have the same and they're not like my mother. I don't have words to describe the magnificence and I know it's late. I shouldn't have woken you, but I just *had* to share it with someone. And you know who I am, what I have inside me. Outside of Josette, Valentine and Lavinia, you're the only one. And I know I can trust you with all of it."

"Yeah, you can," he replied with a smile, but there was a firmness to his tone that I liked very much. This he coupled with resting a hand on the side of my waist and giving me a squeeze. "And seriously pleased you woke me up to share, sweetheart, and totally stoked to hear you dug the experience."

I nodded up at him enthusiastically, not sure what "stoked" meant, but I did know what "dug" meant, thus affirmed, "I did, Noc. I very much did."

He looked down at me with an indulgent expression.

We stood standing close, staring at each other and touching lightly for some time before I realized neither of us was speaking.

Suddenly feeling awkward, I cast a glance at his disheveled bed, took my hand from his arm and stepped back, forcing Noc's hand to fall from my waist.

My eyes to the rug at my side, I stated, "I woke you, now I should let you sleep."

"We could go raid the kitchens," he curiously suggested.

I looked back to him. "Pardon?"

"Babe, you don't look any less wired than you did when you walked in here. That means raid the kitchen, or hitch up a sleigh and go joyriding through Fyngaard, or find ourselves a bottle of whiskey and get slaughtered."

I was definitely peckish.

And I always enjoyed a lovely libation.

"I choose the first and the last," I shared.

To that, Noc's smile went white and wide, and promptly after he strode from the room into his dressing room. He came back wearing one of his attractive, long-sleeved shirts that had no buttons (and I'd discovered all of them were of an oddly stretchy material).

He handed me a ball of wool that I realized were a pair of his socks just as he sat on the couch by the fire and pulled his own ball of wool open.

"Put those on to keep your feet warm," he ordered.

He was concerned about my comfort, did something about it, and that something was as intimate as me wearing his clothing.

There was a loveliness to this I shouldn't allow myself the opportunity to feel.

I did not delay even a second in sitting beside Noc to pull his socks on my feet.

When I had the over-large, warm wool on, he was up and I was too, as he'd grabbed my hand and pulled me that way.

"Let's go, sugarlips."

I rolled my eyes at his irksome endearment.

But I said nothing.

My hand in Noc's, we went to raid the kitchens and get "slaughtered" on whiskey.

This we did.

And I enjoyed every second.

Better, with delight he did not hide from me for a second, Noc did too.

12

DR. ZHIVAGO

Franka

It was time.

Weeks I had waited to get on with things—as Noc would say, close the book on my old life and start the first chapter on the new—and it was finally time.

But now that it was, I didn't want it to be time.

This was, I knew, because I was standing at the window of my bedroom looking down at Kristian's and my sleighs being packed. Ahead of them, more sleighs were being readied to take Finnie and Frey, Cora and Tor, Circe and Lahn...and Noc to Sudvic to start Noc's adventure.

We would be parted for months.

I did not want that.

Anything could happen in months. Months was a long time.

He could find a young beautiful maiden in Hawkvale, fall in love, decide to stay in this world. Or he could wish her to live in his own and bring her back with him.

Or he could think on me and wonder why he was so kind and friendly, supportive and caring, teasing and sweet, and use the time to grow distant so that when we met again, I had none of him at all.

A knock came at the door, and I was so deep in my thoughts, I jumped and turned to it, mouth opening to call to the person beyond to enter.

My mouth shut and tightened, out of habit mostly, because I needn't have bothered with the effort of parting my lips.

The door was already closing behind Noc.

I watched him saunter to me, grinning. "All the action's downstairs, sugarlips."

"I have seen sleighs packed before, many times, starting from the moment I could cipher," I reminded him. "It's hardly fascinating."

Noc stopped in front of me and looked out of my window. "If it's not interesting," he said to the window before turning his attention to me, still grinning, "why are you watching it from up here?"

I stared into his face, his extraordinary eyes, remembering suddenly every moment from that first he'd walked into the sitting room to make me feel better after Minerva and her companions were bested, all of our moments layering, interweaving, making me feel warm...

And bereft.

"I fear I'll miss you," I whispered and watched his grin die.

"Frannie," he whispered back, getting close, putting a hand to my waist and sliding it to the small of my back.

"You've been very kind to me. You...you've..." I shook my head and gave him the honest truth, "You've changed my life, Noc." I drew in a swift breath and carried on even more swiftly, "And no matter what comes for both of us, I cannot abide you leaving without telling you how much it means and just how very grateful I am."

He lifted his other hand, curling his fingers around the side of my neck as he dipped his head so his handsome face was near.

"What's gonna come for both of us is I'm gonna do my thing and you're gonna have quality time with your family. After that, we'll meet in NOLA. Then the first thing I'm gonna do after feeding you pizza is get you drunk on hurricanes."

I felt confusion at his final word but did it no longer finding it irritating. Weeks with Noc and having this feeling, I'd grown accustomed to it. Not to mention, he had great patience and I enjoyed his frequent amusement when I asked for clarification.

"There are hurricanes in Fleuridia," I shared. "They're so bad, seamen who can sense them and dogs that have been trained to do the same are quite valued, for most people pack their carriages and move far inland to avoid them and the death and destruction they often cause."

His eyes lit. "It's a weather phenomenon, sweetheart. But in my world it's also a drink that will fuck you up."

"I'm assuming your usage of 'fuck you up' in this instance is a good thing," I guessed.

"Hell yeah," he confirmed, again with an upward curve to his lips.

I lifted a hand and put it on his chest. "Then I'll look forward to that, Noc."

I'd barely ceased talking when his hand went from my neck to mine on his chest where he folded it tight in his hold and held it there against the soft wool of his thick sweater.

"I want you writing me," he demanded, and at his demand, I stared.

"But, you'll be far and wide. Any missive will—"

"I don't care if the news is three months old when I get it," he interrupted me to say. "I want you writing me and I'll write you too."

Oh.

We'd correspond.

How delightful!

I pressed my hand against his chest. "You have my vow, I will share all the ridiculously boring things that are happening to me as I await the birth of my brother's child, and you can share with me all you've seen, heard, tasted and experienced as you travel the depth of a continent in a parallel universe."

This time his eyes flashed with humor.

"I got a feeling you'll find ways to liven shit up," he told me.

He would be right.

I would be learning how to use my magic, for one, something he knew as I'd told him.

But the truth was, I was me. I wasn't, but I was.

And I wasn't about to abide boring.

"We shall see," I replied.

He got even closer to the point our bellies were brushing through our clothes.

I held my breath.

He held my hand tighter at his chest.

"You leave first and you leave soon, baby," he said quietly, suddenly looking rather splendidly fierce. "I'm gonna walk you down there and I'm gonna give you a hug in front of everybody and I'm gonna act like I feel, which is that this part is gonna suck because I'm gonna miss you too."

He was going to miss me.

Why did that make me feel so much better?

"I have never been...hugged, in public that is," I shared.

Again, his eyes flashed with humor. "Glad I get to break that seal."

I felt my brows draw together. "Break that seal?"

It was then I felt my face freeze as he studied my brow only briefly before he dropped his forehead to mine, and instead of answering my question, he muttered, "Yeah, I'm gonna miss you too."

"Noc," I whispered.

"You be good," he ordered.

Being good would be boring.

But that was me now. I'd eschewed my wicked ways.

I had no choice but to "be good."

Ulk.

Though, I'd find ways to be good without being boring (I hoped).

"I will," I promised.

"Write me," he went on.

"I already promised that," I reminded him.

He behaved like I didn't even speak.

"And when the green mist clears, baby, we're gonna have a fuckin' blast."

I wanted that. I was very much looking forward to going to his world, especially these last few days after I'd shared I'd made the decision that I would and he'd explained much more about his world and what would be awaiting Josette and I there.

I wanted it more now because it would mean Josette and my adventure would finally begin and Noc and my separation would be over.

"Yeah?" he prompted when I said nothing.

"Yes, Noc," I replied dutifully.

He pressed his forehead into mine before he pulled away, looked out my window and murmured, "It's time."

I drew in a sharp breath at the sharp pain those words caused but tried to hide it as I cast my gaze in the same direction to see he spoke true.

And unfortunately Josette was outside, cloaked and ready to go, peering up at the palace in the direction of my room.

If I didn't move, she would be forced to run up to fetch me. A waste of time and energy.

Thus, I put one hand to the window, pulled slightly away from Noc, waved to her with my other and pointed down, indicating in a way I hoped she read that I would be right down.

She waved back, hopped twice on her boots and then whirled, causing an outward waft of her new, lovely cranberry wool cloak that was lined with sunshiny-gold rabbit fur.

Her new clothes were perfection not only because they suited her, but because she made no bones about the fact she was enjoying having them.

Although, according to Noc, she wouldn't be able to wear them in our new world when we got there.

This mattered not. I was screamingly rich. I'd buy her another wardrobe in just months' time and I'd delight in it.

It was a shock, but it couldn't be denied, acts of generosity felt very, *very* good.

On this thought, Noc drew me away from the window, my hand in his still held to his chest, but my arm was now tucked to his side as he led me out of the room.

Apparently, what needed to be said had been said. We were both quiet as we walked down the hall toward the stairs.

I found my feet lagging, Noc's doing the same, and the silence became uncomfortable as we made our way down the stairs.

And as we walked across the grand entry, I had to force myself to put one foot in front of the other rather than drag them or come to a stop entirely, and the silence had become heavy with melancholy.

"Gods, I've grown maudlin," I declared, staring at the door and only faintly sensing a footman coming forward with my cloak and hat.

"Yeah, goodbyes suck," Noc agreed.

He let me go so I could accept my cloak on my shoulders and he awarded me with a cheeky grin when I'd pulled my hat over my forehead.

"Dr. Zhivago," he whispered.

"I beg your pardon?" I asked, yanking on my gloves.

"Straight up, would seem impossible, but you're a fuckuva lot more gorgeous even than Julie Christie," he continued whispering. "And you don't know it, sweetheart, but that's saying something."

Through his words I'd grown solid. I had no idea to whom he was referring, but his tone and the look on his face made the depth of his compliment sparklingly clear.

This meant I did something I'd never done in my life.

In an effort not to be overwhelmed with the emotion I was feeling, I swatted his arm like a spoiled child or a flirting debutante and accused, "You're making this more difficult."

"My apologies," he said through a smile, taking hold of me again and heading us toward the front doors that footmen were opening for us, going on to say, "Let's get your ass in that sleigh."

Noc guided us out into the glorious cold only for me to find myself at the bottom of the palace steps having additional new pleasantly unpleasant experiences.

These being bidding *adieu* to Queen Aurora, Dax Lahn, Circe, Finnie, Frey, Tor and Cora, all people I would not again see, not soon, and perhaps (especially in the case of Circe and Lahn), not ever.

This meant for some unfathomable reason, in getting (and giving) many public hugs, the one I had with Circe was the longest.

And it felt good as well as bad, both coming from the fact it wasn't only me who seemed not to wish to let go.

"Say hey to the other Circe for me," she said in my ear.

"This I'll do," I promised.

"And don't be hard on yourself like you're so good at being," she instructed. "The crap time is over. Now's your time to let go and have fun."

"Of course," I replied, wishing to do as she instructed, but knowing from experience it would not be easy as the women had now been telling me this for some time. "As for you, I wish you a pleasant pregnancy, ease of birth and much joy when that bundle arrives."

She pulled away but didn't let me go to inform me, "The birth couldn't be worse than the last. Then again, I shouldn't say stuff like that or I might jinx myself."

Jinx?

I didn't ask.

I just gave her a small smile.

She gave me a big, bright one and finally let me go.

I could now say that holding affection for others, and having that returned, was quite a lovely feeling, going so far as admitting I treasured it, them, *all* of them (even Lahn, who was daunting but he could be quite amusing and gentle, both definitely endearing).

I could also now say that it had severe drawbacks for I had never, not once, lingered in leaving a place at all, but certainly not because I was saddened to leave the people there behind.

Noc had given me my first hug and he also came in to give me the last before he held my hand and (unnecessarily, but I did not pull away...oh no, I did not) steadied me as I made my way into my sleigh beside Josette who was already seated, ensconced under the furs.

"See you soon," he told me softly once I, too, was under the furs.

I looked into his blue eyes.

It would not be soon.

It would be too bloody long.

"Yes, soon," I agreed.

He leaned in. I held my breath. He kissed my nose. I let my breath go.

He moved away and did it decisively, shutting the door to the sleigh behind us.

"Ready?" Kristian called.

I tore my gaze from Noc to nod to my brother.

He nodded back, turned ahead, snapped his reins and shouted, "*Heeyah!*"

I leaned forward and grabbed our reins from the hook in front of us and followed suit.

I didn't wish to do anything inane such as wave or gaze lingeringly behind me, for I knew all too well what either would communicate.

So I didn't wave and I didn't look behind me, my gaze lingering on Noc.

Instead, I looked behind me and waved once with a flick of my raised hand to indicate my final farewell to them all.

But I did this with my eyes locked to Noc.

He lifted his hand back.

I felt my throat get thick.

It was then I turned away and stared resolutely at the back of my brother's sleigh, thinking I should have asked to have Timofei in our sleigh with us, not only because I enjoyed my nephew's company, but also because he would be a pleasant distraction.

"You're taken with him," Josette said as we left the Winter Palace behind.

"Mm..." I murmured.

"As in, everyone knows you're taken with him, but the truth is, you're *very* taken with him," she went on.

"Mm..." I repeated.

"As in, no one knew if we'd ever be away, you having to say goodbye to him and he to you," she stated. "Everyone suspected such an event would take hours, even days, or longer."

I looked to her. "There was talk of this?"

"I think it was Princess Cora who said something like there was a good chance Master Noc would drag you by your hair up to his bedroom, and if that occurred, they wouldn't see either of you for weeks."

Alas, that did not happen.

And truth be told, I doubted it ever would.

I struggled with, but could not deny, I was attracted to him.

His feelings in return were genuine and warm.

But not once had he ever given indication they were anything more.

I turned my attention back to where we were heading. This, I determined in that moment, would be my focus. Look only where I was heading. One minute to the next. One hour to the next. One day to the next.

And hopefully before we knew it, our true adventure would begin.

That adventure including being back with Noc.

For even if I had him only as my first real friend (outside, strictly, Josette, that was), my feelings for him were such I'd take that.

I'd take anything to have Noc.

Josette reached out and touched my wrist briefly. “We’ll be with him again soon.”

“Yes, we will,” I agreed and snapped the reins, for Kristian had done the same and was going faster.

Although I’d agreed, I knew it would not be soon enough.

~

Ten days later

“It’s your crystal ball.”

I stared with some distaste at the large, shining crystal sphere sitting on its bed of sapphire velvet that Valentine had just presented to me.

A crystal ball.

How cliché.

Was this *really* what magic was about?

Disappointing.

“There will be many implements you’ll acquire to assist you in brandishing the magic you have inside you. You’ll find your way with all of them. You’ll find your favorite. This,” Valentine indicated the crystal, “is mine.”

I looked from her back to the globe.

Well, this was my journey. This was who I was. And one could not say I wasn’t utterly delighted to experience the minimal magical experiences I’d had and the time I’d spent with my sister-witches.

In other words, I needed to keep an open mind.

Therefore, I lifted my hand and did so only to touch the cool glass.

When I did, a frisson of pleasure started at the small of my back and chased itself up my spine, over my shoulder, down my arm and through my fingertips, and inside the crystal ball I saw a wisp of the most beautifully-hued azure rise of smoke inside it.

Everything about me grew warm, inside and out.

Never, outside the color of Noctorno Hawthorne-of-the-other-world’s eyes, had I seen anything so exquisite.

“Indeed,” Valentine murmured. “You’re a natural.”

I stared at the smoke curling and suddenly had the uncanny desire to wrap my arms around that shining orb and hold it to me close, warm it with my body, memorize the feel of it against my breast.

I couldn’t deny it.

Even as cliché as it was. I’d fallen in love.

~

Two weeks later

"Oh. My. That's quite interesting."

I spoke these words and continued to look in my crystal ball as I did, delighted I'd learned this very useful skill from Valentine.

I was right then watching the Dax Lahn of the other world. He was wearing clothing that was unusual, but not unattractive. His hair was short, cut to a length it curled around his collar. And he didn't have a beard. But there was no mistaking he was as his twin by the forbidding look on his face.

"Is he angry?" I asked.

It took a few moments to realize I did not receive a reply.

I looked to Valentine who was sitting with me but her eyes were distant and aimed at the carved leg holding up the table.

"Valentine," I called, and her attention came to me, then to my crystal.

She looked back to me. "It seems you've mastered that."

I had. It wasn't difficult.

It was, strangely, second nature.

As Valentine instructed, all I had to do was what I'd always done in the little experimentation I'd attempted.

Tap into the current that was continuously vibrating through me, allow the quickening, and for crystal ball gazing, simply send out to the ether what I wished to see. Then, with a swirl of sapphire smoke, it appeared.

"I have," I replied, wishing to whisk away the other world Lahn from my orb and conjure up visions of Noc, who would undoubtedly have set sail on Frey's galleon by now and be nearly to Hawkvale, if not already there.

But this I would not do. It would be intrusive. I would not wish someone watching me without my knowledge. Thus, I would not do that to Noc, as much as I wanted to see his face, share in his adventure, even if I had to do it gazing in a crystal ball.

Valentine made no reply and again seemed distracted, something that was out of character for her.

From the moment we'd arrived in Älvkyla two weeks ago, she'd attended me six times.

In those times, I'd learned what an astral plane was. I'd learned how to put myself in a trance to travel along it in order to communicate with her as well as Lavinia. I'd been given my crystal ball and taught how to use it. I'd learned how to focus my thoughts (through chanting in my head, this Valentine shared was casting spells) and my power in order to move small objects, at first lifting them from where they lay, and advancing to moving them across the room to me.

It was not slow going. I felt the instinct born, if not bred, in me, and Valentine sensed it as well.

She was just teaching me how to manipulate it. She was teaching me how not to let it control me. She was also teaching me not to fear it.

This last was important, for with each passing lesson, I felt the power rising in me and it would be easy for it to grow out of control.

However, I was safe with Valentine. And I was safe with my power. I simply needed to become accustomed to it, nurture it...

And wield it.

In our other sessions, she'd always been fully engaged.

Now she was not.

"Is there something on your mind?" I asked.

Her eyes tipped to me. "Perhaps our session will be short today," she replied, not, I noted, answering my question.

This I found annoying.

And oddly insulting.

"Are you my sister?" I requested to know rather abruptly.

"Of course," she replied immediately.

I nodded. "I do sense we have somewhat of a kindred spirit. I'm independent and had to be due to life circumstances. You're quite the same for reasons you haven't shared and do not need to if you don't wish. What *I* wish is to make certain you know, should you need to discuss anything, I'm not only here to be trained. I'm here to offer anything you need of me, and you'll have it if I can give it."

Her distraction cleared, she studied me closely and came to a decision.

"You know I wish to maneuver the Circe in my world to be with the Dax of that world," she stated.

"I do," I confirmed.

"And you know both Circes are witches, quite powerful ones," she went on.

"I know that as well."

"Thus, Circe sensed my preliminary operations and blocked them."

"Ah," I murmured, seeing her issue and hoping I, too, would sense it if someone was meddling in my life.

"I have made some further efforts, she's still blocking me," Valentine shared.

I didn't quite understand.

"You can't find this surprising," I noted.

"It isn't. But it's frustrating, for this will undoubtedly mean two things. One, any interference I, and it is my hope that will be a *we*, wish to conduct will have to occur not through your training, as I'd hoped, but when we return to my world, which will mean a delay I don't much like."

"And?" I prompted when she said no more.

"And such interference will need to happen traditionally."

I arched my brow. "Traditionally?"

"By means of..." her lip curled, "non-magical *matchmaking*."

I didn't try to swallow the amused chuckle that came through my lips.

Valentine didn't find it humorous.

She stated, "It's common."

"My dear sister," I whispered, feeling my lips remain curved as I held her eyes. "It is *not* common. Not the way *I* do it. I've made many a match, in the past doing it in order to amuse myself by severing the results of such efforts at a later date. But this..." I kept smiling. "An intrigue. One I can look forward to. And I do. I very much do. And I can promise you, you will too."

One could not say this made me happy.

One could say this made me utterly *ecstatic*.

I could continue with my plotting and schemes.

But in doing so, I could do it for entirely different reasons, which I knew by witnessing the other world Lahn in my crystal, would be far more fulfilling.

I did not think of Noc's tryst with Circe. I hadn't mentioned it. He hadn't mentioned it. No one had mentioned it, and I found I could handle it that way.

What I could not do was think about what might happen when we were all together again in the same city in another world.

So I didn't think about it.

"It would seem when we reach our world, the teacher will become the student," Valentine remarked.

"You will enjoy my lessons," I declared proudly. "Not as much as I'm enjoying the fruits of yours, but you will enjoy them. That I promise."

Finally, Valentine's preoccupation gone, she smiled.

"Now, let us study this man," I suggested, using my hand to indicate my crystal. "We'll need to know as much about him as we can so we'll be prepared the moment I arrive in the other world."

"This study will not be difficult."

"He has no magic to block our regard?" I asked.

"No, he's highly easy to watch," Valentine answered.

To that, I smiled before we both turned to my sphere. And we watched.

~

Noc

One Month later

Standing on a balcony of Tor's palace in Bellebryn, the sun warming through his clothes, the breeze from the emerald waters of the Green Sea making a place that was the sheer perfection of a goddamned, real-life fairytale even more perfect, he bent his head to the thick sheet of expensive paper in his hand.

It was a letter that had just been delivered to him by Tor (Noc was careful how he went about the palace and the city, considering he looked just like its ruler, without the scar, and so they arranged it so Cora was with him if he went exploring—the scar meaning he had to wear a big hat that was completely ridiculous, but at least it didn't have the totally ridiculous feather most of the other men's hats had in that country).

Tor had also told him that in order for that letter to come through royal post—something that meant missives arrived a lot faster than normal post, Aurora kindly having allowed Franka to take advantage of that—she'd had to have written it within weeks of him leaving.

This meant Noc read the letter with a smile on his face, that smile there for more than just getting his first letter from his girl.

My dearest Noc,

Damn good start.

There is much to say but not much I can write, I'm sure you understand my meaning.

She was not wrong about that.

But he got from her tone her witch training was going well.

As you know, Valentine has been keeping me company a great deal. I enjoy her presence and our many conversations.

Yep. Her training was going well.

Noc's smile deepened.

Brikitta has begun to show, and as such, she's ordered her clothing from when she had Timofei in her belly out of storage.

You can rest assured I shared with her this was preposterous and demanded she go into Älvkyla with me to requisition a new wardrobe.

She explained this was quite the waste of coin as she would need a further selection of garments for when she grew more with her child.

I explained that I was ludicrously rich (as, now, was she, thanks to me, but I didn't have a burgeoning family to look after) and my sister was not going to be wearing the fashions of more than two years previous while she nurtured my future niece or nephew

(I've decided on niece, and Brikitta has secretly agreed with me, Kristian will be happy with whatever, but as a man, he is very bad at hiding that he wishes another son).

Of course, Brikitta, who I've noted has a highly unattractive stubborn streak, flatly denied this request, and when I went into town and ordered her clothing myself, she complained to Kristian.

Kristian brought his wife's concerns to me. To say he was not interested in them and therefore did not squander much time in attempting to convince me to change my mind would be quite the understatement.

Thus, Brikitta's new garments started arriving yesterday.

She looks quite fetching in them.

Kristian agrees.

Brikitta does too, but she has not admitted this aloud.

Though, Timofei has found his way to share he much likes them as well.

He is, of course, becoming brighter and brighter as the days pass. I'm no clairvoyant, but I feel fairly certain he will be Head of the Drakkar House when it's his time. Ousting one of the Frey's direct line to do so will be quite the achievement, but mark me, this will surely happen.

There's not much else to tell, except both Josette and I find it highly amusing that Kristian and Brikitta's servants have taken to calling her "Mistress Josette" due to the fact I treat her with such familiarity and we often share breakfasts and even lunches together.

I have not disabused them of the notion of doing this. She's far superior to any I've known in her profession, so this show of respect is due her.

At that, Noc started laughing.

Only Franka could make treating a servant with equality seem like she did it with superiority.

As I feared, there is naught else to share.

Though, I do look forward to receiving your communiqués.

And I very much hope you're enjoying your adventures.

Now, I shall bid you farewell until my next undoubtedly titillating missive where I'll regale you with news of the next set of garments I'll press on Brikitta, and perhaps how I liked, or disliked, the soup I'd taken at lunch.

Until then...and until we meet again,

Always yours,

Franka

Since he'd sent a letter from the port city in Lunwyn (the part of it that used to be Middleland), and he'd used Finnie's dispatch to do it, Franka should be getting his letter any day now, if she hadn't already gotten it.

That didn't stop him from walking into the room behind him, his bedroom in this huge palace that Disney animators would freak over, and go right to the desk in that room.

He sat.

He pulled out paper.

And he shared news that might be more adventurous than hers, but she wouldn't think so since she'd seen it and done it all before.

That didn't stop him either.

In fact, he wrote three pages of the stuff.

Then he sealed it and found Cora so she could send it.

This she arranged before she gave him a hat and took him to Tor's horse, Salem, an outrageously handsome animal (and one who could talk to him, right in his head, if that shit could be believed).

Before getting to that world, Noc had been horseback riding twice in his life.

He'd been on a horse a shit ton since they left *The Finnie*—Frey's kickass galleon that was straight from a pirate movie—in Bellebryn's port.

And off he went with Cora, having to pretend to be Tor until they left the city and galloped across a countryside where the air glittered.

Fucking *glittered*.

It was amazing.

He missed Franka. He missed just looking at her, but he missed more how damned funny she was, how cute she could be and how her trusting him the way she did, the way she showed she did, the way he knew she didn't give to anybody (but maybe Josette, and perhaps the dead Antoine, but Noc didn't go there) made him feel.

But he sure as fuck was glad she'd made the decision she'd made.

Because he wouldn't have known what he was missing.

But he was sure glad he didn't miss it.

And he had it.

But in the end, he'd have her too.

~

Franka

Two and a half months later

Hey there, Sugarlips,

I should not smile. I really should not. He was incorrigible. Even in the written word.

I nevertheless smiled.

I'm guessing you know Finnie and Frey have returned to Lunwyn since they should have gotten there a while ago and brought my last letter with them.

He was correct in this. They had.

Finnie wanted to continue on with me, but Frey wanted her home. She's getting along in her pregnancy and he wants her close to a doctor he trusts. That didn't go over real well with Finnie. She thinks like we do in our world, obviously, and most women work until they practically go into labor...

How bizarre!

And dangerous!

...and they had a big blowout about it. Frey won. Not because Finnie agrees with him that advanced pregnancy makes a woman invalid, when it doesn't. But he's a dude and dudes tend to express worry through anger and bossiness. She's been with him long enough to know that so they took off and passed me off to Achilles, Apollo's cousin (in case you haven't met him, tho' with the incestuous way those Houses are, you probably have) who, with some of Lo's other guys, we went through Hawkvale and now we're in Fleuridia.

Gotta say, I'm not much of a fan of south Lunwyn. There's a bleakness to it that's actually pretty, in its way, but it's also depressing. I can see why that asshole, Baldur, didn't like what he got in the cutting-a-country-in-two bargain. Doesn't excuse him being an asshole, but I can see that.

Bellebryn and Hawkvale, I don't have to tell you, are fucking amazing. There's a lot of beauty in my world and you'll see that, I'll make sure of it.

But there's nothing like this. It's so pure, it's like magic. It almost doesn't seem real and the fact it is makes it even more beautiful.

It also makes me wonder what my world was like a hundred years ago, two hundred, a thousand. Was it like this? Did we fuck it up with all our garbage?

If we did, you'll see how much that sucks.

What's worse is that we're still doing it.

I won't get into that.

What I'll say is, Fleuridia is my favorite, outside Lunwyn.

Oh my.

He felt the same as me!

It has the magic and the beauty of Bellebryn and Hawkvale, but with sophistication. The food here is unbelievable. The wine, even better.

He was quite right!

People are friendly, but not in your face about it (that could be me having trouble getting around in Bellebryn and Hawkvale, looking like Tor—here, some look at me with curiosity, but most people don't pay me any mind at all, and gotta admit, that's a relief—I don't know how Tor does it, that's gotta suck).

Lahn and Circe went on ahead ages ago because Lahn, like Frey, wants Circe at their house in Korwahn when she's getting closer to the time. They asked me to meet them there and from what they said about Korwahk, I'd like to go.

But it's gonna be hard leaving here. We're headed to Benies to hook up with Apollo and Maddie. I figure my time is getting short, at most, I have three months left and it takes forever to get anywhere. We'll see. I'd like to take in all I can, but if Benies is half as awesome as the rest of Fleuridia is, I gotta spend some time eating and drinking my way through it. So maybe we can talk Valentine into sending us to Korwahk some other time. It'd be good to catch up with Lahn and Circe and meet their new arrival after he or she shows.

He was right again. That would be good.

And I liked how he said "talk Valentine into sending us" because he'd said "us."

Though even as much as I liked it, I wondered at it.

What did "us" mean to Noc?

What did it even mean to me?

Those questions gave me the unusual sensation of my heart fluttering in my chest at the same time dread settled heavy in my belly.

I set both aside and refocused on Noc's missive.

One other thing I gotta do is make sure Valentine transports the five cases of wine I've bought from the vineyards we're stopping at along the way. Have a word with her about that, would you? And just to say, sweetheart, the way me and the guys are going, by the time this letter gets to you, that could be fifteen cases of wine.

This would mean I'd have Fleuridian wine in the new world.

And Noc to share it with (for it didn't even occur to me that he wouldn't share it).

Excellent.

Okay, not much else to say. Glad to read you're getting on with things and you're liking doing that. Looking forward to getting the full scoop, baby. Feels like time has flown at the same time it feels like it's dragging. There's a lot I'd love to know that's going on with you and can't wait to hear it.

Now, I should go. We make Benies in two days but only if I get my ass to bed so I can climb on that damn horse tomorrow and hold on. Achilles doesn't fuck around with taking in the countryside. At least my ass is used to sitting that horse and doesn't hurt so goddamn much (along with the rest of my body) at the end of the day. I'll miss a lot from this world when I leave it, but I sure as fuck will be happy to see a car.

I grinned at the letter and read Noc's last.

So I'll end it here. Still miss you. It'll be good to see you again, Frannie.

Take care of yourself, your family and Josette. Say hey to them all for me.

You, me and a slice of pizza, babe.

Soon.

Lotsa love,

-Noc-

Him and me and a slice of pizza.

Soon.

Very soon. Brikitta had grown quite heavy with child (even if she was such stylishly, her pregnancy wardrobe was stunning, if I did say so myself).

The wait for my new niece (I hoped) or nephew (I would not be disappointed) I felt was close to over.

Yes.

Soon.

Noc.

Me.

And pizza.

~

One Month later

The midwife at the other end, as Brikitta sweated and grunted and moaned and gritted her teeth audibly in a highly unladylike manner, I had the dubious (at that point) honor, at Brikitta's request, of attending the birth and holding her hand through it.

It was a hand I'd feared she'd break, for it seemed she was tiring greatly, but her strength had not been affected in the slightest.

And it was at that juncture I feared she was tiring greatly for the midwife kept summoning her to push, her entreaties seeming more and more urgent, and my sister-in-law was drenched with sweat, her hair, her shift, the bedclothes, and her face had gone from red and pained to drained of color, and the pain had drifted from her eyes, a vagueness setting in.

"She mustn't lose consciousness," Hilde, Brikitta's sister, who'd arrived two weeks ago to be present at this very moment, hissed.

I looked across the bed to her, a woman assuming the same position as I, on her feet, bent double, holding her sister's hand. Her expression had been joyful and encouraging these last hours, now it appeared anxious and borderline panicked.

I then looked to Brikitta and saw not only her eyes had gone vague, her head was lolling on her shoulders.

"She must *push*," the midwife pressed and the urgency was gone.

Fear was threading her tone.

And that fear threaded through my veins.

"The baby's just about to crown, I can feel it," the midwife went on. "She needs one, hearty push. If I can get hold of him..."

"*Her*," I snapped, not for myself (solely).

My sister-in-law wanted a girl.

My brother didn't care, but Brikitta had confided in me she longed for a baby girl that she could dress and Kristian could dote over and Timofei could love and protect.

I had no idea if the child was a girl. I was not a seer (I'd tried, I'd failed), as Valentine was not.

But I had hope.

"Whatever it is," the midwife snapped back, "make her push. If we lose her now, we could lose them *both* now."

"That is not happening," I shared haughtily, watched her open her mouth to speak, but I turned my head from hers, tightened my hand well beyond the strength Brikitta had been using, feeling her bones and flesh crunch in my grip, and I bent over my sister. "Awake!" I commanded.

Her eyes fluttered and her head again drooped.

I yanked her hand hard so her back left the bed, Hilde cried, "Franka!" but Brikitta focused on me.

"Look at me and push," I ordered.

"I'm so tired, Franka," she whispered.

"I'm quite certain you were tired of me being an unceasing bitch for five years, but you never let me beat you," I retorted.

She blinked at me.

"Push," I charged.

"I don't...have much...more..."

I yanked her again, heard Hilde's surprised cry, but my maneuver had the desired results. The fading Brikitta focused again.

I put my face square in hers.

"Push, sister. I'll not have you leaving us now. Not now. Not ever. Today, you bring my brother more joy. You bring it for yourself. And you bring it for *me*, and I get what I bloody well want. So you're giving me a bloody niece. Now...*push*."

"You...are very... mercenary," Brikitta forced out.

"I'm a Drakkar," I retorted. "Now, I'd be happy to have a conversation with you, sister. But before that, if you'd be so kind—"

I didn't finish as, before I could, her hand crushed mine, she bared her teeth as she gritted them, the blood rushed to her face, and she bent forward, groaning.

"I see the head!" the midwife cried.

Thank the gods!

I looked that way and saw the same, covered in Kristian's dark hair.

I again turned to Brikitta. "She's got Kristian's hair." I watched her eyes flash. "Keep going, my beautiful girl."

She nodded and kept pushing.

Back and forth I looked as more of the baby came through, Hilde's encouragement mingled with my own, and finally on a tortured cry that I was sure, if my brother heard it (and the last time I checked, he was pacing the hall outside this very bedchamber door so he would), would send him into a deathly fright, the rest of the baby came out.

"It's a boy!" the midwife whispered excitedly.

Brikitta slumped against the pillows.

I drew in a long breath, let it out and sat down on the bed, still holding her hand as Hilde let the other one go to dash around with bathing cloths and blankets, clucking and cooing, and murmuring, "How beautiful, so beautiful."

Through this, Brikitta stared at what was happening at the end of the bed, an exhausted smile shading her lips, a look of deep contentment eclipsing the fatigue that shadowed her eyes.

It took time, but eventually feeling my gaze, she gave me hers.

When she did, I felt my eyes get moist.

I sniffed and decreed, "A boy. It seems you'll have to do this again."

Her eyes grew wide then her exhausted laughter filled the room.

I smiled before I leaned forward, kissed her forehead, let her go, got up and walked out of the room in order to tell my brother he had a new son.

Noc

Darling.

Noc turned in bed.

Noc, are you there?

His eyes shot open and he sat straight up. He looked around the room that had no furniture (except that bed) but still, with the patterned metal mirrors and weave work adorning the walls and other shit like that, it kicked ass.

The moonlight shone through the opened windows and he saw nothing.

Noc?

Fuck, that was Franka's voice.

"Frannie?" he called into the empty room.

You're there.

He didn't know where her voice was coming from, his head or disembodied in the room.

He also didn't give a shit.

It was just fucking great to hear her voice.

"I see you've learned some wielding," he remarked.

Her voice held humor when she replied, *If it would not take great magic, I'd be standing by your bed.*

He would not mind that at all.

Months had passed. Her lover was not freshly dead. She was no longer in the throes of grief. Her parents had not just been discovered to be the fuckwads they were, and Franka was not trying to find ways to cope with the massive changes that meant, healing from mental wounds as well as the physical ones her father had unleashed.

It was time they had a conversation.

Though, he'd wait until he had her on his turf and not do it when she was somewhere else and just coming to him in his head (or whatever).

I have a new nephew, she shared.

"Fuckin' hell, baby, that's awesome," he said as he laid back in bed and crossed his hands behind his head.

It is, she agreed.

"Everyone good?" he asked.

Yes. The baby is healthy, loud and robust. Quite heavy, he gave Brikitta a tough time, but she persevered. He's also quite long, so he, too, will be tall like his father. A full head of hair. All his fingers. All his toes. Brikitta is tired, but she's got plenty of people around to look after the child so she can get some rest. I nearly had to cast a spell on Josette to make her forget for a time we had a newborn in our midst. She quite fell in love.

He thought of her and the frequent time she spent with Tim.

"And I'm sure you're not interested at all," he teased.

They've named him Frantz.

Even, however she was coming to him, he could hear the emotion thickening her voice.

"Baby," he whispered.

He said no more, giving her a minute to pull her shit together because that was Franka. She wasn't about falling apart.

She took that minute and said in a crisp voice (total Franka, bullshitting to cover), *He's quite handsome.*

"Babies aren't handsome, sugarlips, they're cute."

I thought you said I was cute.

"You are. Babies are a different kind of cute."

And baby is what you often call me.

He chuckled.

There are parts of your patois that are very clever. There are parts that make no sense. She paused before she finished, *And now, after I take a week or so to get to know my new nephew, be certain Brikitta is well and recovering, and sort out Josette and I, I'll learn much more.*

"Yeah, you will," he agreed.

Are you...?

He waited for her to finish, but she didn't.

He turned to his side, wrapping a hand around his pillow and using both arms to curl it closer.

Like it was a woman.

Like Franka was there.

Fuck, he hoped the saying was right that time healed all wounds.

If it didn't, he'd wait for her to heal. He'd help her do it.

But he'd also be right fucking there if she was.

"I'm ready when you are, babe. Korwahk is fuckin' nutty. I dig it to visit and explore, but I'm not sure how Circe made the decision to live here forever. Interesting. But still fucked up. Knew she loved Lahn in a big way. Now I know the woman *loves* her husband seriously, 'cause she's not only cool livin' here, she's totally in her element. It's like she's lived here all her life."

I would like the opportunity one day to witness her in her element.

"We'll figure that out. First, next time you see Valentine, let her know we're good to go and have her get in touch with me so I know when that's gonna happen. I'm good to go too, but that doesn't mean I want green smoke to surround me and suddenly be gone before I say goodbye."

I'll be certain she forewarns you.

"Thanks, Frannie."

And I must go. It's late here and I wish to check in once more with Kristian and Brikitta before I'm abed.

"Right, sweetheart. Glad you floated into my consciousness and gave me the good news."

I'm not in your consciousness, Noc, she informed him snootily, *I'm gliding on an astral plane, though without my body. I've simply tuned in to your plane. You have my conscious as I'm in a trance. But I don't have yours.*

"You do know that makes no fuckin' sense whatsoever," he stated.

I'll explain it more thoroughly over pizza.

Fuck yeah, she would.

"Right, go to bed, baby. And see you soon."

Yes, Noc. Soon. Sleep well.

"You too, Frannie. Later."

Uh...well, um...later.

He grinned and could actually feel it when he lost her.

Kristian had named his kid Frantz.

Noc liked the guy. Now he liked him more.

He drew the pillow closer and closed his eyes.

A week or so.

Then he'd finally be home.

And so would Frannie.

13
Welcome Home

Franka

"By the gods! Look at your garments!"

I whirled from the window, twisting my ankle as I did so and nearly crashing to the floor.

Just managing to prevent myself from doing something that incredibly mortifying, I stood blinking rapidly as I stared at Josette who was rushing through the door.

She was not dressed as me in preparation to be transported to our new world.

No, Valentine had brought her something very much different.

She was wearing trousers like Noc's (he'd told me they were referred to as "jeans"). Up top she had on something that was frilly but skimpy. On her feet she had...

I shook my head as I took them in.

They were indescribable. I didn't even know what they were made of. There was a sole that looked squishy and two straps that led from the juncture of her first and second toe along her foot, exposing the rest of it.

And that was all.

"They're called *flip-flops*," Valentine drawled, strolling in after Josette. "They seemed very...*her*."

Josette stopped a foot away and sprung up and down on them, saying, "They're very comfortable. But odd. I was walking and one came right off, flying halfway down the corridor. I have to scrunch my toes to keep them on."

I could see this.

However, as strange as her shoes were, in fact her whole outfit (for a woman), she had it much better than I.

Before leaving to see to Josette, Valentine had painstakingly instructed me as I painted my face with a variety of brushes and wands, decreeing through it, "You'll need to experiment in future, and when we're in my world I'll take you to an artist to share further techniques."

I did this utilizing what Valentine said was "makeup or cosmetics, *chérie*."

Although this took some time, and I wasn't a complete novice (many in my world painted their faces with rouge or lip tint, powder on their eyes, kohl to line their lids, pencils to fill in brows—this happening everywhere, though it was worn especially heavy in Fleuridia), I was enchanted not only by the results but by the quality of the elements Valentine had provided. In my world, they were far more rudimentary.

But after that, Valentine had given me some other-world undergarments (which I liked very much), as well as a swatch of material and a curious metal band. She'd then glided out of the room to see to Josette and give me time to change, stating with a wave of her hand toward a box on a chair, "Those are your shoes, *ma petite sorcière*."

Examining the garment she'd given me, I realized I simply had to shrug it on like a coat. It wrapped around the front and closed not with frogs or buttons, but with a belt, the belt being the metal band.

The material was quite soft and I could tell it was excellent quality. It was also a sumptuous cream, a color I'd never worn, but it seemed to highlight the natural olive tone of my skin, not to mention deepen the color of my hair and bring out the same in my eyes.

All this was fine.

What was slightly concerning was the fact that the hem was uneven. One edge of the coat-like dress hung longer than the other, which aesthetically was quite pleasing, but it still seemed to be a mistake in construction.

This I could live with because everyone knew, if something was aesthetically pleasing, that was all that mattered.

What was most concerning was the location of the hem, this being at my upper thigh.

Yes.

My *upper thigh*.

Everything beyond was exposed.

Bare.

I could be risqué. I could even take that to extremes. In fact, there was a time I enjoyed taking it to extremes and reveling in the reactions that would get. And I had not been out in society for some months but I had a feeling that was a part of me that had not changed.

But this was outlandish.

Indeed, there was a good possibility that when I walked, the flaps of the short coatdress would fan out and show *everything*.

A woman had to have *some* mystery, most assuredly. *That* mystery particularly.

And this could not be so different in the other world. If that was the case, surely Valentine or Noc would have told me.

Even generally, I was not a woman to hide her charms. Because of this, the plunging neckline of the long-sleeved dress did not concern me. And I was not a woman who had a problem with adding flair. Therefore, the peculiar belt that seemed made of shiny gold I liked quite a lot.

But I had never in my life exposed my legs as such to anyone but a lover.

And this did not get into the shoes.

They were like Josette's in the sense that they, too, were constructed of a very small number of straps (precisely, three). One across the toes that was somewhat wide. Two that came up from the sides of the heel and wrapped around my ankle, those being exceptionally dainty.

They were also shiny gold, which was lovely.

But the heel included a golden spike at the bottom back that was elegant to gaze upon, but it had to be at least four inches tall, therefore standing upon them forced me to my toes.

Needless to say, walking was nigh on impossible.

However, it explained Noc's statement about "spiked heels" from many months before.

Indeed it explained it *literally*.

One could not deny (and I myself had admired just this in the full-length mirror) that the dress did wonderful things for my figure and the shoes did miraculous things to my legs (and bum).

But what would Noc think of me, seeing me in such attire?

And what would he think when I took one step toward him and fell flat on my face?

"How are you going to walk on those *shoes*?" Josette cried my thoughts out loud, injecting a goodly dose of the concern I myself felt in each word.

"Carefully," I answered.

"I can imagine," Josette muttered, still staring at the shoes. "Though, they're very pretty. But I can't imagine other-world women walk about on them much. Instead, they must sit and have them gazed upon admiringly, don't you think?"

What I thought was, to get to any seat one had to walk on them. So, although I very much wanted off my feet at that moment, I, and any woman wearing such footwear, was out of luck when the necessity arose to ambulate.

"Do tell me you've practiced walking, Franka," Valentine said. "We're set to leave soon. Noc is already at your appointed meeting place, waiting."

My body jolted because my heart leaped so at her words I feared it had torn right out of my chest.

"I've practiced," I replied and took a step, then another to show her.

I'd gotten quite good at balancing while standing. And I was becoming adept at slow steps.

A natural gait would take some doing. Much longer than the time I had.

It might take days.

Or weeks.

Though I would prefer to wear what I was used to, superb quality slippers, and not wear those kind of shoes at all.

Suffice it to say, for myself and for Josette, we should have requested other-world garments and footwear some time ago so we could become accustomed to them.

It was too late for that now.

"Well, practice some more," Valentine ordered. "I'm taking Josette and I'll come back for you."

"What?" Josette asked on a whirl from facing me to doing the same with Valentine.

"I beg your pardon?" I queried on narrowed eyes.

"I'm taking Josette to my home. She can settle in. I'll come back for you as you'll be going somewhere else and at that somewhere else, Noc wants only you," Valentine replied.

Noc wanted only me.

My belly clenched.

"No offense, *chérie*," she said to Josette. "But you're not invited to their reunion."

"That's quite all right!" Josette chirped, no longer showing concern we'd be separated upon entry to this parallel universe and turning bright eyes to me.

"Circe is coming around to take Josette out to dinner," Valentine carried on. "This while I finish up some of my own business here and make my final return home. Then, of course, I'll be around should she need anything."

I wanted to see Noc. I wanted to see a Noc that didn't invite Josette to our "reunion." I missed him and had been waiting for months to see him again, and now that wait was over.

But I *needed* to see to Josette.

"I think it's best if Josette and I travel together and stay together, at least for a time," I informed Valentine. "When we both become accustomed to getting around in our new world, then we can go off and do things alone."

"Nonononono," Josette said swiftly, shaking her head in a negative to strengthen her words. "I'll be just fine."

"See," Valentine lazily swung her hand Josette's way. "She'll be fine."

I looked to Josette. "My dear, this is our adventure, and I'll emphasize the *our* in that statement. It's my responsibility to look out for you. I can't leave you to your own devices the instant you get there."

"Mistress Valentine is taking care of me," Josette replied.

"Indeed I am, and it's all sorted," Valentine added, quite definite about that, and I knew she was as she lifted her hands, and without delay, the room started to turn green.

I knew what that meant.

I took a step toward her. "Sister, this needs to be discussed. Josette is my charge and—"

"Practice on those heels, Franka," Valentine cut me off to advise. "You have fifteen minutes to make certain you don't take an embarrassing tumble the first time you see Noctorno."

The very thought of that arrested me and the workings of my mind for a moment before I realized the room was becoming greener and I needed to act with haste.

I lifted my own hands, certain there was no way to beat Valentine's magic, but I had to try...for Josette.

"Valentine, listen to me..." I began as clouds of blue started swirling through the green.

"I'll be fine," Josette promised.

Valentine stepped closer to her.

I ignored her. "Valentine—"

She smiled her smile that *I* had perfected (back in the day).

And then she and Josette disappeared, the green drifted away and there was nothing but the floating clouds of blue that had no purpose for I'd called them up to beat back the green and that magic, as well as Valentine and Josette, were gone.

I dropped my hands and the clouds vanished.

"Blast!" I snapped, too loudly. "Blast," I whispered, my eyes darting to the door in hopes it didn't open.

I'd already said my farewells to my brother, sister and nephews. These were not moments I relished, at the same time I knew I would never forget them and the warmth and love they communicated.

But during them, Kristian and Brikitta shared they were worried about my upcoming adventure. Previously they both were all for this it, but now that the time had come, they were getting cold feet. Especially when they learned communication between worlds could be difficult.

If Kristian heard aught amiss—say me shouting, "Blast!"—he'd come running, even more concerned, and I didn't want to have to say farewell to him all over again.

Once was enough.

Noc had been right.

Goodbyes sucked.

It would be worse if my brother saw me in this dress.

He might not allow me to go at all (though he'd have a time of it stopping Valentine from doing anything—the woman, I'd found, was a force of nature, literally).

Annoyed at Valentine, but knowing she was correct, I did not want to take a tumble in front of Noc, I started walking tentatively again in those beautiful but bloody uncomfortable (and dangerous) shoes.

I found to my distress (and some shame) that as the minutes passed and I moved around in those shoes, not only did my feet hurt more and more, but I thought less and less of Josette, what she was now experiencing and the fact I was not experiencing it with her as we both had thought we would.

No, I thought more and more of seeing Noc again.

With me in this dress.

And these shoes.

And just seeing...*him*.

I shook my hands feeling my palms perspiring as I tried a faster pace, finding my footing.

Damp palms due to fretfulness.

Unthinkable.

Ah, but what had happened to the Franka Drakkar I once knew?

You do know the answer to that, Antoine noted in my head.

I stopped dead.

I hadn't heard him in months. Even before Noc left me. Definitely not after.

She never actually existed, Antoine's voice carried on. *A part you played,* mon ange, *beautifully. But you've quite literally taken off the costume and face paint, put on new, and are now ready for a different role. The role, to be banal, of a lifetime. The role of you just being...you.*

I turned my head and saw myself in the mirror.

Was that me, the woman with her hair flowing unhindered, her cheeks pink with excitement (and what Valentine said in her world was fittingly called "blush"), her eyes bright with nervousness, her breaths coming fast from anticipation?

I always loved your legs, Antoine murmured.

"*Mon cœur*," I whispered.

Farewell, my Franka. I'd bid you be happy, but I don't need to.

"Why?" I asked.

You'll see.

Those simple words made a tickle run down my spine.

He said no more.

"Antoine?" I called.

He didn't speak to me, and in my soul I knew he never again would.

"Antoine," I whispered, feeling not-so-oddly pleased the last I heard of his voice, he sounded happy.

But mostly I felt uncertain that I was facing my greatest adventure, and in doing so had long since let him go and was moving on.

That greatest adventure was not going to a parallel universe where women were referred to as infants (of a variety of species) and wore death-defying shoes.

That adventure was living life from that point on simply as me.

Franka Drakkar.

A woman prone to generosity (even if I had to force it on those who were stubbornly opposed to it), outgoingness and sociability.

And also a woman who was a practicing witch.

On this thought, the room filled with green.

I turned to where I sensed her joining me and Valentine appeared right there.

She cocked her head to the side. "Ready?"

I was.

And I was not.

"How odd would I seem if I went to your new world in my own attire?" I queried.

"Nothing is odd in New Orleans," she answered. "This is one of the vast number of reasons it's the greatest city in my world...or yours."

"Then I—"

"Rubbish," she stated before I could even finish my thought, lifting her hands, the green of her magic returning.

"Valentine," I snapped.

"Come closer, *ma petite sorcière*."

I came closer but repeated on a sharper snap, "Valentine!"

She smiled again as I sensed the room receding and then there was nothing but her magic shrouding us.

I did not find this alarming.

What I found alarming was her smile.

It was another one I'd perfected many years ago.

And it was the one I'd indulge in when a fine bit of conniving was about to come gloriously to fruition.

"What have you done?" I demanded to know.

I got no answer.

Instead, suddenly, I had earth beneath my feet, bright lights, loud noise and movement everywhere, and I was experiencing an odor so foul, it would have turned my stomach.

It did not because it did not have my focus.

My focus was on the fact that Valentine had gone.

And right in front of me, Noc was standing.

I stared up in his extraordinary blue eyes and watched his head jerk in surprise at my abrupt appearance.

My.

He was right there.

Right there.

An inch away.

So *there*, I'd barely have to sway and I'd brush against him.

"Frannie," he whispered, saying the name he gave me with unhidden affection and relief.

Bloody hell!

I was going to burst into tears.

"Noc," I forced out.

"Frannie," he repeated.

Yes. Drat it all!

I was going to start weeping within moments of starting my grand adventure!

Bloody *Noc*.

Slowly, his lips formed one of the grins I so adored and he raised a hand. In it were long strings of shiny beads, gold, purple and green. He lifted them over my head and settled them around my neck.

They appeared like they'd be heavy, but as his hands moved away, leaving them behind, they were light.

Light and bright and festive.

"Welcome home," Noc said, and my eyes shot from the beads dangling down my front to Noc's. "*Laissez les bon temps rouler.*"

How odd, he was speaking Fleuridian. He'd never done that before.

At that point, before I could ask after this, it seemed he became aware that there was more of me that had been transported, not just my face.

He leaned back an inch as his eyes traveled down my body and I watched his expression begin to change.

Gods.

I had nothing against harlots. I'd fallen in love with the male variety of a harlot and had happily acted as one myself without shame.

Now, however...

"Valentine selected it," I stated quickly, referring to my attire that Noc was right then gazing at fixedly. "I can be risqué, but—"

"Fuck," he muttered.

I went silent at the timbre in his voice.

His eyes moved, made it to my feet, and slowly, they traveled up.

Halfway to my face, it came as a growl.

"*Fuck.*"

It had been some time, but his tone was not lost on me.

In entering the period of my recent (prolonged) celibacy, I had declared I was done with that part of my life.

Of course, Noc changed all that, and if I was honest, he did it months ago.

But if he had not, he would have done it with that one word, the look on his face as he said it, and the tone with which he uttered it.

And it would seem, in but seconds, any questions (lamentations, anxieties, fears, trepidations) I had about what would become of Noc and me upon our reunion, he answered.

In one word.

Even if that word and the way he said it had answered it, what he did next *really* answered it.

That being the fact I suddenly had his hand at the small of my back.

It didn't press in.

It *hauled* me in and I was plastered against his long body.

The instant I was, his other hand dove in my hair, tangling and gripping.

There was no pain at his touch. Thus the gasp that came from my mouth and drifted across his descending lips was indication of an altogether different feeling.

I closed my eyes after his lips crushed down on mine.

It was not instinct but instead a driving need that made me lift my hands and filter my fingers in his thick, soft hair to hold him to me.

And it was not generosity but pure greed that made me open my mouth to invite him inside.

He accepted the invitation with a low snarl down my throat, his head slanting, his hand at the small of my back gliding around and curving at my hip so he could hold me closer to him, all as he deepened the kiss.

He tasted good. Fresh and warm and spicy.

He smelled good, all of those same things.

And he *felt* good.

Like coming home, and I knew the feeling even though I'd never felt that *in my life*.

I burrowed into him as I accepted the invasion of his tongue, his talented workings scuttling along my skin, from my hair to my toes, gathering specifically between my legs, forcing me to press my hips to his, grind them against him, seek something I *needed*.

Intimacy.

Connection.

Just Noc.

I pulled one hand from his hair to wrap my arm around his neck, going up further on my toes to push even closer.

I did not hear the calls or whistles or shouts.

But vaguely, only because of what happened after it came, I heard, "Serious, dude, get a freakin' room."

Noc broke only the connections of our mouths and we panted at each other's lips, our gazes sultry and hooded but locked as he muttered, "Great fuckin' idea."

And then I was teetering for a moment, bereft of Noc's hold.

But only for a moment.

His hand closed around mine and he turned, dragging me behind him.

The earth beneath my feet was paved with an odd, continuous (though uneven and broken in parts) stone, but I couldn't really pay attention to it or any of the rather active, raucous, loud and smelly goings-on around us.

I had to concentrate on walking on my heels.

This did not go well.

I tripped, emitting a faint cry, caught myself and called out, "Noc, I—"

He stopped, yanked at my hand so I completely lost balance, but did it falling toward him. He released me but only to bend at his waist whereupon I had his shoulder in my belly. Promptly I was *on* said shoulder, one of his arms wrapped around the backs of my thighs, and we were advancing through the street at the great speed Noc's long strides afforded us.

"You *go*, brutha!" someone shouted.

"Right the fuck on, man!" someone else shouted.

"Oh my God, I think I just had an orgasm," someone further said.

The first two were male voices.

The last was a woman.

I could pay no mind to this. Noc was marching down the crowded street and the way he was doing so—as I put my hands to the sides of his waist and peered around him to the front—I saw the throng part to ease his way.

He made the mouth of the road, turned left and kept striding down a slightly less populated, but much wider, avenue.

All I could see were the contraptions on the road.

Automobiles. Cars. Trucks. All that Noc had described, but far more fanciful in real life, vied for space on the thoroughfare.

By the gods.

He couldn't be telling it true.

It *had* to be magic.

I stared at this until Noc stopped moving, bent, put me on my feet, took my hand and looked into my eyes.

"You think you're good to go now?" he asked.

I didn't know the answer to that.

But I was with Noctorno Hawthorne of the parallel universe. Thus there was only one answer to anything he requested.

"Yes," I whispered.

He nodded shortly and resumed walking (quickly), pulling me with him.

Fortunately, we didn't go far. There was a door to our left that Noc turned toward, pushed through, and he continued pulling me along with him as we walked through what appeared to be a large, elegantly-appointed, rather elaborate entrance hall.

He took us directly to a long, tall desk, behind which a man and a woman, oddly (albeit different sexes) both attired in what looked to be poorly-fitting uniforms, were standing.

"May I help you, sir?" the male asked, looking from Noc to me and back to Noc.

"A room," Noc stated. "King-size bed."

The man cast his eyes down at the desk and his fingers started tapping on a peculiar apparatus that had letters and numbers on it.

I stared, transfixed.

"How long will you be staying?" he queried, not lifting his head (which, distractedly, I found rude).

"The night," Noc answered.

"Two people?"

"Only two."

"We have availability," the man declared, looked up and gave Noc a courteous smile. "How will you be paying?"

Noc let my hand go to pull a billfold out of the back pocket of his jeans, and I watched all that happened next with fascination.

I stopped watching when Noc shoved the billfold back in his jeans, took a tiny envelope from the man and grunted, "Thanks," when the man invited us to "Call should you need anything and enjoy your stay."

Then I again had my hand in Noc's and he was towing me toward a wall that had four shining-gold double doors (that couldn't be real gold, surely), all inexplicably situated close together.

He stopped me near them, reached out and depressed a button in the wall between the doors.

I watched him do this.

I stopped watching when that hand came right to my face, cupped my jaw and forced it back so I was looking up at him.

My, but he was handsome.

"We're about to get in an elevator, baby," he declared.

I had no idea what that meant.

I also did not care one whit what that meant.

I only cared about the heat in his beautiful eyes.

"We'll walk into a little box, you'll feel it move. It takes you up and down automatically so you don't have to use stairs. We'll be going up," he explained then asked, "You get that?"

It occurred to me vaguely that with the variety of things he shared that they had in that world—motorcycles, automobiles, these...*elevators*—much of it doing things "automatically," that there might be a reason Noc ran around the Winter Palace frequently to "keep fit."

If one didn't even have to climb stairs in this world, such inactivity could make one quite unhealthy.

This thought, vague as it was, flew from my head as a *bing* was heard and I looked in that direction.

A set of the golden doors was sliding open in a way that made me stare in shock, but I had no time to recover. Noc's hand left my face, grabbed mine, and he pulled me to them, through them, and we were as he said, in a little box.

And that box was really quite little. I'd been in privies that were larger.

Not to mention, Noc told me it was going to move.

Upward.

Taking us with it!

I felt a frisson of panic gather at the small of my back and my eyes shot to Noc's.

"Noc, I'm uncertain—"

My attention shifted instantly to the doors as they slid closed.

My heart bolted up to my throat and my body locked.

Then my back hit the wall of the box, Noc's body pressing it there, and both his hands were at my jaw tipping it up.

Before I could draw in a breath, his mouth crashed down on mine, his tongue slid inside and the panic disappeared.

There was no box.

There was no world.

There was only Noc, his touch, his taste...*him.*

He kissed me even as I felt my belly fall (and it wasn't only because of his kiss).

He kept kissing me even as I heard the soft *whoosh* noise of the doors opening.

He stopped kissing me to grab my hand and pull me down a carpeted hallway that was wide and elegant and exceptionally brightly lit.

I was breathing with difficulty, trying to focus on walking without falling, something that was not easy considering my focus wanted to be on the tingling occurring at my lips, along my skin, and between my legs.

He stopped us at a door, pulled the tiny envelope the man gave him out of his front pocket and opened it. He then took a flat, rectangular doodad from it, touched it to a space above the door handle, and I blinked in surprise as I heard a whirring noise at the same time a section at the top of the area Noc touched with the doodad lit green.

"My word," I whispered, staring at the green light.

How could Noc say this world had no magic?

It seemed to be everywhere!

Noc opened the door, pulled me inside and stopped us both.

He touched something on the wall and the space we were in illuminated.

Just.

Like.

That!

And there was more magic!

"My *word,*" I breathed.

He took a placard that was hanging from the back door handle and suspended it from the front, pushed the door closed, flicked a metal doohickey at the jamb that looked like a rather clever door latch that could not be opened from the outside (an excellent safety feature in this, what appeared to be, large public inn), and then he caught my hand again.

Before I could take in where I was and all that had happened, I was standing at the foot of a large bed, my back to it, Noc standing in front of me.

I looked up at him.

"Noc—"

"Shut up, baby."

I blinked up at him.

He twisted at the waist, and with a flick of his fingers, he flung the doodad across to a bureau behind him. It landed on the top, but even before it did, he'd twisted back to me.

"Noc—"

He lifted his hands to my jaw again and I quieted.

"Missed you," he said softly.

I stared into his eyes.

He did.

It was written right there, right there for me to see.

With a wide variety of other things.

All of which I loved.

"And I you," I replied.

"Done missin' you, and really fuckin' glad I am," he stated.

Still staring deep into his eyes, I did nothing but nod.

I was done too and I was very, *very* glad I was.

"Yeah," he muttered like I spoke my words aloud, his gaze falling to my mouth.

"Noc." I said his name with a different purpose this time, swaying toward him.

"Shoulda known that mouth would be sweet," he murmured.

I had the feeling Noc needed to take hold of me somewhere other than my jaw, for if he kept speaking words like that while gazing at my mouth, my legs were going to give way.

He dipped his head so I could feel his breath caress my lips.

"But in all the time I spent wondering how sweet it would be, never in my wildest dreams would I imagine it's as sweet as it is."

Yes.

He needed to hold me elsewhere or I'd crumple at his feet.

"Noc," I whispered yet again.

He didn't kiss me as I expected him to do.

Wanted him to do.

No.

His hands went from my jaw to my bottom, his fingers clenched in, and I gasped when I was lifted up.

With no choice, my legs curled around his hips, and in no time he'd entered the bed on his knees and placed me on it.

He then placed *him* on *me*.

It was *then* he kissed me.

And it was then something happened that had never happened to me.

I had exceptional skills at making love. I'd made a practice of it to the point I'd made an art of it. My approach to it was considered, deliberate, unhurried. A climax was not an occasion to rush to but a sensation to shape and manipulate, and when reached, to revel in...*languidly*.

Noc did not make love like this.

Further, Noc did not do what I selected lovers in the past exclusively to do.

This being allow me to lead the festivities.

Noc took over.

He also was not considered, deliberate, unhurried.

He kissed deeply, demanding much in return in a way it was impossible not to give it to him, *desire* to give it to him, have that become the entire reason for your existence. He did this with his mouth, his tongue, his teeth and his hands.

Those roamed everywhere, as if he'd been starved of human touch the entirety of his life and he was making up for that in a matter of seconds.

I couldn't keep up. I couldn't slow him down.

And I didn't want to.

His taste, his touch, everything he was doing was drawing out extraordinary sensations I couldn't control.

Beauty beyond imagining.

In an instant I needed more.

In the next instant, I *craved* it.

Without warning, he tore his mouth from mine and pushed up to his knees between my legs in the bed.

I stared up at him, finding myself panting, my body singing, watching the beauty of his face now carved with passion, but noting his hands had lifted to unbutton his shirt.

I took that as a cue to release my belt.

I did so, the heavy metal slid to the sides, and without its fastener, the soft material of the dress parted, exposing the undergarments Valentine had given me.

They were, incidentally, the only part about my attire (at the time) that I liked unreservedly.

Cream lace so delicate, it was a miracle of construction. Shiny, soft satin that was a marvel at the seat and along the gusset (but not at the front, that was lace) of my panties as well as at the bottom of the cups of my brassiere.

They were divine.

One look at Noc's face told me he felt the same way.

"Goddamned *fuck*," Noc growled with such ferocity, I stilled.

And if what we'd done before was *not* unhurried, deliberate, considered, I was about to learn the meaning of lovemaking entirely void of these concepts.

And enjoy every fiery second.

He tore the shirt from his shoulders, tossed it aside, and in a blur of movement I felt his arm drive under me, pulling up at the middle of my back.

I cried out in surprise at the unexpected arch but my next cry was much different when Noc used his other hand to drag down the lacy material of the cup of the brassiere. Then Noc's mouth was fastened to my nipple, drawing in.

Harsh.

Strong.

The force of the pull tore from nipple to clitoris, buzzing there with such intensity, I had no thought. I felt the beads he'd given me glide up and rest lightly at my throat but the extreme sensitivity of my skin made them feel like I was held there by a caressing hand.

I moved instinctively, the fingers of one hand into his hair to grasp him there, the other one dragging my nails down his back.

At this touch, Noc released my nipple, his lips speeding up my chest, my neck, over my chin to my mouth, my back still arched at his arm's command, his lips now to mine, his eyes molten.

One look in them and my body became the same way.

"Every inch of you, fucking gorgeous," he ground out. "Saw it. Knew it. But now it's goddamned *mine*."

Those words drove right up to my womb.

He didn't allow me to reply.

He kissed me. His hands roamed all over me. He ended the kiss but only for his mouth to move to my other nipple and he dragged it in, drawing deeper, forcing me to arch myself as the hunger for any touch from him took over, feeding on itself more and more the more Noc gave.

I touched him too, the silk of his skin over the hard of his muscle. I attempted to get my mouth on him. I tasted his neck. His shoulder.

But I couldn't seem to concentrate. Control my body's movements. Focus on what I could do that might bring Noc pleasure.

I just touched, nipped, kissed, licked, dragged, clawed—wherever I could reach, however I could find purchase.

Everything I took, everything Noc gave drove me deeper and deeper into the abandon, deeper and deeper into the oblivion where nothing existed.

Nothing but Noc and me.

A puff of breath shot from my lips as he readjusted his body so he could tear my panties down my legs but he immediately resumed his position between them. Having caught one of my ankles in his hand, he put his lips to it and dragged them down the inside of my calf, my thigh, all the way to the heart of me.

I watched, holding my breath, quivering, dripping with wet between my legs, my nipples hard stones tormented by the very air touching them, thinking I'd never witnessed anything as beautiful as Noc putting his mouth to me like that.

He kissed me above the triangle of hair between my legs and then lifted his eyes to mine.

"Need to be inside you, baby."

Thank the Goddess Adele.

"I think I may need that more," I pushed out, nowhere near the position of being embarrassed that I admitted that need out loud, but even if I didn't, my voice betrayed it.

His sultry face grew even more sultry as he pushed up to his knees again, reaching behind him.

It caused me some confusion when he again pulled out his billfold.

I lost this confusion when I watched, fixated, as he unearthed something from it and held the square packet between his teeth.

I did this fixatedly because he was then unbuckling his belt, unfastening his trousers and pushing them down his hips.

All that had gone before was hurried, even desperate.

But it seemed his movements now were taking years.

His cock bounded free and my lips parted.

The length, more than average, though not ridiculously so.

The girth...

My.

Suddenly my mouth started watering.

"Noc," I whispered urgently.

"Two seconds, Frannie."

He rolled the sheath he'd unearthed from an unusual wrapper on his thick shaft.

Watching this, I started squirming.

"*Noc,*" I demanded.

He covered me.

But he did not enter me.

I continued squirming, wrapping a leg around his hip, an arm around his waist, diving my fingers into his hair, all while looking in his eyes.

"You need—" I started.

I did not go on when he framed one side of my face with his hand.

I stopped squirming when his other hand found mine, his fingers laced with my own, and he pressed the back of my hand into the bed, bearing his weight into it.

"Other leg around me, sweetheart," he whispered.

I did as told, staring into his eyes.

"Guide me," he commanded quietly.

I didn't ask what he meant.

I knew.

And I did that too, instantly drawing my arm from around his waist to push my hand between us and wrap it around his beautiful shaft.

I felt and heard his breath leave him in a gust at my touch, saw the flare in his eyes, and I rubbed the tip of him through my wetness, doing this for him and for me.

"Fuck, you feel good," he murmured, his teeth gritted.

"You do too," I panted, catching my breath as I stroked the tip of him over my clitoris and then I took him down.

The moment he was there, his hips pressed in.

I drew my hand away, circling his waist with my arm again.

But he didn't invade. I had nary an inch of him and there was much more than that.

"Darling," I whispered.

"Look at me," he demanded.

"I am, my dearest."

"Don't stop lookin' at me."

"I won't," I promised.

Slowly, his eyes holding mine captive the entire time, Noc slid inside.

Gods, the beauty Noc gave me. So much.

And now so much *more*.

It took great effort not to close my eyes at the glory of him, arch my neck, center everything on the magnificence of the feeling of him filling me, connecting with me.

Noc and I becoming one.

Instead, I watched the beauty *he* felt as he seated himself inside me, and I hoped I gave him the same, and more.

His thumb swept my lips and the fingers of his other hand laced in mine squeezed.

"Gonna take you now, baby."

I nodded.

"Don't stop lookin' at me," he ordered.

"I won't," I vowed.

He moved—out, then in.

I bit my lip and stared into his eyes.

His mouth trailing the inside of my leg had been the most beautiful vision I'd beheld.

Until now.

He moved again, out...in.

"Noc," I whispered.

"Faster?" he asked.

"Please."

He gave me what I wished.

And again. And again.

Faster. Faster.

More. And more.

Deeper. Harder. His gaze holding mine. His breath escalating with my own. His body driving, mine jarring. His hand clenching in mine. The fingers of his other moving back, tangling in my hair to curl against my scalp. My legs circling his hips tighter, the heels of my shoes spiking into his thighs.

All of a sudden, his nose touched mine and his tone was low and fierce when he gritted, "Fuck, *fuck*, you're so goddamned beautiful."

"You are too," I gasped.

Out and in. Out and in. Eyes locked. Fingers clutched. Legs wound. Out and in.

"Every inch of you," he grunted.

My fingers convulsed around his.

Something else convulsed as well, repeatedly, and my legs got tighter.

His deep groan sounded against my lips and radiated *everywhere*.

Too good.

I was at my end.

"Darling, I'm—"

"Hold on, baby, look in my eyes."

My entire body tightened. The sensations overwhelming, I watched a muscle dance up his cheek in reaction to feeling it at our intimate connection, and his eyes fired further.

I couldn't do as he asked.

"*Noc*," I cried urgently.

"With me, sweetheart. Come with me."

Wishing to give him what he wanted, I drew in deep breaths, arching into him, my hips undulating to meet his thrusts, the nails of my hand at his back pressing in and clawing, all in the attempt to give, to take...and to hold on.

"Darling," I begged.

"Look in my eyes."

"*Darling*," I pleaded.

"Don't lose my eyes, Frannie."

I was going to fly apart.

"I must," I implored.

"Let go," he grunted.

And only then did I lose Noc's gaze because I came apart.

The explosion was life changing. Obliterating everything I was in burst after burst of sheer pleasure, leaving nothing but the me I was with Noc. The me I was connected to Noc. The me I was with his fingers laced in mine, his body still thrusting into mine, driving me into the bed, the mighty noises of his simultaneous orgasm blazing along every inch of me.

I found I'd lifted my head and was whimpering into his neck through my climax, then panting into it as I kept hold on him exactly as I was as he continued pounding into me, his grunts no less potent, only drawing my nails from his flesh to soothe with my hand where they'd grazed the small of his back.

I was settling into my afterglow but Noc was still thrusting and grunting, music to my ears, when a tug on my hair told me I needed to lower my head.

I did so and I barely got it to the pillow before Noc's mouth was on mine.

Only when he'd begun to drink from me did he slide inside and cease moving.

I continued to hold him tight.

He broke the kiss, shifted and buried his face in my neck.

And I held him tight.

I stared at the ceiling, feeling Noc's warmth, his weight, smelling the spice of his skin, glorying in the stretch of his cock embedded deep inside me, allowing my breath to even as I felt his breath do the same.

I didn't know what came over me, but the moment he started nuzzling my neck with his mouth, his hand clenched in mine relaxed only so his thumb could caress the apple of my palm, I blurted, "Does this mean I won't get pizza?"

Noc stilled completely.

I did the same beneath him.

Now, whyever did I ask that?

Why?

He lifted up and looked down at me.

I opened my mouth to say something, anything, willing to cast a spell to take us to the beauty of what we were sharing but seconds ago and not the awkwardness and stupidity of what I'd just said.

I didn't have to do that.

Noc was my Noc.

My savior. My friend.

Now...my lover.

He just gave.

In other words, we'd shared beauty but seconds ago.

And he gave me more.

He did this as he burst out laughing and he did not come close to getting it under control before he was kissing me, laughing into my mouth.

Bar none, it was the most beautiful moment of my life.

Bar...

None.

Even the climax he'd just given me at the same moment he'd shared his own.

So, of course, I kissed him back.

Fervently.

Alas, he eventually had to lift his head so we both could breathe, but I was delighted to see he was still smiling broadly when he did.

"They deliver," he declared.

"Pardon?" I asked.

"Pizza places. They deliver. So the answer is yes. You're gonna get your pizza. Though I'm not gonna get you drunk after that because you're gonna eat, I'm gonna eat, then we're gonna fuck until we can't keep our eyes open anymore. Then we're gonna sleep. We'll wake up. We'll fuck again. And then I'll take you home but only so you can change clothes so I can take you to Café du Monde to get beignets."

"You've used this word often, my dearest, but I'm afraid I don't understand how you're using the word 'fuck' now."

He flexed his hips into mine, his semi-hard shaft made its presence known (not that I forgot it was there), and he did this dipping his face so the tip of his nose touched mine.

"*Fuck*, baby. We're gonna fuck. And we're gonna do it a lot."

"You mean," I whispered, "make love?"

"We'll do that too."

I blinked.

"I don't—" I started to tell him I didn't understand, but he interrupted me by lifting up, pulling out as he did so, but also moving me at the same time that in the end he was sitting on the side of the bed and I was straddling his lap.

"Pizza first," he announced. "While we wait for it, I'll explain fucking versus making love. Though, I might not explain it," he gave me a grin I'd never seen before, one I felt tighten my nipples, "I might demonstrate. Then we'll do both until I wear you out. We got a plan?"

Until he wore me out?

I felt goose pimples raise all over my skin.

"I, uh...well..."

How did one answer that question?

I decided on, "I suppose so."

The arm he had around my waist dropped, he lifted the skirt of the open dress I still wore and cupped one cheek of my bare behind.

"You got something else you wanna do?" he murmured, his eyes on my mouth.

I was in an entirely different universe. There were likely billions of things we could do.

"No," I answered immediately.

His gaze found mine.

"Then we got a plan," he stated.

"Yes, Noc," I replied. "We have a plan."

He grinned before he surged up and set me on my feet.

And promptly, he pulled his jeans over his arse, bent and kissed the tip of my nose as he yanked the edges of my dress together (a fruitless endeavor, the belt was in the bed) and then he set about putting that plan into action.

14
TEN TIMES

Franka

After Noc gave me a dressing gown to put on that the inn supplied (an unusual but lovely amenity), sat me down at the side of the bed and took off my shoes (a tenderness I would not soon forget), he divested me of the beads he'd bestowed on me and guided me to the small room attached to our chamber.

I stood in it with him blinking my eyes against the unnatural brightness.

"Right, basics," Noc declared, and he sounded like he was about to impart something important, so I attempted to focus on him through the glare.

He was moving to the only chair in the space, and it didn't look comfortable.

"Toilet," he stated. "Self-explanatory," he went on.

This was not true.

Until he lifted the lid.

By the gods.

It was a commode.

"Do your thing, use that." He pointed to something that looked like rolled tissue fastened to the wall. "When you're done, hit this," he finished and depressed a lever.

Water noises filled the room and I stared in astonishment as the water in the bowl disappeared while other water whooshed around the sides, undoubtedly making it so anything that was deposited in said bowl vanished without a trace.

Pure brilliance!

"Extraordinary," I breathed, watching the water swirl.

There was a grin in Noc's voice as he grabbed me about the back of my neck, yanked me into his side and continued, saying, "Sink," while taking us to the basin. "Hot, cold," he stated, twisting knobs that made water flow rather forcefully into the basin *without pumping*.

"By the gods," I whispered, unable to tear my eyes away from this glorious spectacle.

"Left's always hot," he carried on, turning off the left knob.

Always...*hot*?

But how? I saw no fire.

I didn't get the chance to ask, Noc kept speaking.

"But it doesn't come out that way at first. That said, Frannie, be careful because hot sometimes can get *hot*. Right's always cold."

I raised what I knew were rounded eyes to him.

He looked into them, burst out laughing and turned me fully into him, wrapping both his arms around me.

He then dropped his face so it was close to mine, stopped laughing but continued smiling, his eyes dancing, and he said, "You look like that over a sink and toilet, beautiful, the next couple of weeks are gonna be a goddamned *blast*."

If the little I'd already experienced was any indication, he was far from wrong.

But I wasn't thinking about the commode and basin (or not entirely about them).

"Indeed," I replied, staring right in his eyes.

He continued smiling as he said, "Now, I gotta go out for a bit. I didn't expect our reunion to go that way and didn't come prepared. Need to pick up some condoms. Also gonna grab some cold beer. I'll order the pizza, leave some money in case they deliver it before I get back, take off and do that. Fast as I can, I'll be back. But I'll show you how to work the TV before I go so you have something to do."

I didn't want him to go.

Though I could use a cold beverage.

"What are condoms?" I asked.

"Protection." At my blank look, he explained further. "What I put on so I could have you and not give us both somethin' we don't want right now."

His answer didn't exactly make sense until it dawned on me.

"Oh, the *sheath*," I said.

He nodded, pulling his face from mine slightly, but he was still smiling. "Yeah. The *sheath*. I need to go get more of those."

He certainly did.

"I approve of your plan," I shared.

His smile got bigger and his hold on me got tighter.

"Take you with me but seems you haven't quite bested the challenge of walking on heels."

His words confused me.

"I've been walking on my heels for decades now, Noc, as anyone who can ambulate does. It's walking on spikes that's a challenge."

"You're right," he said through a low chuckle, then dropped down again but only to touch his mouth to mine before he guided me out of the small chamber. He did this saying, "Now, the TV."

He then introduced me to the TV.

And it was *extraordinary*.

~

I HEARD the door open and the only move I made from my highly inelegant position of sitting cross-legged on the bed (something Josette was prone to do during our breakfasts, something I belatedly realized was quite comfortable) was leaning forward to watch Noc walk down the short hall.

"Darling, you cannot imagine what's happening on this screen," I stated, flinging an arm out in disgust toward the television, an apparatus I'd been "channel surfing" (Noc's term of what he'd taught me to do) since he left.

He walked into the chamber, his eyes taking me in before he shifted them to the television while setting a number of bottles in a rather ingenious carrier on the bureau and tossing a rustling scrap of something with it.

"You're watching *Chopped*?" he asked the television.

"I am indeed," I affirmed before I declared, "And it...is...*outrageous*. It's clear these chefs are highly trained and dedicated to their craft. Why that bespectacled man would pit them against each other, giving them no time at all to create culinary masterpieces but expect *just that*, I do *not* know. Then those three awful people sit in judgment of the dishes the chefs create, knowing the limitations they worked under, even *watching the process*, and still being unforgivably rude after they were gifted with the opportunity of tasting the results. I understand the challenge of giving the chefs odd ingredients to work with. But the rest is beyond me. It seems senseless, and at times it's cruel."

"TV programs where talented people are pitted against each other and then rude people judge them is a big thing in this world, sugarlips. Cooking. Singing. Dancing. Even falling in love is television sport."

At this statement, my brows drew up and I turned my attention from the screen to him, asking, "Falling in love?"

He nodded, but did it saying, "Though, I don't watch those."

"That's absurd," I declared. "People *wish* to watch this drivel?"

He came toward me, mouth quirking. "Babe, I totally dig this program. I even DVR it. Never miss an episode."

I couldn't believe it (not the part about DVR, I had no idea what that meant). The concept of Noc enjoying this form of entertainment. He didn't have an ounce of rudeness in him.

"Truly?" I asked.

"Yup," he answered, right before he lunged and I found myself hauled up the bed.

No longer sitting inelegantly, or at all, I ended Noc's maneuver on my back with Noc on me.

And I couldn't see the TV.

"No pizza?" he asked softly.

"No," I answered breathily. "They've yet to arrive."

His eyes dropped to my mouth. "Right, then we're makin' out until it comes."

I had no idea what that meant.

What I did know was that on the program the appetizer round was over and they were getting into entrées.

"Noc, I'm rather hoping the female chef will beat out the males and they're just starting the entrée round."

He looked back to my eyes. "Frannie, making out means kissing, hot and heavy, with groping, and a lot of it."

"Oh," I whispered and made an instant decision. "I'm sure the female will triumph. Instead of watching her emerge victorious, let's do that."

Noc grinned at me again while his head descended.

Then we did that.

"So?" Noc asked.

"What?" It came out garbled as my mouth was full.

It was bad-mannered.

I simply didn't care.

Pizza was *sublime*.

He tipped his head to the magnificence I was shoving in my mouth. "You like it?"

"It's quite good," I replied, still chewing, but even so, I took another huge bite of the scrumptious doughy, spicy, cheesy miracle in my hand.

"Quite good," he muttered, shaking his head and reaching toward the box on the bed between us.

At his alarming movements, I darted out a hand and grabbed his wrist.

Swallowing, I cried, "Noc, that's the last of it!"

He looked up at me. "Yeah. And you hoovered through your half. That slice is the last of my half."

This was unfortunate because it was true.

Fair was fair, and apparently, along with generous, outgoing and social, the Franka I was seemed to be fair.

This meant I let him go, requesting, "Can we order another?"

At this, Noc's eyes grew big. "Frannie, this one was a large. Usually, three, four people eat this amount."

I stared down at the sad, now empty box before again turning my attention to Noc.

"Can we have more tomorrow?"

He grinned at me, reached out, hooked me behind the neck (again, something he seemed fond of doing, something I was fond of him doing) and pulled me to him for a peck on the lips before he let me go.

And promptly denied me.

"We're havin' étouffée for dinner tomorrow."

"I want this," I announced, lifting up the remains of my slice.

Amusement unhidden, he stated, "Trust me. You have étouffée, you'll want that."

I had no choice but to trust him. He had this world's coin. I did not. I couldn't pay for my own pizza even if I figured out how to order it as he'd done this one.

On this thought, I shared, "I want my next lesson to be about the telephone. And along with that, the ordering of food."

Noc chewed, swallowed, crinkled his eyes at me with his humor and said, "After beignets, first order of business is gettin' you and Josette your own cells. So tomorrow, we'll get on that."

"Thank you," I murmured, taking one of the last bites of my pizza. Deciding to turn my mind from the dismal fact there may be only two bites left, I looked to Noc and queried, "How many sheaths did you procure?"

"Box of ten."

I blinked.

Rapidly.

And my voice was pitched higher when I inquired, "Can you perform that often in one night?"

Noc's body moved, the bed moved with it, and I recognized the laughter as his voice vibrated when he replied, "They come in boxes of ten, sweetheart."

I sounded somewhat strangled when I pressed, "That doesn't answer the question, my dearest."

"How the fuck you can make 'my dearest' sweet and hot, I do not know," Noc muttered.

"Noc!" I snapped, beginning to panic, for I was a skilled lover, but the way Noc made love I was relatively certain *I* couldn't perform ten times in one night.

His eyes glinted as he asked, "You not up for ten times?"

Was he jesting?

He had to be jesting.

"I, well...that would...that is, I've never—"

I stopped speaking (or, blast it all, *stammering*) when Noc reached out, took the last of my pizza from my hand and tossed it into the box.

I glared at it, turned my glare to him, but the remains of his pizza had joined it and he was shoving the box off the bed.

This accomplished, before I could protest his cavalier treatment of our pizza, he pulled me into his arms and rolled me over him so I was again on my back and he was on me.

"No, baby," he admitted quietly, "I can't perform ten times in one night."

"Oh," I said quietly in return, not certain if I should be relieved or disappointed. Just knowing a certain area in my body probably would not stand up to that challenge, even if I wanted it to.

He swept his mouth against mine.

"But you're gonna come ten times in one night," he declared.

My breath caught.

"One down," he whispered, his hands beginning to move on me, "Nine to go."

"No—"

I didn't finish saying his name.

Noc kissed me.

~

"I WANT YOU INSIDE ME," I begged.

Noc, naked on his knees behind me, me naked on my knees in front of him, his arms around me, one hand at my breast doing delicious things, one hand between my legs doing *scrumptious* things, his mouth at my neck suckling, nipping, kissing, he slid it to my ear and nibbled my earlobe.

Oh my.

I made my position clear.

"*Please*," I gasped, hips grinding into his hand, feeling his hardness press into my bottom, wanting that for my own.

"Next go," he whispered into my ear.

I almost didn't hear him. My climax was gathering powerfully, preparing to overwhelm me.

"Noc, *hurry*, take me. I'm about—"

His finger at my clitoris circled faster and harder.

"Come, Frannie," he growled in my ear.

He didn't have to make the demand. At the workings of his finger I acquiesced, my head flying back and colliding with his shoulder, my body trembling violently in his hold, my hands shooting to his to grasp them in order to stop their machinations because I was learning there was such a thing as too much pleasure. I was experiencing it at that very moment, and it was going to devour me.

At my climax's end, tenderly, Noc lay me on my back, covered me with his big, warm body, his hands trailing soothingly along my skin, his mouth again at my neck.

When I had control of my breath, I put my hands on him, loving how he felt, his warmth, the power at my fingertips that was a part of Noc and yet seemed a contradiction with all his understanding, thoughtful, humorous, teasing gentleness.

It was on this thought his hand traveled over my hip and in.

I drew in a sharp breath and turned my head just as Noc lifted his so our mouths were nearly touching.

"Two," he murmured, and I shuddered under him at that word, what it meant *and* his fingers trailing through my most intimate part. "So wet," he whispered, "can't wait to taste that for three."

"You," was all I had in me to reply.

"Later."

"Noc—"

He kissed me. He used his tongue. It was magnificent.

But it was too short.

"Later," he repeated against my lips, and before I could utter a word, his lips moved down my body.

Noc eventually tasted me.

He took his time. He demonstrated extraordinary skill.

And in the end, I got three.

~

We were naked and abed, Noc on his back, head and shoulders up on stacked pillows, me cuddled into his side.

The room was dark, lit only by the misty blue sparking up from Noc's bare chest.

I had his hand in mine and was guiding his big palm under the sparks.

Together, we lifted them up and I turned his hand with my own, circling the shimmers until they formed a ball.

Willing that ball to do as I wished, I pulled my hand away and said softly, "All yours, darling."

Noc continued circling it, replying, "What do I do with it?"

I looked at his face and experienced something profound, seeing its handsomeness lit by the beautiful blue of my magic.

At the sight, I felt my body melt more deeply into his side as I replied, "It's just a plaything. It has no power to harm. Toy with it. Or you can disperse it by drawing your hand through it. You can set it on the night table to return to later. Or, throw it across the room, and if you do that, it'll travel back to you as it's yours. I gave it to you."

Lazily, he drew his hand back, the ball followed, and he tossed it across the room, the blue-arced streak it made, utterly gorgeous (if I did say so myself).

It flew nearly to the wall before it stopped and slowly made its way back.

When Noc took it, he circled his hand around it several times before he curled his fingers into a fist, only his forefinger out, and he twirled the ball on his finger. Eventually, he reopened his hand, drew his fingers through it and it disappeared, leaving us in darkness.

Without delay, he turned into me, gathering me in his arms.

"You know you're the shit?" he asked, his deep voice deeper with obvious pride.

I knew he thought that.

I adored that he thought that.

And I *loved* that tone in his voice.

"I've done quite well, Valentine says," I shared softly. "Though now she says she's nothing more to teach me except, how she phrases it, 'in the field.' This means I need practical experience to advance further. And I'll tell you, Noc," I went on, cuddling even closer, "I'm quite excited. It's fascinating, magic, learning to wield it, understanding my power, how to use it, how not to abuse it. Although I missed you gravely while we were parted, Valentine showing me what's inside me and all I'm capable of doing...I'll never forget our times together and be forever grateful for all she's done for me."

"You missed me gravely?"

I stared at him through the dark and stiffened.

He pulled me closer. "Babe, before you freak you let that out, you gotta know already I missed you gravely too."

His words meant much to me and from the moment we were reunited he had not hidden that they were true.

Even so, for the first time since I came to his world, reality intruded and I wondered at the wisdom of this impetuous shift in our relations.

Outside Josette, Noc was my truest friend.

Indeed, the only other friend I had in my world, Frey's mother, Valeria, I didn't even explain that I was leaving so it went without saying I didn't bid her farewell.

That said, the last I'd heard from her (some months prior), Frey's father had officially severed ties with her—meaning ending their marriage—not an unwelcome happenstance for Valeria.

She was currently residing with her longtime paramour, an almost grotesquely wealthy merchant, who was still just a merchant.

Obviously, the old Franka would think that, but I was right then lying abed with a naked city watchman who had treasure, this was true (he'd told me he accepted a reward for his part in ending Minerva's plot), but no House and no title, and I did not care a whit. Therefore, I no longer cared if Valeria's love was a lord, a merchant or a laborer.

Valeria, however, struggled with his lack of position. Until she had no choice but to accept it once her husband finished with her.

My friend of the other world was one to be very present when things in her life were not going well, in order to have someone with whom to complain about them.

In the rare occasions she was happy (prior to becoming the kept woman of a wealthy merchant), she'd all but disappear.

Thus, I knew she was deliriously happy. So much so, I barely heard from her, such was her contentment.

This did not negate the fact that I cared about her, she cared about me, and I'd left our entire world behind, with her in it, without even a goodbye.

What kind of friend was I, doing that to Valeria?

And what kind of friend was I, jumping into bed with Noc without thinking of the repercussions that might have?

"Frannie?" Noc called my attention back to him.

My stiff body stiffened further. "Perhaps we should—"

He interrupted me. "No. We shouldn't."

His penchant for interruption was beginning to peeve me.

"You keep interrupting me and I'm not fond of it," I shared irritably.

"You haven't complained before now," he replied. "And that's probably because it led to things like me going down on you and you had no problem with that. Now you got somethin' to say that I can feel by your change in mood doesn't need to be said, not right now, but for some reason you feel like fuckin' this up, and I'm not gonna let you. But you're not used to not getting what you want so suddenly you're 'not fond of it.'"

First things first.

"Going down on me?" I queried.

"Makin' you come with my mouth," he explained.

Well, that certainly was *going down*, for Noc's part. He just was so good at it, it made me fly high.

"That's explained," I went on then carried on. "Now I'll note if I have something to say, I'd like to be able to say it. And truthfully, I can't believe I even have to make the request."

"Not if you're fuckin' shit up," he returned.

"I'm not 'fuckin' shit up,'" I retorted.

He rolled into me so I had some of his weight at my hips, his long legs tangling in mine, and he lifted up on a bent elbow so he wasn't looming over me but he did have the dominant position.

This, my guess, though I wouldn't ever know for certain, was a ploy often used by Frey, Lahn and Tor when their wives were doing something which they had every intention of containing, and such an occurrence happened in bed.

This, I also found irritating, at the same time I found it titillating.

And that was even more irritating.

Blast!

"You wanna talk about this." He pressed his hips into mine. "Us. Where we are. What we did. How it came about. And you wanna do it because you're freaked, thinkin' it happened too fast or it was the wrong direction for us to go, or whatever the fuck."

I didn't get the opportunity to confirm this was exactly what I wanted to do, he continued speaking.

"It didn't happen too fast, Frannie, it took too fuckin' long, in my opinion. And it wasn't the wrong direction. At least for me, I'm right where I wanted to be since practically the minute we met. You were in a bad place. I had to see to you. I did that. That's done. You're not in that place anymore so we're moving on and this," he again pressed his hips into mine, "is the direction we're moving in."

In truth, his "it took too fuckin' long, in my opinion" made me want to jump from the bed, shout with glee and perhaps dance a little jig.

Not to mention all the other delightful things he said (practically the minute we met!).

I was a much-changed Franka Drakkar.

But I was not *that* changed.

Therefore, instead of jumping from the bed, I asked crossly, "And I have no say about that?"

He was silent a moment before I could feel the tremor of his amusement shaking his body as he reminded me, "Frannie, baby, I've made you come three times, you're lying naked pressed to me and think I permanently got indentations in the backs of my thighs from the spikes on your heels. And before you latch on to that," he said the last swiftly, "that is not a complaint, nowhere near. Your heels could scar me, which they didn't, and taking that memory with me wherever I go would be fine with me. But you did not fight any of that, and, just pointing out, you *still* aren't. With all that, you wanna make a case you're not good with this direction?"

This was all true (though I was concerned about the indentations, Noc clearly didn't mind, but those spikes appeared lethal, I hoped I caused no lasting damage).

And I absolutely did *not* want to make a case that I was not good with this direction.

I didn't admit that.

I stated, "I'm not pressed to you. You're pressed to me."

"Fair enough," he granted. "Three minutes ago, though, babe, you were pressed to me."

This, too, was true.

I snapped my mouth shut and fought grinding my teeth.

I saw his shadowed face get closer and I could see the white of his teeth.

Hmm.

How could I forget how bloody *annoying* Noc could be?

"So, to be clear, the direction you wish to go is that we have relations?" I asked.

More trembling of his body (and voice) as he replied, "Yeah, sweetheart, I wanna have relations."

"And what of tomorrow and the next day?" I pressed, pushing back the hope and pulling up the haughty.

"I'll amend. We've had relations. Tonight, we're gonna have more relations.

And after we leave this room and get along with our lives, we'll *continue* to have relations, repeatedly and often."

This was most promising.

In order to confirm, I stated, "To end, you wish our direction to be about you being open to have sex with me."

Unexpectedly, his mirth swept through the room with such speed, I froze against him in reaction to the change.

"You really asking me that shit?" he demanded, his voice low and there was a tremor to it, but it certainly was not humor.

It was anger.

Noc had never been angry at me.

Not once.

I didn't like it. Not at all.

I was concerned about the wisdom of my response, but the veracity of it couldn't be denied as I'd already "asked him that shit."

"Well...yes," I said hesitantly.

"You think all I want is your pussy?"

I wasn't certain I'd heard him correctly.

"I beg your pardon?"

"You think all I want is your pussy."

The first was uttered as a statement that was also an incredulous question.

The second was uttered just as a statement.

An insulting one.

I lost my concern at his anger and got that way myself.

"Well, I should hope not," I snapped, pulling out from under him, undecided about what to do once I was free of him, though focused on doing just that.

However I was with Noc. He was a man. A dominant one. A strong one.

Not to mention, he already had his arm around me.

It being thus, he simply used it to drag me right back where I was.

"I need to use the commode," I lied.

"You so do not," he returned.

"You're correct. I *don't* need to use the commode. I need a moment away from you for I'm angry at you and my temper is formidable. It being so, I've found it best, if I can't use it to an advantage, to absent myself when it flares."

"Franka, to make things clear, just in case the impossible is happening and you're missing any of this, what I want from you is not just sex. It's anything you got to give to me. Including your formidable temper. So, babe, if you got somethin' to say, say it. And if you don't mind, it'd be cool you started with telling me why *you're* pissed when you just said straight out that you thought all I wanted from you was being open to fuck you."

By the gods!

How on earth could he think that's what I said?

"I did not say any such thing," I rejoined.

"You did."

"I did not."

"I got a good memory, but I don't need it seein' as it wasn't even two minutes ago you said, 'you wish our direction to be about you being open to have sex with me.' Are you denying that now?" he asked.

"Of course not," I answered.

Noc pulled slightly away, the temperature in the room decreased and that chill frosted his words as he commanded, "So again, explain to me how it is you're pissed when you just said all I'm angling for is your pussy, which means you think that's all I've *been* angling for when it comes to you."

Bloody hell!

He'd lost his mind!

"I did not say that, Noc," I snapped.

He pulled away further and his voice started rising when he returned, "You fuckin' did, Franka, and you just fuckin' *confirmed* you did."

My voice was rising too. "I did not, Noctorno!"

"Do not call me that," he gritted between his teeth.

"Do not claim I mean ridiculous, offensive things when I don't," I retorted.

"Then tell me what you meant," he ordered.

"You're fond of me," I bit out.

"Yeah," he bit back.

"You missed me when we were apart."

"Uh...*yeah*, been over that. What's this—?"

I interrupted him. "And you're very aware I felt the same for you with both. So, my assumption, indeed my *hope* would be that what we had would remain. Being fond of each other. Enjoying each other's company and therefore spending a goodly amount of time in it. But our direction...*now*...is *the addition* that you wish to be open to have sex with me."

He had no reply to that.

This was not a surprise.

He'd jumped to conclusions, he should have known better and, again, I had no direct experience, but I would assert it was a good guess that a man such as him—regardless of the profoundness of his ability to be gentle and kind—would have an overabundance of pride.

So when he was wrong he would not be eager to admit that.

This was something that angered me even more.

And because of that, I did not keep my mouth shut.

"I can't imagine how, in all the time you've spent with me, Noctorno, that you would ever consider I'd think such about you. I have a midnight soul, it's true, but light shines upon it every once in a while. I feel its warmth when it does and it means everything to me. *Everything*. So much of everything, you've given me your light and there are precisely five beings I'd take a lash for...Kristian, Josette, Timofei, Frantz *and you*."

"Frannie—" he whispered, his tone much changed.

But I was angry.

In other words, there was no stopping me.

"And just in case *you* missed any of it, I thoroughly enjoyed your lovemaking. I've never had the like. It's abandoned. It's somehow freeing. You make even when I'm giving something to you about you giving something to me, and I don't know how you accomplish that, but it's a thing of beauty. So, to be honest, even if I didn't have all the other parts of Noctorno Hawthorne that you've given me, parts I cherish, I would not mind in the slightest that all you wanted was my pussy."

He again did not reply.

I had nothing more to say, and since he wasn't letting me go, I was forced to wait it out for it was undignified to struggle.

As I waited, I started making plans, doing this in my head. These being finding Valentine with magic, demanding she come, take me to her and Josette, and that she do this immediately. If she did not, I'd do it and she'd not yet taught me how to spirit myself. She told me not to practice without her either.

"The results, *chérie*, if you did something wrong, could be drastic," she'd warned.

If she didn't do it, I still was going to. I didn't care if I ended up in oblivion (for a spell, that obviously wouldn't do for eternity).

Suddenly, it occurred to me that Noc was no longer pulled away and the temperature of the room was no longer chilled by his mood, this making me focus on his shadowed face again.

It was as if he felt my focus, for the instant I did, he asked, "You done?"

"With what?" I queried.

"Telling me off."

"Yes," I answered.

"And while you were seething after you did that, did you plot my murder, visualize beating the crap outta me or make your plan to contact Valentine and have her come and get you?"

This question made me recall a conversation I'd had with Cora months ago where she was describing, at some length, the investigative prowess of the "police" in her old world. I knew nothing of the skills or duties of the city guard and had never had any interest (though, when Cora was speaking, I was all ears).

What Cora said about this was impressive, and not simply because I knew Noc engaged in these activities and I thought everything about him was impressive.

However, having a naked man in bed with you and being in the middle of an argument with said man who also had what appeared to be significant powers of insight, was vexing.

"I'll be contacting Valentine," I shared.

"No you won't."

Gods.

How very Noc.

I sighed and looked to the dark ceiling.

"Midnight soul?" This question came not with the nuance of humor that had been threading his tone but with something solemn.

I looked back at him.

"You are aware you're in bed with Franka Drakkar, not my twin of this world, aren't you?"

It was then I wondered about my twin in this world, something I'd never thought to do.

Gods, I hoped she didn't live in this very city. How awkward would that be, running into her?

"Babe, you wanna focus on me, or are you dialing up Valentine?"

I did as he not-exactly asked and focused on him.

"I'm not 'dialing up' Valentine."

"So you wanna focus on me? Seein' as we're havin' a kinda important conversation."

He was right.

Drat.

"I'm focused on you, Noc," I assured.

"Midnight soul?" he pressed.

"Yes?"

Abruptly, all I could see was a shadow, that shadow being his face, which was a breath from mine.

"Is that what you think you've got?"

I felt my brows draw together, but since he likely didn't have night vision along with his awesome powers of deduction, I stated my confusion.

"You find this surprising?"

"Frannie, you took your brother's beatings since you knew that was an option."

To that, it was me who had no reply.

"That's the most selfless thing I've ever known," he declared.

Why, oh why did we have to get into this?

However, in all fairness to Noc, we needed to do just that. If he didn't already know from things the others told him, he needed to know who he had naked and lying abed with him.

"You know I've done terrible things, Noc," I said quietly.

"I know you've acted like a complete bitch to keep people from getting close, Frannie. But that doesn't mean dick."

"I'm of my parents, and even midnight has a hue. Their souls are void."

"Your dad is an arrogant prick," he returned. "Your mom, I don't know, but the minute she lost her power she lost herself, so the only thing I can think about that is that her power *was* her, that and the position her husband gave her. He's an asshole. She's worse, because in the end she's actually just nothing and really always has been."

This was all very true.

Which made me wonder why he would question my assertion.

"They made me," I reiterated.

"They did and that's the miracle of life, babe. Some people get good from good. Some people are good and make bad. And some people are like your folks. They're wastes of space and they created you and your brother, who are absolutely not."

I adored that he thought that way.

It was just that it simply wasn't true.

"You don't know the person I was."

"I know what you said to Maddie, right to her face. Lo told me. He knows your story now, Frannie. Like everyone else, he's changed his tune about you. That said, he's *still* pissed about that and he'll never forgive you for it because that's the guy he is. He loves his wife, you wounded her, he's never gonna let that go. And I get that, what you said to her was not nice. It was nasty."

To be honest, though I wouldn't share this verbally at that juncture (or maybe ever), his example was a poor one.

I did not know Maddie very well. She'd gone before all had happened at the Winter Palace with me. But I still did not quite understand her and Apollo's relationship.

It was none of my business, this was true. And it was without doubt I shouldn't have spoken my mind to Madeleine.

However, the circumstances were dire, my lover was being tortured by malevolent witches, I was in the middle of being caught committing treason against my country, and, at least in that instance, I felt I should have some leeway.

"It was also the way you had to be because of what those parents of yours did to you," Noc concluded.

Suddenly afraid to touch him, but needing to do so, I lifted my hand and wrapped it around his jaw before I said quietly, "Noc, I fear you're making excuses because you hold feelings for me and this allows you not to see me for *me*. Or the me I used to be before all that occurred."

"Franka," he replied instantly, shifting so he was completely on top of me, his hands gliding all the way up my back so he could use both to cup my head, "no offense, baby, but that's complete bullshit."

Noc.

Bloody annoying.

Even in moments like these.

My hand still at his jaw moved to his shoulder and shoved as I snapped, "It is not."

"It's what you tell yourself so you don't lose hold on everything you know, and I get that, sweetheart. The way your reality has shifted the last months, all you've known gone in a blink, that's gotta be pretty fuckin' scary. But everyone knows it was all an act. It was always an act. They know the real you. The only one who doesn't is *you*."

This was a refrain I'd heard before.

He was right about the new Franka.

But he was also very wrong for the new Franka was just that.

New.

"It's impossible for people, including you, Noc, to know me better than me."

One of his thumbs started drawing soothing circles on the skin under my ear (which felt nice) while his other hand shifted and he started stroking my jaw with that thumb (which arguably felt nicer).

He did this while he murmured, "See I got more work to do to get you out of that bad place." His thumb at my jaw shifted further and he rubbed it across my lips before he dropped his head and did the same with his own lips. Once he'd done that, against mine, he stated, "But I'll get to that later. That's too heavy for now. And anyway, it's time for number four."

Number four?

Had he gone mad?

"Just to say, after arguing with you and all the rest, I'm really not in the mood for another orgasm," I shared waspishly, saying words I never thought I'd *ever* say.

Especially about orgasms delivered by Noc.

He nipped my lower lip with his teeth.

I couldn't stop it...

I shivered.

"Bullshit," he whispered, his amusement in that one word abundantly clear.

"You do know you're bloody annoying," I declared. "And *that* part of you I do not cherish, Noctorno Hawthorne. *That* part of you I also did not miss. Not even slightly."

That was all a lie. I missed every part of him. Including him being irksome.

"Mm," he hummed against my lips, and, drat it all!

I shivered again.

"You don't care that at times I find you annoying, do you?" I asked.

"Baby, you cherish me. Don't give a fuck there's some parts you don't. That shit's gonna happen." He slid his mouth to my ear and whispered, "Just fuckin' thrilled there are parts you do."

"I see," I told the ceiling, "that I should learn when to shut my mouth."

He slid his lips back to mine and stated, "Now is not that time."

I started to say something and didn't finish because Noc was kissing my open mouth and doing it deeply.

And then he set about proving that it was, indeed, bullshit that I was not in the mood for another orgasm.

Apparently, I was.

In fact, apparently, I was in the mood for two.

Noc's hands insistent on my hips, he murmured, "Faster, sweetheart."

I did not move faster.

Sitting astride him, I gazed down at him lying on his back before me in the faint early morning light and took my time moving up and down on his shaft, shifting my hips or torso minutely to change the angle, give him a surprise, offer him more, all while I watched his enjoyment.

As did he, watching me do my work.

His fingers dug into my flesh.

"Frannie, baby, faster."

I again didn't go faster.

That night, I'd had eight orgasms. He'd had one. I could take all the time I needed to give him the depth of pleasure I was right then intent to give him.

Moving at the same speed, I bent over him, trailing a hand lazily down his chest. My hair falling over my shoulder and brushing his pectoral, I squeezed my walls around his cock, filled myself with him and started undulating.

"Fuck, Frannie," he gritted, his eyes aflame, his fingers now biting into me.

"Allow me to give you something, darling."

"You been givin' somethin' to me but givin' more of it about now would be good, baby."

I smiled at him.

His gaze dropped to my mouth and his body under mine went utterly still.

I found that an odd and disturbing reaction.

Then, with a surprised cry, I found myself again on my knees but no longer straddling Noc with his shaft inside me.

I was facing the headboard, forced slightly to bent by Noc's chest in my back. He had a hand between my legs, finger at my clitoris, his other hand was angled across my chest, those fingers curled around the side of my neck.

And he was driving his cock inside me swiftly and brutally.

Oh.

My, my, *my*.

The pad of his thumb pressed up under my jaw, forcing my head back to his shoulder as he kept taking me violently, pounding into me.

Amazing.

His lips at my ear, he grunted, "Want number nine."

"Noc," I forced out.

Loving the feel of his cock slamming into me, the power of him surrounding me, the dominance of him having mounted me, I raised a hand to brace myself against the headboard so I could get more out of his thrusts.

"Come on, baby," his finger at my clitoris started twitching dazzlingly, "give me nine."

I felt the tingles ripple up the fronts of my thighs and I started to push myself back to meet his drives, gasping with effort and pleasure through each.

His thumb at my jaw slid in, over my lip and inside my mouth.

"Suck," he ordered.

I suckled and the instant I did, the power of his movements intensified.

The taste of him, the feel of him, I moaned against his thumb, my body bucking with the orgasm that suddenly crashed over me. Jarred by his increasing thrusts, I pulled hard on his thumb in my mouth and burrowed my head in his shoulder, experiencing glory.

"That's nine," he grunted, sliding his thumb out of my mouth to wrap his hand fully around my jaw, "now give me ten, Frannie."

"Noc," I panted, still in the throes of number nine.

He kept at me, finger at my clitoris and cock driving deep.

"Fuck, you should see you taking me," he groaned, and if it was possible (which it was since he did it), he started taking me harder. "Your tits. Your face. Your cunt. Goddamned beautiful."

I heard him. I loved the words.

But I was in the middle of marveling about the fact I could feel another climax coming so I couldn't reply.

"This, baby," he stated, his fingers at my jaw holding tighter, "what we're doin' right now, is *fucking*."

"I...like...fucking," I pushed out.

"Good," he grunted, slamming inside.

Good was an understatement.

"Next time, I'm doin' you in front of a mirror."

At his enticing words, my arm flew up and back. I caught his hair in my grip and gave him number ten, even after all he'd given me that night, not to mention just climaxing, orgasming violently in his hold.

"There we go," he growled then drove inside, grinding, and I heard and felt his grunts sound against my shoulder as he climaxed inside me.

After some time, when heartbeats and breathing had slowed, Noc wrapped one arm around my belly, the other hand he moved to again curl around the side of my neck and he took me with his cock leisurely, tenderly. So beautiful.

So Noc.

After offering that intimate caress, he slowly pulled out, laid me on my back, kissed my belly, my chest, my chin and looked in my eyes.

"Right back," he murmured.

He was good on his promise. Leaving me to dispose of the sheath, he returned and I was in his arms under the covers, my back to his front.

I was also half asleep.

"Figure we got maybe four hours before we have to check out," he muttered into the back of my hair.

"Check out?" I mumbled.

His arms around me tightened and he answered, "I'll explain later. Now, sleep."

My drifting eyes drifted closed and stayed that way.

My mouth did not.

"Noc?" I called.

"Yeah, Frannie."

"All of the parts I do," I told him.

"What?"

"All of the parts I do," I repeated.

He burrowed his face into my hair and pulled me deeper into his arms, murmuring a sleepy, "Sorry, baby, I don't get it."

"All of the parts that make you, I cherish," I explained. Vaguely I felt his warm, languid body go solid all around me. "It's only when you're being bloody-minded that I tell myself I don't. But I cherish that too, because it's you."

I finished by finding one of his wrists at my midriff, wrapping my fingers around it and giving it a squeeze.

Promptly after accomplishing that, I fell fast asleep with Noc's body still solid behind me, his arms holding me tight.

15
DASHBOARD LIGHTS

Noc

"What does this do?"

"It counts how many steps you take and you can input what you've eaten, what exercise you've done, how much water you've drunk, and it tracks how far you've walked, how many calories you've burned, how long you've been active, things like that."

Complete silence.

Then.

"And what does this do?"

"Uh, well...it's a scale."

"A scale?"

"A scale."

"What sort of scale?"

A different kind of silence, then...

"You step on it and it tells you how much you weigh."

"Why would you need to know that?"

"Um..."

Noc was having trouble not busting a gut laughing.

He really should intervene. The sales guy at the phone store probably made squat. He didn't need two parallel universe women asking him a million questions.

Though, Josette was the one asking the questions. Frannie was standing tucked close to his side, her arm around his waist, his arm around her shoulders. She was being quiet and watching her girl take in her new world and doing it with a sweet, sexy smile on her face.

From what he'd experienced since taking Franka to Valentine's so she could change clothes and get ready for the day, then taking both her and Josette out for beignets, Noc knew the guy was in for it. But it was so hilarious, and Josette was having so much fun, he couldn't bring himself to stop it.

He'd learned that day when she'd cried out in Café du Monde, "By the goddess Hermia, there are Maroovians *everywhere*! Isn't it *divine*?" that Josette was into Black dudes seeing as, as far as Noc could tell while in their world, people from Maroo (as well as some from Keenhak) were Black.

And the sales guy was a good-looking Black dude.

Another reason Noc didn't intervene.

Though, after realizing she was attracted to Black guys, he'd spent some time in the car explaining political correctness to help her out in not putting her foot in it. He just had to hope Josette took it in from her place in the back with her nose pressed to the window and her mouth hanging open.

"Never mind," Josette said to the sales guy. "Where are you from?"

"Uh, where am I from?"

"You know, what country on this planet?"

The guy looked from Josette to Noc and Franka, got no help, so he looked back to Josette.

"America," he answered.

Josette turned to Noc. "That's where we are now, right?"

"Yeah, babe." Noc's voice was shaking, "That's where we are now."

Josette turned again to the sales guy and declared, "You're very handsome. We don't have many handsome men like you where I'm from."

The guy's eyes got huge then they dropped to Josette's impressive rack.

At that, Noc had to take half a step back (taking Frannie with him) and bend at the waist a little to alleviate the pain in his side from controlling his laughter.

"Darling," Frannie murmured but said no more, and he could hear in that one word she thought it was hilarious too.

"I'm uncertain what the etiquette is," Josette went on. "Where I'm from, I'd just ask you, after you're finished with your duties, if you'd like to meet me at a pub for an ale and then take me to your bed." She again turned to Noc as he made a choking noise. "What do you do here?"

"Uh," he pushed out, "not that...exactly."

Josette took in Noc's position, expression and tone, and not stupid, she interpreted all of them.

Which meant she returned her attention back to the guy, murmuring, "Pity."

"Jesus, where are *you* from?" he whispered.

"Not here," Josette gave him the understatement of the decade, looked to the display of stuff at her side and asked, "What's that?"

"Same as the other band but it has a clock on it and monitors your heart rate," the guy answered, sounding strangled.

"Now, why on earth would you need *that*?" Josette asked.

"Young fellow," Franka called before he could respond, and Noc swallowed a bark of laughter at the words she chose.

Josette and the sales guy turned their attention to her and when they did, the sales guy again had big eyes, probably because he'd never been called "young fellow" in his life.

Franka went on, "We're here for telephones. As illuminating as this is, perhaps we should move on to that part of our expedition."

"Right this way," he said quickly and moved even quicker. He started his spiel before they got to the phone section. "We have a wide selection, a number of plans, different data options, our coverage is the best in the country and—"

"I'll take that one," Franka declared, pointing at a rose-gold iPhone.

"Yes, pink!" Josette exclaimed. "I'll take that one too." She whirled to Franka. "We'll have twin telephones, Franka! Won't that be *divine*?"

"Indeed it will, my dear," Franka murmured, again sounding amused.

The salesman stood in the midst of a sea of phones and looked to Noc.

"Let's just go with that, yeah?" Noc suggested.

"Right," the guy mumbled.

"To make this easy on you, they're probably not gonna need more than three gigs on the plan," he told him. "They're also not gonna need the larger storage capacity on the phone."

"Gotcha," came the reply. "I'll go get 'em now."

And he took off.

Fast.

"Well, that's somewhat rude," Josette muttered, eyeing him as he went and looking put out.

"My assumption from his earlier reaction is," Franka started, and Noc looked to her, "regardless of the fact that the women wear far less clothing, as do the men on some occasions, the sexual mores here are more stringent than they are at home, am I correct?"

Since he still had her in his hold, Noc curled her into his front, enjoying watching that slim, gorgeous neck of hers arch further back to keep hold of his gaze as he answered, "Not sure I can answer that question accurately. Didn't go on the prowl in your world, sugarlips."

She nodded smartly, sharing, "Josette told no tales. In our world, it's not unusual for a young woman, or man, to approach someone they find attractive and offer to share their bed. Flirting is sometimes utilized, but it's also often abandoned. No use wasting time when you can discover quite quickly if both parties desire the same thing. Is this not done here?"

He fought a grin as he shook his head and added, "Nope."

"Oh dear, was I rude?" Josette asked, sounding horrified.

Noc looked to her. "I figure he's never gonna forget today, not in a bad way, and right about now he's trying to decide if you saw his wedding band so he can take it off, come back out and take you up on your offer."

"Wedding band?" Franka asked.

He looked down into her beautiful face, still unable to decide if it was more beautiful made up or not.

When he did he thought of seeing that face for the first time in months the night before.

He also thought of all the brilliance that came after.

Especially the brilliance of what she'd said right before she drifted to sleep in his arms.

He then forced himself to stop thinking about this because, if he didn't, he'd drag Frannie to his Suburban, take her to his new place and not give a shit they were leaving Josette behind. And that would not only not be cool, Josette was not like a babe in the woods.

She was like a kid in a candy store.

And that was worse.

"The band on his left ring finger," he shared. "If a man has a band there, that means he's married."

"How marvelous!" Josette cried. "And what an excellent idea." She turned to Franka. "If our men wore bands, a woman would know and she wouldn't have to walk into a pub and unexpectedly have some wench accost her, tearing at her hair and clothing and spitting in her face."

Clearly, this was something that had happened to Josette.

Christ.

Franka, already relaxed into his body and his hold, relaxed deeper while noting, "I never did quite understand the impulse of the wronged wife going after the lover. If the lover knew about the wife, all's fair and I bid her strength in every pull and as much spittle as she can produce. If she didn't, why tear at her hair and spit in her face? The lover was wronged as well, perhaps not as wronged as the wife, but she was wronged. The wife should be tearing at her *husband's* hair and spitting in *his* face." She tipped her head back and looked to Noc. "Do you agree? Or are vows of fidelity not practiced here as Cora and Circe shared they were?"

"They're practiced," he replied. "And I agree. A dude cheats, his wife cuts off his dick, my thoughts, he's got no place to complain."

A sweet, happy light lit in Franka's eyes at his words.

"His dick?" Josette stage-whispered to Franka, she turned to her girl and Noc lost that light.

But he'd had it, he liked it and he was good with that.

Midnight soul.

Not even fucking close.

"I do believe, with that term, that Noc's referring to a man's member," Franka stage-whispered back.

And Noc was again fighting laughter.

"They vow fidelity here?" Josette asked.

"They do," Franka told her.

"Odd," Josette mumbled.

Noc was surprised. "You don't in your world?"

Frannie looked back up at him. "As they speak an ancient tongue, no one actually knows what the Vallees are saying during the marriage ceremony, even, in some cases, the Vallees. But my understanding is, no. Fidelity is not vowed in the Dwelling of the Gods when a man and woman are officially wed. Expected by the lower classes, definitely." Her mouth tightened. "Expected of the females of all the classes, also definitely. Expected from the males of the Houses, no."

"I take it you don't like that much," Noc observed.

"What's expected for one should be expected for all," she replied.

Noc again beat back laughter as he curled her closer and dipped his face to hers. "Listen to my Frannie, just a few months ago you were all about class, conservative to the core. Now you sound like a socialist."

"I've no idea what that means but the teasing light in your eyes and the grin on your lips I *have* seen on a variety of occasions. As such, I *do* know what *they* mean and they make me think I should be finding you annoying right now," she returned.

"Not today, baby," he murmured, giving her a squeeze. "Today started great, it's going great, and it's going to keep going that way so let's get along."

"With delight," she agreed. "But only because you called me 'my Frannie' and it's the first time you've called me anything, outside Franka and sweetheart, that I like, so it's put me in a good mood."

Noc liked that she liked that.

And he liked that she looked almost as good in jeans and a designer tee as she did in that unbelievable dress she'd worn last night. He liked that she wasn't letting the heels beat her and she had on another pair (or it could be that Valentine had only supplied those and Frannie had nothing else, Valentine wasn't at her place when they showed that morning and didn't return before they left—not that he'd ask about Frannie's shoes, but he would express his gratitude).

He also liked that she dug beignets so much, after she'd swallowed her first bite, she'd kissed him right at their table at the very crowded Café du Monde like they had their own private room. She did it long. She used her tongue. And she tasted of dough and powdered sugar when she did it, which made a fucking great kiss even better.

Further, he liked having her curled close. He liked that not only because he liked her curled close, but because she *was* close and not half a continent away on a parallel universe so he *could* curl her close.

And onward from that, he liked that he had his Frannie back so she could act uppity and cute, making him want to laugh, which he did right then.

But more, he liked all that knowing she'd be in his bed that night, and after he did what he was going to do to her there, she'd sleep in his arms again.

Oh yeah.

He liked all that.

A fuckuva lot.

"I've heard you chuckle, of course," she said, her voice lower, meant only for him, and as she studied him her eyes were warm. "But I've never seen that particular look on your face."

"That's a happy look, sweetheart," he told her. "Though, I've been happy around you so let's just say it's a *seriously* happy look."

One of her brows went up. "Happy to be home?"

"Happy we're both home."

His words made her melt into him, doing it lifting her hands from where they were sitting light on his waist to rest them on his chest and giving him a sexy smile that he took as her being happy too.

"Here they are," the sales guy cut into their moment, and Noc tore his gaze from Franka, feeling her turn slightly in his arms, but she didn't take her hands from his chest nor did she turn in a way she'd lose contact with him at all.

He liked that too.

He also liked the glance he caught of Josette watching them with an expression on her face that couldn't be interpreted as anything but ecstatic.

He had her best girl's approval.

He wouldn't have cared if he didn't.

But it didn't suck that he did.

They set up the phone plans and got the phones, doing it using credit cards in Franka's and Josette's names that Valentine had left behind for them in envelopes that also included driver's licenses, social security cards, passports and debit cards.

The cop in Noc *didn't* like that. But there was no way around it. They didn't exist in this world and they were going to be living there. This meant it had to be done so they didn't have to live off the grid like criminals.

He still didn't like it.

Regardless, Noc wasn't a cop anymore. Valentine had returned him to that world a week ago so he could get his shit sorted, find a place to live, move his stuff that was in storage into his new home and start his life so he'd have all of that out of the way when Frannie showed.

But when Valentine had brought him home, she'd given him a choice. She could pull strings to get him a job on the force or he could work with a private firm who she contracted with to do jobs for her. They'd seen his résumé, talked to his captain in Seattle and received a referral from a valued client (Valentine). They wanted to meet him.

After he sat down with them, he had an official offer within an hour.

All this was done within two days of arriving home.

The pay was three times more than working for the city, he had a lot more autonomy, his hours were more flexible, and he liked the two guys who owned the agency.

He took the job.

He started in two weeks. Two weeks to get Frannie settled. Two weeks to settle *them*.

And then back to life, one with Franka in it.

All was good.

Better, the plans he'd made to wine and dine Franka in order to talk her around to his way of thinking about where they should take what they had, he didn't have to spend time doing because they took it that way the night before.

Now he could spend his time wining and dining her and end that with her beautiful face, great hair, fantastic body and adorable attitude in his bed.

Which meant all was *great*.

They were walking out of the store, Frannie again tucked in his side, arms around each other, when she asked, "What's next for our day?"

"I'd like to learn to operate one of these conveyances," Josette declared, her attention on the cars parked outside the store.

"Think maybe you should give it a few days before you get your first driving lesson," Noc replied, saying a few days, meaning a few months.

"I'd like a luncheon repast of pizza," Frannie announced, and Noc smiled.

His girl liked her pizza. That was not in question.

And that was something else Noc liked.

"Pizza? What's that?" Josette asked.

"You have to experience it to understand the wonders of it," Frannie answered.

Noc felt his smile getting broader.

"Circe took me to what she called 'a boil' last night," Josette shared. "She said it's quite the done thing here. It was very unusual. After boiling the lot of the food, they drained it and dumped all of it on a table and you ate it with your fingers. The food was delicious and it made eating fun. Though, while consuming it, Circe said her favorite food from this world is tacos. She explained what they were to me and they sounded most odd but also most delicious."

Franka had wobbled on her heel when Josette started speaking.

As Josette kept talking, Noc tightened his hold, and after she righted herself, murmured, "Good?"

It seemed she wasn't meeting his eyes when she replied, "Yes, good."

"What do you think for next?" Josette carried on. "I agree with luncheon. As delicious as those morsels were at the café this morning, I'm *starved*. So this pizza? Or tacos? And I should make it be known that I'd be happy again with a boil. The shrimp here are exceptionally succulent. And their *petites homards* are almost as flavorful as home."

"Tacos," Noc decided, watching Franka's profile, all he had since she was keeping her face averted.

She didn't only seem to be avoiding his eyes, she was also suddenly stiff, and he didn't get it.

"I'm happy with that," Josette decreed. "Franka?"

"Fine," Franka said softly.

Noc beeped the locks to his SUV and Josette skipped to it excitedly.

She dug riding in cars, as in *really* dug it.

Franka didn't feel the same.

He steered Frannie to her door but didn't open it.

He turned her into him in a way she had no choice but to look up at him.

When she did Noc knew she was hiding something.

"Everything okay?" he asked quietly.

"Fine," she repeated, moving to pull out of his hold and turn to the car.

He curled her closer and her gaze that had skidded away came back.

"Babe, you sure?" he pushed and added, "Cars are safe, sweetheart, and I'm a good driver."

She nodded but made no verbal reply.

He looked into her eyes.

She was totally lying.

"Frannie, what's up?"

"Nothing, Noc, though I am hungry, so perhaps we can move along to luncheon?"

"We have that word, Frannie, but it's mostly called lunch here."

"Ah," she murmured, her gaze again sliding away.

He didn't like her weird change of mood, the suddenness of it or the fact she was lying about it. It could be she was nervous about taking another ride, she hadn't taken to being in a vehicle like Josette had done. It could also be she was embarrassed by her misstep on her heels. Frannie didn't make many missteps. She wore her dignity like armor and didn't do embarrassment very well.

It could be something else.

But Josette was in the car. It was time for lunch. Then he had to get them somewhere they could charge their phones and he could teach them how to use them.

After that, he'd be leaving them so Frannie could get ready, and he could go home and do the same, because he was taking Frannie out to dinner.

Noc decided to give her space now and talk to her then.

At that moment, he moved in and touched his lips to her temple.

His touch got him her eyes again and the remoteness he'd seen a moment earlier wasn't totally gone, but some of the warmth had come back, and he knew it'd all be good.

Franka could go into her head. He'd find a way pull her out.

He reached beyond her as he shifted her out of the way of the door, muttering, "Climb up, sweetheart."

She did.

He shut the door behind her, rounded the hood and took his two otherworld girls to find tacos.

Not surprisingly, tacos were a hit.

THE DOOR to Valentine's place opened and Noc stood still, staring down at Frannie.

Jesus, but Valentine had good taste.

"Fuck, baby, you look beautiful," he said quietly, staring at her dress.

It was a little black one made of lace. One shoulder had lace over it. The other was bare. The material under the lace looked nude. And the fitted skirt was short so her long-ass legs went on forever, especially in those pumps that showed her toes and had bows.

Her hair looked amazing, poofed out and falling over her shoulders in big soft curls.

And she'd become a master with makeup in a very short time.

"Josette is enamored with the gadgets called 'curling irons,'" she declared when his attention fixed on her hair. "We have something like this at home, but of course they're not heated through a string that's pushed into a wall."

Noc shook himself out of it, moved into her, rounded her waist with an arm and shuffled her in, grabbing the door and throwing it to behind them.

"Encourage that obsession, Frannie," he advised, dipping his face to hers.

"My hair is extremely..." she seemed at a loss for words but settled on, "*large*."

He grinned and dipped the half an inch he had left for his lips to hit hers.

"You work it," he murmured there.

"I assume that's good," she murmured back.

"Mm-hmm," he replied then he pulled her close with both arms and took her mouth.

He felt her fingers circle the back of his neck, but only vaguely.

It was all about her tits pressed to his chest. The feel of his hips snug in hers. The smell of her. The taste of her mouth.

Noc slanted his head and deepened the kiss, bending her over his arm, wondering if he was hungry or if he'd be good just feasting on Frannie.

The thought made him break the kiss, but he didn't pull away too far.

He liked to watch from close as she swam up from one of his kisses. She took her time opening her eyes like she was still lost to his mouth and didn't want to admit it was gone. And her gaze—usually so sharp, alert, guarded, missing nothing—was open, vulnerable, giving everything.

"Much as I want more from that sweet mouth of yours, sugarlips, we don't stop, we'll be goin' right to my place and not the restaurant."

A flare of interest sparked in her eyes before she nodded, pulled away, ducked her head and smoothed her skirt along her hips in an agitated move that exposed the effects of his kiss.

A move that was so fucking feminine and so goddamned hot, he felt his dick start to get hard.

"Okay, maybe you should stop moving," he said.

Her attention shot to him. "But...why?"

"Frannie, you're making me hard and I'm not even touching you anymore."

He watched it glide over her face, the smug satisfaction that softened her mouth, hooded her gaze.

"Fuck, now just lookin' at your face, I'm gettin' hard," he grumbled.

"You need to control yourself, Noc," she purred.

"Think back, baby. Not sure those words would have come out of your mouth last night."

He saw the pink hit her cheeks even as her eyes narrowed. He liked both. Enough he didn't even bother to try to control himself from reaching out a long arm, hooking her at the waist and pulling her to him for a quick touch of the lips.

"Josette settled in for the night?" he asked when he lifted his head.

"Yes, but I'd like to say farewell."

He nodded. "Let's get to that."

"She's watching the television," Frannie told him, detaching from his hold. But the instant she did, she reached out a hand, captured his and took him down Valentine's hall.

"Way Valentine lives, looks like the witch business is good," he observed, this not being the first time in the last week he'd been to Valentine's place. One that looked expensive on the outside but it actually hid the opulence of the inside that managed to be both lavish and utter class.

"She's said that her secretary has set up some tours of homes for Josette and I over the next several days. I'm hoping she finds much the same for us as this is more than adequate." She stopped and looked back to him. "I know you have a good deal to attend to yourself, darling, after having just returned home, but if you could find time to accompany us and give your opinions, I'd be grateful."

"I'm there, Frannie," he promised. "But did you see Valentine?"

She gave him a small smile at his promise, but at his question she only gave him a short nod, turned ahead and kept walking, sharing, "She was here briefly, thus our understanding of the existence of curling irons. She said she has much to do to catch up." It was quieter and reflective when she finished, "She seemed very distracted."

Before he could ask after that, she was stopping them inside a door.

Josette was on the couch in that room, shoveling popcorn in her mouth from a bag, her eyes glued to the television where *Interview with a Vampire* was playing.

"Josette, my dear, Noc's arrived and we're about to be away," Franka called.

Josette turned her head to them.

"This food says it's flavored with cheddar but it's not any cheddar I've ever tasted. That said, it's the most delicious thing I think I've ever eaten, outside tacos," she declared.

After tacos, while they were waiting for the phones to charge, Noc had taken them grocery shopping. He'd bought them a cart and a half full of food. He'd also subscribed them to Netflix and showed them how to pull it up on Valentine's TV so Josette would be set while he and Frannie were out for the night.

He didn't know if Netflix had *Interview with a Vampire* in their queue. Though, it being that movie, maybe local stations played it on a continuous loop.

"The creatures in this program *drink blood*," she went on. "It's gruesome and *wonderful*."

"I'm delighted you're enjoying yourself, my sweet," Franka said with a smile in her voice. "Now, you have all our numbers in your telephone and remember how to use them in case you need anything, yes?"

"Yes, Franka."

Noc put a hand to the small of Frannie's back and started to move her out of the door as she bid her girl to "Continue enjoying your evening."

"You enjoy yours as well, and hello and goodbye, Master Noctorno!" Josette called.

"It's Noc, babe. And here it's really *just Noc*," he told her, giving her a smile even if his words were firm.

"Noc," she said on a huge return smile then gave a swift wave and looked back to the TV.

Noc guided Franka down the hall. She stopped at a table to grab a black clutch. He nabbed the wrap that was thrown over a chair and draped it around her shoulders, kissing her neck while he did it, doing it to touch her, have her taste on his lips, but earning himself another look of soft satisfaction that he felt in his dick.

When he had her ready, he took her out to his car.

While they walked, she said, "You look very nice as well, Noc. Most handsome, or more than usual."

He pulled her closer with the arm he had around her waist, murmuring, "Not surprised my Frannie likes me in a suit."

"What you're wearing is called a suit?"

"Yup."

"Clever, seeing as it suits you."

He chuckled, beeped the locks and helped her up into his Suburban.

He'd learned the times she'd been in it to start it up and then take her hand.

Even when he did, he felt her tenseness come fast, fill the cabin, and he saw her other hand move out and latch on to the grip on the armrest at her door.

"You'll get used to it, sweetheart," he said quietly as he hit the gas, not wanting to call too much attention to it.

His Frannie, she had pride. She'd appreciate the assurance but not so much him pointing out she needed it.

And he knew he was right when she said nothing but her fingers flexed in his hand.

They were on their way when he brought it up.

"We can get you different shoes."

He felt her gaze on him when she asked, "Pardon?"

He glanced at her then back to the road before he answered, "Different shoes. Ones without high heels like all the ones you've been wearing since you got here."

"Do you not like these kinds of shoes?"

"Oh yeah, I like 'em," he told her, gave her a squeeze of his hand and dropped his voice. "But, baby, until you're used to walking in them, you can wear other stuff. I'll take you guys to a mall tomorrow. Josette'll like that and I figure you will too. And since Valentine took some of your stash, converted it to cash and opened you both bank accounts, you got a shit ton of money to spend, so you can have some fun."

"I'm perfectly fine in the shoes Valentine bought me, Noc. I'm growing accustomed to them. And just to say, I had time this afternoon to go through the things she procured for me and there are five similar pairs in my chamber and they're all very lovely. I'm looking forward to donning them."

He wondered if she'd lose the way she talked the longer she was in his world.

He hoped she did, she'd fit in better and he didn't want her to feel awkward.

He also hoped she didn't because it was so Frannie.

"You can have both," he said.

"I like what I have," she replied.

He gave her hand another squeeze. "Babe, what I'm trying to say without saying it is that today, when we left the phone store, you tripped and then went funny on me. I don't know if that's why you went funny, could be you're not used to riding in cars and you weren't looking forward to getting back in mine. But whatever it was, I noticed it, and whatever it was, I want you to know I'm here to look out for you. So let me do that."

She didn't say anything and this lasted so long, he glanced to her from the

GPS he'd programmed, something he needed because a week in NOLA was not near enough to know how to get around.

His eyes went back to the road and he noted gently, "Nothin' to be embarrassed about, Frannie. Again, just lookin' out for you."

"I know," she murmured.

"You wanna keep the heels, I am not gonna complain. You look great in them."

She was silent a moment before she said, "It isn't about the shoes."

"Right," he replied. "Then you'll get used to being in cars. Seeing them. Hearing them. The speed they can have. The number of them there are. Coupla weeks, it might help if I take you somewhere open with no one around and show you how to drive. You're in control of the car, you'll understand it better and maybe be better sitting in the passenger seat."

"It's not about your vehicle either, Noc."

That caught her another glance. "Then what was it about?"

She didn't answer.

"Frannie, you shut down on me for a while there. You bounced back at lunch, but I've been in your world. I know how freaky it is when everything around you is new. It can be overwhelming. And I can't look after you if you don't share what's on your mind."

At first she didn't say anything and Noc was about to prompt her when she spoke.

"Is it safe, having a discussion while you're operating this machine?" she asked. "All the lights, knobs, wheels, levers, it seems a lot to look after."

He gave her hand another squeeze, but let it go thinking that maybe she'd feel more comfortable if he was using both of his to drive until she got used to riding around.

He did this while he answered, "I've got a lot of practice. Been driving a car for twenty-two years, officially. This is not counting my dad teaching me how to drive at fourteen, with my stepmom having a conniption that he did it, and me joyriding with the guys numerous times before we got caught and Dad put a stop to it."

"Joyriding?"

"Taking a car out without permission and driving it around. Legal age to drive is sixteen. We were not legal."

"You're thirty-eight years of age?"

She sounded shocked and that bought her another glance.

"Yeah," he confirmed.

"Odd how I didn't know that," she murmured.

"Babe, we're off the subject. To confirm," he said with a grin in his voice, "I can have a discussion while operating this machine."

Even after he confirmed, she didn't say anything.

"Frannie," he pushed.

"I know," she said softly.

But she didn't say anything else.

"You know what?" he prompted.

He felt her eyes on him when she stated, "About you and the Circe now in this world."

Fuck.

He didn't have to ask what she knew.

He knew what she knew.

Fuck.

He glanced at her again. "How do you know?"

"I saw you...that night, I..." There was a long hesitation and then, "I was coming down the hall. You were both in her door. It was obviously, er...*after*. I could...well, I could tell what had occurred. I retreated. Not much later, you walked into the sitting room and..." Another long pause before she finished, nearly on a whisper, "You know the rest."

After they got their phones, Josette had mentioned going out to dinner with Circe and Franka had tripped. Clearly, she did this not because she wasn't used to her heels. Clearly she did it because this was on her mind.

"I...well, I..." she went on uncertainly. "I considered this often when we were parted. Of course, I could not know what would happen upon our reunion. I will admit, as I'm sure you can gather, that I was desirous of that being the path we took and you're very aware that I'm happy we've taken it. But I couldn't assume it would be what would happen. What I knew was you'd been intimate with Circe. You two, well...you suit. She's here. You're here. And I'm—"

Noc cut her off with words he hoped would set her mind at ease. "It was a one-time thing. We had that one time. Now it's done."

Again with the silence before, very quietly, she shared he had not come close to setting her mind at ease.

"Noc, what we have, it's very new. I understand I have no claim on you. You need give me no promises."

Fuck.

That time, it was him that was silent and he was that way looking for a place to pull off.

He found it, indicated, swerved carefully into an open parking spot at the side of the street, put the truck in park and turned to her.

She was holding tight to the door grip and staring with big eyes through the windshield.

Apparently, he hadn't swerved carefully enough.

"Frannie, look at me."

Slowly, she tore her eyes from the window and turned her head his way.

And before he could even open his mouth, she opened hers and the words suddenly spewed out, but this time they came without hesitancy and they came fast.

"I just want you to know that isn't why I agreed to do what I agreed to do with Valentine in regards to Circe. To take her from you. To create a clear path for me. That was not my intention at all. Those are no longer my ways. Well, they are, obviously with what Valentine and I are planning. A little intrigue. Some conniving. But not for sport. And not to harm. Our meaning is kind. It's actually the natural order of things, in a way. But if you intend to continue on with her or, have, well..." she swallowed and it looked painful, "*already* started things up again on your return, that's not my business. Or it is, in the sense that I should know so I can tell Valentine and we can stop doing what we're doing so you can have a chance or, erm, whatever...with what you intend with Circe. And I will just...you and I will simply—"

"Stop talking," he gritted.

She did as told and looked relieved to do it.

Noc took a deep breath and endeavored not to lose his mind and fuck up like he did the night before.

When he got his shit together, he stated, "Okay, I'm gonna make this crystal clear right now, Frannie, so we don't fall into this again. That means I want you listening close, baby. Are you listening?"

"Yes," she whispered.

"Right. Good. Here it is," he began, took a big breath and gave it to her. "On a night months ago, after me and a bunch of folks I did not know saved a world, no matter what happened just before, I sat down to wine and whiskey with a beautiful woman, and by the time I watched her walk out of that room, she had me wrapped around her finger."

He heard her intake of breath, but he kept talking.

"She didn't know it, and obviously *still* doesn't know it, but since that day, it's all been about her. That her being *you*."

"Noc." His name came husky and sweet, it was gorgeous, he loved hearing it, but he still kept at her.

"And now I'll take the time to share that I'm not that guy. When I'm with a woman, *I'm with that woman*. I expect her to be with me too. If I have a woman in my life, it's about her, getting to know her, seeing where things are gonna go and focusing on only that. It's not about playing the field, being sure to keep myself open so I don't miss anything or getting as much pussy as I can. It's about her and me. Right now, I'm with a woman. *Very* with her. And in that current scenario, Frannie, I'll repeat, that her is *you*."

"All right, darling," she said soothingly.

"I'm not done."

By the dashboard lights, he watched as she closed her mouth.

He did not.

"So what I do with my time *is* your business, and what I do with my dick is *definitely* your business, is that understood?"

A quick nod with her "Yes."

"And I expect the same from you. I'm in your business, and that beautiful body of yours, Franka, is only for me. You still with me?"

Now her "Yes," came breathy.

He loved hearing that too.

But he still kept at her.

"And to demonstrate what I'm talking about, no one has gotten what I'm gonna share with you, and no one is going to get it except you. When I say that, I mean I haven't shared and I'm not going to share with anyone but you. I expect you to keep this between you and me as well because it's only your business due to what you mean to me, who you are in my life, where I'm hoping what we got is gonna go. Other than that, it would be only Circe and my business."

He gave her a chance to let that sink in, she indicated it did by slowly nodding, and then he kept going.

"She approached me. You could call it coming onto me, because mostly, in an inexperienced way, it was. I don't know why she did. Maybe she was feelin' it after helping to save the world. Maybe she was beside herself the world had been saved and she wanted to celebrate. Maybe it was just the time for her to do it. I don't know what it was and I didn't ask. That's only hers. I did know about her. Valentine told me everything about everybody before she took me to that world. So I knew what her approach meant, how huge it was, and what an honor it was she picked me. Serious...and I am not saying this shit to make you feel better, it's just true...she's not my type. She's gorgeous and we shared something that was intense and all good, but normally, I wouldn't go there. I went there with her because I knew what her choosing me meant for her and I'd just put my life on the line to help save a continent. I was feelin' in the mood."

"Of course," she whispered when he took a breath.

"That's it," he continued. "Before we took it there, she made it clear she wanted no more and I made it clear I was down with that because I felt the same. We parted friends. We're still friends. She's phoned since I've been home, but I've been too busy to catch up with her. But again, she's just a friend, that's all she is and that's all she'll ever be. We got what happened between us in our history and it means something to me. It was a beautiful moment in my life, her trusting me like she did, and I hope I gave that beauty back to her. But then it was done. And by the way, to make something else clear, you *are* my type. That hair. Your eyes. That fuckin' mouth of yours. Your neck, which is the most beautiful thing I've seen on any woman. The uppity cute shit you got going. Totally my type."

When she got it that he was done speaking, she said softly, her words carrying a shit ton of feeling, "Thank you for sharing all of that with me."

"You don't have to thank me, Frannie. The gig is, you should expect that shit from me because that's who I am to you. I'm yours. I'm your guy. And there's nothing of mine that's not yours to have."

She leaned his way as far as her seat belt would let her and put a hand his knee.

"I, well...that means everything to me, Noc, and I wish you to know you should feel the same way about me."

"I already do," he returned.

He saw her lips tip up and he wanted to kiss her, looking at her face, the relief there she didn't hide, the emotion she had for him she also didn't hide, feeling her hand curl on his knee.

But they weren't done.

"Now we got that clear, what are you and Valentine planning to do with Circe?"

Her hand disappeared from his knee and she leaned away.

He caught it before it was out of reach and pulled her back, resting both their hands on his thigh.

"You just told me there was nothing of yours that's not mine to have, sugar-lips, so spill," he demanded.

He watched her bite her bottom lip.

"Frannie..." he warned.

He watched her let her lip go and she drew in a deep breath.

On the exhale, she said quickly, "The Lahn of this world lives in this city."

Noc's eyes went directly to the ceiling of the cab as his lips muttered, "Christ."

"It's the natural order of things," she defended.

He looked back to her. "The natural order of things would put me with the Cora of that world."

Her upper lip curled.

She knew of Cora of the other world. The woman made the shit Franka pulled all her life to keep people distant look tame. Cora of the other world wasn't just a bitch. She was a cunt.

She was also dead, and Franka knew that too.

"Well, that doesn't bode well for our futures," she murmured, her eyes drifting away. "And I must say, I have thought on this before last night and quite often today and it troubles me."

"Babe," he called.

Her attention came back.

He studied her face.

Then he said, "You don't know."

"What don't I know?"

Shit.

He released his belt so he could get closer to her, curved her fingers around his thigh and lifted that hand to hold her at the side of her neck.

"You...the you of this world, sweetheart, she passed years ago. A boating accident when she was seventeen."

Her gasp was audible.

"Yeah," he said gently. "Valentine told me last week."

"That...I..." She shook her head and it took her time to get it together. "This news...it's peculiar. Before, I was concerned about running into her and how awkward that might be. But now, knowing this, all I feel is sad."

"That's because it's sad, knowin' a girl had her life cut short before she even got a chance to start living it. Fucks with my head, knowin' that girl looked just like you."

"Yes," she agreed quietly.

"As sad as that is, Frannie, it still balances shit out."

"Pardon?"

"You and me. My destined mate of that world is dead. The you of this world is also sadly passed. Think Valentine told me this just so I'd know, because of that, there's balance."

"Oh," she whispered, and that was all she gave him after that mammoth piece of news.

He grinned and teased, "Yeah. Oh."

"Well, that's one thing we don't need to worry about."

He kept teasing. "Yeah, strike that off the list of non-existent shit we should worry about since this just works between us, what we got, so we really don't have anything to worry about unless you make it up."

Her eyes narrowed.

He leaned close and touched his lips to hers.

When he pulled away he ordered, "Leave Circe alone."

She drew both of her lips between her teeth.

"Seriously, Frannie, let her live her life."

She let her lips go. "Valentine thinks—"

"I don't give a shit what Valentine thinks."

"But, I agree and—"

"Then you'd be wrong."

Her eyes narrowed again.

"You're interrupting me, Noc," she warned.

"Babe, this is serious," he returned.

"You are correct, it is," she retorted. "Very serious. And being serious, I wish for you to explain to me, right now, why Circe is not allowed her happiness. Of the players in this game of universe hopping, Finnie and Frey have found their bliss. Circe and Lahn of Korwahk. Tor and Cora. Maddie and Apollo. And I daresay, when you aren't being vexing, you and me. So what of the Lahn of this world and the Circe of the other? Are they not to find their bliss?"

"If that's gonna happen, let it happen."

"Even if it were to happen without intervention, by the time they get together, Noc, the Circe and Lahn of the other world will have at least three children, that being if Circe doesn't deliver twins on her husband again, making it four. The Circe and Lahn in this world already have to catch up. There's no time to waste."

"You tell yourself that and Valentine tells herself that so you can meddle, seein' as you're both addicted to it."

She pulled away from his hold, saying archly, "And let us see, Valentine has meddled in precisely *three* relationships, my clothing and shoes yesterday being not an unintentional fashion selection in the slightest. She planted me where she planted me the *way* she planted me knowing precisely what the results would be from her machinations. You may disagree, for reasons unknown, but from the results...including Finnie and Frey, Maddie and Apollo, and you and me...I would estimate she's quite skilled at what you call her *meddling*."

Shit, she had him there.

"And do you think for even a moment that Valentine or I would wish Circe harm or *do* that first thing to harm her?" she demanded to know.

"Frannie, calm down," he urged. "Of course not."

"Then I fail to see your problem with our plan."

He didn't like it. But she was right, which meant he had no choice but to live with it.

"Just, whatever you plan to do, be careful," he muttered.

She pulled away even further and snapped, "But of course!"

"Baby, she's spent her entire life being used and violated by men. I'm the only man she's ever chosen of her free will. I'm protective of her and it's partly because of that, partly because I'm human, and lastly because I'm a man and I fuckin' hate that my kind has put her through a lifetime of shit. You say you're gonna fix her up with a huge dude that I can't imagine looks any less scary in this world than the other, I'm gonna react. Cut me some slack."

"And cutting you some slack would mean allowing you your erroneous reaction, which was insulting, and forgiving you for it even if you haven't admitted you were in the wrong and apologized," she returned.

Noc fought a grin. "Yeah, that'd be what cutting me some slack means."

"All right, Noctorno, I shall 'cut you some slack.'"

He didn't need to fight a grin anymore.

"Babe," he said shortly. "Making something else crystal clear right now, something I don't want to tell you again, I do not like being called Noctorno."

"I have heard you say that, repeatedly. But it *is* your name, it's a regal, manly name, and when you're being vexing it's mostly when you're being very much *a man*, and a high-handed one to boot, so that's how I'll refer to you. And I will admit I'm not beneath using something I know annoys you to do just that after you've annoyed me."

Noc sighed.

Franka held his gaze.

"It's good you taste so goddamned sweet, or even with all the rest, you might not be worth it," he muttered.

"I do hope you jest," she bit out.

"Just finding things that annoy you that I can use after you've annoyed me."

She glared at him.

Then she burst out laughing.

Noc stared at her.

Fuck, he'd never seen or heard her laugh like that. Not like that. Totally giving into it. Totally giving him all of it.

Christ, even her laughter sounded like a purr.

Beautiful.

She was still doing it when she undid her seatbelt and erased the distance between them, putting her laughing mouth to his and sliding her hand up his thigh.

"I do believe you need to feed me, darling. I'm quite famished."

He couldn't stay ticked. Not after what she just gave him and now, with her mouth on his, hearing the humor in her voice and seeing her eyes dance in the dashboard lights.

"Best get you to some food, then," he muttered, brushing his mouth against hers.

He was about to pull away when she caught him with her hand cupping his cheek.

"We balance worlds," she said softly.

He felt those words in his gut.

"Yeah," he replied softly.

"You're my type too, Noc, even though I didn't know it until I met you," she shared.

Fuck.

That did it.

They had a booking. They didn't have the time to sit in his SUV and have a conversation.

But it was important and it had to be had.

So they had it.

Now they did not have time for him to make out with her the way he wanted to make out with her to show his appreciation of not only how she ended an argument, but what she'd just said.

But it was important.

So he took that time.

They were twenty minutes late for their reservation.

The busy restaurant sat them regardless.

And Noc was not surprised that every man followed Frannie with his eyes as she passed, which meant no way in fuck he could wipe the satisfied grin off his face that all that was her was all his.

He was also not surprised his Frannie liked shrimp étouffée better than pizza.

By a lot.

16

MY COMMAND

Franka

"Noc?"

"Mm?"

Gods, I loved it when he made that noise.

I also loved how he held my fingers laced in his.

But in that very moment what I loved most was how he was lazily circling his thumb on the inside of my wrist, even if he did it as he drove (seeing as it was my view that it was probably far safer to operate his vehicle with two hands).

We were just then heading to his home after an utterly sumptuous dinner, the like I'd never had. Such flavors. Complicated. Rich. Spicy. Decadent.

This world seemed rushed. It was loud. It did not smell very good. I found it disconcerting there were only glimpses of nature here and there—along avenues, trees growing up from stone pavements. Although there was great beauty in (some) of the architecture, I was uncertain how I felt about the overall look, sound and smell of the place.

But the food was wonderful.

And Noc's company...as ever, there was none better.

"On our journey to dinner, you mentioned your father and stepmother," I noted.

"Yeah?" Noc prompted when I said no more.

"Although I know a good deal about King Ludlum and his history, that's history from the other world. Due to circumstances being what they were, you know all about my family, and unfortunately in the case of my parents, you've met them. In discussions, you've mentioned your family but you haven't shared much but anecdotes."

Noc, ever generous, did not dillydally in giving me a reply.

But regardless, I thought with a smile, as he'd said, what was his was mine and therefore what he did was not dillydally in giving me just that.

Pieces of him.

All of which were mine.

"Probably won't surprise you it's all the same," he said. "My dad's name's Ludlum Hawthorne and he kept the tradition of saddling his kids with crazy-ass names that'll have one purpose, they'll get real good at fighting because every asshat in school that gives them shit about their names'll get a fist in his face."

"Oh dear," I murmured, rethinking, if this was his lot since schoolyard days, of using that very same thing to annoy him (even if it was deserved).

"Yeah," Noc confirmed. "It wasn't fun, but they learned and eventually word got out and it ended. So I got a brother named Dashiell, known only as Dash or he gets even more pissed than I do when you call me Noctorno."

"Right." I kept murmuring.

"And our youngest brother is Orlando, we call him Orly. He got the short end of the stick because Noc isn't great but it doesn't totally suck. Dash is actually kinda cool. Orly is just bad."

I squeezed his hand as a soft chuckle escaped me.

I didn't chuckle long.

This was because he said quietly, "Same for our moms."

I clutched his hand because I knew the wretched story of King Ludlum and the loss of not one, but *three* loves of his life.

Noc went on with his own story.

"Mom died in childbirth with me. Dash's mom died of pneumonia. And Orly's mom was with us longer than the Orlando of your world's mom made it, but she eventually died of breast cancer. She was the one who got pissed about Dad teaching me how to drive."

I turned to him as best I could with the obnoxious, but apparently mandatory, belt restraining me to the seat.

"I'm so sorry, darling."

"Yeah," he muttered.

"Perhaps I shouldn't have brought it up,"

"Nope," he said on gentle shake of my hand, "you wanna know, ask."

I looked out the window in front of me. "I shall, my dearest, but we've had a lovely night. Knowing the way of our two worlds, I should have assumed that would be the case and picked a better time."

"Babe, she was great," he declared. "Only mom I had and she was a good one. She's gone and I miss her. Think about her every day. And she deserves that. She deserves me talking about her. Keeping her alive that way. She took on my dad and two boys. Gave my dad another son. Gave us a brother, good kid, grew into a good man, proud he's my baby bro. She made our family better and Dad didn't suck at lookin' after his boys. I was little, but I remember he did it all and gave it his all. But when Judy showed, we *really* had it all."

I looked to his profile. "Even if her time with you was cut short, I'm pleased you had that."

"I am too," he replied quietly and kept sharing. "Only thing I'd change was the way we lost her. Dash's mom, Christina, I was too young, don't remember much. Seemed like one day she was there, next she was gone. I know now it took a while, by that 'while' I mean a couple of weeks, but truth was, her pregnancy was a difficult one, she never recovered from having Dash, so when she got pneumonia, it was the worst thing that coulda happened. But I was a little kid, all I felt was confusion and a lot of bad shit I didn't get and then it got worse. Judy, Frannie..." he paused, and through it the air in his vehicle became heavy, "*fuck*."

He suddenly stopped speaking and I didn't start. I just held his hand, turned my eyes from him to give him his time and stared at the road ahead of us.

He eventually continued, his voice thicker so I held his hand tighter.

"She fought it. She gave it her all. Kept strong the whole time. Still amazes me how she'd come home from treatment, her and Dad would disappear in their room, but we heard her puking, crying. God, the way she cried, Frannie, I can still hear it. So exhausted. Never heard anything like that, like she didn't have the energy to do it but still couldn't stop. Fucking hated hearing her cry like that. Wouldn't want Judy to cry ever, but never like that."

After gifting this awful beauty to me—awful, what had happened, beauty, Noc sharing the depths it made him feel—he took another moment and I did too, swallowing against the sadness that seemed to coat my throat in a layer of acrid dust.

"Next day, she'd be over it," he eventually carried on. "Even on the days she actually wasn't, she was in the kitchen giving us shit and making us some of the magic she made there. The cancer kicked her ass in the end, though, and that pissed me off. It still pisses me off. She fought so fuckin' hard, she shoulda won. But it beat her and that wasn't right. It wasn't how it should go. Not for Judy."

His last was hoarse.

He cleared his throat and finished softly, “Not for her.”

I didn’t have any idea what “breast cancer” was, but in my world we had terrible illnesses that were prolonged, nightmares for those who fell to them, much longer nightmares for those who had to watch them struggle and carry on with those memories.

Apollo’s first wife, I’d been told, had such an illness. Many believed it was the reason he mourned her so tremendously after she was lost. He’d been marked not simply by her passing but by being forced to experience, at some length, the excruciating torture of how she’d passed.

I was one who believed just that.

“Your father now?” I queried gently.

“Lost three good women, he’s not gonna try again. He’s got a lady friend. He says it ‘isn’t like that,’ but the only way it’s ‘not like that’ is that he refuses to marry her. Like having Lud Hawthorne’s ring on your finger is a curse, and I get why he thinks that and it’s none of my business so I don’t go there. She’s down with that. She loves him. She’s good with taking him as he feels he can give himself to her. They live together. Her name is Sue. She makes him happy. She’s a good cook. She’s smart enough not to try to be a mom to three grown men who lost their real moms in an ugly way. But she doesn’t hide she cares about our dad, likes it when we’re around and wants us to quit dicking around because she loves kids and she wants grandkids. ‘Even if they aren’t blood, the more the merrier,’ she says. Seeing as she has two already from her own kids, it’s just me, Dash and Orly who are taking our time. Last, she’s wicked funny. You’ll meet her. You’ll like her.”

By the gods, I’d meet her?

I’d meet a woman who was pressing her not-exactly-but-still stepsons to give her grandchildren, Noc being one of those stepsons?

Dear goddess!

“My mom was named Amara.”

My panicked thoughts vanished at his tone and my gaze immediately turned to him.

“Only thing I got of her is pictures, but she was beautiful, Frannie. Most beautiful woman I ever saw, until I met you.”

I felt it again, as I’d felt it several times with some of the things he’d said when he’d stopped his vehicle and gave his words to me before dinner.

My eyes starting to sting.

“If I have a baby girl, first one I have, I’m naming her Amara,” he declared.

It was the most beautiful name I’d ever heard.

I swallowed in an effort not to expose the emotion I was feeling before I shared, "I think that's lovely, Noc, and your mother's name is even more so."

His thumb stopped absently stroking and his hand tightened around mine, pulling them farther up his thigh where he'd been resting them.

He did this as he murmured, "Good you're on board with that."

"On board?" I asked.

"You agree," he explained.

I turned to face forward again, feeling the alarming sensation of my heart swelling.

A beautiful baby girl with Noc's unusual blue eyes named Amara.

My word, did anything sound sweeter?

"You want kids?" he asked quietly.

"That was not my future," I answered in the same vein.

"How's that?"

"Anyone I loved was in danger."

His thumb started stroking my wrist again as he reminded me, "That's not the case anymore, Frannie."

"I know," I whispered.

"Then I'll repeat, you want kids?"

I wanted a little girl with beautiful blue eyes and black hair named Amara.

And this desire, the like I'd never allowed myself to have, bubbled up my throat. A throat having been ravaged by emotion that night, that feeling grew, built and blocked it so it wasn't my choice not to speak.

It was an impossibility.

"Frannie?" he called.

It took effort to clear the blockage.

I did it, but even so, my voice was not as I'd ever heard it when I replied, "It's just occurred to me how much my life has changed since that night in the buttery." I felt my fingers curl deep into his, not at my direction, but automatically as I continued speaking. "How free I actually am. How my life and my future are truly, for the first time, my own."

"I'm hopin' that's a good thing, baby, and it doesn't freak you, because it *is* a good thing and you should rejoice in it," he advised.

I looked to his handsome profile and announced suddenly and with not a small amount of fervor, "I want children, Noc. Girls. Boys. As many of them as I can have, stopping only when I feel like I cannot give them the love and attention they deserve if I had another."

He again stopped stroking my wrist so his hand could clasp mine, but this time it did it fiercely, causing a twinge of pain.

"Good to hear," he murmured.

That was his wish as well.

My.

It would seem I had to pull myself together or I'd be crawling all over him in this vehicle, and if I did such it would mean certain death.

Therefore, I demanded, "We must cease talking about this or I fear the results would be calamitous."

"And why's that?"

"I wish to kiss you," I shared, but didn't stop at that. "And do other things to you, and you may have demonstrated you can concentrate on more than operating this contraption, however, I would hope my crawling into your lap to deliver a kiss would not be such a thing."

"You're right," he replied with humor. "You crawled into my lap and kissed me while I was driving, sugarlips, it's likely the results would be calamitous."

"Then let us get to your home and swiftly, Noc," I ordered. "For I have need of a *digestif*, your lovemaking and a soft pillow. I'm afraid after the events of the last two days, I'm quite fatigued."

"Your wish is my command, gorgeous," he muttered.

I looked forward, murmuring myself. "What a lovely thing to say."

More muttering from Noc. "Fuck, you're cute."

I made no reply. I no longer had qualms he thought that of me. Indeed, it pleased me.

We spoke of nothing earth-shattering, and fortunately our journey wasn't much longer before Noc executed an alarming maneuver of stopping in the street then going backwards at a disquieting angle in order to park very close to the edge of the pavement.

I did hope he was correct and I'd grow accustomed to his, as he called it, "SUV."

Though I suspected I would (I *was* still Franka Drakkar), I also suspected it would take some time.

"We're here, babe," he said as I felt the vehicle's engine cease running, and then I heard him open his door.

But I looked beyond the pavement to "here."

I heard Noc's door slam as I whispered, "Oh my."

It was a home unlike any I'd seen before. There was dim light coming from the inside that I could see vaguely through the front windows of the house and the window over the door. The night hid the color his home was painted, but I could see that the woodwork was white. And there was a lovely, black, wrought iron fence before it spiking up proudly from the edge of the small lawn.

There was also a vast amount of intricate millwork along the portico and railing.

And among the three windows at the front of the house, the middle one was made of rather simple, but quite lovely, stained glass.

It was tidy. It was immensely attractive. It had personality. It was in no way grand or overwhelming, but instead well-tended and welcoming.

All very Noc.

He opened my door as I unleashed myself from the seat and he took my hand, assisting me to alight his vehicle.

I saw then the pavements leading to his home were made of brick.

A lovely touch.

"Shotgun house," Noc stated as I continued to take in his home while he guided me there. "Told Valentine I was going to move to NOLA, I wanted to live in something that was NOLA. Only other thing it had to have was me bein' able to own it and live in it fast as money could change hands. Her agent found this for me and it rocks."

He'd opened the iron gate, led me through and was taking me up the steps as I asked, "Shotgun?"

He looked down at me. "Right. Forgot. You don't have guns in your world." He took me across the small veranda and let me go to stop at the door, explaining, "A gun is a weapon. Fires a bullet, or a small projectile, fast, faster than the eye can see. The bullet travels straight from the barrel to the target. There's change in its trajectory due to distance and wind, but it's minimal. Not sure you were in a state to notice it, but it's what I used when I did my thing against those witch bitches on your world."

I was not really in that state to notice. However, I did recall, vaguely. Obviously, there'd been other things on my mind.

He opened the door and I saw through to acres of gleaming wood floors, a brick fireplace with a beautifully carved wood mantelpiece that was freestanding in a room that went on the length of the house. Sitting room first, fireplace delineating it from a dining room and then the this-world kitchen was entirely visible at the back.

As was the back door.

"Shotgun," Noc said, drawing me in, "means you could stand at the front door and shoot a shotgun straight through the house right out the back door."

I looked up at him as he stopped us to close and latch the door behind him.

"Why would one do that?"

He took my hand and drew me deeper into the space, grinning and answering, "They wouldn't. That's just a nickname for these kinds of homes. Places like this were built because it gets hot. When it does, you open the doors, a breeze can get through when you do, cooling the space."

It could, indeed.

Clever.

"Also," he went on, "they're narrow so you can fit a bunch of them on a street. This one was a double-barrel. That means it was two houses once that shared a wall. Someone renovated it, pulling them together. The length that's now communal space was once all there was to the house, but now I also have three bedrooms and two baths."

He stopped us in the kitchen, which was long, but narrow, and had a number of quite impressive cupboards, which included a kind of cupboard-esque/counter-esque seating area in the middle.

He let me go and turned to a cabinet door, opening it.

"Will whiskey work for your *digestif*?" he asked, putting odd emphasis on *digestif*, like that word amused him.

"Yes, darling," I murmured, taking in his furnishings and décor.

Not surprisingly, it was all very masculine. Somewhat like a high-born member of a House would decorate a hunting lodge, but with this-world differences, obviously.

I felt Noc touch my waist and turned from my perusal of his abode to him to see him offering me a glass of amber liquid.

I took it and barely did so before he moved into me, maneuvering my position then pinning me with my back against the counter.

I felt my lips curl up.

"Like it?" he asked quietly.

"Very much," I answered. "It's very attractive. Very masculine. Very inviting. Thus very you."

He shook his head slightly, his eyes lighting, his chin dipping, saying, "My Frannie has a way with a compliment."

"I share this trait with you," I replied.

He bent closer, his movement taking his nose a whisper away along the side of mine, his lips *right there*, before he lifted away and took a sip of his drink.

I drew in breath, delighting in his tease and taking a sip from my own glass to calm my reaction.

Marvelous, this world had excellent whiskey and Noc had the taste to procure it.

"Frey," he said suddenly.

"I beg your pardon?" I asked, confused at this and thinking our next activities would be quite different and have not a thing to do with my cousin in the other world.

Noc focused on me. "Frey and Finnie. They're together. Having babies. But the Finnie of this world, Valentine says, is a lesbian so she's not gonna be finding her Frey."

"A lesbian?" I asked.

"She likes only women."

"Ah," I whispered, feeling my lips curl again, for the rumors had been rampant, with most refusing to believe it, but I just *knew* the deposed Winter Princess was a *guenipe*. "A *guenipe*," I stated.

"Say what?"

I focused on him. "We call them *guenipes* in my world. Most usual, for women and men to prefer the same sex, or both sexes, as a matter of fact. Most undesirable when the woman happens to be the Winter Princess and responsible for carrying on the royal line."

He nodded. "I can see that."

I took another sip of his excellent whiskey and noted, "This does not offer balance of the worlds for she would not be likely to carry on any line here either."

Noc shook his head. "Nope."

"Perhaps I'll look into my crystal ball tomorrow, find the Frey of this world. Not," I added swiftly, "to spy on him or meddle. Simply to assuage my curiosity, and I'm guessing, yours."

He grinned. "Crystal ball."

I understood his amusement and returned his grin. "I know. It seems absurd, this being precisely what I thought at first, but it's most useful."

Noc had no comment to that.

He had something else on his mind.

"You done with your *digestif*?" he asked, tipping his head to my glass.

I was not.

And yet I very much was.

But in response to his question, reading the look in his eyes, thus what was on his mind, I lifted my glass slowly, took a sip just as slowly, and removed the glass from my lips at my leisure, all this staring into his eyes and watching them heat as I did so.

When the glass was away, Noc dropped his head again, his nose coming close enough it *almost* touched mine. Dipping it under and around, his lips so *very* close, his heated eyes unceasingly peering into my own.

"You like to tease, baby?" he whispered.

"Perhaps," I whispered back.

It seemed he was moving in to take my mouth, and I held my breath, but just as he got near enough to capture my lips, he retreated, again only a whisper away.

I tipped my head back, wishing to erase that whisper, but Noc changed course, lazily running a phantom trail with his lips along my jaw, my cheekbone and back to my lips, right there, but not there enough.

My heart was beating a swift tattoo, the area between my legs tingling, growing moist, and I swayed slightly into him, wanting to remove even the limited distance we had.

But Noc put his drink down on the counter behind me, his hand spanning my hip and holding me steady.

And away.

I felt his lower lip brush mine, but the touch was so light, it was like a dream.

Thus, I felt my nipples strain the material confining them, a pleasurable discomfort.

"You tease too," I accused softly.

"Mm..."

This he murmured as his face got even closer.

But not close enough.

Gods, he was better at this even than me!

And it was marvelous.

I put a hand to his stomach and drifted it up.

"I would very much like you to kiss me, darling," I requested.

"Yeah," was all he said as a reply.

"Now," I demanded, swaying closer, and he allowed the touch of our bodies but didn't give me his mouth.

"Now?" he asked.

"Now," I repeated.

He ran the tip of his nose along the flare of my nostril and then adjusted so I could feel the hairs of his brow brush mine.

My breath started to get heavy.

"How much you want my mouth, Frannie?" he asked.

"Quite a bit," I answered, trailing my hand around his side to his back and up to his shoulder blade, pressing in.

He resisted.

I felt my panties dampen.

"Noc," I breathed.

"Say please," he ordered.

My eyes narrowed even as my womb convulsed.

"You're very bad," I admonished.

"You think you ask pretty you won't get your reward?" he inquired.

That was an excellent point.

"Say please," he urged, giving me the barest trace of his mouth. I sought more, but he denied me. "Say it, baby."

There was nothing for it.

"Please, Noc," I pressed my breasts into his chest, "may I have your mouth?" I whispered, and I got my reward from the burn in his eyes even before he gave me my real reward.

"Absolutely," he growled, and then he gave me what I asked for.

I was so attuned to him, I nearly dropped my glass in an effort to clutch him to me the instant I tasted his tongue, forgetting I even held it.

Fortunately, Noc had more presence of mind, and before the kiss heated, my glass joined his on the counter.

My arse also joined the glasses on the counter when Noc suddenly yanked up my skirt, lifted me and planted me there, pushing in, forcing my legs open, rounding me tightly in his arms so my intimate parts were pressed to his hardening ones and his mouth devoured mine.

When I was grasping his hair, whimpering down his throat and grinding my hips into his, he lifted his head and looked down at me with eyes ablaze.

"Ready for bed?" he asked.

"Absolutely," I breathed.

Noc grinned.

Then he lifted me off the counter, put me on my feet, yanked down my skirt, took possession of my hand and pulled me out of the kitchen.

~

"No, please," I begged.

I was close. So very close.

As I had been, time and again, repeatedly, while Noc spent what felt like *ages* taking me in a heady variety of positions, some of them I didn't know existed.

And as he took me, touching me, kissing me, nibbling, biting, licking, suckling, thrusting inside me, he brought me to the precipice of climax.

And then he'd pull out, whip my body into a new position and start all over again.

This time, I was on my back, Noc between my legs.

But he'd pulled out and was hooking me behind my knee. He lifted that leg across the front of his body, forcing it to the other side. He found the back of my other knee and bent that in line so both legs were angled the same, inner thighs pressed together, the outside of one leg pushed to the bed, but my hips were twisted to the side, my arse and pussy offered to him.

I caught his gaze as I tried to catch my breath.

He imprisoned my gaze while his other hand wrapped around his cock, he found me and drove inside.

My lips parted, my eyes closed and my neck arched.

"Look at me," he grunted, thrusting deep.

I forced my eyes to open and again found his.

"Twist at the waist, Frannie, hands over your head, press them against the headboard. I wanna watch you move with me."

I didn't hesitate even a moment to adhere to this command.

His eyes dropped to my breasts that were surging with each plunge.

"Fuck yeah," he groaned, putting a hand in the bed at the small of my back, arm straight, giving him leverage, as he removed his other arm from the backs of my knees and shoved his hand between my legs, finding my sensitive nub.

I lifted my top knee higher to give him better access and my entire body spasmed.

"Noc," I gasped, my back arcing, the pleasure rippling over me, driving me down into his thrusts.

"Whose cock are you taking?" he asked.

"Yours," I forced out.

He drove home and ground inside.

I whimpered.

"Whose?" he demanded to know.

I stared into his striking face, which was now harsh with pleasure, and knew the answer.

"Mine," I whispered, beginning to tremble not only with what he was doing to me but the force of his meaning.

He started thrusting again.

"Whose pussy is this?" he bit out.

"Yours, darling. It's yours," I gasped, my trembling turning to tremors.

"Fuck yeah, it's mine."

"My love, I need to climax," I begged and only vaguely watched something fierce, frightening and exquisite brand itself into his features.

"Say that again," he ordered.

"I need to climax," I repeated.

He bent at the elbow so he was closer to me, not interrupting his thrusts but adding pressure with his fingers between my legs.

"All of it," he growled. "Repeat all of it, Franka."

"My love, I need to—"

"That's it," he grunted, driving deep, circling hard, the pleasure overtook me, lifting my back from the bed, forcing my head into the pillows, his name a pant of bliss through my lips. "Yeah," I heard him groan. "Yeah, Frannie." He sank in fully and whispered, "Yeah," as I felt his body strain into me and the deep, intoxicating sigh of his release.

After the sensations chased themselves away, I relaxed into the bed, opening my eyes and watching Noc as he lifted his head, which had fallen after his orgasm, and he gazed at me as he stroked inside, tender and sweet before he pulled out.

And then I watched as he moved down.

He bent to my hip, touching his lips to it. Along my outer thigh, halfway to my knee, another lip touch, and onward, to the side of my knee for another one.

He shifted and I continued to watch as he gently pulled his hand from between my legs where he'd been cupping my sex in an intimate touch since my climax. He rested it on my knees, keeping me twisted sideways in the bed, but he brushed his lips along the side of my torso. Up, to my ribcage. Around, to between my breasts.

Then his weight was pressing into my hips as he looked into my eyes, his somnolent, sated—such beauty—and he said quietly, "Do not move an inch, Frannie."

"Your wish is my command, darling."

A blaze of something I couldn't quite decipher flared in his eyes before he gave me a tender grin, dropped his head again to kiss me between my breasts and he retraced his path along my body before he left the bed to go to the privy attached to his bedchamber.

I would know why he didn't wish me to move when he returned, extinguished the light on the nightstand behind me and then entered the bed, fitting himself at a curve to my length at the back. Pressing into me to reach a long arm to the light in front of me, he put that out, then pulled the covers up over us and settled in, an arm around my belly, snuggling me closer.

But he said nothing.

He just held me and he did it close.

I felt his warmth. His strength. His affection for me. All of this simply lying on our sides, his arm around me.

"Thank you for a lovely first day in your world, Noc," I said.

"My pleasure, sweetheart," he replied.

"Dinner was delicious," I shared.

"Yeah, I got that, seein' as you didn't say shit to me until you cleaned your plate. Thought, when you got done, you were gonna pick it up and lick it."

I did, actually, have that urge. Fortunately, I was able to quell it.

I didn't respond to his commentary as it was slightly vexing and I was in no mood to be vexed.

Instead, I said, "Thank you for being so kind and patient with Josette."

"Not hard," he told me. "She's sweet and funny and you mean the world to her."

I had a feeling it was the last part that caused Noc to show her his generosity of kindness and patience.

On this thought, I wondered how I had lived the life I had and in the end it led me to Noc.

I desired an answer to that question at the same time I thought it best not to question it.

No.

I should, just to experience it. Nurture it.

Revel in it.

Noc pressed closer. "What's on your mind?"

"What makes you think something's on my mind?" I asked.

"'Cause we had four hours of sleep last night, a busy day today, I just came hard, gave it to you harder, and you said you were tired before we even hit my house. And now you don't sound it, don't act it and you don't feel it," he said his last with a squeeze of my middle.

"Cora told me police in this world were quite intuitive," I mumbled, wondering if that boded well or ill for me and thinking, in most instances, it would be the latter.

"We are," he confirmed. "Though I'm not a cop anymore, but in ways I'll never shake, once a cop, always a cop."

I stared into the dark a moment before turning in his hold.

He shifted his position to allow me to do this but he did it keeping me in the curve of his arm.

"You told me Valentine was going to get you a position with this city's guard," I said.

"She was."

I was shocked at what I read this to mean.

"And you've decided, with the treasure bestowed on you in my world, to be a man of leisure?"

I was shocked at this idea because the Noctorno Hawthornes of *both* worlds were no men of leisure. So much not, I couldn't credit it, wondered at it and was troubled by it, the last in regards to it possibly having something to do with me.

"No," Noc replied. "With that I paid my way eating and drinking through four countries in your world, bought twelve cases of wine in Fleuridia, my new Suburban and this house, which, with the reno on it and the neighborhood it's in, wasn't cheap. But I put the bulk of it away, because I've learned in life shit can happen and it does, without fail, so you gotta be prepared. A good way to be prepared is have more than a million dollars' worth of gold illegally converted into cash, which is then illegally invested in foreign investments that, if I take any out, I'll get back in cash so the IRS won't cotton on I took a trip to a parallel universe that made me a millionaire, an explanation they won't buy. This means I gotta keep that windfall on the down low in order to avoid a prison sentence, because no matter how smart you think you are, the IRS will catch you. And I actually *did* earn that treasure in a parallel universe, but they won't believe it, and since I don't have an explanation they *will* believe, I gotta break the law."

I had opened my mouth to ask, but I didn't need to bother, Noc answered me.

"And the IRS is the department in the government you pay taxes to, sugar-lips. They frown on anyone not doing that and they get pretty nasty when that happens."

"Tax collectors in my world are much the same," I shared.

"I bet," he muttered.

"Although I will take this opportunity to note I'm delighted to hear that you acquired so much Fleuridian wine, your explanation does not negate my question."

"Sorry, Frannie, what I'm sayin' is, that money is not gonna be used so I can be a man of leisure." I could hear he found something about that amusing but he didn't explain what that was as he continued talking. "I decided not to take a job with the 'city guard,' but instead work for a private firm that pays more, is more flexible with hours and will hopefully offer an interesting caseload that's not like I'm used to so I'll be doing something different, all of this giving me a needed change of pace."

"And this is desired by you?" I queried.

"I didn't know it was until Valentine gave me the option, but from what the guys who own the firm told me about what they do, it is." I heard his head move on the pillow as I felt him dip his face closer to mine and his voice was reassuring when he continued, "It's good, sweetheart. It's what I want. I'm lookin' forward to it."

"Well, then that's fine," I replied.

"Glad you're down with it," he muttered with amusement.

I was down with it but only because he was.

"Now," I carried on, "I'd like to know, when you said, 'shit can happen' and then stated it does, 'without fail,' what, precisely, you mean."

His reply was instantaneous.

"Your parents abused you, probably in terms of mental and emotional abuse, since birth, but the physical shit hit at age five. The only mom I knew got cancer, fought it hard, and died anyway. Your boyfriend was kidnapped by witches and tortured to death. Your world almost was taken over by evil forces. During an investigation, I hooked up with an other-world woman who eventually led me to her this-world twin, someone I connected with, meaning I got roped into helping save your world. What, precisely, I mean is that shit can happen, crazy shit, shit that's in-fucking-sane, and it does. Without fail."

This could not be argued.

That said, I had a curious feeling he was not sharing all with me.

I looked into his shadowed face, and due to the hour, the mood, and our location, decided that perhaps now was not the time to press that.

He'd said everything that was his was mine to have. He was Noc, therefore I believed him.

But that didn't mean I needed to demand everything from him immediately.

"Are you tired?" I asked.

Another smile in his answer of "Baby, wasn't ten minutes ago, you can't have forgotten I did all the work."

Well!

"This is correct," I retorted. "I also have not forgotten that you did all the work regardless of my attempts to, at first, share that endeavor, and then later beg you to *stop* doing all the work and provide me with what you were working *toward*."

"Yeah," he murmured warmly. "I didn't forget that either." He tilted in and touched his mouth to mine where he said, "You beg real pretty, sweetheart."

Blast, but he had a talent for titillation mingled with vexation.

However, it was the first part that made me involuntarily press my body into his.

In response, Noc drifted his hand down my spine and cupped the cheek of my bottom with it, saying, "You gotta let your man get some rest, sugarlips. Then he'll give you what you want and be able to do it the way you like it."

"I was not requesting more, Noc," I returned.

"Your mouth wasn't, but your body was."

I said nothing for this was true and there was no denying it.

"You gonna let me sleep?" Noc asked.

Him sleeping would mean him not annoying me.

Or exciting me.

"Yes," I answered.

"You gonna sleep?" he asked.

I had things on my mind, particularly the "shit" in Noc's life that had hit without fail, shit that was not his stepmother dying, something which quite clearly had wounded him deeply, a wound that had not healed, nor ever would.

"Yes," I lied.

"Sleep now and then mall tomorrow," he muttered. "Get you more clothes so you can leave some here."

This was an excellent plan.

I snuggled closer to him, saying softly, "That sounds good."

"Show you and Josette around the kitchen. How to use the stove, microwave, shit like that." He continued to plan, the drowsy beginning to permeate his tone. "She at least knows how to use a microwave, she won't have to eat popcorn from a bag if she's hungry."

"That also sounds good," I replied.

"We'll find out the schedule Valentine has set up for you to look at places and—"

I interrupted him. "Darling?"

"Yeah?"

Running a hand soothingly over his back I whispered, "Sleep. We can plan tomorrow, tomorrow."

"Right," he mumbled, his hand at my arse curving around to bury itself between my hip and the bed, this pulling me even closer. "'Night, Frannie."

"Good night, my dearest."

"My dearest," he muttered. "My Frannie, so fuckin' cute."

I held him and stroked him and felt his big body loosen against me, his head falling forward so his forehead rested on mine, his hold relaxing but the tilt of his body in sleep meant I took on some of his weight.

And gloried in it.

I felt replete from a lovely dinner, delightful company, meaningful sharing, excellent whiskey and exquisite lovemaking. Much had happened in a short time and my body and mind were exhausted because of it.

Even so, it took me some time to find my own peace because, no longer wrestling with the many changes in life I'd endured, I could finally focus on something that wasn't me.

And what I focused on was that fact that the man whose bed I lay naked in, whose naked body lay rested against mine, the man who had stolen into my heart and captured a large portion for himself that I knew, no matter what the future might bring, would always be his...that man was still a mystery.

And that troubled me.

Deeply.

17
EVERY SECOND

Franka

"I'll drop you off, do some shit," Noc declared. "Text me when you're almost done, I'll come back and get you. But, just to say, they cut off too much of your hair, I'll lose my mind. Be warned and make sure that doesn't happen, sugarlips, because that shit goes down, I promise you it won't be pretty."

Noc and my plans made over the breakfast he'd offered me that morning (he called it bagels and cream cheese, I called it delicious) had been thwarted for the day.

This meant Josette and I now stood in the rather elegant entryway of an establishment where Noc had taken us due to the fact that Valentine had left a note with Josette. This note proclaimed she'd made an appointment for us to take care of our persons in a this-world way. This in the form of us going to a "spa" to have our hair "styled," our brows "shaped" and our nails "done."

They've been informed you're both new to these experiences so have been instructed to have a care with you, my chéries. *They've also been paid and tipped. All you need to do is enjoy.* She'd written.

Although I did understand the concept of having my hair styled, the rest of it was entirely foreign to me (and Josette). Even if Valentine had shared with the staff that we were "new to these experiences," we were, indeed, *new to these experiences.* I didn't want anyone near my hair (which Noc had just declared a rather healthy interest in), my nails (unless that person was Josette, she was quite talented with filing and shaping, not to mention taking care of my hair), but mostly my *brows* (what did one do to brows?) not knowing a thing about it thus having no choice but to appear just that way.

In other words, gauche *and* daft.

I was neither.

Nor was Josette.

This wouldn't do!

Damn Valentine. It was irritating in the extreme she'd brought us to this world, championed doing just that and disappeared after we'd arrived.

"I...well, Noc..." I got myself together and requested, "It would be most appreciated if you'd accompany us through our, erm, assignations here."

Noc got closer, smiling encouragingly, saying, "You'll be good, sweetheart. And you'll like it. Women do this kind of shit in this world all the time and they love it. It's considered a treat."

"I'm certain it is," I mumbled. "It would still—"

He cut me off by taking my hand, tugging it and giving Josette a look as he moved us a few steps away.

He turned his attention to me and lifted both hands to either side of my neck before dropping his face to mine and saying only for my ears, "Okay, baby, first, hair. When they get you in the chair, they're gonna ask you what you wanna do with it, maybe recommend things you might wanna try. Be firm you want it trimmed only. They'll do that. They might wash it, blow it dry with a handheld, electric blow dryer and style it. When they get to your brows, they're gonna..."

He then patiently, and rather thoroughly, explained all that was to happen to Josette and myself at that "spa."

"To end," he concluded. "I'm a dude. Dudes these days do this kinda thing. Have pedicures. Get shit shaped. I am not that kind of dude. I'm also not the kind of dude that hangs with his woman while she has it done. If you're anxious, I'm here, won't step a foot out that door if you need me to stay. But if I didn't think it would all be good, I wouldn't even consider leaving. Do you understand what I'm saying?"

I nodded. "I understand, Noc."

"So you want me to stay or can I go?"

I stared into his eyes as his words tumbled in my head.

I am not that kind of dude.

You want me to stay or can I go?

Can I go?

But he would stay.

For me, he would stay.

"I'm exceptionally fond of you, Noctorno Hawthorne," I blurted.

His face blanked momentarily in surprise before the blank vanished and his gaze took on a heat I'd only thus far felt from him during loveplay.

"For future reference," he rumbled, "you look at me like that while you say shit to me like that, you do it in a place that at the very least has a relatively private broom closet so I can take you there and fuck you against the wall."

I swayed into him, lifting a hand to clutch his shirt to help hold me up as his words coursed up my legs to target the area between them.

This they did.

With precision.

"Yeah?" he pushed on a growl.

"Yes, Noc."

"Now, do you want me to stay?"

"No, darling. I think Josette and I can manage."

"Right," he muttered, sounding perturbed, looking stimulated, and dropping his mouth to mine for a hard, closed-mouth kiss before he lifted an inch away. "Text me when you're almost done, I'll come get you, take you both to lunch then the mall. Good?"

I nodded. "Good."

He looked over my head and then at me. "You'll love it, sweetheart. Just relax and have fun."

I nodded again.

His heated gaze shifted just to warmth. "I can go, but only if you let go of my shirt."

"Oh!" I cried, letting him go and watching my hand smooth his attractive shirt against his chest.

This was a mistake, seeing as his chest under his shirt was so warm...and so hard.

I pulled my hand away.

"Late lunch, early dinner, we tuck Josette away, back to my place for another marathon," he stated roughly and again I lifted my eyes to his.

Warmth gone, heat back.

"Marathon?" I asked, fighting against melting from his heat.

"Do you have those in your world?" he queried in return.

"Running? Yes, there are games in Hawkvale where athletes from all over the Northlands—"

"Our marathon will not be running," he promised.

My "Oh," that time was much softer.

"Fuck, she says 'oh' and I'm in danger of coming in my pants," he groused, looking annoyed.

I felt my eyes round before I felt my lids get heavy and my mouth get soft.

I watched as Noc took in my look and appeared to grow even more annoyed.

"Gone," he grunted abruptly. Lifting a hand to snatch me around the back of the head, he bent it down, kissed the top, tangled his fingers in my hair and pulled it back. He bent in again to brush his lips against mine. "Text me," he demanded, let me go, and then he sauntered rather aggressively to and out the door without even glancing at Josette in farewell.

This was rude, but I didn't have it in me to consider that as I was at that moment memorizing his aggressive gait because it was such an agreeable sight, I never wanted to forget it.

Once I realized I was staring longingly at the door, I shook myself out of it, turned and saw the woman behind the desk who had greeted us as we'd walked in, as well as Josette, were both staring at the door.

Longingly.

This made me smile.

Exultantly.

I moved toward Josette.

The sooner we had our this-world treat, the sooner we'd again be with Noc.

So it was time to get started.

~

"Look at this. Look...at...this!" Josette demanded, striding into the lounge with its comfortable furnishings that was the waiting area of the spa.

I looked at this, "this" being her flipping her hair out at both sides with her hands then shaking it with her head tipped back.

She did not have a man who demanded her hair stay long so it had been cut to be just longer than her shoulders and styled in soft curls that were most becoming. Not to mention, as if by magic, blonde streaks had been added, changing the color but a nuance, but that nuance was most appealing.

She righted her head and smiled hugely at me.

"It's a miracle!" she cried.

It was, indeed, a very attractive hairstyle.

"You look lovely, my dear."

She got close to where I was sitting, bent over me and started plucking carefully at my hair with expert attentiveness. "Gads, Franka, I see what they've done. Released some of the buoyancy by cutting layers into the length to take off the weight. *Extraordinary*," she breathed, leaned back and examined my face. "And your brows are quite lovely, arched like that. All in all, I must say, you look even more beautiful than normal," she declared. "Mas...I mean, *Noc* will be even more enamored with you when he sees you."

I had no doubt this would be true.

And the reason why was not my hairstyle, which was really quite lovely, a change but not much of one, however it made an impact. Or my brows, which were always arched but the delicate sweep of them now was most effective.

It was simply because Noc was enamored with me and it seemed anything I did made him more so.

I tucked that thought safe close to my heart and smiled in a way I knew how it felt having it there showed on my face.

And it did, for Josette asked, "He's lovely to you in all ways?"

"He's more than lovely to me in all ways," I answered.

"I knew he would be," she whispered. "And this makes me happy."

It did me as well.

I didn't share that.

I reached out a hand and took hers, giving it a squeeze.

"Franka? Josette?" a woman called.

We both looked to her standing at the mouth of the area we were in.

"Time for mani-pedis!" she exclaimed, as if she'd said, "Time for you to select your sapphire the size of your palm!"

Josette, my sweet adventurer who greeted every new experience with excitement and delight, gave me an eager look then rushed to the woman.

I pushed up from my seat and followed more slowly, doing it realizing, for some reason, I'd taken on this other-world adventure with trepidation. Perhaps because nothing had gone well for me in my past and I could not imagine a future where I could expect even a modicum of that and I was living in unconscious dread of when my luck would turn. Perhaps it was because I was Franka Drakkar and I had not yet gotten used to the new me, I feared I'd lapse into the old, and it would be me who would drive away all the good I seemed to be earning.

I followed Josette and the woman slowly, also realizing this was foolish and feeling my shoulders straighten at the thought.

Antoine had been right.

Kristian had been right.

Josette had been right.

And Noc had been right.

The four people I had allowed closest to me knew me better than I did myself.

The new me *was* me.

As such, it didn't *seem* I was earning anything.

I simply *was* earning it.

So I should bloody well enjoy it.

As I felt a smile curve my lips, my step increased and I sallied forth on my next adventure of allowing someone (not Josette) to shape my nails.

It was not hand to claw combat with a bear.

But it was *my* adventure, *my* life.

I was going to cease fearing it.

I was going to embrace it.

Every second.

"By Hermia," Josette whispered loudly from her place beside me, her entire body vibrating from the apparatus that was inside the seat that whirled and kneaded, tapped and pounded against our backs. "Another miracle," she whispered, waving her pink-tipped fingernails my way.

I'd noted, with some envy, Valentine's varnished nails, something we did not have in our world.

Now, both Josette and my nails were the same, shaped and varnished, and the ladies were attending our feet, an utterly sublime experience.

Josette had chosen pink.

I had selected a rich burgundy, the color of my favorite Fleuridian wine.

"We must come here every week, Franka," Josette carried on whispering.

This, once Noc taught us to drive a vehicle, we would do.

"Agreed," I declared.

She again smiled hugely.

I looked down at the woman sitting on a low stool at my feet.

"Hail, young woman," I called, her head twitched, and she tipped it back to blink at me. "Can you please inform me of when you're close to finished?" I requested. "Not," I went on quickly, "that I'm not enjoying your ministrations. I am. Thoroughly. Just that my, well...erm..."

I looked to Josette and lifted my brows, uncertain how to refer to Noc.

She shrugged.

Ah well.

I turned back to the woman at my feet. "My *lover* requires me to text him when we're nearly finished so he can collect us. We've both enjoyed our time here, tremendously. But I, for one, am quite famished and he's to take us out to luncheon." At her continued stunned expression, I amended, "*Lunch* and I'd rather not delay in waiting for him to arrive by texting too late."

"Are you in character for some play or something?" she asked when I stopped speaking.

"In what?" I queried in return.

She stared at me.

She then inquired, "Are you from England?"

I stared back at her.

It was not lost on me I was much different in manner and speech to those of this world. Until I found my footing, at times such as these, an explanation might be required.

Therefore, I gave her one.

"We both are from Lunwyn," I shared, flinging a hand Josette's way. "It's a land far from here. Though we speak the same language, things are much different there."

"I've never heard of that," she turned to her compatriot on a stool at Josette's feet. "Have you heard of it?"

That woman shook her head.

"It's very difficult to get to. Quite, *undeveloped*, as it were, in comparison, of course, with your," I threw out my other hand again, indicating the soil under the floor on which we sat, "America."

"Right," she said. "Okay."

"So, to end, are we nearly finished?" I asked.

"Yeah, uh, just, you know, the massage and polish. Maybe twenty minutes. But you should probably text now."

I nodded. "My gratitude."

"Right," she mumbled then went back to my feet whereupon she commenced massaging them and my calves.

Marvelous.

I had to request another who worked at the establishment to help me liberate my phone from my reticule so I didn't spoil my varnish and it was not easy poking at it with wet nails.

I accomplished it, a whoosh noise happened telling me it was sent, the phone sounded in my hand, making both Josette and I grin at each other like schoolgirls, but my grin deepened when I saw Noc's name above a little bubble that was underneath my little bubble.

BE RIGHT THERE, SUGARLIPS, it decreed.

Ah Noc.

My Noc.

A goodness *I* earned.

The best there could be.

~

HALF AN HOUR LATER, I was not thinking such kind thoughts about Noc.

I was grinding my teeth.

This was because he was laughing his arse off, doing it carrying me to his vehicle, with me wearing brightly-colored, flimsy, weightless pieces of nothing that looked like the footwear Josette had been wearing since she donned this-world clothes, except much less substantial.

I had been shuffling along, rather gracelessly (to my utter despair), holding my shoes and my bag, until Noc took pity on me and swung me up in his arms.

He didn't take that much pity considering he did it as I'd mentioned, laughing his arse off.

Apparently, after a pedicure was complete, you either had to wait some time for your varnish to dry or you were to arrive in footwear that would not demolish the efforts your pedicure person put into making your feet look better than they ever had. Something you'd paid no mind to all your life. Something that seemed, from the moment the last brush of varnish went on, crucial to existence.

This bringing of the appropriate footwear being something I did not do.

Noc walked me out to his car, opened the door while still carrying me, and ducking us carefully to avoid slamming us both into the roof, he deposited me in my seat.

Through this, I had ignored his existence, a difficult task considering he was carrying me, but one I pulled off with aplomb (in my estimation), until that moment when I could no longer do so since he placed his hand on my jaw and forced me to look at him.

He was still laughing.

This meant I began glaring.

"We'll get you some real flip-flops for the next time you go to a spa," he said, continuing not to put the slightest effort into quelling his mirth.

"I've been in your world not but two days and I still can say with some authority I am *not* a *flip-flop* person," I announced haughtily.

His waning laughter burst forth yet again, and he felt, for some reason, the need to kiss me even while allowing the full force of his hilarity to continue to flow.

This he did.

When he ended it, he was only chuckling.

Regardless of the fact that his laughter tasted lovely on my tongue, I was still glaring.

He took in my glare and that made him no less amused.

"Will it help if I say you look cute, even shuffling like an invalid?" he asked.

"No...it...will...*not*," I snapped.

Noc. Still no less amused.

"How about if I tell you, three hours ago, someone asked if you could get any more beautiful, I woulda said it was an impossibility, but I've been proved wrong?"

"How about if I tell you, if you remove yourself from my vicinity, perhaps I'll no longer wish to kick you somewhere unpleasant?" I returned with false sweetness.

"Is it vanity, baby?" he queried, now only grinning, which was no less annoying, "Or pride?" he finished.

"It's both," I admitted the complete truth without embarrassment.

He shook his head, the grin remaining in place. "That's my girl. Someone says you're cute and beautiful, you get pissed. Or in this instance, *stay* pissed. Someone asks if you're vain or prideful, you claim that without a second's delay."

"It's true."

"It is, I'm sure," he returned. "But you're still cute and you're definitely fuckin' beautiful."

I decided that was a good time to share something important.

This I did.

"I think, with this conversation, that it's clear that even you, who I hold dear, cannot cajole me out of a pique by saying lovely things. That even for you, my piques, as they always have been, run deep and are lasting and require me having time to fume before they naturally die away. So I think that you need to kiss me, but do it swiftly, then exit my vicinity, drive me and Josette somewhere in order to feed us and do that immediately."

"Even me," he said instead of doing as I asked.

"Even you," I confirmed.

"Even me."

Something in the way he said that pulled me out of my irritation and fully into that moment.

When I arrived at that moment I saw that Noc held no humor. He was looking into my eyes, his shining with a light so beautiful, my soul lit in such a way it felt it would never go dark again.

"Even you," I whispered.

He held my gaze and worlds could have collided. Millennium could have passed. Stars could have fallen from the sky.

Nothing could have intruded on our moment.

After some time (I fear, rudely, a good deal of it), a subtle clearing of her throat brought our attention to the fact that Josette (wearing flip-flops and having some experience in them so she had no issues) had followed us and she was currently sitting in the back of Noc's vehicle.

This broke the moment, causing Noc to lean in, touch his mouth to mine, but after he'd done that, instead of doing the rest I'd demanded, he put his mouth to my ear.

"All my life, thirty-eight years, *only* you," he whispered there before he promptly moved away and closed my door.

With frozen body but shifting eyes, I watched as he walked around the front of his car, what he'd delivered in my ear settling with the flutter of butterfly wings around my heart.

"I love him," Josette whispered into the confines of the car. "Love, love, love him," she went on, and before Noc opened his door, she finished, "For you."

I did too.

By the goddess.

I...did...too.

~

"My word, Franka, have we arrived in the lap of the gods?" Josette asked reverently.

I didn't answer, though if I had, my answer might have been yes.

Noc did.

"No, babe. It's just the Nordstrom shoe department."

Slowly, her head turned and her gleaming eyes lifted to Noc.

"Can I—?" she started.

"Have at it," he told her, tipping his head to the vast area beyond us filled with tables and shelves covered in a dizzyingly delightful spectacle of this-world shoes. "You find something you like, let me know. I'll get you a salesperson and we'll sort you out."

"I love you," she breathed, eyes still gleaming.

I pressed into Noc's side, my lips curved into a deep smile.

Noc chuckled.

Josette hesitantly approached the first table of shoes, staring at it reverently, her manner one of care, such as you would approach a large chest tumbling over with such treasure you couldn't quite believe your eyes.

Noc used his arm about me to curl me to his front. I took my gaze from Josette and brought it to his.

"I cannot believe I'm asking you this," he began. "I'm thinkin' I'm breakin' a seal I'll regret. But you ready to learn how to shop?"

This confused me.

"Why would you regret this?" I queried. "You and I both are criminally wealthy. In this world, that would be literally. Thus, I can afford to spoil myself, and Josette, without worry."

His lips twitched before he answered, "Right. Probably good I explain. We're gonna do this today. We're gonna kick the shit out of it. We're gonna set you and Josette up. Fill my Suburban with stuff that you dig that'll make you girls happy and make you feel more comfortable here. And until you two can get around on your own, I have a feeling I'll be doing that more than once. But just to warn you, when you get used to getting around by yourselves, you can ask me to go shopping with you once every five years. No more, but you could go with less. And if you feel like buying me shit, have at it. I have a feeling I'll get off on watching you trying on clothes and shoes. I *never* get off on having to buy shit for myself."

There was so much there, I had no idea how to begin.

I wanted to comment on the "once every five years," but I suspected my best play with that was to let it lie and hope that I had many opportunities in my future to hit this quota.

So I focused on something else.

"You don't enjoy purchasing garments for yourself?"

"Nope."

I was even more confused.

"But, you always look so nice. Your selections are most attractive. They suit you completely. So much so they'd indicate you get great enjoyment out of making those selections."

His eyes warmed at my words, and when I was done uttering them, he replied, "I failed to mention, Sue, my dad's woman, likes to shop. Christmas and birthdays are off the hook. It makes Dad apoplectic. He keeps telling us we're wearing his retirement. That doesn't stop her. I haven't catalogued it all, but I'm pretty sure nothing I've worn since I've known you I bought for myself."

"Interesting," I murmured.

His arm got tighter in a manner I wasn't certain I liked.

When I caught the look on his face, I knew I was correct in having that feeling.

"And, just to put it all out there, Cora, the dead one, bought me a ton of shit when I was with her working undercover on that illegal gambling gig I was investigating."

"Ah," I whispered, quite in the know about this as it, too, had been shared with me (carefully) by the lovely and alive Cora, not to mention Noc had not spoken of it at length, but he also had not shied away from mentioning it before.

"Frannie," he called, regardless of the fact I was right there.

"Yes?" I asked.

He was studying me closely. "Not that this is for Nordstrom shoe department, and I can make sure Josette is good for a while so we can go get a coffee if we need some alone time to hash it out, but things have changed with us and," he kept studying me, "you seem down with that."

"Well, I am," I shared.

He looked dubious. "You are?"

I pressed closer.

"I am not your first lover, Noc, and you are not mine. It would be unkind to make you feel uncomfortable and definitely not contrite for having lovers before me, or further, making you feel unease in mentioning them when you speak of your life. But more, it would be a waste of words and emotion for both of us in going over such when it's history. We're together now and it's only our future that interests me, not a study of the past we can do nothing about."

He grinned. "Just in case you forgot, gonna remind you that you're the shit, sugarlips."

I smiled back. "Indeed I am."

He bent and gave me a brush of the lips, lifted his head and queried, "Can't believe I'm askin' you this, but you want more shoes?"

I couldn't believe he was asking that either.

Thus, I didn't answer.

I just broke free, took his hand and entered the lap of the gods.

I OPENED THEN CLOSED the mirror which was actually a cupboard in Noc's bathroom.

I did it again.

And again.

I smiled to myself at the ingenious use of space that included a charming hidden compartment and then opened it again in order to put the bottles I'd purchased at the mall inside it.

These bottles included cleanser, something I would need to use on my own face to rid it of the paint without Josette at Noc's to assist me (and this, oddly, elated me).

Also moisturizing lotion, which the woman who sold us our cleansers shared with us was a *crucial* element in our "skincare regime," this moisturizer having two varieties, day and night.

And then there was toner, something which was explained, but I still wasn't quite clear on its purpose, just that it was vital to my skin appearing "healthy" and required Noc to take us to a place called a "pharmacy" so we could buy "cotton wipes" in order to use it.

The perfume I'd purchased I'd set on the counter surrounding Noc's basin. The bottle was far too attractive to be hidden away in a compartment, no matter how clever that compartment was.

"It's called a medicine cabinet."

I jumped at Noc's voice and turned to see him leaning in the doorway, watching me, a look of soft satisfaction on his face.

I felt my spirit settle into that look and asked quietly, "Why is it called that?"

"You put what you put in it just now, but it was invented back in a day when there wasn't much of that stuff. Mostly it was where you stored medicine."

"Ah," I murmured, watching him and not moving because he was not moving, just standing in the doorway, leaning his shoulder into the jamb, his eyes gentle on me.

It was, of course, after our trip to the mall and Noc had returned Josette to Valentine's, where she assured us she was quite happy to experiment with her newly-acquired skills with the microwave in order to make her supper that night and again watch the television. "Where I learn much of this world," she'd said.

I felt some guilt, however, for I knew she was saying such with only a hint of truth. Mostly, she wanted to be certain Noc and I had time together.

This was her adventure too, and as such she shouldn't be spending it sitting in an empty house (for Valentine again was not there upon our return or even when we'd left), eating alone and watching a box, no matter how interesting what played on it was.

But for now, I was back at Noc's where he said he'd make me dinner while I put away the purchases I'd made to keep at his home and where I'd be sleeping.

Needless to say, Josette and I very much enjoyed our time at the mall. We'd done as Noc said we'd do, filling his Suburban to the brim with our bags.

In other words, there was a good deal for me to put away.

And I had been doing just that while Noc had been in his kitchen cooking.

I was surprised he had these skills but only because, in my world, a man such as him would have servants to do these things for him.

In this world, it seemed everyone cooked for themselves, which I found most odd and vaguely alarming for there might come a time when I was expected to do the same and I had no desire to do so.

I didn't think much on that. I thought simply of going through my marvelous purchases and putting them away while I smelled the pleasant aroma of Noc's efforts filling the house.

"Is dinner ready?" I queried when Noc said nothing and continued not to move.

"Not quite," he replied.

I tipped my head to the side and asked carefully, "Is all well?"

He looked to my perfume bottle on the counter and back to me.

"Absolutely."

He said this firmly, but his manner was peculiar.

"You seem in a strange mood, my love," I whispered.

With a suddenness that was astounding, his energy filled the room, wrapping me in its warm embrace with such fierceness, it almost made me gasp.

But even as this happened, his reply was calm.

"No, baby, just enjoying our first night of normal."

"Our first night of normal?" I inquired.

"Life can't be all drama and adventure, Frannie," he replied. "Travel between worlds. Trips on galleons. Dinners with a queen. For us, it's gonna be this. Your shit in my medicine cabinet, your perfume on my bathroom counter, dinner in the oven, a glass of wine waiting for you in the kitchen when you're done putzing around."

"You've poured me a glass of wine?" I asked, for some reason thinking this was the height of thoughtfulness.

"Yeah, sweetheart. I know how you like to unwind."

He did. I always had a glass of wine prior to dinner as well as during it.

He looked to the empty bags on the counter and back to me.

"You need any help?"

I shook my head. "No, darling. And I'm almost finished."

He raised a hand in a casual gesture and dropped it. "Take your time. Made shepherd's pie. It needs to bake, but even when it's done it can rest until you're ready."

I smiled at him. "Thank you."

He nodded, his gaze sweeping me from head to foot and back again before his beautiful lips formed a tender smile and he moved to leave.

"Noc?" I called.

He stopped and looked into my eyes.

"This new normal is lovely," I told him. "And it being what our normal shall be, I look forward to much more of it. And you know I always enjoy spending time with you." I felt my face soften and continued, "Especially when we have time alone. However, I do feel I should look after Josette and not leave her in her own company quite so much. I know she's content with giving us time," I hastened to add. "But until she finds her footing in this world, is able to get out, do more for herself, meet other people she can spend time with, we're all she has, especially with Valentine absenting herself. I—"

He lifted a hand again, this time higher. "Say no more, baby, I hear you. I know she's bein' cool for us. But you're right. We gotta see to her. I'll take you both to Bourbon Street tomorrow night. Have fun, get you hammered on hurricanes, have more fun. Sound good to you?"

I knew his use of "hammered" was not what it seemed so I nodded.

"Is that all?" he asked.

It was not all.

I wanted to tell him that his world was advanced. The telephones. The televisions. The cars. What we'd been introduced to that day: escalators. And so much more. All of it was impressive. There was so much of it, it was astonishing. There was so much more to learn, myriad amounts, and the idea of that was exciting, as each new discovery had been. There was almost nothing similar between our worlds and he'd been right, because of that, this was the grandest adventure we could take.

Even so, from what I could tell, regardless of the delicious food, the conveniences, the wonders of manicures and pedicures and the existence of Nordstrom shoe department, I preferred my world. The simplicity of it. The quiet of it. The clean of it in look and smell. The unmolested beauty of the landscape you could see all around, even in the cities, something you couldn't see here no matter how far you looked, unless you were close to the water and even then it was often cluttered with boats and bridges.

That said, there was nowhere on this earth, or my own, I'd prefer to be but standing in his bathroom with Noc but feet away.

"Babe?" he prompted.

I shook my head and did it shaking myself out of my thoughts.

"Yes, darling, that's all. I'll join you shortly."

He nodded, tipping his lips up slightly, and he turned from the door.

I watched him disappear and took a long breath.

I let it go, turned back to the empty bags and began folding them away.

I SAT ASTRIDE Noc, my torso up, my eyes on my fingers, which were trailing lazily through the dark hair scattered to perfection on his chest. I then trailed them down, my thumbs dipping into the ridges at his stomach, tracing each box, taking their time. And again up, my fingers worshipfully brushing along the grooves of his ribs.

My touch was light, not meant to be stimulating, we'd both found our pleasure (for my part, Noc had guided me there twice).

No.

I had a sated Noc on my hands, our first night of normal coming to an end, and I found myself in the position of being able to enjoy simply touching him, learning him, stroking him, giving to him.

I drew an idle line over his pectoral and shoulder, running the tip of my middle finger down the outside of his arm, murmuring, "You're quite talented in the kitchen."

And he was. His shepherd's pie was simple fare, but it was also rich and flavorful.

"Give you and Josette some lessons," he said and my gaze darted to his. "We can all cook together. And when it's just us here, you and me can do it."

"Cook together?" I asked.

He held my gaze and repeated after me, but not in a query. "Cook together."

"Mm," I mumbled noncommittally.

There was silence as I averted my attention (and hopefully his) to drawing my other finger from the inside of his elbow, up his biceps, over his shoulder and down, where I flattened it over the bulge of his pectoral.

A pectoral that was slightly shaking.

I again looked to his eyes.

They were laughing.

"You have no intention of learning to cook, do you?" he asked.

"Erm," I hedged.

"Babe, people cook here."

"I had guessed that with the kitchens being an integral part of the home, open, right in the living space. Even Valentine's home has an enormous space off the kitchen with sofas and lounges, which makes the area appear communal."

"That's because the kitchen is the heart of the house."

It was not.

The parlor was.

Everyone knew that.

Though, apparently not in this world.

"Interesting," I mumbled, and didn't even try to hide I thought it was not.

His pectoral shook under my hand again.

I wished to roll my eyes but I didn't.

"Frannie, we're both stinkin' rich, you way more than me, which means you could probably hire a cook. But you shouldn't because cooking is fun."

I could not imagine this was anywhere near the truth, therefore I made no reply.

However, I did put it on the list in my head of things to see to, to discuss hiring a cook with Valentine, once I'd found a home, of course.

"Right, I'll be the one who cooks," Noc declared, and my attention refocused on his face. "Just want you sittin' there with me, drinkin' wine and doin' whatever when I do it because I'm thinkin' from your attitude it'll also be me cleaning up. That means, to earn your meal, you gotta keep me company."

At his behest, after dinner, we'd left the dishes in the sink.

It hadn't even occurred to me he'd eventually have to tidy them and it definitely hadn't occurred to me he might wish me to assist.

I added a housekeeper to my list of new acquisitions.

"You can take the girl outta the House but you can't take the House outta the girl," he muttered, smiling broadly while watching me closely. "Everyone's blood is red. Your blood is the red of the Drakkars. If it wasn't, it'd be blue."

My brows drew together. "Blue blood?"

"Royals, nobles, back in the day, *way* back in the day," he began, "didn't get out much. Common folk, they were in the sun. Worked there. Walked where they had to go because they didn't have carriages or sometimes even horses. Couldn't avoid it. The whiter the skin, the more noble someone would seem. Their veins were visible, looked blue, easy to see through that pasty-white skin. Blue bloods."

"So this is a slang word for your aristocracy," I surmised.

"Yup," he affirmed.

"I much like being in the sun. My skin becomes an attractive shade when I am," I shared.

His pectoral started shaking again. "Although I look forward to the day I'm introduced to you in a bikini, I bet you've never worked in it."

"Of course not," I huffed, for I had not worked a day in my life and did not intend to.

Practicing the craft didn't count. That was simply who I was, and when I began to earn alongside Valentine, I would accept the money, of course. Money *was* money and the more of it you had, the better everything was. But they'd be paying me, essentially, for being me and doing what came naturally, something I had no issue with.

His smile remained fixed even as his lips ordered, "Fuckin' kiss me, Lady Franka."

This I could gladly do.

And I set about doing just that, sweeping both hands up his chest and bending over him.

Resting my breasts to his chest, he circled me with an arm low at my back, his other hand drawing languid patterns on the skin of my outer thigh, and I kissed him.

It was as lazy as our mood, slow and deep.

And it was delicious.

When I lifted my head I saw a contentedness in his eyes, the tranquil lines in his face, both making him more handsome than ever, which was quite a feat.

His expression settled in my soul as I traced his collarbone and shared softly, "You often tell me of my beauty, but I wonder, do you know the greatness of yours?"

"No one has run screaming when I walked into a room," he joked.

I pressed closer, running a light caress along the cords at the side of his neck, smiling at his jest. "This undoubtedly is true. Though it minimalizes the sheer perfection that is you."

His eyes sparked, his hand at my thigh gripped and his arm at my back slanted up so he could tangle his fingers in my hair, all this as he growled, "Frannie."

"It's true," I stated. "It makes me feel most fortunate."

The intensity ebbed as his lips quirked. "And why are *you* fortunate, babe?"

"You chose me."

"You chose me," he returned.

"Yes, but you're perfect and I am not."

He shook his head on the pillow. "I'm not perfect, Frannie."

"Yes, you can be vexing, but mostly, you're perfect, and physically, and this is always in the eye of the beholder so you cannot argue it, my dearest, so don't try, you're most definitely perfect."

For a moment he continued to hold me as he had.

But then suddenly, I felt him still under me.

"Noc?" I called.

"You're also perfect, you know," he whispered, a curious tone to his voice making my belly pitch.

"As you are the beholder, I can't argue that either," I replied in a manner that shared openly I couldn't argue it, but I also didn't agree.

"You're perfect, Franka," he declared, firmness now in his voice that was almost scolding.

I bent to him, touched my mouth to his and moved a hint away before I whispered, "Thank you, my love."

"Do not think you can get away with that shit."

I blinked at his words, the abrupt and unexpected change in his mood and lifted my head further.

Noc rolled so I was no longer atop him, but he was atop me.

He didn't allow me to become accustomed to our new positions before he asked, "This part of that midnight soul garbage you're determined not to let go?"

Oh balls.

Not this.

"Darling, we've had a lovely day and a *very* lovely evening. Let's not ruin it with such talk."

"That gonna be your gig every time I bring it up?" he asked.

I smiled up at him, wrapping my arms around him. "I hope so, as it would mean we'd have many lovely days."

"Franka, don't be sweet and cute, which right now is sweet and cute and pissing me off."

It wasn't me behaving in a way that would piss someone off.

It was Noc for we were both enjoying our togetherness and now he was ruining it.

On this thought, my eyes narrowed. "Can I request that if this is so important to you and you wish to discuss it, that we do it at a later date?"

"And when would that date be?" he asked back.

"I don't know except for the fact it would be *later*."

He stared down at me, appearing perturbed.

Then, abruptly, he lifted himself, readjusted his legs so it was he straddling me, and he whipped me to my belly.

I drew in a sharp breath.

He pulled his knees in so they were clamped to the outsides of my thighs and now he was not only straddling me, but imprisoning my lower half for the weight of him settling on me, the power of him restraining me, I couldn't move.

This was not meant to be stimulating.

This was something else that I knew I was not ready for, then or perhaps ever.

"Noc," I hissed.

"This is perfect," he stated, running a flat hand over my bum.

"I'm pleased you think so, now—" I tried, attempting to pull myself up.

Noc's hand in my back pushed me down and again I gasped in surprise.

I felt his other hand dive deep, shoving between my legs, and suddenly he was cupping my sex.

"This is totally perfect, Franka."

"Noc," I pushed out.

His hand left my back and tangled in my hair.

"This is perfect."

"Cease, you don't have to—"

Both his hands left me and went to the bed on either side of me.

This was not what made me stop speaking.

He'd shifted his hands so he could lower himself to my back.

"And this is perfect."

I grew still.

I felt him move even if I couldn't quite feel what he was doing. My guess was that he was running his lips along a scar.

One of many.

I closed my eyes tight.

"You feel that, Frannie?" he asked.

"Please get up," I requested.

He did not get up.

What he did was move upwards so his mouth was at my ear.

"You don't, do you, sweetheart?"

I opened my eyes but looked only at the pillow. "Again, I'll ask you to get up."

"You know how you're perfect?" he queried.

I knew the glaring evidence of my imperfection was right in front of his eyes but I did not point that out to him for I didn't wish to and he could bloody well see it for himself.

I remained silent.

"You don't feel much at your back. I gotta go hard if I want you to know I'm touching you there. And the reason that's perfect when you think it's imperfection is that they took that from you. They crippled you here. This will never be the same," he said, and I could feel him running his hand down my back, putting pressure into the touch so I could experience it. "*They* did that, Frannie. *They* took that. And you survived."

"Yes, I am aware. I was there each time," I returned cuttingly, beginning to get angry at discussing something I did not wish to discuss, and he very well knew it.

"You survived."

"I am aware."

"They did not survive."

I quieted.

"They're beaten and broken and as good as dead. Their lives are over. You, though, you're here and getting pedicures and worried about making your girl eat dinner alone, carrying these marks not as their brand, but your badge of honor because you survived. I know. I know the elves could have healed you, taken this away." His hand soothed deep down my back. "I know Frey offered that to you. And I know you refused. That makes this perfect, that you took from them what they did to you and twisted it into something that was *yours*. Something that was beautiful. Something that means you're a fighter. A warrior. Victorious. And you wear their mark as your medal of valor."

I held my breath, no longer angry.

Now I was fighting trembling.

Noc continued talking.

"You don't think you're perfect, but you are, Frannie. Every inch."

My voice was frail and wavering, I hated it but for the life of me I couldn't strengthen it, when I begged, "Please stop talking."

He shifted and I felt his teeth sink into my skin at my shoulder blade. The sensation was there and gone before I felt him smoothing the area, pressing deep with his thumb.

"I look at this and see beauty. I touch it and love how it feels. I taste it and it tastes as gorgeous as the rest of you."

Gods.

He was undoing me.

"Stop talking."

He slid his knees out, straightening his legs, covering me with his big body, his weight bearing into me, his flawless chest with its perfect array of hair pressed into the mess of my back.

Putting some of his weight in one forearm in the bed, he shoved his other arm under me at my belly and held me close, his mouth back to my ear.

"You say my light shines on your soul, do you think for one second you'd be in my bed right now if your light didn't warm mine?"

I again closed my eyes tight and it came through my lips before I even knew I had the thought.

"I want to be that for you."

"*Fuck*," he bit out. His word scoring into me like a lash, Noc lifted, turning me again to my back. Insinuating his hips between my legs so they opened to accommodate him, I felt his palm cup my cheek and heard his demand. "Open your eyes."

I did as commanded.

"The first I knew of you, you loved a man so deeply, you put your life on the line twice, first committing treason, which I know in Lunwyn is a hanging offense, and then facing those witches. Does that come from a soul that's midnight?"

"Noc—"

"You don't know it, don't see it, but even before your relationship shifted, you treated Josette with more care and respect than any of those people treated what they considered their inferiors, save Cora, Circe and Finnie, who aren't from there and don't know how to act the blue blood even though they now are. And don't think she didn't know it, Frannie. Don't think Josette is here for whatever you pay her or for an adventure. She's here *for you*. She's here to be *with you*. She's here because, to her, you're family. Is that kind of loyalty earned by a dark soul?"

He *really* had to stop because I felt them brimming and I knew I wouldn't be able to hold them back.

Especially when Noc saw them and shifted his hand at my cheek so his thumb swept below my eye. Releasing the tear into the pad of his thumb, he skimmed the wet along my temple as he dipped his face close.

"You grew up without any love," he whispered, and gods, *gods*, I saw it in his eyes as well. The bright gathering there, his own wet gleaming. "I have no fuckin' clue how you survived, baby. I've known love every day of my life and I cannot imagine the man I'd be if I didn't. If my life was void of it. If I had to find my way without that as the single-most prevalent guiding force from the minute my mom died giving me life to this moment with you. I could only hope that I'd become what you've become against every odd. A woman starved of love her whole life and yet so fuckin' full of it, she'd stand holding a hook with blood running down her thighs just so the brother she adored wouldn't have to do it. You don't have a midnight soul, Frannie. Your soul is so bright, I look too close, I'd be blinded."

"Please." My voice broke, I swallowed and finished on a return whisper, "Please stop talking, my love."

"I will you answer this. Do you have a midnight soul?" he asked.

"Apparently not," I continued whispering.

And apparently, I actually did not.

"No, you do not," he affirmed. "Am I gonna hear that again?"

I shook my head.

"You gonna think it?"

I shook my head again (though it was perhaps more hesitant than the first).

Noc, of course, did not miss it.

"You think it, baby, you give that shit to me and I'll remind you what makes you. We got a deal?"

I nodded.

"Promise me," he demanded.

I drew in a trembling breath before I gave him what he asked.

"I promise, darling."

He let that drift between us before he dipped closer and spoke again gently, his thumb caressing the apple of my cheek.

"There is not a single soul on this earth who has not done things they regret, Frannie. Multiple things. Years of doing stupid shit or mean shit or thoughtless shit or whatever. It's part of growing up. It's part of life. It's part of surviving. Everyone makes mistakes. Everyone finds their way. You were who you had to be. It's just the way it was. And now it isn't that way and you aren't that way either. You said earlier it's our future, not the past that interests you. But you're still livin' in the past, sweetheart. Let it go. Be with me. *Really* be here with me. Because I love you here, baby, and what we got, it's a beautiful place to be."

He was right.

Very, very right.

That was that past. That was the way it was and now it wasn't that way anymore.

I wasn't that way anymore.

I was free to be the real me.

"You're right, Noc."

"I know."

The arrogance of his words made me give him a shaky grin.

His other hand came to my opposite cheek and he swept the tear that dropped there across that temple.

"I dislike weeping," I muttered.

"God gave us a variety of ways to get hurt out and do it clean. Blood cleans a wound. Tears clean a different kind of wound. You might not like it, Frannie, but you shouldn't stop yourself from doing it. Clean the wound so it can heal. Then move on."

By the gods, I really could take no more.

"You do know you're demonstrating my earlier point, being handsome, having a magnificent physique, being thoughtful, kind, patient, intuitive and wise, all this meaning you're rather perfect, do you not?" I noted.

Noc continued his acute study of me before his expression cleared and his lips tipped up.

"You wanna think I'm perfect, sugarlips, be my guest. My point was never about arguing yours."

This was true.

But I was done.

"Can we go to sleep?" I requested.

"Are you tired?" he asked.

I actually was.

Exhausted.

It seemed coming to terms with your wonderfulness took a good deal out of you.

I nodded.

His voice quieted. "Then yeah, gorgeous, you want, we can go to sleep."

"Are you tired?" I queried.

"Not so much."

"Then—"

"You're down with it, I'll turn on the TV. I watch, you sleep. You can't get to sleep with the TV on, I'll turn it off and read. Cool?"

I nodded.

Noc dipped in for a lip brush, but when he was done, he pulled only slightly away.

"That was heavy, you okay?" he asked gently.

I nodded, though in truth I wasn't.

But I suspected I would be.

"Gonna be a hard promise to keep, the promise you made me, but want you to keep it, Frannie."

I drew in a deep breath and let it go.

"I'll keep it, Noc," I promised again.

His face again assumed a version of the sated contentment he'd had before. It did not run as deep but it was still there.

He was pleased.

Which made me pleased.

He dipped in for something much deeper than a lip brush before he rolled off me and rearranged us, the covers, and turned off the lights, but he turned on the television that was resting on a cabinet at the other side of the room beyond the end of the bed.

He lay with head and shoulders propped on pillows, holding me tucked close to his side, my cheek to his ribs.

I held him around the stomach and stared at the perfect hair on his chest, feeling his finger again drawing languid patterns, this time on the skin just below the small of my back.

Healthy skin, where I could feel his caress and what he wished it to communicate to me.

And I felt his caress.

But more, I felt what he wished it to communicate.

I was there, *really* there, with him, where he wanted me to be, where he liked me to be, a good, safe, healthy place. And he wanted me right there, and a man like Noc would not chose a woman to be right there if she did not deserve to be.

The sound of the television strangely did not distract me from falling asleep.

Strangely, it and Noc's warmth, his nearness, his touch, his simply *being* and being with me lulled me to sleep.

And when I slept, I slept deep, snuggled up to sheer perfection.

18

FALLEN FOR ME

Franka

I sat alone at a table in one of Valentine's sitting rooms, looking into my crystal ball that sat atop its lovely pillow of sapphire-blue velvet.

I was trying to concentrate, but although I'd been in it now for a full five days, I didn't know this world enough to understand the visions I was calling up.

Not to mention, I had on my mind the fact that the three homes Valentine's agent had shown us the day before were not to my, Josette's, or even Noc's liking, something, in our depth of discussion of each we'd had over dinner the evening before, had become clear.

We had another "showing" that day, and my mind was also on that, as I was finding more with each passing day the need to settle, not only myself but Josette.

Valentine had no opinion on the houses we'd seen since she was not there to view them with us.

In fact, I had not seen her since she introduced Josette and me to the wonders of the curling iron. Our only communication was through texts, notes she left and messages delivered to us by her secretary or the man who was her caretaker.

This irked me, greatly, and the longer it lasted the more irksome it became.

Yes, one could say that our time had been full since our arrival, so our need of Valentine's presence was not great. There was much to do, see and experience, and Noc was being lovely with offering us all of that.

This included his promise of taking Josette and me to Bourbon Street the evening before last, a place I knew was where I'd been spirited to upon entering this world due to the familiarity of its noise, but mostly its smell.

"Spilled booze, puke and bodies, baby, all baked in the sun," Noc had explained the smell. "In other words, the aroma of a really fuckin' good time."

I did not agree.

That was I did not agree until he introduced Josette and I to hurricanes, which were *delicious*, and jazz, a music that was *extraordinary*.

Halfway through hurricane one, we'd commenced having great fun and met the many fast friends around us who were a delight (and who I would not then remember even if they walked up to me and offered me an embrace, such was the potency of hurricanes, something which Noc told us to stop partaking of at one, and Josette and I had each had three).

Through this experience I was realizing that my preference for my own world was partly my loyalty to it as well as my familiarity of it.

Fleuridia was much different than Hawkvale, which was much different than Lunwyn.

But they all were marvelous, in their own way.

As was this world, it's liveliness, fast pace, music, food.

I simply had to open my mind to it.

And being on Bourbon Street, there was no way you could keep your mind closed. You became one with the mood, that mood being revelry and frivolity, and were swept away by it. And one could most assuredly say being swept away with revelry and frivolity was a joyous thing.

But even if we had not liked what we had seen during the house showings we'd had, Josette and I would eventually find a home and then we would need to settle into the new lives we'd chosen. It couldn't all be shopping, eating and frivolity.

It could, of course. We were wealthy enough to have this. But then it might become boring, and when frivolity became boring, what did you do after that?

So settling into the lives we'd chosen it was.

And for me to do this required Valentine.

Not to mention, we had plans for Circe and the Dax Lahn of this world and there had been no time to waste...now there was even less.

It was on that thought I sensed someone in the hall. I turned in my chair and saw Valentine walk past the doorway.

"Sister," I called.

It was unlikely she didn't hear me but there was a moment when I thought

I would have to rise from my chair and follow her before she finally retraced her steps and filled the doorframe.

"Franka," she greeted.

I sensed immediately all was not well.

This was not by look.

It was by feel.

I stood, examining her closely. "Are you well?"

Valentine walked but a foot into the room and lied, "I am."

"We've not seen much of you," I noted carefully.

"I'd been spending a good deal of time in your world," she stated. "This means there's a good deal to see to now that I've returned to my own."

A likely explanation.

But not a truthful one.

Before I could ask after it, her eyes dropped to my crystal and came back to me.

"You practice?"

I shook my head. "I'm searching for Frey."

She nodded. "Of course. You're curious, as you would be. The child is born. A girl. They've named her Alyssa Aurora Eugenie."

I blinked at the brusque delivery of this important news.

"Frey and Finnie's child has been born?"

"Yes. As has Circe and Lahn's. A girl. They've named her Andromeda." She offered me no opportunity to make comment, she carried on, "Tor and Cora have not yet been delivered of their joy, but it could be any day now. And as you know, Apollo and Madeleine have had their Valentine."

I could not believe what I was hearing.

"I knew no such thing," I shared.

Her head twitched, but she replied simply, "Well, they have."

"When did all this news come?" I asked.

"Circe and Lahn, just yesterday. Finnie and Frey, I found out later that it was occurring as I was spiriting you to this world. I'm afraid I was lax in keeping track of Madeleine but discovered that wonderful news prior to your departure from your world. I'm afraid I was also lax in sharing it."

She was *lax* indeed!

"Did you not think we would wish to hear this news?" I queried, tamping down my annoyance due to her queer demeanor.

"You're hearing it now."

I studied her and repeated, again carefully, "Things are not well."

"They are," she returned and again shifted her gaze to my crystal before looking back to me. "And I'll note, if you wish any news of the others, you simply have to seek them out yourself. You've been busy, this I know. But I'm not a messenger, my sister. If you want to know," she tossed a hand lazily toward my crystal, "look."

She was correct.

She still could have told me.

I let that go and shared, "I actually wasn't looking for the Frey I know. I was looking for the Frey of this world."

Her brows rose. "And why would you do that?"

"Curiosity," I replied. "Noc has explained that the two worlds are unbalanced in regards to that part of the equation. Noc and I both are interested in understanding, as we provide a kind of balance to the loss of Cora and the loss of the me of this world, how the situation with the Frey of this world and the Sjofn once of my own balances between the universes."

"The Frey of this world was in need of money to start his own custom furniture business," Valentine began to explain instantly. "Thus, some time ago he sold his sperm to a sperm bank. Perhaps a rash thing to do, but with his IQ and other charms, a smart one, for he was unsurprisingly remunerated very well for it. This sperm was selected by Sjofn and the lover she's married since coming to this world, and it has been selected twice. They have a son, Viktor, and a daughter was just born to them, Alyssa, both children Sjofn carried. Quite the coincidence, unless you understand the destiny at work."

I stared at her.

She carried on.

"To fully assuage your curiosity, Frey of this world lives in Boise, Idaho with his wife, who is barren. His custom furniture business is quite the success now that he's put a goodly amount of time, effort and talent into it. He sells furniture across the country. And they're raising three children, all of Vietnamese descent who they adopted from that land. He's quite happy, quite in love and quite proud of his family, having no idea he has a son and daughter of his seed, nor will he ever know. However, Sjofn does know as she's seen photos of the donor she selected, which was one of the reasons she selected him. If possible, balance must be maintained and that is not lost on our deposed princess."

"Well, that answers that," I murmured, and it did, even if some of it I didn't quite understand.

"Now, if that'll be all..." she trailed off doing it moving out the door.

If that'll be all?

I hadn't spoken directly to her in days!

I took a step toward her, calling, "Valentine."

She stopped, turned to me and again lifted her brows, doing all with clear impatience.

"There are things we must see to," I told her something she had to know.

"Agreed, and we shall, after I see to the things *I* need to see to," she returned.

"Can you perhaps share when you feel this would be?" I requested.

She tipped her head to the side. "Do you not have enough to occupy your time?"

"Of course I do, however, in the case of Circe and Lahn—"

"Yes," she interrupted me quickly. "If you'd like to carry on with that, be my guest and keep me apprised."

She finished that again turning to leave.

"Sister," I said sharply, keeping tight hold on my displeasure.

And concern.

She turned back on a sigh.

I held her gaze steady. "Things are not well."

I saw her jaw tighten. "I'll not answer that again."

"Things are not well," I repeated.

"Franka, I have little time for—"

I took a step toward her and quieted my voice. "I know things are not well. I don't know *what* is not well, but I know whatever it is is troubling you. And you need to know I know, so you'll also know I'm here to listen and help should you have the need."

She turned her head away and it appeared she was collecting herself before she turned back and the remoteness was gone.

I did not have the Valentine I knew returned when she again gazed at me, but at least she'd removed the shield she'd been holding up against me.

And what I saw made my breath catch, I couldn't quite read it, but I most assuredly didn't like it.

"You're right, *ma petite sorcière*," she said softly, "things are not well. I find I'm experiencing something I had not thought I ever would. And I'm having some difficulty finding my way around it. I wish to do that on my own, but," she lifted a hand when I opened my mouth, "if I should fail to find that way, I will take you up on your offer."

I nodded and pressed no more. I knew women of her ilk, for, until very recently, I was just that kind of woman.

"You're also correct," she continued. "You're here and our plans for Circe and Dax Lahn need to commence. I just...I simply..." Again it seemed she was collecting herself before she finished, "This is not something I can do right now."

She'd been seeing to her business, but she could not see to that business.

That business.

I studied her carefully, and at what I finally read, I felt my throat constrict.

By the gods, she'd had her heart broken.

Gods, the despair I now saw hidden deep in her eyes was that she'd lost a lover.

I took a step toward her, whispering, "Valentine."

I saw her body brace. "Please, Franka, don't."

I stopped moving.

"All will be well," she lied.

I nodded and assured her of the only thing I could in that moment, or at least all she would allow.

"I shall begin with Circe and Lahn. I'll keep you apprised."

She dipped her chin. "Thank you."

Before I could utter another word, without a glance back, she swept from the room.

I stood staring at the empty doorway for some time, my heart heavy for my friend, feeling some frustration her pride forced her to block the efforts of help of those who cared about her.

And it was not lost on me that perhaps, in the past, those who cared about me felt the same with my prideful ways.

If this was the case, it was good that Noc had delivered me of that on our first night of normal, for now I knew the pain of having pain without allowing oneself to seek solace was much akin to the pain of caring about someone who refused solace offered.

I heaved a sigh and moved back to my crystal ball, fluttering a hand over it to clear the blue smoke that drifted through it and called up the this-world Lahn.

When I did, regardless of how often I'd observed him, I found myself surprised at just how easy he was to observe.

Unlike losing my concentration earlier in attempting to understand the life of the this-world Frey, I got quite lost in watching the this-word Lahn.

So much so, I jumped when I heard Noc's voice saying, "Ready to go find a house, sugarlips?"

I looked to the door to see him sauntering through.

Therefore, I smiled and rose again from my seat.

He walked right to me, smiling back, rounding me with an arm and dipping his head to mine to drop a closed-mouth kiss on my lips.

After delivering me that morning from his home so I could have breakfast with Josette and he could leave to give her and I time to spend together, as planned, he'd returned to take us, what he referred to as, "house hunting."

We'd been apart perhaps three hours.

I'd missed him.

"I'm ready, darling," I answered.

His arm around me gave me a squeeze and I could feel him preparing to let me go, but I placed a hand to his chest to forestall him.

"Before we go, you must know I have news," I shared.

"And that would be?"

Standing close together, I told him all I'd learned.

His joy at Finnie and Frey, Lahn and Circe and Apollo and Maddie's news was unhidden, this one of the many things I loved about him.

There was no subterfuge with Noc. He did not feel it made him more of a man to hide his emotions. It was a thing of beauty, a gift he bestowed on anyone who was fortunate enough to witness it, and I treasured it for just that.

But when I told him of the Frey and Sjofn of this world, he burst out laughing.

When his mirth settled to chuckles, he said, "Well, that takes care of that."

"Although I do believe I can put it together, can you explain what a sperm bank is?"

He grinned and explained.

When he did, it was I who burst out laughing.

When my mirth had settled to chuckles, I wondered if I looked upon him with the warmth that he was right then looking at me after he did the same.

I hoped so.

"This world has many conveniences," I observed. "*Many*."

"Yeah," Noc agreed through a grin. "Now, after we look at places, we'll go to the mall again. Get baby presents. See if we can wrangle five minutes with Valentine so she'll deliver them."

"What a lovely idea," I murmured, not at all surprised that Noc had had it.

I had not shared with him about Valentine except to tell him I'd seen her and she'd given me the news I'd imparted on Noc.

I wouldn't either, unless he asked about it.

That wasn't what sisters did.

And I finally had sisters. I needed to take care of them.

And this, however I needed to do, specifically with Valentine, I would do.

~

"This is revolting," I said under my breath to Noc.

"This is suburbia, Frannie," he replied under his breath to me. "You told the agent you wanted greenspace, you aren't gonna find much of that in a city."

I tore my gaze from the personality-less room of what had been referred to as a "model home," though my understanding of the word "model" did not reconcile with anything to do with the home we were in, and looked to Josette.

She felt my regard, turned to me and curled her lip.

I looked to the agent who was pretending she wasn't trying to listen and stated, "I'm sorry for taking you so far away from the city to show us this property, but I'm afraid it won't do."

She forced a smile and moved my way, saying, "Well, now we've seen four properties so perhaps you can share what you liked, and didn't, about each, and maybe I can narrow my search."

What I liked was Noc's home and not because I wished that for Josette and me.

I liked it because there was great beauty in having all that was Noc surrounding me, making me feel safe and warm and peaceful, none of which I'd ever had. I loved being in his home in a way I knew that could be my home, far less grand than any I'd ever known, but indisputably far better as well.

But I couldn't request from Noc that he allow Josette and me to live with him.

Firstly, because it was far too small. For Noc and I to have what I wished Noc and I to have when we had our alone times, Josette obviously could not be with us.

Secondly, because this was an intimacy I felt—for some unfathomable reason I still understood as accurate—was one Noc needed to invite.

And he would not do that with Josette accompanying me.

However, I was Franka Drakkar and I knew what I liked.

So I shared it.

"The brick walkways of the first property you showed us, as well as the drive and garage, for Mr. Hawthorne will need somewhere to keep his vehicle that's safer than the street for when he's with us, as will Josette and I when we acquire our own conveyances," I declared.

The woman stared fixedly at me, something she did often when I knew she found my speech odd.

I ignored it and carried on.

"The wrought iron around the veranda and balconies of the second, with the large tree in front that offered shade, its two stories and lovely cornices and ceiling roses. And the privacy and maturity of the garden in the courtyard of the third." I drifted out a hand. "Alas, I've nothing to share that I like of this, except the large lawns, which I do believe I may need to relinquish in order to have other things that are priorities."

"I like to find my clients exactly what they want, but I will say that's likely," she muttered.

"And lastly, proximity to Mr. Hawthorne, which I should have said first," I finished.

At this, Noc slid an arm around me and pulled me close to his side. Therefore, I returned the gesture.

"I can work with this," the agent said.

I should hope she could, she was being paid to do just that.

"I'll sort some listings. Do you have a direct email or would you like me to continue sending them to Ms. Rousseau's assistant?" she asked.

"Send them to me," Noc answered. "It'll all go faster that way. I'll get your number from Franka and text you my email."

"Excellent," she replied.

"Not to hurry us along or anything," Josette began. "But are we done here? Just because, you see, Noc said we're going to the mall after this and there was that blouse I decided against that I haven't been able to get out of my mind since. And I was hoping it'd still be there."

"We're done here," Noc decreed, looked to the agent and lifted his chin. "Thanks for your time, and you send us some listings, we'll be in touch."

"My pleasure. I hope to see you again soon."

Josette and I also gave our farewells and Noc guided us out.

We were in his SUV when he shared, "Babe, you don't have to live in the city. You want nature around you, I'm sure they have places that might not be close but they're not far."

"Yes, but you're in the city," was my reply.

"Yeah, but I'm also not getting to you by sled, sweetheart," he returned with humor. "It won't take half a day to make an hour's drive."

I turned from viewing the road before us to look at Noc and only then did I repeat, but more definitively this time, "Yes, but *you* are in the city."

He glanced at me and back to the road, but even with only having his profile, I watched his expression warm before he said, "Gotcha."

I nodded smartly, looked behind me to smile at Josette, who smiled back, and then I looked back to the road.

~

I WAS ENGROSSED in my perusal of a very attractive dress hanging on a rack in the mall when I heard Noc make a noise.

I looked up to him to see that his expression was no longer vacant (this being because I knew he was bored out of his mind, for we did not simply pick up some baby gifts and Josette's blouse, we became distracted by other things, so our quick trip to the mall was nothing of the like).

Now he looked alert and I turned to see what he was regarding.

It was Josette, skipping toward us, waving her telephone and looking joyous.

I couldn't help it, her demeanor made me smile.

My lovely Josette, she so enjoyed the mall.

She stopped on a sway and cried, "I have a dinner date tomorrow!"

My smile died.

"I beg your pardon?" I queried.

"Say again?" Noc asked.

"Glover," she stated, rolling up to her toes, and back, and again, grinning like a lunatic. "That man we met on Bourbon Street. You know. The large, tall, handsome Maroovian-non-Maroovian one with the lovely smile?"

I knew no such man.

"No, I do not know," I stated.

"That guy, baby, the one Jo was talkin' to for, like, two hours," Noc explained.

I turned to him, vaguely remembering, and back to Josette when she started talking.

"He gave me his number. I texted. He texted back. We've been exchanging them, like, *bunches*. He's been being very sweet. I was looking at the jeans over there," she tossed an arm behind her but didn't turn that direction, she kept grinning at Noc and me, "and he called and asked if I wanted to go out to dinner tomorrow night. And I said *yes*!" She nearly shouted her last. "Isn't that *divine*? He's coming to pick me up at seven at Valentine's."

"He's doing nothing of the sort," I spat.

Josette blinked and her smile faltered.

I felt Noc move closer to me.

"I'm sorry?" Josette whispered.

"Am I to understand he's arriving at Valentine's home to put you in a car and take you for a meal?" I inquired.

"Yes," Josette kept whispering.

"That's unacceptable," I declared.

Josette blinked again and her shoulders fell.

"Frannie—" Noc started.

I jerked my head his way. "It's unacceptable."

"You were drunk and unnecessarily flirting with me so I think you missed she's into the guy and he was *way* into her," Noc replied.

"I do not care," I retorted and again turned my attention to Josette. "I forbid this to happen."

"Franka," Noc clipped as Josette's entire expression fell.

I again looked to Noc.

"Josette was not a common servant with no one to look after her even when she *was* a servant," I bit out. "She's a young woman of means with family who cares for her. Thus, he will behave like she is as such, which means he will behave appropriately. In other words, he'll arrive at Valentine's home at seven tomorrow to sit with us for drinks and dinner. Through this time spent with him, I'll understand what he does to make his living. I'll ask questions to ascertain his moral character. I'll observe his behavior toward Josette. And only *then* will I allow the *possibility* of a future *dinner date*. This being after he's proved himself a gentleman in his intentions toward Josette once we've spent some time with him and he has our approval."

Noc stared down at me.

I looked to Josette.

"Telephone him back and share this," I ordered.

Josette stared at me.

"Sweetheart, that's not how it's done in this world," Noc told me.

I returned my gaze to him. "This matters not to me."

"The dude is gonna think you're crazy, worse, he's gonna think Jo's crazy, and he's totally gonna beg off."

My brows snapped together. "Why on earth would he do that?"

"Because, Frannie, this is not how it's done in this world," he answered. "A guy likes a girl, he texts her, calls her, asks her out, takes her to dinner, gets to know her better. They like each other, that keeps happening. Beyond that," his eyes slid to Josette and back to me, "we won't go there right now."

I considered this information.

Then I turned to Josette and decreed, "Fine. Then telephone him back and share that Noc and I will be attending this dinner with you."

Josette's mouth dropped open.

"Frannie..." My name from Noc's lips was shaking with mirth.

I scowled at Noc, finding nothing amusing.

"*What?*" I clipped.

"You can't invite yourself on a double date if the guy didn't ask us along, especially on a first date."

My voice was rising. "Why not?"

He shook his head, his amusement plain. "You just can't."

"Then who's going to look after her?" I demanded to know.

Noc's amusement didn't leave but the warmth in his expression heightened.

"We'll make sure she texts us, tells us where she is, how she's getting on, when he brings her safe home." He looked to Josette. "That cool with you?"

"Definitely!" she chirped.

"It's not cool with me," I put in, and Noc looked to me.

"He's not asking *you* out," he noted.

I continued scowling at him before I made a decision. "All right, then we shall go to this same restaurant and sit at another table so we'll be close in case anything untoward happens or I observe something that displeases me in his behavior, or Josette needs me."

Noc started chuckling as he got close and curved an arm around me.

Tipping his head down, he said quietly, "Right, Momma Bear, the gig is, you're gonna have to let your little cub explore on her own eventually. I met the guy. We talked for a while. He seemed good to me. If he wasn't, if I got a bad vibe from him, anything, I'd be the one throwing a wrench in on his action. But what I got from him, I liked. And what Jo got from him, *she* liked. So you're just gonna have to stand down."

I did not wish to stand down.

I stared into Noc's eyes.

I turned my head toward Josette and saw the hope and excitement shining in hers.

Blast!

"Tell him he has you home by ten," I demanded.

Noc burst into laughter.

Josette's face became wreathed in smiles.

With the side of his fist under my chin, Noc turned my face to his and tipped it up so he could drop a short kiss on my lips.

When he finished doing that, he looked to Josette.

"I'll talk her into letting you have until midnight," he said.

Well!

"Now I gotta teach you two something else women do in this world," Noc continued, no longer sounding entertained, now sounding beleaguered. "That being the fact that a woman has a first date with a guy, she uses it as an excuse to buy a new outfit. You both got more new outfits than you can get through in a month. But I'm thinking none of them at this point are the right one for dinner with Glover."

"You're correct, Noc, I've been going through all of them in my head since I said yes, and Frannie, we *must* find something he will *most* like to see me in," Josette declared.

Gods, now Josette was calling me Frannie.

I sighed.

But she was quite right.

Nothing we'd bought previously would do.

Thus, it was time to get to work.

"Have you lost your mind?"

Much later, after Josette had insisted Noc and I have an evening alone together, we left her at Valentine's and returned to Noc's where I now sat on the sofa staring up at him standing in front of me holding one glass of wine (mine, which he had halted in delivering to me after I'd said what I'd just said) and one bottle of ale (his).

"No, I have not," I pointed out the obvious.

"You are not gonna do that," he declared, still standing several feet away from me and not offering me my glass. "More, *I'm* not gonna do that, but *you* definitely aren't gonna do that so to make myself perfectly clear, *we* are not gonna do that."

"May I have my wine, darling?" I requested quietly.

He looked down to his hand like he forgot he was holding it before he took the last step toward me and offered me my wine.

I took it and immediately sipped.

"Confirm you heard me, Frannie," he demanded, not sipping his beer, instead glowering down at me.

"Come sit beside me," I invited cajolingly.

"Nope," he shook his head. "I gotta cook, but I'm not doin' that either until I know we're both on the same page with this."

"Noc, my dearest, I *am* quite good at this," I assured. "I've had years of practice and I can't imagine the skills I have do not translate to this world. I've watched carefully and I've planned everything precisely."

"Right, this is the deal, babe," Noc returned tersely. "You go into an attorney's office, any attorney, but definitely an attorney known as the fuckin' *Savage*, of all fuckin' things, create a distraction in hopes that I'll be able to follow you and go unseen into his office to hack into his computer to get his schedule so you can set something up so he runs into Circe, you're an accessory to the crime *I'm* committing. A crime the fuckin' *Savage* will lose his fuckin' mind about if one of us is caught. And you do not piss off an attorney, Frannie.

My guess, and I'm betting a pretty damn good one, you especially don't piss off one known as the Savage."

"It's a crime to look at someone's, erm...computer diary?" I asked.

"It's a crime to break and enter, even if you don't do any breaking in order to enter, and it's also a crime to help yourself to unauthorized access of a private or business computer."

I thought of all the many times I had found my way (stealthily, I will admit) into someone's study to peruse their engagement diary (or into another room to view an altogether different kind of diary) and shivered at the idea of it being a criminal act.

"Find another way," Noc demanded as he turned and prowled toward the kitchen.

I pushed up from his sofa and followed him, explaining, "I'm uncertain how to do that if I don't know where he'll be. In my crystal ball, they're always tapping at their computers, but obviously they don't dictate aloud what they're tapping. I can hone in on it, but when I succeed, I don't understand what I'm seeing, and most of the time, by the time I acquire the vision, the screen doesn't display the diary since the person I'm watching has moved on to something else."

He opened his refrigerator, sticking his head into it and replying to its interior, "This is not my gig, baby, it's yours. Find another way."

I stopped at his counter-esque/cupboard-esque area (known, Noc explained, as an "island," which it was, in a small sea of kitchen) and shifted my bum up to one of the attractive stools there, murmuring thoughtfully, "Well, from what I know of this towing business where Circe works, such a service would be needed if I could arrange for Dax Lahn's vehicle to be incapacitated."

I heard the slam and rattle of the refrigerator door closing and then Noc muttering, "And now she plans vandalism, at best, destruction of property, at worst."

I narrowed my eyes at him.

"Are all aspects of intrigue illegal in this world?" I snapped.

"Uh, yeah," he fired back, coming to a stop opposite me at the island.

"This is most exasperating," I shared, doing it most *exasperated*. "I simply wish to plot a love match. How can that be a crime?"

"Again, Frannie, I'll suggest that you just let be what's gonna be. If they're fated for each other, that shit is gonna happen. Just let it happen and try to be cool even if you hate the bridesmaid gown she'll eventually choose for you."

His words took me out of our conversation.

"Bridesmaid's gown?"

"You're gonna get to know her, she's gonna get to know you. Fact is, she texted me yesterday to suggest we all get together for dinner, including Valentine and Josette. We should do that. We do that, she gets to know you, she'll love you. She's awesome so you'll do the same. When she falls in love with this guy, gets married, she'll want bridesmaids, and I suspect that time comes, one of them will be you."

"What's a bridesmaid?"

He gave a slight shrug that, with his broad shoulders, still was a powerful one.

"You wear a fancy dress and walk down the aisle in front of her before she gets married. As far as I can tell, this position has three duties. One, to get the bride slaughtered during the bachelorette party, and by slaughtered I don't mean dead, obviously. I mean drop-dead drunk. Two, to throw a shower for her so, and I'm speaking from the viewpoint of the man here, she gets really fuckin' good lingerie and not a bunch of mixing bowls for the kitchen. And three, to hold her wedding bouquet when her new husband puts the ring on her finger."

Fascinating.

"A wife gets a ring too?" I queried.

He shook his head but said, "No. She gets two. The engagement ring, usually a diamond, but it can be whatever, just as long as she loves it, and the wedding band."

One thing was quite clear about the difference in our worlds, the bestowal of jewelry upon marriage was one I very much liked, the significance of the symbol *and* the fact the wife gets a diamond.

"I see you like that idea," Noc observed, and I stopped thinking of diamonds and focused on him to see he no longer looked annoyed but now amused.

"Any idea that includes diamonds I'll like," I replied.

"I bet," he muttered, his eyes crinkling, then he declared, "Choices. Steaks. Chops. Hamburgers. Or spaghetti. Got potatoes I can do up whatever way you want and veggies. Also got frozen garlic bread and salad. Just gotta know which way you want me to go."

"I'll eat whatever you wish to cook, my love."

"Good answer," he said, turning back to the refrigerator.

He started taking things from it and piling them on the island before me when I reminded him, "We have yet to fall upon a solution to this problem, for, I shall assert, we won't be leaving Circe and Lahn to the fates."

"*We* aren't fallin' upon anything, sugarlips," he returned. "Again, this is your gig, not mine."

"I'm afraid I'll need your assistance, darling," I shared. "I cannot yet drive and I have yet to acquire any skills with a computer. I'll definitely need you for the first, I'm sure, and I may need you for the last."

"Frannie, I'm not gonna be your wheel man either."

"Wheel man?"

"The getaway driver after you go off and commit a crime."

Balls!

"You're not being very helpful, my love," I pointed out, seeking patience.

"And you're finally getting my point, sweetheart."

We stared at each other over the island for long moments before Noc broke the silence.

"You think you can help out by cutting up a tomato for our salad?"

I was aghast.

"They're slimy," I declared with revulsion.

"You eat them," he returned.

"I eat them. I don't *touch* them. I eat escargot too, but I don't touch those either."

At my words, Noc burst out laughing, doing it rounding the island and arriving at me whereupon he captured my head at the sides in both hands, tipped it back and delivered a very deep, very wet, very long kiss on me.

He lifted away and looked into my eyes. "Cora, the dead, was a pain in my ass. Every minute I spent with her and then everything I learned about her was not good. But I'll always be thankful for the day she crossed my path, because her doin' that led to you sitting right here being you. If you told me I was gonna fall for an uppity, blue blood, snobby chick who won't even slice a tomato, I'd tell you you were crazy. But here you are and thank fuck for that."

My heart was fluttering, my knees were trembling (even seated!), and I feared I was about to burst into tears or fall from my stool in a dead faint.

I could certainly not do either of the last, and to cover how all he'd said made me feel, I ordered, "Stop being charming after you've denied me something I very much desire."

His hands slid down to the sides of my neck. "Baby, you can't best the challenge of setting up Circe and Lahn in this world, then you better hang up your gloves as the heavyweight champion of scheming."

My back straightened. "I'll do no such thing."

"Then time to get creative," he dared.

I glared at him. "You don't think I can do it."

"What I think is, you can't drive. You've no idea how else to get around. If you commit a crime, I'll spank your ass, after I bail it out of jail, of course. You don't know how to use a computer, and even if you did, no way you're gonna acquire hacking skills in a matter of hours. You do know how to use a phone, but you still peck at it biting the side of your bottom lip with concentration, so I'm not thinking you'll be surfing the web on it anytime soon. And last, for whatever Valentine reason Valentine has, she's left the building so you're flying solo. Although you probably could do this blindfolded with one hand tied behind your back in your world, in this one, you're just gonna eventually have to give up and let nature take its course."

"I do not *give up*," I retorted.

"Then this is gonna be interesting," he decreed.

"And I *do not* peck at my phone biting my lip," I carried on.

I mean really. How gauche!

"You texted Josette when we got home to tell her we got here safe and to make sure she was good, and you bit your lip the whole time you did it," he shot back.

I feared he spoke truth.

Thus, I harrumphed even as I made a silent vow to cease doing such immediately.

Noc grinned.

I went back to glaring.

His grin became a white smile.

I returned a different kind of smile and informed him, "You do know, darling, that when I'm perturbed, I'm not in the mood for intimacy."

He didn't hesitate a moment with his rejoinder.

"You do know, baby, that you trying to use denying me that body of yours as punishment for me not giving you your way means, after you suck me while I play with you for a really fuckin' long time, you're gonna have to beg *real* pretty for me to make you come."

Vexing.

And titillating.

Blast!

I stopped smiling insincerely at him and again glared.

"You're good, you know it," he murmured, his eyes dropping to my mouth. "But don't think for one second I don't know you want what I just said and you want it now."

We'd enjoyed our lovemaking quite thoroughly since it began, but I had yet to taste him there.

I'd wanted to do it before his threat.

And he was drattedly correct. I wanted it more now.

I did not deny what he said or confirm it. Mostly because I knew denying it would eventually be proved wrong and that would be irksome and confirming it would make him smug, which would be equally irksome.

So I did neither.

When he again looked into my eyes, I said, "It's good to know you don't fight fair."

"Like you had any intention of ever fighting fair," he replied.

"Of course I didn't," I confirmed blithely.

His smile came back. "That's my Frannie."

"Indeed it is," I stated arrogantly.

In a dizzying shift, his mood changed from audacious to tender as he agreed softly, "Yeah, indeed it is."

After that, he tilted in and took my mouth. This time it was short, not deep, but very sweet.

When he moved away, he murmured, "Gotta feed my girl."

I drew in breath and nodded.

He let one hand slide lingeringly along my jaw as he removed both. And while he walked away, to hide my response to his words and caress, I took a fortifying sip of my wine.

If you told me I was gonna fall for an uppity, blue blood, snobby chick who won't even slice a tomato, I'd tell you you were crazy. But here you are and thank fuck for that.

Well then.

Fine.

So he wouldn't assist me in making a love match of Circe and Lahn.

And yes, Valentine was no longer there to lead the charge because she was nursing a broken heart.

And it was true I was in a new world and had only been in it for five days. I knew very little, and of the very little I knew, much of it were things I would need to know in order to carry out any plan (should I eventually fall on one that wasn't unlawful).

But Noctorno Hawthorne had fallen for me.

Fallen for me.

So I figured I could do pretty much anything.

And so I figured I would.

~

"*Frannie.*"

Noc had made a mistake.

In all our lovemaking, at which he was exceptionally talented, and *dominant*, he had not yet allowed me to demonstrate the fullness of *my* skills.

And thus, when I finally got my mouth on him, I was able to do just this.

Needless to say, I was very good at it. And thus, needless to say, Noc had become consumed by it and had thus been unable to bring to fruition his earlier plan.

Even though his voice communicated something very clearly, I was *much* enjoying what I was doing. The taste of him. The weight of him. The rigidity. Each ridge and vein tantalizing my tongue. Each grunt and groan urging me to move faster, draw deeper. The feel of him straining to hold his control.

"Baby," he gritted, and I raised my eyes to his from where I lay curled between his widespread legs, his knees up. I felt the wash of wetness at the heart of me witnessing the darkness in his face even as I carried on and he reached out to me, his fingertips skimming my cheek on their journey to glide into my hair and cup the side of my head. "Warning," he finished thickly, in a way it was clear he could not force out more.

I felt my eyes turn lazy (or lazier), did not heed his warning but instead increased my ministrations.

"Right," he bit out and it happened.

Without losing purchase of his cock in my mouth, he shifted to his knees, drawing my head up with his hand fisted in my hair so I was no longer curled between his legs but up on my hands and knees.

And then I was no longer in control of pleasuring his shaft.

He was thrusting it into my mouth.

Yes.

Noc.

Dominant.

And *divine.*

I closed my eyes and moaned, feeling my inner thighs tremble.

"Fuck, shit, *fuck*," he grunted, his one hand staying fisted in my hair, his other one cupping my head to assist in holding me steady. "Take me, Frannie."

Oh, I'd take him. Any way he'd give himself to me.

Including like this.

Especially like this.

I moaned around his cock and reached a hand between my legs, my finger just skimming through the wet to where I needed it when Noc forced out, "Unh-unh."

He then pulled out of my mouth, reached down to me, and with a hand at my wrist yanking me up, he cast his other arm around my waist, lifting me so my naked body collided with his own.

With no choice, I rounded him with my legs. When I did, he fell back to his calves, held me to him with his arm at my waist, leaning our bodies and reaching with the other hand to the nightstand.

He opened the drawer so violently the lamp on top tumbled and fell, coins clinked and dropped to the floor, things I didn't know what they were came out of the drawer, all this before Noc straightened us, coming back on his knees and handing me a condom.

"Fast," he growled.

I looked into his eyes, shivered in his hold and nodded my head quickly.

My fingers fumbled, but I went fast, finally rolling it on his beautiful shaft successfully. I barely had it to the root before Noc shoved my hand aside, wrapping his around his cock.

He found me and drove inside.

I grasped his shoulders as my spine formed an arc, my head falling back. The low moan ripping from my throat, he pummeled me with his thrusts and I did my best to hold on for the ride.

"God, fuck, *fuck*, my Frannie, so goddamned *hot*," Noc rumbled, beginning to lift me and drive me down to meet his lunges.

I righted my head with a snap and lifted my hands to the sides of his neck, gripping him there, my forehead hitting his, my body lurching at his command.

"Fuck me, Noc," I demanded.

"I am, baby," he grunted.

I seized his jaw in both hands, my voice throaty. "Fuck me, my love."

He stared into my eyes. His flaring, burning, *blazing*, he fell forward so I was on my back in his bed, Noc covering me. With me stationary and Noc able to center all his power at his hips, he *fucked* me.

It took no time at all before I came, dragging my nails down his shoulders, crying out loudly, clenching my legs around his driving hips, lost in Noc. His filling me, claiming me, fucking me in a way no one could come after him, no one could have me again. I was no one but his, he was no one but mine, destined to be together, connected, balancing...bloody...*worlds*.

I heard it, felt it, the tension, the increased rhythm, the shorter strokes.

My climax began to fade and I opened my eyes just in time to see the beauty of Noc's head slanting back sharply, the veins in his corded neck popping, the quick succession of grunts that led to a low rumble. I watched, fascinated, feeling him pour this beauty inside me, wishing there was no barrier to keep me from absorbing it, until his head fell, and he buried his face in my neck.

I held his weight and stroked him while the tension in his body released, and finally I felt the workings of his mouth at my neck as he rested himself on a forearm in the bed, his other arm curved under me, around me, the fingers idly caressing the skin of my hip.

I turned my lips to his ear. "I want you."

For a brief second, Noc grew still then he lifted his head and looked down at me, smiling.

"Babe, still deep inside you, on top of you, not sure how much more of me you can get," he teased.

I moved a hand to his face, mine, I knew, was serious.

"I hope you feel it as little as me, but even so, I don't like it there. I don't like it between us. When you give me your seed, I want it. Even if it doesn't take root, I want it in my womb. I want it to be a part of me. Thus, I need to ask Valentine to return to my world and acquire some pennyrium for me."

Noc said nothing.

But he no longer looked teasing. He was staring at me in a way I could not decipher but it warmed me to my toes.

"Noc," I called when his silence lengthened.

"I wanna go the distance with you."

My body around his tightened and I opened my mouth to speak.

He was not done.

"I wanna make a baby with you."

I clamped my mouth shut.

Noc did not.

"I wanna make as many as we can as long as they know we love each of them with everything we are. I don't give a fuck if you've got my baby growing in you year after year until your body won't do it anymore." He drew his attention to our continued connection by flexing his hips. "If I could, I'd fuck you for hours, days, goddamned years, nonstop. I want part of me in you every breath you take. I can't do that so I want it that any time your mind wanders, you think of me inside you however that can be. My cock taking you. My cum buried deep. My kid growing in your belly. What that means. What we got. What we made. What we built between us. The fact that I love you so fuckin' much, I'd commit treason for you. I'd perpetrate crimes for you. I'd go to prison for you. I'd break my back to give you everything you wanted from cutting the damned tomatoes in your salad and pouring you a glass of wine to wrestling the world into my arms and laying it at your feet."

I lay under him, frozen.

Then I burst into tears.

Loud, obnoxious tears.

Noc pulled out (alas) and rolled us to our sides, gathering me into his arms, holding me close, his hand stroking deep at my back, his other arm tight around my waist as I sobbed against his chest, my body shaking uncontrollably with the power of emotion sweeping through me.

And with deep regret, this happened for a long time.

And with even deeper regret, when it began to subside, I started hiccoughing with the wealth of emotion still needing to be expressed.

I loathed crying.

And worse, *hiccoughing.*

Ulk.

The mortification.

"So, to end," Noc said, and I kept my face buried in his chest, feeling his voice rumble even as I heard it, "I don't know what this pennyrium stuff is, but an easier fix is to get your ass on the Pill so I can be inside you without a condom. In other words, I'm down with that until we decide no birth control is needed and whenever that happens, I'm down with that too."

I tipped my head back and gazed upon him with watery eyes.

"I love you," I whispered.

"Thank fuck," he whispered back.

"I'll cut tomatoes for you," I shared.

I watched his wavy mouth smile as he stopped stroking my back and tightened both his arms around me.

"No need to make that great a sacrifice, sweetheart," he muttered.

"I have a golden soul," I told him softly.

His arms flexed so powerfully they pushed all the air out of me before it seemed he forced them to relax.

"Yeah you do," he finally replied.

"I have a golden soul," I repeated.

"I know, baby."

"I have a golden soul," I said again, and he opened his mouth to speak, but I carried on. "I know this because the gods in my world and the God in yours would never tether a soul that was anything less than golden to the perfection that is you."

"Fuck," he growled, rolling me again to my back with him on me.

"I love you, Noc," I breathed as his weight pressed it out of me.

"Fuck," he growled again.

And then he kissed me.

We had need of several condoms that night for our avowals commenced the belated sexual marathon Noc had promised days before.

And dawn was kissing the sky when, exhausted, sated and deliriously happy, I let all my weight settle into the man who lay under me, holding me close, taking my weight, my worries, my demons, my dreams.

The man who showed me my golden soul in a way I knew truly I carried it inside me.

The man who loved me.

~

THE NEXT EVENING, I stood at the back of Valentine's foyer, arms crossed on my chest, giving my best forbidding stare to the intensely handsome (I had to admit) Glover as he put a hand to the small of Josette's back to start to lead her out the door.

He smiled at me and shared, "She'll be in good hands."

"She better," I retorted, moving forward and catching the door before he could close it so I could continue to glare at them as they moved down Valentine's walk in order to be absolutely certain I'd made my point.

He nodded, his lips now just quirking, and I moved my gaze, my face softening, when Josette looked back and said, "'Night, Frannie."

"Good night, my sweet," I bid.

She looked ahead as Glover moved them both forward.

I knew he did not intend for me to hear it, but I had honed exceptional eavesdropping skills in my lifetime, so I heard it when he spoke after he had her halfway down the walk.

"Your sister's kinda protective, yeah?" he asked.

"Er, well...we've been through a lot together," Josette replied quietly. "And she loves me."

"Right," Glover returned, not sounding disgruntled, sounding pleased.

Although I quite liked the fact that Josette understood my feelings for her, and the fact that Glover was not put off by a protective family member, I harrumphed.

"Shut the door, sugarlips," came from behind me.

I turned to see Noc leaned against the wall at the side of the entry to the hall appearing like he didn't know whether to come fetch me or let loose his hilarity.

"I'll see them safe in his car," I returned.

"Shut the door, baby," he said softly.

I liked his soft so I stepped out of the door and shut it.

Only then did Noc come to me.

Putting his hands to my hips, he pulled me close and tipped his head down.

"So, my guess, we're hanging here until you know she's home all right," he noted.

"Yes," I confirmed.

He grinned and murmured, "Momma bear."

"You say this as a tease you think might get a rise out of me when I have no issue you think this way at all."

"Just to say, not teaching you how to use a gun considering you're like this with Josette, it'll be you and not me the boys will have a problem with when our daughters start dating."

I could actually feel myself blanch.

Noc burst out laughing, hauling me into his embrace as he did it and putting his mouth to mine.

"Christ, I love you," he said there through his mirth.

"Thank fuck," I replied and lost Noc's dancing, happy eyes.

I did for he was kissing me.

Obviously, I kissed him back.

19
CREATIVE

Franka

"We have little time, Josette," I warned as Josette handed over money to the friendly gentleman with the odd accent he said he had because he was from "Ay-tee." A gentleman who was the driver of what Josette had told me was a taxi.

A boon.

While I was spending time learning the fullness of my love for Noc, and his love for me, Josette had been watching the television and fiddling with her telephone.

Noc had been correct three days previous. I knew little of this world.

But Josette was a quick study.

"Just a minute, Frannie," Josette replied, sounding like she was concentrating. "I need to work out the tip."

"The what?" I queried.

"I'll explain later," she muttered.

I looked to the watch on my wrist that I had purchased the day before when Noc had been driving Josette and I to a vacant parking lot where he could safely begin to teach us how to drive, and through the window of his Suburban I'd seen a jewelry store.

Of course, I'd demanded he stop immediately, for I had not seen an entire store in that world devoted to jewelry (that wasn't in a mall displaying paltry offerings) and obviously this was something we needed to experience without delay.

My watch was thin, with a black strap and what the sales lady explained was an "art deco," white gold and diamond face. Whatever "art deco" meant. I simply thought it elegant.

Josette's was white and rose gold with a mother of pearl face. It was not trim but quite big, almost like men's watches, but even so, it was most attractive.

Both watches cost over fifty thousand dollars, at which Noc shook his head and said (not to anyone, certainly not me), "Way she's going, she'll be out of treasure in a month."

"No I won't," I declared. "Valentine says the this-world value of my treasure equals nearly half a billion of your American dollars. If this is so, I could buy Josette and myself ten watches and not run out of treasure."

Noc gave me a look that said without words I should cease speaking.

The sales lady made a noise that sounded like she was choking.

I thought my best play at that juncture was to smile at her, and, of course, hand over my credit card.

Our driving lesson was not as successful as our trip to the jewelry store.

It was not me who was having difficulty mastering the controls of the car. In fact, it all seemed quite intuitive. Noc had even given me a pleased kiss after my lesson and declared me a "natural."

No, Josette was quite erratic, went too fast, and her turns, even watching while standing outside the big vehicle and well away, were terrifying.

Noc said I could probably start practicing on real streets after a few more goes "behind the wheel."

"Sorry, Jo, but it's gonna be the parking lot for you for a while," he'd told her.

She didn't seem to mind. She was just happy to be learning.

And regardless, her head was in the clouds due to the fact that Glover was attentive and amusing, and "oh so clever, Frannie, you wouldn't believe!"

I didn't believe.

I would have to see for myself. Something, I noted, I had not been invited to have the opportunity to do as yet even though they'd had their second date last night, dinner and Josette's first movie.

So I wouldn't feel left out, Noc took me to my first movie as well (though he had not, as I requested, taken me to the same exact movie as Josette and Glover's movie).

It was insanely loud, the sound seeming to beat into my body.

Regardless, it was a rather interesting way to tell a tale, inflating images so they were humongous and all you could pay attention to.

In the end, I got used to the incessant loudness and quite lost myself in it.

Though, I was still peeved, for it was played in the dark, which meant we could have easily gone to the same one as Josette and Glover and done this without detection.

But Noc had no time for my pique, ordering rather firmly, "Just let her enjoy herself, Frannie, and keep out of it."

It was hateful to admit, but I had no choice but to do just that.

Now, we were in a vehicle sitting at the curb outside the building where Dax Lahn had his office, and our time to see to what needed to be seen to was short.

"Right, good, thank you," Josette said to the driver and looked to me. "We can go."

I threw open my door and stepped out.

Josette followed me, slammed the door and wasted precious moments being friendly and waving at our driver as he drove away.

I took her waving hand and pulled her with me.

"Come. We must make haste. This staff meeting they have has already started. It can last upwards of an hour, but I've no idea how much time we need, though I fear the more the better and it's ticking away rapidly."

"All right, all right, I'm coming," Josette murmured, flipping and flopping behind me while my high heels clicked on the pavements, my thighs straining the most becoming, but quite tight skirt I was wearing that hit me at my knees, my filmy blouse billowing with the swiftness of our gaits.

I had hit on the perfect plan, for when they had this meeting, all working there attended so the office was practically deserted, save the big room where they sat, and we could easily reach Dax Lahn's office without them seeing us.

As we entered, I did not take time, as I had done often, to admire the fact that Dax Lahn had selected an older, rather handsome building in which to house his offices.

No, guiding Josette with me, we quickly moved to the elevators, called one, it whooshed us to the appropriate floor and let us out.

Outside the elevator, I took in a deep breath and let it go, turning to Josette and advising, "Deep breath, Josette. Calm. Serene. The key to being somewhere you aren't supposed to be is behaving like you have every reason to be there."

She nodded.

"Deep breath," I repeated, noting she hadn't taken one.

I watched her do that, gave her a small, reassuring smile, and turned in the direction we would need to take to get to Lahn's office.

Since I was very good at this, we had no issues entering the rooms that housed Lahn's business nor getting to his office. It was as I'd known it would be, deserted with everyone in the meeting. We hadn't seen a soul all the way to our destination.

We entered his personal office and went immediately to the large desk that was carved attractively and made of beautiful wood.

I stood at its side and looked to Josette, sweeping an arm toward the contraption lying closed on its top.

"There it is, Josette, let us find his schedule quickly so we can just as quickly leave."

She looked to me then to the contraption then to me.

"It's closed," she stated.

I examined it even though I'd just seen it.

"It" was called a "laptop." Noc had one. I had requested he show me how to use it just last night, but he'd grinned and shaken his head, asking, "You know I'm not stupid, right?"

My reply had been a heated, "Of course! How could you ask such nonsense?"

He'd simply shaken his head again and said, "We'll get into computers after Lahn bumps into Circe on the street somewhere and they fall in love at first sight." And after delivering that, he'd walked away.

Most irritating.

Though, he'd walked away to get the wine bottle and refresh my glass so my irritation couldn't last long without it becoming mulish.

Which was also irritating.

In Lahn's office, I turned back to Josette.

"It is, indeed, closed," I confirmed.

"On TV, when they close it, that means turning it off," she explained. "Always when they're finished doing something of great import on it, they slap it shut and sit back contentedly."

"Well, we shall open it as we have yet to do what we need to do that's of great import. We'll shut it again when we're done."

"No, I mean, if I open it, it's like turning it on. And a lot of the time, when people on the television are doing what people like us are doing now, they open the ones that have been closed, and they're immediately foiled in their activities because they have to get by the password."

I stared in shock at the computer, asking, "Does it speak?"

"Not that I know," Josette answered.

I looked to her. "Then how can it ask for a password?"

"You tap it in."

Of course.

I'd seen Noc tapping on his own.

"Right, well, we—"

It was then, I sensed it.

I stopped speaking and froze, not including my eyes which I felt grow big.

Then I stepped close to Josette and whispered, "Keep quiet."

"What the—?" A deep, perturbed voice came our way. "Can I help you with something?"

Josette made an "eep" noise as she turned to face the door.

I was already facing the door, and thus I saw Dax Lahn walk through it and stop.

I had forgotten how large he was.

Oh balls!

We were going to be arrested before we'd even managed to open his laptop and now Noc was going to have to retrieve us from jail.

He'd said he'd spank me if this was to occur, and I might not be averse to a spanking from Noc on certain occasions, but I suspected the one he'd wish to deliver after liberating us from a cell would not be the kind I would like.

"Again," this came as a growl as the large man took a threatening step toward us and stopped, "can I help you with something?"

This was what I did and did well.

So this was what I needed to do.

"You can indeed," I declared, lifting my chin. "You can explain to us why you're so late for our appointment, Mr. Lahn."

His head tipped slightly to the side and that was threatening too.

In Korwahk, the sight of Lahn doing this might cause someone to relieve themselves immediately and maybe run for their lives.

The repeated "eep" Josette made gave me the understanding this same reaction could come on this world too.

"Sorry?" he asked.

I stepped forward. "Franka Drakkar. We were to meet at ten. It is not ten. It is," I looked at my watch irritably, "twenty *passed* ten."

"I'm sorry, Ms. Drakkar," Lahn stated, glancing at Josette then back to me, "I didn't have a ten o'clock appointment today."

"You certainly did and it was with me," I retorted.

"I'm afraid I didn't," he returned.

"I'm afraid you did," I rejoined.

He took in our positions in the room and again caught my eyes.

"Is there a reason why you're standing so close to my desk, Ms. Drakkar?"

"Since we weren't even greeted, we've hardly been invited to sit," I snapped in full affront.

He seemed to examine the top of his desk before again returning his attention to me.

"If you weren't greeted, how did you make it to my office?"

"I *do* know who you are, since I made an appointment with you," I declared. "I also know you're the founding partner of this firm. When we were not seen to upon entry, where else would we go and look for you but the biggest office? I can't imagine you'd give it to an underling," I noted with disdain and finished, "And I see I was correct."

"All right then, you're Franka Drakkar, may I ask who this is?" He tipped his head to Josette.

"Josette Aubuchon, my assistant," I told him.

"And maybe you'll explain to me what our appointment was to discuss," he pressed.

I sighed with impatience, but answered, "My donation to First Mother House."

That took him aback even if I could only barely see the slight jerk of his chin.

"First Mother House?" he queried.

"Yes, as I explained over the telephone, I'll be donating one million dollars to it and you were going to assist me with this as their legal counsel."

I was hoping that was a dramatic enough amount to take his attention from finding us in his office, and I was hoping I was using words I'd heard while observing him correctly.

"One million dollars?" he asked low and disbelieving, answering my question about the amount of my donation.

"Yes," I confirmed.

"First, Ms. Drakkar," he stated, moving a step farther into the room, but doing so, I noted with some alarm, still blocking the door. "My assistant would not make a meeting during this day or time because this day and time is always blocked. Second..."

He took another step and I felt the fear start wafting from Josette.

I wished I could put a hand to her or give her a glance to calm her, but I needed to remain in my play, for if I did not, I was afraid the results would be disastrous.

Lahn continued speaking.

"I would remember any possible meeting with a woman who intended to give one million dollars to First Mother House. And last, your donation does not require legal counsel."

Drat.

I needed time and sought it.

"If the fullness of our meeting was communicated to you, you would know this was not true."

"The fullness of our meeting *wasn't* communicated to me, so perhaps you'll explain how I can assist you in giving a donation to a charity when you can simply write a check and put it in the mail?"

How could he assist me, indeed?

How could he assist me?

How?

Blast!

"The donation needs to be anonymous," Josette piped in.

Excellent!

I fought the urge to give her an embrace.

"This, too, can be done without legal counsel," Dax Lahn stated.

Bloody hell.

"Do we have attorney-client confidentiality?" Josette asked, sounding authoritative.

I looked to her and saw her staring right in Dax Lahn's eyes.

Ah, my Josette. Such the clever girl.

And a brave one.

"You aren't a client," Dax Lahn pointed out.

"Yes, of course we're not," I snapped, jumping on Josette's track. "Because we have not yet *had our meeting*."

"I must admit I'm getting impatient," he shared, appearing just that, and it was unfortunately quite frightening, even for me, and I'd been caught in a variety of delicate situations I'd had to talk my way out of. "And I have things to do. So now you've got one minute to explain to me why you're in my office. If that explanation doesn't satisfy me, I'll be phoning the police."

I glared at him.

He held my glare.

Then he said, "Fifty seconds."

Gods.

There was nothing for it.

I raised my hands to the buttons of my blouse and started to undo them.

"Frannie," Josette hissed.

Dax Lahn lifted a hand, his face now carved in stone.

"Do not make another move," he ground out.

I turned my back to him, lifted my blouse and dipped it over my shoulder, feeling it fall down my shoulder blade and partially down my back.

I raised my other hand and swept my hair to the side.

The air in the room went still as I heard Lahn's shocked, "Jesus Christ."

I pulled my blouse back up my shoulder instantly, redid the four buttons I'd undone and turned smartly to him.

"I am from somewhere else," I proclaimed. "This somewhere else is far away. In order to leave that place, I had to do terrible things. The man who did this to me..." I drew in breath through my nose and straightened my shoulders. "I have a good deal of money. It's not strictly *legal* money, but it's *mine*. I *earned* it. I have quite enough to care for me and Josette, who looks after me in a variety of ways and has done for some time, and I have more. *Much* more. I wish for it to do good. However, I need to use great caution when I use that money so certain people cannot locate me and certain governmental departments don't..."

I trailed off, drew in another breath and shook my head in disgust, looking to Josette.

"Come," I demanded. "It's clear we've made an error in our selection of worthy organizations."

Both Josette and I began to stomp past him, for my part demonstrating openly the height of the insult I felt had been delivered, when I saw his arm come out and heard his, "Ms. Drakkar...Franka, wait."

I halted and turned my head to the side and up (and this up was *up*, Noc was tall, Dax Lahn was a veritable giant).

"My apologies," he murmured. "Something must have been missed."

"I fear it was, however—"

He gestured to the rather smart leather chairs in front of his desk. "If you'll take a seat."

I lifted my chin further for a different reason. "I'd rather not."

"Perhaps we can start again," he suggested.

I turned fully to him, feeling Josette close to my back.

"I fear this would not be wise on my part. We do not have this client confidentiality as we're not clients of yours, but I do hope with the part you play with First Mother House you'll understand there are women with certain needs and I am one of them, so you'll do me the respect of behaving accordingly."

"Of course, you have my word, but—"

I interrupted him, my thoughts on Noc's future employment and what he might do in it.

Therefore, I said, "We shall not *start again*, for it's without doubt you'll be setting someone on investigating the veracity of my statements and when you do, you'll find that I exist. Josette exists. And yet, if your investigator probes deeply enough, you will find we do not. I think you understand my meaning with this. Thus, you're likely to feel that the reliability of my statements isn't exactly reliable. However, one does what one has to do, and Josette and I did just that. I shall not share who I was in a previous life or where I lived it. And I'll not invite further verbal misuse, or other, at your hands should we speak again and you doubt my story."

He moved closer to us, not that close, but it was closer.

When he did, I felt Josette nearly tuck herself in my back.

Dax Lahn didn't miss her movements, undoubtedly read them both correctly and incorrectly, but he'd already stopped, getting close so he could drop his voice very low.

"You are not the first in your position, Franka, to feel the need to falsify her identity."

"I'm sure that's true," I retorted. "And I'm equally certain this is a dire state of affairs for I'm also certain that I'm far from the last. Thus me wishing to give a substantial donation to someone who's doing something about it."

"If there's someone, outside Josette, who can corroborate what you say, just one person, then—"

Bloody hell, was I going to do what I needed to do?

Love was on the line.

I had no choice.

"Noctorno Hawthorne," I declared.

His head twitched at hearing Noc's name, which gave credence to Noc saying it was most unusual here.

Then again, it was unusual in my world too. It was simply that a prince had it, and whenever it came to royals, that was that.

"He's a police officer from Seattle who...well, there was..." I affected an uncomfortable swallow and softened my voice when I went on, "He was lovely with me. And he and I, we..." I looked demurely away and then back to see what I saw many a time from the my-world Lahn when he regarded his Circe (though with obvious differences as this Lahn was regarding me).

A tender warmth of features that I felt settle around my heart.

If I had not known I was doing the right thing (and I already knew that), I would have known in that moment.

"He's here, with me, and Jo," I carried on quietly. "He is not living under... he's himself. And if you were to look into him, contact him, he would verify all I've said to you today."

"Can you give me a contact number so I can phone you when I've had that verification?" he asked gently and finished respectfully, "I hope you understand the need for it."

I opened my mouth to answer, but Josette stepped around me. "You can deal with me on that."

He nodded to her, took us both in and then we pivoted to watch as he sauntered to his desk.

My, but he was *most* watchable.

More so in person.

He pulled a pen from his inside jacket pocket, put it to a pad on his desk and lifted his gaze to Josette. "Your number?"

She rattled it off in a way that made me wonder if I should memorize my own.

I didn't think long of that.

Instead, I thought fast.

First step done, it was time for the next one.

I just didn't expect the first one to happen as it did so I had no idea what should come next.

"Thank you," he said when Josette was done and straightened from his desk. "I know it's an inconvenience that we weren't able to see to our business today, and it would be my pleasure to take you both, and Mr. Hawthorne if he's available, out to lunch as my way of apologizing when we meet again to discuss your situation and how best to bestow your gift on First Mother House."

I had, for once, not thought fast enough.

Fortunately, he'd given me the perfect plan.

I did my best not to allow my mouth to curve in a triumphant smile and declared, "Dinner."

His brows pulled together. "Sorry?"

"Dinner," I repeated. "Drinks, for us first, to go over business that should only be between us. And if you'd please invite the director of First Mother House to dine with us after drinks, I'd like to meet her. I'll make another donation, not anonymous, but generous, to explain her presence while we dine. The anonymous one can be made when all the arrangements have been seen to."

"Actually, that's a great idea," he stated.

I knew it was, seeing as Circe wanted us all to meet for dinner and we would be doing just that.

With Dax Lahn in attendance.

He carried on, "Patricia is an amazing woman and she'll be best at explaining just how much good your gift will do for the women, men and children who find themselves in need of First Mother House."

Then he imparted upon us a genuine smile.

Josette beside me made a noise like a stifled moan.

I pressed my lips together.

"I'll look forward to that," he said, lifting an arm. "And now, I'll walk you to the lobby."

Josette touched the back of my hand and whispered, "I need to call a taxi."

"I'll do that as we walk," Lahn offered. "We have a service. The least I can do is get you home after wasting your time in coming here."

Not to mention, his "service" could offer him the information of the locale of where we'd been deposited.

I had no idea what reputation Valentine had in New Orleans. My sister-witch was exceptionally cunning, so I had no doubt she made certain it was excellent.

I was still going to lead them to Noc's house.

He might be angry.

But then again, he could have helped. I'd asked. He'd refused. He'd told me to get creative.

And one could say the last ten minutes were most creative.

I smiled slowly at Dax Lahn and accepted.

"That'd be lovely."

"YEAH, UNH-HUNH, YEAH."

Noc was pacing his kitchen, head bent, hand wrapped around the back of his neck.

Josette and I were perched atop the stools at his island, watching him.

I caught myself biting the side of my lip and ceased doing that as Noc made a turn, dropped his hand, lifted his eyes to me, and at the look in them, I felt a not-altogether-pleasant curl in my belly.

"Right," he said into his phone. "Tomorrow's good. We'll meet there. No problems. Yeah. Later."

He finished speaking and took his phone from his ear, his eyes still locked on me.

"Just to put your mind at rest, sugarlips, I just made a meet with one of Dax Lahn's investigators to corroborate your story."

"I, well, erm..." I began.

I looked to Josette.

She felt my gaze and returned it with wide eyes.

I turned back to Noc.

"Thank you, darling. That will be most appreciated," I finished.

"And so you know," he continued like I didn't say anything, "Lahn contracts with the firm I'll be working for to do his investigative work. So essentially I'll be having a meeting with my boss tomorrow to let him know my woman is filthy rich but on the run from an abusive relationship and living under a false identity."

It took much to remain impassive in the face of this dire information, but I did so, saying, "Is that going to be troublesome, my dearest?"

"No, since I've given them permission to investigate me in order to clear myself for the job. This means, now that you're in my life, they'll likely investigate you, so now I have a plausible excuse why the woman in my life has falsified identification documents, somethin' guys the caliber of these are gonna find out in about two seconds."

Well!

That was a windfall!

"How lovely. Two birds," I murmured.

"Two birds, my ass." Noc did not murmur. "Really fuckin' good luck."

That worked too.

Noc turned his attention to Josette.

"I gotta worry about this one's shenanigans," he gestured to me. "With this shit today, now I gotta worry about you jumpin' on her bandwagon?"

"I'm sorry, Noc, I don't know what jumping on a band—" Josette began.

"Oh for fuck's sake," Noc interrupted her to say to the ceiling, visibly at the end of his patience.

I decided to move us past this part as it seemed all had settled quite well and now it was time to move on to the next part.

"As soon as this is sorted, we're having dinner with Lahn, or Dax, as he's known here. You will, of course, need to invite Circe to this dinner," I shared.

Noc dropped his eyes to me. "Did you hear me when I said this was your gig?"

"I heard you when you said you'd do anything for me," I replied quietly.

Yes, that wasn't fighting fair.

But love was on the line.

That was the one time anyone had to agree it was all right not to fight fair.

"I just...need to text Glover," Josette murmured and slid off her stool, moving out of Noc's kitchen.

I watched her go, and when she was in the living room, I again looked to Noc.

"I'm not asking you to break any laws, be my wheel man. I'm asking you to affirm I am who I am and I have the money I've offered his charity. And I'm asking you to ask Circe to dinner. That's it."

"And I'm gonna affirm you are who you are and I'm doin' that part because I got no choice but also because you got half a billion dollars, you can give a million to a domestic violence shelter. Circe, I'll give you her number. I'll show at this dinner. But I'm not gonna be the one who leads her to the Savage."

"Noc—"

He took a quick step to stand opposite me at the island.

"Do anything for you," he whispered. "Anything you ask. Call Circe. Set her up for an ambush. Right now what I'm askin' *you* to do is not ask me to do that. I am who I am to her. That means something to me. She trusts me. That means even more. So please, babe, I'm askin' you. Don't ask me to do that."

I nodded immediately. "I'll phone her and you don't have to be at dinner."

"I'll be there if only to keep your ass out of whatever hot water you might get it in and to be there for Circe if she freaks way the fuck out you're throwin' her right to the wolves."

Dax was frightening but I'd seen his tender streak.

He was no wolf.

I did not share my insight into Dax Lahn's character.

I said, "I think that's wise."

Noc drew in breath through his nose.

I sat still and said nothing as he did that.

When he released it, he declared, "I cannot believe you waltzed into his office and told him off for missing a non-existent meeting with you."

We had told him the story.

All save the part we were intending unauthorized access to Dax Lahn's computer.

We did not (as far as I knew) break any laws.

Noc didn't need to know we'd intended to.

"You told me to get creative."

"Well, Frannie, you succeeded in that."

I held his gaze and asked softly, "Are you angry at me, my love?"

"Fuck no," he replied instantly. "Why would you think that?"

"You seem," I flipped out a hand, "irked."

His lips twitched. "Irked isn't angry, gorgeous. Irked is irked."

"So you're irked, not angry."

"Yeah, the woman I love confronts the most vicious attorney in the city, she succeeds in her objectives and comes away unscathed, I'm not freaked because she's good. I'm not angry because she's good. I'm irked because she's a lunatic."

My spine snapped straight. "I'm not a lunatic."

He shook his head and returned, "This is an argument I don't think we should have when I'm hungry and need food...or maybe ever."

I decided we shouldn't have it, maybe ever, because I was also hungry.

But further, I was pleased Noc was not going to get more than irked about what Josette and I had done, making me feel like I'd gotten away with something that day, *twice*. Therefore I felt it best to quietly enjoy my success and move on.

"Thoughts on dinner?" Noc prompted.

"Pizza!" Josette cried from the living room.

Noc grinned in that direction and then he transferred that to me.

"Good for you?" he asked.

He didn't have to ask.

It was pizza.

I still answered. "Most definitely."

He jerked his chin up to me, expression no longer irked, just sweet.

No.

Just Noc.

"Get on your phone, Frannie. You can't slice a tomato, but you can learn how to order a pizza."

I instantly exited my stool to get my purse to find my phone, for it would be no hardship to learn how to order a pizza.

None at all.

20
I'M IN

Franka

"I'm thinking about beauty school," Jo declared in Noc's bathroom where I was leaned forward across his basin and putting on my lip gloss while she twitched and flipped strands of my hair that hung around my face, tucking pins more securely in the large chignon that rested at the side of my neck.

I shifted my eyes to hers in the mirror.

"Sorry?"

"Beauty school. I wish to go to one. After Noc teaches me how to drive, that is."

I straightened, slid the wand into the gloss and turned fully to her.

She dropped her hands.

"Sorry?" I repeated.

"You know, for something to do," she stated confusingly. "I've always enjoyed doing your hair, best part of what I do. You have lovely hair." She grinned. "But it's even more fun here with curling irons and straighteners and smoothing elixirs and—"

"Jo," I cut her off.

"What?" she asked.

"Explain fully what you're talking about," I ordered.

"I need employment," she declared.

I felt my head give a slight jerk with my surprise. "Whyever do you need that?"

It was then I saw Josette's head jerk.

"Whyever do I need that?" she parroted.

"That was my query," I confirmed, and at her look of bemusement, I explained, "You can imagine my confusion since you're already in *my* employ."

"There are showers here," she said.

"There are," I agreed.

And there were. Delightful rainfalls in the bathroom that were made more delightful when Noc led me to his and we both bathed together.

"And you enjoy doing your own face paint, I mean...erm, makeup."

"I do indeed."

"And they have washing machines for clothes. And irons that get hot by plugging them into the wall. You don't have to suspend them over fires."

I knew nothing of this, really, in this world or my other.

Noc had shown us how this was done, of course, in his pursuit of introducing us to as many things as he could before he had to go to work (something that would happen that Monday, two days away, something that I was not looking forward to because it would take him from me).

He was rather diligent in this endeavor in the hopes we'd be able to get along by ourselves when we'd be on our own.

But obviously, considering the subject matter, I paid scant attention.

"This isn't explaining, Jo," I informed her.

"Frannie," she leaned a hip against Noc's basin, "we're staying here, aren't we? In this world."

"Yes, unless you don't wish to remain," I replied hesitantly.

"I do wish to remain." Another grin. "I like it here. But eventually you'll have the things you do with Valentine. And you'll be with Noc. And I'll be—"

"With me," I finished for her.

She scooted an inch toward me and her expression turned gentle.

"Frannie, what I'm trying to say is, nearly everything is much easier here. It takes no time at all to do the things I do for you. I can't sit around all day playing on my phone, watching the television and waiting for Glover to text when I can care for your clothes once a week and have that done in but hours, and I can arrange your hair in no time."

She had a point.

"And people have employment here, jobs," she continued. "Even wealthy people on the television have employment."

"You have a job," I reminded her.

"I do, but the only people I know are you and Noc, Circe, a little bit, and

Valentine, and I don't know her very well either. If I go to beauty school, I'll make friends. If I get a job, I'll meet people."

She had a point about that too.

"So," she forged on, "once I learn to drive and can get around on my own, I'll go to beauty school and arrange hair as my employment. I'll continue to take care of you, of course," she hastened to add. "But then, once I start making this-world money, I'll be able to get my own place to live and—"

She'd been making excellent points.

However, this last one alarmed me enough for my voice to rise as I interrupted her with, "Your own *what*?"

"My own place to live."

I raised my brows. "And why would you need *that*?"

She opened her mouth to speak but got naught out when we heard, "Everything okay in here?"

I turned to see Noc at the doorway to his bathroom. He was wearing another suit. He looked decidedly handsome.

I would tell him that later.

I would also react later to the way his gaze became fixed on the lovely, feminine, flowy and elegant, but somewhat revealing (due to its slash from whimsical ruffled neckline to beltline) red dress that I wore.

Now, there were other things to attend to.

"Josette wishes to go to beauty school in order to obtain employment arranging hair *for other people*, doing this to make a living with the objective of eventually finding her own home," I declared like I was saying, "Josette wishes to go on a violent rampage, murdering scores of people in the name of Meer, our god of war."

It appeared to take physical effort for Noc to tear his eyes away from my dress. They moved briefly to Josette before returning to me.

"Baby, take a deep breath and think for five seconds about what you're saying," he urged quietly, going on, "And while you do that, think of how many people in your world get to pick the jobs they wanna have, getting paid well enough to do them that they're able to afford places to call their own."

I didn't need five seconds to think on this. I had no idea how many of such people lived in my world who were able to do that. I didn't even care.

I just knew if Josette wanted that, I wanted that for her.

And she was saying she wanted that.

I drew in a breath and I did it turning to her.

"You do this knowing, when you leave me, if aught happens you don't like, for instance you begin to feel lonely, you always have a home with me," I declared.

Her upper lip started quivering.

"Do not weep," I warned, feeling my own nose stinging.

The words were trembling when she returned, "I won't."

Noc interrupted our moment. "Right, before you two ruin your makeup, meaning you'll have to wipe it all off and put it on again, can we get the hell outta here and get this fucked-up dinner done?"

I turned again to him as Josette said, "I'm ready. I just need to go grab my bag."

She squeezed out of the space while I took in Noc's expression.

Tonight was our dinner with Dax Lahn and the director of the organization he supported.

A dinner I'd arranged that Circe would attend.

She was attending, however she didn't know Dax would be there.

I knew Noc was not anticipating this evening with glee.

Now, studying him, I saw he was actually dreading it.

I moved to him, placing a hand on his chest, swaying close.

"You don't need to go," I told him softly.

"We've had this discussion," he replied.

"We have, but Josette and I can easily take a taxi—"

He shook his head, his jaw getting hard. "You're not gonna be sitting at a table with this Savage guy without me sitting right beside you."

My Noctorno.

So protective.

"I don't know him," he carried on. "That means I don't trust him. And that means you *or* Jo *or* Circe are not gonna be sitting at a table with him unless I'm there. And since you all are gonna be there, I'm gonna be there."

Oh, *my Noctorno.*

So protective of *all* of those who had a place in his heart.

I smiled up at him.

"Babe, that dress, that smile, your perfume, your hand on me, knowin' I can get right to your nipple just sliding a hand inside that slit because I can tell you're not wearing a bra, you want this done tonight, you best go get your bag too. You don't do that and fast, you're gonna be bent over the sink, Jo is gonna get an earful and we're gonna be way fuckin' late," he growled.

I felt a lovely tingle as my eyelids lowered and my smile changed, but, wisely, I moved away from him to enter the bedroom where my reticule was on the bed.

I did this deciding to share with him that I'd very much like to engage in the activity he'd threatened me with.

However, I'd do that later too.

I was making sure I had everything I needed, screwing the cap shut firmly and sliding the lip gloss I still held into a side pocket of the little clutch when Noc spoke again.

I looked to him as he did so and saw he'd turned my way and was leaning his shoulder to the doorjamb, watching me.

"You wanna tell me why Valentine has all but disappeared?"

I did.

Yet I didn't.

"She's seeing to business, Noc. She'd been in my old world training me for some time. Being home, there's much she needs to catch up on."

This was not a complete lie, for Valentine had told me that same thing.

I watched Noc's regard turn penetrating.

"Just to say, gorgeous," he started in a low tone, "anytime you keep somethin' from me, no matter what it's about, you better have a really fuckin' good reason."

"She's lost a lover," I whispered.

I saw Noc's body come alert as he bit out, "Fuck. Breakup? Or...*lost*?"

"I don't believe he's *lost* lost," I answered. "Just lost to her. She's quite heartsick."

That, he looked like he didn't believe. "Valentine? Heartsick?"

I nodded.

"Fuck," he repeated, quieter this time.

"I, well, women tend to—"

He shook his head, pushing away from the jamb and coming to me. "Say no more, Frannie." He made it to me and put a hand to my waist. "That's you lookin' after your girl. I don't need to know her business. In other words, you keepin' her situation to yourself is a really good reason."

He understood.

And I loved that.

I smiled up at him again.

He looked to my smile then he dipped his head and put his lips to it.

When he lifted away, he asked, "You ready to go?"

"I have been for several days now, my dearest." I tipped my head to the side. "Are you?"

He gave a slight shrug, stepped away but grabbed my hand and pulled me toward the door stating, "As ready as I'll ever be."

We collected Josette.

Noc helped us both into his SUV (for Josette was wearing heels as well this night and she actually needed his assistance as she didn't have near as much practice as me).

Then he drove us to the restaurant where Dax Lahn would meet his Circe.

I sat mostly in silence as we rode, listening with half an ear to Josette chattering and Noc interjecting every once in a while.

I did this because I was relishing my anticipation for what was to come and tamping down my impatience that it would not come faster.

There was nothing better than the time before your carefully laid plans played out.

In other words, I could not *wait*.

I AIMED my behind toward the seat as Noc held out my chair for me.

Drinks and final explanations to Dax out of the way, my generous donation would be anonymously forwarded to First Mother House in the next week.

We'd met Patricia, and a check Noc showed me how to write for fifty thousand dollars that I'd be presenting to her that night was in my bag.

All seemed to be going well.

Dax was being friendly and respectful.

And after some circling of the savages, Noc and Dax seemed to settle in with each other.

I wasn't certain if Dax had worn him down and gained his trust with his manner, but Noc was no longer eyeing him with unhidden intensity. This was something that Dax, at first, seemed to take as his due (likely as he'd expect I would share the awkwardness of our first meeting with Noc and Noc would react to that). When his friendliness to Josette and myself didn't diminish Noc's focus, it caused Dax's alertness to increase until the sheer maleness wafting around us felt like it might cause me to choke.

Josette did very well at hiding it (from all but me, then again, neither man was paying much mind to Josette, considering they were using so much of their own to size each other up), but I saw she found this amusing.

I did not.

Although it was attractive, from both men, especially Noc because I knew why he was behaving in such a way, it went on so long, it was also trying.

Fortunately, Patricia arrived. We met her. She was lovely. Her addition to our party meant the men were forced to be outwardly civil to each other. And not long after we were told our table was ready.

The problem was, Circe had not yet arrived and she was supposed to do just that ten minutes ago.

I sat but tipped my head back to look up at Noc who was standing behind me with his hand on my chair.

"I think I may need to text someone, darling," I murmured.

"Leave it," he said.

"Noc—"

He bent toward me.

"Circe got a crystal ball too?" he asked in a voice only I could hear.

Oh balls.

Would she look into it to see us, or where we were to have dinner to ascertain what she should wear (something I would do), or for *any* reason, therefore see Dax and decide not to come?

"Perhaps," I answered.

"Then leave it," Noc repeated. "If she figured out what you're up to, we'll put that fire out later. Now, I'm hungry. I want to eat. I want this night done. And I want you in that dress at my house, just you and me."

I pressed my lips together.

He touched his to my jaw, straightened, pushed my chair to the table and then took his seat beside me.

I set my purse on the table beside my place setting, noting that, as Noc and I spoke, Dax had helped Josette and Patricia to their seats. Now he was watching Noc and me both closely.

When his regard finally settled only on me, he did not look alert and attuned to any action of the other alpha in his proximity.

His look was kind and warm, clearly communicating he was pleased I had such a protector after all he'd assumed I'd suffered.

Taking in that look, I gave him a small smile, hiding the triumph I felt inside for he was *just perfect* for Circe at the same time hiding a far more irritable thought.

This being...where the bloody hell *was* Circe?

"We seem to have an extra chair," Patricia noted.

"Yes, we do," Josette said quickly. "I forgot to mention, we invited a friend of ours. I hope you don't mind. We thought she, too, would be interested in the work you do."

Patricia smiled at Josette. "I don't mind. I'd shout about the First Mother House from the rooftops if I could."

I smiled at her benignly as she spoke.

Then I felt something. Something sudden and something fierce. It made me look away from Patricia and cut my eyes to Dax.

When I did, I felt my insides seize.

"Shit, fuck," Noc muttered under his breath.

He felt it too.

Or saw it.

Or both.

Dax had been in the process of flipping open his menu.

He was no longer in this process.

Indeed, I didn't think he even knew he held a menu in his hand.

Indeed, I didn't think he even knew he was seated at a table in an eating establishment with company.

His eyes were locked at a point across the room.

And his expression was...

Well it was...

Savage.

I felt another tingle as I tore my gaze from him and looked across the room.

At what I saw, I nearly crowed aloud with delight.

Circe was wearing a champagne-colored dress with a tiered skirt made of the most extraordinary lace, an unusual embroidered bodice and very thin straps. It was delicate, chic, but flirty.

And obviously expensive.

Someone had been using their treasure well, and it wasn't just me.

Her hair was down in a tousled riot of curls that fell over her shoulders and even in her face.

Which was what she was seeing to as she moved toward our table, flipping her hair out of her eyes in a manner I'd seen several times from women espousing hair products during what Noc explained were "commercials" on the television.

Her makeup glinted with peachy-bronze beauty.

She was *divine.*

That was, she was divine until she got her hair out of her face, started to drop her hand, looked fully at our table with a smile, and obviously just then noticed one particular member of our party.

Thus, she tripped.

Badly.

Her bag held in one hand went flying, her other hand went out to find purchase to save herself from falling and caught on a seated, elderly man's shoulder.

He cried out in surprise as he took some of her weight.

Noc grunted, "Shit, *fuck,*" and I felt his movements.

I looked his way to see he was pushing his chair back, preparing to go in aid of Circe.

He was too late.

Dax was out of his seat and charging in her direction.

He didn't even know she was coming in ours.

I looked to Josette.

She felt my regard and looked to me.

I smiled.

She let out a giggle.

"Are you all right?"

At his rumble, my attention returned to five feet away where Dax had one hand (now unnecessarily) on her waist steadying her, the other one held her clutch, which he'd clearly collected on his way.

Circe had her head tipped back, staring up at him, wide-eyed with lips parted, taking the clutch from him and doing this like her hand was moving through molasses.

Enchanting.

However, in his care, Dax misinterpreted her look for he moved into her protectively, bent his neck and cast his concerned gaze down to her feet, asking, "Did you twist an ankle? Are you hurt?"

Circe stared mutely at his profile.

He looked again to her.

"Do you need some ice?" he queried.

She remained silent, staring at him.

Then, suddenly, she appeared to get visibly woozy, her torso swaying gracefully (if a bit drunkenly), and in order not to collapse at his feet, she lifted a hand and placed it on his biceps.

At her touch, they both froze.

In fact, it felt like the entirety of the room froze.

I held my breath.

They gazed into each other's eyes.

Circe started swaying again.

This time...

Forward.

I felt my lips curl up in what I knew was undisguised glee.

I barely heard Dax's next.

But I heard it.

"Honey," he whispered, a teasing lilt to his deep voice, most assuredly a man who knew his effect on women, and right then most assuredly pleased he was having that effect on Circe. "You need to speak."

"You're..." Circe trailed off but began again. "You are..."

Not taking his one hand from her waist, Dax raised his other in the (minimal) space between them, an offer for her to take it in greeting.

"Dax Lahn," he introduced at the same exact time she breathed, "*Mine.*"

I saw his very broad shoulders straighten with surprise at her assertion.

Then I saw the color drain from her face.

"Shit, fuck, *fuck*," Noc bit out low, the vicinity of his voice telling me he was standing behind my chair.

"I'm sorry," Circe said, swaying again.

This time back.

Drat!

"So, so sorry. So...very...*sorry*," she chanted, her cheeks now flaming.

She took a hasty step away, out of Dax's hold, glanced at our table and then turned on her attractive champagne-colored, spike-heeled sandal and dashed gracefully (thank the Goddess Adele, no trips, or worse, falls) out of the restaurant.

Drat!

I quickly pushed back my chair, aiming it away from Noc who was still standing behind me. I rose and darted after her.

"Frannie," Noc called on a clip.

"Do you know her?" Dax asked as I passed him.

I kept darting even as I looked over my shoulder and assured, "Give me but a moment. We'll be back."

I only caught half a glance at Noc, and seeing in that scant second his expression, I had a feeling he might also offer spankings for other reasons.

I couldn't think of that.

I had to get to Circe, calm her down and then get her to our table, smooth things out and do what clearly would be minimal work at finishing making a match.

I made it through the seating area, the bar, the reception and out the front door.

I looked right.

No Circe.

I looked left and saw her rolling up on her toes with impatience as she shouted after the black-short-pants-white-shirt-wearing fellow who took Noc's SUV when we'd arrived and drove it away (Noc's explanation: a "valet").

"Please hurry!" I heard her cry after him. "It's an emergency!"

Blast!

"Circe," I called.

She whipped my way, looking at me, beyond me fearfully, then at me, all in a blink of an eye.

And then her beautiful face grew hard.

I hurried to her (as much as I hurried, it was undignified to do thus, so I didn't do it, shall we say, *noticeably*) and I was three feet away when she jabbed a pointed finger at the restaurant and accused, "This is what Valentine was up to and I can see she roped you into it too."

I stopped walking and started speaking, "Circe, we—"

She leaned toward me, jabbing her hand again at the building, and hissed, "I made a fool of myself in there."

Ah.

That was her concern.

I smiled at her. "You absolutely did not. You couldn't have made a more effective entrance if we'd practiced it."

She leaned back, her face still set. "Yes. However, we *didn't* practice it because I had no idea what I was walking into."

"I think it's pretty clear it went better this way," I shared as if I was a teacher instructing a student.

"You do?" she asked, but she didn't wish an answer for she immediately did that herself. "Well I don't."

I didn't understand.

"He's clearly taken with you," I noted. "And he's thus and you barely spoke a word."

"Has it occurred to you I don't *want* him to be taken with me?" she shot back.

How absurd.

I'd simply witnessed what had happened in there.

She felt it.

"Circe, you may try to convince yourself—"

I only got half of that out and stopped talking altogether for she was talking over me.

"No. It hasn't occurred to you, or Valentine. If it had, you wouldn't have orchestrated that debacle I was just forced to perpetrate."

It was then I felt the tickle of unease in my belly.

"My dear, that was not a debacle. It was—"

"*Humiliating*," she spat.

I swung back at the emotion in her tone then took a step forward, directing a hand her way.

"Please, let me expla—"

She didn't even allow me to finish.

"No explanation needed," she snapped, looked high above my shoulder and a change came over her face that cut straight through to the bone. "Did you know?" she asked, her voice no longer angry, but broken.

Oh no.

"Circe," Noc said gently.

"You knew," she whispered, the expression on her face now one of a woman betrayed.

Bloody hell.

Keeping my focus on Circe and not looking at Noc, who I felt now at my back, I shook my still-raised hand, stating swiftly, "He tried to talk me out of it."

Her attention sliced to me, she hid the hurt and her face twisted. "Of course he did. He's not that kind of man. But you're just that kind of woman, aren't you?"

The verbal strike came so unexpected I couldn't stop myself from reacting physically, doing this like I'd been slapped.

"Circe." Her name from Noc's lips now came as a growl.

A disappointed one.

And a warning one.

She turned her gaze to him. "She is," she bit off. "And you should know that." She looked to me. "I know all about you. Baldur used to talk about you. He thought you were magnificent. Any time he mentioned you it seemed he was half in love with you."

This was not a compliment.

Far from it.

And the idea of King Baldur, the Loathsome-But-Thankfully-Now-Dead finding me magnificent turned my stomach nauseatingly.

"I see you think what happened in there was not what actually happened in there," Noc returned, "seeing as Lahn is right now prowling the foyer like a caged animal, looking for any excuse to march out here to check on you."

Her pallor rose instantly as her eyes darted toward the doors to the restaurant.

This was not the right thing to say.

I stepped closer to her and immediately tried to soothe her fears. "He won't. Noc will go to him." I looked up at him. "And now might be a good time to do that, darling," I suggested.

"No fuckin' way," he denied.

"I'll be all right," I assured him.

"You always are," Circe cut in. "Wreaking havoc then blithely going on your way."

I returned to her.

"My intention tonight was—" I began to explain.

"Your usual," she intervened. "Malice. Wickedness. Toying with human beings just for sport."

Without telling my feet to do so, at the force of her vitriol, I took a step back and ran into Noc.

His hand fell warm and reassuring on my waist.

I did not feel reassured.

"Your car, ma'am," the valet said.

Circe didn't hesitate marching to her car where another black-short-pants-white-shirt-wearing young man was holding open her door.

"Circe, let me drive you home," Noc called. "You're upset. I'll get you home safe and we can talk while I do." His voice dipped and his fingers on me squeezed as he said, "We'll call you and Josette a taxi."

"Absolutely not," Circe refused, swinging around the opened door to her car.

"It's not smart to drive in your state," Noc told her.

"I die in a fiery crash, that's on her too," she retorted, jerking her glorious head of hair my way before she folded into her car and slammed the door.

Noc pulled me out of the way even if we were of a safe distance, not to mention on the pavement, as she raced off in her vehicle starting fast and going faster.

I stared after her.

"You wanna tell me what *in the fuck* is going on?"

Still unrecovered from the altercation with Circe, I did not want to turn at Dax's angry voice.

I had no choice but to turn at Dax's angry voice.

Noc did it with me.

And oh yes.

Dax was angry.

My.

"Didn't take a mind reader to see she was distraught and you let her get in her car and drive away?" Dax asked Noc incredulously and more than a little hostilely.

"She wasn't in the mood to let cooler heads prevail," Noc returned, doing this bitingly. "And now I gotta get my girls, my car and go after her to make sure she gets home okay."

"Yeah, you do that, but do it knowing I'll be wanting an explanation about why I feel like I've just been played and worse," he lifted a long arm and stabbed a strong finger in the direction Circe roared off, "*she* was."

"Fuck, shit, *fuck*," Noc swore.

"You standing there being pissed is not making sure she gets home okay," Dax informed him impatiently.

"Go get Josette," Noc ordered to me.

Oh no.

I looked up at him. "I think I'd rather not leave you two alone."

"Go get Jo, Frannie."

And let the man I love get torn apart by a savage in front of an elegant other-world restaurant (or, he could try, Noc could likely defend himself quite well, still, they both could get hurt in the process)?

Categorically...

No.

I stared up at him and didn't move.

He growled, no words, just the noise.

It was attractive.

But the look on his face meant this mingled with not a small amount of downright terrifying.

He turned back to Dax.

"Circe is a friend of ours. Frannie met you. Liked your manner. Liked the look of you. Liked your involvement with First Mother House. I'll say no more about that, but I'm thinkin' you're a bright guy and you can put two and two together to understand why she orchestrated a fixup between the two of you at the same time you can put it together why Circe reacted violently to that, especially when it's clear she took one look at you and was into you."

"Are you...fucking...*shitting me*?"

As this ominous rumble came from Dax, I took a step back, my hands on Noc to try to make him take a step back with me, but he didn't budge.

"So now you know what that was all about," Noc went on. "And we'll be sorting that out. You can tell me how pissed you are right now after you name your first son after me," Noc stated audaciously and again looked at me. "Now, baby," he dipped his face to mine, "go...get...*Jo*."

His tone invited no other response but the one I gave him.

"I'll just go get Jo."

He straightened.

I started on my errand trying not to look like I was moving as hurriedly as I was.

Something made me stop when I'd come alongside Dax (not *close* alongside him, just alongside him, I had something to say, but I was no fool).

Slowly, he stopped scowling at Noc and turned his scowl to me.

"She's the most delicate thing you'll ever hold in your hands. You'll win her. She'll reward you for the effort. But mark my words, if you ever hurt her, I'll fucking *annihilate* you."

He no longer looked fierce. His chin had jerked back into his neck and he looked stunned.

He likely wasn't used to being threatened.

I did not pause to take in the incongruity of the fact that, even stunned, Dax Lahn was immensely attractive.

I hurried without appearing to hurry to collect Jo.

I DASHED up the steps of Valentine's home in my spiked, red heels.

"Frannie," Noc called after me.

I didn't say a word or slow my gait.

I kept charging up the stairs.

"Goddamn it, Franka," Noc clipped.

I made the upper landing and stomped angrily to Valentine's magic room.

I had collected Jo at the restaurant. We'd driven to Circe's. Even if we'd seen the lights on from the outside, we'd gone into her apartment building. There we'd ascertained she was quite all right when Noc knocked on her door and it burst into a sheet of magical, golden flame that caused no harm to the door but blew a wave of heat in our direction that needed no words to share Circe wished us to go away.

We went away.

The drive home was silent.

Noc took my key to Valentine's house and let us in the front door silently.

And I'd made my ascent to her magic room quickly, but also silently.

I flipped the switch and a charming lamp with a jade-green glass shade lit on the table that held her crystal ball.

I went directly to it and touched my hand to its cool surface.

Imbued with her magic but being touched by mine, a striking, if obviously confused, drift of teal smoke formed inside it.

"Franka," Noc said from the door.

"Valentine," I snapped at the ball. "Come. Now."

I touched the crystal again feeling the emotion swell in my breast, the rush of power wash over my skin, barely keeping hold on the guilt clawing inside me.

A waft of cyan smoked the orb.

My magic was winning.

If anyone touched my crystal and filled it with their magic, I'd lose my mind.

I was hoping Valentine felt the same.

"Valentine," I hissed. "Come to me. *Now*."

"Frannie, sweetheart," Noc said from close, his voice now calming.

I looked to him and was not surprised to see the entire room colored blue.

"My magic, at this moment, is not under my control, therefore it would be safer if you absented yourself," I told him.

"Baby, you need to calm down," he replied.

"You do indeed," Valentine declared, and both our eyes went to the sound of her voice.

She'd arrived, and the minute I saw her, she lifted her hand, waved nonchalantly, and the blue cleared away as did the residual emerald smoke that heralded her arrival.

"You also need to explain to me why you interrupted me in what I was doing and practically *pulled* me away," she demanded irately. "Calling to me on an astral plane is one thing, Franka. Dragging me bodily from my pursuits is another."

Now that was a shock. I had no idea I had the power to do that at all, much less do it to a witch who had the awesome power of Valentine.

I did not make a comment on that.

"I orchestrated a meeting with Dax and Circe this evening," I informed her.

She crossed her arms on her chest. "Yes, I'm aware of that. I felt a disturbance in the force."

Noc made an agitated movement at my side, but I was focused on her flippancy (and wouldn't understand just how flippant it was until Noc explained it by making me watch a very fantastical, but quite excellent, film, wisely doing this sometime later).

"I thought you said you were talented in intrigue," she remarked.

"And I thought I had a partner in this particular intrigue," I returned.

Her face shadowed. "You're quite aware I'm not available for this project at this time."

"And now I'm quite aware that affecting schemes in this world might end in a woman operating a vehicle while excessively agitated. Doing this rather than rushing from a room to a sleigh or carriage, at worst, but usually to a fainting couch where she can play out her drama, or in this case, understandable emotion at what she perceives as a betrayal, without putting her life in danger behind the wheel of a car."

It was then I saw the real Valentine, for she looked stricken for a moment before she hid it.

"Perhaps we should allow some time to pass before we again take up the reins on this endeavor," she suggested.

"Absolutely not," I returned, shaking my head and taking a step toward her. "The die has been cast. You weren't there. It could be the disturbance you felt wasn't her upset at the betrayal she thought was committed against her, but instead the moment she clapped eyes on Dax Lahn. Or it could have been the moment he touched her. *Or* it could have been the moment *she* touched *him.* That was, before she fell apart and rushed dramatically from a crowded restaurant. Oh, and this was *after* she nearly fell flat on her face the moment she laid eyes on Dax. All of this, incidentally, happening over the approximate expanse of thirty seconds."

"It seems you *are* clever with intrigues," Valentine murmured admiringly.

Well!

It was safe to venture I'd had enough.

I took another step toward her, the manner in which I did causing Noc to slide an arm around my stomach from his position at my back and waylay me.

So I stopped.

"As difficult as the road that lay ahead of us is, that *us* including Circe, we must carry on before she uses the bleakness of her past to harden her heart to a future of promise," I proclaimed.

"I see what you mean."

That was the only response Valentine gave.

"Valentine, I would say I need you, but *I* don't. *Circe* does," I snapped. "I'm aware the time is not right for you, but I'm afraid, my sister, you need to see beyond your own sorrow in order to lead our other sister from hers."

I watched her mouth tighten and knew this was due to the fact I uttered those words while Noc was in the room. I sensed she was a private woman. The very idea of Noc understanding her current plight would not be welcome.

I could not worry on that. She would endure.

Circe, however, had had enough enduring to last a lifetime.

"Respect, Valentine, what's going on with you is not my business, but you gotta know Frannie is right," Noc thankfully entered the conversation. "What happened tonight was fucking brilliant and a complete disaster. You don't strike while the iron is hot, he'll lose her. And I can tell you right now it's taking all that man's got to convince himself not to call his investigators to find her so *he* can find her. And when he does that, drag her to his beach house or mountain condo or whatever that guy's got that's remote so she can't run away and then convince her she's the one, not having the barest inkling he'll be scaring the absolute shit outta her. That is, if he hasn't already called his investigators."

And the real Valentine made another appearance.

"*Merde*," Valentine whispered.

Finally.

We were getting to her.

"And, just sayin'," Noc carried on, "he tries that shit, it's gonna be a lot of explaining on *her* part when she makes her door a sheet of magical flame to ward him off. A man thinks his drive for a woman has made him so insane he's seeing things, like doors bursting into flame but not catching fire, he'll back off *real quick*."

"*Merde*," Valentine said louder.

Excellent.

We'd gotten to her.

"I think it best at this juncture to let Circe alone," I declared. "For the night, at least. We cannot let her retreat, but we need to allow her to lick her wounds. You, however, need to see to Dax. He needs to be controlled. In case you haven't absorbed all we're telling you, to say he's taken with her, and was upon clapping eyes on her, is an understatement. I don't know what Lahn felt when he saw his future golden queen walking in that hideous parade. But I can now say I hold no surprise he chased her down on his steed and claimed her on the rocks of Korwahk before nary a word was spoken."

"I'll see to Dax," Valentine stated. "You and I will speak more tomorrow."

I felt my body relax and replied, "Thank you."

"And I'll say something now, Franka," she stated in a severe tone. "You must beware how you wield your power. Allowing your emotions to control it rather than your mind can have catastrophic consequences. I've told you this before. I won't share it again."

I made no response, for she had shared this, thus her admonishment hit true.

"Is it all, erm, good up there?" Josette called, and the sound of her voice told me she was likely at the foot of the stairs.

"All good, Jo," Noc called back. "Be down in a minute."

"Right," she yelled.

I stared as Valentine started to disappear in a billow of green.

"Valentine," I snapped, feeling we were not yet done.

"I'll see to Dax. Until tomorrow," she said and disappeared.

"Bloody *hell* that woman is vexing," I bit out.

"Babe."

I glared at where Valentine had been for a long measure then turned in his arm.

The instant he had my eyes, he asked, "You okay?"

"What, pray, happened tonight, my dearest, darling Noc, that would make you think I was even *near* feeling okay?" I asked back.

"Right, well that answered that," he muttered but did it watching me closely.

"I miscalculated," I declared. "Appallingly."

Noc didn't utter a noise.

"I thought, with Circe's approach and, well...activities with you at the

Winter Palace, she was ready to move onwards in healing. Valentine felt the same. It would seem we were wrong."

Noc remained silent.

"Unspeakably wrong," I went on.

Noc did not confirm, or alternately make an effort to appease.

He said nothing.

And nothing was *not* helping.

"Noc," I prompted.

"You're on that. You'll sort it," he stated. "I don't need to go over it because I can tell you're upset and anyway, there's no need. You were there. You saw it play out."

This was all true.

"But Circe lashed out," he continued. "At *you*. Maybe understandable but still unacceptable. So shit went south tonight with Circe. Whatever. Only thing I give a shit about right now is, she cut into you. I didn't just see, I actually felt those cuts slice deep, so *are you okay*?"

His words the night I came to his world rocked through my brain.

I know what you said to Maddie, right to her face. Lo told me. He knows your story now, Frannie. Like everyone else, he's changed his tune about you. That said, he's still pissed about that and he'll never forgive you for it because that's the guy he is. He loves his wife, you wounded her, he's never gonna let that go.

He loves his wife, you wounded her, he's never gonna let that go.

And then...

So shit went south tonight with Circe. Whatever. Only thing I give a shit about right now is...are you okay?

I was Noc's Franka, like Maddie was Apollo's, Finnie was Frey's, Circe was Lahn's, Cora was Tor's.

I was Noc's.

He had that woman to love we spoke about so many months before, sitting at a fire, drinking whiskey.

And that woman was *me*.

"You really do love me," I whispered, staring into his beautiful blue eyes.

His head jerked, his brows snapped together, and his look turned decidedly ominous.

"You doubted it?"

"No, darling," I went on softly. "I'll rephrase. You love me, you *really* do."

"Uh, well...yeah," he replied.

I melted into him, wrapped my arms around his waist and answered his question the way he wished it to be answered.

"I cannot say that her words felt good. What I can say is that she was on the defensive and feeling things I cannot begin to know how they feel. Her attack on me might not have been warranted, but in my estimation not only was it understandable, it was acceptable. I made a grave error in planning. It was her that suffered for it. So yes. It might have hurt, hearing what she said, but I'm standing here in the arms of the man I really love who really loves me in return. So I'm okay."

He examined my face, I knew, to ascertain I was telling the truth.

His face and frame relaxed when it came clear I was.

All but his arms, they tightened, drawing me closer.

"One thing I can say for tonight, she put her hand on his arm, thought that the windows in that restaurant were gonna blow out," he said.

"You felt it too?"

"Think they felt it in the parallel universe."

I smiled up at him.

"Means I'm in," he stated.

I blinked up at him.

"Pardon?"

"Baby, wasn't lost on me, seeing the way Frey was with Finnie, the other Lahn with the other Circe, hell, knew it way back when Tor came tearing into this world to come get Cora, this love between worlds business is extreme."

At that, I just stared up at him, still confused.

"And tonight proved it," he finished.

"Yes," I agreed.

"So I'm in."

I tipped my head to the side. "You're in?"

"Gonna help you make a match between Circe and her savage."

He was going to help!

Delightful!

My smile that time was far bigger.

He dropped his head so his face was close to mine.

"And just so you know, when I mentioned that love between worlds business, I was talkin' about hittin' the door to my bathroom and seeing you in that dress. But what happened between Circe and Dax capped it."

At his first statement, I slid my hands up his back.

After he finished his second, the fingers of both were in his hair.

So of course I used them to pull him to me and kiss him.

But because he was "in," he was going to help me make a match, I let him take over the kiss.

Well, because of that.

And for other reasons besides.

~

In the mirror, I watched Noc shove his face into the side of my neck, feeling the shudders thunder through his powerful frame with his climax.

I had already had mine. Therefore, in the throes of my afterglow, I was able to fully enjoy a visual of how our passion overwhelmed my beautiful Noctorno.

Prior to leading me to his bathroom, Noc had only taken off his suit jacket.

And he'd only taken off my panties.

This before he'd taken me, both of us facing the basin, my skirt about my hips.

And right then, I had a hand braced against the counter and a vision of my face flushed, Noc's lost in my neck, only his thick, dark hair could be seen. I could feel his warm breath against my skin, see his hand in the slit of my dress, feel his fingers cupping my breast, his other arm out straight, his hand covering mine beside the basin.

And his cock, obviously, was still thick and hard inside me.

We were separate and we were one.

We were beauty.

I felt his fingers weaving through mine at the counter as I felt his lips brush my neck.

Then I watched him lift his head and press his jaw against the side of mine, his glorious eyes moving over us in the mirror, the expression in them not hiding he felt as me with what could be seen.

Finally, those stunning blue eyes caught mine.

Noc said nothing.

I said nothing.

We just held each other's gazes in the mirror before he slid his hand out of my dress and lifted it to my jaw.

He needed no words to share what he wanted.

Therefore I gave it to him, turning my head and offering him my mouth.

He took it.

We kissed languidly but greedily, like kings and queens assured of their power, their treasure their reign, nevertheless indulging sumptuously in the lap of luxury that was theirs by right of birth and the grace of the gods.

When Noc finally broke the kiss, he whispered, "Ready for bed, baby?"

I nodded.

Only then did he break the connection of our bodies, but soon enough he sought it again, tangling himself in me in the warmth of his bed.

And there we slept.

21
JUST A GUY

Noc

Noc knocked on the door and stepped back just in case it went up in flames, or maybe shot magical laser beams at him.

He was there because he and Franka had had a meeting with Valentine that morning, he'd been briefed about all things Dax Lahn, and Noc had volunteered to go smooth things over with Circe.

He wasn't looking forward to the task, but he was the man for the job mostly because, if she'd slept on it and was still pissed at Frannie, after all she'd said the night before, no way in hell he was setting up his woman to face whatever Circe felt like dishing out.

Valentine had assured them she was seeing to Dax. She didn't share how she was doing this. Noc also didn't ask because he really didn't want to know.

As he waited outside Circe's place, the door didn't explode.

It also didn't open.

He got close again, knocked again and stayed where he was, saying through it, "I know you know it's me. What you also gotta know is, until I see you're all right, I'm not leaving."

She made him wait, but she finally opened the door.

Cutoff jean shorts, a little tee, bare feet, hair wild, face makeup free, fuck, Dax was going to like every version of Circe.

"I'm all right," she snapped and started to close the door again.

Noc lifted a hand to hold it open.

She didn't push it. Instead, the battle she waged was with her gaze, trying to stare him down.

He didn't just take it.

He pushed back, but only verbally.

"She meant no harm. She wants good things for you. She's lived the life she felt she had to live to keep herself safe. That's not her life anymore, but she's used to doing things a certain way. But now she's doin' those things for good. She just doesn't have it down how to go about doin' that yet. She's not the woman you said she was last night, Circe. Valentine told me she's kept you in the loop about what's been going down with Frannie, so I figure you know it. But even with all that, she shouldn't have played it that way. She fucked up. She knows that now. And she's gutted, babe. Kicking her own ass and worried as shit about you."

Circe could only hold the attitude for a few seconds before she looked away and stepped away, opening the door further, inviting him in.

He went in and saw, with the little she had, she had good taste. But even with the treasure she'd been given, she wasn't about pimping out her space.

Noc moved to the middle of the small living room and stopped, turning to her.

Circe followed him and leaned the side of her thigh against the arm of her couch where a cat instantly appeared, rubbing its side against her skin.

She did not ask Noc to sit. She did not offer him coffee.

She just dropped a hand to scratch the ruff of her pet and held Noc's gaze.

He laid it out.

"I should have stopped her. I knew it wasn't the right play. I told her that, she was determined. I still should have stopped her."

"What's done is done," she stated shortly.

"It I,s but you gotta know, I felt how it made you feel last night and I'm sorry about the part I played in it."

Circe, unsurprisingly not a woman who would carry a grudge in the face of an open apology, visibly lost some of the attitude and repeated, "What's done is done," but this came far more gently.

Right, they were beyond that, now it was time to lay more shit out.

"We need to talk about Dax."

She straightened from the couch, going instantly wired.

"There's nothing to say."

He took only one step toward her before he stopped and pointed out, "I don't get, at the same time I do, why you'd be in denial about what went down last night. But I wouldn't be a friend if I didn't try to pull you out of that."

"You and Franka are proof that there are differences between our two worlds and they still carry on. This being so, I understand why Valentine and Franka would think this needs to happen between me and that man. But it's also obvious that it actually doesn't."

"True enough," Noc replied. "But that doesn't explain your reaction to him last night, or his to you."

She looked away.

He kept at her.

"Circe, babe, please don't shut me out. I'm here to talk to you, but I'm also here for you to talk to me. Share with me. Give me whatever shit is holding you back from something I know rocked you in bad ways last night. The thing is, it also rocked you in good ways. *Really* good. I can't know, but my guess is that the good parts are what are holding you back. And knowing all that's in play here, I would be no friend at all if I didn't try to help you see that good as just what it is."

When she again gave him her attention, her face was a mask and her eyes were angry.

Even so, she couldn't hide they were also haunted.

Fuck.

"There is no way you can understand where I am with this."

"No," he whispered. "No," he repeated, letting all he was feeling out with that one syllable and seeing the anger dissolve, but also seeing the wounds surfacing. He fucking hated what he saw but he didn't give up. "I can't know. But I know what's there. I know why *you're* there. And it kills me there's not a fuckin' thing I can do about it."

"No one can do anything about it, Noc," she said quietly.

"This guy can."

She blinked up at him.

"I was not that guy," Noc went on. "We both knew it. I could not be that guy for you. I knew and you knew. We both understood I was not strong enough to handle all that happened to you. Not for the long run. So what we had was what it was because we both knew I couldn't be the guy for you to give you what you needed."

Now she was staring at him with big eyes that showed she was confused and he didn't get that.

But he didn't ask after it.

He stayed on target.

"But this guy, Circe," he kept at her, "this guy is not any guy. He's an attorney. He's a good one. Not a fighter. A warrior. He's wealthy and he earned that, he didn't get born to it. And he does pro bono for a domestic violence shelter for no reason than that's his mission. And he buys a ten thousand dollar table at their gala event, leaning on all his attorney buddies to do the same. That was how we got him there last night. He probably could be doing a hundred things on a Friday night. He was not doing those things. He was there facilitating a donation from Franka."

She seemed surprised at this information, but said, "Noc, his commitment to that says nice things about him, but it has nothing to do with me. Now what I'd like to talk about is how you feel about—"

He interrupted her.

"What I'm saying is, we're not talking sympathy. We're not talking empathy. We're talking about a man who respects women, knows how they should be treated and does something about it when that shit doesn't happen," Noc informed her.

She shut her mouth.

Noc kept going.

"No one can look at that man and not think he has his head up his ass about his looks, his money, his talents. He's confident, but that's not what he's about. What he's about is, he's all that, and he's still the man he is for women."

"Again, this is all very nice to know about him, but, Noc, it has nothing to do with me."

"Not sure how you see it that way when the minute he saw you, the world faded away."

That was a blow she didn't expect. So much of one, she took a step back.

"And Circe," he pushed, "when you saw him, your world did too."

"I was simply surprised to see Lahn there," she bald-faced lied.

He gentled his tone when he shared, "This wasn't about Lahn. You knew that man was not Lahn. This was about Dax. All about Dax."

"Noc—"

"I did not like this idea," he stated. "When Franka shared what she and Valentine were up to, I didn't like it at all. And she never talked me around to liking it. I was there last night to look after her, because I didn't know this guy, and to look after you, because she was determined to throw you in his path. Then I saw him with you, Circe, and no way in fuck I'd let anyone get near you I didn't trust. But I saw him with you and here I am."

"Noc—"

"I want you to be happy. Franka does. Valentine does. Hell, *everyone* does. The only one standing in the way of that is you."

"I like my life," she asserted.

"Are you happy?"

"Yes, of course."

It was the truth.

And it totally wasn't.

"Are you really happy, babe?" he pressed.

"I'm far more content than I've ever been," she replied. "I'm my own woman. I say where I go and what I do and who I'm with. I have friends. I love this city. I have my power back and it's all mine."

"Content isn't happy," he noted.

"It's better than anything I've ever had."

"Okay, I hear that," Noc conceded but didn't let up. "And it sucks that's true. But it's a far cry from what you deserve."

"Noc, there's a good deal to say about being content in your life."

"I've got Frannie. I fell in love with her. She fell in love with me. She's here and it's not good, it's great. I've got a house I dig and serious money in the bank so I not only don't have to worry about just covering emergencies, I'm set for life. And last, I've got a job that pays me more than I ever thought I'd make. So I'm in a position to say that contentment works, but happy in a good place, a fantastic city, with good friends, a good job and a woman I love to share my life with is a fuckuva lot better."

"I see you won't understand what I'm trying to say," she remarked, beginning to look agitated.

"I think it's the other way around," he returned.

"Can't you just let it go?" she requested.

"After what I saw last night, what I can say is, I want to do that for you, because you want it from me. And I totally cannot do it, also *for you*."

"Noc—"

He knew she wanted him to let it go.

But he saw what he saw last night. He felt it.

So he just couldn't.

"This guy has got it in him, Circe. He can be that guy for you. He might be the only one in two universes who can be. He's a warrior *and* he's a protector. You know where I'm at with you. I wouldn't say that if I didn't feel it in my gut, it's true."

"Noc—" she tried again.

But he kept going.

"And the most important thing about it is, you so rocked his world last night just looking at you, I know he'll take it all from you. He'll hear it and he'll get it and I mean *all* of it. Who you are. The power you have. What happened to you. Where you're from. He won't care if you tell him you're from the moon. The man I saw last night, babe, he just wants you."

"He terrifies me," she blurted.

That was unexpected.

Noc fell silent.

Circe looked beyond him, drew in a visible breath then looked back at him.

"He terrifies me," she whispered.

"Why?" Noc whispered back. "He's not Lahn. He's not from a place they rape women to make them their wives. I can see you looking at him and seeing only that. But that isn't who he is."

"It's not that. I saw Lahn with his Circe and I know even Lahn isn't that."

"Then what is it?"

"He's everything."

Again, unexpected.

And again, Noc fell silent.

"He's meant for me," she kept on, doing it not sounding hopeful, sounding terrified. "He's mine."

"I think from what I saw last night, you're right. He is," Noc agreed.

"I have never, not once, been happy," she told him.

Noc felt that slice through his gut.

"Circe."

"I have never, not once, except long ago in a time that seems so far away it's like it was a dream, the time my parents were alive, I have never felt love."

Christ.

She was killing him.

"Babe."

"I know I have friends who care deeply about me. That's not the same."

It wasn't.

It wasn't the love of a man.

It wasn't that love growing into family, be it a family of two or the family those two made.

"I want him," she admitted.

Finally, they were getting somewhere.

He moved close, saying, "Circe, all I've been saying means you can have him."

She shook her head. "I finally escaped Baldur, only to be set upon by pirates, passed amongst them like a toy. I escaped them, only to be put into the Wife Hunt in Korwahk. At my end, I spirited myself away, only to put my twin in my place where she was promptly violated."

"That worked out," he reminded her.

"But it could have been disastrous," she reminded him.

"It wasn't," he stated.

"It could have been, and the point is, Noc, I don't have very good luck."

"You are not wrong about that, Circe, and now you're at a crossroads. You can live safe, which means you live half a life, or you can keep trying your luck, because serious as shit, babe, you're long due for a windfall and I see it right within your reach. You just gotta reach for it."

She looked hopeful before that melted to uncertain.

"What if he doesn't want me?" she asked almost shyly.

Noc fought a grin.

"Babe, were you conscious last night?" he asked back.

Again with the hope that went uncertain.

She lifted and dropped her free hand. "I'm a witch. I'm from another world. I've had...things have been done to me..."

She trailed off and Noc reached out and took her hand.

"Those things were done *to* you. Those things don't *make* you. You are what you've always been, Circe. A beautiful, strong, caring woman. You took all that was piled on you and never gave up. You escaped Baldur only to end up in a situation that was just as bad. You got kidnapped and landed in another bad situation and you still didn't give up. You found a way to get out. That could have gone really bad, but it didn't, and in the end, the woman you switched with is happy, in love, making babies and her father thinks of you as his daughter. You got all that because you had every reason to give up and you never did. Don't give up now. You've got so much to give, babe, the lucky one in this scenario is not you reaching out to Dax. It'll be Dax, if you find the courage to reach."

"You're very sweet," she murmured.

"Maybe. But mostly I'm very right."

She gave that a moment to sink in before she stated, "This remains to be seen but there is something you're wrong about and that's that you couldn't be 'that guy' for me."

Shit.

What?

He made himself stay close, holding her hand, hoping like fuck he hadn't read what went on between them months ago wrong.

He saw a small smile touch her mouth before she shared, "I don't mean I wanted that between us, and it wouldn't matter because, you'll remember, you didn't want that either. What was understood then is understood now. But you speak like you're not the kind of man strong enough to be 'that guy' who can be all he needs to be for a woman who needs him to be just that. But if you weren't, then Franka would be in a very different place right now and not looking like the gold of the sun shines through her, when before she looked weighed down by the blanket of eternal night."

That made Noc release her and step back.

At his movements, her brows drew together.

"You are that man, Noc, you must know this," she said gently.

He shook his head. "I was just the guy who happened to be there when shit went down and looking back, I was half in love with her already, so I'm lucky this is where we ended up."

When he was done speaking, she stared at him, murmuring, "Lucky?"

He ignored that and carried on. "But we're not talking about me."

Before he could say more, Circe butted in.

"We weren't. We are now."

"I'm here right now for you," he asserted.

"Then good. Thank you. So I'll make a deal with you, Noc. I'll think about not playing it safe. I'll think about trying my luck. But only if you'll think about the absolute rubbish you just handed me."

Noc felt his head jerk and his jaw tighten.

"You're right, I know her story," she said softly. "And I need to speak to her. I was..." she gave a short shake of her head, "not myself last night. I was cruel even knowing she didn't deserve it. I will...I'll apologize. But Noc, it's impossible for me to understand how you can come here championing this man for me not knowing you're that man for Franka."

He was getting impatient.

"Again, Circe, we're not talking about me."

"You said this Dax would be the one who would be lucky if I took a chance. I wonder, if I asked Franka, who *she* felt was the lucky one between her and you."

"She can think that it's her but I know the truth."

She studied him closely, doing this speaking.

"I had everything, a loving family, a magical gift, and it was all swept from me by a cruel and twisted man. Your Franka, I can't even think on it, Noc, knowing from her first breath, she had nothing. Until she had you."

His words were tight when he stated, "Not gonna repeat myself, Circe."

"I can't believe you don't see what's inside you," she whispered, her gaze searching.

"I'm just a guy."

"You are not just a guy," she stated firmly.

He was done in a way they both were going to be done.

"All right, I'm the guy who made it all good for Franka," he lied. "There it is. Now I said that, our deal. I'm going from here to my woman, and if you give me the go ahead, when I get there, we'll call Dax and ask him to dinner tomorrow night. At my place. Me, him, Franka and you."

"You only said what you said about yourself so I'd make that deal," she accused.

She was correct.

Noc didn't confirm that.

He didn't say anything.

Suddenly, what he'd just suggested hit her and her concern for him fled as anxiety again took hold.

"Your decision, your life and I stand by whatever you decide," he said. "I'll make Franka do it, and if I can pull it off, I'll make Valentine do it. But I don't think I have to go on record to say, if you don't come to dinner tomorrow night, don't try your luck one last time and do it for a shot at happiness with this guy, I think you're making a big mistake."

"I'll come to dinner," she replied in such a soft voice he almost didn't hear her.

So relieved, he couldn't stop himself, he reached out and pulled her into his arms to give her a tight hug.

"That's the right decision," he said into the top of her hair.

"I hope it is," she said into his chest.

He lifted his head and she leaned back but he didn't let her go.

"It is," he assured.

She pressed her lips together, still visibly anxious.

"Come early," he urged. "Sit with Franka. Talk to her. Get to know her. Drink some wine. You'll be in a safe place with *your* people around you looking after *you*. You feel uncomfortable or anything, we'll take care of you. I promise you that, Circe. Swear."

"I believe you."

He gave her a squeeze and then slowly let her go, murmuring, "Good. Now I gotta get to my truck to call Frannie and let her know it's all good. She's pretending she's got it all together, but she's freaked as shit things got messed up last night and she's worried about you so I gotta get that off her mind before I get the rest of this show on the road."

She looked like she wanted to say something but thought better of it before she smiled at him and started toward the door.

He followed her.

She opened it and he moved out, turning to say, "I'm seriously glad you opened the door, babe."

"I'll tell you later whether or not I am."

She'd pulled up her courage and was showing him a brave face.

He was glad for it because he didn't hope he was right about this world's Dax Lahn.

What he saw last night he knew he was right and he wanted that for her.

"Early," he said. "I've texted you my address, show at four. I'll be cooking.

Franka will be watching me do it and talking to you. We'll ask him to be there at six."

She tried to hide her nervous swallow and nodded.

Noc lifted a hand, wrapped his fingers briefly around the side of her neck and gave her a smile.

"See you tomorrow," he said as his goodbye.

"Tomorrow, Noc."

He turned to leave and took two steps but stopped when she called his name.

"You can think what you want, but I know. Franka and I have different stories, but we were both left in the same darkness," she said quietly. "So I know. If this man is that man for me, *I* will be the lucky one. And you being the man you are, the only man for Franka, so is she."

Before he could say a word, she shut the door.

He stared at it for a beat and then he didn't give it another second.

Or another thought.

He walked to his Suburban, got in and made a phone call.

FRANKA WAS PACING.

Noc was leaning a hip against his island, phone to his ear, listening to it ringing, focus on Frannie.

"Baby, calm down," he urged.

She stopped instantly, caught his eyes and hers narrowed.

"Calm? This man might have spent the last sixteen hours convincing himself we're insane and he wants nothing to do with us, including Circe. Valentine has made certain he doesn't go after her and he hasn't, but she doesn't have the power to read his thoughts."

She'd counted the hours.

That was cute.

He didn't have a chance to further reassure her.

The phone stopped ringing and a man answered with, "Lahn."

"Lahn, this is Noc Hawthorne."

"Did she get home okay?"

Noc dropped his head and grinned at his feet.

He hadn't spent the last sixteen hours convincing himself they were insane.

Noc saw Franka's hand land on his chest and he lifted his eyes to her, still grinning.

Her shoulders sagged in relief.

"Hawthorne," Dax bit out. "You there?"

"Yes, I'm here and she got home okay, pissed as hell we tried to set her up, but okay. Went 'round and talked to her this morning. She's not been in a place for a while to take a shot at certain things, but I pointed out she's gotta find that place. In other words, we'd like to know if you'd come to dinner tomorrow, my place, Frannie, me and Circe. Six."

"Text me your address, I'll be there."

Noc nearly burst out laughing.

His efforts at not doing that made his next words sound choked.

"Will do."

Frannie pressed in at his chest and gave him wide what-the-hell-is-going-on eyes.

He rounded her with an arm.

"Tomorrow," Dax grunted.

"Yeah, man. See you then," Noc replied.

Dax hung up.

Noc dropped his phone from his ear and started chuckling.

"What?" Franka asked.

"He's coming to dinner."

She lifted her other hand to his chest and pressed both in, beaming and declaring, "By the gods, this pleases me."

Noc was pleased too, but he was more pleased seeing how much she was.

She remained pleased for about two seconds before she got down to business.

"No Fleuridian wine tomorrow, Noc," she bossed. "I don't want her thinking of home. Not the good of Fleuridian wine and definitely not the bad she was treated to there. I want her head firmly in this world."

"Aye, aye captain," he said on a grin.

Her eyes narrowed again.

"This is no jest. We have to plan this carefully. He's taken with her, but we're her people. He mustn't think less of her because he thinks less of us. To that end, what are you making for dinner?"

"I thought—" he started.

"Fillet steak *en croute* with pâté and sautéed mushrooms," she demanded.

Noc beat back his chuckles.

"Babe, I'm not making beef Wellington."

"That's what that's called here?" she asked.

"Uh, yeah, and it's tricky and a pain in the ass. I'll make steak, though, and fire up the grill."

"That's acceptable," she agreed. "We'll serve it with *patates royales*."

"What the fuck is that?" he asked.

"I don't know," she answered. "It's potatoes, and I would say cream, salt, pepper, other things. They're mashed to creamy goodness then piped into fluffy parcels and baked—"

"Frannie, I'm not pipin' shit into fluffy anything and not just because I have no clue how to pipe."

"They're delicious and elegant," she returned impatiently.

It was time to nip this in the bud.

"Right, gorgeous. You got a choice of loaded baked or mashed or we can go out tomorrow and buy a deep fat fryer so I can fry some frozen French fries. I'll grill some asparagus. And this is New Orleans, there's gonna be about seven thousand places we can go to find really fuckin' good desserts and even better rolls. That'll be our mission for the rest of the day. If you want, you can buy a couple four-hundred-dollar bottles of wine and a kickass whiskey, which, my guess, is this dude's thing. And that's what we're doing without me having to pipe anything or wrestle with pastry dough. You with me?"

She wasn't with him and she shared that by declaring, "My ideas for the menu are far more impressive."

"And if you want, instead we can spend the day finding a chef who'll haul his ass to my house to make them since I'm not doin' any of that."

She glared at him.

He fought the need to kiss her.

He won the fight but did it wrapping both arms around her, pulling her closer and dipping his face to hers.

"He's into her, babe. He's not gonna even taste anything we put in front of him. We could serve him a box of cardboard painted like a beef Wellington and he would probably eat it. He has no clue the forces that are drawing him to Circe. He's also a man who doesn't care. His gut says go for it, he's going for it. He'll handle this. He'll do all the work. We're just gonna be there so she's in a safe place in her head to let him."

She looked appeased and acted it, snuggling closer.

"And she was good with you earlier? She seemed bolstered?" she asked.

"Told you that, baby. She's a little freaked, but she's powering through it."

Frannie started fiddling with the collar of his shirt, her eyes dropping to her fingers to watch.

"Also told you she feels bad about what she said to you," he reminded her.

She raised her eyes but kept her fingers at his shirt. "She shouldn't."

"I know you think that, but that's who she is." He bent his head closer to her. "Before we go to the market, you wanna call her? Check in?"

Her eyes lit with a cautious light.

"Do you think she'd welcome that?"

He nodded.

"Then it would please me to do this before we go to the market."

He gave her a squeeze. "You got her number in your phone, babe."

She gave a short nod that time, rolled up on her toes and touched her mouth to his before she pulled away.

She went to her purse sitting on his island, its location meaning she was all the way on the other side of it before she spoke again.

"After I ascertain all is well, I'll ask her opinion about the menu."

Noc grinned.

His little schemer.

She could connive all she wanted.

Circe wasn't going to taste anything either.

Hell, what he saw last night, he wouldn't be surprised if Dax swept his dining room table free of dishes and food, and Circe climbed up herself necessitating Franka and Noc giving them some privacy.

This meant he was doing his woman on the dining room table that night.

If anyone was going to fuck there, it was going to be him and his sweet little schemer who broke the seal.

22
HAPPY?

Franka

"Not that one, the one you had on before," Josette declared.

It was late the next afternoon and Jo and I were lounging atop Noc's bed, Valentine standing at its side behind us, as Circe stood in the doorway of Noc's bathroom having just shown us the third outfit she'd brought to wear for our dinner with Dax.

"I prefer the first, that little dress you showed us is very flattering," I stated.

"I'd prefer not to be here," Valentine murmured from behind us.

I rolled partially to my back and aimed a glower at her.

She visibly sighed and crossed her arms on her chest.

"Isn't the dress too revealing?" Circe asked, and I looked back to her.

"Precisely," I answered, and it was, though only legs, arms, shoulders, a hint of cleavage and nearly all of her back.

"It's a dinner at Noc's house, don't you think it should be more casual?" Jo asked me. "This one seems, for this world, *businessy*." She flung an arm out at Circe who was now wearing a slim skirt, a satin blouse and a rather becoming pair of what was known in this world as "pumps." "The jeans and cute little blouse say *confident* and *at home*," she went on.

"The jeans have rips in them," I pointed out.

"It's the fashion here, Frannie," Jo returned. "You've seen it, surely."

"I have and it's beyond me," I replied and carried on, "Why would anyone wear anything that was torn? It makes no sense. Furthermore, those jeans don't go all the way to her ankles and they're ill-fitting."

"They're skinny jeans and they're cropped. That's the way they're supposed to be too," Josette rejoined.

"And both, as well, are beyond me," I asserted.

"Yes, well, Circe has a fine arse and those jeans do wonders for it," Jo shot back. "Now, you also have a fine arse. So I suggest you put them on and saunter out to see how Noc reacts when he sees you in them. Then you can say it's beyond you."

She had a point. Circe's bum looked spectacular in those jeans.

And although my legs, neck, mouth and hair were my best features (this I didn't think because of conceit, but rather because Noc told me), I also had been made aware that I had a rather alluring backside (this Noc had *demonstrated* to me).

Perhaps the jeans weren't a bad idea.

"That blouse," Valentine stated. "With the jeans and those pumps. Undo at least one more button on the blouse, or if you feel you can carry it off, two. The thin gold necklace that comes to the point at your breastbone and dangles in chains that you were wearing when you arrived. The hoop earrings you wore with the first outfit. And for the love of the goddess, wear your hair down. You've an extraordinary face, neck and collarbone, but that hair should not be hidden. Not tonight."

"By Hermia, that would be perfect, casual but still dressy as well as unique," Jo breathed with keen approval.

I turned my gaze from Valentine to Circe, envisioning this ensemble in my head and thinking that Valentine was onto something.

Circe caught my eyes.

"I approve," I declared.

Josette sat up in the bed, bounced on her bum and clapped, crying, "It's unanimous!"

A sudden, alarming expression stole over Circe's face.

I tensed.

She muttered, "I may be sick," and dashed into the bathroom.

I looked only briefly to Josette then to Valentine before I pushed up from the bed and dashed after her.

I closed the door behind me as I entered to see she was standing before the toilet, deep breathing.

I did not get close but I did not stop far.

"My dear," I said softly.

She looked to me.

"I don't know..." she shook her head. "I don't know..." she repeated, drew in a breath then forged on, "It's silly, ridiculous even. I saw him. I saw his face. The look in his eyes when he gazed at me. I *saw*. And I don't understand." She threw her hands out at her sides helplessly. "Why am I so nervous?"

"Because you've been taught not to want anything at the same time being taught that every second of your life can only bring you to new levels of pain, so you've been taught not to hope," I answered. "Now, there's hope. More than hope, a promise. And it frightens you."

"Yes, that's it," she murmured, looking to the toilet.

"Step away from there," I ordered gently.

I watched her struggle to calm herself as she did as she was told and came closer to me.

I took both of her hands.

"I understand this feeling," I shared. "Perhaps not precisely as you're feeling it, but I can assure you, when the threat that was always looming from my parents was swept away, I could not find it in myself to comprehend how to live a life without that threat darkening every moment."

Her fingers squeezed mine as she whispered, "I'm sorry for that for you, but I'm also glad to hear of it for that's exactly how I feel."

"Baldur is dead," I reminded her, both necessarily and unnecessarily.

"I know this," she replied.

"You have powerful allies, not only in this world, but in our old one."

"I know this too."

"I know you do," I said. "And I know such abundance is hard to come to terms with when your life was so void of it before." I tightened my hold on her and gave her a small smile. "I also know that you *will* come to terms with it. Alas, you need to go through these feelings you're going through. But eventually it will either sink in or something extraordinary will happen to make you understand it to the depths of your soul."

She tipped her head to the side. "Was it Noc that helped you understand that?"

I nodded. "Noc, indeed, most definitely. But also others. My brother. Valentine. Frey. But Noc was the catalyst. He was dogged in making certain I saw myself for who I was, not who I was forced to be. And his efforts made me open to what the others were offering me. All of which showed me the me I was meant to be. And he was all that even before we became what we've become. He was that just simply being my friend."

"He was in love with you from the beginning, you know."

At this unexpected statement in the course of our discussion, I blinked as my body gave a start.

"He shared this with you?" I asked.

This time, she nodded, and it was then I noted that our time in that bathroom was no longer about me reassuring her. She was studying me closely, her mind intent on something that was not the arrival in two hours of Dax Lahn.

"He says when all that happened to you happened, he just happened to be the one who was there for you, and since he was in love with you, or on the path to just that, he was lucky what grew of it was what you both have now."

Although this delighted me, and troubled me, I dropped her hands and moved slightly away.

"With what you have with Noc, should you be sharing this with me?" I queried.

She shrugged one shoulder, her gaze still fixed on me. "Perhaps not, strictly speaking, as I'm his friend. But when I've not been making myself sick with nerves considering all that could go wrong tonight, I was thinking about his words, perplexed by them enough to find them disquieting. And they were disquieting enough I feel the need to share them."

I understood her disquiet.

However, I did not feel comfortable discussing them with her.

Circe did not have the same discomfort.

"I shared that I understood very much what you might be feeling in finding a man like him in your life. He not only disputed it, he refused to discuss it."

That was not troubling.

That was distressing.

"Are you aware he has these feelings?" she asked, and the tone of her voice made my attention sharpen on her.

Circe may have lived through much but she'd been sequestered, indeed actually imprisoned through most of it. She hadn't lived in my world where, to survive, one had to become adept at interpreting every look, mannerism and intonation.

Thus she didn't know she was not hiding from me that this conversation was not about Noc.

It was about understanding in her heart that I would see to Noc.

Thus, I proceeded cautiously.

"I hope you understand, with a man like Noc, not to mention your and my own relationship being new, that I'm feeling some discomfort discussing something with you I wouldn't even discuss with Josette."

Her look turned guarded when she replied, "Of course."

"He's mine," I stated.

I saw her frame tighten.

I carried on.

"I'll see to him."

And I would.

And it would seem I needed to cease dillydallying and do just that.

She continued regarding me closely before her mouth softened and her eyes warmed.

"I'm glad."

"Now," I said crisply, making it clear we were finished with that subject, "are you to change now or wait for closer to when Dax arrives?"

"Now," she answered. "If I wear this blouse, I need to redo my makeup because I've done it in bronzes and it needs to be pinks. That'll take time."

The blouse was a lovely shade of blush.

In other words, she was quite correct in that.

I began to move away, murmuring, "I'll leave you to it."

"Franka," she called when I'd nearly made the door.

I turned back to her.

"I'm happy you're happy," she said. "And I'm happy you're making *him* happy."

I dipped my chin. "Allow me to return those sentiments with you and Dax."

Her lips curved in a hopeful smile.

It wasn't radiant, but as with any time hope made an appearance, it still had a magnificent gleam.

I returned it and walked out of the room, closing the door behind me.

"Am I released from my enforced role as fashion critic?" Valentine asked the moment the door clicked.

"Indeed," I answered.

She didn't hesitate to stroll out of the room.

I watched her contemplatively as she did this, wondering if there was aught to be done about her heartbreak.

After she'd disappeared from sight, Josette began speaking.

"Back home, when one of the other maids had her heart broken, the girls would request free evenings. We'd then take her to the local pub, pour ale into her and help her find someone to bed her in order to erase some of the pain and remind her that her prospects were not limited to just the one who foolishly didn't take care of the gift he'd been given," she noted.

And in her noting this, I noted Jo was far more perceptive than I imagined (and I knew she was perceptive), for I had not breathed a word about Valentine's predicament.

"I do believe that Valentine is not just one of the girls," I replied.

"Too bad," Jo muttered, looked to her watch and shot off the bed. "Glover's to be here to pick me up in five minutes! I need to go check my hair!"

And with that, she darted out of the room.

Although happily available to give fashion advice, Josette had long since had plans with her Glover. They were going to a park and having a picnic, Josette's request for their Sunday afternoon and evening. And Glover, who did not strike me as a picnic sort of man, had acquiesced.

Noc was not a picnic sort of man either, but I knew he'd not delay even a second to give me that should it be my desire.

These were my thoughts as I walked into the kitchen to see Noc sliding the steaks we were to consume into some kind of container filled with some sauce that looked revolting but was making the kitchen smell divine.

"Shit," he said as I appeared, and I focused on him to see him focused on me. "Not good you're coming from Circe and you got that look on your face."

"Circe will be attired charmingly and is quite all right," I informed him.

His mouth quirked before he asked, "So what's with that look on your face?"

"It has occurred to me I might be forced to actually like this Glover man for Josette."

Noc burst out laughing.

I slid on one of the stools, enjoying watching him doing this at the same time deciding that it was most assuredly a day where an early glass of wine was in order.

I then watched him put a lid on the steaks, still chuckling, and continued watching as he turned to the refrigerator.

His manner was relaxed.

His expression was not content, not with that smile.

He was happy.

But as I watched, and did it closely, after having the conversation with Circe that I'd had, I noticed something for the first time. Something that my dearest love had so deeply hidden, the glimpses he'd given me of it had not penetrated my conscious. Something that made my stomach twist so violently, it was a struggle not to jump from my seat and rush to the bathroom.

Because what I saw was that it was not I who was convinced I had a midnight soul.

It was my love who was drowning in the darkness of what he thought was his.

~

I WAS IMPATIENT.

And angry.

What on earth was the man doing?

I didn't care.

I'd had enough.

"Noc, my dearest, I'm worried about the potatoes," I declared.

I sat with Circe at Noc's attractive outdoor table that was made of iron and had striped pads. A Circe who had long, slender fingers to the stem of her wine-glass, twisting it this way and that. A Circe who was sitting with me—*alone with me*—while the men stood by Noc's gleaming steel grilling apparatus on the other side of what Noc called his "deck."

Dax had been there precisely twenty minutes.

I'd counted.

And he'd said precisely twenty-nine words to Circe.

I'd counted those too.

The rest of the time, he drank from the bottle of ale Noc had given him and chatted.

With Noc.

I stood as Noc turned his gaze to me.

"The potatoes?" he asked.

"Indeed," I snapped, glaring at him, then at Dax.

I rearranged my expression to give a reassuring look to a visibly stricken (from fear at my leaving as well as taking Noc with me) and anxious Circe (making me consider magical castration or at the very least impotence if Dax didn't *pull his bloody finger out*). Then, trying not to stomp (and failing in this endeavor), I moved into the house.

I did not go to the potatoes, which I was sure were roasting splendidly in the oven where Noc had placed them.

I went to the living room, whirled, put my hands to my hips and tapped my toe, watching Noc approach me slowly.

Noc got close and asked, "You okay?"

"No, I am not," I stated the obvious.

"What's the matter?" he asked.

What was the matter?

Was he blind?

"That's the matter," I bit out, pointing a finger toward the back of his house. "Dax has barely spoken to Circe. And, I don't believe I have to impart this information on you, but I shall do it regardless, he's not here to fall in love *with you*."

Noc got closer and dipped his voice lower. "Babe, he's playing it cool."

I felt my eyebrows shoot up. "It's hardly time to do that!"

He got even closer, putting a hand to my waist, ordering sternly, "Calm down and keep your voice down."

"You're a very good cook, but I'll also share that he's not here to partake of your talents in the kitchen." My voice rose again. "Circe is freaking!"

He did one of his eyebrows-raising-slow-blinks and asked, "Freaking?"

"Yes. Freaking. She's being quiet about it, but I can feel her unease."

"Freaking," he said again, his lips twitching.

Was I seeing what I was seeing?

My brows snapped together. "Did I miss something amusing?"

His lips were still twitching when he lied, "No."

I couldn't be dealing with Noc's inappropriate humor.

I had bigger things to deal with.

"Speak with him," I demanded.

He slid his hand from my waist to the small of my back and got even closer, taking my hand in his other and lifting both to set them on his chest.

"Okay, you were there the other night and that night, Circe *really* freaked."

"Yes, indeed, I *was* there so you don't have to remind me of this occurrence," I agreed.

"You think his best play is to get here and come on strong?"

I'd not heard the terminology "come on strong."

Still, it was not lost on me.

Neither was his point.

I pressed my lips together.

"He's giving her some space," Noc told me.

"He needs to stop doing that," I told him.

"He will, when the time is right," he said.

"That time was fifteen minutes ago," I retorted.

"Just let them play it out," he advised.

"Noc, my darling, if he thinks she's going to approach, he'll be waiting until the world stops turning."

He bent his neck so his face was close to mine.

"He's not waiting for her to approach, sweetheart, he was waiting for us to check on the potatoes."

I stared at him.

"You think he's not in her space right now, or as in it is he can get without flipping her out?" Noc asked.

I leaned a bit to the side to look down Noc's long house toward the back door. I could see nothing from there. I could hear nothing.

I returned to Noc. "Let's go to the window in your bedroom and peer through to check on them."

More twitching of his lips before he denied, "We're not gonna spy on them."

It was then, something else occurred to me.

"You've put the meat on the fire. What if what they have to do takes too long and the steaks burn?"

"Babe, do you give a shit you eat a burned steak tonight?"

Of course I did. Steak was delicious, I liked my food and I particularly liked a medium rare steak.

Burned would be abysmal.

Of course, I would eat a burned steak should Dax be seeing to things.

I just wouldn't like it.

I made a decision.

"You may not wish to spy on them, but I'm going to," I declared, pulled from his hold and moved around him.

"Frannie," he called.

I kept walking, careful to keep my eyes on the back door should one of them appear in it and see me.

This didn't happen so I was able to duck into Noc's room.

I quickly made my way to the windows, and just as quickly—and expertly—situated myself in a location where I could see but it would be difficult to see me.

I lifted my hand and parted the slats on Noc's blinds.

I peered out.

Noc was correct. Dax was no longer standing by Noc's grilling apparatus. He'd gone to the table where Circe was sitting.

He'd not only gone to it, he'd pulled a chair around the table so that it was near hers, and sat in it.

And he was not only sitting in it, he was turned at the waist, his intent to share she had his entire attention, as she continued to fidget with her wine-glass shyly but seemed to be doing this while speaking to Dax.

This being a Dax who was very much all ears, appearing like every word she spoke was a Sjofn ice diamond dropping from her mouth.

My.

I felt Noc come up behind me, seeing out of the corner of my eye as he opened his own slats to peer out.

He did this grouching irritably, "I can't believe I'm doin' this shit."

I ignored that and whispered, like we were out on the deck and not separated by distance and the outer wall of a house, "He's made his approach."

"Told you," Noc did not whisper back.

"He appears enamored," I noted.

"Are you surprised?" Noc asked.

"No," I answered. "Just pleased he's no longer 'playing it cool' and is now showing his interest."

Circe stopped speaking, Dax's lips moved as he said something, and we watched as Circe's body gave a surprised start before her head bowed back in a graceful way and we heard the dulcet tones of her humor drift through the windowpane.

Excellent.

Dax grinned at her as she did this and his grin did not waver, nor did he hide the intensity of his pleasure when she ceased laughing but did so turning more fully to him, adding leaning toward him in her chair.

Dax reciprocated this gesture by leaning toward her.

At this, she seemed to brace but visibly forced herself to relax as they continued conversing.

"The steaks are totally gonna burn," Noc muttered.

"We'll leave them be and go buy more," I suggested.

Dax said something amusing again, for Circe laughed again, this time doing it reaching out a hand to touch his forearm that was resting on the arm of his chair.

He did not grin as he watched her laugh.

He looked down at her hand on him and immediately twisted his arm so he could lace his fingers in hers.

In return, Circe instantly stopped laughing.

I held my breath.

"Fuck, bold move and too soon," Noc remarked tersely.

I let my breath loose on a chant, "Don't let her go. Don't let her go. Don't let her go."

Circe stiffened, moving her torso away a bit.

Dax did not let her hand go and leaned in deeper, pursuing her, even seated.

She dipped her chin, turning her head and further hiding her face with a fall of hair.

Dax was speaking to her as she did this and continued to do so as she kept her face averted.

He did this for some time.

Noc and I remained silent and watchful for that time.

And then I drew in a sharp breath as Dax lifted his hand, touched gentle fingers to Circe's jaw, and forced her to face him.

"Fuck," Noc growled.

Dax kept speaking.

I held tense.

After moments that felt like eternities passed, she nodded, a warm, relieved look washed over Dax's face and he dropped his fingers from her jaw but continued to hold her hand and his place in her space.

"Now we really gotta check on the potatoes," Noc muttered.

I took my hand from the slats and turned to him.

He was so close I felt my arm brush his chest as I did so. Also as I did so, he took his hand from the slats and looked down at me.

I gazed up at him, all of a sudden stunned.

He was so beautiful. Sheer perfection in every way.

It wasn't the first time I'd noted that, but now that I'd sensed his pain, I couldn't help but feel the silenced throb of it beating under the surface.

This made me sway into him at the same time wrapping my arms around his waist.

Noc returned the gesture.

"A few more minutes and I'll go out and intervene. Give her some respite so she can catch her breath," I told him.

"Think that's a good plan."

I nodded and rolled up to my toes to touch my mouth to his.

When our lips parted, I didn't roll completely back.

I held his gaze and shared the love I had for him in mine.

"Thank you for your patience with this," I whispered.

"Baby, do anything for you, but helping you guide Circe to happy is not a hardship."

I pulled an arm from him, lifted my hand and cupped his cheek, running my thumb along the edge of his bottom lip.

"Yes, I know that, it's very you. But thank you all the same."

He didn't respond. He just shook his head as if to negate the compliment I'd paid, dipped it and brushed his lips against mine.

"I need to check the potatoes," he said when he'd lifted away. "And you need to give our girl a breather."

I nodded.

Noc's arms gave me a squeeze.

I squeezed him back.

He drew his arms from around me but took my hand and held it, even though we were simply walking to his kitchen.

I waited inside it, watching Noc do something peculiar, this being poking the potatoes with a fork.

I didn't ask after this partly because I didn't care, but mostly because I had other things on my mind.

These other things being that I felt I'd given it enough time.

So I went out to see to "our girl."

~

"FRANNIE, GET AWAY FROM THE WINDOW," Noc ordered.

"They can't see me," I retorted.

"Don't you think you've spied on them enough?" he asked.

I looked from the window, having been watching Dax and Circe as they stood on Noc's front porch, to Noc.

"No."

"He might kiss her," Noc said, leaning against the brick at the side the mantle of his fireplace, his expression cross, his eyes on me.

"Good," I replied, turned back to the window and peered through the blinds. "I don't want to miss that."

I was barely able to swallow my surprised cry when, seconds later, my hand was seized and I was yanked bodily from the window.

I was then twirled, pinned with legs to the arm of the couch and finding myself falling, ending with my back to the couch and Noc on me.

"Leave them alone," he demanded.

I caught my breath and decided not to be annoyed by Noc's machinations (or titillated by them) and further annoyed at perhaps missing Circe and Dax's first kiss.

Instead, I decided it'd be just the thing to dissect the entire evening.

"Once Dax broke the ice on your deck, they barely looked at either of us all evening."

Noc stopped looking severe and started grinning. "I know, gorgeous. I was there."

"And when we were in the kitchen refreshing drinks and they were hidden behind your fireplace and they'd been standing so very close and had to separate when we arrived, Dax was so infuriated we broke their moment, I thought he was going to aim a punch at you."

Noc kept grinning. "Yeah, Frannie, caught that too because *I was there.*"

"She came well into herself," I remarked. "She was most amusing. And then she'd be bashful in all the right ways. It was delightful how she often couldn't meet his gaze and that becoming blush would hit her cheeks. Dax couldn't take his eyes off her."

"You're determined to do the blow by blow," he murmured in defeat, still handsomely grinning, therefore, I knew, not minding a bit.

"Of course," I returned. "The only thing better than a successfully executed plot is commending yourself at length on your genius at successfully executing a plot."

Noc started chuckling, doing this rolling toward the back of the couch and adjusting us so we were both sitting up but with me tucked so closely to his side, I was nearly on his lap.

I gave a sidelong glance in the direction of the door and murmured, "I hope he's asking to see her again."

"He's so totally asking to see her again."

I refocused on Noc and smiled.

I then proclaimed, "This will mean we'll need to take her shopping for the perfect outfit. None of this attempting to decide something from garments you already own."

"A woman doesn't need a new outfit for every date," Noc decreed.

He was very wrong in that, but I sensed I'd never convince him of it so I didn't try.

"All I know is," Noc went on, "if Circe wants something new, she'll have to take you. I start work tomorrow so *our* trips to the mall have become *your* trips to the mall." As an afterthought, he finished, "Which means we need to find more time to get you back behind a wheel."

"I do believe it would be beneficial if Josette or I were able to traverse the city on our own, and I do think, at first, that will need to be me," I agreed.

"You down with that?" he asked.

"I quite like driving. Your interstates are somewhat alarming, but we'll work up to that."

He gave me a proud smile. "Yeah, we will."

The door opened and both of us turned to it, me having to twist exceedingly to look over my shoulder, Noc simply having to turn his head to look over my other one.

Circe was inside.

And oh.

My.

Word.

"He so totally kissed her," Noc whispered in my ear.

He so *totally* did.

She seemed barely awake. Sleep walking.

And dreaming good dreams.

"Circe, babe, you good?" Noc called quietly.

For a moment, she was lost in her own world and neither Noc nor I said anything for it was clearly a good place to be.

Suddenly, she started and looked to us.

"I'm sorry, what?" she asked.

"Did he kiss you?" I asked back.

"Frannie," Noc clipped.

"I...he was..." Circe stammered and then started beaming. "Yes."

My *word.*

"I take it he's a talent with that," I noted.

She glanced at Noc and bit her lip.

"No offense taken, Circe," Noc muttered to her unuttered words, sounding amused.

"This is, um, awkward," she glanced to me and back at Noc. "You are, of course, a very good kisser."

I took no offense either to her saying without saying that she thought Dax was a better kisser, and I felt it safe to say, should a woman have comment on this about my man, it would be me who would.

"Of course," I agreed. "And I could assure you that Dax could kiss me and I would say that same thing. But I wouldn't be looking like you after he'd done it."

"I'm glad you understand," she said, obviously relieved.

"Did he ask you out?" Noc queried.

"Tomorrow night," she told him, moving to Noc's armchair and sitting on it, but only on its edge, like she needed to be at the ready to burst from it given any good reason.

"Not letting any grass grow," Noc said under his breath.

But I found this concerning.

"This gives us very little time to go shopping for an outfit," I declared then asked, "Where's he taking you?"

"Well, he's cooking for me at his house," she answered.

I stiffened.

Noc made a noise like he was choking...

On laughter.

A kiss on another man's porch.

Dinner at his home the next night.

Circe would be bedded by this time on the morrow, I was certain of it.

Therefore, plans needed to be laid as soon as possible.

"It's imperative you take off work tomorrow, and first thing when the doors at the mall are opened, we're entering them."

Circe looked confused.

"I have a lot of clothes, Franka."

She probably did.

However, at the mall we'd be seeing to that.

But our primary mission would be undergarments.

I was thinking pink. *Pale* pink. With a good deal of delicate lace.

"Humor me," I ordered.

She studied me and moved her study to Noc.

He must have communicated something to her silently for her face relaxed, and when she looked again to me, she was smiling.

"All right, I'll take the day off."

"Excellent. And now for a *digestif*." I twisted to Noc. "You've been cooking and hosting for hours. I'll go get them," I offered.

"I don't fuckin' think so," he replied.

I stared at him, surprised not only at his words but at the ferocity with which he'd uttered them.

He rose but bent deep, putting his face in mine.

"I take care of my girl," he declared, straightened and looked to Circe with a far less fierce expression. "All of them," he finished and sauntered away.

Well, he definitely did that.

I watched him go and continued to watch him, doing this knowing I wore a supremely smug look on my face and not caring a whit.

I did this until I felt Circe's regard.

The instant I caught her gaze, I asked, "Happy?"

Something settled on her face and it took her a moment to reply. When she did, it was so quietly, I nearly didn't hear.

"So this is what it feels like."

I leaned her way, fully her way, dropping to the cushions of the couch to rest my weight in my forearms.

When I did, she shifted further to the edge of the seat and leaned toward me, perched precariously there as we assumed the pose of girlfriends in this world and any other.

"You see," I whispered, "it's so beautiful, when it's yours, it's difficult to believe it's real."

"Yes, Franka, I see," she whispered back.

"He was lovely to you when we left you to yourselves outside?" I asked.

"He was..." she shook her head, "He's so large, it seems impossible to believe, but he's so gentle, it's startling."

Oh yes.

I was very right.

Just like in the other, Dax Lahn of this world was absolutely perfect for his Circe.

"Please tell me he used his tongue with the kiss," I begged.

A flush hit her cheeks but her eyes lit. "He did." She leaned forward, nearly toppling off the edge before she gave up and I had to sit up as she situated herself close to me on the couch.

We immediately bent our heads together.

"He tastes...I don't know, does it seem odd when I say he tastes like, well, like...*man*?"

How delicious.

"It most assuredly does not," I replied.

"It's the best thing I've ever tasted," she breathed.

My eyes slid to the kitchen when I shared, "I know precisely what you mean."

She let out a giggle before she strangled it.

I took her hand, my body shaking.

I couldn't hold it back. Laughter burst forth.

And to my utter delight...

Circe's followed.

23
EXCUSES

Franka

Early the next morning, a gods-awful racket sounded, jerking me from my slumber as dread set in that that sound could only herald the end of our world.

I shot bolt upright in bed.

As abruptly as it started, the sound stopped, and I turned fearful eyes to Noc to see him stretched toward his nightstand, touching the clock there that I'd learned was illuminated by a magic known as "electricity."

"By the gods, darling, what on earth was that?" I asked.

He rolled back to me, looked at my face and grinned a heavy-eyed grin before he curled up and wrapped his arms around me, pulling me down and rolling me to my back with his weight on me.

"It's an alarm, Frannie," he answered.

"I could tell that. Why was it sounding?"

"To wake me up. I gotta get ready for work, and before I go in to do that, I gotta drop you at Valentine's."

This alarm contraption was clearly another amenity of this world and a needed one considering Noc did not have servants to wake him at the appropriate time.

Which gave rise to questions about how the servants in my past had woken at the appropriate time in order to do the same for me.

"Babe."

I moved my focus from my thoughts to him.

His lids were still heavy with sleep but the look in his eyes was not sleepy in the slightest.

"Fuckin' you first," he declared, his head descending. "Start the day right."

Oh yes. That would indeed start the day right. I knew this as a fact since Noc was a man and men on the whole tended to wish to start any day as such. It was just that Noc was the kind of man who did not wish something to happen, he *made* it happen.

He did so every morning and it absolutely started each day right.

This he set about doing right then, and I would learn that prior to his going to his place of employment he would need to see to both our pleasures in limited time.

Noc had skill with this and it wasn't the first time he'd demonstrated it to me.

However, it was the first time he'd situated my legs up his chest, my ankles to his shoulders, his hands in the bed for power and control, his eyes devouring me, his body positioned so my eyes could do the same.

This they did.

Deliciously.

"Fingers to your tit and clit, baby, wanna watch you help me take you there," he growled his order, pulling out half way and circling while I positioned my hands as I'd been told.

His gaze dropped to them and he pulled out to the tip before he surged in and stayed.

My.

So lovely.

As lovely as it was, I needed more.

From Noc, I always needed more.

"Please move, darling," I breathed.

"Pull at your nipple," he demanded.

I gave him what he wished at the same time giving myself a bolt of beauty from breast to womb. The latter convulsed and I heard his grunt as it did. I dug my ankles into his shoulders uncontrollably.

I had more difficulty focusing on him when I repeated on a gasp, "Please, darling, *move*."

He did as asked, going faster now and putting all his weight into one hand so his other could cover mine, his fingers over mine at my nipple, squeezing and pulling.

He needed do no more.

I ground into his strokes, my back arching, my lips parting, and it quickly overwhelmed me, doing what Noc always made it do, consuming me.

"Keep at your clit, keep coming, baby," Noc grunted, still driving deep and forcing my play at my nipple with his fingers.

"Noc," I pushed out, continuing to toss on the waves of the climax he was giving me.

He made my fingers twist my nipple while he pulled and kept thrusting.

"Don't stop coming," he groaned.

"I...won't," I promised, because I wasn't.

I'd climax forever for him, if he wished, and do it gladly.

"Fuck," he bit off. "*Fuck*," he rasped.

He pulled my hand from my breast, forced his torso through my legs so they slid off his chest and he landed on me, burying his shaft deep and letting me watch the glorious spectacle from up close as his head snapped back and his own pleasure consumed him.

I rounded him with my limbs, twitching gently with the aftershocks and then stroking him through his.

When they'd left him, he dropped his mouth to mine and kissed me.

After he'd lifted his head, he asked quietly, "You wanna snooze while I shower and do your thing after I drop you at Valentine's or you wanna get ready with me?"

"You'll be away from me for the first time in this world that'll last any amount of time, my dearest, heralding this being how it will continue to be. What do think I want to do?"

His face grew warm as he cupped my cheek in his palm and ran his thumb along my cheekbone.

"If that's what you want, we gotta get a move on, sweetheart."

I nodded.

Noc kissed me again.

After, we got a move on.

Early that evening, I nearly sprang from my seat in exaltation as, finally, after at least an hour of doing everything in my power to call it up, a vision formed in my crystal ball.

It was of a fine-looking, blond-haired, blue-eyed man with a tall, well-formed frame and a highly attractive manner.

Valentine's lost lover.

It was no surprise she had good taste.

It was also no surprise she was clearly blocking me.

What was a surprise was that I broke through.

And now I somewhat understood her heartbreak for he was exceptionally handsome.

However, I could read no more because the image was fading fast, my blue smoke mingling with green taking it away at the same time I felt a presence join me.

At who I knew that presence was, I turned from my crystal and watched Noc sauntering in the room.

He smiled at me, glanced at my crystal ball then returned his smile to me.

I rose from my seat and offered him my own smile.

"Hello, darling. How was your first day with your new employers?" I asked.

He arrived at me, rounding me with an arm and bending his head to touch his lips to mine, all before he replied, "Paperwork. Meetings with clients. Going over cases they're assigning me. Not exactly fun but they aren't fucking around. They want me in the field tomorrow so I'll be getting to the good stuff right away."

I had no idea what "the good stuff" was, but seeing as he'd described it thus, I lifted a hand to his biceps and murmured, "Excellent."

Noc again looked to my magical orb, his smile having dimmed, his eyes speculative when he returned his attention to me.

"You spyin' on Circe?" he queried.

I felt my frame stiffen slightly in affront as my mouth tightened. "Of course not."

"Then what are you up to with your crystal ball?"

"Although time has passed, it would seem Valentine is not healing from her heartbreak so I was looking into that situation," I shared.

Noc turned his gaze to the ceiling and declared there, "She's barely done meddling with one, she's starting in on the other."

I put my other hand to his chest and gave it a slight push, again earning his regard.

"She's suffering," I stated.

"Give it a rest," he returned.

"If I can do something—"

His arm tightened and his other hand came up to cup my jaw. "Baby, *give it a rest.* Circe is Circe. Sweet and loving and unable to hold a grudge. Valentine is an entirely different animal. I told you the play you made with Circe wasn't the right one and we both know how that went. Not gonna back down on this. Valentine will lose her mind, you insinuate yourself in her situation. She means something to you. She's a good woman, even if she doesn't like to let that show.

Don't fuck with this. Straight up, Frannie. Don't. You do, she'll carry that grudge, if she can make it happen, she'll do it magically from beyond the grave. And what I mean by that is you'll lose her."

I felt my mouth tighten again because he was probably right (probably).

Noc noted my nonverbal acceptance of his statement and changed the subject.

"You get Circe sorted at the mall?"

I nodded, moving past what we'd just discussed and I did it excitedly. "Yes, we bought her the most *divine* set of underwear. I'm quite certain Dax will be most affected when he uncovers—"

Noc took one arm from around me and held it in front of me, palm out. "Stop right there. That's woman shit. I don't need to know about Circe's underwear or what you figure Dax will do when he sees it. I'll go on to say that if she shares what he actually gets down to doin', I don't wanna know that either."

I decided to say no more.

Noc decided the opposite.

"I'm hungry and don't feel like cooking or hanging at a restaurant so you good with Chinese takeaway?"

I had no idea what Chinese takeaway was.

I still nodded.

"Josette with us?" he inquired.

I shook my head. "Glover's picking her up soon to take her to dinner." I made my thoughts clear on the subject of my next with my tone, "She's spending the night tonight at his place. As she did last night."

Noc grinned.

I did not.

Noc noticed my lack of enthusiasm for this and his grin got bigger.

However, he made no mention of it and simply said, "Then let's get home."

Home.

Yes.

I wanted to go there.

But only because that was where Noc wanted to be.

For me home was a different thing.

For me, home was simply Noc.

~

I LIKED CHINESE TAKEAWAY.

Very much.

The utensils Noc had great skill in using to eat it I did not like because they were awkward. But I was determined to master them because Noc said, "You should eat any food the way it was meant to be eaten. Chinese doesn't taste the same with a fork. Trust me, it's better with chopsticks."

It was excellent as it was.

Therefore, I was definitely going to master chopsticks.

Dinner consumed, minimal cleanup achieved (I'd even helped, but as it was simply rinsing plates to put in the dishwasher, this was not difficult), we were lazing, cuddled on Noc's couch, watching what he called a "crime drama."

I was inattentive to this drama.

Instead, I was what I'd been on and off all day.

This being completely at a loss as to how to broach the subject in a meaningful way (this being in a way I could change his thinking entirely on the subject) of the issues I knew in my soul were coloring Noc's world.

Or more to the point, the way Noc viewed himself in our world.

Issues I had no idea from where they stemmed.

When approaching this same subject with me, Noc faced it head on and made me do the same.

I did not think this same approach would be welcomed by him.

I just knew I had to find an approach.

But for the first time in my lifetime, prying into someone's affairs, their emotions, their past, was not coming easy.

Which made matters worse, since this time was the most important I'd ever faced.

"She's gonna be fine."

Noc's words pulled me from my reverie and I turned my head to look at him where he was snuggled into me, his front to my back.

"Sorry?"

His expression was gentle as was his tone.

"Circe, sweetheart. You don't have to worry. She's gonna be fine."

I knew this. She was with Dax. He'd sink a blade in his own heart before he'd do that first thing to make her *not* fine.

However, I hesitated sharing this with Noc since I didn't wish him to know what actually *was* on my mind.

"You're a million miles away, but you can come back home. She'll be good," he continued to assure me.

"Of course," I murmured noncommittally, feeling some guilt I wasn't assuaging his concerns by sharing the truth.

"You can call her in the morning," he stated.

I nodded.

I also studied his face.

He liked that I was concerned about Circe (he thought). He liked being nestled with me on the couch watching TV.

And he loved me.

He was in what I thought was a Noc Mood. A sweet one. An attentive one. A gentle one.

A mood that might be conducive to a certain kind of discussion.

I should face the issue head on. Tell him what I saw in him. *All* I saw. Then ask him to share with me the pain he was holding, pain no longer hidden.

But it would seem I had the courage to commit treason for my country. I also had the courage to face three witches who could have obliterated me with a blink. And I had the courage to leave my entire world to travel to one that was all new to me.

But I didn't have the courage to do one thing to force Noc to face whatever caused his pain by making him share that pain with me.

Blast.

"I'll call her in the morning," I told him.

"Good," he muttered.

"I love you," I blurted, and his head gave a slight, surprised jerk before his eyes warmed and he bent his face closer to mine.

"I love you too, Frannie," he whispered.

I wanted to use that opening to find the right words to erase whatever was causing him harm without making him face it. To share with him all he meant to me and make him know he could release it just like he'd given that same gift to me.

I had many talents in many areas.

This just wasn't one.

And I found it immensely frustrating.

Noc took us out of the moment by bending even deeper and kissing my nose.

He then turned back to the TV, lifting the remote to rewind the action to when he took his attention from it.

He was interested in this program.

Thus, now was not the time.

But I had to find the time.

And I had to find a way.

I just didn't know how to do either.

~

THE NEXT AFTERNOON, the phone to my ear, the fifth time I'd called, I finally connected.

"'Lo?" sounded in my ear slumberously.

"Well?" I demanded.

"Frannie?"

I was no longer annoyed yet another person was addressing me thus, this time Circe.

I had other things on my mind.

"Yes, Frannie," I confirmed, even though I knew my name came up on her phone like all the names of the callers came up on mine and I didn't need to do so. "I've been trying to reach you all day," I snapped.

"Sorry. I've been busy," she told me.

"You don't sound busy. Are you napping at work?" I asked, not entirely incredulously. Circe seemed rather industrious. However, it could be that she was exhausted for a particular reason.

"Well, I'm not at work."

I glanced at my watch, surprised, for I'd learned working hours in that world were eight in the morning until five in the evening (normally), and these were Circe's hours. And right then, it was a quarter after three.

"Is something amiss at your employment?" I asked.

"No. It's just, I didn't go into work today."

I had no reply.

Her voice dipped when she said, "Dax hasn't either."

Oh my.

"Right," I stated smartly. "Carry on," I bid and concluded with, "Goodbye."

And I hung up.

Then I started chuckling.

Still doing it, I reengaged my phone and called Noc.

"In other words, like I said," he began after I relayed this information to him, "she's not only fine, she's *more than* fine."

I could not argue that, didn't even want to, so I said nothing.

"We done gossiping about Circe?" he queried with humor in his voice.

"For now," I replied.

"Right," he said. "Later, babe. Love you."

"And I you."

We hung up.

I was, indeed, done gossiping about Circe.

To Noc.

But I moved from where I was to Valentine's kitchen to find Josette, who was practicing her this-world culinary skills.

Because I was not actually done gossiping about Circe.

News this good was news too good not to share.

Two days later, in the afternoon, I moved through a room in the home the agent was showing us, feeling it.

Feeling everything.

She'd found it.

It was perfect.

I had my phone to my ear and it was ringing.

"Sweetheart," Noc answered.

"I think we've found it," I whispered, having removed myself from Josette, the agent and Valentine, who had driven us to the showing.

"It's good?" he asked.

"It's perfect, darling. The courtyard. The ceiling roses. A magic room for me. And many bedrooms."

He was silent a second before he asked, "How you feelin' like fillin' those up?"

My voice dropped lower. "You know how."

"Tell the agent I wanna see it. I got shit on with the job on Saturday so it'll have to be Sunday."

"I'll do that."

"Josette like it?" he queried.

"Yes," I told him.

"Valentine with you?"

"Yes."

"What's she say?"

"She said, 'it'll do.'"

There was amusement in his voice when he replied, "So she likes it."

"That's my read."

"Right. Good. I'll look at it Sunday and we'll discuss your offer."

"Excellent, darling. Now I'll let you get back to work."

"Okay, sweetheart. Valentine dropping you at my place?"

"No, her caretaker is giving Josette and me driving lessons after this. Then he's dropping me at your place. Josette is making dinner for Glover at Valentine's. Trying her hand at her skills in the kitchen. Valentine is absenting herself. She hasn't shared where she's going."

"Not a surprise," he muttered. "I'll see you when I get home then, yeah?"

"Yes, Noc."

"Later, babe. Love you."

"And I you, my darling."

He rang off.

I took the phone from my ear and turned my attention again to the room in which I stood.

Yes.

Perfection.

The room was. The house was.

I was not.

Noc had started his cases and this meant he woke us earlier. It also meant he came home later. And he even took phone calls and worked on his laptop after getting home.

He made it clear he did not mind this. He was enjoying his work, he made that clear too. It was not exhausting, it was invigorating.

I liked that for him. I drank my wine and watched the television or read a book I'd found at his house that was quite interesting and let him do what he enjoyed. And when it was time for me, I let him enjoy me.

Therefore, obviously, with his new job and the satisfaction he got from it, now was not the time to bring up whatever was festering inside him, shadowing his soul.

It was an excellent excuse.

But it was still an excuse.

I knew it.

I just didn't know how to get past it.

~

THAT SUNDAY, Noc stood in a bedroom upstairs in the home I was considering purchasing.

The room in which I'd made my decision just days before and given him a call.

It was right now where a little girl slept. Pink walls. An elephant motif. Not frilly but still girly. Absolutely adorable.

It was the last room I allowed him to enter.

The courtyard was lovely, elegant, private and serene, mature plants, with a handsome, built-in grilling apparatus I knew Noc would love (and he did).

My magic room would be a sunroom, bright and cheery, seeming outside when it was in.

The master suite, as it was known here, was luxurious with a separate shower and bath, both utterly divine.

And the kitchen was large and stylish, but welcoming, making Noc's assertion that it was the heart of the house very true.

I liked all those things.

But I'd decided this house was the one based on this room.

He was staring at a stuffed elephant on the bed.

"Darling?" I called.

His eyes came directly to me.

"I love it," he stated. "We're offering."

We were offering.

He liked his house. I did too.

But this tall, stately, elegant, spacious place was going to be our home.

I felt my throat close.

Amara would sleep there.

Right there.

I knew it just looking at him.

I felt my face get soft and I smiled.

Noc's face didn't get soft. The look on his was fierce.

Even so.

He smiled back.

~

"FRANNIE."

"Yes, darling."

"Sugarlips, I'm home."

"Yes, darling."

Silence.

Then a shaking, "Babe."

"Yes, darling?"

I did not see the hand that came to the apparatus I held in my own.

What I saw on the television screen was the action pausing.

My eyebrows shot together, I twisted my neck to the side, bent it back and glared at Noc, who was smiling down at me hugely.

"I was making record time!" I snapped.

"Babe," he replied.

"Do you know how many efforts it took to *get* to that time?" I demanded to know.

"Babe," he repeated.

"You paused me!" I continued to snap.

"Babe," he said again, this sounding clogged, likely due to his visible hilarity.

"I'll never get that run back!" I groused and did it loudly.

"Love you. Think it's cute as all fuck you're Franka Drakkar and Franka Drakkar is a woman who'd be so into a fuckin' video game she wouldn't even look at her man when he came home from work. But just sayin', I just got home from work and I want my woman not only to look at me but greet me with a smile and give me a kiss, my preference, with tongues, even if it messes with her record time while it looks like she's racing a fake race car in a make-believe video version of Monaco."

I felt instantly contrite, set the apparatus aside and pushed myself up from his couch.

I then fitted myself in his arms, wrapping my own around him, lifted up on my bare toes and gave him a kiss.

With tongues.

When I rocked back, both of us held on.

"Welcome home, my darling," I said softly. "How was your day?"

"Best part of it happened just now," he replied in my same tone. "Though, that isn't strictly true since what you gave me this morning edges it out."

I didn't give him anything.

In bed and with everything else, it was always Noc doing the giving.

I melted into him.

"See you introduced yourself to the PlayStation," he noted.

"I didn't. Josette did before she left in a taxi to meet some friend of Glover's. They're at an establishment that has wine and paint. I don't understand what that means, but she reports she's going to be drinking and painting on a canvas, even though she's never painted a thing in her life."

"That's strange," he noted.

"I agree," I replied. "But she seemed excited about it."

His arms gave me a squeeze. "Maybe you should have gone with her."

Was he mad?

"And missed time with you?"

That didn't get me an arm squeeze.

That earned me another kiss, this also with tongues, and it lasted longer.

When he lifted his head, he stated, "Dinnertime. Past dinnertime, actually. So you got a choice. I can throw some burgers on the grill or we can order pizza."

I liked burgers.

But pizza beat out everything.

Except, perhaps, lobster, but Noc didn't offer that.

And regardless, as I glanced to his entertainment station, I saw it was well after seven in the evening.

He didn't seem fatigued, but he'd left for work before seven that morning, thus I didn't want him cooking.

What I did want was whatever he wanted.

"You chose, darling," I said.

"Feelin' like a burger."

"How can I help?" I asked.

He grinned at me stating clearly that any help I may be able to give wouldn't be much help at all, but he then let me go, took my hand and guided us to the kitchen.

"When it's time, you can get out the chips and condiments. I'll do the rest."

These were things I could do.

I could also get him a beer, which I did. And I could open my own bottle of wine, I was relatively certain (I had watched him and a number of servants open a vast quantity of them), which I started to try to do but was halted.

"Babe, no," Noc muttered gently, ceasing his endeavors of opening up a package of meat to take the wine bottle and opener from me.

"I can pour myself wine, Noc," I told him.

"You snap open a beer for me, that's sweet, babe. But I get you your wine. Deal?"

I supposed.

Thus I also nodded.

He got me my wine, leaving me nothing to do but sit at the counter and watch him form hamburgers with his hands.

I found this fascinating, but mostly because Noc had beautiful hands and I'd watch them do anything, including manipulating meat.

As had become the norm, he didn't tell me much about his day because he wasn't at liberty to share too much about his cases.

We nevertheless found many things to chat about, as we usually did. How the purchase was going with my house. How Valentine seemed to be coming back to herself, still melancholy, but she'd begun discussing the things I would be doing with her and taking an interest in showing Josette and I our new world. How I'd be going to what was referred to as a "gynecologist" the next day to see about "birth control." And how Circe and Dax had not spent one evening apart since our dinner that was now a week and a half ago.

He went out to fire up the grill and I remained seated, ignoring the fact that it had now been a week and a half since that evening Circe and Dax had come for dinner, and in that week and a half I had found excuse after excuse to set aside the fact that I had *not* found the right time or the right way to approach Noc about my concerns.

He made this easy due to the fact he seemed most content with absolutely everything. My being a part of his life, in his home and bed. Spending time with Jo. Being involved in his new cases.

You had to look to know he carried pain.

But I'd looked.

So I knew.

I just wasn't doing a thing about it.

What I was doing was becoming quite adept at ignoring it or making excuses that it wasn't the right time to do anything about it.

On that thought, his phone that he left on the island rang just as he was walking back in from outside.

I looked to it, saw on the screen the word DAD, then I looked to Noc, stiffening.

"Your father," I told him.

Noc, who was always so very *Noc,* appeared delighted his father was calling, didn't hide this and went right to the phone.

I was not delighted.

I was pleased he clearly enjoyed hearing from his father.

But it was a father I would one day meet, of this I was certain. And when I did, I would need to impress him and even make him care for me, and this I was not certain I could achieve.

"Hey, Dad," Noc answered, moving to the refrigerator.

I slid off my stool and began to gather the detritus of meat wrappings to throw them away.

"Yeah, it's good. Like it. Caseload is way lighter than on the force, means more focus. Respect the men I work for. Team's tight too," he stated, coming out of the fridge with a tomato.

I pressed my lips together at the sight of the tomato and went to the cupboard for chips.

"She's good," he said softly. "Lookin' forward to you meetin' her."

I felt my shoulders tighten as I selected my favorite variety of chips (one I noted was Noc's too), barbeque.

"What?" he asked, his voice changing.

That was to say, changing significantly.

I turned to him, chips in hand.

He had his phone to his ear, but his eyes were riveted to the tomato he'd placed on the island and he was now unmoving.

"No, I didn't forget," he stated, and his tenor was deteriorating.

I stood still and kept my attention on him.

"Yeah, I will," he declared, and I read his next as interrupting his father when he carried on swiftly and curtly, "Told you I will. So I will." There was only but a brief pause before, "We'll see about it next year." Another brief pause and then, his voice lower, somewhat conciliatory, but still tight, he said, "I know it means something to you, so like I said, we'll see about it next year." There was a small measure of silence before he went on, "Yeah, it's about Frannie bein' here and me startin' the job, and like I said, I'm sorry I couldn't make it this year, but it's the way it is."

Slowly, I made my way to the island and stopped, standing opposite him, finding it troubling that Noc, always attuned to me, *always*, didn't lift his head to watch me do this or even when he sensed me arrive.

"I know it's the first time I missed it, Dad, but I got a lot goin' on," he continued. "Next year, we'll see about it. But you know I got things in my life now where it isn't just all about me. I'm not there for one, so it isn't as easy for me to be there seein' as I'm all the way across the country. And if I got time off, I gotta share it the way *we* wanna share it, Franka and me, not just me makin' the decisions."

I was reeling from learning the information through his conversation that it was clear Noc had already told his father about me, but I had little time to recover.

What he'd just said quite obviously did not go over very well with his father, and I knew this when Noc's back shot straight, forcing his eyes to aim away from the island.

But they stared unseeing beyond me.

"I know what it means to you. Of course I fuckin' know," he growled infuriatedly, and shockingly disrespectfully.

I stood still, silent, stunned that Noc could sound like that at all much less aiming it at his father.

"Yeah, it's a tough time for us all, Dad, and I get that. I get it for you, probably now more than ever, havin' Frannie. I get that for Dash and for Orly. What I keep tryin' to get *you* to get is that the way you deal with it might not be the way we all wanna do that." There was another moment of silence before he declared, "Dash is like you. But Orly is like me. And not to dig the knife in deeper, but to make my point, he's also like Judy." A very brief pause before, "You get my point, you totally get it. Don't make me say it."

And then there was a very long pause as I watched, fascinated and horrified, as emotion twisted Noc's beautiful features. Ugly emotion. Pain so deep, witnessing it wounded *me*. My heart squeezed, my stomach lurched, and it took everything for me not to round the island and envelope him in my arms in the effort to absorb his pain, take it deep inside me so it was something he'd never again feel.

But he wouldn't want that. Not in that moment. Everything about him screamed it.

So it cost me, but I stayed put.

"Okay, I'll say it. She'd hate this shit and you know it. Every fuckin' year, Dad, we do it for you and because Dash gets somethin' out of it. But it's mostly for you. I want you to have what you need. But you know Judy would fuckin' hate it. Thought it every fuckin' year, kept it to myself. Talked to Orly about it. He kept it to himself. You pushed it. Now you're hearing it. Judy'd think that shit was fucked up. And my guess, deep down you know it."

I realized I was holding my breath, drew in a deep one, and held that.

"Think that's a good idea. We'll leave it at that and talk more later. But like I said, I promised I'd do it here. And I'll do it here." A very short pause before, "Right. Love you," he pushed out tersely. "'Bye."

With that, he hit the screen of his phone with his thumb and tossed it with a rather volatile clatter on the island.

Then he scowled at it.

"Darling?" I whispered.

He turned his scowl to me.

I swallowed at the range and depth of emotions in it—anger, frustration and hurt.

"Is everything all right?" I queried carefully.

"You been standin' right there, gorgeous, and you don't know the answer to that?" he asked, his tone edged sharply with sarcasm.

What did I do now?

I'd never had this Noc.

I didn't even know there could *be* this Noc.

I decided to start with something benign.

"You've told your father about me?" I asked.

"Love my dad. He's not a colossal dick like yours, so I fall in love with a woman, she's all but livin' with me and I see my future with her in it, he's the first one I tell."

This delighted me in all ways except the tone with which he shared it.

"You hadn't shared that with me," I told him quietly.

"Well, sorry, babe. Now you know," he replied shortly, grasped the plate with the burgers and stormed out of the kitchen to the deck.

I drew in breath and followed.

Before I even got close to him, he warned, "Not in the mood to talk about it, Frannie."

I stopped and stared at his back, noting his movements of putting the burgers on the flame were stilted, but noting this only vaguely.

My mind raced for something to say.

It seemed to take eons, but I finally caught on it.

"I'm here for you when you are, my love."

"Right," he bit off.

"Like you always are for me."

"Yeah," he stated dismissively.

He wanted no more words said.

Yet I sensed I should not leave it at that.

I hesitated a moment before I admitted, "You're clearly feeling something upsetting and I want to help, but I don't know how."

He turned, dropping the lid on his grill, and growled, "You can help by opening up the chips. I'm fuckin' hungry."

He then prowled right by me and into the house.

I kept my eyes to the grill, deciding the next day I was going to start practicing slicing tomatoes at Valentine's.

I could open a packet of chips.

But it was becoming clear that after experiencing the exquisite glow of realizing you'd found the man you'd love for eternity and he'd found you right back, life intruded.

I needed to be brave and face that life head on. I needed to be able to cope with whatever came at me. But more, at Noc.

I needed to learn to do what he did.

Support. Nurture. Care. Understanding.

And I had no skills in those areas.

I couldn't even slice his tomato.

But I could learn to slice a bloody tomato.

And I had to learn it all.

Noc pulled me down on his cock, I gasped at the silken violence of it and watched as he came.

We were both seated, me in Noc's lap, my legs wrapped around his hips, his legs stretched beyond me.

He'd already given mine to me. So in his moment, I simply held him in my arms, and when his head fell forward, his forehead resting on my shoulder, I buried my face in his neck.

"I love you," I whispered there, and for once, words of such grave import felt like they meant very little at all, for I knew I should be giving him so much more.

He turned his lips to my skin and kissed me before he whispered back, "Love you too, Frannie."

His words did not feel the same as mine.

They felt like they gave me everything.

With nothing further, he pulled me off him, set me gently in the bed and exited it, not going to the bathroom before he twitched the covers over me.

Nurture.

Care.

He was back in no time, pulling me into his embrace, burrowing into me, holding me tucked close, my back curved into his front.

He said nothing, and after a short period of time, I sensed him drift to sleep.

I did not.

He'd held his mood throughout the evening, therefore I was surprised with his continued distance when he'd instigated lovemaking.

I was surprised, but I did not demur.

It was what he needed, what I always wanted, and last, it was the only thing I knew how to give.

He deserved more.

I did not know how to give it to him.

But as I lay in his embrace, feeling his strength and heat swathing me, protective and fortifying even in his sleep, I knew the time I allowed excuses to delay me were over.

There would be no more excuses.

I needed to give my Noctorno more.

24

AND I YOU

Franka

"Franka."

The sharp tone pulled me from my musings and I focused on Valentine where she sat opposite me in her magic room in her home. She was staring at me irritably.

"Did you hear a word I said?" she queried with the same irritability.

Unfortunately, I had not.

"I beg your pardon. I have a number of things on my mind," I shared.

"This has not escaped me," she retorted. "However, I take the needs of my clientele very seriously, and as I'm offering you your first assignment, regardless that it's as simplistic as casting a love spell, it's important for you to be very clear on the client's needs."

"Of course," I murmured.

"To make a point that needs not be made, it wouldn't do for you to erroneously cast a spell on the employer our client hates, even if he's rather handsome and exceptionally wealthy, when it's the maintenance man she's secretly in love with," she continued.

"Yes, obviously," I replied.

She gazed at me. "Not that I wish to become involved, but is everything well with you and Noctorno?"

It was not.

Oh no.

Definitely not.

One could say, tragically accurately, I had not been dealing with things well.

But last night I made things worse.

Starting the morning some days ago after his father's phone call, Noc had decided that he was going to ignore what occurred. He'd swept away the distant mood he'd treated me to the evening before and again became Noc.

This was, until he came home that evening and I attempted to broach the subject.

"Told you last night, not in the mood to talk about it," he'd replied brusquely.

"Will there be a time you'll be in the mood?" I'd inquired hesitantly.

"I am, I'll let you know," he'd stated conclusively.

And the subject, according to Noc, was done.

I will admit, my approach was weak and I'd allowed him to dismiss the discussion mostly because he again became aloof and I didn't like it. Indeed, it frightened me enough I knew it would take some time for me to gather the courage to try again.

Therefore I gave it that time (again weak, gads!)

That time included the weekend.

A weekend where Noc worked on the Saturday, but it was the first he'd done so in a way I felt he was doing it to avoid me.

But after a morning driving lesson on Sunday (where he allowed Josette to go on actual streets and where I had the hair-raising—but eventually I'd settled into it—experience of driving on a freeway), he'd relaxed. This meant I felt my Noc with me again as we spent the afternoon and evening drinking and munching on a variety of food in a bar with Glover while watching some sport on television.

I told myself as the days passed that I was allowing Noc time to cope in his head with whatever had gone on with his father, so when I approached him again he'd be more conducive to such.

But mostly I was bolstering my courage.

This I'd decided was bolstered enough last night, a now-unusual evening when Noc came home from work before six.

It started out well, considering I'd perused his cupboards and had managed to arrange (quite artfully, to my way of thinking) some crackers and slices of cheese on a plate for him to nibble on with the beer I'd opened for him when he got home.

I did this, for nearly every evening he arrived home and declared he was hungry. Although I couldn't cook a splendid meal for him, I could do something to assuage his hunger.

Noc had put a slice of cheese on a cracker, doing this with his arm around my shoulders, holding me tucked to his side, and declaring through a smile, "Next thing I know, I'm gonna be coming home to beef Wellington."

I couldn't stop the face I made, one likely of revulsion mixed with terror, which made Noc emit a deep bark of laughter before he kissed me quickly and pulled away, putting the cracker and cheese into his mouth.

As he munched, I decided to broach the subject later, when he had a full stomach and thus would be in good humor for a variety of reasons.

He was indeed in good humor.

I made note of that and decided henceforth to be certain there were a variety of nibbles in the house I could arrange artfully on a plate for him to be treated to when he came home.

Alas, his good humor vanished the moment I mentioned his father's call.

"You need to let up on that, babe," he'd stated tersely, drawing away from me where we were snuggled on the couch, Noc sitting with feet up on the coffee table, me nestled into his side with my legs curled beside me on the seat.

His terse tone brooked no further discourse.

Even so, I knew I could not be weak. I could not give up. Not on Noc.

No more excuses.

"There are things, darling, that I think we should discuss and they aren't entirely what occurred during that call with your father. However, I sense that there was something there—"

"Franka," he started, taking his feet from the table, and the frigid way he said my name not only made me snap my mouth shut, it made my insides freeze. "You've made an art of sticking your nose in shit and I see you've decided to stick it in this. What I've been sayin' that you've not been hearing is that this is not somewhere you can go."

I didn't wish to persevere.

But I had to.

"I thought you said what was yours was mine."

"And what I'm sayin' now is that *I* don't even want this, so I'm sure as fuck not givin' it to you."

That didn't make sense.

"Noc—"

"Let it go, Frannie."

"But—"

His face transformed to granite, and having that hard look aimed at me, my throat closed.

"I'm warning you. Let...it...*go.*"

And with that, he left me on his couch and prowled to the bedroom, his closing of the door behind him telling me I was not invited to follow.

I did not follow.

I sat still on the couch, staring at the door, hearing his words.

I'm warning you.

Warning me of what?

Let it go.

The coward in me wanted to do that.

But I knew I shouldn't.

Some time later, when I'd gathered the courage to join him in the bedroom, I found it dark, and as far as I could tell, Noc was asleep.

I joined him in bed and didn't wake him.

But I did curl into his back which was turned to my side of the bed.

He did not shift to further accommodate my cuddle.

It was the first night we did not end the day making love.

And it was the first night I did not sleep within Noc's embrace.

Thus, it was not a surprise I was awake hours later when he woke, doing so without the aid of his alarm.

He did not turn into me.

He got out of bed, doing it cautiously as I feigned sleep, and he went to the bathroom, prepared for work, and left the bedroom—and the house—leaving me abed undisturbed.

And thus, we had the first morning when we started a day without making love.

However, after I'd dragged myself from his bed, I'd found a note propped on the coffeemaker that read:

Sugarlips,

Coffee's good to go. All you have to do is flip the switch.

Just call Valentine to come get you when you're ready.

See you tonight.

Love you, babe.

-Noc-

Although the note started and ended in ways that were heartening, he'd made his point very clear.

His warning was understood.

It was now my decision to heed it or proceed as planned, even if, in truth, I had no plan.

"Franka!" Valentine snapped, and again brought me back to reality.

"My apologies, I not only have much on my mind, I slept little last night." I attempted to excuse my rudeness.

"Are you prepared to take on this assignment?" she asked.

"Will I have your oversight?" I asked in return.

"Of course," she answered.

"Then yes, I'm ready," I told her.

She studied me another moment before stating, "You didn't answer my question about Noc."

"All is well," I lied.

She knew I lied, I could see it in the shrewd look in her eyes, but I held her gaze, my chin lifted, my meaning clear.

She had her business that wasn't mine, even if I wanted to be there for her to assist in any way I could.

I had mine.

She gave in. "We'll work the spell tomorrow."

I inclined my head.

She tipped hers to the door. "I suggest you watch this maintenance man and ascertain the best way we can make an approach without detection. We need to be close to cast a love spell and he should be alone. He doesn't simply get stars in his eyes, seek out our client and sweep her off her feet. My work is much more subtle than that. Therefore, yours will be too."

I nodded and stood.

Having been dismissed, and glad for it, I made my way from her magic room to head to the room below where my crystal ball was waiting for me.

I'd nearly made the door when she called, "Franka."

I turned to her.

Her gaze locked to mine.

"All will be well," she said quietly.

I hoped she was correct, but the first time since Noc entered the sitting room I was in at the Winter Palace months ago, I felt my hopes would be dashed.

I said not a word and swept from the room.

I went to my crystal ball, but when I got there, I did not call up this "maintenance man" (whatever that was).

I stared at it thinking other thoughts.

Dismal thoughts.

Fearful thoughts.

Insecure thoughts.

Doing all this finding myself entirely unable to stop it or the growing emotion that rose up inside me, making me feel useless and unworthy of the man who loved me enough to steer me beyond a lifetime of pain when I could not offer the same.

Therefore, when ten digits appeared in my crystal ball, I was startled.

I knew not what they meant or even how they appeared.

I had not called for them (whatever they were).

However, they didn't go away.

I continued to stare, and as I did the handbag I'd placed on the table by my orb jumped in its place.

This meant I jumped in my seat and stared at that.

My handbag skipped again and I heard a distinct buzz that I knew came from my phone.

I released a relieved breath as I understood what was happening and reached for it, for I was simply getting a text.

I pulled the phone out of my bag and activated it.

However, there were no notifications of a text.

My eyes slid to my crystal ball and a frisson of awareness slinked up my spine.

My ball was telling me something.

My *magic* was telling me something.

And what I knew was my magic was *my* magic.

Good magic.

So wherever that magic led me to, in my bones, I felt it safe to follow.

I touched the phone button, went to my keypad and entered the digits from my crystal ball.

Sitting straight in my chair, I lifted the phone to my ear and listened to it ring.

Shortly into this, a man's voice boomed, "You got Lud."

Lud?

Who was Lud?

"Yo? Hello?" the voice called.

Lud.

Oh no.

Lud!

As in...*Ludlum*.

The digits were for Noc's father's phone.

Balls!

"One more time, someone there?" he asked.

"Hello, Mr. Hawthorne?" I said it as a question even if I knew the answer.

"Right, darlin', no offense, your job ain't fun, but I'm not a big fan of marketing calls so do me a favor and take me off your call list."

"Mr. Hawthorne," I stated but couldn't, for the life of me, decide what to say next.

"Will you do that for me?" he asked.

"This is Franka," I declared.

He said nothing and I thought he'd disengaged.

"Mr. Hawthorne?"

"Franka?"

I nodded swiftly even if he couldn't see me. "Yes, Franka. Franka Drakkar. Er, Frannie. I'm Noc's...I'm, erm, Noc's...well, I'm just Noc's," I introduced stupidly.

Gods!

"Interesting way to put it," he muttered, sounding amused, and then suddenly he did not sound anything of the sort when he asked, "Is my boy okay?"

"Yes, yes, he's fine. Absolutely. I mean, yes. He is. In most senses. Very fine. I mean to say that.... Actually, what I mean is, he's quite well. But he's also..."

Drat!

Why didn't I disconnect the moment I knew who it was?

There was nothing for it, I hadn't, so I had to go on.

"He's also, well...*not*."

"Damn," he muttered, seemingly knowing precisely what I was saying. "Uh, sorry, honey. I mean, darn."

"Cursing does not offend me," I shared.

He was back to muttering. "Knowin' my boy, that's probably good."

He was right about that.

Abruptly, I got cold feet (not that they'd ever been warm).

Damn my crystal ball.

"I need to apologize. I'm rethinking the wisdom of calling you," I told him even though I hadn't actually called him knowing I was doing any such thing.

"No, I'm thinkin' it's probably very wise you called me."

I didn't know what to say so I didn't say anything.

"Let me guess, he's not in a very good mood these days," he said.

"Well, I think that I'm...what I mean to say is, your guess would be correct, but I do believe it's me who's putting him in that mood."

"Frannie, honey, it is one hundred percent not you."

Again, I had no idea what to say so I remained silent.

"He gets this way on the anniversary," Mr. Hawthorne relayed.

The anniversary?

"The anniversary of what?" I queried.

"Judy passing."

Even sitting, I had to brace my hand to the tabletop to steady myself.

Judy. His stepmother. The only mother he'd known.

The mother he'd been forced to watch die.

"We had a thing," he went on. "The boys were young when it happened and it was me who made the decision, and Noc didn't agree with it so we had a go 'round about it. He shared how he felt and he was clear on that, even then. This being she didn't wanna be buried, but I wanted somewhere to go where I could be with her. Where the boys could be with her. So I buried her. And every year, day she died, I get my boys together and we go there to be with her. Take some lawn chairs and lay 'em out. Bring her flowers. Sit with her. Throw back some bourbon. Talk about her. Have her with us for a while."

I thought this lovely and horrible, in equal measures.

Noc's father kept speaking.

"Noc wasn't a big fan I went against Judy's wishes and didn't cremate her. And he's also not a big fan of going to see her. Know it. Maybe should let it go. But it's the only time I got with my family back together, all of us, and it may be me bein' selfish, but I don't care how old he is. I'm still his dad. And she's the only mom he had. So I feel he should give me that. Me and Judy. He should give us both that."

It took a moment for me to do it and my voice was not my own when I replied, "I cannot say you're wrong about that, Mr. Hawthorne."

"Lud, Frannie. Please call me Lud."

"Lud," I whispered.

"Knew he wasn't gonna be able to come this year, made him promise to do somethin' to remember her there. Reckon she's with all of us all the time, the only way she can be. So told him I want him to find a pretty, peaceful spot, just be quiet and let her be with him. He said he'd do it. Maybe he's just humoring his old man, but gotta say, as much as I know he doesn't like it, still hope he does it. And because I'm stubborn and love my boy and my wife, the first one I still got, thank the Lord, the last one we lost and it broke us in a way it took a lot of fixin' and we still ain't right, I want him here next year. Want him to bring you. Want Judy to meet you."

Want Judy to meet you.

I'd never felt more honored.

"I think...I think, sir, she already knows me quite well," I shared carefully.

And hopefully.

Further hoping she liked what she knew.

"I think you are not wrong. Looked after Noc while she was breathin' in a way there's no way she'd quit even after she'd stopped. He found you, she'd definitely start lookin' after you."

I said nothing, lost in the glory of knowing after his mother died giving Noc to this world, to me, he had another who looked after him at the same time feeling the loss he'd endured when she went away.

"You there, Frannie?"

"I just...need a moment," I murmured stiltedly.

He gave me that moment, but in his, he said softly, "Damned you do."

"Sorry?"

I heard him clear his throat before he replied, "You do. Heard it in Noc when he talked about you. Now I hear it in you. What I hear pleases me, Frannie, reckon you know that, just reckon you don't know how much. And it makes me look forward even more to meeting you."

I knew what he was saying and I was beside myself with happiness he understood my feelings for his son.

But even if I had more information about what was happening, I didn't comprehend the fullness of it.

Before I could broach that, Ludlum Hawthorne declared, "Obvious this is worryin' you and thank you for givin' that to my boy. And thank you again for doin' the right thing and callin' his old man to have a chat about it. But I got it from here."

Oh no.

I knew what "I got it" meant and I didn't have a good feeling about Noc's father having anything if it had a thing to do with all this.

"Um...Lud—"

"We'll hash it out and get ourselves sorted. Don't you worry," he assured without assuring me in the slightest. "No doubt you know we got a lotta love in our family, but that doesn't mean, four men, all of us pigheaded, we don't clash. We do. First time you see it, I can understand it'll worry you. But you'll also see we get over it. We learned over and over again, doin' that the hard way, to hang on to what we got. And just so you know, anniversary passes, he comes back to himself. My advice next time, just wait it out. He'll be good as new in no time."

"Can I just say, Lud, that—"

He cut me off like he didn't hear me speak.

"Now I gotta go. Bad timing, Sue's dragging me out to lunch with her bridge cronies. Twice a year I gotta go to this lunch, and if they didn't raise buckets of money for cancer research, I'd be on my boat with a rod in my hand. But I'll say, regardless of the subject matter, sure was good to talk to you. Next time we do it, I'll make you giggle. I'm a comedian. A good one. And don't listen to Noc or Dash or Orly when they say my material stinks. They don't know what they're talking about. I'm damned funny."

"I'm sure you are," I replied swiftly but didn't get the rest out swiftly enough as he spoke again.

"Now you take care of yourself, honey, and would say take care of my boy but seems to me you got that down."

He was so very wrong.

He was also so very much not done.

"And maybe Sue and me'll get on a plane so I can give you a hug in person and she can size you up for whatever outfits she's gonna buy you come Christmas. If they're not your thing, just give 'em to charity but don't say anything to her. Only way I'll say it's fortunate you live across the country, you won't have to dress up in the stuff she buys and she won't see you not doin' it. She gave the boys all Christmas sweaters three years ago and pouts that they refuse to wear 'em. Won't listen to a word I say on the subject that those sweaters are butt-ugly and laughable besides. Noc's has got a reindeer stitched on it with a bell for a nose, for chrissakes. I mean, who in their right mind thinks a man is gonna wear a Christmas sweater with a reindeer on it with a bell for a nose? Love her to bits, she's a damn fine woman, but that don't mean she don't got some crazy ideas."

I had no earthly idea what he was talking about.

I also had no intention of asking. My anxiety was building and I needed to stop him from "hashing" anything out with Noc, and I needed to do that *now*.

To my grave misfortune, I didn't get the chance to get into it, for I heard him shout, not at me, "I'm ready, sweetheart, just on the phone with Noc's Frannie!"

Gods.

"Yeah, Frannie!" he kept shouting. "Noc's girl!"

Gods!

"No," he said, again not to me, "I'm sayin' goodbye. You get on the phone with her, you'll talk for a year."

"I will not," I heard a woman say. Then I heard, this time to me, "Well, hello! Nice to meet you."

Oh...

Balls.

"I, um...well, right...hello to you too, Sue," I pushed out.

"What a wonderful surprise, you calling," she declared.

"Yes, well, erm..."

"I cannot *tell you* how *delighted* I was to hear Noc had finally found someone. But really mostly when we heard how very taken he is with you. Lud told me the way Noc speaks about you, we should be careful and not flip out when we watch you walk on water."

This surprised me (as well as parts of it thrilling me) because I couldn't imagine in this world where magic was hidden that Noc would share I had it for I doubted it would be difficult to do just that.

Though why I'd ever wish to walk on water, I couldn't fathom.

"That's lovely, but could I speak with—?" I attempted to ask.

"We can't *wait* to meet you."

"And I you," I hurried out but had no opportunity to say more.

"Wonderful," she declared. "Now, I must let you go because Lud is giving me the evil eye seeing as he doesn't want to go to this lunch and I'm making him, so I best not chat with you for a year and prolong his torture. We'll talk more later. Lud's got your number in his phone now, I'll call you."

By the gods.

What had I done?

"I'll look forward to that," I (somewhat) lied.

"Lovely. And I can't let you go without telling you that you have *such* a beautiful voice. I can't wait to see pictures. Noc told his father you're effin' gorgeous, though he used the actual F-word, to my everlasting distress. If you're as pretty as your voice, you must be something. Tell Noc to send some photos, quick as he can."

I heard her pull in a deep breath, but she did even that fast and I got out nary a sound before she carried on.

"Okay, must run. Again, so nice to meet you. Take care, Frannie."

"You do the same," I forced out, sounding strangled.

"Give that to me. No, give it to me. I wanna say 'bye too," I heard in the background. Then in my ear came from Lud, "Take care of yourself, Frannie. And don't worry about a thing, I got this. 'Bye, honey."

When Noc said he "had" things, I'd learned he spoke truth.

I didn't mean to cast aspersions on his father, but I had grave fears in this instance it was not the same.

Helpless to do anything but, I bid, "Goodbye, Lud."

He disconnected.

I stared at my crystal ball and watched the digits fade away until there was nothing but a lazy billow of smoke.

"Perhaps I don't adore you," I snapped at it.

The lazy billow of smoke cleared and showed me a picture of Kristian and Brikitta sleeping, Frantz peacefully at rest in a cot by the side of their bed.

Blasted ball.

"All right, so I do adore you, I'm just annoyed at you."

The vision of my family wafted away.

I drew in breath and knew exactly what I had to do.

This I did without delay so I wouldn't lose my nerve.

I phoned Noc.

For the first time I'd done this, he did not take my call.

It went to his voicemail.

Surprised and disturbed by this, I simply said after the tone, "Could you call me at your soonest convenience, darling?" and disconnected.

But I feared his not picking up was another part of his warning.

Or, worse, that he was right then speaking to his father.

However, even if it happened through my magic and not my machinations, I'd set something in motion and I needed to alert him to that.

Thus, I found the maintenance man and allowed some time to pass while observing him before I called Noc again.

He again didn't answer.

I did not leave a message. But I did struggle to keep the panic at bay while trying to decide whether or not to send a text.

I decided I should do all to be open about what had occurred so I sent a text.

It read:

Darling, I've had a conversation I need to share with you. Please call me.

This went unanswered as well.

And hours later, when Noc should have picked me up from Valentine's as he normally did when I was not already at his home after he was finished with work, he did not do that either.

Which meant I knew I should have heeded his warning.

A warning the love I felt for him dictated I could not heed.

And as I purloined the keys to Valentine's car and went out to nick the actual vehicle, I knew I had to go to him immediately.

And face the consequences.

Noc's Suburban at the curb in front of his house, it took me seven (yes, seven) tries to maneuver Valentine's car in a spot two houses up from his, the only spot open on his street.

In the end, my parking efforts weren't exactly perfect. The back wheel was up on the pavement when I decided the deed was well and truly done. I left it at that, simply relieved I'd made it there in one piece, and doing my best to ignore my dread, I got out of the car and walked to Noc's home.

The door was barred against me, however I didn't knock.

I also didn't bother to dig out my key.

Magically, I turned the lock.

And then I walked in.

I saw immediately Noc leaning against the side of his island, an open bottle of whiskey on the counter, his fingers wrapped around a glass.

Oddly, he appeared to be waiting for me.

I drew in breath and made him wait no longer.

Tossing my bag to the couch as I passed, I approached him.

When I made the very edge of the kitchen area, I stopped because he spoke.

"How'd you get here?"

"I helped myself to Valentine's car," I shared carefully.

This, I found instantly, was not careful enough, for his face grew tight.

"You drove yourself?" he asked.

"I did, my love," I answered.

"Thought you'd spirit yourself," he remarked in a manner I could tell was deceptively casually.

"As you know, I've not learned how to do that," I reminded him.

"You haven't learned how to drive a car by yourself, but you did that," he pointed out.

"I—"

"You're here safe now, but swear to fuck, Franka, you do that again, shit will happen."

I knew immediately whatever "shit" he was referring to I did not want to happen.

I allowed that to pass and tried to begin again.

"Noc, we need—"

He pushed from the island but moved no further as he interrupted, "For a woman who's made an art of being attuned to every nuance of someone she's meaning to play, seems you're not cluing in real well on how to play me."

I suffered that blow and forced my voice to conciliatory when I replied, "You must know I have no wish to play you, Noc."

"No? So you called my dad just to say hi?"

"I didn't mean—" I began to explain.

But Noc wanted different explanations.

"What'd you do, babe? Sneak out of our bed when I was sleeping and copy his digits from my phone?"

"Of course not," I whispered.

"Magic," he stated.

I didn't confirm.

Instead, I again attempted to explain.

"It wasn't my intention—"

"Right. Let's be clear about that. I don't give a fuck what your intention was. You weren't gettin' what you wanted so you called my fuckin' *dad*. A man you have not met. A man you don't fuckin' know. A man you got no business talkin' to until the time I thought it was right to give him to you. That was not cool, and I'm thinkin' I don't gotta tell you that. I'm thinkin' that's the same in your world or mine. So I'm thinkin' you fuckin' know it."

I tried to take the situation in hand.

"There are a variety of things we need to discuss, darling."

"No there aren't and think I made that clear already."

I took a step toward him and the pain slashed deep when his expression shared unmistakably an approach was far from welcome.

Therefore, I stopped.

But I didn't stop myself from speaking.

"Valentine warned me that I needed to control my emotion in regard to my magic," I shared. "And what's been going on between us was weighing heavily on my mind. So, as I sat beside my crystal ball, fretting over this, your father's number appeared in it. I didn't ask for it to appear. It just appeared. And I swear to you that's the truth."

"So you called it."

"I called it not knowing who I was calling."

"But you called it. Found out who it was and talked to him. And Sue, I'll fuckin' add."

"Yes, but Noc, once I knew who it was, I could hardly hang up."

"Maybe not, but you could also have just said hey, introduced yourself and not fuckin' brought up your gig with me and the shit you're tryin' to insinuate yourself into."

I bore that blow too and endured.

"I can assert that you've made your feelings clear on this subject, my darling, however I'm uncertain I've done the same. There are things that are concerning me."

"I'm gettin' that, seein' as you were totally okay with bringing them up with my dad."

I shook my head and tried to steer us elsewhere.

"He explained to me about Judy, the anniversary, and I understand where both of your thoughts rest on that matter. What I don't understand is why you didn't feel open to share yours with me."

"No, what you don't understand is that I didn't fuckin' *want* to share that shit with you."

"I do understand that, Noc," I said quietly. "I just don't understand why."

"You don't wanna know why."

"I do."

"No, Franka, you don't."

I took another step toward him, stopped and stressed, "I want everything from you."

His words were implacable when he replied, "Trust me, you don't."

"Please Noc."

"Let it go."

I shook my head, took another step and stopped. "I can't."

"You can. You won't."

"I see your pain," I whispered.

"Yeah?" he asked, his voice actually snide.

My Noctorno.

Snide.

Regardless of the shock it caused he even had that in him, I persisted.

"You helped me through mine, my love, I want to guide you from yours."

At that, but a brief moment elapsed before he burst into laughter.

Laughter that held no mirth.

My body locked at the foulness of the sound and the odious feelings it made me feel.

When he stopped, my words dripped the ache I felt inside as I remarked, "You don't think I can do it. You did it for me, but you don't think I have it in me to do it for you."

I knew just how far he'd drifted from me when he had no reaction to the torment in my words, replying unemotionally, "I see you want that, Franka, and part of me digs that from you. What I do *not* dig is that you won't fuckin' listen when I tell you this is somewhere you can't go."

"So you can force me to see my golden soul, but you wish me to allow you to live in midnight?" I pushed.

At that, with a sudden violence that was so startling, my entire body jumped, and I had to fight cowering when he took his glass and threw it across the kitchen where it crashed against the cupboards on the opposite wall, the glass shattering, the whiskey splattering.

And then came the thunder, the force of it making me wince.

"*They took me from her dead body,*" Noc roared.

I stood utterly still.

"She was dead before I took my first fuckin' breath," he declared.

Oh gods.

Gods.

He was talking about his mother.

"Darling," I breathed.

"I was born in midnight and it was in the middle of the fuckin' day I made it into the world," he bit out. "You think you can take that from me?"

"Noc," I whispered, edging toward him.

I stopped when he declared, "She never held me. She was dead before I was alive. Dead to give me life. I'm no doctor. I don't know the research. I don't know what infants can feel. All I know is, I was a baby and I knew he loved her. Fuck, Franka, my dad loved her so fuckin' much, it tells me the man he was that he had the courage to give it another go, *three times,* because with what I felt from the minute I was born I wouldn't think the man had that in him, that's how much he loved her. That's what I felt. I also felt just what he felt that he lost her. From my first breath, I felt his loss and I felt his love for me and that's *all* I felt. And then that loss happened again. And then it fucking happened *again*. And I had to fucking *watch*."

"My love—"

"You think you can take that from me?" he clipped.

"I—"

"There are no heroes, Franka."

I closed my mouth.

"I know that," he declared. "I learned that. Killed my own fuckin' mother bein' born, and I prayed to God every damned night Judy was sick, askin' him to let her win. Begging for that shit. She fought so fuckin' hard, she deserved it. But it was more. The woman she was, there's no reason I could get why she'd be forced to take that pain. Why a woman like her would be taken from us. I didn't understand what we'd done to deserve that because she sure as fuck didn't do shit to deserve it. But she didn't win. And we had to watch. We had to watch her waste away. We had to see her pain. And there was not one fuckin' thing any of us could do about it."

He gave me that, shredding me with it.

And then he blasted me with, "You know what makes a hero, babe?"

Slowly, I shook my head.

"What makes a hero is the one that's left standing when the others are dead. Or the one that gave his life so the others could live. That's a fuckin' hero."

Cautiously, I said, "There are other definitions, Noc."

"Those are the ones that matter."

I couldn't argue that.

"My mother was a hero," he declared.

Gods, he was killing me.

"My love," I whispered.

"The way she fought to stay with us, Judy was a hero too."

Standing in front of him whole, I still felt like I was bleeding.

"That being a hero, Franka, who would want to be a fuckin' hero?" he demanded.

"You were a wee babe when you were born, darling. You couldn't have saved your mother."

His head twitched in disgust. "You think that makes it easier?"

I persevered. "And you were still but a boy, even if that boy was growing to a man, and certain illnesses can bring low the greatest of warriors, as evidenced through your Judy."

"And you think that makes *that* easier?"

"What I think is you hold guilt for things that were beyond your control."

"No shit?" he asked sarcastically. "Became a cop because I wanted to save the world seein' as I couldn't save my mom. I couldn't save Judy. Fuck, I actually helped save a goddamned world. It didn't help. I could lift a gun and shoot that fuckin' bitch of a witch and help save countless lives. But I was totally helpless, in Judy's case forced to sit back and actually watch, completely unable to do fuck all to save either one of them."

I stared right into his eyes, right into the heart of his anguish, and finally understood.

And what I understood gave me rapture.

"So you hold on to your midnight soul and refuse to let it go."

"It's got hold of me, Franka, and there's no way to escape it."

"Good," I whispered.

His chin jerked into his neck and he did one of his slow blinks.

"Midnight is beautiful," I told him. "And it's at its most beautiful in you."

I watched his body lock.

"Oh, but the gods do so love me," I shared softly. "To give me a man who would allow his soul to be taken over by the darkness of night, for he's a man who loves so deeply, he lost those who had his love, was cast into the shadows, and he refuses to crawl to the light."

I stopped speaking and Noc said nothing. He just stared at me, and I saw the cords of his throat convulse with his swallow.

Then he dropped his head.

I moved forward quickly.

Getting close, fitting my front to his, I lifted both my hands to his cheeks and peered up at him, bearing the agony in his face, now understanding what he was hiding behind his closed eyes.

And relishing the honor it was to have both.

He stood, not touching me, not speaking.

I stood, holding his beauty in my hands, and I did this silently.

This lasted an eternity.

Then he whispered, "I fuckin' hate this goddamned anniversary."

Finally.

I had not seen his pain weeks ago simply because I'd had reason to look more closely.

I'd seen his pain because now was the time when it forced itself to the surface.

"You miss her," I whispered back.

He opened his eyes.

I saw the wet gleam and I was honored to have that too.

"Yeah, sweetheart, every fuckin' day."

I slid my thumb along his cheekbone. "I love you for that."

He closed his eyes, drew breath in through his nose, and when he opened them again, contrition shifted into his gaze.

He lifted one hand to my jaw and returned my gesture. "Been a fuckin' dick."

I shook my head, but said, "It's my joy to take every part of you."

He shook his head in return, his lips twitching. "My Frannie. Should've known. She takes the good but she's always been better at takin' the bad."

"Indeed."

All of a sudden, my arms were forced to circle his shoulders when his hand disappeared from my jaw. He caught me up in a tight embrace and buried his face in my neck.

"Love you, baby," he declared there.

"And I you."

He pressed his face deeper in my neck and his voice was gruff when he went on, "She would have loved you too."

I closed my eyes at more rapture.

But I said nothing.

I just held on to my love.

And I basked in the beauty of midnight.

25
Never Far

Franka

Noc had chosen the place.

He'd also chosen the time.

We walked there together in the moonlight.

When we got to the spot he wished to be, standing amongst the shadows of trees dripping their moss gracefully, he turned me in his arms and bent his neck to touch his lips to mine. After, he tucked my cheek to his chest and rested his on top of my head.

I had one arm around his back, but the other hand I rested on his biceps.

I did this for two reasons.

One was to touch him, obviously.

The other so I'd know when it was time.

We remained in each other's arms as the minutes on my watch ticked by.

And I watched through the moonlight as the second hand warned me the time was nigh.

Only then did I step slightly from Noc's embrace.

Keeping hold of him with my arm around him, I swept my other down then up in a wide arc.

And from my fingers, a flock of doves flew, their gossamer wings glittering among moonbeams, the tips of their feathers trailing delicate shimmers that dropped in an exquisite fade to the earth.

They flew direct toward the waning quarter moon and disappeared in its light.

It was midnight.

My favorite time of day.

And it was the anniversary of Judy's death.

When the least I could do was make doves fly.

My gaze turned to Noc to see him staring into the sky where the doves had disappeared.

I gave him a moment to spend with Judy.

Then I whispered, "It's time to go home, my love."

His eyes drifted down to me.

I saw pain that would never fade.

As it should be.

But I also saw peace.

"Yeah, sweetheart. It's time to go home."

Holding hands, we made our way to his car, leaving moonlight and magic behind.

However, Judy stayed with us, for I was certain no matter what day it was, or what time, the love Noc had for her, the love she'd earned, she was never far.

EPILOGUE
EVERY WAY LOVE CAN BE

Franka

"I would say that's a job well done," Valentine noted.

We stood, Valentine, Lavinia and I, on the pavement across from the restaurant where the maintenance man and the woman who'd loved him from afar, the woman who had loved him so much she scrimped and saved to buy his love for her in return, were sitting at a table at the window, eating hamburgers.

Their first date.

I was aghast.

Surely, my magic said more than *hamburgers* for a first date.

"I find this highly disturbing," Lavinia murmured.

I did as well.

I mean, *hamburgers*?

Valentine and I turned our attention to her.

She shifted her attention from the couple to us. "All the beauty you can make with your magic, you use it to meddle in people's lives?"

"We give them what they want," Valentine replied.

"And that man," Lavinia gestured to the restaurant across the street, "did he want her?"

"He does now," I shared the obvious.

Lavinia rolled her eyes skyward.

Even though we'd just started, Valentine made it known that she was quite done talking about this.

"We've a booking at Arnaud's in half an hour. Noc, Dax and Circe are meeting us there. We must be going."

Lavinia sighed and we all moved to where Valentine had parked her car.

"These conveyances, I cannot get used to them," the other-world witch muttered as we did.

"I felt the same," I shared. "As you seem to enjoy spending time in this world, we'll teach you how to drive. Trust me, it'll make it better."

Lavinia cast a horrified glance my way.

I smiled a small smile.

The car made a noise while its lights flashed, telling us the doors were open.

Valentine headed to the driver's side, speaking.

"That job complete, having been away, I have many lined up, Franka," she said to me. "Are you ready for your next?"

This one was hardly a challenge.

And it ended in *hamburgers*.

I was very much ready for my next.

"Of course," I replied to her over the roof of the car. "Do you have one in mind?"

"Yes," she stated.

I studied her face and the look on it made a thrill gather at the small of my back.

"Your next client seeks revenge," she whispered.

I held her gaze, and at her words, my smile was still small.

But it spoke volumes.

Korwahk

"STOP DROOLING, SUGARLIPS."

"Mm?"

"Babe."

"Yes?"

A shaking "Frannie," mingled with an arm tightening around my shoulders, curling me to Noc's front meant I was forced to tear my eyes from the Korwahk warrior.

Oh so many moons ago, I'd briefly met him back in Fyngaard, although after the troubles he'd quickly been away home.

He was one of Lahn's most trusted lieutenants.

His name was Zahnin.

And his ferocity of appearance was a match for Lahn's. I'd found him most frightening, and as lovely as many things on him were to gaze upon, at the time I did not admit to the relief I felt when I heard he was gone.

But now, here, in his homeland in its capital city of Korwahn, standing on its Majestic Rim, awaiting the ceremony that was soon to commence, he was with his wife.

And his children.

Before Noc pulled me away, I'd been watching the little boy crawling up his long, stout leg while Zahnin was tickling, squeezing and throwing up in the air his baby girl, catching her as she giggled uncontrollably. And she kept doing so while he blew kisses into her neck.

Then, easily tucking her in his long, strong arm, he'd bent to haul up his toddler son, the boy going up shrieking his glee, and the warrior juggled them both against the large expanse of his bare, brown-skinned, painted chest, to their abandoned delight.

Through all this, his exceedingly pretty Fleuridian wife, Anastasie, stood pressed close to his side, both her arms wrapped around his middle, and looked on with unconcealed adoration.

Of her children, of course.

But mostly her husband.

I could understand this.

His smile was white and wide, transforming his face.

There was no fierceness there, not now.

Only love and happiness.

Something that veritably beamed from him when he'd finally turned his attention from their children and gazed with open and frank devotion at his wife.

Right then, I looked up to Noc and saw no fierceness either.

His smile was white and wide, but it didn't transform his face.

My Noc always showed me his love and the happiness I gave him.

And the devotion he gave to me.

Thus, I melted into his body.

"Would be jealous you're pervin' on that guy if you didn't wake up happy to be back in your world and feelin' the need to go down on me," he noted.

I frowned.

Noc kept smiling. "You told me a year ago that I'd be in an adobe house that had running water only because it was fed direct from a river, that house in a parallel universe, waking up in that place to get the best blowjob of my life, I'd be intrigued, but I'd think you were crazy."

"This is hardly the topic for discussion on a day like today," I snapped. "Circe and Lahn haven't invited us here for you to be rude."

He dipped his face closer to mine, still smiling. "Babe, first, no one understands a fuckin' thing I'm sayin' seein' as no one speaks English. And second, you think there aren't gonna be a lotta blowjobs goin' around today, you're very wrong. Weddings make people horny."

Well!

"That may be so, but you don't *discuss* it moments before the joyous festivities begin." I admonished. "Regardless if people don't understand you, that wolfish look on your face speaks volumes."

His wolfish look got even more wolfish (which I had to admit, though not to Noc, was most attractive). "If they had airplanes here, I'd hire one to skywrite how good my woman is at giving head."

Although I was most pleased I could pleasure him so thoroughly in this way, I batted his chest.

He started chuckling.

At that moment, a hush fell over the crowd.

Noc lifted his head and we both turned our attention to the colossal lip of sand-colored rock that jutted out over the city of Korwahn creating its Majestic Rim.

There we saw Korwahk's Dax Lahn, his chest and back painted in blacks and golds, striding to the clearing before us where his throne and that of his queen were sitting.

The Golden Queen Circe was at his side, in extraordinary regalia, including a band of glittering golden feathers around her forehead.

And loping next to her like a trusted pet (something I'd found last night when we'd arrived and I was introduced to it that it was) was a large, grand white tiger.

Following them, under a drooping shade of golden silk, was a young couple, the pretty, plump woman beaming happily, the lean, tall man at her side looking serious.

The shade was held up on four poles by four young women, all practically skipping in their excitement.

Coming up the rear was a regiment of Korwahk warriors, all wearing black and gold paint.

Just off to the side of the clearing, Lahn and Circe's three children were being looked after by Circe's friends, Narinda and Nahka (women I'd also met last night), who had their own children with them, this large brood easily managed considering Narinda's husband, Feetak, and Nahka's husband, Bohtan, were keeping a stern eye on the crew.

Circe and Lahn made it to their thrones just as Diandra, Circe's best friend, a kind and exceedingly attractive Valerian woman (which meant she spoke Noc and my language), sidled up next to us.

I looked to her and returned her smile before my gaze shifted back to the rim to see Circe seated in her throne made of white horns.

The honor guard had lined up behind her.

Lahn's throne, made of massive black horns, was empty, for he did not seat himself. He stood, hands on hide-covered hips, looking like he was scowling down at the couple who were now situated in front of their king and queen, facing each other, the four women still holding the shade over them.

"Iykoo!" Lahn boomed.

"Kneel," Diandra whispered in translation.

I at once had the urge to kneel, but as the throng around us did not, I stayed where I was, in the curve of Noc's arm, and watched Jacanda, Circe's trusted slave girl, kneel across from her soon-to-be-husband, Derahn.

The instant they settled on their knees, a collective gasp came from the crowd as a shower of flower petals in the colors of yellow, orange and deep pink fell from the underside of the awning held over them, raining down on the couple below.

Feeling my lips quirk, knowing that was the queen's magic, I looked from the couple to Circe, seeing her mouth curved up in a soft, indulgent smile, her eyes glued on her slave who was also her friend.

And I noted it again.

Since arriving the day before, I realized in her home, she was the Circe I knew. My friend. A woman from my new world living in a savage land in my old, a woman who was giving and amusing and kind.

But when she walked out of her home, she was the Golden Warrior Queen of Korwahk.

It was her way that this distinction was rather vague.

But it was nevertheless unmistakable.

Now she was queen.

And she was a sight to behold.

Even so, I tore my gaze from her to another sight that was always one to behold and saw her husband, his torso twisted so he could look at his wife.

When he turned back to the couple, he was shaking his head but doing it quite clearly fighting a smile.

Lahn was not one for flower petals.

But he liked that his wife was.

He became serious again when he regarded the subjects kneeled before him.

Then he opened his mouth and started speaking.

Diandra translated as he did.

"Today, the slave Derahn takes to wife my queen's servant, Jacanda. Today, he gives his oath that he is now her possession. She owns his body. She owns his spirit. She owns his seed. And today, the queen's trusted servant Jacanda gives her oath that she is now Derahn's possession. He owns her body. He owns her spirit. He owns her womb. They will take no other until death. They will be owned by no other until death. Derahn will sow children into Jacanda and he will offer protection and guidance to the family he creates until his final breath. Jacanda will deliver him these children and offer nurture and care to them and Derahn until her final breath."

As Lahn paused, there seemed a stirring of the warriors both behind Circe and Lahn's thrones as well as those painted for the ceremonial day who were standing amongst the crowd (including, I noted with a sidelong glance, Zahnin, who had transferred his children to his wife, and was now looking much more alert and back to fierce).

My gaze returned to Lahn as he spoke again.

"And they will do this as free man and woman..."

The stirring around us increased as Noc's hold on me tightened because this stirring was not only of the warriors, but also the entirety of the crowd.

Lahn spoke through it, I had no doubt noting the feel of the gathering, but ignoring it entirely.

"Owned from now to their death by no merchant, no man, no warrior. Owned only by each other. This is my decree. This is the decree of my golden queen. And this will be done. As their oath is now done and they are man and wife to each other from this day until they burn on their pyres."

I shifted my gaze to the couple to see that this declaration of freedom was another gift bestowed on them that was a far sight sweeter than flower petals falling. They were staring up at their Dax in open-mouthed wonder.

Apparently, slaves were rarely freed in Korwahk.

"And as a gift to Jacanda," Lahn roared on while Diandra translated, sounding surprised herself (a secret well-kept, clearly, for Diandra was much beloved and trusted by Circe), "a loyal slave to your queen, a slave who has stood by your queen's side in womanly ways that mirror the actions of a warrior of the Horde to his brother, it is the will of your king and his golden queen that every merchant, man and warrior give liberty to those who serve them with steadfast allegiance."

I felt my frame stiffen.

Was he...?

I stared.

By the gods, Lahn was freeing the slaves!

The stirring increased as did the tightness of Noc's hold, and a shocked murmuring broke out amongst the crowd.

"It is our will, the will of your king and your queen," Lahn thundered over the low sound. "It is the seal of the Golden Dynasty. Fidelity is rewarded. Freedom is granted. We build the Korwahk the prophets have foreseen and that Korwahk will flourish and thrive under the reign of the Golden Dynasty," he suddenly lifted a hand and beat it to his chest, "*my* Golden Dynasty. The dynasty pouring forth from my seed planted in the fertility between the legs of *my*," another chest pound, "golden warrior queen."

My eyes shot to Circe to see her rolling hers at Lahn's bold assertions.

But she was doing this grinning.

Lahn just kept speaking.

"All of those within our borders that your Horde protects from this day walk free, and they do it vowing allegiance to the sand and rock of this proud country."

There was more murmuring amongst the gathering, but as I glanced around, held close in Noc's hold, I noticed it was only murmuring. To my shock, although this was a declaration that would change the fabric of their daily lives, most everyone (but the warriors) looked surprised, no one looked angry.

This was undoubtedly because every warrior amongst them had clearly been told this was happening today and they not only wore their paint, they wore their large swords at a slant across their backs.

I'd thought this was all ceremonial.

I realized then it was not.

So apparently, when told to free your slaves, you were quite all right with that because your alternative was to demur and have a Korwahk Horde warrior carve you asunder.

I felt this was an appropriate reaction for a variety of reasons and turned my attention back to Lahn when he again started speaking.

"It is the way of my wife's people that you kiss to seal your oath," Lahn said, now only speaking to the couple. Then he ordered, "Do that now."

I heard Noc chuckle as I felt him relax, and it took a moment for Jacanda and Derahn to pull themselves together, but once that moment was over, they hesitated no further and fell into each other's arms.

The kiss was not chaste.

Indeed, it was so not chaste it didn't end at all but continued with Derahn twisting Jacanda to her back on a bed of petals on stone, covering her with his body, and a cheer rent from the crowd.

Suddenly, golden panels until then unseen (in other words, Circe conjured them), fell around the couple, hiding them from view.

"That, sugarlips, is precisely why weddings make people horny," Noc murmured amusedly in my ear.

I twisted my neck and gave him a vexed look.

His gaze drifted upward and his lips muttered, "Fuckin' hell."

At his words and a new shout from the crowd, my gaze drifted upward too.

And there, arcing over the gathering, indeed the entirety of the Majestic Rim, glinting like it dripped pixie dust, was the brightest, clearest, largest rainbow I'd ever seen.

I again looked to Circe who now sat by her husband. Lahn had taken his own throne and was jerking his head tersely to a hovering servant, telling her without words to pour the libation she'd brought for his wife first.

She scuttled over to Circe.

I watched her accept the chalice of wine like she was taking a glass offered to her while she was seated at Noc's island.

And I knew.

Lahn did not free the oppressed of his country.

His wife did.

She did by talking her husband into doing it.

Oh yes, the golden warrior queen of Korwahk was quite something.

"Seems we weren't invited just for a visit with the excuse of the wedding of some chick we didn't know," Noc remarked, bringing my eyes to him. "Seems we were here to witness something really fucking cool."

It would seem he was correct.

"I wish the others were here," I replied, meaning Frey and Finnie, Tor and Cora, and even Maddie and Apollo (these last two for Noc, I didn't think they liked me much, but my Noc liked them).

"If they were, I wouldn't have an excuse to take you to Fleuridia, Bellebryn and Lunwyn," Noc returned.

"True," I murmured.

"Babe," he called, even though I was right in his arms, looking into his eyes.

"Yes, my darling?"

"Feel like sealing our own oath?" he asked, his stunning blue eyes now dancing.

"I always feel like sealing our own oath," I answered with the gods' honest truth.

Noc smiled down at me.

Then he kissed me.

Unfortunately, for the sake of politeness, he ceased doing this when Diandra's husband, Seerim, and her daughter, Sheena, joined us, carrying resin cups filled to the brim with Korwahkian wine.

When I took mine from Sheena with a soft, "*Shahsha*," ("thank you" in Korwahkian) the pretty girl grinned at me.

"I can see Lahn has it going on," Noc said to Diandra, who looked confused for a moment but her lips still moved, uttering Korwahkian, translating for her husband and daughter. "Not many leaders, no matter they can tear a man's head off with their bare hands, could pull that off by just saying it's gonna be done."

Diandra kept talking, and when she was finished, Seerim started.

Diandra translated.

"There will be uprisings. This is only the beginning. The Horde has been warned and they are aware. It will not be this easy. What it will be, eventually, is the legacy of the Golden Dynasty."

"Don't doubt that," Noc replied.

Diandra translated what Noc had said then shared her own words, "It helps matters, I'm certain, that all the rulers of the Northlands have declared their alliance with this new creed and will block trade with merchants from Korwahk who won't follow it. Rulers who have also vowed they're prepared to ride with the Horde for those who take up weapons in an effort to defy it."

In other words, Queen Aurora (with the support of Frey and Apollo, no doubt), Prince Noctorno, King Ludlum and whoever was ruling Fleuridia now (I was out of the loop, I'd heard there was a coup in the last conversation I'd had with Cora through my crystal ball, but it was no longer my world so I didn't pay it much mind) were on board with Lahn's decree.

"Not bad backup," Noc muttered.

Diandra nodded.

Sheena said something and Diandra looked toward the thrones before saying to us, "Our Dax and Dahksahna wish our presence."

I looked to the thrones too and saw now that the king and his queen had been reunited with their family.

Thus Circe was waving us her way even as she seemed to be attempting to control a very active Andromeda in her arms (this effort failing as she was also holding her chalice of wine and the child very much wanted to launch herself at the white tiger, who was engaged in the activity of licking the baby's leg).

This was happening while Lahn had his dark-haired toddler Tunahn riding his broad shoulders, the boy peering at the expanse before him like he already ruled the people milling about in it.

But his golden-haired daughter, Isis, had plastered her front to her father's massive chest, blurring his paint, which was now smudging her golden garments, and giggling while she pulled at his beard.

Lahn felt no need to appear kingly with his daughter pressed to him, pulling at his beard. He'd just wrapped his strapping forearm under her bum, held her to him, and smiled wide into her beautiful little face.

"Time to attend the king and queen," Noc said in my ear, putting a hand to the small of my back and starting us that way.

He was right, of course.

In a way.

But really, it was time to be with our friends and celebrate a momentous occasion.

The first new creed as proclaimed by The Golden Dynasty.

I took a sip from my cup as I moved, and thought, *May it be one of many.*

Fleuridia

I PLUCKED a piece of lavender as I ambled down the lane beside Maddie.

I'd asked for this stroll.

Now I didn't know how to go about the business of why I'd done that.

During our visit to my world, Noc wanted to see everyone, including Apollo and Maddie.

I'd said no words against it, even if I felt no small amount of concern that I knew Noc would be welcomed, but I likely wouldn't.

This did not occur. Both Apollo and his Maddie were very cordial with me.

Cordial.

Not friendly.

It was clear they most enjoyed seeing Noc.

But they were very poor at hiding they were not the same with me.

Apollo was formal and terse, if not outwardly unwelcoming.

Maddie was hesitant and watchful.

We were only staying but days before being spirited to Bellebryn as arranged (and paid for) with Valentine, and I had thought to simply get through it and then move on with our holiday.

What I didn't factor was the fact that Noc was as he was.

Highly perceptive.

At first, he seemed keen on the course of attempting, with his good humor and easy manner, to sweep away the awkwardness.

When this didn't occur, and regardless that I tried to hide my discomfort, he started to get frustrated.

Then angry.

I feared he'd demand words with Apollo, and before he did something like that, altering a relationship I knew they both enjoyed in a way they would cease doing that, something had to be done.

And I had to do it.

Thus, I'd asked Maddie on this stroll.

And I couldn't begin to know how to sort through the matter at hand.

I just knew I must.

For Noc.

And, to be quite truthful, for Maddie.

I stopped, twirling the stem of lavender in my fingers, and called quietly, "Lady Madeleine."

She stopped too, having walked on several strides, and turned back to me.

I decided to face it head on.

"When I said what I said to you at Brunskar, I know my words harmed you," I declared.

"Franka," she said my name uneasily.

"This has been made very clear to me," I shared.

She seemed at a loss before she replied, "Things were very...*emotional* at the time."

"They were indeed," I agreed. "This does not erase the harm that I'd done."

She took a step toward me, saying again, "Franka."

"Those I care about, who care about me, call me Frannie."

She stopped and stared.

"Even if I would never speak it aloud, until now, I've always admired Apollo for many reasons. His service to my country is one. Another is the love he has for his family."

She looked to be fighting turning her gaze away and she won, holding mine steady but saying nothing.

"This man I've long respected, it's good to see him again happy," I declared.

A startled warmth moved through her gaze as she took the last step toward me, reaching out to wrap her fingers around mine.

"That's kind of you to say," she replied quietly.

"Perhaps, but mostly it's true," I returned.

Her lips curved.

"It may be the damage my words caused make it so we cannot have what I have with the others who've found love across worlds," I carried on. "But my Noc has grown to care about you both. So, although it is not mine to ask anything of you, for him I do so regardless. And what I ask is that we endeavor to get past the awkwardness between us so that Noc can enjoy his time, time which is rather brief, with the two of you."

"I know what happened to you," she whispered.

I fought lifting my chin and replied, "I know you do."

"My ex, the other Apollo, Pol, beat the absolute crap out of me, doing it repeatedly. Once doing it, and I lost the son I carried."

I blinked in shock and distress.

"When I went to my parents for help," she continued, "my father closed the door in my face."

"By the gods," I breathed.

She nodded and went on to tell her startling tale of woe.

"I went on the run and I didn't let anyone close to me. Not for ages. Not until Apollo."

I said nothing.

"In other words, Frannie. I get you." She looked beyond me, back up to the grand manse in the countryside of Fleuridia she shared with her husband, his children by Ilsa, and their little Valentine, and again to me. "The awkwardness was because, well, even having changed, you're kind of intimidating and I didn't know how to broach it with you." She gave me a grin. "I'm glad you knew what to do."

"Well, I'm..." I cleared my throat, "glad too."

Her grin became a smile, she moved to me, coming to my side and hooking her arm through my own.

Thus, she moved us again forward. "So now, tell me. I'm dying to know. How did you react to my old world? I have to admit, I'd love to take Lo there. See how he feels about airplanes and Jacuzzis. You have to tell me everything. What did you think the weirdest thing was? And the most wonderful?"

I shared this with her and she threw her head back and laughed when I told her both were my introduction to the glory of toilets.

And from there, Lady Madeleine Ulfr and I wandered a lane lined in lavender.

And as we did, we became friends.

~

Noc

"She's much changed."

Noc didn't take his attention from the window as he watched Frannie and

Maddie wandering down the lane, arm in arm, heads bent together even when he felt Apollo come to stand beside him or when Apollo said those words.

"No, she's not," Noc replied

"I knew her well before you, my brother," Lo stated carefully.

Only then did Noc give the man his eyes.

"No you did not."

Apollo Ulfr held his gaze.

Then he lifted his chin.

Both men turned their attention back out the window.

And they stood watching the women they loved wandering a lane, their skirts and the fields of lavender waving about them in a gentle breeze, their bodies bathed in sunshine.

~

Lunwyn

I WAS RIDING Noc's cock, both of us sitting up, our eyes locked, when his arm clamped about my hips and he held me down, full of him, and shifted to his knees.

He then dropped me to my back, covering me and again moving inside.

Through this, my gaze on his never wavered, nor did it when his hand found mine, linking our fingers and pressing them into the bed as his other hand moved, pushing deep, up my spine, the back of my neck, to curl against my scalp.

"Don't stop lookin' at me," he growled.

"I won't," I whimpered, arching into him, our position, his words, neither lost on me.

Like our first time.

Exactly.

"So goddamned beautiful," he grunted as his thrusts picked up speed. "Always so goddamned beautiful."

"Darling," I breathed, grinding into him, moving urgently, the need nearly overwhelming me.

"Hold on, Frannie. Not yet. Look into my eyes."

"You have me," I whispered, and he very much did, now in every way.

My hands were roaming his skin, hungry.

His strokes gathered power as he drove into me.

I moaned, losing hold.

Noc felt it.

"Don't lose my eyes, baby."

"I...won't, my love," I gasped.

His face darkened, his fingers in mine clenched, I felt the metal at one biting into the webbing and he groaned, "Now, Frannie. Let go."

As the sound of his climax powered through the room, the softer wisps of my own filtered through it and I arced into him, pulling him deep, clasping him to me, and Noc poured himself inside me, unhindered.

I was shuddering through the final glorious moments when he collapsed on top of me, sinking his face into my neck.

I took him happily, memorizing the feel of him I'd already never forget, the smell, the sound of his harsh breathing whispering against the skin under my ear.

In these times, we never needed to speak.

And this time, so different, but yet the same, this was something we still did not need.

However, Noc felt something had to be said.

And he said it by raising his head, taking off some of his weight, and then lifting our hands he still had laced together.

He brought them to his lips, his eyes on me, and kissed the large Sjofn ice diamond there that nestled perfectly with the plain gold band underneath.

He wore a band as well, on the hand that still held my head.

I'd slipped it on under the bemused eyes of a Vallee in a Dwelling of the Gods just an hour before.

His gesture was all that needed to be said from my new husband to me, his new wife.

And for long moments as we gazed at each other, his handsome lips to the beautiful rings he'd bestowed on me, that was all that was said.

Eventually, Noc pressed our hands to his chest and in the most profound moment of my life (and I'll note all the others on that list carried memories of him too), he declared, "We are *so* gonna piss everyone off that we eloped on a parallel universe and we didn't invite anyone from this world or the other."

I felt my face form a scowl at his mentioning a discussion we'd already had.

One which we ended in whole-hearted agreement (of a sort, Noc was much the champion of being married, doing it in my homeland, something that he knew meant much to me, and it being rather private—he was not quite the champion of going it totally alone, but he'd given in...for me).

"This is not their moment, Noc."

"Not sure Sue's gonna see it that way," he replied. "Or Dad. Or Dash. Or Aurora. Orly. Finnie. Frey's gonna give me tons of shit. And I don't even wanna think how Jo is gonna react."

"She's dealing with her own emotion concerning that odious Glover," I snapped and Noc's brows rose.

"Odious? How's Glover odious, sugarlips? It was *Jo* who dumped *him*."

It was indeed.

She'd explained this days prior to our being spirited away for our holiday, stating, "I tried, Frannie. I really tried to see it in him. But watching you and Noc, he didn't have it. So in the end, he just didn't do it for me."

She was falling into our new-world language, then again she would as we'd been in that new world now for many months.

She was also quite right about taking her leave of Glover.

If he didn't do it for her, it was time to scrape him off.

"It isn't easy dumping someone, Noc," I shared. "She feels awful."

"She should. He was totally gone for her. And he was a good guy."

"Not good enough, this, I will note, I *always* knew."

Noc shook his head but did it grinning.

He was still grinning when he declared, "We need to have another ceremony when we get to Rimée Keep."

"Whyever would we do that?"

He didn't answer, he kept on his bent.

"And we need to have another one when we get home."

"The deed is already done," I pointed out.

"Right, *you* tell Sue she can't wear a crazy hat to some shindig," he returned. "And by the way, being married here is not legal at home and we get a tax break for being married."

"We'll have a ceremony at home," I stated instantly.

Another grin from Noc as he muttered, "That's my Frannie. If she can keep her money so she can spend it on herself or anyone else she wants to lavish shit on, she's gonna do it."

"I do not mind your government knowing we're eternally joined. As you say, if I felt it prudent to part with the money it would cost, when we returned home, I'd hire an operator of an airplane to write it in the sky."

That did not get me a grin.

That earned me Noc dropping his mouth to mine and giving me a deep, wet, heated kiss.

When he finished it and our eyes opened, he whispered, "Franka Hawthorne."

That name.

Such beauty.

"That's me," I whispered back.

His face started to grow soft when, suddenly, we both stiffened.

This was because the room was tinted green.

Noc rose alertly to an outstretched arm, causing me to press my lips together to stifle the pleasured moan for we were still joined and his movements were far from unpleasant, doing this growling, "You've gotta be shitting me."

I pushed up to my elbows and turned my eyes to where my senses were guiding me.

And there, on the table by the window of the lovely inn in which we were staying, was an elegant tea service set out, its porcelain painted in a stunning motif of emerald green.

From the spout, wafts of smoke drifted from the heated brew inside.

Along with a glitter that was unmistakable.

I felt a slow smile form on my lips as the green tint of the room faded.

"Fuck, is she here?" Noc bit off.

"She's not here," I answered him and his eyes came to me. "But she knows we're wed and has left us a present."

"A present?"

I put a hand to his warm, wide chest. "Are you fatigued, my love?"

"Are you crazy, gorgeous?" he returned, but didn't wish an answer. He kept talking. "It's my wedding night and I'm feelin' the need to beat my record."

My brows drew together. "Your record?"

"Ten times, babe," he stated, causing a rather delicious tingle at the memory. "Tonight, I'm gonna go for fifteen."

My attention drifted to the tea.

He would best that.

Oh yes he would.

Splendidly.

And I would best my record of three.

Oh yes, I most definitely would.

And I'd do this *splendidly*.

It was time for some tea.

~

"So *this* is a bridesmaid dress," I murmured, staring down at myself.

I was of a mixed opinion.

The design was very fine.

The color—a pale pink—did not a thing for me.

Cora, wearing her own dress, the same exact one for reasons I couldn't fathom, came to me.

"It is," she confirmed.

"It's the same as yours," I told her something she already knew.

"It's that too."

"I must say I don't quite understand why we need to be dressed identically."

"It's just the way it is," she stated.

"In your old world," I told her. "We're not in your old world. Since both Finnie and Circe are bound to this world everlasting, in order that they can be her bridesmaids, my-world Circe is marrying Dax in Lunwyn."

"Yeah, but she's giving him his kind of wedding seeing as they're doing the Justice of the Peace thing when they get back home."

I knew of this "Justice of the Peace thing."

But for Noc and I to "make it legal," at the inflexible demands of his step-mother, my dearest Jo (who was, indeed, *very* vexed Noc and I had wed without her), and even Valentine (who had reunited with her lover amongst great drama and had become quite the romantic, in a detached way, of course) we had not gone to a Justice of the Peace and then gone somewhere else to have some cake, as Noc shared with them at first we would do (to a calamitous uprising).

We'd had a "shindig."

A *large* one.

I got a very fabulous dress out of the situation and we were showered with gifts that were all very lovely, even if we could afford to buy them ourselves. Not to mention, having this gave us an excuse to go on what was called a "honeymoon." This we did in a tranquil place filled with astounding beauty called the "Caribbean" where we were able to make love on a blanket on a sandy beach with the sea lapping at our toes (amongst other places, a number of them).

The door opened and my brief conversation with Cora was interrupted when my husband entered the room.

All eyes, including mine, Cora's, Maddie's, Finnie's, Circe's, Aurora's, Josette's, and the bride—the other Circe (attired in a dress that was *far* more becoming than my own)—went to him.

His eyes came to me.

I saw his face go soft, his gaze drop to my gown and his lips tip up before his attention turned to the bride.

A bride he was "giving away."

Although this was said to be against all tradition, Jo was not only my maid of honor at our other-world ceremony, she'd also walked me down the aisle and placed my hand in Noc's.

She'd done this sobbing.

Like a ninny.

Gods love her.

"Is he ready?" Circe asked Noc as he approached.

"Babe, you don't haul your ass into that sanctuary and soon, Dax is gonna tear in here and drag you down the aisle himself," Noc answered.

Me and my friends all gave each other knowing, delighted looks.

Circe gathered her skirts and her bundle of adela tree twigs and bustled to Noc, declaring, "Then we must go. Dax impatient is not a good thing."

"Dax impatient to make you his wife is probably a great deal worse," I shared.

Circe gave me big eyes.

Even so, I noted they were glowing and happy.

Oh yes.

Yes.

I did *so* enjoy when a carefully crafted scheme succeeded.

At Finnie's command, we all collected the arrangements of flowers we were to hold in our hands, and we lined up in order to start the proceedings.

I was the last in line before Circe and Noc.

Jo had been my maid of honor but Circe had also stood up with me.

And I was to be Circe's maid of honor and Josette was also to stand up with her.

And an honor it was.

Indeed.

As we'd been told (and actually practiced the night before, for reasons beyond me—we were all walking down an aisle and then standing at the front of the pews, listening as the Vallee droned on and on, it was hardly worth the military-style drilling Finnie forced us through), we filed out and did as we'd practiced.

We all got to the front and took our places opposite Dax, who was standing alone wearing a well-cut suit, looking impatient (and looking that frighteningly).

He was scowling down the aisle (like Circe was going to do anything but maybe throw decorum to the wind and run down the aisle to him), waiting for the doors Noc and Circe were to come through when something not practiced happened.

This was Frey's booming voice ordering, "Stand!"

I looked to Jo at my side and then watched as the meager audience (the outside of the Dwelling was heavily guarded, there were two Noctornos, two

Dax Lahns and two Circes in that room and it wouldn't do for anyone who shouldn't to see that).

After all stood, suddenly, filing in from the side, came Frey's men. As they moved along the back wall to the aisle, Frey fell in in front of them.

We then saw Apollo's closest soldiers following Frey's, led by Apollo.

When they traversed the aisle, Lahn and Tor got out of their pews and joined the men.

They marched up the aisle before Noc even guided Circe into the sanctuary.

When they made it to the front, they lined up around the bridesmaids and to the other side around Dax, turning and standing almost what appeared to be at attention, watching as my husband finally guided Circe into the room and slowly walked the bride down the aisle.

I reached out a hand and found Jo's, hers already searching mine.

We held on as we watched Circe's lips quiver while she made her approach, taking in the assemblage in front of her, a woman who was once violently stripped of everything, her family, her virtue, her freedom. She'd had no one to whom to turn. No one she could trust.

And now she had the armies of four countries at her back and six sisters at her side.

I felt my own tears welling when suddenly, the room filled with green.

"Fabulous." I heard Frey mutter sardonically.

I understood his lament.

Valentine did very much like to cause a drama.

But I heard this at the same time I heard on the other side of me, Circe's wondrous, whispered, "Oh my *God. Pop.*"

And then I saw an older man who'd formed from a rise of green mist move out of a pew toward Noc and Circe, who had just made it to the middle of the long aisle.

"If you don't mind, son," he said to Noc, his eyes never leaving Circe, "I'll take it from here."

"Who's that man?" Jo whispered to me.

"My dad," Circe whispered to Jo.

Both Josette and I cut our gazes to Queen Circe who was openly weeping.

And hugely smiling.

We looked back to Circe as Noc took one look at the bride, dipped his chin and stepped aside.

The man I would eventually know as Harold Quinn walked his other-world daughter to her groom, grinning like a lunatic, his eyes filled with pride as they rested on both the daughter he claimed and the daughter he made before he guided the bride to the man she loved.

Noc moved to stand by Lahn and Tor.

But before I turned to the couple to watch them wed, I caught sight of her standing in the shadows at the back.

She was wearing a fabulous dress of jade green.

Love is everything, I heard Valentine's voice whisper in my ear. *Every way love can be.*

And then, a cat's smile flirting at her lips, she faded away in a beautiful drift of jewel-green smoke.

~

New Orleans

"I SAY, I've kept you up long enough. It's time for me to find my bed...and my wife, and you yours," Kristian stated.

Noc, sitting outside with his brother-in-law, having a whiskey while Kristian enjoyed a cigar, nodded.

It was definitely time.

He liked the man but he liked his wife better.

They rose from their padded chairs and lifted their chins at each other as Kristian moved through the courtyard toward the carriage house at the other side where Franka had created a guest suite.

Noc left the bottle and glasses where they were on the table between the two chairs and walked into the house.

He went through it, knowing the doors were locked, the windows closed and latched.

He checked them all just the same. There were precious beings sleeping under his roof, a number of them, and it was the man he was that he'd make sure they were safe.

At the top of the stairs, looking up and down the hall, he saw no light coming from under the door to the master suite, or any of the others.

Except a dim light coming from under one in the middle of the hall, a door that led to a room that was painted pink.

He felt the grin hit his mouth but his body jerked when a different door, the one right beside him, opened.

Noc's father blinked sleepily at his son then grunted, "Damned bladder."

And then his dad lifted his hand, patted Noc's shoulder, and walked the opposite way, toward the bathroom.

Noc walked toward the light.

He put his hand on the handle and turned it, opening the door a crack, doing it silently.

He stopped it at just a crack when he heard his daughter speak.

"Really, Momma?" Amara was asking in her little girl voice.

"Really, my sweetest love," Frannie replied.

"Daddy did that?"

"Yes, my darling, your father did that. He did that and more. So much more."

There was a beat of silence before Amara declared sleepily, "Mm, I believe it. Daddy's so sweet."

Noc grinned again.

"He is that, beautiful Amara Judith," Frannie agreed. "He's also something else."

"What's that?"

"He's my valiant."

Noc's body locked.

"What does that mean?" their daughter asked.

"That means, precious girl, your daddy is my hero."

Noc closed his eyes and rested his forehead on the doorjamb.

"He's mine too," Amara declared.

Noc's throat closed.

"I know, baby," Frannie cooed. "Now it's very late. I've told you your story. It's time for you to go to sleep."

His daughter's sounded dreamy as she shared, "I can't wait to find my valiant."

Frannie's tone was crisper when she returned, "We'll talk about that in thirty years."

Amara's voice was higher when she asked, "Thirty?"

"Go to sleep, darling."

"I'm not gonna be thirty-six when I get married."

"Amara, my love, *sleep*."

"All right." Noc heard his girl mumble.

At that, Noc moved from the door, down the hall and into his and Frannie's room.

He went straight to the window.

He didn't pull the curtains closed.

He stood looking down at their quiet courtyard with its riot of flowers, all of it lit by moonlight.

He heard her enter behind him.

"Has Kristian finished his cigar?" she asked his back.

"Yep," he answered the window.

"Foul things," she murmured and the door clicked.

Noc stared at the courtyard.

Frannie came right to him, circling him with her arms and fitting herself to his back.

"I love having the house filled with family," she whispered.

She was talking about Dad and Sue, Kristian and Brikitta and their three boys visiting.

She was also talking about their own five kids.

Four boys.

One girl.

Amara right smack in the middle.

"Noc," she said softly, "is everything all right?"

He looked from the courtyard to her hands at his stomach, her diamond blinking faintly in the moonlight. He felt her breasts pressed to his back, the belly she'd nurtured his five children in tucked to his ass.

He could smell her.

He could feel her power contained but still emanating through her.

And it took no effort at all to pull her face up in his mind's eye, that delicate neck, her beautiful mouth, her gorgeous hair.

Her arms around him tightened.

"Darling? Are you okay?"

Noc took her wrist and pulled it to his side, forcing his wife to circle around to his front.

She kept hold of him, and when he stopped her, she tipped her head back to catch his eyes.

He let her wrist go and lifted his hand to cup her jaw.

Holding her there and drawing his other arm around her to pull her close, he dipped his face to hers and studied the woman he loved, so goddamned beautiful, even more right then, lit by moonbeams.

"My valiant," he whispered.

He saw those beautiful blue eyes of hers warm.

And then he saw them grow bright with wet.

She lifted up on her toes so that fucking amazing mouth was a breath from his.

But she didn't kiss him.

She whispered back.

Two words he never believed.

Two words he knew she believed down to her glorious soul.

"My hero."

The End

This concludes the Fantasyland Series.
Thank you for reading!

If you enjoy being in my parallel universe, you can return to Hawkvale with my novella *Gossamer in the Darkness.*

And I invite you to explore the next adventures in The Rising.

GLOSSARY OF PARALLEL UNIVERSE

PLACES, SEAS, REGIONS IN THE KRISTEN ASHLEY'S FANTASYLAND SERIES

Bellebryn—(place) Small, peaceful, city-sized princedom located in the Northlands and fully within the boundaries of Hawkvale and the Green Sea (west)

Fleuridia—(place) Somewhat advanced, peaceful nation located in the Northlands; boundaries to Hawkvale (north and west) and the Marhac Sea (south)

Green Sea—(body of water) Ocean-like body of water with coastlines abutting Bellebryn, Hawkvale, Lunwyn and Middleland

Hawkvale—(place) Somewhat advanced, peaceful nation located in the Northlands; boundaries with Middleland (north), Fleuridia (south and east) and the Green Sea (west) and Marhac Sea (south)

Keenhak—(place) Primitive, warring nation located in the Southlands; boundaries with Korwahk (north) and Maroo (west)

Korwahk—(place) Primitive, warring nation located in the Southlands; boundaries with the Marhac Sea (north) and the nations of Keenhak (southeast) and Maroo (southwest)

Korwahn—(place) Large capital city of Korwahk

Lunwyn—(place) Somewhat advanced, peaceful nation in the farthest reaches of the Northlands; boundaries to Middleland (south), the Green Sea (west) and the Winter Sea (north)

Marhac Sea—(large body of water) Separates Korwahk and Hawkvale and Fleuridia

Maroo—(place) Primitive, warring nation located in the Southlands; boundaries to Korwahk (north) and Keenhak (east)

Middleland—(place) Somewhat advanced nation with tyrant king located in the Northlands; boundaries to Hawkvale (south), Fleuridia (south), Lunwyn (north) and the Green Sea (west)

[The] Northlands—(region) The region north of the equator on the alternate earth

[The] Southlands—(region) The region south of the equator on the alternate earth

Winter Sea—(large body of water) Arctic body of water that forms the northern coast of Lunwyn, filled with large glaciers

KEEP READING FOR MORE FANTASYLAND

Gossamer in the Darkness

Their engagement was set when they were children. Loren Copeland, the rich and handsome Marquess of Remington, would marry Maxine Dawes, the stunning daughter of the Count of Derryman. It's a power match. The perfect alliance for each house.

However, the Count has been keeping secret a childhood injury that means Maxine can never marry. He's done this as he searches for a miracle so this marriage can take place. He needs the influence such an alliance would give him, and he'll stop at nothing to have it.

The time has come. There could be no more excuses. No more delays. The marriage has to happen, or the contract will be broken.

When all seems lost, the Count finds his miracle: There's a parallel universe where his daughter has a twin. He must find her, bring her to his world and force her to make the Marquess fall in love with her.

And this, he does.

Gossamer in the Darkness is available now.

KEEP READING FOR MORE KRISTEN ASHLEY FANTASY

The Rising Series
The Beginning of Everything
Book One

Once upon a time, in a parallel universe, there existed the continent of Triton. The land was filled with beauty, but it was also splintered by war. Out of the chaos grew a conspiracy to reawaken the Beast, a fearsome creature who wrought only tragedy and devastation. The only way to stop him was to fulfill an ancient prophecy: Triton's four strongest warriors must wed its four most powerful witches, binding all nations together and finally bringing peace to the land.

This is the story of their unions: the quiet maiden Silence and the savage king Mars. The cold warrior Cassius and the fiery witch Elena. The steadfast soldier True and the banished beauty Farah. And the pirate king Aramus and the mysterious queen Ha-Lah.

Their unions will not be easy, but each couple must succeed, for the fate of their world is at stake....

Keep reading for more of The Beginning of Everything.

THE BEGINNING OF EVERYTHING
PROLOGUE

The Prophecy

Once upon a time, in a parallel universe, there existed an abundance of beauty and riches on the continent of Triton.

Yet for millennia, the peoples within it knew nothing but mistrust and oppression and war.

Peace was not the destiny chosen by the rulers.

Differences were reviled.

Subjugation was observed.

Conflict was sought.

One cold night in Sky City, broken from centuries of exploitation, finding themselves without an alternate course, the women gathered their magicks and made the ultimate sacrifice.

They slayed the men who were their masters.

Leaving their sons and gathering their daughters, they fled the city and created The Enchantments of the Warrior Sisterhood of the Nadirii.

In the magical, green, sunny forest of The Enchantments, mighty trees charmed by their witches grew tall and strong, providing treehomes for the sisterhood of the skilled warriors of the Nadirii. The sisterhood welcomed all who beseeched their Enchantments to escape their oppressors and thus grew and thrived through loyalty and trust.

And earned the wrath of men who sought to collect them.

The rest of Triton grew fractured, splintering into different realms.

There were the sun-drenched dunes and mountains of the wealthy, wanton and barbarous southern region of Firenze whose mines of jewels, northern fields of spices and rare silk made them the richest nation of Triton.

And their riches were coveted by others.

Then there were the wet, fertile, wooded forests, dells and plains of the virtuous northwest region of Wodell, whose sheep produced the best wool on the planet, and whose crops and orchards fed the continent.

And whose people tired of war and chafed under a weak king.

Further, there were the black crags of the northern shores and the rolling fields inland of the cultured nation of Airen, producing olives and wine and the best leather and weapons on the continent.

And populated by men who had not learned.

And there was the island continent of Mar-el. Its barren shores of rock and beach forced its people to live by the sea and become fishermen, sailors...and pirates. But within its boundaries, there was a secret.

And its peoples remained removed from the rest by decree of their king.

Last, there was the Dome City. Known for its resplendent golden domes, the city-state was the place of the religion and practitioners of Go'Doan. The priests and their mysterious female acolytes held fast to three sacred missions: education, healing, and most of all, extending their beliefs.

But even after the Night of the Fallen Masters that saw the birth of the Nadirii...

Dissension, assassination, rebellion and conflict reigned across the continent of Triton.

And then there were those...

Those who would see the dominion of all in all lands, the peoples of the nations of Triton cowed to their whims and controlled by new masters.

And it was those who conspired to reawaken the Beast, a fearsome creature who wrought tragedy and devastation across the continent who had been vanquished centuries before.

Foreseeing this, a powerful coven of witches proclaimed the prophecy.

Triton's four strongest warriors must wed its four most powerful witches, binding all nations together.

There is the quiet maiden, Silence, born of Wodell.

And the savage king, Mars, born of Firenze.

And the cold warrior, Cassius, born to Airen.

And the fierce witch, Elena, born to the Nadirii.

And the steadfast soldier, True, born to Wodell.

And the banished beauty, Farah, born to Firenze.

And the pirate king, Aramus, ascended in Mar-el.

To make the crusading Ha-Lah his queen.

If these men and women could see beyond their differences of culture and history, pride, politics and pasts—and love could prevail—their strength and magicks would flourish...

Then, they could face The Rising.

And perhaps defeat the Beast.

The time has come.

He has been awakened...

And he is rising...

The Beginning of Everything is available now.

About the Author

Kristen Ashley is the *New York Times* bestselling author of over eighty romance novels including the *Rock Chick, Colorado Mountain, Dream Man, Chaos, Unfinished Heroes, The 'Burg, Magdalene, Fantasyland, The Three, Ghost and Reincarnation, The Rising, Dream Team, Moonlight and Motor Oil, River Rain, Wild West MC, Misted Pines* and *Honey* series along with several standalone novels. She's a hybrid author, publishing titles both independently and traditionally, her books have been translated in fourteen languages and she's sold over five million books.

Kristen's novel, *Law Man*, won the *RT Book Reviews* Reviewer's Choice Award for best Romantic Suspense, her independently published title *Hold On* was nominated for *RT Book Reviews* best Independent Contemporary Romance and her traditionally published title *Breathe* was nominated for best Contemporary Romance. Kristen's titles *Motorcycle Man, The Will,* and *Ride Steady* (which won the Reader's Choice award from *Romance Reviews*) all made the final rounds for Goodreads Choice Awards in the Romance category.

Kristen, born in Gary and raised in Brownsburg, Indiana, is a fourth-generation graduate of Purdue University. Since, she's lived in Denver, the West Country of England, and she now resides in Phoenix. She worked as a charity executive for eighteen years prior to beginning her independent publishing career. She now writes full-time.

Although romance is her genre, the prevailing themes running through all of Kristen's novels are friendship, family and a strong sisterhood. To this end, and as a way to thank her readers for their support, Kristen has created the Rock Chick Nation, a series of programs that are designed to give back to her readers and promote a strong female community.

The mission of the Rock Chick Nation is to live your best life, be true to your true self, recognize your beauty, and take your sister's back whether they're at your side as friends and family or if they're thousands of miles away and you don't know who they are.

The programs of the RC Nation include Rock Chick Rendezvous, weekends Kristen organizes full of parties and get-togethers to bring the sisterhood together, Rock Chick Recharges, evenings Kristen arranges for women who have been nominated to receive a special night, and Rock Chick Rewards, an ongoing program that raises funds for nonprofit women's organizations Kristen's readers nominate. Kristen's Rock Chick Rewards have donated hundreds of thousands of dollars to charity and this number continues to rise.

You can read more about Kristen, her titles and the Rock Chick Nation at KristenAshley.net.

facebook.com/kristenashleybooks
twitter.com/KristenAshley68
instagram.com/kristenashleybooks
pinterest.com/KristenAshleyBooks
goodreads.com/kristenashleybooks
bookbub.com/authors/kristen-ashley

Also by Kristen Ashley

Rock Chick Series:

Rock Chick

Rock Chick Rescue

Rock Chick Redemption

Rock Chick Renegade

Rock Chick Revenge

Rock Chick Reckoning

Rock Chick Regret

Rock Chick Revolution

Rock Chick Reawakening

Rock Chick Reborn

The 'Burg Series:

For You

At Peace

Golden Trail

Games of the Heart

The Promise

Hold On

The Chaos Series:

Own the Wind

Fire Inside

Ride Steady

Walk Through Fire

A Christmas to Remember

Rough Ride

Wild Like the Wind

Free

Wild Fire

Wild Wind

The Colorado Mountain Series:

The Gamble

Sweet Dreams

Lady Luck

Breathe

Jagged

Kaleidoscope

Bounty

Dream Man Series:

Mystery Man

Wild Man

Law Man

Motorcycle Man

Quiet Man

Dream Team Series:

Dream Maker

Dream Chaser

Dream Bites Cookbook

Dream Spinner

Dream Keeper

The Fantasyland Series:

Wildest Dreams

The Golden Dynasty

Fantastical

Broken Dove

Midnight Soul

Gossamer in the Darkness

Ghosts and Reincarnation Series:

Sommersgate House

Lacybourne Manor

Penmort Castle

Fairytale Come Alive

Lucky Stars

The Honey Series:

The Deep End

The Farthest Edge

The Greatest Risk

The Magdalene Series:

The Will

Soaring

The Time in Between

Mathilda, SuperWitch:

Mathilda's Book of Shadows

Mathilda The Rise of the Dark Lord

Misted Pines Series

The Girl in the Mist

The Girl in the Woods

Moonlight and Motor Oil Series:

The Hookup

The Slow Burn

The Rising Series:

The Beginning of Everything

The Plan Commences

The Dawn of the End

The Rising

The River Rain Series:

After the Climb

After the Climb Special Edition

Chasing Serenity

Taking the Leap

Making the Match

The Three Series:

Until the Sun Falls from the Sky

With Everything I Am

Wild and Free

The Unfinished Hero Series:

Knight

Creed

Raid

Deacon

Sebring

Wild West MC Series:

Still Standing

Smoke and Steel

Other Titles by Kristen Ashley:

Heaven and Hell

Play It Safe

Three Wishes

Complicated

Loose Ends

Fast Lane

Perfect Together (Summer 2023)

Printed in the USA
CPSIA information can be obtained
at www.ICGtesting.com
LVHW090746181023
761214LV00014B/24